A TIME
TO ACT

A TIME TO ACT

S.J. KNIGHT

To order additional copies of this book, contact:
Xlibris
1-800-455-039
www.Xlibris.com.au
Orders@Xlibris.com.au
636662

A junior version of this book by the same author
is available for younger readers, under the title:
The Torchbearer *by S.J. Burke (ISBN 0-949457-00-0)*

Other biblical novels by S.J. Knight:

A Time to Hear

> *(ISBN 978-0-85189-164-4)*

A Time to See

> *(ISBN 978-0-85189-185-9)*

A Time to Speak

> *(ISBN 978-0-85189-197-2)*

Also:

A Time To Hear: A Musical Stage Play

> *(ISBN 978-1-5144-4214-2)*

An illustrated musical adaptation of the book for the stage with full script, directions and music scores.

For information contact:
sjknightworks@gmail.com

ACKNOWLEDGEMENTS:

Cover photography: Front – R. Bracey, Back – D. Knight

Chapter Six: sketch taken from a work in the public domain (Wikimedia Commons) – Watercolour by Tissot, James (1836-1902) Reconstruction of Jerusalem and Herod's Temple (*Réconstitution de Jérusalem et du temple d'Hérode*)

Chapters Ten, Twenty-two, Forty-three: original glass plate photographs by R.E.M. Bain, 1894 *(public domain)*

Chapter Twenty: original photograph, unattributed, 1896 *(public domain)*

Chapter Forty-seven: original photograph – Nigel Moore

All other chapters: original photographs – David Knight

AUTHOR'S NOTE

This is a work of fiction, not exposition.

Set against a background of scriptural and historical fact,

much of it is imaginary, but the man himself is not.

His passion, faith and humility are well documented,

but how he came to be who he was, can only be conjectured.

This is how it might have been.

S.J.K.

Chapter One

A SMALL pair of sandals pelted down the wide street. Puffs of dust rose into the hot Cilician sunlight, lazily trailing young Deborah's running feet. At the far end of the street, citizens of Tarsus were emerging from the cool synagogue, blinking in the sudden dazzle. Observing the custom of leaving a place of worship with slow and reluctant steps, they straggled sedately down the road, blocking the way, while the little girl dodged through the crowd as politely as she could, feverish impatience battling with deeply ingrained habits of respect. A long-bearded Pharisee with a tense expression was the last to step out of the synagogue porch.

"Father!" Deborah waved wildly.

Forgetful of dignity, Rabbi Benjamin sprang forward, catching his excited daughter in his arms. "Your mother?" he demanded anxiously.

"Safe!" she panted happily. "She's safe – they're *both* safe – and, oh, Father – it's a boy!"

The rabbi gasped and tears sprang to his eyes. "A boy! Safe! My wife *and* my son! Ah! Praise the Eternal for His mercy – that today He gives without taking! A son, at last, a son!"

Abandoning his customary gravity for the first and last time in his life, and in complete defiance of tradition, Rabbi Benjamin picked up his robes and actually ran all the way home.

The scarlet, crumpled scrap of life beat the air with his fists, squalling defiance, his tongue quivering inside tiny gums from the force of his shrieks. The frantically wailing little face was mottled with waxy smears, his cheeks and narrow shoulders were lightly furred with dark hair, and truth to tell, in this state he resembled more an ugly imp than the pretty baby his sister had been hoping for, but nobody cared. He was here, not only alive, but kicking and screaming – and with a singing heart, his tall father held him reverently aloft as a thing of precious beauty, like a priest presenting a perfect Wave Offering in the Holy Temple across the sea.

"Just look at him, Anna! And hark at the noise he makes – I declare it's bigger than he is! Too impatient even to wait his full time, yet he's ready to take on the world! Surely this time all will be well – may it please Almighty God."

Deborah's mother smiled, but hesitantly, and a touch of fear was in her eyes. When the infant had been placed so warmly wet and spluttering on her gasping breast she had burst into thankful tears, sobbing only one question to the midwife, "Tell me the truth, if you fear God! – has he come to stay?"

As a woman who had already lost four little ones, she could take nothing for granted, and the midwife's robust optimism was hard to accept.

Now she said tremulously to her husband, "He is so early, Benjamin – so very tiny – and he struggled hard for that first breath …"

"You would be a lot more worried had he *not* struggled," the midwife interrupted firmly and cheerfully as she took the raging mite from his father. "Once he gulped it in – why, he hasn't stopped screaming. Oh yes, this one's hungry for life! See how he fights to escape before I've even tied the swaddling bands! Undercooked and undersized, I grant you, but strong. I doubt he'll ever outgrow his big sister here, but he'll last the distance, is my opinion, and I've seen plenty come and go in my time."

Deftly she imprisoned the flailing red arms and vainly scrambling legs to her satisfaction, before handing him back to the rabbi, who was holding out his arms impatiently. Suddenly recalling that she was in the presence of an elder (however unorthodox it might be to have him in the birth room!) she asked respectfully, "And what will his name be, sir?"

Benjamin looked down proudly at the piteously protesting bundle, studying his new son's face thoughtfully, pretending to consider, but a name had been chosen in prayerful hope long ago. He straightened up with a smile and returned the swaddled infant to his wife to nurse, whereupon it snuffled into silence.

"His name will be Shaul, after my father, may he rest in peace." He laid his right hand on the child's head. "May Adonai God grant him long life and make him memorable among our people!"

He laughed exultantly. "And truly my son has a good start – nobody will easily forget someone called Shaul ben Benjamin ben Shaul, of the tribe of Benjamin! And surely, since the days of Israel's first King, the two names belong together."

The symmetry of it appealed to him, as did the touch of humour, but he was also laughing for joy that the son who had been so long in coming, was now here – fragile in appearance, perhaps, but alive and very determined. In God's mercy, surely he would grow to bless his family and carry on his father's name! Meanwhile, a smiling Anna shook her head indulgently at her husband's high humour, though inwardly sighing over such a very long way of addressing such a very small baby, but Deborah hastily put her hands over the newborn's delicate ears, so he could not hear such weighty expectations.

"But *King* Shaul was nearly a giant, Father!" she protested at once. "Head and shoulders above any in Israel! And the baby may not grow up any taller than me!"

"Well, pray God he will be head and shoulders above King Shaul in faith," said her father firmly, "and that he will have the true heart of a king, if not the impressive stature! Shaul of old began well, but sadly lost his way. I have often wondered how it came about. If being used to imposing his will on herds of unruly asses, led him to treat men the same way … rather than leading them with compassion, as a shepherd leads a trustful flock … Yet he seemed so humble at first! Did his elevation go to his head? Or was his initial self-effacement but a morbidly excessive shyness – which being an absorption with self is the exact opposite of real humility … ?"

Anna rolled her eyes at the midwife, who turned to hide a smile. Of course, the man was a Pharisee and of a philosophical turn of mind, but for him to hold forth at her bedside at a time like this … ! Nevertheless Anna answered her husband mildly.

"Perhaps as a youth he was not taught spiritual wisdom at his mother's knee." She caught Benjamin's eye, adding with a smile, "Or his father's."

"Praise the Eternal we need have no fear on that account, my dear Anna. Our Shaul will be given proper grounding and guidance in spiritual matters, just as my father gave me."

"I don't remember him," Deborah said, dropping a kiss on the baby's head. "Was he tall too?"

"Not really," her father answered with a smile, "but he was a wise and loving man, may he rest in peace, and I am only sad he is not here today to see his name continued in his only grandson."

Anna tenderly stroked the damp little head in the crook of her arm, and added softly, "And even aside from that, it is truly fitting, my darling – the meaning is the most important thing, and your new little brother was indeed *Asked of God*. For a very long time."

Deborah grinned, shaking her head. "But, Mother, he really is such a very *little* little-brother – so until he grows big I will have to call him '*little one*'."

"Then he will be *Paulus*!" said the midwife approvingly. "A good Roman name, befitting a new citizen of Tarsus."

Benjamin and his wife exchanged amused glances. They had already chosen Paulus as his *praenomen*, for its convenient similarity to his Jewish name. And perhaps unconsciously they hoped it would remind their son to avoid the false pride of his ancient namesake.

"He is a child of two cultures after all," Benjamin admitted. "A Hebrew, and yet a Roman citizen. But I will raise him as a son of the Covenant – a Pharisee – and a Shaul!"

Anna lifted her tiny son to her shoulder and patted his back gently. "Paul-Shaul," she whispered, nuzzling his downy cheek. He hiccupped, and screwed up his face in what his sister chose to believe was a smile.

"He likes it!" she laughed.

Now it only remained to be seen whether the midwife's confident words would come to pass, and meanwhile every milestone in his progress was celebrated. First he must survive eight days to the all-important circumcision. Given the alarmingly small size of the child, this was a task before which Benjamin understandably quailed, instead calling in the most experienced rabbi in the synagogue, and asking him first to determine whether there might be a lawful case for delaying it another week.

Having examined Benjamin's son, the rabbi admitted that this would be quite the smallest babe upon which he had ever operated, but assured the nervous parents it would be quite safe, and so it was that Shaul Benjamin of Tarsus was circumcised according to the Law of Moses, on the eighth day.

Several days of misery and fever followed, with the babe too distressed to suckle properly. The midwife was recalled and appealed to at once, and she, Anna and even young Deborah united in patient nursing of the little sufferer day and night. By dint of their assiduous care and many earnest prayers, he rallied, though Anna continued to brood anxiously over her precious son in the night watches.

As she yearningly held him to her breast, at times she would catch herself compressing her lips, frowning in concentration, somehow attempting to will her own strength into his little body. Whether this was approved by the angels she had no idea, and she could only hope that if it was wrong, she would be forgiven.

During those weeks she spoke quietly, doing everything gently, seemingly afraid to laugh. Around the child she moved lightly, almost on tiptoe, as if walking on eggshells, unable to shake a panicked feeling that she must not stop holding her breath until he should survive his first thirty days. Then, should the worst happen, *me genoito!* – perish the thought! – at least the child might be given a funeral with proper mourning, instead of a mere burial and painful forgetting.

Her almost superstitious fears were understandable, but the midwife's confidence gently rebuked them – the babe's colour returned, he was now feeding well, and though he still looked like a skinned rabbit, squalling for hours each day and continually fighting sleep, he was bright, alert, and extremely lively for a child scarcely out of swaddling clothes. Cheerfully assuring Anna that she was not needed any more, the midwife left, and the family began to breathe more easily.

It had almost seemed like tempting fate to do it any earlier, but as thirty days was the maximum time the city allowed for registering a birth, Benjamin now gathered the required seven witnesses and strode off proudly to the city's office of municipal records.

"Father's name, nativity and citizenship status?"

"My name is Benjamin, son of Shaul. *Praenomen*, Praxis. *Cognomen*, Timaeus. Native of Tarsus, and Citizen of Rome."

"Citizen of Rome as well, eh? And you a Jew? Freeborn or purchased?"

"Freeborn. Citizenship granted to my grandfather Timaeus."

"Documents?"

"Yes, here is his Table of Manumission."

"H'm ... seems he served a noble household. *Livius Atticus*, no less – still on the University committee, aren't they? *Thirty years teaching ... faithful services rendered to his master's sons ... and their sons in turn...* Sooner him than me. I can't get mine to listen to a word I say. Thirty years of trying to get anything through the thick skull of a schoolboy would drive me to drink." The official skimmed the parchment, paying particular attention to the seals stamped upon it. "And your own proof of citizenship?"

Taking an inscribed wooden *diptych* from a protective linen bag, Benjamin handed over the flat hinged case – a copy, provided by the state, of his own birth record. The man flipped it open casually and read the words inscribed on the wax, tilting it to the light to ensure it had not been tampered with.

"Looks in order." The official handed it back and dipped his pen. "Name of child, Shaul. *Praenomen*, Paulus, you said? Very well, name of mother, then have your witnesses step forward. Pay the fee on your way out. Collect your son's diptych at the end of the month."

Chapter Two

STRONG and lively, the infant Shaul fought off every ailment of babyhood and thrived despite the miasmic port-side air of Tarsus – but he was the last child of his mother to do so. Two more little ones came and went without drawing breath. A third arrived with limp waxy limbs and a slack mouth.

Gentile acquaintances whispered and shook their heads. In their families she would not have been permitted to survive the day, for infanticide was accepted practice when unfortunate or unwanted newborns were weakly, or deformed – or female. But Jews were strange people with a strange god – treasuring their children, not as their own possessions, but as his everlasting heritage – and the child was actually yearned over! Well, there was no accounting for personal beliefs – live and let live in these modern times, they shrugged.

Though hard to feed from the beginning, the babe survived the first essential thirty days and therefore might be acknowledged as a daughter not a mishap – yet she remained sickly and unresponsive. Young Deborah was old enough to enter fully into her parents' distress, but her little brother was confused by the oppressive sadness which settled upon the family like a grey mist.

Night after night the small boy lay awake, listening to stifled sobs, hearing low murmured voices. Day after day he watched his father become more grave, his mother more haggard, his sister less patient.

Once he heard angry voices arguing in the street. A half-blind old woman who eked out a living by begging and fortune telling had taken to sitting opposite their house, spinning lumpy black yarn on a cracked spindle from scraps of dirty fleece, muttering continually to herself and croaking dismally to passers by. This was her real trade, since she was paid more for silence than for her words. Neighbours murmured that she was bad luck at best and had the Evil Eye at worst, and poor Anna shuddered whenever she saw her.

The noise waking little Shaul from his afternoon nap, the child scrambled up on a stool to peer down from a window. He was greatly startled to see his father below in the street, waving his arms, harshly demanding that the old woman beg elsewhere. The boy rubbed his eyes, half wondering whether he was dreaming. Was this the same father who told him to be respectful and kind to women, to old people, and even beggars? And why was his mother crying down there in the courtyard? Perhaps she was unhappy because Father had forgotten his own words. Perhaps she was afraid that now he might be unkind to *her*. What if he was? What then?

"Women suffer much in this world because of the harshness of men," Benjamin had said firmly on more than one occasion, with scant regard to the tenderness of his son's years. "Take care that you are never one of those men. A Godly man is compassionate to all."

Yet here he was, urging a feeble old beggar woman away from their house while she heaped shrill curses upon his head. The contradiction made the little boy's head swim. Below, his mother was still weeping and now he could hear his sister trying to comfort her as in the street the loud argument went on and neighbours began to join in.

Agitated beyond bearing, the child put his hands over his ears, but he could not block out the raised voices and heated words – then all at once his father came stamping back through the courtyard, slamming the gate with a final bark of warning.

Suddenly dizzy, the little boy slid off his stool, down from the high wide window sill, deeply troubled and trembling, huddling below on the cool floor till the room steadied. He had never seen his father so angry – but yet – even in his wrath he had still given the old woman money. Shaul had seen him do it. It made no sense.

Still, that night when relating the story of brave Daniel in the lion's den, Benjamin seemed the same as always: growling like the lions to make him laugh, tickling his face with his long whiskers when he kissed him good night, as kind and affectionate as ever.

The next day the old woman was gone from their street, and did not return. Little Shaul wondered much, but eventually the disturbing incident faded from his memory, leaving only a faint imprint of confused anxiety. It was just one more puzzle which belonged to the shadowy grownup world.

At times, visitors came to the house with their own children but he found them loud and quarrelsome and shrank from their rough play. Babes in arms he observed curiously, especially their noise and liveliness.

He did not understand why his new sister did not grow and squirm and babble like other people's babies but remained as limp as their newborns and rarely cried. He would sometimes be allowed to hold her, nuzzling her pale cheek, toying with her cool, inert fingers and toes, telling stories to her as gravely as a rabbi. Other times he would hang over her basket chattering nonsense while the uncomprehending dark eyes, so large in the wan little face, stared solemnly into his.

When she was around six months old, the little boy's attentions brought an unexpected reward. Engrossed in narrating to her a fantastical tale of his own invention, he suddenly startled himself with an unexpected sneeze so violent his eyes watered – and the corners of her mauve-tinged lips lilted into a tentative smile. Entranced, he forgot his story at once, determined to prolong this rare response.

Chanting the children's game of *Five Little Beans* he gently pinched and wiggled her thin toes one by one, while her dark-lashed eyes crinkled up happily – and suddenly she gave a gurgling chuckle. His mother and Deborah dropped their sewing in shock, but there it was again! Unmistakeably this time she actually giggled, her narrow chest and flat stomach quivering with the unfamiliar and delightful sensation.

Deborah leaped up, nearly strangling her triumphant little brother in an exultant hug, while her mother, overwhelmed, scooped up the babe and through a rush of tears, cried out excitedly to her husband. Within a half hour the whole neighbourhood had crowded in, praising God and rejoicing that Anna's precious, feeble nursling had finally laughed for the first time, and that her four year old brother had made it happen.

Small Shaul was hugged and kissed and made much of while everyone fussed over the child to make her laugh again, but only the boy could do it, and do it again he did, to everyone's delight, until the little one began to cough, and Anna, her eyes softened with glad hope, decreed that there had been quite enough excitement for one afternoon. So the neighbours drifted home again, with final caresses and words of praise to little Shaul. Young as he was, he never forgot the glowing pride and pure happiness of that day.

The next morning, however, dawned a day of cold darkness – equally unforgettable – for the babe had failed to wake. She had left them that one brief and tiny gift of joy and now she was gone.

The adult grief all around him bewildered the boy. It was like a crushing black cloud ... it stifled him ... he felt he could not move or breathe. His thin body felt icy, but there was a strange burning feeling in his small chest and in his scrawny little throat. His mother seemed to be somewhere very far away, his sister sobbed herself sick and his father seemed to be stricken dumb.

After the burial, again the wakeful hours, the suppressed sobs, the anguished whispers overheard in the dark. Worst of all came on a night when the child tiptoed by moonlight in search of his mother's comfort, only to freeze as he came upon his father brokenly praying by a dark open window, his face turned beseechingly to the starry, windswept heavens.

"Oh, Master of the Universe, what have I done? How have I sinned that such sorrow has come upon my beloved family? Adonai God! How often I pleaded that she would grow stronger, and yet still she did not thrive. But did I not accept Thy will? Even as I accepted Thy will for all our lost babes who have come and gone, some which never saw the light! Have I ever railed against Thee as did Job of old? Have I not always striven to trust Thee and so be content in whatsoever state I am placed?"

The voice crumbled and faltered, the head bowed and the strong shoulders shook. Then with determination the dark face was lifted up again, distorted with grief and weirdly splashed with flickering shadows.

The child shrinking by the door gripped the wooden post in a spasm of anxiety. Was this really his father?

"Truly I praise and thank Thee for the precious children I have left, and for my beloved wife, and for all my blessings, indeed – but grant me this one request now, Oh Lord Almighty, and let there be no more little ones to break our hearts! Forgive me, for I am sorely conflicted, my God! In Eden Thou ordained a union for joy, yet surely it is better for a man to bear his burdens alone than to marry and beget continual grief …"

The silent child crept back to his bed, feeling guiltily uneasy to have trespassed on his father at such a time. He did not understand all the words, but nevertheless they sank deep into his soul.

Chapter Three

YET private anguish was just that – private. After the prescribed period of mourning, custom required that grief must be left behind and life go on, and so it did. Benjamin's anguished prayer being heard on high, the weary shadows of sadness crept out of sight, and the rest of Shaul's early childhood was a happy one.

The midwife's prediction continued to hold good as he navigated the perils of infancy, growing from a stringy toddler into a wiry child. The boy was indeed hungry for life – almost as if to make up for the other brief lives which had too easily slipped away.

His moods were often passionate, whether for good or ill, and his eager mind was filled with curiosity. Perhaps this accounted for the rather un-childlike look in his deep brown eyes, a look which seemed directed inward rather than to what was around him. Neighbourhood women who had seen much of life nodded their heads knowingly and privately pronounced him an 'old soul', though wisely they did not say such things in his mother's hearing.

Although always slighter than others of his own age, Shaul's thin brown body was full of an intense energy which seemed hard to contain. When trying to express himself on anything about which he felt strongly, the child would shake with deep tremors unless he was free to pace and fidget to his heart's content, often waving his hands emphatically.

Despite this peculiarity, his liveliness, less physical than mental, was not of the boisterous kind – he moved quietly, softly, often on tiptoe. His father said teasingly it was to make himself taller, his sister said dismissively it was for sheer stealth, and his mother said defensively it was because he took after her own father, who had short hamstrings. Privately she thought he took after him in other ways too – such as his frequently unseeing gaze, and an odd habit of touching and fingering objects as if reassuring himself they were really there. She worried a little about his solitary nature, regretting there were no tribes of cousins to take the edge off it. But that was the price of her being an only child and marrying a man in the same situation. With their parents gone there was no extended family left.

Still, perhaps it did not matter as much as she thought. The boy was not particularly interested in other children, finding them dull or incomprehensible. He was quite content with the company of his sister, blissfully unaware that pastimes she taught him so dictatorially might be 'girl games'. He did his best to oblige her, but at skipping and hopping he was a dismal failure. Even in more boyish occupations such as throwing and catching he did not fare much better, and he could barely kick a ball without falling over.

Only in games with words did he excel. Nonsense rhymes, clapping games, tongue-twisters, counting songs and riddles he was always quick to learn; and Anna was grateful that during long winter days when they were shut in by icy winds sweeping down from the Taurus mountains and dreary rain which lashed inland from the sea, her children's voices could be heard giggling, singing or chanting happily rather than quarrelling or whining with boredom.

At other times however, like most mothers, she would much rather have them outside.

"Son! Get out from under my feet!" Anna tripped over the small body on the tiled floor. "What are you doing down there?"

A pair of large, intelligent dark eyes looked up at her reproachfully. "I *have* to be down here – it's where my feet are!"

The small boy resumed his investigation of two big ants, which were fighting over a crumb in a crack of the dark red tiles.

"Ants," he commented thoughtfully, shifting obligingly to allow Anna to get to the table where she was making bread. "Why do they have six legs and spiders have eight?"

Above him, Anna turned the dough over with a slap. "I don't know," she replied absently. "It's just the way God made them."

A puff of flour drifted down and sifted into the boy's dark hair. He watched the pale specks powder the floor and carefully drew lines in it, studying the way the flour heaped up on both sides of his finger. Another ant appeared from under the table leg and crawled onto Anna's sandal, up her toe, over the instep. Shaul watched with interest as it began to march across the leather straps towards his mother's ankle, wondering whether it would try to make the jump to the hem of her robe.

"That's funny!" he commented. "Ants don't eat people, do they? So why –"

"Why-why-why?" his mother interrupted with a smile. She straightened, tucking a wisp of black hair under her headscarf, leaving a floury smear on her cheek. "Always why! Always questions!"

Benjamin walked in. "He thinks, Anna! He thinks! Shaul, your mother is just teasing you. Ask away, my son – never be afraid to ask questions!"

Shaul uncurled his body from its investigative crouch and got to his feet. "I was just wondering," he said, peering over the table top and poking experimentally at the soft dough. Anna smacked his fingers automatically.

"Wondering what?" Benjamin encouraged.

Shaul licked flour from his fingers and said idly, "Oh, I just wondered why that big ant was crawling up Mother's leg."

Anna gave a squeal, snatched up her skirts and slapped hard. Shaul saw the squashed insect drop to the floor.

"Now I'll never know," he complained forlornly. "If you had just left it alone …"

"Deborah!" Anna called firmly, and in she skipped with an enquiring look. "Take your brother out, there's a good girl!"

Deborah snatched Shaul's hand and swung it gaily. "Come on, Paul-Shaul! Let's go down to the harbour!"

"Be careful!" Anna called as they scampered off. "Remember what happened to Alexander the Great!"

"Yes, Mother!" they shouted back dutifully, giggling. She trotted out this old warning every time. Just because some foolish conqueror in the olden days swam in the Cydnus when it was full of snow-melt and nearly took his death of cold!

Benjamin put an arm around his wife's shoulder. "Worry, worry! Deborah will take care of him!"

The harbour was a favourite play-place, not particularly close to home, but time and distance meant little to children bent on enjoying themselves, and they set off happily.

Playing guessing games and chanting silly rhymes as they went, the two were in no hurry, and it was a little while before they passed through the outer of the twin walls which embraced the city. Scuttling through the busy sea gate they came at last to where the cold, clear waters of the Cydnus flowed into the Rhegma Lagoon before debouching towards the sea. Here, ancient engineers had capitalised on this natural advantage, deepening the lagoon into a large safe harbour and widening the channel to the coast. Their skill and determination had established Tarsus as a major port and greatly prospered the famous city.

Scrambling and picking their way past many hazards, the children were soon safely ensconsed in their usual spot between a crumbling tumble-down wall and a jumble of old packing cases strewn with straw. A faint breath of rancid oil and stale wine hovered in the air. It came from a continually replenished heap of stained pottery shards – cracked or broken *amphorae* which had not survived their sea journeys.

The children rummaged through them to find useful pieces. The thick slabs they would play with, the thinnest and cleanest they would take home to scribble on, or for their mother to use for notes and shopping lists. She had a basket in her kitchen especially for these *ostraca*, and the children were proud to be her suppliers.

Shaul's particular pleasure in this pottery playground was to sort his chosen pieces by size, shape and colour. Sometimes Deborah would trifle with them, wantonly mixing up his neat little collections to goad him into doing something else, but his agitation would soon have her relenting and helping to restore them. Her idea of fun was more in finding the tapered ends, using their conical shapes to create tiny fanciful playhouses amid curly weed gardens with tottering stick fences.

The boy was not interested in fashioning such domestic scenes. He sorted and arranged his pieces just for the satisfaction of bringing order out of chaos. He liked feeling their texture and sniffing their smell; the contrast of smooth, oil-shiny pieces with the ridged ones furry with sediment of wine; he liked the look of the slender salvaged handles like neat bundles of bones; and he liked the dry scraping sound of the shards as he carefully layered a stack of them into an uneven tower.

Now came his only artistic concession, as he darted out to the water's edge for a fat shell to crown his achievement. The sharp wind stung his eyes and made his nose run. As he finished delicately placing his shell, Deborah grabbed his free arm just in time to stop him smearing a sleeve across his face, and handed him the well-washed rag which small-boy experience had taught her to keep in her sash.

"Blow!"

Shaul blew and handed back the ragged cloth. He leant back happily and stretched, absorbing the mixture of sensations, smells, sights and sounds – all woven together in a potent charm which never failed to entrance him. Only at the port was such a delightful and satisfactory combination to be found: the warmth of the sun, the grittiness of sand and crunch of water-worn stones, the sticky mud where the bank was silting up … the rustle of reeds marching into the shallows, the breath of breeze, the brackish tang in the air … the mewing and screeching of gulls squabbling over the rich pickings of the man-made harbour, the sibilant plash and swish of small waves on rocks, the creaking of ropes and slapping of sails, the wooden grumbling of heavy boats nuzzling and bumping the wharf.

Sharp whiffs of tar cut through the thick smell of rotting water weeds, and intriguing aromas wafted here and there – wine, spices, dried fish, resinous wood, cheeses, livestock, and the occasional split cask of *garum* – the pungent, fermented fish sauce relished throughout Caesar's dominions by all except fastidious Jews. Closer to the boats the children could make a fine game of guessing cargoes with their noses, but today they were happy to stay out of the wind, watching from a distance the swarm of deck hands loading and unloading a procession of bales, boxes, bottles, barrels and bundles.

All around was the busy confusion of the port – the groan and thud of heavy nets laden with goods coming and going to different parts of the Empire; the rattle and clump of mud-laden, bucket-swinging dredges which kept the harbour mouth open; the drum-like echoes from dockyard warehouses; the snatches of foreign song (and swearing) from sailors in salt-stiff tunics, who clambered about, efficiently hauling anchor stones, coiling thick wet hawsers, tarring timbers and hemp ropes, or attending to patched and faded sails of different colours.

From time to time came the warning shouts and boisterous laughter of men skilfully guiding the simplest and most temporary of vessels – ungainly rafts of heavy logs, floated down the Cydnus from forests high in the Taurus mountains.

Little Shaul observed everything with equal interest, but to his sister, the rigged ships held the most fascination when there were passengers, and she stared, intrigued, at them all, trying to guess their stories. Some were leaving, their nervous faces unhappy as they clambered on board a rocking vessel, attempting emotional farewells while being shouted at by irritable ship masters. And some were disembarking, many unfortunates still looking pale and ill as they staggered off to endure boisterous reunions which meant little compared to the blessed relief of being on dry land again. But there was also light-heartedness, with joking and spurts of laughter in the air – not a lot, for the port was a serious place – just enough to lift the spirits of travellers, workers and onlookers alike.

"I wonder where they're all going," Deborah sighed dreamily, as they watched several well-trimmed vessels slip out of the harbour, sails cracking in the gusting wind. "And what it's like when they get there. Perhaps one of them is going to the Homeland! How I would love to see it – especially Jerusalem! Father saw it when he was a boy but I don't suppose he'll ever take us on pilgrimage. Some of my friends have fathers who go every Passover – imagine that! But he says Mother is too afraid of the roads and he gets too sick in a ship."

A startling thought occurred to her. Could he be afraid of the sea? She shook it away with scorn. Surely fathers were not afraid of anything!

"One day *I'll* sail away on a big ship," her small brother boasted adventurously. "I'll find out what it's like, then I'll come back and tell you."

"One day is too far away." Deborah could not resist an opportunity to tease him. "Why don't you run down right now and see if they'll take you on board as ship's monkey!"

The child's narrow face crumpled in immediate distress and she made remorseful haste to soothe him.

"I'm only joking, Paul-Shaul! Oh, don't cry, you silly! Look – I'll teach you the new clapping game I just learned. But promise you won't tell," she warned quickly, knowing her mother regarded this one as slightly dubious.

Forgetting his tears the boy sat up expectantly, first nodding then shaking his head obediently, and then with a grin began to copy his sister, slowly at first, then more surely as they clapped and clicked and flapped their hands in complicated combinations, chanting in time:

"Who shall I marry? Who is for me?
Find my love and you will see
A tall brown woman with blue-black hair
A foreign tongue and a green-eyed stare."

"Oh no, my boy, you pay good heed
A Jewish wife is what you need.
Turn around and flee away
She won't be worth the price you'll pay!"

"How much will you pay?" cried Deborah, getting to the exciting part of the game.

"Three *sestertii!*" he shouted excitedly.

"No, no!" she objected. "More than that or it's no fun!"

"Twenty?"

"That's better! Now remember, it's *slap, clap, left, right, knees, chest,* and *bump together.* Let's see how fast we can do it! Ready? Go! *One sestertius, two sestertii, three sestertii, four...*"

Each time of course the chant must increase in pace, and so they clapped and counted faster and faster until they were tripping over words and actions and giggling so much they accidentally knocked over their pottery creations, and finally went home, still laughing.

When the mosquitoes were too thick at the harbour, or when the colourful, noisy bazaar which was their other favourite haunt was too hot, the two liked to wander off to the University. This fine seat of learning had a reputation equal (Tarsians said, *superior*) to any in the world, including the famous universities of Athens in Greece, and Alexandria in Egypt. On a hot day, the shaded marble-columned walkways and lush peaceful gardens were a pleasant change from the hustling market-place, or the windblown grit of the bustling harbour.

Deborah leant her cheek against the coolness of a glossy stone block which commemorated some long-forgotten benefactor, and drowsily fanned herself with a palm leaf.

"Father says people come here to study from all over Cilicia," she murmured. "How sad it must be to have to leave your home and family to get an education."

She looked over towards a group of young men who sat clogging a narrow flight of steps, comforting a distraught friend while vociferating passionately among themselves – and sighed somewhat romantically. They were in fact telling their friend he was a fool to have backed the wrong horse (especially when it was his turn to buy the beer), and arguing over who would pay for lunch, but fortunately for Deborah's softer feelings, she could not hear that, and continued to regard them with innocent sympathy.

Little Shaul was lying on his back on the cool grass, chewing a flower stem, his eyes half-closed against the glare. He rolled over, spat out the stem and waved his small brown hand towards the imposing group of buildings nearby.

"One day *I'm* going there."

"What, you?" his sister scoffed with amusement, her pensive moment vanishing at once.

Shaul rolled over and snatched the palm leaf. "Yes, me!" He tickled her nose with the scratchy fronds.

Deborah snatched back her fan and pushed him away. "Go away, pest! It's too hot to argue! Anyway – you've got synagogue school to get through first."

A few weeks later, Anna put the finishing touches to a new felt cap she was making and settled it on her son's head.

"There!" she smiled, satisfied. "Now put on the new coat I made you last week, and, Deborah – hand him the wax tablets Father brought home last night and we'll see how he looks as a schoolboy."

When Shaul was ready, Anna called Benjamin to see. He looked at the child with a proud smile.

"*Shalom*, my rabbi!" Shaul bowed, practising.

"*Shalom*, my disciple!" he replied gravely, and they laughed. Benjamin hugged his small son. "Tomorrow we will walk to synagogue together – me to teach, you to learn – and we will leave the women to their cooking pots, hey? And afterwards you will walk home on your own like a big boy, because I will still be working, you know. Unless you want your sister to come and fetch you?"

"No, no, I can do it all by myself!" the child said, rather indignantly. "But will you really be my teacher, Father?"

Benjamin smiled, shaking his head. "No, my son. I'm far too impatient to teach infants!" he said, quite untruthfully. "Why, they tremble at the mere length of my beard! But don't worry. You have met the *Chazzan* many a time, eh? Remember little old Chazzan Lemuel? He's the good man who keeps the synagogue clean and prepared and in perfect order for us all to use, and he only appoints the kindest of men to help him instruct small people like you."

"You'll be reading in no time!" Deborah promised recklessly.

"And writing!" Benjamin added firmly. Unlike many fathers, he was not content for his son to have the ability to read sacred scriptures without the means to communicate them further. Though there was no disgrace for the average man in being unable to write, (after all, what were market-place scribes for?) the rabbi's plans for his son went beyond being satisfied with a basic education. No offspring of *his* would ever have to rely on paid scribes! Even his wife and daughter could read and write (having been taught somewhat furtively), which being most unorthodox was not bruited about – but of course a boy must go to school! And not just any Greek school, either. There would be time for secular learning later, but Holy Writ would be the only text from which *his* son would learn the fundamentals.

Among Jews hungry to learn, there was no need for the supervision of a pedagogue, and so with Benjamin setting out as usual to conduct the senior men's classes, father and son walked off the next day, hand in hand.

Sitting cross-legged on the floor in the middle of a large class of other wide-eyed, apprehensive beginners, small Shaul was relieved to find that what his father had told him was true, and that learning was made pleasant for the youngest boys. To begin with, they wrote the Hebrew alphabet in honey on their waxed boards. The children cleaned off the letters by licking them. It was fun, and gave meaning to the words the scribes would recite from the scriptures – *The words of God are sweet, like honey to my taste.*

Shortly afterwards the honey was exchanged for a pointed stick which scratched letters in the dark wax. Each boy kept tucked in his belt a smooth stone with which to polish out mistakes (preferably before the teacher noticed). After school the shiny pebbles made handy markers for various games of fun and skill scratched in the dirt. Shaul soon learned to clean his afterwards – having found that a dirty tool of correction made more of a mess than it fixed.

Rabbi Benjamin's son enjoyed school. That is, he enjoyed learning. He did not relate very easily to the other boys, being hampered by a strong sense of the fitness of things which was naturally at odds with normal childish pranks. Something of an oddity himself with his strange little habits, he was often baffled by the behaviour of others. Should the whole class be punished for the misdemeanour of one pupil he would be equally furious that any boy should flout the rules, and that any teacher could be so unjust. The rest of the pupils, far more pragmatic, laughed off his red-faced indignation as self-righteousness, an unjust taunt which scorched his sincere young soul.

As well as these obstacles to his peace of mind, early in his schooldays another form of suffering was imposed upon the child. With two Shauls in his class, the teacher must add their father's names to distinguish them. This was customary, and not even worth remark for the other boy, who rejoiced in the unremarkable name of Shaul ben Micah, but for Shaul ben Benjamin it led to all kinds of raillery which the new pupil found very hard to take. Already knowing Rabbi Benjamin ben Shaul, the bigger boys soon realised with delight the scope for entertainment in his son's name. *Shaul ben Benjamin ben Shaul!* It was too funny, in their eyes, and the other boys followed where they led.

"Shaul ben Benjamin ben Shaul ben Benjamin ben Shaul ...!" became a favourite taunt of mockers who would keep up the ridiculous chant until they saw his face flush crimson and his jaw clench – or until they spied an approaching adult – whereupon they were quick to laugh an insincere apology, "Sorry! I lost count!" The strain of such persistent derision told upon the rabbi's son, and he was too young to pretend indifference.

Those who disliked him – being secretly envious of his scholastic powers while openly scornful of his bodily insignificance – soon learned how to make the most of their opportunities. Often, outside of class they would block his way and before he could pass, demand his name in such jeering tones that more than once, paralysed by a trembling mixture of dread and confusion he answered with a stammering, "Shaul ben Shaul!" making them howl with unkind laughter. To his distress, their circular repetition of his name somehow stuck in his head, sometimes running around and around and around like a dog chasing its tail until he almost sobbed with frustration.

He did not tell his family of these ordeals, however. The very idea of doing so disturbed him. Rightly or wrongly he had a sense that it would be disloyal to admit that the name so proudly passed down to him was frequently a source of deep misery.

At least when safely in class he could be touched by no-one, and meanwhile the very intensity which had provoked the ridicule saw him progressing far ahead of the ridiculers. This private satisfaction increased his confidence, until at length their snide phrases no longer tortured him, fading from his mind if not altogether from his experience.

As time passed, although his burning sense of justice was never far away he learned to distance himself, to keep his vexations better hidden. Mixing with older children taught him to modify his peculiarities, outwardly at least, though he was still reluctant to make friends outside of his small, safe family circle.

Unsettled by chaos, the growing boy was calmed by order and found the increasing strictness of the more advanced classes helpful rather than onerous. As well, he was gradually becoming adept at using his tongue as a weapon, and his blistering responses to those who attempted to needle him eventually led to them choosing to avoid provoking his annoyance – most of the time. As a result, school now became less painful, even as the work became harder.

However, this did not prevent him escaping into daydreams like any other restless boy on sweltering summer days ... drowsy days when massed voices droning rote-memory passages could not drown out the longing to escape to the chilly shallows of the rapids just up-river of the city ... to paddle hot feet, to be splashed by refreshing waterfalls, to dip into little pools ... and to sprawl dreamily on baking rocks to warm up … before getting deliciously cold and wet again! Nor did his growing confidence make the lessons themselves any easier to master, especially now that numbering exercises and Jewish history were added to the subjects of reading, writing and speaking Hebrew.

Sand neatly smoothed on the floor at the scribe's feet made a writing surface big enough for all the class to see, but of course, a boy had to be sitting up straight and craning his neck to follow the workings of such an exercise. For a fidget like Shaul, who preferred to learn by listening (while wriggling all he pleased), sitting so rigidly was an ordeal only to be endured by escaping in his mind … whereupon should the subject be dull and his thoughts vivid, he would tend to go to the opposite extreme, becoming so still that sometimes his legs went to sleep.

His unpredictability was enough to drive his instructors to distraction, but they could not deny his intelligence; which however, had certain limitations.

"Make a note of this!" Bending down, the teacher wrote with his finger on the ground. His penetrating gaze roamed the class sitting cross-legged on the floor before him. "Shaul ben Benjamin!"

There was a smothered giggle from the front row and an unwise whisper of, *"Ben Shaul ben Benjamin ben Shaul ben –* Ow!" The miscreant rubbed his leg and shamefacedly followed the teacher's sternly pointing stick to slouch out of the room, as Shaul, who had been gazing through the high narrow window at softly inviting clouds drifting in a hot blue sky, came back to earth with a jolt.

"Yes, rabbi?"

"No doubt you know this lesson so well you can afford to be present in body and absent in mind?" the teacher said with ominous politeness, tapping his long pointer casually against his stool and sighing to himself. This strange boy's memory for words and facts was phenomenal, but why, oh why, would it not extend to the abstract matters of *Arithmos*? If only he could beat it into him, he would! But alas, pain did not sharpen young minds, and discipline, while essential, must always be cautionary not punitive. Thus it was written. Somewhere. Probably. He sighed again and reminded himself to be patient.

"You will come to the front and complete this sum," he directed firmly, though privately without much hope.

Groaning inwardly, Shaul uncurled his legs and obeyed, with only a wince and a slight stagger betraying the furious pins and needles which were now attacking his feet. He frowned at the figures written large on the floor, his mind a blank. "Forty and nine," he traced in the sand, guessing. There was a sharp rap on his outstretched hand. Shaul rubbed his smarting knuckles.

"The answer, please?" asked the scribe calmly of the class, neatly erasing the error with his palm.

"Fifty and one," the other boys chorused virtuously, and a few smug looks were exchanged. At least here the rabbi's son did *not* excel!

Shaul humbly brushed the sand smooth again, wrote the correct numbers, stumbled back to his place and sighed. *Arithmos* was not his favourite subject.

Chapter Four

"WELL, you should have been paying attention!" Deborah snapped unsympathetically when Shaul related the woes of the day. She had spent hours unsuccessfully rummaging through hot and dusty bazaars for a particular copper fire shovel her mother wanted and was feeling out of sorts. "If you tried as hard with your numbers as you do with your history, you'd be the head of your class!"

Shaul propped his chin on a lean brown hand and said dreamily, "History! I don't mind trying in history. It's not even trying. The things the Eternal has done for us! We must be the *best* people in the world!"

"*Some* of us might be!" she corrected with a short laugh, her habitual good temper already reasserting itself. "But just you remember," she could not resist adding in the superior tone of an elder sister, "Father says that *everything* you do at school should be done well, as a service to God, not just things you *like* to do. That's no sacrifice."

Shaul lazily flicked his reed pen at her. "That's easy for you to say, isn't it! You don't have to do sums – just a bit on your fingers at the market – and your life's easy, just women's work, fussing around the house, directing servants, wasting hours in the bazaar –"

Deborah jumped up with a cry of dismay at the blob of ink on her brightly embroidered shawl. "Now see what you've done! It took me days to stitch this pattern!"

Immediately contrite, the boy leapt out of his seat, upsetting his stool, which went over with a crash. "I'm sorry! But it's only weak stuff – watered down dregs, that's all! Look, give it here quickly and I'll pour water on it – that will get it out!"

Angrily Deborah pulled off the pretty garment. Shaul snatched up a stoneware jug next to a washbasin on the corner table and hastily tipped the contents over the inky embroidery. His expression suddenly changed. With a fearful glance at his sister he set down the jug with a bang.

Deborah, crossly rearranging the soft folds of her *chiton* overdress, turned impatiently as she pinned and clasped the last *fibula* to her satisfaction. "Well, is it coming out?"

Her brother looked at her apologetically. Deborah marched over to look. "Shaul!" she wailed in anguish. "Pomegranate juice!"

Although Shaul continued to complain about arithmetic, he enjoyed the challenge of increasingly demanding lessons, and worked hard. Long passages from the Holy Scriptures had to be memorised and repeated perfectly. Every square Hebrew character had to be perfectly formed. The very letters which formed the words of the sacred texts were to be respected.

"Remember," Benjamin would tell his son, "the whole purpose of learning Hebrew is to praise Adonai God in His own pure tongue!"

"Does God speak Hebrew, then, Father?" Shaul asked once, greatly daring, and wondering about it for the first time.

His father looked shocked. "What else would He speak?! Greek? Latin? The very idea is impious. Back to your work, my son, and no more irreverent questions!"

Shaul needed no encouraging. From his family he had inherited a love and reverence for his Creator, and though the process of learning was often tedious, he attacked his work (all except arithmetic) with a kind of hungry ferocity. The power and beauty of the words which soaked into his soul awakened an even deeper joy and pride in his Jewish heritage. There was no doubt in his passionate young mind that he would – he *must* – grow up to be like his father, a devout Pharisee, a fine teacher, a learned interpreter of God's Holy Law. If only he could study with the best of the best! But that would mean Jerusalem in the Homeland, and that was so far away.

As he and Benjamin walked home after synagogue they would discuss the lessons together. They made an odd pair, the tall, sedate Pharisee and his slight, fidgety son; but their love for the things of God was mutual and genuine. So entranced was the boy by the wonderful things his father told him and read to him from the sacred scriptures, that phrases such as *The Law of Moses!* and *The Faith of our Fathers!* sounded in his mind like the clarion call of silver trumpets, while words like *Holy Writ* seemed to hover in the air, hushed and reverent, wrapped in a protective cloud of incense. Their special tangibility to him was a comfort. It was to be many years before he realised that other people did not see the shape and hear the sound of hallowed words in the unique way he did, and though it faded somewhat as he grew, it lingered as a quirk of his senses which never quite left him.

Always a precocious student, blessed as he was with a quick ear and almost unnaturally retentive memory, Shaul was still only a boy when

Benjamin enrolled him in classes at the University for the purpose of improving his Greek.

"But, Father, why?" he protested, half laughing. "I admit my Hebrew is rather slow still – but only because I take so much care with it – and I only scrape through in Aramaic, but my Latin is passable, and my Greek is sublime!"

"Naturally," Benjamin said firmly. "Not only is it your mother tongue, but your father," he shrugged modestly, "has an accent as pure as any in Athens, or so I have been told …"

Shaul grinned, but a moment later his face fell as Benjamin continued fiercely, "However – the way you *write* your Greek, my son, is very far from sublime. It is, in fact, a disgrace! Chicken scratchings! Beetle tracks! A man must guess every second word! And what use is that? You can speak eloquently enough, oh yes, you converse like a sage, for all your untried youth – and so enthusiastically that it is hard for others to get a word in edgeways. But you must also communicate by letters, is this not so? And your spelling …!" Benjamin rolled his eyes in pained exasperation. "I cannot have a semi-literate son follow me into the family business! You will be sending sailcloth to Arabians and tents to Phoenicians!"

"I doubt it, Father," the boy replied confidently, ignoring the jibes about both his penmanship and his un-childlike eloquence, which he had heard before. "I am going to be a teacher at the synagogue, like you!"

Benjamin raised his eyebrows. "Only a teacher? It is a commendable thought, my son, but a Pharisee is not paid for his work – else why do I spend half my days at the warehouse up to my beard in shipping lists? While it is true that we who are rabbis find ourselves freely bestowed with lashings of respect, unfortunately we can't *eat* it! I was blessed to inherit the warehouse and a means of supporting myself – and later a family – in a way which did not compromise my passion for the Law. But if you do not care for a merchant life, then you will have to learn a trade, Shaul. I do not mind *what* trade – so long as it is not legally unclean, of course – for Adam himself was a gardener, and working with your hands is an honourable occupation. But you must choose one which does not fret the life out of you, so that you may calmly study and teach as a good Pharisee should."

"I had forgotten," his boy admitted, crestfallen, dismayed at the harsh realities which now intruded upon his splendid dreams. "Do you want me to take up an apprenticeship, Father?"

"No, no!" Benjamin replied with a smile. "Not yet! Your education comes first! And you must do better with numbers, eh? Afterwards we can worry about how you will make a living. But don't forget, my son, never allow your ambitions, however noble, to overshadow your responsibilities. If a man is not willing to earn his bread, he does not deserve to be supported."

Shaul nodded obediently, but his father had not finished with him yet, and Benjamin's eyes suddenly lit up. "Now that I think of it," he added enthusiastically, "it would be an excellent idea for you to take extra tuition in Aramaic – and Latin too. Not to speak of some philosophy and literature and so forth. Oh, yes, it is the wisdom of men, I know, and not of Adonai God, but if a Jew wants to be successful in this Gentile world, whether in business or in making proselytes, he needs to understand how others think."

"Oh, Father!" Shaul groaned.

But Benjamin's mind was fixed. Having persuaded the University to admit his son at what for anyone else might have been a foolishly young age, he was determined Shaul should make the most of it. Before he knew it, the boy found himself in the lofty halls of higher learning – and despite his professed reluctance, developing a keen interest in his new studies. In the mornings he studied ancient poets and philosophers, and during the long afternoons he valiantly scratched away under the basilisk glare of Tarsian tutors who delighted in complicated rules of grammar, spelling tests and long vocabulary lists.

As for his writing, it all changed on the happy day an elderly scrivener, working among dusty scrolls and codices in the university library, looked up to scowl at some heavy sighs which were disturbing his concentration. They emanated from Shaul, who was rubbing a sore neck and shaking a cramped hand as he laboured over a long session of copying. The old man shook his head at the youth and beckoned him over. Pointing out that there was no need to gouge his sputtering letters as if using a stylus on wax, he instructed him to keep his nibs well trimmed, hold the pen as lightly as possible and only caress the page, letting the ink – "*Good ink, mind!*" – do the work. The days of aching arms, ruined reeds and mangled quills were over! Shaul could not believe he had struggled so long with what should have been obvious. This single piece of advice dramatically improved his writing almost overnight. Now he could write easily for hours, and before much longer even Benjamin had to admit that his son had developed a quick, neat hand of which anyone could be proud.

His improved penmanship was no help to him, however, in those many evenings when the boy wearily ploughed his unsteady way through problems in arithmetic, overseen by Benjamin, who seemed determined to make his son as competent as himself, and preferably as agile as Grandfather Shaul.

"My dear old father! Such a nimble numberer! May he rest in peace," Benjamin would sigh, "if only because he cannot see how you strangle your sums! Else surely he would be rolling in his grave."

Benjamin was the kindest, most patient of fathers and meant well, but on this subject, as his wife chided him fruitlessly, he became extremely tiresome and repetitive.

Shaul the younger could not help wondering whether Shaul the elder had *really* been as 'number nimble' as he was made out to be; glumly wishing that he had been named for his *mother's* father, Asahel (who had owned a carpet workshop) instead. Then one day he realised that had this been so, Benjamin might have required him to be good at selling carpets, which could have been worse. Actually, it *would* have been worse, far worse, for then he would have to calculate fast enough to bargain skilfully – on top of persuading someone to buy! The mere thought turned him cold.

Though he was something of an academic prodigy – that is, in letters, not numbers – Shaul's tender age and strict upbringing inevitably made him withdrawn around other students, who were nearly all so much older. As a result he had little to do with campus social life, except for participating in occasional contests of *Calculi*, a grid-and-counter game relished by youths who loved to pit their wits against each other. One of his opponents, a young Jew impressed by the boy's intelligence, took him under his wing and introduced him to the more complex strategies of *Latrunculi*. Despite soon being outstripped at the game by his quick-minded pupil, Joseph ben Asa Nahath wasted no time in establishing himself as a good friend.

A Levite from the prosperous city of Salamis on the Isle of Cyprus, Joseph was also of a tender age to be at university, but being tall, confident and very independent in outlook, he seemed far more mature than his years. Well liked by Shaul's family, he was good humoured with a mischievous teasing streak, a wealthy student who was generous and pleasant to everyone and popular even with the tutors. He did not talk much about his own family except to complain that his father had been rather thoughtless in naming his firstborn Asa, after himself. Joseph and his sister Mari having arrived much later, Asa their brother was often assumed to be Asa their father – and took unfair advantage of it, or so Joseph felt. Later, the senior Asa took the name of his own father, Nahath, as a surname, which reduced confusion to some extent. Sibling harmony was restored, but Joseph was left with the opinion that families could be difficult, and most unusually for a Jew seemed determined to avoid creating one of his own. As a result he had something of a task to dodge various beady-eyed mothers (and sometimes fathers) who saw in him a potential catch for their daughters. He eluded them all, saying impressively to Shaul, "Just remember, my friend, there is more to life than domesticity and begettal!"

Being very good with numbers, Joseph made a point of trying to help his younger friend with the arithmetical problems which Benjamin, being concerned for Shaul's future, set him from time to time. It really did not help that Benjamin continually exhorted his son that he owed it to the memory of the Nimble Numberer and Founder of the Family Business (*'My-dear-old-father-may-he-rest-in peace-if-not-rolling-in-his-grave!'* and so on), to attempt more than the mere basics of calculating. 'Not to speak of' – alas, Benjamin did so frequently – the fact that it would render him more useful and less likely to be cheated by the unscrupulous, in whatever trade he later undertook.

Occasionally Shaul – and therefore, Joseph – would have a rare triumph when for a brief duration something clicked into place in Shaul's comprehension of a calculating process, and a beautifully worked sum rewarded them both with a correct answer. Shaul would bask in his father's astonished approval and accept the accolade that perhaps Grandfather Shaul might recognise him as a descendant after all. Meanwhile Joseph would be muttering, "Truly, thou art a *Shaul bar Shaul!*" into his ear in tones of such mock awe that eventually a tussle must ensue.

This good-natured foolery went far to taking the sting out of Shaul's earlier sufferings with his name. It even ceased to matter to him that Joseph being more accustomed to speaking Greek or Aramaic than Hebrew, invariably used the Aramaic *bar* ('son of') instead of the Hebrew *ben* – most of the time, anyway. Once Shaul would have found the trivial inconsistency agitating; but from the older youth, his first real friend, he was already learning the boyish art of nonsensical banter, and even that there was merit in being able, just occasionally, to laugh at himself.

For all his light-heartedness, Joseph had a decidedly commercial inclination and never missed an opportunity to trade. Apart from their games of strategy, his favourite form of recreation was to forage odd little stalls at the bazaars for interesting (but often somewhat worthless) items, for which he would invent amusing and sometimes outlandish uses, before selling them on to delighted fellow pupils for a neat profit.

How he did it was something of a mystery to Shaul, who did not have a commercial bone in his body. Sometimes he would listen to Joseph and his father happily discussing trade and attempt an interest, but the truth was that it turned him either bored or impatient. Inevitably his eyes would glaze over and he would twitch and fidget and sigh until his father would dismiss them both, or his mother would clap her hands and chase them outside, urging them to throw a ball, run races, or swim, or wrestle – anything other than talk!

"Can't you romp like normal boys?" she would scold, though with a smile lurking.

But Joseph not being prone to physical exertion and Shaul not seeing much point in it for its own sake, they would invariably end up wrestling in a different way, either in board games, or debates. Shaul, who found great satisfaction in thrashing out a matter, delighted in having such a fine opponent to hone his skills. Both quick thinkers and good with words, the two often battled over such mock-serious topics as 'All Sailors Are Not Superstitious', or, 'All Cretians Are Liars'. This last was a favourite, being a famous puzzle in logic, known as *pseudomenos logos*, posed by an ancient Greek philosopher and poet, Epimenides – himself a Cretian. They never resolved it, tussle as they would over his paradox, but then, neither – in the last six hundred or so years – had anyone else! But that did not stop them enjoying their debates.

It was not surprising that Shaul soon fell into a way of debating with himself, whether mentally to clarify his thinking, or in discussion to prove a point. Deborah admired him for it, saying it saved her the trouble of asking all the questions because he would ask them first and then answer them. Joseph boasted with a self-deprecating twinkle in his eye that it was purely due to *his* influence, while Benjamin privately assumed much of the credit – after all, it was the Pharasaic way to learn through question and answer!

Anna however, kept her own counsel, rightly believing that Shaul was too introverted to be readily influenced by anyone. She understood her boy – that he needed method and order in his thoughts just as in everything else, and that he had found this was the surest way of establishing his own premise or navigating an argument.

Nevertheless, Joseph did impress Shaul in one respect, in that he demonstrated an easy confidence of which his shorter friend was sincerely in awe. Would *he* ever have – or inspire – such a thing? Perhaps it was the older boy's generosity – not just of silver, but of spirit – a warmth and acceptance of other people … and young Shaul, who was inclined to be prickly, glumly wondered how he did it. It seemed nobody could help liking Cypriot Joseph.

Despite his habit of making money, the young Levite was not at all avaricious, and though he saved a little for reinvesting, and some for sharing delectable treats (toasted almonds in particular being his favourite), more than half his profits ended up in the synagogue Poor Box. Neither did his studies suffer, even though he did not seem to take his education as seriously as Shaul. For such a young man he had a charmingly avuncular manner towards all, young and old, and not an enemy in the world. The other students chaffed him with the nickname of 'Uncle', even those who were older, which he accepted with a lazy grin. He seemed quite proud of it.

All this puzzled Shaul. He was used to holding his breath when harsh taunts about his physical appearance were flung at his back by sneering street urchins. Yet the same urchins would crowd around Joseph smiling and holding out their grimy hands. Joseph told him not to take it personally.

"I don't, either, you know. Cupboard love, that's all," he shrugged. "They have to survive somehow, you see. If they thought such a scrawny young fellow as you had something to give they'd watch their tongues, no doubt."

Shaul snorted crossly. He had never aspired to be popular, but it was unpleasant to be actively disliked, even despised – especially by the despicable!

Joseph squinted at the shadow on his friend's upper lip. "Maybe when the whiskers win their struggle to survive you'll get more respect!" he suggested – and ducked a flying cushion so unsuccessfully that Shaul cheered up at once.

Outside of his friendship with the comfortable Joseph, Shaul remained socially aloof, preferring to read or dream and follow his own thoughts without distraction. *His* idea of the very best pastime was an intense discussion with his father, and many a night the two of them lingered on the rooftop (Shaul usually tormenting some long-suffering cushions, or pacing up and down the while) until the neighbours irritably hushed them or his mother threatened to lock them out.

Taking increasing pride in his son's growing understanding of the scriptures Benjamin finally ceased plaguing him with arithmetic, much to the relief of everyone concerned. If worst came to worst the boy must rely on an abacus – or his fingers! There were more important matters to teach a son growing to manhood – such as wisdom, self-governance, and sound spiritual discernment.

One such instructive evening, Benjamin recited a passage from his favourite psalm, telling his son that it was the best guide to life he would find.

"Better than the Commandments?" Shaul was shocked.

Benjamin considered. "In a way. You see, the Commandments tell us what to do and what not to do. But King David tells us *why*. If we don't know that, what good is the rest of it?"

Shaul was confused. "Obedience, of course! Surely that is essential, even when we don't know why. That is something you've taught me from childhood!"

"True, but how sad is a child who never grows up? We must not remain little children when the Eternal has given us so much more to know and love and understand. That would be ungrateful and foolish, spurning His gifts. David knew that we must go beyond mere blind obedience, and that means making an effort to understand, to accept and love what God loves. Then our obedience is more than outward show, because it comes from the heart."

Shaul groaned as he plucked at a sadly threadbare cushion. "Didn't the prophet Jeremias say the heart of men is full of deceit?! Yet David was a man after God's own heart, wasn't he – so how did he manage it?"

"Oh, I do not deny that it is always a struggle, even for the best of men. We all have what *we* want warring with what *God* wants. But I think the key is in the passage we have just recited together – David stayed truthful in his heart, so the Eternal, who *is* Truth, could work with him. He did not pretend to himself, or God or anyone."

"*Except* for the sin with Bathsheba," Shaul protested, thumping the dog-eared cushion by way of emphasis, "when he pretended to *every* one!"

"Yes, except for that – and it nearly killed him. He never made the same mistake again. So remember, my son, obedience is the start, but understanding is vital. If we do not understand the 'why', how can we, like David, tune our hearts in honest sympathy with our God? Now, repeat the words, and perhaps they will mean more to you."

"*Adonai, who shall ascend your mountain? Who shall stand on your sacred hill? He who walks blamelessly, who works righteousness, and who speaks the truth in his heart.*"

"There, you see? *Who speaks the truth in his heart!* That's true integrity. And the rest shows the actions of a man who is too aware of his own faults to point the finger at others: *He speaks no slander, does no evil to his neighbour, nor bears a grudge against him.* Yet he is discerning: *He despises the vile but honours God-fearers.* He is faithful: *He swears to his own hurt and does not change.* He is compassionate, honest and just: *He does not charge usury, or accept bribes against the innocent.* And the conclusion?"

"*He that does these things shall never be moved,*" Shaul answered slowly. Joseph – the words reminded him of his friend – confident, benevolent, devout Joseph. No wonder he had such comforting steadiness about him! It struck him for the first time that perhaps it was not just his friend's nature, but his choice. *True integrity.*

Hugging his cushion he frowned, muttering the psalm over again, thinking hard. Suddenly his eyes lit up. "Why, Father – all the Commandments are right here in this psalm anyway!"

"Aha! You see it!" Benjamin was proud of his son's perception. "Yes, trust King David to interpret the spirit of the Law – and express it so personally – he is a great comfort, I have always found."

Impatiently his son sprang up and began to pace the roof, mangling the cushion as if he would wring answers out of it. So intense was his concentration that he did not even remember not to go too close to the edge, where the parapet guarded an alarming drop to the courtyard below.

"But what of the Oral Law, Father? The collected wisdom of learned Pharisees? Is that not also about interpreting the Law?"

Benjamin scratched his beard. "Well, you know, my son, that has immense value of course. I would not be a Pharisee if I did not think so, though just between you and me I do not subscribe to the view that it is superior to Moses. However, unlike David's poetry, it deals more with examining *actions* than *intentions* –"

"So King David would not make a good Pharisee?!" Shaul interrupted, startled.

Benjamin cleared his throat. "H'm, well of course he lived in an age when prophets could be consulted directly, and the Spirit of Adonai God was with him, so he could discern spiritual matters more clearly, no doubt than even the most learned of us."

Shaul sighed. "And you have told me yourself that for every great man's opinion there is another which contradicts it!" Throwing down the persecuted pillow he stamped around it like Jericho. "What are we to do, then?"

Benjamin stood up and stretched wearily. "Hear this, my son. Heretical as it sounds, there are times when Godly compassion and common sense is less harmful than the most scholarly conflict. Come now – stop that prowling, you're making me dizzy – your mother is calling."

Shaul never forgot that conversation, and he locked the most striking words of that psalm, like internal phylacteries, deep within his heart:

Adonai, who shall inhabit your tabernacle?... He who speaks the truth in his heart ... who swears to his own hurt and does not change!

The months flew past. Shaul enjoyed his time at the University and was almost sorry when his studies there came to an end. Not long afterwards, Joseph returned to Salamis, but within a week had put pen to paper to tell Shaul of his mother's sudden death, and that his father was moving the entire household back to his birthplace in the Homeland.

Joseph's next letter was even more of a shock, for writing only three months later from a place called Cana, which he described as a stuffy little backwater, he told his Tarsian friend there would be no more confusion concerning who was the head of the family. Sadly and unexpectedly Asa Nahath was no more, and now Asa the younger had taken his place in earnest. An advantageous marriage was already being arranged for their sister Mari, while Joseph had been put to work in the family import business. Writing with uncharacteristic bitterness, he asserted that only his old nurse Esther, now serving as Mari's handmaid, understood how very miserable he was.

Shaul hardly recognized his once cheerful friend in these unhappy lines. He wrote back, but both of them being preoccupied and youthfully self-absorbed, their correspondence petered out over time. Shaul, however, with the next stage of his ambitions to pursue, had no time to be lonely.

As only the best students were accepted for training in the Jewish Oral Law, he returned to his synagogue lessons, revising and studying hard in the men's classes, proud that he was now no longer a mere schoolboy but a youth counted as responsible under Mosaic Law. He supposed that he would be undertaking formal rabbinical training in due course, but nothing definite seemed to have been arranged. He did not know that Benjamin and Anna had higher hopes for their son than even the best synagogues of Tarsus could furnish. Fearing disappointment, they had not yet revealed their plans to Shaul, or to Deborah, who was soon to leave them. A marriage had been arranged for her with a prosperous merchant from Jerusalem and her future seemed assured.

Shaul, with nothing yet said about *his* future, felt suddenly adrift. Deborah had been his most faithful friend all his life. Together they had played and argued, studied lessons and caused mischief, laughed and talked over everything. Now she was grown up. She would leave the family home and go far away to the Land once proudly known as Israel, now divided up into territories with Greek names and governed by the authority of Rome. To Jerusalem! Oh, he had long decided that when he was fully a man, he would take his sister on wonderful pilgrimages to the Holy City, with or without their parents – but had he imagined she would ever go there without him? Still less, for ever? Shaul buried himself in his books, refusing to count the days until her departure.

"Shaul, are you *still* studying?" Deborah whispered, coming into his room late one chilly spring night. In the yellow pool of light from a small oil lamp, Shaul was slumped over his table.

She shook him gently. "Wake up, little brother!"

The dark head jerked up. "I'm not asleep."

Then she saw his face – the damp streaks glistening on the thin cheeks so lightly stroked with dark hair. "What is it, Paul-Shaul?"

He rolled up his parchments and tied them slowly. "A daughter's duty is to care for her parents," he said defiantly, not looking at her.

"Yes, in want or old age," she answered gently but firmly, kneeling down beside him. "They are neither old nor destitute and they have you. Tomorrow I marry Simeon ben Gabbai and become daughter to his parents too. They *are* old, and he is all they have. I will be a comfort to them. And if the Eternal so blesses us, there will be children to bring us all greater happiness."

She put a loving arm around him and rubbed her cheek affectionately against his shoulder, not minding his silence. "We have had a good long childhood together, haven't we, Paul-Shaul? If Father had not been so particular about finding me the right man, I might have been married years ago."

Shaul looked critically at his sister. "Can you love him?"

Deborah reached for a blanket from Shaul's bed and threw it around his slight shoulders. "I would not be a true daughter of the Faith if I did not try to honour and respect my husband," she answered.

Shaul toyed with his stylus, digging long brown curls of wax from the tablet before him. "I said love."

Deborah smiled, and shrugged. "He is a good man, and kind. He loves the Faith. Yes, I will love him, in time. Were those tears for me?"

Her brother shook his head, but another drop suddenly slid down his face. Deborah stopped it with a finger tip.

"Taste," she said softly, touching it to his mouth. "See, it's salt. Tears wash away bitterness, Paul-Shaul – so never be ashamed to shed them."

Her brother attempted a dismissive laugh, averting his head as more traitorous drops escaped his brimming eyes to trickle down past his nose. He sniffed desperately, lifting his forearm to his face. Deborah clutched his arm in horror. "Shaul – don't you dare!"

He laughed, more surely now, and at once showed her the crumpled cloth in his other hand. "Sorry! You don't have to fuss over me – I'm all right. I'm just envious that you will get to the Homeland before me, that's all." He blew his nose fiercely, though his throat was choked and his eyes continued to fill, for he knew she did not believe him for an instant, and neither did he.

"Here, a wedding present," he added roughly, handing her something wrapped in a scrap of linen and tied with a blue cord. "I was going to give it to you tomorrow, but you may as well have it now. May it bless your new home."

"Shaul!" It was an intricately carved cedarwood *mezuzah* case, polished with sweet oil and lined with finest leather. "Oh, but how could you afford such a lovely thing?"

"Someone Father knows – Gaius Maximus – needed some fine copying done, so I did it, and he paid me what he thought it was worth."

"You must have done it very well then, this is beautiful work!"

"I thought you would like it. But you must find a proper scribe from the Holy Temple to write the lines of the *mezuzah* itself. He will purify himself before he copies the sacred words of the Law, lest the blessing be nullified."

"Thank you, my dearest, precious brother!" she responded with great emotion. "Simeon will take care to have it respectfully affixed to our door post, and we will treasure it always!"

Deborah hugged him tightly, swallowing her own rush of tears. How she would miss him! *May God watch over you, Paul-Shaul,* she thought, *and let us meet again some day!*

Chapter Five

IT was less than a year later when Anna hurried to meet her son as he walked home from the warehouse where he had been assisting his father's storeman in making up accounts – acting as *amanuensis* supposedly because of his neat penmanship, but in reality because he was far less reliable as a tallyman.

And as Benjamin was fond of reminding him, though Tarsus had been immune from Roman taxes since the time of Caesar Augustus, Tarsians themselves were not immune from those which were locally imposed – and that meant keeping careful accounts or suffering unpleasant consequences.

Thus enjoined to take great pains with his accuracy, Shaul was always relieved to escape after his stints of copying bills in the warehouse. Now as he took a deep breath of fresh air he was surprised to see his mother excitedly hastening up the street towards him.

"Mother! You should not hurry in this heat – is anything wrong?" Shaul fanned his mother laughingly with his parchments, for her face showed joy, not distress.

"No, my dear, I must not say a word! Your father has great news for you!"

"Then why does *he* not run to meet me?"

Anna smiled. "He is gathering the neighbours that they may share in our happiness!"

"Perhaps Deborah and Simeon are expecting a child," Shaul guessed. For their sake, he hoped so, as Simeon's gentle, elderly parents had since died, and there were no other relatives in Jerusalem.

Deborah had written cheerfully enough of new friends she had made, but nothing could be quite as secure and comforting as your own family, Shaul thought, as his mother excitedly bustled him through their gate into the leafy courtyard of the welcoming house. There stood his father, beaming all over his face as he warmly beckoned Shaul to his side, calling for quiet from the gossiping neighbours clustered around. Anna stood beside them with shining eyes while Rabbi Benjamin unfurled a sheet of creamy yellow parchment, a large seal in black wax dangling brokenly from its eagerly-snapped string, and held it proudly aloft.

"This, my dear friends, is a letter from Judaea," he began, his voice heavy with emotion. Shaul was now certain of his earlier guess, but Benjamin cleared his throat and continued, "It is a formal statement of enrolment, confirming that following stringent testing and strong recommendation by our Synagogue Elders, our beloved son Shaul has been accepted for training as a Pharisee – in Jerusalem!"

There was an immediate, delighted outbreak of admiring exclamations … and then Shaul's mouth went dry as his father added triumphantly, "Under the grandson of Scholar Hillel himself – Rabban Gamaliel!"

Everyone gasped and chattered and congratulated. Shaul, dazed, hardly heard them. His heart was racing! To learn at the feet of Gamaliel, renowned for his wisdom, descendant of Hillel, the great interpreter of the Law – it was such an honour!

Anna hugged him proudly. "You will stay with Deborah, my son! How happy she will be to see you!"

How he got through the intervening days Shaul could never tell – it was all a blur of excited preparation, until there he was on the wharf, with his beloved parents tenderly pressing final instructions and little gifts upon him. Benjamin embraced his son, and hung around his neck a small cylindrical leather case stamped with a simple design.

"What is this, Father? A new way to wear phylacteries?" Shaul attempted a laugh. "Wait – no, don't tell me it's an amulet!"

"In a way, it is, for it may afford you protection in unforeseen circumstances. Inside is an official copy of your birth registration, certifying that you are a Roman Citizen. The old wooden diptych is much too awkward a thing to travel with, and might be damaged or stolen."

"Thank you, Father. This is a valuable gift."

"Oh, yes, indeed. Your father had to pay good money for that piece of papyrus, so don't you dare lose it," Anna hugged her boy for the tenth time. "We gave one just like it to Deborah too, when she left. The case appears worthless so as not to attract thieves, but rest assured, the document itself is folded small, rolled up in waxed linen, and sealed for protection. You see, here, it is laced all the way round so it cannot come out unless you cut the stitching."

"Of course, you may never need to produce it," Benjamin said calmly, "but the world is a wide and ever-changing place, and a little precautionary wisdom is always in order."

Tenderly Anna kissed him, bravely resisting a maternal urge to cling to her boy and sob. "God be with you, my dearest, darling son." She smiled through her tears as fondly he returned her kiss, hugging her tightly.

"Yes indeed, my boy!" Benjamin's voice was not quite steady. "If God is with you, who can be against you, eh? Now, work hard!"

"That I promise!" Shaul embraced his father with with a ferocious hug which betrayed the mingled apprehension and excitement he was attempting to hide beneath an air of calm maturity. "I will make you proud of me."

Benjamin mopped his eyes and cleared his throat. "Ah my son, I am so proud of you already I am in danger of a mortal sin. There now. Go forth and do valiantly!"

To Shaul, the rest of the goodbyes to family friends and neighbours, the blessings, the promises to write, the waving of hands, the confusion of finding his place in the vessel, the short passage down the choppy Cydnus to the river mouth – all happened in a daze. All too soon they had left the relative shelter of the shore and the vessel had hit the Great Sea – which was hitting back. The next thing he knew was the sudden terror of clinging to a heaving deck, losing his breakfast over the side, and hoping he would not follow it to the bottom of this fearful deep. A blustering wind churning up the waves, the ship seemed to behave like an excited dog, plunging its nose eagerly into every foaming crest, joyously tossing lashings of spray over its back, and flinging itself vigorously from side to side as if attempting to throw its unhappy passenger headlong into the depths. Why, oh why, he asked himself bitterly, had he ever imagined that a sea voyage must be a delightful adventure?

He survived however, though somewhat to his amazement, for even after the sea calmed, every roll of the ship convinced him it would turn turtle, and many times was he cursed by the busy sailors as he instinctively ran from one side to the other in a fruitless compulsion to counterbalance the vessel. It was a relief to all when the pale slightly-built youth finally tottered down the gangplank at the magnificent, man-made Sebastos harbour which served the wealthy port-side city of Caesarea Maritima.

In no time at all he was captured, along with his box of belongings, by one of the many vociferous carters thronging its twin loading wharves, whereupon he was whisked away to Jerusalem – or so he enthusiastically if less than accurately wrote in his first letter home, the seventy miles of trundling up to the holy city in a wagon being rather more tedious and less speedy than he admitted. It was in fact a two day journey, and though he had expected to feel many lofty emotions during his first night on the Homeland soil, all he felt was exhaustion. He was too weary even for the discomforts of a roadside inn to keep him awake, though the next morning he found himself with a dawning appreciation for his father's dislike of travel. Still, what did that matter now, for Jerusalem was up ahead!

Jerusalem! A riot of thick limestone walls and buildings – dazzling white at noontide, glowing gold at sunset, shining silver under moonlight! A sprawling, exuberant city steeped in history, filled with noise and colour! Shaul loved it. To tread the very soil that God had chosen – to breathe the very air King David had breathed – it was intoxicating, wonderful!

How fascinatingly chaotic in character it was – sitting firmly astride its four hills, perched defiantly and almost precariously above its surrounding ravines! How different was this restless, landlocked city from sedate, spacious, orderly Tarsus beside its famous harbour! Yet in some respects they were similar, in that both cities showed Rome's military presence; and among the well-to-do, Greek customs of dress and behaviour were well established. Just as in Tarsus, lofty viaducts and aquaducts laced the city together, serving the needs of the populace, while in the wealthy quarters were private pools and lavish pleasure gardens. Jerusalem too boasted a superb display of Graeco-Roman architecture, which drew gasps from many a village-dwelling Judaean who came to the ancient capital for the solemn adventure of religious festivals.

However, such structures were neither novel nor awe-inspiring to a youth who had grown up in a grand city like Tarsus. Shaul was unimpressed by the Hippodrome which gave enormous crowds the spectacle of chariot races and lewd Greek theatre – and which was uncomfortably close to the Synagogue of the Freemen he attended with other ex-patriot Cilicians. As for the obscenely Hellenic Gymnasium, that was equally offensive to all devout Jews, and even Herod's imposing Palace did not pique Shaul's particular interest. It was the essential Jewishness of the place, its essential Hebrew soul he was looking for!

Benjamin's descriptions of how Jerusalem had looked in his youth, and the impressions that Deborah had attempted to convey in letters, were utterly inadequate to prepare the young man for what he experienced in the city of his forefathers. The dry, healthful air was invigorating in comparison to the humidity of Tarsus, and the place continually surprised him – the glow of its buildings in the mellow late-afternoon light, the craziness of its staggering streets in the lower city, the suffocating congestion of festival times, the sprawl of houses and shops wherever you looked, with hundreds of synagogues large and small scattered among them, and terraced vegetable plots sprouting in the most unexpected places.

There were streets full of industry; the gossiping Street of the Tailors, the delicious Street of the Bakers, the sour Valley of Cheesemakers, the noisy Place of the Coppersmiths, the bright gleams of the Brazier's Bazaar, the bleating Sheep Market, the rank Fish Market, and innumerable others, including a crooked little square with several cave-like, luridly lit workshops to which Shaul was drawn in fascination, asking many questions of the busy artisans within. There over small intense fires, exquisite glassware was created; melted and blown and fashioned by master craftsmen from blocks of raw glass brought in from afar. Finished pieces were arrayed outside the shops, where strings of colourful beads hung swaying in the breeze, tinkling and tapping against each other, catching the light, enticing the eye. Some were fine and fragile, iridescent, winking in the sunshine; others were heavier, patterned, textured, inviting to the touch and tempting as sweetmeats.

Shaul fingered the thick, polished edges of cloudy goblets, luminous as gems on display. He squinted through translucent platters for the charm of seeing the street turn dreamlike, distorted in shades of cobalt and aqua. It gave him a queer sensation of being under water in some lost drowned city of antiquity. Carefully he set down the dishes with a dull chink which reminded him of the pottery shards he played with as a child. He bought two little perfume bottles, bright as jewels, as gifts for his mother and sister, and marvelled at how the torture of fire could turn mere sand of the seashore into objects of such beauty. It seemed a fitting allegory of God's chosen people, lifted up from the sands of Egypt and smelted in the furnace of the Eternal – the Divine Master Craftsman at work, fashioning a people through many tribulations to be His precious treasures, individually beautiful, uniquely reflecting His light.

And surely out of all places, this place, this Holy City, was His crucible. Shaul could almost feel it. Here, the arms of Adonai God were about His people, here, where the scarred, ancient walls of Jerusalem soared high and strong! Yes, those walls were old friends, for he knew them intimately, and every one of the city's descriptively named gates, from the inspirational writings of Prophet Nehemiah – no matter how many wars, no matter how much pillage, tearing down and rebuilding had happened since then. Jerusalem abided forever! And the fact that he, young Shaul of Cilicia, stood right here, right now in the midst of its antiquity, was a witness to the faithfulness of Adonai God and His covenant with His chosen race.

How amazing it was to be able to walk around the city as he had done so often in imagination, to admire those walls, to number those gates! Now he could live out the ecstatic urging of the psalm: *Walk about Zion and go all around her! Count her towers! Note well her bulwarks! Admire her palaces! Tell it to the next generation after you. Cry aloud and shout it out, you who inhabit Zion, for great is the Mighty One Who is in your midst!*

Yet even as he sang these words under his breath with delight and paced out the length and breadth of the Holy City, the young man recognised that the soaring towers and private palaces before him were built for and by foreigners; they were not testaments to Israel's former strength, but to her present weakness. The Mighty One who was Israel's God, was no longer in the midst of them, as once He had been, for the *Shekinah* glory of the Eternal had long since departed as His prophets had warned; and in the Temple's veiled Holy of Holies, the resplendent heavy draperies hid, not the ancient golden Ark of the Covenant — but the fact that it was no longer there.

Yet appearances were to the contrary. On the east side of the city rose the impressive height of Mount Moriah, its gigantic plateau a monumental stage where so much of Israel's history had played out before wondering eyes. Here was the sacred site where Patriarch Abraham had been willing to sacrifice his only son; where repentant King David had witnessed the avenging angel stay his destroying sword; where Solomon's Temple had been raised in glory; where after many destructive years Prince Zerubbabel had laboured over a humbler replacement; where invaders had desecrated the rebuilt House of God, and valorous men had fought until they seized it back! And now — on the same ground, dominating the city, there stood its supplanter in shining, glittering splendour, thrown into artistic relief against the darkly verdant groves of nearby Mount Olivet.

All his life he had wanted to see it – but even as he looked at the magnificent architecture all around him, the rabbi's son was conscious of a faint, sneaking sense of dismay. Everyone knew what force had driven this colossal project.

It was a far cry from the religious fervour which had raised the Tabernacle in the Wilderness. No Aholiab and Bezaleel had been divinely inspired with special skills to fashion it. Neither had its contents been crafted from the devoted spoil of Israel's enemies, such as King David had stored up to build a house for the God Who had given the victories. There was no goodwill furthering the work as in the building of Solomon's Temple, when a Phoenician king had supplied materials, labourers and superior artisans – not merely for gain, but for love of David, and respect for his God.

But as for this present Temple, so long in building and still unfinished, there was no love involved in its construction. No jealousy for the name of the Eternal, no determined zeal such as had seized the returning exiles from Babylon who rebuilt God's House when it lay waste. No such ardent spiritual passion had sanctified *this* structure.

Herod the Great had built it. Glorious and beautiful as it was, fit for the purpose as it was, honoured, even, as it was, it was still Herod's Temple. A lavish complex designed with the genius of apparent simplicity, it was constructed on a bewildering scale, accommodating thousands upon ten thousands of worshippers. Ravishing the eye with its beauty, with its breathtaking sweeps of open courts, terraces, cloisters and flights of steps, it was a new wonder of the world, firmly planted – forever, so it seemed – on massive retaining walls of monolithic limestone blocks to rival the pyramids of Egypt.

All its magnificence notwithstanding, the uncomfortable fact remained that all this glory reflected the ambitions of a despotic and ruthless ruler who had sought to aggrandise and memorialise himself through spectacular public works. This modern crown of ancient Jerusalem, this vision of incandescent marble and glaring gold, like fresh mountain snows splashed with a host of scintillating suns, this resplendent Temple of God had been raised by a grubbing, godless Gentile. Craving public acclaim, he had attempted to engineer gratitude and approval from subjects who justifiably despised him. An Idumean! who had clutched at Jewish acceptance by marrying into its aristocracy – the noble house of the beloved Maccabees – which he then proceeded systematically to destroy. A king called Great, but never Good, whose long reign had been distinguished by the blood of thousands, young or old, who had provoked his wrath or insane jealousy.

In his early years he had executed more than half the members of the Great Sanhedrin, yet later, to buy loyalty, he had tiptoed around Jewish religious sensitivities to the extent of training a thousand priests as masons, so that work on the holy sanctuary might not risk defilement. The depth of this piety might be measured by his order that when he died, the leading Jews of the country should be rounded up and killed so that the whole nation might mourn – for he knew they would not weep for him. And this Temple was a product of that man.

All this and more went confusedly through Shaul's mind as he gazed upon the sights before him. Still, his heart could not help but rejoice at the numbers of black-robed Pharisees, with deeply fringed borders to their garments and conspicuous phylacteries lashed to their right arms and foreheads, praying on street corners; at the numbers of white-garbed Levites, with their neat linen caps, coming and going around the Temple precincts from their quarters on the nearby promontory of Ophel. His spirits lifted at the sight of purposeful priests in snowy calyx-shaped turbans – their plain linen ephods wound high with broad, intricately woven sashes tied with long trailing ends – traversing the terrifyingly high and narrow Royal Bridge over the Tyropoeon Valley. Such an ambitious structure! Such ease of movement from the High Priest's palace, across the ravine! Could King David, forever scrambling up and down the slopes of his citadel, only have seen such a thing! For Mount Zion, his ancient stronghold, to be so loftily connected to the great Temple for which he had so passionately made preparation ... surely such an amazing vision would have inspired another psalm, perhaps poetically contrasting the narrow path of the viaduct with the wide street so far beneath.

How appropriate was it, how graceful its arches, and how beautiful the whole scene! It seemed to express the solidity, the extraordinary immovability, the unquenchable flame of the Jewish Faith. A sudden throb of emotion caught in Shaul's throat. There was no doubt that even the most sumptuous synagogue in Tarsus could not produce such an intoxicating sensation of perfection, of rightness, of belonging, of knowing that *here* a whole nation, the Eternal's chosen people, worshipped Him in unity.

Thus his conflicting reservations about its builder sat uneasily with his admiration for the work itself; but eyeing with approval the dutiful worshippers thronging the broad public way below the bridge, he reminded himself that it was the heart of the individual worshipper which mattered more than the place. Did not Naaman the Syrian of old beg the indulgence of Prophet Elisha when he must worship in a foreign land? And Jews of the *Diaspora* - those dispersed from the Homeland? Did not all of them, his own family included, also worship in a foreign land, perforce? So he put his discomfort to one side and entered the staggeringly large courts of Herod's Temple with as much equanimity of conscience as he could muster.

There, over the course of many visits he watched the incessant movement around him, the ebb and flow of worshippers to its Courts, the work of the porters, the guards, the pervasion of priests and bustle of busy Levites, the sharp-eyed money changers and clamorous sellers of convenience offerings – doves, lambs, kids, meal and oil and wine. He was awed by glimpses of the High Priest in his richly appointed costume for glory and beauty, which was more gorgeous than he had imagined in all the years he had read about it. He was uplifted by the clear voices of boy singers mingling with the rich tones of the men's chorus; exhilarated by the Hebraic melodies sounding from massed musical instruments; stirred by the smells of incense, burnt offerings, and the sacrificial smoke arising in clouds above the marble courts; and deeply moved by observing and being part of the nation going about its worship … and so it was that gradually the dark drop of doubt began to disperse in the suffusion of heady emotions filling his breast.

No matter who had built it, or why – this was the place where Adonai God had decreed He should be worshipped, and here He *was* worshipped. Surely to worship Him obediently in humility and sincerity was all that God had ever asked, otherwise many faithful men down the centuries would have been cut off from their Maker through nothing but sheer circumstance.

So he gave himself up to accepting how things were, and in time the shadow of Herod faded from the Temple, its courts, its porches, its ceremonies and music and beauty. Now he could take pride in it, now he could rejoice as he marvelled at the fitness of its situation, this man-made place of worship so aptly overlooking the Creator's own handiwork – just over the intervening Kidron Valley – where rustled the beautiful trees and peaceful gardens gracing the ever-green slopes of Mount Olivet.

Chapter Six

SHAUL never forgot the impact of celebrating in this awe-inspiring sanctuary all the Holy Days and festivals of that first year – the days when he was a wide-eyed and eager young student among sage men and priests, avidly participating for the first time in his life in the complexities and richness of Temple services, so very different from worship in the synagogue. The first time he caught sight of the High Priest in full ceremonial garb left him almost speechless with emotion. To see in the flesh that splendid costume, something he had only read about, only ever imagined! And now, he was here, seeing it with his own eyes.

The Day of Atonement in particular affected him as it never had before. What a privilege to be in Jerusalem for *Yom Kippur*, this, the holiest day of all! To be *here*, on the one day in the year when the High Priest might pass from the Holy Place through the thick, weighty curtains which hid the Holy of Holies! To be standing in a Temple court amid a sea of sober faces pale with fasting, awaiting the reappearance of the High Priest with his smoking censer of incense in his hand! Alas! that the incense was wafted into an empty space. Alas! that the atoning blood of the sin offerings was sprinkled over only the foundation stone where the lost Ark of the Covenant once sat. There was no beautifully gilded sacred chest, no gleaming four-faced Cherubim stretching protective golden wings over a Mercy Seat … not since centuries ago … yet Shaul could see it all – beauteous and glowing in his mind's eye. It struck him then that this was the only place throughout the ages where any ordinary Israelite had *ever* been able to see it since it was first created and sanctified for the Tabernacle in the Wilderness. Even as it had been carried from camp to camp, the people had seen only a shrouded object. Its continuing existence they had to take on faith. In an indefinable way Shaul felt that to be some sort of consolation.

What he could see before him in the flesh, however, was the concluding ritual of the Scapegoat. Having struggled to a vantage point on the steps, he watched with a deep, reverent thrill, as the High Priest, wearing the simple white linen garments prescribed for the lengthy sacrificial ceremonies of this day, laid his hands upon the head of a live goat. Tapping its hooves restlessly on the pavement the puzzled creature rolled its yellow eyes as the High Priest formally confessed over it the sins of the nation. The national guilt thus symbolically transferred, immediately afterwards the animal was led away amid great rejoicing.

So intense was his identification with the ceremony that Shaul felt a palpable sense of relief as the goat trotted out of the court, from whence it would be taken by an appointed man to an uninhabited place, and there released. What mercy the Eternal showed His people! To remove the guilt of every failing and wrong deed of every individual in the nation, whether confessed, unconfessed or even unrealised – to carry away all their sins, far away into the wilderness, never to be seen again! Truly Adonai God was great, and greatly to be praised, and it was good to be one of His people, His chosen race!

This stirring, solemn day of national contrition produced in all devout worshippers a sombre, reflective mood, but soon afterwards followed a festival which lifted everyone's spirits, and to Jerusalem was sheer delight, as the whole city sprouted with greenery for *Succoth*, the entrancing Festival of Booths. Everywhere a shelter could be thrown up, or lashed together, in the street, on the housetops, on whatever patch of garden, ground or bit of terracing had the space, families made their little tabernacles and camped out in them as much as possible. Everyone managed to squeeze in somewhere, and the houses being emptied, the rustling, fresh-smelling frond-fringed streets were full of people in holiday mood, sociably chattering and sharing food, minding each other's business in the most enjoyable way, and smiles were everywhere.

After this came the rainy season, when the city seemed to sulk, wind-lashed and cold, wet, dank and dripping. Yet the Temple work went on, rain or no, and so did everyone else's, for life could not stop just because the weather was miserable – and it would not last for ever. Quite apart from anything else, the heavy rain was a divine blessing, else where would the crops be? So the wet was accepted with as much gratitude as the dry in its own good season, and in the middle of it all, the dark nights were happily enlivened by *Chanukah*, the Festival of Lights. Memorialising both a notable victory and a rare miracle, it had been added to the Jews' calendar around two hundred years earlier, after their warrior hero Judas Maccabee, 'The Hammer', had wrested back the Temple from the vicious grip of one Antiochus Epiphanes – a Seleucid king who had forced Greek culture upon the Land and ruthlessly outlawed Judaism.

The entire Sanctuary having been polluted by the defiling and bloody work of this abominable ruler, there was only enough untainted pure oil left to keep its golden *menorah* alight for a single day. Nevertheless the lampstand was faithfully lit for the Temple's reconsecration – and according to legend, its light burned for eight days, long enough to prepare a fresh supply. Ever since, upon the anniversary of the Dedication, Jews celebrated in their homes by burning *Chanukah* lights for eight days.

Shaul and Deborah as children had delighted in this festival, singing the victory songs, playing exciting memorial games, and vying with each other for the honour of lighting the lamps. However, it was the one which came next, *Purim*, the Casting of Lots, which was their favourite, bound up as it was with the giving of presents and the thrilling story of Queen Esther in Persia. Brave was Queen Esther! Faithful was Mordecai her uncle! Together they defeated a jealous vizier who had cast lots to determine auspicious days for advancing his scheme to exterminate all Jews. Not until too late did he realize he had cast them to his own destruction. What child would not relish shouting, "Blessed be Mordecai!" or, "Down with Haman!" as the familiar parts were read and noisily re-enacted in homes and synagogues! The Purim celebration may have seemed more rowdy than reverent, but it was still a devout thanksgiving. Even though Shaul was now a young man who had left childish things behind, he still enjoyed cheering Mordecai and hissing Haman, as did everyone, no matter what their age. The triumph of good over evil, and the execution of the villainous Haman and his sons, never failed to strike a chord of deep satisfaction.

As spring approached the city revived, casting off the pall of winter, welcoming the softer rain and the time of almond blossom. *Purim* came and went, and now Shaul experienced the ferment of his first ever Jerusalem *Pesach* – the days of Passover and Unleavened Bread. Commemorating Israel's deliverance from Egypt, it was always a time of expectation and sometimes agitation, for this was the time the ancient rabbis believed would herald the advent of Messiah – and national fervour rose to fever pitch. As devout pilgrims poured into the city from all over the Land, all over the Empire, it was also a time when the Roman governor gritted his teeth and doubled the guards, arrested as many potential troublemakers as possible, and hoped grimly for the best.

This year, however, there was nothing more serious than the usual skirmishes in the street as Zealots needled their enemies, hinted at plots, and gnashed their teeth at any provocation. Undisturbed by anything untoward, therefore, Shaul went to the Temple with Simeon, full of glad anticipation. Having ritually purified themselves, they were now bringing their own perfect Passover sacrifice – a small kid chosen with great care at a market where male yearlings had been examined, pronounced free of blemish and penned for four days according to ordinance. Now the two brothers-in-law stood in the crush of people with their animals, all waiting their turn for a priest who would stand with them as each household representative killed his own animal, catching its blood in a gold or silver bowl, passing it up the line to be flung at the base of the Altar of Burnt Offering. The smell of burning blood and fat was overpowering, and greasy dark smoke rose relentlessly into the air.

As each batch of animals was brought into the Court of the Priests to be slaughtered, silver trumpets blew a piercing triple blast. Down the side of the huge open courtyard, teams of priests and Levites worked steadily to dress the carcasses in accordance with the Law, and hand them back to their owners to carry home, while the inner fat was salted to be burnt on the Altar. All this while, the Hallal psalms of praise were being sung by Levites and Temple singers, the massed crowd of people singing back the responses – sometimes repetitions of the lines of the psalm, sometimes Hallelujahs, sometimes both – switching from one to the other unerringly out of long familiarity.

"When Israel went out of Egypt … Hallelujah!"

Though very willing to sing, Shaul had been floundering, not knowing which response should be sung where. *"When Israel went out of Egypt,"* sang the people. *"Hallelujah!"*

Having made several false starts Shaul took refuge in silence.

"O Lord, surely I am thy servant …" The line was moving along, the sacrificial knife put into the next man's hand …*"O Lord, surely I am thy servant,"* came the response from behind him, someone singing with

great feeling … less than ten men to go … whose hand would do the deed? Surely Simeon's! But Shaul held the leading rope.

"I will not fear what man can do to me …" The kid nudged Shaul's legs and bleated to him uneasily, nostrils quivering with the thick smell of charring fat. *"Hallelujah!"* Glancing down at its trusting ignorant face, all at once he felt his heart trip faster and quickly he looked away.

"I will not fear what man can do to me!" sang the passionate voice behind him. Shaul stared at nothing, agitated to find himself suddenly swamped with emotion. Was that even a *tear* welling in his eye? How so? He was here, gladly, to obey the Law! Beside him Simeon was singing loudly with the crowd, enjoying himself, his eyes on the singers. *"Hallelujah!"* Eight men to go. Seven.

"Save now, I beseech thee, Oh Lord …" The knife changed hands again. The massed voices repeating the words all around seemed to blur and now he could only hear the one behind him. *"Save now! I beseech Thee, Oh Lord!"* Six men. *"Hallelujah!"*

The kid bleated plaintively, nervously, nosing him again, more urgently, dancing anxiously on its dainty hooves. Five! Impulsively Shaul put a hand on the shaggy little head with its nubby horn buds – just as the stranger behind him had the same impulse, and putting out his hand accidentally covered Shaul's with his own. For a confused instant Shaul felt a wave of comfort wash over him, as if he had intercepted what was intended for the kid. Their eyes met, an amused smile, a shrug, and together they soothed the trembling little animal as the Court of the Priests sang around them and silver trumpets blared. Four.

The older man – not so very much older, despite his lined face – nodded at the head of the line. "Not long now." He turned to murmur to his own silent lamb, fondling its soft drooping ears.

Three. Shaul looked suddenly stricken. "Will you change places with us?" he blurted out and the other gave him an unfathomable look. "Gladly," he replied quietly.

Simeon was surprised when Shaul tugged him backwards but he understood completely as his young brother-in-law forced the rope into his hand, urging him almost in panic, "*You* must do it!" He merely nodded. *"Hallelujah!"* he sang with the others, totally unperturbed. Two men.

With a reassuring hand on Shaul's shoulder, the stranger stepped in front. One man.

"Thank you, friend. I was … we are … I am not quite ready," Shaul stammered rather incoherently, and the man turned, his dark eyes searching.

"You will be one day, my brother," he replied, with a curious smile. "Fear not." But now with a nod the Levite was beckoning him forward as he took from the last man the bloodstained knife so long and sharp and sticky. Laying his hands on the head of the lamb the stranger bowed his head, taking a deep breath.

"Blessed be he that cometh in the name of the Lord …" sang the priests and the boy singers. The Levite picked up his golden bowl and held it in position, the man took the knife, straddling the lamb, lifting its head, exposing the soft throat – and suddenly the deed was done.

"Blessed be he that cometh in the name of the Lord!" Shaul muttered the response, not caring whether it was in the right place or not; transfixed as the blood gushed forth; as tears rained down the stranger's bearded face while he cradled the slain creature in his arms. *"Hallelujah!"* sang everyone loudly, and now it was Simeon's turn … but Shaul had gone.

Later, at their commemorative *Pesach* supper, he apologised, feeling like a fool for having been so strangely affected, and in a way he could not even explain. But Simeon merely shook his head kindly. Of course it was understandable for a young fellow who had not been brought up to it. The crowds, the heat, the tension and excitement, the sight and smell of blood, and offal and burning fat; the noise of the instruments and animals and people, the hypnotic rhythm of call and response in the music, oh, all very orderly, but combined with the mass slaughtering it was an overpowering assault on the senses.

The first time *he* had been to the Temple with his own father had been horrific, Simeon said cheerfully. He had made an utter nuisance of himself firstly by throwing up his breakfast and then by passing out cold and his poor father had stumped home crossly with a lamb carcase on one shoulder and his little son a dead weight on the other.

"Poor dear Simeon!" Deborah said, laughing. "Fortunately for you he cooked the right one."

"You'll get used to how things are done in the Temple, in time," Simeon said, "However, you will have to slaughter your own Passover one day, so my advice is to find a good butcher and learn from him – and I know just the man. Since today is only the first of the Unleavened Bread you will have to be patient, but as soon as the holy week is finished, I will take you to him. That is, if you wish. Meanwhile, do not reproach yourself. I would be far more concerned had you found any pleasure in the taking of life."

Nevertheless, Shaul felt he had failed some kind of spiritual test. Was obedience more important than his own emotions, or not? He thought of the psalmist's words, *Who can understand his own mistakes? Cleanse me from secret sins!* A brave prayer, this admission that a man could not always interpret his own heart. How many men would dare ask the Eternal to show them their worst selves? Yet now Shaul humbly resolved to make this prayer his own, telling himself firmly that he could not control a fault unless he knew what it was. Unwittingly however, he did retain a blind spot, in that he stopped short of inviting his *sister* to point out his faults! Truth to tell, it had not occurred to him to ask, but had he been challenged, perhaps he would have replied that she needed no invitation, and perhaps he would have been right. Though Deborah always treated him with the deference due to a man, a brother, and a scholar of the Law, still she retained an elder-sisterly candour which Shaul respected too much to resent. In any case, he knew quite well it was just another fond expression of their long-standing mutual affection.

So Shaul prayed his prayers and privately attempted to face his faults. Despite various struggles with legal jots and tittles both in his books and behaviours he determined nonetheless to serve the Eternal with gladness of heart, for that too was enjoined in the Law – and the festivals so wisely and Divinely appointed were a continual reminder to men to lift their spirits to Heaven, despite all natural attachments to things of the earth.

Only seven weeks later came *Shavuot*, the Festival of Firstfruits also known as Pentecost, celebrating the dedication of the wheat harvest, when the people rejoiced before God with a sense of relief. It was a comfort to know there would be sufficient grain to feed them through the coming year, something nobody could take for granted. The weather had turned very warm and dry, and by this time Shaul, having reasoned himself into taking Simeon's sensible advice, had thrown off his initial squeamishness about blood sacrifices and was attending the Temple whenever he could spare the time from his studies. Not a Sabbath, a High Day, a holy convocation, or a Feast Day did the young man fail to appear in the Temple courts, and the strident sound of its trumpets announcing rituals of worship was sweet music to his heart. It was as if he could not get enough of its unique atmosphere where the beauteous physical met the glorious spiritual. He was drawn back to it continually, sometimes to to marvel at its splendour, sometimes to observe its rituals, and many times to relish deep converse with its learned men.

As for the city itself and its surrounds, at times when his head ached and his eyes were sore from hours of poring over his books, his refreshment was to wander its streets, where there was no shortage of sights to amaze – the gravity of the Tombs of the Kings, the extravagance of cedar-roofed palaces of dignitaries, the exuberance of gardens and limpid sparkle of pools, the contrasting starkness of the lonely Judaean hills in the distance, the extraordinary atmosphere which seemed to make even the commonplace special – truly Jerusalem was a place of wonder!

The wonder wore off eventually, as wonders do, but Shaul never stopped fiercely loving Jerusalem. However, as time went on he could not help seeing much unholiness in the Holy City, and the aggressive commercialism in the great Temple disturbed him greatly.

Chapter Seven

DEBORAH had welcomed Shaul with a fierce joy that betrayed her loneliness, for Simeon often travelled on business, and they had no children. She had made many new friends since coming to the Holy City, and was never idle, but as she said feelingly to her husband, there was nothing quite like having someone with whom you could comfortably share an old joke or those odd little family phrases, without having to explain things in tedious detail. And close as she had been to her parents and various girlhood friends in Cilicia, there was, after all, nobody quite like Shaul. Not only was he a continual fount of scholarly information (both useful and otherwise) he was one of the few people with whom she could enjoy an intelligent argument without the slightest touch of rancour. Always excepting Simeon himself, of course!

How grateful she was to have her beloved brother close by her side again! It was almost like it used to be back in Tarsus, except that now Shaul seemed to be more the older brother than the younger. But Deborah only smiled over this, as proof that he had grown up – in spirit, if not so much in body – at last. The men in a family were always in charge, and now that Shaul was no longer a boy, he took his position very seriously. In fact, he took everything very seriously. Strongly conscious of the hand of God in his life, Shaul determined to be worthy of his studies. Much as he loved the city, when stalking through the narrow streets to classes in the early morning, he was resolutely deaf and blind to the distracting, alluring bustle about him.

In class he endured long hours of concentration, seemingly ignorant that such a thing as physical comfort existed – so enthralled by the mental landscapes which opened before him that he even mastered his natural restlessness, channelling it into vigour of thought.

In this new discipline his early training proved to be invaluable. He had already developed sound study habits, and his background in languages gave him confidence with words. Conversations with his father had long familiarised him with the major works of former scholars, and in the intense classes Shaul flourished where some were left behind. His quick mind, reliable memory and boldly rapid responses served him well in many a session of testing questions where students competed for mastery and recognition.

Yet pride did not enter into his thoughts, only deep satisfaction – a sense that there was order, and an answer for every question, if it be sought with enough diligence. Sitting at the feet of the great man, avidly he snatched up his teacher's words, stamping them on his memory, tracing on his mind the patterns of reasoning and logic that were the mark of a Pharisee.

He was the delight of Gamaliel's heart. The first master of Jewish Oral Law ever to be honoured with the title of Rabban – *Our Teacher*, Gamaliel was growing old, and in the almost fanatical devotion of young Shaul to Pharisaism he saw real hope for a successor.

Watching him, the venerable Pharisee mused, "He is still very young … but experience in life will add wisdom to his knowledge … in time – yes, in time, he may yet become Rabban Shaul!"

Less liberal than his father, Shaul adopted the strictest standards of the sect, intent on correctly following every practical interpretation of the words of Moses as approved by the doctors of the Law. He did it gladly, wholeheartedly and sincerely, confident that he was honouring God, creating some sense of divine order in a lamentably incoherent state of religious affairs, and providing an example to the worldly and ignorant.

His sister soon became accustomed to the constant hand-washings, customs, restrictions and prayers. She even grew used to the regulation of her personal liberty by her young brother, who was scrupulous about certain requirements of female seclusion, no matter how inconvenient it might be.

"He always seems to know exactly what is permitted, denied or demanded by the Law on every occasion!" Simeon grumbled.

"So he should!" Deborah replied proudly.

During those years she supported her brother to the full, and behind closed doors soon established herself as an invaluable study partner. Of course it was not customary for Jewish women to be educated, but Tarsus had been a long way from Jerusalem, and even a Pharisee might defy tradition. Her father had warned Simeon before their betrothal that Deborah had been raised in a Hellenist home where she had been taught far more than how to run a house. Benjamin had explained with touching frankness that this had come about because he had privately despaired of a son to whom he could impart his knowledge. After all, he shrugged, for a long time Deborah looked like being the only child he and his wife would ever raise.

Simeon had at once, and truthfully, assured him that he might have found an ignorant wife anywhere if that was what he wanted; and that he had come a long way to find one who would be not only a woman of faith, but intelligent, useful and stalwart in business during his frequent absences. A virtuous woman such as Solomon had praised in his Proverbs, he said firmly. Listening shamelessly at the door, Deborah and her mother had sighed in relief that they had got away with flouting social normality. Meanwhile Simeon had privately congratulated himself on the double catch of being connected to a father-in-law who was not only a well respected Pharisee, but – wonder of contradictory wonders – at heart, a progressive man!

Now, both of Benjamin's offspring had equal reason to be glad of their father's unorthodoxy. Armed with precious, expensive, and bulky copies of the scriptures, and even heavier codices of scholarly interpretations, Deborah would hear the long passages her brother had committed to memory, throw him questions, take the opposing side in practice debates, and yet understand when he needed to be left alone.

"Wife! I should lock you in the kitchen!" Simeon groaned, though privately very proud of her abilities. "You're as much a Pharisee as Shaul!"

Never one to seek external approval, Shaul was oblivious to the praise of others, for he compared his progress only with his own standards – and Gamaliel's. His self-absorption and the intensity of his studies also rendered the youthful student blind to all hints, plots and traps laid for him by ambitious Jerusalem matrons with eligible daughters. Marriage as a pre-requisite of practical wisdom was an acknowledged duty for any who would set up as a spiritual leader of men, but Shaul was too much in love with his books even to theorize over such an alarming prospect at this stage of his life.

His sister tried to prod him occasionally but the only response she ever had was a sardonic recitation of the clapping game they had played as children.

"Who shall I marry? Who is for me?
Find my love and you will see.
A tall brown woman with blue-black hair
A foreign tongue and a green-eyed stare."

Deborah found it most irritating that her brother was able so easily to keep ducking his adult responsibilities, and gave him a dose of sisterly sarcasm.

"Oh, ho, funny indeed! That's a dangerous answer for such a very short man," she mocked, when he had been more annoying than usual. "Especially one who's afraid of heights! As if *you'd* ever love any such woman! You'd have to stand on a chair to kiss your wife."

Shaul only waved her away airily and stuck his generous hooked nose back in his books, suppressing a grin. In all future provocation, he continued to irk his sister with the same teasing answer. Eventually the mere mention of matrimony was enough to set him off, should Deborah be so unwise as to give him too meaningful a look at some socially critical moment. No longer bothering with the rhyme, he would merely start tapping out the rhythm – until finally she gave up all hinting as a hopeless task.

Perhaps it was just as well, she sighed to herself. If he ever married, be she tall or short (and certainly it would be far easier to find him a tall wife than one shorter than himself!) his wife would be a lonely woman, for once deep in his work, Shaul, forgetting meals, manners, and sleep, had no concept of the passing of time. He was quite capable of emerging at midnight from his industrious mining of dusty scrolls, hungry, in a mood to talk, and wondering where everyone was.

Where he would have found time for a wife was hard to imagine – but it was equally hard to imagine how any wife of his would have found time for her own duties – for when in the mood, Shaul would follow

Deborah or Simeon or anyone who showed the faintest interest, from room to room or wherever they went, meanwhile sustaining a relentless one-sided discussion on his latest topic. Many a time had Simeon, in a moment of non-attention which he called self-defence, turned around and almost tripped over his enthusiastic brother-in-law, who continued to hold forth oblivious to all else. His family was used to it, but others took time to adjust.

One day it happened that the husband of Deborah's closest friend invited Shaul to dinner. As so often was the case in these matters, the invitation had come about through some feminine conniving of which the males involved were quite innocent. The fact was that Joseph and Chavera, his much younger second wife, were very wealthy and had four daughters to marry off.

Chavera had already confided in Deborah that she was worried about her girls, for they were getting older all the time and who would ever meet their father's high standards? Joseph was insisting on finding sons-in-law who would be not only devout, but also intelligent and well educated, while being neither too poor nor too *old* for his daughters. As Chavera despairingly told Deborah, this was rather a lot to ask of *one* man, let alone four of them!

"You see," she explained, "my dear Joseph always frets himself lest his greater age and gravity should become a heavy burden to me as time goes by, which of course is utter nonsense, but he is such a thoughtful man, and he fears that fate for our girls. But there is far more to it than that, alas. I have only been able to give him daughters, but having lost his own little boys so tragically, he still craves a *son*, you see."

Her usually laughing eyes dimmed with tears. "It is not just because he is a member of the Sanhedrin that he wants a respectable son-in-law with all those good qualities. Pride has nothing to do with it, you know. What he wants is a young man who will be part of our family and affectionately call him Father – a good young man he can mentor, and love!" Chavera wiped her eyes. "Preferably one such paragon for each of our daughters," she added with a sad laugh.

"Yes, of course," Deborah said gently. It was no secret that many years ago, Joseph had left his home town of Ramah in heartbreaking circumstances. Others too had also found it hard to go on living in the districts around Bethlehem where their precious children had been so brutally slain. In Joseph's case, it was a horror later compounded by the loss of his first wife. Haunted by her failure to protect the newborn at her breast and the toddler hiding in her skirts, she had slowly lost her mind ... and a year later, drowned herself. All Joseph had left of those days were his nightmares, and under his sleeves some thick scars, the legacy of a *gladius* blade which had rendered futile a desperate fight to save his sons. Intense, solitary years of rabbinic study in Jerusalem had followed. Only later had come marriage to the blithe-spirited Chavera, which had brought joy and healing to his wounded soul.

"Of course, we don't want your brother to be *suspicious*, Deborah dear," Chavera said, giving herself a little shake and smiling again. "So I will suggest to Joseph that he asks Rabbi Nakkai too. Joseph mentioned in passing the other day that Nakkai seems to be quite impressed with young Shaul, and thinks he will go far. That is a good opening, don't you think? And don't worry – I will make sure that the girls are present for as long as I can contrive to keep them in the same room!"

Thus were their plans made, and now it only remained to be seen how they would succeed. The invitation duly arrived, and Deborah excitedly confided to her brother that she knew Rabbi Nakkai had also been invited to dine with Joseph's family. Shaul was honoured to be included in such wise and exalted company, she added happily. He was certain to learn much from them, and surely they must be interested in his prospects, or he would not have been asked.

Shaul was not particularly sociable, but this argument was hard to resist. Yielding to his sister's urgings, accordingly he went – and was gone half the night. Simeon calmly went to bed, but Deborah sat up anxiously awaiting his return and mentally swithering between twin visions, one appealing, one appalling.

Was he still talking to the girls' parents, being so admired, approved and mutually attracted to one daughter or another (Deborah did not mind which, they were all satisfactory), that they were even now happily negotiating a betrothal? Or was he lying bleeding in a dark alleyway on the way home, having been overthrown by a runaway horse, or kicked by a camel, or stabbed by a Samaritan? At last her patience was rewarded, when she heard the gate at a dismal hour, and ran herself to open the house door, her anxious eyebrows interrogating her brother even as he touched the *mezuzah* - his own gift - on the doorpost and kissed his fingers.

Of course she would not interrupt the devotion he would now murmur, though she herself did not take things so far. The touch and kiss was enough for most people – a respectful acknowledgement of the holy words within the *mezuzah's* decorative case – and certainly enough for a busy woman who was forever running in and out during her busy day. If she stopped to recite the *Shema* every time – even an abbreviated version as some did – she would never get a thing done. But Shaul was not most people. Therefore she waited as calmly as she could (wondering whether he had smiled upon either Hadassah, Abigail, Achsah *or* Miriam!) while he went through the entire lengthy ritual without leaving out a single, formal word.

"Hear, O Israel, Adonai is our God, Adonai is One.
Thou shalt love Adonai thy God with all thy heart,
And with all thy soul, and with all thy might.
And these words that I command thee this day, shall be upon thy heart.
And thou shalt teach them diligently unto thy children,

And thou shalt talk of them when sitting in thy house,
And when walking by the way, and when lying down
And when rising up.
And thou shalt bind them for a sign upon thy hand,
And they shalt be for frontlets between thine eyes.
And thou shalt write them upon the doorposts of thy house, and upon thy gates."

"I've been fretted half to death, wondering where you were!" she whispered rather crossly as soon as he had finished. "You're so late! Is all well?"

"Of course it is. Why are you still up?" Shaul touched a finger to his lips and tapped her affectionately on the nose. Taking the lamp from his impatient sister he stepped inside, looking fresh still, and beaming while she questioned him about his evening. A lovely family, he told her sincerely, who had been so fascinated with what he had to say about the relative merits of *Haggadah* and *Halakah* expositions, that they had simply refused to let him leave. Unfortunately Rabbi Nakkai could not stay long and was clearly full of regrets to be missing the full discussion.

As for Rabbi Joseph, there was not a high and mighty bone in his body, Elder though he might be. He had rarely interrupted, and without standing on ceremony had treated him just like a member of the family. At the door he had even mumbled some sort of parting joke about wishing Shaul could stay with them long enough to see him into the new tomb he was having built, and telling him exactly where it was, "just in case".

This last comment Deborah hugged excitedly to herself, refusing to countenance the possibility that it might just be a nonsensical product of the Elder having too much wine, or that his tone might have been somewhat ironic. Surely, rather, it was a significant remark (one most appropriate to any prospective son-in-law) and showed great promise! Heaving a happy sigh of relief, she collapsed into bed, to whisper triumphantly into her husband's ear that Shaul was really becoming more sociable at last, and who knew where it might end?

The next day she called on her friend, full of smiles, eager to hear from her lips what good company Shaul had proved to be.

"Dear Chavera! Thank you so much for your kind hospitality to my brother," she said confidently. "He had a delightful evening."

At first Chavera tried to answer politely but soon abandoned the attempt in favour of speaking with freedom, her eyes dancing with merriment.

"Oh, Deborah, dear, he is the most fascinating young man – far too high-souled and clever for us to keep up with – but in all honesty it was a *dreadful* evening!" She rolled her eyes and began to chortle. "He talked and talked and we couldn't get rid of him! The only thing I understood was something very pithy and exhortational, about making the right decisions in life, so at least I can't say the night was *entirely* wasted."

"I'm glad to hear it," said poor Deborah, watching her friend collapse into giggles. "What did he say? Obviously he was not making the best decisions himself at the time!"

Trying unsuccessfully to compose herself, Chavera flapped her hands helplessly, chuckling, "No, really, it was very good. He said, *'It's easy to make decisions when you know your values.'* Now, that *is* something worth remembering, anyway. But after that I have no idea what he was talking about. My poor girls were simply beside themselves, pinching each other black and blue just to stay awake, and eventually I took pity on them and sent them to bed."

Deborah covered her face with her hands and groaned, as her friend continued between giggles, "Poor Rabbi Nakkai has to get up for work at *dawn* you know, so he excused himself with a thousand apologies and left very early. But as for my dear husband, he is not as young as he was and he had been outdoors all day, supervising work on the new family sepulchre. For once he was far too fatigued to keep up a conversation, and with your brother doing all the talking, my poor Joseph kept dozing off and then nearly breaking his neck with a jerk if Shaul suddenly raised his voice to make a point ... oh dear, it really was terribly funny! So you see our cunning little scheme was all quite a disaster in the end. Joseph was absolutely *desperate* to retire, but your dear brother hardly drew breath."

"Oh, Chavera! I am so sorry! But why did you not explain and ask him to leave?"

"What? How inhospitable would that be?! You scandalize me by such a suggestion – or you would if I could keep a straight face! No, we just hinted as strongly as we could, and sent all the servants but one to bed."

"Oh dear, Shaul is impervious to hints. You need to tell him things very plainly. He never minds, you know."

"Impervious is the word. My shameless husband yawned and yawned until I thought he would break his jaw, then disappeared and returned in his *night* clothes! Eventually our clever manservant saved us by something of a subterfuge, naughty as it was. (Though I have my suspicions about who might have suggested it while out of the room.) He actually snuffed all the lights behind our backs and churlishly told us that they had run out of oil and he would *not* be crashing around in the dark to find more! I don't know *what* your brother thought of such impertinence, but at least it forced him to go home, else he would still be there talking while we all quietly expired around him."

Here her mirth won out and as Deborah could not help seeing the funny side in spite of herself, she joined in until the two of them had laughed themselves into hiccups.

Nevertheless, she was utterly mortified! Simeon positively roared with delight when he heard the tale, but she hushed him quickly, as Shaul was studying at the other end of the house. Resignedly she told her husband they must simply forget about encouraging her brother to marry, as shocking a capitulation as that might be.

"It wouldn't be much of a life for a woman to live with such a man, for he would either neglect her completely or talk her to death," she said despairingly.

Simeon winked. "*You* seem to manage quite well, my love."

Deborah scruffled his bushy beard affectionately. "M'm – but being a sister is a *very* different matter, much as I love him dearly. For one thing, I'm not stuck with him forever, and for another, I am blessed to have *you*."

"Ah, what a good answer," chuckled her husband, planting a kiss on her cheek, then holding a warning finger to his lips as Shaul himself, muttering over a thick codex, walked past the open door, appearing and disappearing like a mirage. They listened to his soft steps stalking the corridor and his startled grunt as he hit the wall at the far end. Deborah smothered a giggle as the quiet padding footfalls returned; again he appeared and disappeared without noticing them, and the pacing up and down continued.

Simeon smiled and shrugged. He was extremely fond of his brother-in-law, despite his peculiarities, and was proud of him too, and if this was how Shaul learned, then this was how he learned. At least there was no need to hound him to his studies – they were like meat and drink to him. But it would not be for much longer, for though a Pharisee should never stop studying, never stop learning, his discipleship at the feet of Gamaliel was nearly over.

They all were excited at the prospect, particularly because it augured a longed-for family reunion. Benjamin had written (with not a word about his demanding duties in both synagogue and business, or his general detestation of travel), to promise that when Shaul at last graduated from the School of Hillel, his parents would visit Jerusalem! There they could rejoice with them all and offer sacrifices of thanksgiving together at the Holy Temple – and even stay for the next Passover.

So Simeon and Deborah made many happy plans, and Shaul worked even harder at his books, longing for the moment when he might write exultantly to his proud parents and tell them their son was now a rabbi, a respected teacher of the Law.

Finally, the day came. Shaul went to the old Doctor of the Law in the morning as a disciple and strode home that evening as a graduate, Rabbi Shaul, dark eyes shining and a prayer of thanks in his heart. He could now take his place in society as a Pharisee should, instructing and guiding others to keep God's holy precepts! He would teach, and counsel, and perhaps even take up the kind of missionary work he had once discussed with Gamaliel, making full proselytes of God-fearers among the synagogues in far-away lands. Perhaps – or perhaps not, as these days he was not quite so sure of how he felt about it. The work itself was worthy, and he did not fear the travel, but appreciating the finer legal points of the revered traditions might be too much for people not raised with Judaism, and would it really be the best use of all his hard-won rabbinic knowledge?

Then the daring thought struck him that one bright day he might even be elected to the Sanhedrin – the highest honour – and become one of the nation's seventy two respected leaders of religion! A position usually reserved for grey beards, it seemed a long way off, but surely by industry and faithfulness to his calling he might achieve it sooner than anyone might expect. In that position, yes, he could really glorify Eternal God all the more, by guiding the faith of the nation, dispensing His divine justice, helping His people serve their Creator as they should!

Elatedly he hurried through Simeon's spacious house, looking for Deborah. He found her on the rooftop, standing still and quiet as the stars that blazed overhead ...

She turned, her face pale and set in the shadows. Wordlessly she handed him a letter. Shaul tilted the black writing towards the moonlight and read it slowly. He rolled up the letter, tucked it in his girdle, and drew a deep, unsteady breath.

"The Eternal One gives, and He takes away," he said carefully, though his voice did not seem to belong to him any more. "Blessed be His name."

Quietly he led Deborah into the house.

Chapter Eight

SHAUL returned to Tarsus to put his father's affairs in order, and to oversee the welfare of his mother, who was ill for a long time with recurring bouts of the fever that had taken Benjamin. Deborah sent them letters with Simeon's shipments which came to Tarsus from time to time. She reported that curious unrest was brewing in Jerusalem. A strange, ascetic, and solitary Levite had set up in the wilderness of Judaea as a prophet, somewhat after the fashion of Elijah. There he was predicting the coming of Messiah, and baptising Jews in the Jordan. Everyone was flocking to hear his powerful preaching.

Shaul, who had recently contracted fever himself, shook his aching head. Baptising proselytes was one thing, but baptizing *Jews?!* What madness was that? What the people needed was good, sound instruction in the Law! He shrugged when he heard that King Herod had executed the man.

Despite his own intermittent ill health, Shaul was kept busy. He had been asked to fill his father's place in the synagogue, he had the responsibility of his mother on his hands, and he was learning a trade. To take over his father's warehouse did not suit Shaul, whose restless spirit already felt confined at the sudden narrowing of his horizons. He also had justifiable reserves about his ability to handle the financial complexities involved. Instead, he leased out Benjamin's dry goods business, which provided Anna with a small but steady income, and apprenticed himself to an old weaver who had supplied cloth to his father for many years. There was no shortage of work available for a Tarsian tentmaker.

Some twenty-five miles behind the city of Tarsus stretched the east-west backbone of Asia, hundreds of miles long, heaping up vast swathes of the continent into massive mountains. These were the Taurus Ranges, wild and bitterly cold for long periods of the year. Here large flocks of goats grew long protective coats of thick hair, from which was woven a strong black fabric. Called *cilicium* after the region, it was particularly prized for tentmaking, since it had the peculiarity that when wet it swelled to become waterproof, and when dry it shrank, allowing air to pass through the weave. As well as tenting, cilicium had a great many other uses, from horse-blankets and coarse tunics to sails and rope, and being much in demand was exported all over the Empire.

Under the guidance of the master weaver, Shaul painstakingly learned his trade – how to set up looms and weave, how to mend and even make his own equipment. He also learned how to spin thread, though to begin with he always felt uneasy as he struggled with his lumpy black yarn. This he put down to his overpowering desire for perfection, for if ever he felt the long-cast shadow of a dismal old woman spinning prophesies of woe in the street, he did not recognize it as such. All he knew was that he must improve quickly, and as he did so, and his work produced smooth, strong threads his sense of anxiety faded.

Always keen to become more proficient, always eager to learn something new, Shaul took pride in every aspect of his work, and to his master's surprise and delight everything he did was quick yet painstaking. His soft scholar's hands soon became hard, his fingers sore and roughened with a thousand stabs as he mastered the art of using a large needle. This had an unexpected side effect which though minor took the young man a long time to accept without agitation.

Despite physical weariness, in the evenings Shaul had never stopped studying and writing, and it was not until too late that he realized many a fresh needle stab had become permanently ingrained with ink. Inadvertent though it was, to this over-conscientious Pharisee it was a humiliating betrayal of the command against making marks in the flesh. Though few would even have noticed the dark spots, from then on, having been made acutely aware of the hazards of combining his two occupations, he was very much more careful with both his ink and his needle. As a result he quickly became adept at stitching, and just as well, for there was plenty to do.

Now half Shaul's time was spent weaving, the other half in neatly sewing the heavy black lengths of material together for tents and awnings. Smaller pieces were sold for tool bags and sacking, floor coverings, or window shades – and some were destined to become burial bags for the dead. He learned something of leather craft as well, making his own protective palm guards which allowed him to force thick needles and lashings through the stiff fabric.

His master's eyes glinted at this developing skill, and he reminded Shaul that good money was to be made if he cared to branch out into leather tentmaking for the Roman army. This however Shaul would not do, extending his new craft only so far as to mend his own sandals, make his own phylacteries, and repair small household items. He also learnt patience, as he listened to the old man's tales over and over again.

"Did I ever tell you of the time the great Egyptian queen Kleopatra sailed into Tarsus to meet General Marcus Antonius?" he would ask with relish, as his eyes lit up with distant, well-burnished memories. "Only young, I was then, but –"

"You *saw* that?" Shaul had interrupted incredulously the first time. "You remember it?"

"Oh, who could ever forget such a momentous occasion! It was talked of for years! I was with my family in the market when all around people began eagerly pointing and running, and suddenly we were running too, down to the harbour as fast as we could to see what was happening. Men and women were pouring out of the city, crowding the water's edge, and I cried bitterly as I tugged at my mother's skirts, for now I could hear the sweetest of music drifting across the water, yet all I could see was a forest of bodies."

Shaul could not help grinning. "Aha, so you saw nothing after all!"

"Aha yourself, you young doubter, for my mother lifted me up with a kiss, and perched me on my father's shoulder and then I saw more than most, I'll warrant. Coming up the Cydnus with people excitedly following on either bank, was a sight so unbelievable it seemed to be straight out of a fable – a glorious, flower-strewn barge with purple silk sails – yes, silk *and* purple! Imagine! Its stern was gold, and its oars silver – now what do you think of that? How they flashed in the sunlight, rowing in time to the ravishing sound of flutes and harps which filled the air! Well might you marvel and so did we – it was all so magical, like a myth, a mirage! – but that is not the half of it.

"Closer it came, through the harbour mouth, with clouds of perfume and incense wafting to our astonished noses. Then, as the vessel slid towards us, we stared, gaping, at the crew so skilfully handling the ropes and rudder. Never did anyone see such sailors! – for all of them were beautiful children in the guise of godlings; every boy was a gilded Eros, and all the girls were bedecked as Nereides and Graces. Oh, such a spectacle! It seemed the gods themselves had come to Cilicia, and we were all speechless with amazement!"

Shaul smiled to himself. The story of Kleopatra's entry into Tarsus was a favourite with market-place storytellers, and no doubt much had been exaggerated over the years – but old Sempronius had not quite finished. The shuttle lay motionless in his hand as he lost himself in the past.

"Ahhh, yes! We all gasped, from the youngest to the oldest, for there ... bedizened with jewels and languidly draped upon a bed of the finest cushions ... a breathtaking vision within a vision! ... surely the Goddess of Love herself lay before us!"

"Are you sure, master Sempronius? I have heard some say she presented herself as Isis, one of her own deities."

"Isis?" Brought back to earth with a bump, Sempronius sniffed impatiently. "So, you would correct me, would you, and you a mere stripling? Pah! I tell you, we Tarsians hailed her as Aphrodite, and others said Venus, but that her mission was as Goddess of Love is beyond doubt, as later events proved, for everyone knows the General was well and truly seduced. It is true, of course, that I was far too young – alas – to fully, ah, *appreciate* that side of it, at the time. My excitement must have been purely childish, you understand. But when I shut my eyes I can still see her – an exotic, painted woman, gorgeously arrayed and glistening with gems, lolling under a golden canopy, fanned by golden boys. Even her body seemed to be golden, her skin glowing through gauzy draperies which fluttered in the breeze. I could hardly believe she was not some mystical creature of legend ..."

"Legendary indeed," Shaul agreed, but the old weaver had caught the amusement in his voice.

"Oh, I see – you think I am inventing, eh? Leading you on with a fine story just to watch your eyes bulge, eh?"

"By no means!" Shaul hastened to assure him. "But, forgive me, my master, surely you are rather too young to remember this event?" He bit his tongue before he could add, "Let alone in such detail!"

Sempronius frowned dubiously. Perhaps this was a compliment. Yes, no doubt that's what it was. But now he was confused. "I remember it clearly!" he said with a firmness he did not feel.

"Why, then, herein is a curious thing," Shaul replied politely. "You must be far older than you appear to be, for otherwise you could not have seen these marvellous events with your own eyes."

Sempronius scratched his head thoughtfully with his shuttle. "Could I not?" He put it down with a clatter, and counted several times on his fingers. "Well, perhaps you are right! But how is this? It is so clear to me! My father, my mother, my grandfather – we spoke of it so often on long winter nights!"

"Ah, then, no doubt that is why, and surely it is a credit to them that they have passed such wonderful memories, so wholly intact, into your safe-keeping."

"Well, well," Sempronius shook his head regretfully, looking lost. "I have shared my story many a time, for I have no sons to pass it on in their turn, and nobody has ever questioned it. But I did not mean to mislead anyone. All this time, it was so vivid, so real to me." He shrugged, with little sigh. "My mother's arms were soft, my father's shoulder hard … I recall that well enough, and that I was happy. Yes, I could have sworn I was there."

Shaul felt a sudden stab of guilt. What right had he to high-handedly rob an old man of a private treasure of such value, simply for the sake of satisfying his own compulsive passion for accuracy?

"It is of no matter," he said quickly, feeling rather ashamed. "You have described it so well that now I feel that I too was there! And you must tell me again, another time, until I remember every detail. Then perhaps it will be my turn to pass it down to others."

With a relieved chuckle, old Sempronious clapped him on the back, his cheerfulness quite restored. And as he took Shaul at his word, the tale was oft retold. It was not long before Shaul knew it by heart, and at the first mention of Kleopatra or General Marcus Antonius, his mind would slip free.

Working with his hands gave him time to think, to meditate, and, inevitably, to worry. Deborah's letters were not frequent, as she relied on Simeon's shipments to Tarsus to carry them, but of late they had become increasingly excited. The new wave of religious fervour begun by the Baptiser had not died with him. It was being continued by a very unorthodox preacher from the back streets of Nazareth, way up in the mongrel territory of Galilee, who was travelling the land, attracting vast crowds of the common people with his philosophies. At first Shaul smiled cynically when he read this.

"Such frauds arise from time to time," he wrote back to his sister. "They cheat the trusting and quietly disappear."

But he grew concerned when she replied that the man, far from disappearing, publicly engaged in verbal battles over interpretation of the Law of Moses with learned men – scribes and lawyers, Sadducees and Pharisees alike.

"And what is this unschooled fellow, anyway!" Shaul spluttered indignantly. "A mere woodworker!" He overlooked the fact that he himself was 'a mere tentmaker'. After all, *he* was above all else a Pharisee. *He* had studied at the feet of Rabban Gamaliel.

Tales of miracles – curing of incurable diseases, magical provision of food for the poor, and even raising of the dead! – came not only through Deborah's letters, but also by word of mouth from the superstitious merchant seamen who passed through Tarsus. Shaul found it incredible that his sister appeared to be increasingly tolerant, and worse, even influenced by such blasphemous lies.

One day he stormed into his mother's room, where Anna increasingly spent most of her days. The maidservant shrank into a corner at the sight of his scowl. Shaul was master in this house now and his moods were unpredictable, especially when he was unwell.

"Just listen to this, Mother!" Shaul jabbed fiercely at the letter in his hand. "*The Sanhedrin wants the Rabbi Jeshua* – look! She actually calls him *Teacher* now! – *wants the Rabbi Jeshua to be denounced as a traitor to the Roman Empire. If they do not succeed in pressing this charge, they will seek grounds to stone him for blasphemy.* Seek grounds?" He flung down the letter in disgust. "How is it they have to *look* for reasons when they have plenty already? Do you realise, Mother, that he actually claims to be the Messiah of Israel? The promised Saviour of our people? Your own daughter calmly reports this, yet says nothing against him!"

Anna held up a thin hand to calm him. "You are far away, Shaul. It is unwise to condemn a man you have neither seen nor heard. And as for your sister … how can you forget those years in Jerusalem when she studied by your side? I believe she knows the Law and Prophets as well as you, my son! The very fact that she does not denounce him outright herself, should make you think twice."

"She is emotional and unstable!" Shaul strode impatiently around the room. "Now that she is at last with child, it seems she is incapable of sensible thought." He made a dismissive gesture. "I do not blame her!"

Anna looked out of the window to the cool courtyard where a lazy fountain splashed in the shadows. "Ah, yes," she sighed. "You think just like a man!"

Shaul stopped pacing. "I hope I think more like God, Mother. It is what we are called to do!"

Anna shifted the pillow restlessly beneath her white hair. "You misunderstand me, son, which only proves my point!" Suddenly, she raised herself on an elbow and blurted out, "But what if – what if this man is what he claims to be!"

Shaul stared at his mother unbelievingly.

"Only think!" she continued breathlessly, her face flushed with excitement. "To be privileged to see the coming of the Messiah! In my lifetime!"

Alarmed, Shaul knelt beside her. "Be calm, Mother! You must not agitate yourself!" He took a damp cloth to cool her hot forehead. "You are ill – you are not responsible for what you say! When the true Messiah appears," he murmured soothingly, "he will reveal Himself first to the spiritual leaders of our nation – to those who are best fitted to receive him and humbly serve as his ministers! I pray God it *will* be within your lifetime."

Several months later they received two items of news. The carpenter from Nazareth had met his end, and Deborah and Simeon had been blessed with a son.

Anna died soon afterwards, content in the knowledge of Deborah's happiness. Alone and bereft in his empty boyhood home, Shaul wondered dazedly how his heart could feel so frozen when grief burned within him like hot coals. He had sorrowed deeply over Benjamin, but this somehow was different. All his adult griefs were freshened in Anna's death. It was as if he had suddenly lost, not one overshadowing shelter, but three – a father, a mother, and that indivisible identity summed up in the word *parents* ... and for all his unshakeable faith in God's word the Resurrection Day seemed very far away. He sought comfort in his memories, but one alone persisted in taking precedence, striking over and over. Her excited, flushed face, forever repeating the same words. *Only think! Only think! In my lifetime! In my lifetime!*

Shaul was dismayed to realise that an irritating cycle of repetitious thought had taken hold again, but told himself firmly that even if unrealised it was at least a good thought, far better than a schoolyard taunt, and if he did not dwell on it, it would fade the more quickly. Meanwhile, he wrote to his sister, and after observing the correct period of mourning, prepared to return to Jerusalem.

The subsequent voyage being rough enough to render him so totally wretched as to exclude all else, even coherent thought, the cycle was broken, and Shaul was able to watch the approaching Judaean coast with a sense of relief in more ways than one, feeling that some old, inner adversary had been ousted, and pitched overboard to the bottom of the sea.

Chapter Nine

THE colour drained out of Deborah's face as a thin, dusty young man appeared in the doorway. "Shaul! Little Shaul!" she gasped.

In two strides Shaul had her in his arms. Half laughing, Deborah clutched at his travel-stained cloak. "Is it really you?"

Teasingly he showed her the small cylindrical case hanging around his neck. "Proof enough?"

"Perhaps! But are you real?"

"Pinch me and see," he grinned. "Ouch! Brutal as ever – hasn't that infant of yours had a softening influence on you yet?" Affectionately he tugged a strand of her hair.

"Dearest Paul-Shaul!" Deborah hugged him again with a sudden rush of tears, and dragged him to a seat, her mood sobering quickly. "Oh, it's so good to have you here again!" She paused, then asked tentatively, "Tell me just this, before anything else ... did Mother ... suffer ...?"

"She died very quietly, without struggle, praise the Eternal. She sleeps beside Father. May they rest in peace."

"Until the Resurrection of the last day," she responded softly, wiping away tears.

Shaul glanced at her. "Yes."

His arm tightened around her as inwardly he thanked the Eternal that they were Jews, His chosen people, for whom death would not come as the end. To know that though worms destroyed their bodies, yet in their flesh would they see God! Oh, where would they be without that great Hope!

They were silent for a moment. Then Deborah collected her thoughts, and smiled again, squeezing his hand warmly. "Simeon will be so glad to see you again! We've both missed you – and all those noisy late-night discussions we used to have – and there's so much to talk over!" She stood up, motioning to a servant to bring water for her brother's feet. "But now you must wash and eat. Then I will introduce you to little Joshua."

"Joshua? There is no-one of that name in our family. For whom did you name him Joshua?" said Shaul, a little surprised, for he had half expected his nephew to be named after himself. But Simeon was a Judaean, and so perhaps he had followed the local custom of naming a child for a deceased relative. As the last of his family, Simeon had plenty to choose from, and Shaul felt slightly ashamed that he could not remember any of their names.

Deborah hesitated briefly as if not sure how to begin. "I – we – were very afraid, at first, Shaul. Poor dearest Mother lost so many little ones, as you know ... We would not name him at all before he had survived his first month. Then we named him for a very special friend ..." She busied herself with pouring him watered wine from a small pitcher.

As Shaul took the cup it suddenly dawned on him that Deborah and Simeon must have made many friends in the years he had been away. Perhaps she had spoken of them in her letters, and he had not paid enough attention. Noticing people had never been his strong point. Shaul smiled wryly, recalling how that Rabbi Nakkai from his student days used to say that the best teachers were also the best listeners, paying close attention to their audience. It was good advice, if old fashioned, but hard to follow.

Shaul finished his drink, wondering vaguely whether he would come across Nakkai again, now that he was home. Home? Yes, so it felt. It was not that Tarsus had so quickly faded from memory, but there was nothing left for him now in that city. And Jerusalem *was* home to every true son of Israel, no matter where he was born.

Just then there was a muffled slapping sound on the tiles in the *atrium*. A fat, red-haired baby crawled in, looking happily expectant. A long string of dribble swung from his chin, and a soggy cloth trailed behind him, leaving damp smears on the floor. His eyes lighting up at the sight of his mother, he scuttled towards her with great determination.

Shaul grinned. "Aha – at last, someone in the family who's shorter than myself!"

"Joshua!" Deborah wailed. "Oh, you naughty boy! Where's your nursemaid? Oh, Shaul – I did want you to see him all clean and beautiful and just look at the mess he's in!"

Shaul only laughed. He squatted beside the child, tapping him gently on the nose with one finger. "Greetings and salutations, small person," he said politely, but Joshua knew fingers were for only one thing. He grabbed it gratefully and bit hard.

Shaul slipped easily into his old place in the household, and the very first Sabbath after he arrived, Simeon urged him to make his home with them.

"Now that Benjamin and Anna are gone – may they rest in peace – we need you all the more, my brother," he said in his kind way. "We are rather pitifully short on relatives here!"

"Are you not growing your own these days?" Shaul quipped good humouredly.

"We are doing our best," Simeon said with an answering smile, "though it is a somewhat slow way of acquiring *adult* relatives! But, in truth, we should stick together, don't you agree? Unless you have plans for a family of your own, of course …"

Shaul shook his head and pulled a face. "In Tarsus I had my fill of matchmakers, Simeon! Marriage is an honourable thing – it clearly suits you and Deborah – but since you are generously offering me a home, you should be warned that you may be stuck with me. I have always been something of a Job, you know."

"Ah, I understand, you have made a covenant with your eyes, eh? Well, that is a rare and admirable thing."

"Perhaps – but not as admirable as you might think, for the truth is, firstly that I hardly notice anybody when I am thinking, which is most of the time; and secondly, I have never yet seen a woman who made me want to look twice."

He moved restlessly around the room, fidgeting with various objects, picking them up and putting them down again, running his fingertips lightly over the walls and furnishings, as he confessed himself, somewhat reluctantly, as if to get it over with.

"I know full well that it is incumbent upon any one who aspires to spiritual leadership to marry and raise a family. I do not doubt that a wife and the experience of fatherhood must teach a man many valuable lessons, furnishing him with greater wisdom, compassion and understanding so he may better guide others. Yet I am somewhat ashamed to admit that the very thought of marriage makes me feel smothered. No doubt I am too self-centred. However, with the pleasure and honour of being part of your household I may at least learn much by observation."

He smiled a little. "You and Deborah will have to teach me by your good example, and I will have to learn paternal skills through being a good uncle. Just as long as I don't have to deal with anything *sticky*."

"Agreed, gladly!" Simeon said warmly, adding with amusement, "I, too, prefer to avoid the sticky side!"

But Shaul had not quite finished his rare disclosure. He added, "And there is one other thing – I have dreams of travelling throughout the Diaspora one day, encouraging and assisting synagogues to make full proselytes of their Gentile God-fearers; and how practical would that be, exposing a wife and family to the perils of the road? Or leaving them behind while I took risks? Let alone supporting them! As my father once said, receiving respect as a teacher is all very well, but you can't *eat* it."

Simeon laughed, while Shaul permitted himself a smile and a shrug. "If I am to serve my God wholeheartedly, I must be free. You know me by now, I think – I can't do two things at once and do them both properly."

"It's not always easy!" Simeon admitted with a grin. "But it is good that you know your true self at such a young age. That kind of wisdom will save you much hardship in the long run, I am sure."

Shaul stopped prowling, picked up a scroll and began to search for an elusive quotation. "It is too late this evening, but tomorrow I will pay my respects to Rabban Gamaliel, and ask his advice on what I should do here. I'd like to know first hand how the Council is dealing with this Nazarene sect, which still seems to be making trouble. Something will have to be done about it."

"Be careful," Simeon cautioned his wife later that night. "We don't yet know his mind – he has only heard rumours, after all."

"He must know," Deborah answered quietly, "and very soon. I'm frightened, Simeon. He will embrace us, or reject us, one or the other. I know Shaul – there are no half measures with him."

The next day, an agitated Shaul returned from his meeting with Gamaliel, Nakkai and several other elders, a strained look on his face. He stalked through the house searching for Simeon and Deborah. He found them in the airy *triclinium*, a dining room which opened on to a pleasant internal courtyard. Sitting with them were their household servants, and a large group of ill-dressed people who were strangers to him. It appeared they had just finished a meal. Astonished, Shaul drew Simeon aside.

"Who are these people? Do you eat with servants and entertain beggars?"

"Does not the Law command us to befriend the fatherless and widows?" Simeon raised his eyebrows inquiringly, signalling behind his back to Deborah, who calmly took her guests and servants through the courtyard, and with a few murmured words ushered the entire company out of the house by another door. They left quickly and quietly, and Deborah returned to the adjoining room with a thudding heart.

Shaul turned heatedly to his sister. "You have not told me the half of what has been going on in Jerusalem! I had no idea how many have been taken in by the claims of the Nazarene! The people are in turmoil – they even stole his body and declared it had been divinely resurrected! They are not the slightest bit confounded by the fact that he is nowhere to be found, because according to them he has been carried up to heaven – like Elijah, I suppose! Or translated like Enoch, perhaps!"

Deborah opened her mouth but he gave her no time to interrupt, his suppressed anger bursting out.

"It is blasphemy! Blasphemy! I wonder they are not struck down where they stand! But Adonai God must have a purpose in restraining His wrath – if only to see, as in the days of the Exodus – *Who is on the side of the Eternal? Let him step forward!*"

Now his eyes were blazing beneath their heavy brows, and his voice rose in an uncompromising tirade. "Look back through history – it is always the same! A crowd-pleaser is dead so they make a martyr out of him – and all the more do the ignorant and self-deceived seek to perpetuate a memory and justify a crime! The whole Sanhedrin tried to suppress this evil, and they are all despised for it by mere commoners who owe them honour! All despised, that is, except for Rabbi Nakkai – who has actually turned his back on reason and followed the rabble. No wonder he has lost his seat on the Council. Premature senility is the best excuse I can make for him. He even approached me with some nonsense about being born again of water and spirit!

"I told him to his face that I would not listen to such pagan mysticisms. And to think I used to hold him in respect as a man of wisdom! Oh, and did I mention old Rabbi Joseph? When I asked a porter where might be, he looked downcast and merely shook his head, saying I would never see him in these chambers again."

Shaul's mouth twisted in a sarcastic smile as he paced up and down the room. "Naturally I assumed then the rabbi was in his sepulchre – well, perhaps it would be better for him if he was! I knew the place so there I went, minded to add a stone and pay my respects – but if he was ever there before, he wasn't now. The door was rolled away and inside was empty. It made no sense to me, for had he died a while ago his family might already have collected the bones, but there wasn't even an ossuary. I would have thought the tomb was still unused, had it not been for the broken mortar around the opening and a lingering smell of spice. So, to clear up the mystery, I went straight back to Gamalial to ask what *had* become of Rabbi Joseph."

Shaul's face darkened and he began jerkily to pace the floor, chewing his lip, speaking angrily. "And it was then that Gamaliel told me the old man was not dead, but had been *excommunicated!* And for what? For treating a majority decision of the Sanhedrin with contempt! Rabbi Joseph! Did you *know*? Why did you not write me of this?! He and Nakkai had actually conspired to flout the Council by saving the executed Nazarene from Gehenna and burying him like a prince! Joseph's instigation, they say, else Nakkai would be gone too. Oh yes, Gamaliel told me everything. They were watched! They had somehow managed to take him down from the cross themselves, teetering on a borrowed ladder, awkwardly prising out the nails as carefully as if he could still feel it, with borrowed tools such as they had never before used; embracing the naked corpse as it slumped heavily on to them – yet in all their finery they supported it in their arms, covered in his sweat and filth and blood, blasphemously and deliberately defiling themselves on a Holy Day! Unspeakable! Unbelievable!"

Now he strode even more furiously up and down the room, while Deborah and Simeon stood as if turned to ice.

"They are preaching 'Messiah crucified' everywhere – *crucified!* Cursed under the Law! The Messiah? Can you imagine – a despised, degraded, humiliated Saviour? As for the Eternal raising such a man from the dead...where is he now, then? Tell me that! Delivering us from Rome? Is he? Well, is he?? Words fail me! It is utterly incredible!"

He swung around and lifted a clenched fist.

"I swear to God I am on His side!" he shouted passionately. "I will not sit back and denounce this heresy with mere words! I will act! I will bring these followers of Jeshua bar Joseph to justice no matter what it takes! Oh, a cunning man! No doubt he deliberately took the same name as the successor of Moses, so the weak-minded might imagine he led them to some promised land! I thank God he was executed – I am only ashamed that the Council was too timid to stone him as the Law demanded!"

A protesting wail suddenly rose in the air.

"You've woken Joshua," said Deborah faintly. She moved to the door.

Shaul leapt forward suspiciously and gripped her arm. "Joshua! Jeshua! Named for a very dear friend?" he shouted, almost beside himself.

Gasping, Deborah tore free and fled to her child, leaving a delicate silk shawl ripped in Shaul's grasping fingers. Simeon took a step forward.

"She is as your mother now, Shaul," he said, staying calm with an effort. "As your mother and your sister, if not as my wife, she deserves more honourable treatment from you."

Shaul searched Simeon's face as if he would read his heart. Trembling, he said, "You, Simeon – who are usually so outspoken – you and my sister have said nothing – *nothing* – to condemn the corruption in this city … surely, even you …"

Deborah came running back with little Joshua bundled in her arms and pushed herself between the two men.

"Yes – even us!" she cried defiantly. "It's true! We are followers of Jeshua of Nazareth! We believe that he is the Saviour, the promised Messiah, the crucified Son of the Eternal, now raised to life and sitting at the right hand of God Most High! Can I confess him more clearly? We wanted to tell you everything – all that has happened here – and all the miraculous wonders we have seen with our very own eyes! We hoped to convince you – but you have already closed your mind and hardened your heart."

"No, Deborah!" Shaul paled, his stomach churning. "No – not you! You who have learned the Law and the Prophets at my side – an enemy of the Living God? A blasphemer who deserves stoning – like the rest of them?" His voice rose despairingly.

"*Listen*, Paul-Shaul!" Tears of anguish burned in Deborah's eyes as she reached out to him.

"No!" He shrank from the contamination of her touch. "I have sworn to obey Almighty God and I will not turn back! It is the Law … *Slay every man his brother and every man his companion…* So He commanded! Yes, and someone must be prepared to act upon it! *The family of the rebellious must cast the first stone …*"

"That was for idolatry!"

"For rebellion! For blasphemy! They are one and the same!"

"But I am your *sister*!" Deborah pleaded.

"We are enemies! I have sworn!" he gasped, a sudden wave of dizziness sweeping over him. "Verily, even to my own hurt! I am on God's side …" and he slumped to the floor.

"The fever he had in Tarsus!" Deborah dropped to her knees beside him as she anxiously felt his forehead. "He warned me he was afflicted in this way – it won't pass for some hours – help me, Simeon! I sent all the servants around to brother Nakkai's house for safety."

Together they lifted Shaul to a low couch and covered him with his own cloak, for he was shivering, despite the hot flush on his skin. Deborah knelt beside him, pulling her ruined shawl from between his fingers to wipe away the sweat which suddenly poured from his face. Small Joshua crawled away to a corner and knocked over an elegant Greek vase, but they hardly heard it break.

"The move to suppress the Nazarenes is growing," said Simeon quietly. "Persecutions are coming. The Master told us so himself – that families would be divided."

Deborah shivered slightly as she looked down at her brother. "He *will* bring us to judgement," she said flatly. "I know it."

Simeon gently took both her hands in his. "We must leave Jerusalem at once, Deborah. Shaul will not compromise what he firmly believes is right, not even for you. He may even deal more harshly with us to prove he is not partial."

She leant her cheek against him. "Oh, Simeon!" she choked miserably. "He is so wrong!"

"Then we must pray for God to open his eyes." Simeon lifted his wife to her feet and kissed her. "Now make haste. We must be off tonight before he comes to himself again, and there's much to do. First I must run to Nakkai's and warn the servants. They can flee with us or stay, as they think best. None of them must suffer on our account. And I'll have Nakkai tell the Twelve that the house is to be used for the brethren at their discretion should Shaul leave. I doubt he will want to remain under our roof once he has recovered."

"But meanwhile? We can't leave him like this!"

Upending a box of reed and quill pens on his writing desk, Simeon pounced on a stray stick of lead, and began scribbling a hasty note, recklessly scrawling it in large letters over a fresh sheet of papyrus. "Don't worry. I am already summoning a physician. And I will send someone to care for your brother until he is stronger, just as soon as we are on our way."

Deborah scooped up Joshua. "On our way to where?" she asked wearily.

"Does it matter? Wherever we go we bring the light of the gospel. This is in God's hands now. Take courage, my love. His Son is with us, and the angels are on our side!"

Chapter Ten

SIMEON and Deborah left the city just in time. From then on, persecution against the followers of Jeshua the Nazarene began to gain momentum. At first the High Priest and the Council tried to suppress the teachings of his followers quietly, hoping that the whole affair would die down. But the mushrooming sect of the Nazarenes refused to be silenced.

Shaul was intensely frustrated by the inability of the elders to contain such widespread religious rebellion. The Law demanded the death of false preachers, so there should be no doubt or delaying – only swift action! The ringleaders, Shimon bar Jonah with Jacob and Johanan Zebedee – and all who supported them – should be tried, condemned and executed. He found it hard to accept even the pragmatic words of his old mentor Gamaliel, who was aware that there were plans afoot to dispose of these passionate disciples of the Nazarene. Standing up in the Council, the aged Doctor of the Law soberly advised the assembled members to do nothing in haste.

"Fellow Israelites! We should be extremely careful about what we do with these men. Their sect has a new name, but it is not a new cause. Since the days of the Maccabees there has been no shortage of zealots, self-appointed prophets and messiahs, raising false hopes, stirring up revolt in our country – causing nothing but bloodshed and misery. Even within living memory there have been men who made themselves out to be Somebodies of great import to our long-suffering nation – men such as that Theudas who led astray around four hundred souls, and later there was Judas the Galilean, inducing his band of idealists to resist the Census. All came to a violent end, as even this Jeshua did. What few followers escaped, quickly melted away! The same will happen with these Nazarenes!"

There were grunts and nods of approval. The tall, gaunt old man slowly raised one hand, gnarled and deeply veined with age, his voluminous black sleeve falling back to reveal a bony wrist and narrow black phylactery straps criss-crossing a scrawny forearm. Lifting a warning finger, he cast his hooded eyes around the great chamber, addressing the semicircle of elders with a forcefulness which belied his physical frailty.

"But, mind ye! If what they preach should turn out to be true, then Adonai God will be on their side! Take note, brethren, that these men are not common zealots. They do not preach taking up arms against anyone, and neither do they seek glory for themselves, only for the dead man they revere. Verily, their claims attempt to turn our religion inside out, and we should be deeply concerned! But while they threaten hallowed traditions, rather than national politics, I tell you this: that if you respond with violence you will beget it to our hurt. I say again, if it be of men nothing will come of it, but if it be of God, then you will not prevail – and who would fight against Almighty God? Leave them be – they can do no lasting harm. Time will sort this matter out!"

The room rumbled with muttered responses all around. At the back the elders murmured and argued with each other in low voices, and at the front where their disciples sat cross-legged on the floor, there was much wide-eyed whispering. In the midst of them, Shaul, his eyes like flint, was grimly silent. He could never endorse such reasoning! It was sheer pragmatism! Refusing to see the logic in it, he was sickeningly taken aback to hear such temporising from the master he had held in such honour.

Surely it was willing blindness for Gamaliel to say the Nazarenes were not politically motivated! And even if they were not *now*, how long before they *would* be? Everyone had heard something of the rumours breathed into eager ears and even now circulating throughout the city ... that the Zealots were doing their best to infiltrate the sect which called itself the Way, trying to persuade members to transfer allegiance from their executed leader, to join with them in their various schemes to overthrow the Romans and reclaim the entire Land as their own. To do nothing as Gamaliel advised was only to sit back and wait for another bloodbath.

Meanwhile, far from melting away, the Nazarene movement was growing every day, and Shaul regarded it as a disgrace that swift retribution was not forthcoming. Claims of miracles performed by the executed Jeshua's disciples further infuriated him, while making not the slightest difference to his opinion. After all, even pagans had faith healers! It proved nothing, in his eyes. What mattered far more to him was the perversion of God's holy word to suit the purposes of a minority.

He was still not exactly sure what the group hoped to gain from their stubborn beliefs, or how, since they claimed to be peacemakers not warriors. However the fact that they flagrantly accused the nation's most pious spiritual guardians of murdering the Messiah of Israel was more than enough to fan his wrath. They must be stopped, or surely a judgement would come upon the Land! And if persuasion failed, then the Law of Moses *must* be invoked.

Since Procurator Pilatus, a stickler for correct protocol, had been recalled to Rome, it would now be far easier for the Sanhedrin to do their duty than it had been. The interim governors, turning a blind eye to religious rulings, rarely stirred from the delightful port city of Caesarea Maritima – another impressive work built and ingratiatingly named by Herod the

Great. Not only was it the administrative capital of the province, but its fresh seaside air was far more salubrious than Jerusalem's in more ways than one. Impious men were wont to joke slyly that the only Mosaic evidence in Caesarea was something they might walk all over with impunity. In this they referred to its tessellated floors and paving, a proportion of which showed high craftsmanship and low morality in roughly equal balance. With many such dubious pleasures to hand, the governors' disinterest in the tedious religious animosities of the Jews' holy city was unsurprising – and a distinct advantage as far as the Sanhedrin were concerned. Without an over-zealous Procurator breathing down their necks, this time there would be no need of Roman endorsement of a Jewish death sentence, no arguments about whose jurisdiction held sway!

This last was a significant point which Shaul – not content to leave matters to any moderate greybeards – was at pains to emphasise in all private exhortations and discussions with fellow Pharisees and scribes. If they needed an energetic young man to stir them, to provoke them, to light fires under Nazarene vipers' nests, to smoke out Nazarene scorpion burrows, then he was the one! Did they not see there was no time to lose? This was more than a squabble about interpretations of prophecy! The whole fabric of the Law was in danger if the heretics were not silenced – and upon the Law reposed the security of the nation. Not just spiritually, but physically, for the one led to the other! Surely they must learn from the horrors of the past, from the terrible judgements the Eternal had inflicted upon them for unfaithfulness. Must Jews be exiled yet again, for turning a blind eye to apostasy? The idea was unthinkable! Better to have civil warfare than to lose the Land!

Continually in and out of the Temple courts, Shaul spent his days discussing tactics with fellow Pharisees and lawyers, befriending scribes, even exchanging views, somewhat stiffly, with selected Sadducees. From anything like true companionship he remained aloof, mistrusting human sentiment. Hotly passionate as he was for his cause, his bearing toward individuals remained coolly distant and few cared to cultivate a warmer acquaintance. At night he stalked back to his cramped lodging house – a far cry from the comfort he had been used to all his life – and in his wretched room lit a lamp and immersed himself in his books, thanking God that he could afford to keep them, so long as the trickle of income from the lease of his father's old warehouse still supported him. He studied and planned and made notes, thought hard and prayed harder, with rigorous fasting to discipline his lonely body and clarify his racing mind. He had long been convinced that the body was only something to carry the thoughts around, but there were times when it seemed to have a contradictory voice of its own, which must needs be silenced. And he read widely, both sacred texts and uninspired writings, meditating on the ingenuity of the Maccabees and the persuasive wiles of a certain Judith; the machinations of Rachel and Jacob, the stealth of the Jericho spies and the cool lies of Rahab; the bluffing tactics of Joshua, the double-dealing of Jael, the slipperiness of David, the cunning wisdom of Abigail, the sheer genius of Hushai, the daring, sword-wielding feint of Solomon, and of many more who had by deceptive means conquered great evils down through the ages.

The misery of his living conditions and the estrangement from his loving family was hammered firmly into the background by the repetition of uncompromising aphorisms. *He swears to his own hurt and does not change!* Having chosen them deliberately, he welcomed rather than resisted their continual revolution in his mind. *Belief is Peace!* With his family gone, what else had he to live for except to serve the Sovereign Law-Giver? To keep the flame of Truth burning? What else was there? He would fight for the purity and holiness of the Faith of his fathers! And since this was a holy war, he told himself firmly, he had to be prepared to get his hands dirty.

In populous, sprawling Jerusalem, there were hundreds of synagogues of every size, and Rabbi Shaul heatedly urged the Council to put spies in all of them. Meanwhile he visited as many as he could, attempting to dismantle any sneaking sympathy for Nazarene beliefs before it could germinate into deluded faith. In the Greek-speaking Synagogue of the

Freemen he stirred up many a heated disagreement with the Hellenist Jews there, challenging followers of the Way at every opportunity. And if there was no opportunity he would create one with affronting, damaging imputations. His particular target was a young Nazarene named Stefanos, a powerful preacher who was said to be a great worker of miracles. To Shaul, the only miracle was that the fellow unaccountably managed to frustrate the most rigorously reasoned arguments on every occasion. But such public arguments were only the outward attempts to discredit Stefanos. Beneath the surface of synagogue life many other small fires had been quietly set, and were smouldering nicely, ready to burst into flame when sufficiently fanned.

Passover approached and the tension in the city was palpable. The learned sages had long held that when Messiah came, he would reveal himself at this, the nation's foundation festival of deliverance! It was hardly surprising that there had been all that hysteria over the Pretender the previous year, with the excitable populace waving palm leaves and hailing him with exulted *Hallelujahs* and *Hosannas* as he entered the city! It seemed there was always something brewing at this emotional time of the calendar – but what would happen *this* year? The real Deliverance? Or more conflict? Would the Zealots flash their swords, would there be a Roman blood-letting? Would the Nazarenes make more trouble? Or would there be blessed peace?

Once more there was wild speculation amid the semi-orderly confusion, as pilgrims poured in from all over the Empire, the city was crammed with people, and swathes of tents sprawled over the sward of nearby slopes, right up to the priests' barley field in the Kidron Valley. As usual, it seemed that the whole world had gathered at Jerusalem, and no wonder. If the Restoration was finally to come at Passover – and surely it was close, according to the Prophets – who would want to miss it!

It was at this highly significant time that the hot-blooded young Pharisee, self-appointed defender of the Faith, finally out-did his hated adversary in the Freemen's Synagogue, weaving an argument of such complexity that it became a public interrogation which subtly trussed up the genial, gracious Nazarene with his own words. Oh, Shaul knew full well that this Stefanos was an upright young man in all his ways, an Israelite in whom there was no guile, and whose good works were above reproach! He had not attended the same synagogue for months without becoming aware of this. He also knew in his heart that it had been an unfair contest, a lawyer's victory, won through skilled debating tactics which had little to do with scripturally refuting the young man's beliefs. But what did any of that matter? The fact was, the man was a blasphemer, and however it was done, the end would justify the means. So Nazarene Stefanos was at last hauled up before the full Council on a charge of blasphemy. Now justice would at last be executed! Shaul felt a huge sense of relief which almost overwhelmed his feeling of personal triumph.

Despite this involuntary pride of accomplishment (which he did his best to quash within his breast as an unworthy emotion) it was not all his own single-handed doing, by any means. The Sanhedrin had made sure that there would be no such clumsiness as had marred the trial of Jeshua bar Joseph the previous year, no more awkwardly contradictory witnesses. The campaign against Stefanos had been designed and led by Shaul, but it was a concerted and complex effort. Past attempts to deal judicially with the chief disciples of the Pretender had ended poorly. It was clearly of no use to swoop upon them, gaol them, or forbid them to preach. Inexplicable escapes had happened which their followers rejoiced over as divine miracles. No, this time there had been more thought involved, more caution. Stefanos was an ideal target, looked up to by all Nazarenes, but he was not one of the twelve Galileans who were leaders of the movement. He had no influential friends among the hierarchy of Judaism, and was a late-comer of lower rank, a Hellenist, moving in circles which more rigidly religious men found offensive. If he was accused, it would be easier to push through a conviction. Especially with the right witnesses.

Shaul had done his work thoroughly, engaging apparently blameless men to ferment rumours, men who murmured in the ears of the Synagogue of the Freemen's elders, provoked anxiety among the members, and caused the very scribes who handed Stefanos the scrolls from which to read and reason, to look at him with uncomfortable doubt. Of course, they all loved their dear Stefanos. And his preaching was excellent. Most worthy! But had he introduced the slightest whiff of foreign incense to their place of worship? Was there just a hint that he could do without Moses? That Jeshua the hero of Galilee was perhaps more significant than Adonai God, the Eternal? *No smoke without some fire,* so the word went around in sibilant undertones and it was true enough too – except that the smoke was a mere screen, and issued not from warm-hearted Stefanos but from a hot-headed Tarsian firebrand.

Now Stefanos was arrested. Now the news flashed around the city like lightning. Now the people poured into the streets from all over, hastening towards the Temple precinct. Ever thickening crowds flocked together, assembling outside the great Hall of Hewn Stones, which opened into the Temple grounds at one end and the common street at the other. The double doors to the street were left ajar, a nod to the claim that Sanhedrin Justice was open and above board; and Jerusalem took advantage of it. Filling the porch, clogging the steps, straining their ears to hear, passing along whispers of what somebody closer to the doors had heard, the simmering crowd hissed like a cauldron.

Inside the Hall, the charges were laid, the preliminaries were hastened through, and Shaul had stated his case. The witnesses stepped forward, wisely keeping their statements brief, emphatic, and in harmony with each other. Stefanos had spoken blasphemous words against Moses, against God, and perhaps even more grievously, against the hallowed place of worship. Stefanos had set at nought the Law! Stefanos had declared that Nazareth Jeshua would destroy their holy Temple, and change all the sacred customs which Moses himself had delivered to them!

Shaul looked over to glare at the prisoner, and stiffened with indignation. Was the fellow not afraid? His face was calm, radiant, joyful, as if he had heard something glorious rather than a damning indictment! Was he actually glad to speak in such a notable gathering, proud to have his day in this venerable court of Law? Did he seriously imagine he might coax or contrive an acquittal?

The High Priest stood up slowly. "Are these things so?" he grated ominously, intoning the formal question with frowning deliberation. "The accused will make answer!" Ceremoniously he raised his palm in judicial invitation to the stocky, simple-garbed prisoner, and solemnly resumed his seat.

Sitting with the other witnesses, Shaul prepared himself to listen to the defence, a mocking smile flickering at the corner of his lips as the Nazarene earnestly addressed the Council.

"Men, brethren and fathers, I invite your attention," the young man began respectfully.

"Your deferential manner will get you nowhere!" Shaul thought. These Nazarenes were mostly ignorant commoners, and no matter how slippery Stefanos had been in synagogue, he could not hope to impress the learned Council with fawning speeches. Here Shaul was arrested in his train of thought ... inconvenient honesty forcing him to admit that there was nothing either fawning or ignorant about this Stefanos. Well then, bold and arrogant? No – he was irritated to realise that this did not fit either. Now he was forced to listen to the steady, clear voice intelligently relating the story of their nation from the days of Patriarch Abraham to the days of their first kings ... Relentlessly demonstrating that running right throughout in Israel's history was an ugly common thread of stubborn spiritual blindness ... Reminding them that even in the glory days under David and Solomon, the nation misunderstood the nature of their worship ... Reciting the words of Prophet Isaias which plainly stated that the Most High God did not dwell in buildings made

by man. *Implying* that since this was so, then speaking against a Temple built by Herod could not be blasphemy!

Oh, very clever! Shaul clenched his jaw as he saw a few disconcerted looks flit across faces in the room. Could they not recognize this was an argument of straw not substance? Isaias had been quoting from Solomon's own prayer at the Temple dedication! A prayer which was full of impassioned pleas to the Eternal to hear the appeal of Jews who prayed towards the Temple, even when exiled for their sins. A prayer which God had honoured, for here they were today, in the Land again! If that did not demonstrate the sanctity of the Temple, what did?

All this raced through Shaul's mind, but now – unexpectedly – the Nazarene had paused. The dark eyes flashed over the stern-visaged assembly, and the firm voice was raised at last. Swiftly drawing together the threads of his defence, so suddenly that some gasped, he twisted them into a noose!

"You stubborn men – uncircumcised in heart, heathens in hearing! You are still fighting the Holy Spirit of the Eternal – just as your ancestors did!" Stefanos cried, boldly reversing his position from Defence to Prosecution. Shaul felt a tremor snake through him as the accusing eyes met his. "Are there any of the prophets whom they did *not* persecute? They killed the very men of God who warned that Messiah was coming! Then Messiah came as prophesied – the Righteous One – and what happened? You betrayed and murdered him! You! Who received the Law from the hand of *angels*, and yet have not kept it!"

There was a moment of stunned silence. Then, "Stone the blasphemer!" came a hoarse cry. Shaul sprang to his feet. "Yes! Stone him!" he shouted angrily, but his words were almost drowned by the sudden uproar in the Council – the crash of overturned benches as men ran at their accuser – the air filling with cries, hisses and hurled abuse. Rabbi Nakkai's frantic shouts of protest went unheard. There was no discussion, no vote, no formal passing of the death sentence – and no wonder, for legally, condemnation could not be declared until the day after a trial. Judicial protocol was abandoned and all dignity forgotten. Pushed, elbowed and over-run as he was, Shaul struggled to a pillar and on to its plinth, straining to see over the heads of the unbridled mass, willing Stefanos to recant before the onslaught of sheer fury – not so he might be saved, however, but because it would damage the Nazarene cause far more than an execution.

Strange! Startling! The young man's dark, craggy countenance showed no trepidation, no fear – none! Rather he seemed elated, exalted! His uplifted face seemed to shine as he exclaimed joyfully that he saw a vision of Heaven itself!

"Look!" he cried to the snarling assembly, raising his hands in an ecstacy totally at odds with the mayhem around him. "See! The Son of Man – standing at the right hand of God!"

Shaul stifled a swift, terrifying pang of doubt as another outraged roar rose from many throats – the man was deluded! blaspheming! – he had sealed his own fate! There was none to interfere and this time the righteous judgement of God's people would stand.

Furious elders dragged their victim through the double doors of the Sanhedrin's great Hall of Hewn Stones, down the steps and into the rain-lashed street where hundreds of drenched onlookers had been waiting, heedless of the weather. Realising at once how things stood, excitedly they pressed forward, hurling invective. Most were baying for blood, but a ragged group of aghast Nazarene leaders and sympathisers was shouting protests, pleading, vainly trying to restrain them. As the stocky Stefanos was brutally shoved through the wet press of bodies, it seemed that the pent up tension of the entire city had been unleashed, while grasping hands clawed at him with such savagery that half the clothes were torn from his broad back. Such was the ferocity of the yelling multitude that it forced its way behind him down the street and through every archway all unconscious of personal injury, though people were trampled and bruised and mercilessly scraped against the cold stone walls on either side.

At first Shaul could not keep up in the crush as the cruelly buffeted young man, his tunic ripped to shreds, was swallowed up in the ever-growing, howling pack. Surging around the captive Stefanos like the Jordan in flood, the people of Jerusalem fell in behind him in a triumphant disorderly procession of aggressive, closely packed bodies. The madness of the moment spurring him to run harder than he ever had before, the young Pharisee forced his way to the front, using his elbows mercilessly; and by the time everyone had crammed through the nearest city gate and stampeded down into an area of rough waste ground in the Kidron Valley – slipping on stones, splashing and skidding on wet grass and mud – he was finally ahead of them all.

Springing across the narrow brook and a little way up the slope, he watched men roughly slam the doomed man against a stony outcrop nearby, binding him with his own ripped girdle. The ugly noise of the rabid throng simmered lower and suddenly hushed in anticipation as their eyes fastened on the chief accuser, who stood with wildly hammering heart, trying to regain his breath. Shaul stared fiercely out at the panting rabble, avoiding the eyes of the silent prisoner who stood, dishevelled, also heaving for breath, the darkly matted hair of his naked chest glistening in the rain.

A muscle twitched in Shaul's cheek. After all this time, after all the watching, the listening, the compiling of notes, leading questions and attempts at entrapment, the moment was here at last … a man was about to die, and he, Rabbi Shaul, the Pharisee youngest in years, but hottest in zeal, was the one who had brought him to justice. A stoning! Never had he seen it done. Never had he imagined how it would feel to be standing here, with the power – the sacred duty! – to extinguish a man's life with a word and a signal. His breath quickened again, his mouth dried, his skin prickled, he broke into a sweat, glad of the pelting rain. The eyes of Jerusalem were upon him.

The men flanking Stefanos nodded firmly, and stepped away. Shaul set his jaw and lifted his head with determination, his dark eyes raking the soaked crowd, the restively alert faces – a mass of self-appointed executioners, seething on the other side of the rushing brook. He drew a deep breath.

"On my accusation Stefanos the Nazarene is convicted of blasphemy," he shouted in a stentorian voice, water streaming from his rain-plastered hair into his dripping beard.

"We are witnesses." The men who had supported his claims in the judgement hall, pulled off their sodden coats and threw them down to cover his feet, a token of protection, ritually and publicly attesting to the chief accuser's truth.

"The Council is agreed!"

"No vote was taken!" An angry shout rang out clearly from the other side of the brook. "This is not justice!"

"You are compounding your sins!" roared Rabbi Nakki at the same instant, but the dissenting voices were swamped in the menacing growl of the dense crowd.

"Hold your tongues!" Shaul shouted as if possessed, his powerful voice echoing through the valley. How dare they! The Council had voted with their actions and their condemnation was loud and clear! "The sentence is Death!"

His authoritative demand for silence confused the people. Uncertain as to whom it was directed, they gave no answering cheer, but they knew what would come next. Excitedly stooping to snatch up stones, roused to a pitch of feverishness which they told themselves was righteous fervour, they waited … for the chief accuser must cast the first stone.

With deliberation Shaul took up a rock the size of his fist, gripping it so tightly his knuckles whitened. Even he could not miss at this distance! Now he looked at the prisoner fully for the first time. For a shocking instant, their eyes met, and each darkly tense face might have been a grim mirror of the other. Setting his jaw, Shaul took a deep breath, and though his heart raced so hard he felt faint he drew back his arm, determined to hurl without flinching. Almost as the stone left his hand a distraught girl shrieked wildly to Stefanos – and it missed. Immediately the crowd let fly with a frantic volley of their own, covering the shameful mishap. Dignity, ceremony, formality was thrown to the winds. Normally staid, respectable men scrabbled hungrily for missiles, snatching them even from the brook, dragging off garments that hampered their throwing arms. Shouts and curses rained down with the rocks in a hail of hate, and amid the horrific noise the girl's high-pitched voice continued to scream pitifully, defiantly, calling down a blessing on the doomed man she loved.

Shaul folded his arms and did not lift his shaking hand again. He had done his part. From the higher ground he watched the scene of slaughter, the cast off coats of the witnesses at his feet – outwardly cool, inwardly flinching as rocks smashed the young man's body, spattering crimson into the mud. With shocking suddenness, an image of Deborah flared up before him – his sister, gashed, moaning, battered, streaming blood … he crushed the thought! Family ties were never an excuse for failing to execute Divine Judgement. God first! It was the Law! The Law of God! Justice before mercy!

"Lord, count them Not Guilty!" Startlingly clear amidst the shouts of the angry multitude, the voice of the dying Stefanos rang out.

The Law satisfied, the trembling Pharisee turned on his heel and left, fighting an absurd impulse to run.

Chapter Eleven

SHAUL's earlier ambitions of quietly teaching and helping people to serve their God vanished like morning dew. He had been blooded now, and it could go only one of two ways – either he would be sickened, or he must redouble his efforts. For him there was no question about it. In his passion for right and deep anxiety for his nation there could be no going back, and all the more resolutely did he set his face to his mission of threshing, winnowing and cleansing Jerusalem. Even if no other man stood with him, he must not fail. Godly order must be restored before the spreading religious chaos and confusion led people astray. Had not the Eternal agreed to spare Sodom if only ten righteous men might be found therein? If he did his part, trusting that more faithful ones might be found, perhaps he, Shaul Benjamin of Tarsus, youthful, solitary as he was – yes, he might even be the essential tenth man to stand with nine unknown others! Whatever happened, *he* would stand for righteousness, *he* would act for God Almighty! The fire of his zeal would cleanse the city – even the land, if need be – of corruption.

Around this time a strange and faintly frightening idea began to insinuate itself into his mind, almost against his will. It seemed to jump into the shadows and hide when he ventured to approach it. Now he began to see its shape, and he tingled at what he descried. He had always known his fond parents saw him as their own private miracle, their blessed gift from the Eternal. But could there be more to it than that?

Several years ago the Baptiser of Jordan had made uncompromising prophecies. Deborah had written all she knew, and all she heard of the man. Though Shaul had impatiently dismissed her sometimes incoherent reports, gradually he had come to realise that whatever anyone thought of him, nobody (not even Herod) denied that he had been a Prophet of God … though he did nothing amazing or miraculous. He only talked. He was just a voice – a powerful one which could not be ignored. Yet the Sanhedrin and other learned men had not attempted to silence him, even though he had insulted many of them on occasion. (As for the commoners, being prodded out of their spiritual lethargy could only have been a good thing!) Everyone had still sought him out, for despite his harsh words, it had been thrilling to have a real live prophet in the Land after hundreds of years without one. After all, prophets had always warned, and threatened judgement, and ignored delicate sensitivities – that's just what they did.

What had the Baptiser said? Many things. *Repent. Admit your sins and be baptised.* Sad to think so many Jews today were so degraded in morality as to need the same ritual cleansing as Gentile proselytes! But that was not the thing which was prowling in the back of Shaul's quicksilver mind. *Prepare the way! Before Messiah comes!* Yes! And here it was, the rest of what the Prophet had said, the thought which began to fill his head in all its disquieting enormity: *One would come after the Baptist, to thresh the nation, baptising it with the Spirit of God and fire, fanning the chaff from the land, and purging it with cleansing flames…*

Was it – could it be – that he, Shaul Benjamin of Cilicia, a young rabbi of the smallest tribe of Israel, might be the one to fulfil these words? It almost made him tremble! Was it blasphemous to ask whether he might be the man especially determined for that purpose? Was it for this he had survived a hazardously premature birth? Or perhaps it was simply that he was fit and prepared to take up the challenge? Just as the prophet Isaias had said to his God, *Here am I, send me!* And with the nation purged as the Prophet had demanded, the way would be clear for Messiah! Surely this meshed with what the learned sages had believed for decades – centuries even.

Shaul held his breath as he saw a new future rolling out before him, the glory of it crackling like an illuminating blaze which threw every shadow into bold relief. He broke out in a clammy sweat, and his head swam. He had sometimes wondered what it must have felt like to men of God who *knew* they were living out what had been predicted of them. Moses, Joshua, David, Samuel, Hezekiah, hand in hand with the Eternal! Did it feel like this? *Was* he the One? The more he thought of it, the more terrifyingly clear the answer seemed to loom. He did not care about personal renown, only about divine duty, and the thought he might fall short made him quail. What responsibility was laid upon him! What a mission! To be lax in fulfilling it would surely be to delay the advent of the Messiah! His heart hammered with anxiety.

He told no one of this secret burden, and the bringing of the Nazarenes to justice became his whole life. Regardless even of the Baptiser's words, as a Pharisee, a custodian of Holy Writ, he had an obligation not only to teach but to carry out the injunctions of Moses and the Prophets. Not for him the accusation of Stefanos, *"You – who have received the Law by the hand of angels, and have not kept it!"* Well, they had proved him wrong – they *had* kept the Law, by stoning him. Shaul marvelled at the stubborn faith that forced a man to such a savage death.

"Not faith," he corrected himself forcefully. "The strength of a deluded fanatic!" *Deluded? A man of obvious intelligence?* something within him prodded perversely. Shaking the thought aside he hurried on with his internal discussion. News of the stoning had of course reached Caesarea, where it jolted the interim governor out of his indifference enough for him to reprimand the High Priest. Open executions by unruly mobs, he cautioned, especially in broad daylight, could not be condoned! Did this hint that less public retributions, quietly carried out, might be winked at? Shaul wondered about it, but the execution of punishments was out of his hands.

Once, early in his campaign of cleansing, in a tiny synagogue with barely a quorum, he had stood in for another to assist in a judicial flogging – one prescribed and carefully circumscribed according to rules of synagogue discipline – but never again. He had learned something about himself, then. (*Cleanse me from secret sins!*) He had never struck anyone in his life before. As he wielded the short, triple corded whip his breast was heaving with a mixture of emotions which at first he imagined was a righteous anger soon to be assuaged by the administering of proper punishment. However, it was not so, for with every lash he laid on the bared back of the stubbornly silent heretic, Shaul's anger only grew – and as it burned all the more fiercely, so all the more fiercely did he strike – until suddenly he froze, dropping the upraised scourge in a stark realisation of something akin to panic. Another elder calmly took over without comment, for since the young rabbi was apparently trembling with rage, and therefore unable to perform his duty with appropriate detachment, he had done the correct and seemly thing in declining to continue.

Still shaking, Shaul sought refuge within the cramped little building, deeply dismayed, to pray for forgiveness. Perturbed beyond expectation, he faced the ugly truth that this day he had not been doing God's work but his own, and he was scaldingly ashamed. He had struck in a spirit which was not judicial but purely vengeful. He had taken out his frustration with the whole Nazarene movement upon one man, and a sneaking part of him had even relished his pain. He had compromised with his own passions what should have been a Godly discipline. He must purify himself, and never risk such a thing again!

Beatings were best and most justly administered by cool-headed men who did not allow their emotions to get the better of them. He was not yet one of those men, and perhaps never would be, for such detachment was foreign to him. His particular task was bringing people to trial, examining them and doing all he could to force a conviction for these unconscionable liars, deceivers and fools. He would do the winnowing, the fanning of the chaff, and deliver it to the burning, but the rest must be up to the Sanhedrin. Naturally the Romans were not happy with religious matters infringing their control over executions, but there were ways around that – private retributions, beatings, imprisonments, threats, at the very least – the commandments of God must be obeyed!

Staunchly convinced that to leave the sect of the Nazarenes to flourish was not only to invite Divine Judgement upon the Israel of God but to hinder Messiah's advent, Shaul continued to throw all his energies into stamping them out. With the help of spies and informers, he raided meeting places, ransacked houses, dragged men and women off to prison and oversaw the confiscation of their goods. His fervour ignited others in the cause, but so fierce was his 'purifying flame', as he saw it, that his name soon became solely credited with all devastation wreaked in any Nazarene community, while his reputation as a ruthless prosecutor was spreading like wildfire.

Yet all Rabbi Shaul's skills as a lawyer never once made a Nazarene recant.

The conduct and reasoning of his captives (so uncomfortably like that of the executed Stefanos), their God-centred way of life, and their utter conviction, haunted him at nights. They were so wrong – and yet how could they behave with such frustrating confidence in their rightness? It was impossible that Almighty God could be in this movement – how could a Messiah ever be humbled, disgraced, degraded and forced to suffer! And would the real Saviour of Israel, promised since the foundation of the world, meekly allow himself to be condemned as a criminal, and *executed*? For what reason? Who then would deliver Jews from Gentile oppression and restore the glory days of the Kingdom? It made no sense.

Deliverers of Israel through the ages always fought passionately for their people. Moses, Joshua, Barak, Samson, David! Brave Esther, boldly using her beauty, courage and cunning! Unflinching Nehemiah, defending Jerusalem with a trowel in one hand and a sword in the other – right up to the heroic Maccabees who relentlessly clawed back the Land and the Temple from desolation and sacrilege. It was ridiculous to hail a so-called saviour who couldn't even save himself! The very idea was not only blasphemous but totally illogical.

As for his being raised from the dead, how very convenient for his devotees to claim he was now 'in heaven', for he certainly was nowhere on earth! But even that seemed to be a pointless claim, for what good was a Messiah up there when he should have been down here, throwing Rome out of the Eternal's holy Land and restoring Israel's Kingdom? What was it all supposed to be about? Did his followers even *know* what a nonsensical mess they were making of the Messiah prophecies? Evil traducers, all of them!

And so in the long silent hours of darkness, tossing and turning on his narrow palliasse, in a discomfort which had nothing to do with the stiff straws poking through its thin cover, the young Pharisee would seek assurance in his mental store of scriptures until finally, through sheer exhaustion, he would drift off to sleep. One miserable stormy night, however, with torrential rain roaring over the housetops and gushing down the street, any hope of sleep was abandoned. Having shoved several pots into position as instructed by the lazy landlord who refused to fix the roof, he huddled down in his blankets, trying to muffle his ears against the torture of the continual *splat! sploink! sploink!* which for a while bothered him more than the storm. A sudden creak overhead, a noisy clatter and a whacking thump – and he sprang up again, fumbling to secure the loose shutters which were banging in the wind, ramming home the bar which pinned them safely. With relief he dived back under the warm blankets … and then the thunder began.

Thunder – the sound of raw power. Thunder – the voice of God, and the judgements thereof! Thunder recorded in Holy Writ – terrifying Pharoah in Egypt, the people at Sinai, the Philistines in battle, and Israel for demanding a king like the nations around them. The wisdom writings of Job spoke with awe of divine thunder … and likewise the Psalms. Thunder in the prophecies of Isaias too … so many judgements in that book … such stirring words … such warnings … And people said there had been thunder at that worthless Pretender's crucifixion. Well, it was that time of year, wasn't it? As for Nazarenes claiming that it was a sign of Divine anger – no devout Jew would believe such a report!

Isaias … thunder … warnings … ***Who has believed our report?*** There was a crackling roar in the heavens and with a gasp Shaul jerked bolt upright, skin rising all over in icy gooseflesh, staring at the shuttered window in shock. He had never before been afraid of thunder. Even as a child, to him it had just been a very big and exciting noise, but now all at once he was tingling with terror. *Who has believed our report?* He set his teeth as dazzling sheets of lightning flashed through the leaky shutters and probed under the rough door of his dank room, stabbing the blackness with startling gashes of white light – while weird after-images flung up fractured ghosts of the room at every blink.

Who has believed our report? He shut his eyes but the lightning glared redly through the closed lids until he blocked it out with a pillow over his face, and immediately the words came unbidden, *We hid our faces from him, he was despised, and we regarded him as worthless …* With a shudder he rolled over, curling into a ball, clutching the pillow to his chest, dragging the blankets over his head. *We hid our faces … who has believed?* Again and again the thunder rolled and pealed and echoed in the mighty unseen heavens above. *Who?* Now he was cowering under the covers, hiding like a child, and he could scarcely believe it of himself!

But who has believed our report? It was like some terrible dream. Shaul pressed his fingers into his ears even as he told himself not to be such a fool! *But who has believed our report?* **Who?!** No, oh, no, no, it was happening again, this horrible obsessive repetition of a single thought. He must think about the rest of that passage, quickly! He swallowed. *We have all gone astray ...* Crash! The shutters shook again. *Who has believed?* Once more the lightning splintered into the austere room, so bright and pure that its flashes were visible through the blankets. Think. Think past it. *He was led like a lamb to the slaughter ... silent as a sheep before its shearer...*

Line after subsequent line ran through his head, each one appearing more sinisterly significant than the last. *He was oppressed, taken without justice ... cut off from the land of the living ... died with the wicked and was buried with the wealthy ...* No! No more! Gritting his teeth Shaul took hold of himself at last, thumping his pillow violently, casting his mind around for solid sureties to cling to. But now, mercifully, the wild storm was blowing over as unexpectedly as it came, no longer pummelling silent dark Jerusalem. The thunder grumbled lower and more hoarsely, rolling into the distance, and the lightning lost its fury, its once bright sheets fading, splintering into sharp, staggering little forks as it followed the retreating clouds.

Now the rain could be heard again, down it came, drumming rhythmically on the roof, splattering from sodden awnings, hissing gently on the ground, hypnotically, comfortingly, and Shaul breathed more easily. Rain was substantial, you could see it, and from whence it came. There was nothing mystical about it to frighten you. It was only water. He rolled over with a relieved sigh, allowing his thoughts to drift. *Lamb to the slaughter, cut off from the land of the living, buried with the wealthy ...* such phrases were open to many interpretations. Oh, the things a midnight thunderstorm could do to a man, scrambling his thoughts like eggs, and totally unnerving him! This is what came of not getting enough sleep!

As for those enigmatic words of Isaias, did they not describe the collective sufferings of *'My servant Jacob,'* as the Eternal described His people? And if not, then the passage must represent the dire fate of a righteous servant of God during some dark phase of Israel's history – one such as Samson in the days of the Judges; or High Priest Ahimelech, slain in an evil hour of King Shaul's reign; or perhaps Prophet Daniel being led to the lion's den. Even Stefanos the Nazarene had been right about the persecution of prophets in those dark old days of apostate kings, but thankfully such blatantly idolatrous times had finally passed, just like this appalling thunderstorm. No modern Pharisee would ever scorn a genuine man of God! And had not the whole nation been disgusted with Herod Antipas for killing their baptising Prophet? Mad though some held him to be, the Baptiser had urged people to turn their hearts back to God (not to speak of preparing the way for Messiah!), and *everyone* had honoured him. Herod himself had feared him as a just and holy man – right up to the time he overcame his scruples and beheaded him – but everyone knew Herod was a wicked, unstable man and not a proper Jew anyway, so he did not really count.

If it came to that, this prophecy might even refer to that very same prophet, Johannes the Levite, led out of his cell and slaughtered like a lamb in a pen. Did he not therefore die among the wicked? And though his disciples removed his body, what happened to the head so mockingly presented like a choice dish at the king's banquet? No doubt disposed of somewhere in the palace grounds – was that not 'buried with the wealthy'?

Regardless, never had the Word of God been held in such national respect as it was these days, with so much study and understanding compiled from dedicated scholars who solemnly instructed the ignorant commoners. More people than ever had the benefit of learning from scripture, if they paid attention in synagogue! Even that unschooled wood-worker was reported to have called out, in his final agony, words from a psalm of David: *My God, my God! Why have you forsaken me?* Yes, and well he might, too – God would not help blasphemers, no matter how self-deceived!

As the rain eased to a gentle patter, the persistent, irregular sound of the leaking roof reasserted itself. *Drip, drip, drip. Drip. Drip-drip!* Shaul turned over with an exasperated grunt, and resolving to ignore this renewed aggravation, wearily urged his overtaxed mind through the remainder of the psalm. *Drip. Drip.* Halfway through, his skin began to prickle and suddenly to his dismay he was more wide awake than ever. *The assembly of the wicked have enclosed me; they pierced my hands and my feet. I can count all my bones. They look and stare upon me. They divide my garments among them and gamble for my clothing.*

Was not this exactly what took place at the Pretender's crucifixion? *Drip, drip.* He had heard many reports of that day! *Who has believed our report?* Coarse Roman soldiers had surrounded him, nailing his hands and feet to the cross, and stayed to watch him die. *Drip, drip.* Unlike those executed with him, he had succumbed so quickly there had been no need to break his legs to have it over with before the start of the new Holy day. *Drip, drip.* Meanwhile the soldiers had helped themselves to the garments so roughly stripped from his beaten body, casting lots to decide who took what. *Drip, drip, drip.* Oh, but of course they did, for soldiers always divided their spoil! *Who has believed?* Yes, he had heard about that eclipse, and the earthquake which somehow tore the heavy fixed curtain of the Most Holy place – perhaps by a dislodged beam. But anything might be read into such events of nature. They were no more signs of Divine displeasure than the omens of pagan auguries. *Drip, drip-drip.*

Who has believed our report? As for all the other talk – including that of a frightened centurion who fell to his knees, convinced this was the

Son of God; and most outrageous of all, eerie claims of the dead rising from opened graves to walk around the city, not to speak of – but stop! Enough! *Drip, drip, splat, sploink!* Shaul twitched resentfully. It was all too preposterous to lose sleep over.

Nevertheless, he wrapped his blankets more tightly around his body, shuddering to dispel the deathly coldness that had crept over him.

Who has believed our report? came the insistent whisper one more time, but he shut it out at last, slamming the pillow over his head as if to smother all thoughts which might lead to madness.

"I'm turning as superstitious as the common people!" he thought angrily. "Confused imaginings! Cold chills! Another bout of marsh-fever, more likely!" Any sensible man of education would accept that the psalmist had been speaking metaphorically, using poetic licence. King David was an inspired poet, and used very colourful language which at times was lyrically cryptic. *I can count all my bones* – that was simple. Many times had the wicked surrounded David, and yet he was unhurt – he even died of old age! *They pierced my hands and my feet* – obviously this meant when David's enemies prevented him from action, for instance when he was in hiding from the murderous impulses of his jealous sovereign. And as to *they divide my garments,* this could well refer to the sad division of David's Kingdom after the death of Solomon! Yes, of course that must be it. There was even a precedent in the writings of Samuel the Seer for such an expression. The old prophet himself had used the very same illustration of a divided garment, when he warned the rebellious, high-handed King Shaul that the Kingdom would be torn from him and given to a better man.

A sigh, almost of relief, escaped the young Pharisee's lips. He was not going to slide into some strange mania after all. He was still in control of himself! If only Deborah had remained in Jerusalem, he could have reasoned with her like this. Oh, he should have been more patient instead of losing his head – but, no! Shaul turned over decisively, pulling the blanket over his head once more. He would *not* think of his sister, her affection, her laughter, her encouragement, her piety and compassion. He would not even think of her appalling heresy. She had vanished and that was that. So, he would not think of Deborah or Simeon at all. Ugh, what an abominable night – but praise the Eternal it was over! Dawn was breaking, and he must soon get up. There was work to be done!

So savagely did he fling himself into his self-appointed mission that the fear of his name drove many away from Jerusalem. This did not satisfy Shaul, as those who fled took their gospel with them to spread to other parts of the country. News came of other groups of believers, or *ekklesias* as they were called, mushrooming up in Judaea and Samaria, and even as far north as Damascus, a hundred and fifty miles away. With frustration Shaul realised that by concentrating on Jerusalem he would only chase the disciples of Nazarene Jeshua out to other places where they could preach in peace. The movement was like oil that spread further the more it was heated.

Night after night Shaul continued to toss uneasily on his bed, visited by recurring nightmares where he was fleeing up a hill of loose stones which slid down faster the harder he ran. Often rising before daybreak he would stride the lonely streets, his mind churning. One grey dawn he came upon an abandoned shade booth in a neglected patch of ground – just a crumbling spur overlooking the Kidron barley fields – and this silent lonely place became his refuge.

It was a shock when first he realised that from here he could see down below, over the brook, an untidy heap of stones where Stefanos the Nazarene had died. Yet, though his heart beat faster at the memory, it only spurred his blazing resolve and he felt no regret, only a kind of agitated conviction that he had accomplished a righteous end.

How long this relentless pursuit must go on he could not tell, nor where it would all end. Who can say whether misty visions of Rabban Shaul the Saviour of Judaism, might have drifted through his head, no matter how unsought? If such had presented themselves, he would have thrust them away almost in panic. Dealing with what was in front of him was already more than enough – doing his all, fighting for God, preparing an ignorant, backsliding, pagan-infected, apostacising nation for the Messiah! Shaul was already disabused of the idea that today the nation respected God's word as never before, for now the alarming surge of Nazarene followers surely belied it and their numbers were heaping up like the insurmountable hill of stones in his dreams. To think more than a month ahead somehow revived this running nightmare, which every morning seemed to creep from his head to inhabit his chest all day with a glowering sensation of burning pressure. At least here, in this desolate booth, as morning's first tentative rays of light crept over the horizon, time seemed to stand blessedly still, and he need not plan anything, only exist, and commune with the Creator as best he might.

Staring into the empty sky, with a low wind whining through the loose palm thatch above and swooping down to ripple the crops below, Shaul drew a deep breath, suddenly reminded of when he had first left Tarsus, with high hopes, sailing away on a big ship just as he had once boasted he would. Forgetting his youthful dismay at finding that the deep ocean provoked in him both fear and nausea, he remembered only the light, the space, the emptiness, and a surreal sense of being suspended in time. This was how it felt now – here – like being afloat – flying before the wind, on a rolling ship at sea, free … away from the stifling four walls of his room which at times felt as though they would crush him, he knew not why.

Many a pre-dawn hour he spent in the deserted booth, repeating his prayers, meditating, clearing his mind, before returning home refreshed – to again immerse himself in designing even more effective schemes against the heretics. He had sworn to act, to bring them to justice – sworn to his own hurt, and he would not change, must never change. He knew it was right! Once you knew something for certain, you had peace, and it was the *only* way to have peace.

So why was he so restless?

Perhaps – yes, surely – it was his many sleepness nights, he thought, clenching his teeth, combined with his unvoiced but continued distress and agitation about his sister's defection, which made him feel so disturbed; and that only showed the dangers of allowing emotions and other weaknesses to get in the way of truth! All the rest might abandon the cause, but he, Shaul Benjamin of Tarsus knew he could not and he was right, and when you knew and believed, then you knew where you were. Aware that his thoughts were turning circles yet again, he mentally shook himself, and firmly repeated his affirmation. *Belief was Peace!* Once he had expunged all old, foolish, and slyly traitorous feelings, Peace *would* follow.

But like an unscratched itch, the words of Rabban Gamaliel kept niggling at the back of Shaul's consciousness. *"If this be of men it will come to nothing, but if it be of God..."* Not for the first time, he dismissed the thought impatiently. Gamaliel had merely been extending the Pharisaic philosophy of not 'rocking the boat'. Shaul had been deeply disappointed in this sign of weakness in his once-revered teacher – Gamaliel was getting old and tired. But his former pupil, already known as 'that fiery young rabbi', would never be so weak! Too much was at stake.

Shaul knew believers regularly attended synagogue where possible and attempted to make converts among them, so he now set spies in synagogues all through the Land as well as in Jerusalem. Again and again he arrested men and women – old or young, wise or simple, careless of whether they were breadwinners, nurturers or those who needed them – who stood no chance against his accusations. For years he had trained with the weapons of persuasive argument, and his cunning questions and blatant assertions could force innocent people to contradict themselves before they even realized where he was leading them.

Soon his campaign of annhilation across the different territories of the Land gathered pace. Nazarenes were not safe no matter where they went. With the exception of a dismal discomforting, way up in the town of Cana – where his few captives managed to escape their escort – the young Pharisee was grimly successful, and the prisons were crammed with heretics awaiting their fate.

In his rare moments of self-examination, Shaul knew he had made an error in Cana which he must never repeat. So over-confident had he been that he had allowed personal pride to overtake his spiritual zeal. He knew it was so, for in the swelling triumph of the moment he had completely lost his head, and boasted to a courtyard of Nazarenes that his name was *Shaul bar Shaul*. The fanatical, maddened Shaul was indeed now a man of his own begetting – one who would have been a stranger to his gentle father Benjamin – but those unguarded words had made him aware of a flaw in his nature which made him writhe to recall.

He tried to discount it by reminding himself of his schooldays when relentless boyish taunts caused him to confuse his father's name with his grandfather's; and of how his friend Joseph used to mock-seriously call him *bar Shaul* in Aramaic or *ben Shaul* in Hebrew when applauding him for some limping prowess in numbers. But could such rationalising disguise his ungodly pride in being a self-made man? It was still inexcuseable in his own eyes. He was almost grateful that the raid had, after all, collapsed in a chaotic failure which mercifully and retrospectively swamped that humiliating moment of self-revelation.

"Cleanse me from secret sins," he prayed yet again with deep mortification. But it would be foolish and pointless to waste time in breast-beating. He

would not make the same mistake again, but only allow it to refresh his zeal. Now, with renewed determination, he decided to go even further – to attack heresy in distant areas that would be least expecting it.

With this in mind he sought an interview with the High Priest, seeking permission to examine synagogues in far-off Damascus that might be tolerant of Nazarene disciples. Shaul approached this powerful man with tact and caution. Whichever son or son-in-law of the old High Priest, the notoriously corrupt Annas, might hold the title at the time (for the same family ruled though the individual office-bearers changed), they were all aristocrats, Sadducees, men of great wealth and influence who held themselves above the common herd. Shaul himself, no matter how admirable his learning, had no nobility, no rank, no family, and no highly-placed friends. He was just a humble Pharisee, he admitted (for he must show due deference to the highest Sadducee in the Land even if it choked him), but when it came to dealing with rank heresies and blasphemies – and with the integrity of Judaism at stake! – surely they might work together?

The High Priest was somewhat shocked at the appearance of the young rabbi who petitioned him – gaunt with fasting, his hollow, burning eyes looking as though they never slept, there was a kind of rabid awfulness about him which was frankly disturbing. This fiery fellow, fit as he was for the cause, was surely headed for a crisis. Without friends or family, he could not last much longer. Better use him while they could. Few others had such a solitary and all-consuming passion for the task! Therefore the High Priest immediately gave him letters of introduction to the Damascene synagogues. He even provided him with a company of men well suited to the task of arresting and escorting Nazarene disciples all the long way back to Jerusalem. Once there, they would face trial before the Council, where a variety of punishments awaited them, from excommunication and confiscation of property, to death.

Chapter Twelve

THERE was no fast way to reach Damascus from Jerusalem. Whichever route travellers chose, they must trudge for the best part of a whole week, carrying essential supplies, resting in the worst heat of the day, and often sleeping rough at night. But Rabbi Shaul marched at a great pace, eating up the miles more like a soldier than a scholar, thinking only of the work which lay ahead – all he must achieve for his God. Spurring him on were visions of zealous kings and prophets of old; they passed through his mind fiery with righteous anger – strong, fearless men who stamped out evil in the face of bleating opposition and led the people back – dragged them back – out of sin's murky darkness to the glorious clear light of pure worship.

Heat, dust and weariness Shaul ignored. So uncompromising was he, so obdurate his resolve, that he had his troop rise at first light and only make camp when it was almost too dark to see the road at their feet. Now on the final stretch he was more hotly determined than ever, too impatient even to wait out the full heat of midday, when sane travellers conserved their strength, reposing in whatever shade they could find.

As the high walls of the ancient city came into view, wavering like a mirage in the harsh glare of noon, he quickened his pace, outstripping the tired men with him. This great city was from antiquity, this city had known Abraham! And now it would know Shaul, his lowly descendant, devoted to the purity of Abraham's Faith.

His eyes fixed on the massive gates, his mind was already planning the havoc ahead – when suddenly from the burnished blue sky flared a blaze of white so bright that the sun itself appeared to dim – and the rabbi and his troop froze in midstride, enmeshed, scarce able to breathe, in a shimmering haze of incandescent light.

Flinging up an arm to shield his eyes, Shaul felt a joint-weakening, terrifying awe flooding through him – a deep, spine-tingling awareness of a great Presence … a Presence mighty, unearthly and all-pervading. Gasping, he sank to the ground, stupefied by the heart-stopping aura of Power emanating from the heavens.

And then a Voice thundered through the ringing stillness that enveloped the earth – a Voice resonant, and clear.

SHAUL!

Crouching paralysed in the dust, Shaul could not lift his head.

SHAUL – WHY ARE YOU TORMENTING ME?

With a great effort, the young Pharisee dragged his hands from his eyes and ventured to face his heavenly accuser. Amidst the dazzling burst of light which seemed to stream from his person, stood a man of angelic appearance.

Trembling in every limb, Shaul whispered through dry lips, "My Lord – who are you?'

I AM JESHUA – THE ONE YOU PERSECUTE.

He was stunned – Jeshua – the Nazarene! The Nazarene was of God! It was true! Then – then – what had he done?!!

The risen Christ knew Shaul's mind – the voice softened a little. *IT HAS BEEN HARD FOR YOU TO KICK AGAINST THE GOADS!*

The whips, the goads, the stings of his conscience – how hard indeed had Shaul resisted them! Those doubts that had tortured him, the voice of reason he had tried to drown in the cries of his victims! His thoughts swirled blindly.

He could not think, he could barely grasp the enormity of it all – except for one thing, that Jeshua the executed carpenter of Nazareth was now not only *alive* but imbued and radiant with heavenly power. Therefore this exalted and glorified person *must* be the Son of God. He must be all that the Nazarenes claimed, he must be the Saviour of Israel, he must be the Messiah, the promised heir of King David, of royal blood, to be addressed as Lord! … while as for himself, he, Rabbi Shaul – self-righteous, self-confident scholar that he was – had been unthinkably, appallingly, and humiliatingly wrong.

He shuddered as it hit him – he had even taken pride in the way he had ruined the lives of Messiah's followers, by the hundred – and all the while, in persecuting them, he had been tormenting *him!* The raw realisation of his situation peeled his mind of self delusion, strip by smarting strip. Now he must face judgement! Not the judgement of men, but the judgement of Heaven. Despite his terror, he was aware of a strange sensation of lightness – for whatever was decreed against him, he knew it would be just. If he was only spared annihilation, oh, he would do all he could to atone! Into his struggling thoughts flashed simple words from the Prophets, *What is required of you except to act with justice, to love mercy, and walk humbly with your God?* and he realised he could not earn forgiveness, nor could he bargain for his life. But undeserving as he was, the word 'mercy' gave him faint hope.

Therefore, with shaking voice, he asked humbly, "Lord, what do you want me to do?"

In the intense light, Shaul's eyes began to cloud. He closed them, wincing in painful apprehension as he awaited his fate.

UP – GO INTO THE CITY, came the reply. *THERE YOU WILL BE SHOWN ALL THAT YOU HAVE BEEN APPOINTED TO DO.*

The light faded, leaving the surrounding countryside lifeless and dull by comparison, in spite of the bright midday sun.

Shaul staggered to his feet and opened his eyes. He saw nothing! At his cries of alarm, his trembling companions arose from their abject cowering and ran to help him, dazed and terrified by the unearthly blast of light from which they had hidden their faces. Of the Voice they had understood not a word, for it had spoken in flawless Hebrew, and they knew only Aramaic. Indeed, so overwhelming was their fear and confusion they could not have told what they had heard, and some thought it was thunder.

In a state of utter shock, Shaul was led blind through the towering city gates into Damascus, physically and mentally shattered by the experience. Unnerved by what had happened, afraid of what might happen next, bewildered and shaken by his affliction, his hired men took him to a cheap lodging house before deserting him. What if they were to be accused of being secret Nazarene supporters, of assaulting him to further their own ends? How would they explain matters to all the synagogue officials in Damascus? Let alone to the High Priest in Jerusalem who had paid them! It was the hour of rest, the streets were empty, few could have seen them bringing their stumbling companion in to this place, and they must not lose this advantage! Having assured the hard-eyed landlord that their 'blind drunk' friend was someone important, and had money to pay for his keep, they warned him to keep quiet about it until the man recovered. Then they hastily decamped with the nearest thing they could contrive to a clear conscience (in that they did not dare to rob him themselves), and they melted into the ancient streets like shadows, and were not found again.

For three days the stricken man lay in a darkened room without speaking, eating or drinking. It was as though he were dead.

Prostrate and unmoving on his hard bed, Shaul's churning thoughts were in deep confusion. Several days before, he had known exactly who he was, where he was going, what he was doing, and why. His whole life had been clear before him. Now his neatly constructed world had been turned upside down and inside out. He could hardly comprehend it, even now, that all this time he had been doing exactly what wise old Gamaliel had warned of – fighting against the will of Adonai God.

But he had been so sure! His understanding, then, of the teachings about Messiah had been appallingly at fault. And he a rabbi with years of study and training! It was *himself*, Shaul of Tarsus, who was the blasphemer! And yet, astoundingly, the glorified Nazarene who was Lord Jeshua the Son of God Most High, had taken no vengeance, but actually declared there was work for him to do! Ah, how could any amount of work make up for what he had done? Nothing would restore the lives he had shattered in his bigoted zeal. And this blindness – this horrifying, hopeless darkness that all the blinking, rubbing, and straining to see could not change – was this to be his punishment? Was he never to read joyfully again from lovingly copied scrolls, or gladly write down his soaring thoughts on the beautiful scriptures he had so badly interpreted? Was this blindness a reminder that he had misused his eyes, like Samson of old – not to lust after false women but to pursue false knowledge? Well, the Psalms spoke of Wisdom as a woman, and the wisdom he had devoured with his eyes was definitely false. Yes, no doubt this was part of it.

He had even congratulated himself that he saw more clearly than anyone else. Yet all the time it was an illusion; his spiritual sight had been in utter darkness. But what now? Must he work for the Saviour as a blind man begging his way through life? No doubt such humiliation would be a fit punishment for all his earlier, dangerous pride.

The distraught young man wept many times as he struggled to understand. He prayed silently for forgiveness, beseeching Lord Jeshua to swiftly reveal the guidance he had promised. Too ill to move, too exhausted to speak, and left to himself in darkness, he did not even know where he was, let alone what to do next.

Meanwhile Judah the landlord, who had managed to extract Shaul's name, nothing more, coolly rummaged through the helpless man's belongings, not with intent to steal – for he was not *quite* a thief, despite his tight-fisted double-dealings – but to satisfy himself there really was money to pay for his trouble. In addition to money he found letters. He could read not well, but well enough to decipher various names written boldly upon them, some of which he recognized as belonging to Damascus synagogue elders. By the time he had scrutinized the details of large official seals stamped upon the parchment covers and stuffed the letters back where they came from, it had fully dawned on him that he was sheltering none other than the notorious scourge of the Nazarenes. He did not like the idea at all. What could have happened, for his men to abandon him so furtively? It was clear the man had received some queer shock of some kind, and his eyes were damaged. Had he been cursed by a Nazarene? There were rumours that some of them had the power to destroy! For a brief uneasy moment Judah wondered about his next-door tenant. He was a Nazarene, though a Greek, and also a physician – a strange combination perhaps, but he seemed harmless enough. Anyway, he had been nowhere in sight when the sick man had been dumped on the doorstep, so rudely awakening hard-working landlords taking their midday rest.

Judah looked in on his distressed lodger once or twice but finding the fellow refused all food and water, shrugged his shoulders. If a man wanted to grieve himself into oblivion, that was his own affair, but he'd better not do it in *this* house. On the third day he stumped angrily next door where his tenant, intent on repairing the decrepit hovel Judah had leased to him, was hammering loudly, and told him gruffly that he had a very sick man in the house, and the noise was making him worse.

"And it's not doing my head any favours either," he snapped. "So leave off, will you?"

By now his indifference had succumbed to genuine concern. After all, if the fellow died after sunset Judah would be severely inconvenienced, since tonight was the Sabbath.

"I will see him at once," offered the concerned physician, but when Judah only snorted cynically, he was quick to add with a smile, "No charge to you, landlord, I assure you. As Lord Jeshua said, *Do to others as you would be done by.*"

Lord Jeshua, indeed! Judah eyed him narrowly. "You won't be so keen when I tell you who it is that's lying on the other side of your wall," he said abruptly. "It's the Nazarene hunter."

"What?!"

Judah allowed details to be drawn from him, but refused to allow his Nazarene tenant to attend the man. What if the helpful physician thought to do his beleaguered community a favour and slip him something toxic?

"He won't eat. Won't drink. Won't see anyone. Feverish ... just lies there and weeps, tossing and turning – praying, I suppose. Now, thanks to you, he's turned delirious ... muttering about someone laying hands on him, whatever that means, so I've just about had enough. If he doesn't come good by tomorrow, I'll turn him over to the elders and wash my hands of the whole business. Even if he *has* been cursed, I don't want the glory of finishing him off, thank you very much. I have too many other lodgers who might object."

"Feverish? Delirious? You *must* make him drink!" urged his alarmed tenant vehemently. "Do you want his death on your head?" Throwing down his hammer he ran like the wind to alert his ekklesia of the amazing news, while Judah stamped home again, muttering. What was he expected to do? Throw water down the man's neck and risk drowning him? Take him out back to the bath-house and drop him bodily into the *balneum?* Yes, that would go down well with his customers enjoying a leisurely soak, he did *not* think. *Pah!* Was he a businessman or a nursemaid?!

He raised his eyebrows at the elderly slave he had set to watch Shaul, but the wrinkled old man shook his dirty grey head. No change. Judah sighed heavily. Nearly three days of tension over a man nobody wanted to know. He began to calculate how much he might charge the elders tomorrow for his trouble, after first extracting the full sum on the quiet from the man himself, of course. If he survived till then. Not that Judah cared much one way or another, so long as *he* was not implicated. But a dead man, especially one with such significant connections, would cause prying inconvenience which might scare off his regulars.

His head throbbing, weakened with hunger, panting with fever and dangerously parched from thirst as he was, the emaciated, tortured man in the dark stuffy room nevertheless was not delirious, as Judah had supposed, but had been granted a fleeting vision of help. *A man, a name, an action.* It poured hope into his burning, agitated heart, it quietened his seething, disordered mind, and gradually his anguished prayers became calmer.

"He will come, soon he will come," he muttered thickly, though in the pain and the blackness and confusion he no longer had any conception of the passing of time. Another grim stretch of endurance and he heard the door creak. Feebly he turned towards the sound.

"Brother Shaul," said the unseen visitor calmly, closing the door. "I am Ananias."

"Praise God!" Shaul mumbled clumsily through cracked, bleeding lips, a rush of gratitude pouring as tears from his unseeing eyes. "Even as he showed me …!" He could barely articulate, his tongue stuck to his teeth, his mouth was dry as dust. He felt an arm raise his head, a cup of water pressed to his lips, but his throat glued itself together when he attempted to swallow, and he choked, coughing painfully.

"A little more. Slowly," responded the steady voice, and he sipped gratefully, until finally, hoarsely, he could form words.

"Where – what is this place? How long have I been here? How did you find me?"

"This is a lodging house on the *Via Recta*. You have been shut up three days, but your stay here is over. He who appeared to you on the road, even Lord Jeshua himself, sent me to you." Firm hands rested on the thin, stooped shoulders. "Brother Shaul, by his command you are to receive your sight, and the Holy Spirit."

At once a rush of indescribable well-being flooded Shaul's body with strength, drowning all pain – a blindfold seemed to peel away from his crusted eyes – he could see! There before him in the dim room stood a quiet-looking middle-aged man who returned Shaul's wild-eyed stare with gravity.

"I must confess, young man, that when the Lord told me to come here I was not anxious to obey. You have caused great suffering to his disciples."

Shaul bowed his head as Ananias continued, "Yet he told me not to be afraid. You have been honoured, my brother. Greatly honoured. He has chosen you to be His mouthpiece, to declare his name before Gentiles, and kings, and the sons of Israel."

Shaul looked up in amazement. *That* was to be his task? Surely it was incredible. But so was everything else – yes, incredible!

Ananias concluded, "But you must suffer, in your turn, many things for His name's sake." He opened the door and the late afternoon sun streamed into room, hurting Shaul's eyes. "You must be baptised into his name, Shaul. With this immersion you will identify with His death and resurrection, fulfilling his command, and your past sins will be washed away."

"All the evil I brought on his people … the terrible things I have done to those who loved him…"

"Forgotten. Not literally of course. But struck from the Divine record, you might say. Totally forgiven. He died that we might live! Come – what are you waiting for? In the rear courtyard of this place is water and there is no need to delay even an instant! Then you must straightway renew your strength with a meal – and I know just where one is waiting."

Ananias thought of the small group of disciples, his family and a handful of friends, who were at this moment sharing a Sabbath eve meal, knowing only that he had been called away on a mission for the Lord. Everyone had heard that Rabbi Shaul was headed for Damascus, and most of the other believers had gone into hiding. Only these few had volunteered to carry on as usual and find out all they could in the synagogues tomorrow, and tonight they were meeting to decide what to do next, and how to stay safe. He took a deep breath – oh, they were in for a shock when he turned up with his unexpected guest!

"I am ready." Shaul rose shakily to his feet.

Ananias nodded, and with an arm around the still-dazed Pharisee's shoulders, helped him gently into the light.

Chapter Thirteen

WITH the act of baptism, Shaul's conversion was complete. Never half-hearted in anything, he immediately threw himself into the new work before him. The small group of believers who were the first to meet him were at first incredulous, but the testimony of Ananias could not be gainsaid, and the humble demeanour of their unlikely new brother both astonished and moved them. In company with these disciples Shaul began to tour the synagogues preaching that the crucified Jeshua of Nazareth was indeed the Son of God.

As the extraordinary news spread, the synagogue elders and their staunch congregations did not know where to put themselves. Some were confused, some angry, some were rubbing their hands over what they thought must be the rabbi's latest new plot, which was bound to succeed magnificently. After all, what better position could a spy wish for than to be trustfully embraced in the bosom of the enemy?

Nazarenes all over the city met to pray anxiously over the news. They could hardly believe that this was the same man who had terrorised them such a short while before, and many of them suspected an elaborate deception. The fiery Pharisee had been well known for trapping people into unwitting blasphemy, they told each other nervously, cleverly twisting his questions to find cause for offense. Was this just another way to obtain damning evidence? But it was quickly obvious that this was not a plot to lull disciples into a false security. The bold young man's passionate conviction rang through every word he spoke. He confessed his error openly, repudiating it with honest tears. He had seen the risen Christ! He was witness to the truth of the matter!

Damascus society – Jew, Syrian, Greek, religious, irreligious, or habitually oblivious – was in a ferment, and could talk of nothing else but the bizarre situation in the Jewish quarter, about which everybody had an opinion, and nobody seemed to fully understand. However, within a short period of time, things changed yet again, and the city's gossip was refreshed with even wilder speculations, when the man at the centre of the situation quietly seemed to vanish.

Examining his own heart, communing both with his heavenly Master and with older brethren among the believers, Shaul had soon become aware that the mere strength of his personal conviction, the mere forcefulness of his personal testimony, would not be enough for him to carry out a lifetime of preaching. Before he could feed others, he must first be stronger himself. Even Lord Jeshua himself, devoted as he was to his Father's work from the very beginning, had not begun his public ministry until he was around thirty years old.

Reluctantly Shaul realised that his conversion was too recent, his Pharisaical attitudes too deeply entrenched, for him to be of lasting value to the Nazarene community in this raw state of mind. He needed a time of solitude to resolve his own tumultuous feelings, to unlearn old habits of thought and action, to confirm his new-found Faith, to develop a new way of thinking, and to reach a deeper understanding of how the crucified, risen, yet absent Messiah intended to work with his people.

He had been used to driving people before him, now he must learn how to shepherd, how to lead. As he said wryly to Ananias, he would not be the first man to enrol in this school of experience. Moses and David also had to learn the hard way – how to endure hardship, know themselves, develop compassion and learn Godly patience – before they were fit to care for God's people. Taking these men, and Johannes the Baptiser, the kinsman of the Lord, as his examples, he chose to leave Damascus for the time being and retreat to the deserts where he could be alone.

Once more he took to the road, travelling down the King's Highway, back into Jewish territory, down on the east side of the Jordan, and continuing way down into the bleak hills of Nabataea, he came into Arabia. There he remained for well over two years. There he worked, prayed, and fasted, re-examining the scriptures in the light of his new knowledge regarding the Messiah. There he came to know in a way he had never experienced before, how profound was Belief, and how passing understanding was the Peace which this brought. Oh, truly, it was far beyond anything he had ever comprehended! There, his faith was strengthened, his mind and body prepared for the work ahead of him. There he continued to commune with his new Master, learning more about his mission – and himself.

It was at times a painful business as he unravelled the mistakes of the past. In his misguided zeal, persecuting the Lord's followers, he had confused everything about the Baptiser's message. How had he ever been so self-deceived as to imagine he might be the One to burn up the chaff of Israel, to prepare for Messiah! As if the Saviour could not appear, had an obsessive young Pharisee not done his part?!

Shaul could see his folly so clearly now. The Baptiser's call to make clear the way, to prepare, was an appeal to individual hearts, not a demand for a national heresy-hunt. The separation of wheat and chaff was not for mortal men to arbitrate, and purging the land would be Messiah's own doing. Not now. Later! And meanwhile? Here he was,

Shaul of Tarsus, still full of zeal, and divinely appointed indeed, but for a completely opposite reason – and far earlier than he ever could have imagined. Amidst the carved rock dwellings, red cliffs and striated caves of Nabataea, this was emphasised by the Lord himself, as he taught his servant, revealing an astonishing truth.

You were separated for a holy purpose, Shaul, from the moment of your conception.

From the moment of his conception! His whole life had been a preparation – all the childhood trials, the youthful mistakes and the grown man's misplaced zeal! These were behind him now, but what he had learned from them he must never forget, for now he was a chosen vessel. Yes, chosen by God, and appointed by His Son! – not to be a cleansing flame within the confines of Israel, but to be lifted up – to bear the torch of the gospel to the whole empire.

I have appeared to you for a special task, Lord Jeshua told him. *You will be a minister and a witness for me, and I will deliver you from the Jews, and also from the Gentiles to whom I will send you. You will turn them from darkness to light, and from sinfulness to God, so that they may be forgiven their wrongs and inherit the Kingdom with all those who have faith in me.*

Shaul meditated many hours upon these words. In them was revealed his whole purpose in life, the key to the whole message. He was not just to preach or 'witness' to people – he was to do more. He was to *minister* to others on behalf of his Lord – to serve, help, and care for them. The waster of ekklesias would become a nurturer. Formerly he had destroyed believers, but now he would build them up, in numbers and in their faith.

There was also the warning that trials and persecutions would come on him from Jews and Gentiles alike. But this would not stop him, for he would *turn them from darkness to light*, just as the Lord had done for him, so that Jew and Gentile *together* would share in the blessings of the Kingdom of God. Gentiles! Non-Jews, pagans, the very people all Pharisees avoided as unclean! He was to challenge them to change, to invite them to embrace the Jewish faith in Messiah, and to share an inheritance with God's own people. Most Jews would see this as inviting a fox to roost with chickens! Small wonder then that Shaul must expect the same kind of persecutions he had once inflicted on others.

But had not the Patriarch Abraham been promised that from his family would come one in whom *all* nations of the earth would be blessed? Now the young Pharisee could see that this was no mere figure of speech. The time had come for this amazing next step in God's plan, and he, Shaul of Tarsus, was the one chosen to lead the way. There was no doubt in his mind that an incredible work was ahead, and the time in Arabia was necessary to prepare him; a time of strengthening and revelation from the Master he now loved as fervently as he had once hated.

It was a rare mission, unique! Never before had one man been commissioned as a prophet or preacher especially to benefit Gentiles. Except perhaps for Jonah, sent to the wicked Assyrian city of Nineveh – and he had been so outraged that at first he had refused to go! But even then, the Ninevites had repented to avoid Divine punishment, not to become spiritual Jews. There was never any love lost between Jews and Gentiles – and how they would worship together, sharing a faith which had already divided the Jewish nation itself, Shaul could scarcely imagine.

"Vision!" he told himself, as he paced, sheltering from noon-day heat, deep in the coolness of his stark rock-face dwelling. "Yes, that is the key! *Where there is no vision, the people perish!* I must communicate that at all costs. Oh, but what if I fail!"

Falling to his knees, he bowed his face, gaunt with fasting, to the ground. "Oh, my Lord! My Master! I am only flesh and blood, set about with weakness like any other man ... and men forget so easily! I pray thee – never let me forget the glory which lies ahead!"

A voice he now knew well answered, just as it had once answered him in the Court of the Priests, at a Passover so long ago.

Fear not ...

Suddenly there was a strong rushing sensation ... with a gasp he felt himself caught up as if in the air ... and his eyes were opened to a staggering, shining, awe-inspiring sight – a vision of the undreamed-of, the unheard-of, the unimaginable ... divine, profound, extraordinary, and holy beyond words ... an incredible revelation of heavenly glory, and breathtaking things to come.

Transfixed in speechless wonder, he heard the compassionate, beloved voice again.

You will not forget, Shaul ...

How long it was before he came to himself, he had no idea, but feeling a tingling, gritty sensation down one side of his face he realised he was still – or once again – prostrate on the sandy floor, while soft black night had fallen all around.

The astounding experience had passed, leaving him dazed, elated, and yet deeply humbled.

Of one thing alone he was unshakeably certain, for which he poured out his soul in grateful prayer ... he would not fail, no matter what came. That sacred, unutterable vision would uphold him to the end of his days.

Chapter Fourteen

THE fear of Shaul's name, however, did not disappear when he did. It was rumoured in Jerusalem that he was searching even further afield for heretics. Half-garbled stories of his conversion did not reassure the disciples there for long – they thought it would be just the kind of trap a cunning fiend like the infamous Rabbi Shaul would delight in. The disciples of Damascus remained convinced of his sincerity, but since he had gone away there was no way they could prove it.

Private stories of his miraculous change of heart trickled back to the High Priest, but neither he, his fellow Sadducees, nor the Pharisees knew what to make of them. It seemed impossible that their greatest, most vigorous, and most single-minded ally against the Nazarene sect could have changed sides!

But if he *had*, they reasoned, then it was just as well that he had disappeared! For such a man to turn traitor to his own cause was a serious blow to the High Priest's pride. Perhaps he had been killed by Nazarenes bent on revenge. Perhaps he had lost his nerve and returned to his home town in Cilicia. Who could say? One thing was certain – if he reappeared, and the startling conversion story turned out to be true, then Rabbi Shaul would be the very next man to be hunted down!

As summer faded and the rains set in, the campaign against the followers of Jeshua bar Joseph lost momentum. Without the Cilician Pharisee, it had no leader, no system, and nobody else had the same ferocious, relentless energy. Disciples of the Nazarene were still individually persecuted, especially in Jerusalem, but the wave of nation-wide terror subsided, and for a time they had a measure of peace, for which they praised God and thanked Lord Jeshua.

Two more winters passed before a thin, sunburned traveller with deep-set, far-away eyes walked resolutely through the Damascus gates and slipped through labyrinthian streets to the Jewish quarter, where he knocked at the door of the disciple Ananias. Shaul had returned. Ananias and the others welcomed him gladly. Some had feared his lengthy solitude after so drastically abrupt a conversion might have been too much for him, but in those years he had been led by God, encouraged by Lord Jeshua, and instructed in many things.

Confident in his preparation for the work appointed him, Shaul resumed his teaching. His understanding and love now deeper than that of an impetuous novice, his arguments carried a weight and a power that surprised those who heard him.

The conservative Jews of Damascus were infuriated. They thought the man had safely vanished into obscurity a long time ago and would never dare show his face again. To find him not only back in their territory, but more determined than ever to preach the Nazarene cause and denounce his previous activities against the sect, worried them greatly. As 'good public citizens', they warned the Damascene Governor about him.

"This so-called Rabbi Shaul," they confided, "is preaching another King. Would not King Aretus have some objections to this?"

At first the Governor responded with impatience.

"When King Aretus appointed me Ethnarch of Damascus, I don't recall that he advised me to listen to Jews," he snapped. Such a tiresome, vexatious people, always squabbling about religion! As if it was not bad enough to be continually involved with enmity between Syrians, Romans and Nabataeans!

"What do I care if yet another madman creates yet another sect in your hair-splitting Judaism? Send him to Herod Antipas – he took care of the last supposed 'king of the Jews' – *and* his prophet."

"With respect, Sir, madmen often disguise their politics beneath pious professions of religion. And *this* particular madman is no longer in Herod's territory. He is in our – that is to say, *your* territory, disquieting this peaceful city after a suspiciously long time spent rather secretively in Nabataea – very likely stirring unrest in the province of King Aretus by stealth."

"Ah, indeed!" the Governor muttered crossly. That complicated matters. Aretus was the father of Herod's first wife, but since Herod had divorced her to marry his own sister-in-law, there was no love lost between the two kings. The Governor was caught in the middle.

He could not risk offending either Aretus or Herod by appearing to tolerate a rabble-rouser, no matter what the fellow really was up to. Plots and intrigues were an inevitable part of staying in power but the Governor did not want to find himself on the wrong side.

"Say on," he said wearily to the delegation which was waiting patiently for his response. They too had power, though of a different kind, and they knew it.

"We believe this Shaul of Cilicia to be an unstable troublemaker, intent on fomenting religious discord. He is an aggravator, a dissenter, a promulgator of a banned sect, and a very unsettling influence in our community – all of which has a very bad effect on business," they said blandly. "However, with your help, we believe we can remove this mutual threat to our prosperity and our positions."

So the Governor, conscious of the economy of his city to which these prominent Jews largely contributed, agreed to arrest Shaul Benjamin on sight, and even post sentries to prevent him escaping the city. That done, he would turn the man over for the Jews to deal with according to their law. From the malevolence in their eyes he had little doubt that they had a swift and permanent solution in mind, but that was their affair. His was to maintain the city's peace.

Complimenting their Ethnarch on his diplomacy, the Jewish delegation withdrew, rubbing their hands over gaining more time to apprehend the man who had destabilised their religion. Now they might with great confidence hatch their own plots against him. If they could destroy the obnoxious turncoat, they need not worry over-much about his associates.

Meanwhile, many long miles away in Jerusalem, the High Priest heard of Shaul's return, and his fearless gospel preaching in Damascus.

"All those letters of authority – useless!" he despaired angrily, on realising that it was indeed all true – that his former best ally had returned as his worst enemy. "He is bewitched!"

Shaul knew his former associates had automatically become his bitterest foes, but continued boldly to proclaim *Jeshua the Christos* in the synagogues. However, it was not long before the other disciples realised that the situation was serious.

The core group which was shepherded by Ananias, one Samuel, and a certain Loukanos, made this very clear to their passionate preacher as they sat together in a neat, orderly dwelling. Standing on the *Via Recta*, next door to the lodging house of the disreputable Judah, the place had been repaired and well maintained by the efficient Loukanos. Here he lived and ran his clinic, uncompromisingly preaching spiritual health to his patients while attending their bodily ailments. He was equally blunt with brother Shaul.

"It is not safe for you in Damascus any longer," he said firmly. "We must face the fact and do something about it. We have just heard that the city guards have orders to arrest you, so you must not leave this house until it is dark. Meanwhile you are safe here – you see that mat by the door? Underneath is a hatch to the cellar. If anyone knocks in the name of the Governor, down you go at once. Agreed?"

Without waiting for Shaul's nod, he added, "And that's not the worst of it. The sentries have been issued with your description and are watching the gates day and night in case you slip through."

"And so are various spies working for synagogue elders and men of business," Samuel added grimly.

"Speaking of descriptions," Loukanos cast a clinical eye over Shaul's face, "that rash is becoming pretty distinctive."

He rummaged among a collection of tiny alabaster pots on his dispensing table. "Here, dab of wool-fat, twice a day. And you can try the juice of aloes, too." He looked around. "Sorry. Where were we?"

"Thinking of ways to save my skin," Shaul murmured, meekly accepting the proffered remedy, "all the rest of it, that is."

A few masculine chuckles broke some of the tension in the room, but not for long. Now it was the women's turn, and one by one they voiced their own concerns, telling him what they had gleaned from butchers, bakers, merchants, servants – and from the urgent whispers of secret sympathisers.

Samuel's wife Esther summed it up, her voice insistent.

"Brother Shaul, it is not even wise for you to walk through the souks alone," she said. "They are only waiting for the right moment to slide a knife between your ribs."

Now it was Shaul's turn to experience the same fear he had inflicted on others. It was a sickening feeling which crept up through the bones and writhed in the stomach. Nevertheless he responded soberly, "The Lord has promised to protect me ..."

"Then he will keep his promise, of course," Esther replied, "but you will not expect licence to risk your life unnecessarily, I hope. And if they start with you, they may finish with us."

Shaul glanced at her, chastened. "Esther, you are a woman of wisdom. I am ashamed not to have thought of that myself."

"One man can not think of everything," Ananias said. "We should hear what others have to say. Pass the word. Sunset this evening, at my place."

The meeting at his house that dark, cold night was brief. A single lamp cast its oily glow on concerned faces.

"We should not delay," warned Samuel. "Brother Shaul must be smuggled out of the city."

"None of you must be involved," said Shaul strongly, feeling a flash of independent spirit. "If I am caught, it must be only myself that is taken."

Discussion was brisk, ideas flew to and fro. All sorts of plans were proposed. He should be hidden under a cartload of cabbages. He should be rolled up and transported in a carpet like the legendary Egyptian Queen Kleopatra who supposedly thus inveigled an audience with Julius Caesar. He should be disguised as an old man, or a cripple, or a beggar.

Shaul felt distaste for this latter suggestion – he had once disguised himself in this way to spy on a house of Nazarenes, on the occasion of his first raid in Jerusalem. It had only been moderately successful, but it was not an occasion he cared to remember for any reason.

As he listened to the urgent conversation around him, he felt strange and uneasy – he was used to deciding matters for himself, and it was humbling to submit to having his person discussed almost as if he wasn't there. When finally someone rashly suggested he disguise himself as a woman, he flinched.

"I am a Nazarene now, but I am still a Pharisee – I cannot dress as a woman, even to escape the city. It is contrary to the Law."

"We must come to a decision!" Loukanos said impatiently, raking long fingers through his hair in frustration. "They may grow tired of watching the gates and hunt him down."

Ananias agreed, tapping his foot agitatedly, not even noticing the surreptitious soothing pats that his wife Ruth was applying to his arm. "If they abduct him he has lost all chance to flee!"

In spite of himself, Shaul laughed ruefully. "It seems I must either burrow out or fly over the walls!"

"That's it!" Ruth's eyes lit up. "You must go over the wall! Joseph, my son, take a lamp and fetch those good strong well-ropes from the courtyard."

Shaul's feet tingled at the thought. His fear of heights, and the occasional dizzy spells which still plagued him, did not incline him to be enthusiastic about this idea.

"It's too dangerous." Flavius, an old disciple, shook his head. "The man is a scholar, not a sailor accustomed to rope climbing! The walls are immensely high! No – it's far too dangerous!"

"I agree," said Loukanos crisply. "One slip, or an attack of vertigo, or fatigue halfway down would mean the end."

Someone put in, "And we can't send him away without provisions!"

"Or warm clothing," Esther added, shivering as she huddled herself closer to a tiny smouldering brazier. "It's freezing out there."

"We could lower supplies down to him." Running back with an armful of ropes and cords, young Joseph was already calculating their length. Sepheth, *'Edge'* was his nickname, for he was a sharp thinker. "Yes, they will be long enough, I'm sure."

Flavius shook his head. "It would take too much time. The thing should be done as swiftly as possible to avoid attracting any notice from passing sentries."

Shaul, concerned as he was to leave the city, was relieved to think he would not have to dangle at the end of a piece of rope which might or might not be long enough.

"What is to be done, then?" he asked slowly, looking from one frown of concentration to another. "If I had not already seen the way the guards jab their swords into suspicious bundles I might suggest you tried smuggling me out in a basket of goods, but –"

"Wait!" Startling them all, Ruth sprang to her feet and darted to a tall storage basket that stood in a corner on the earth floor. Snatching it up, she triumphantly upended it before them all. Narrow nubbly lengths of home-spun cloth, fleeces, a spindle, bone needles stuck in coarse reels of thread, a small pair of shears, and strips of half-tooled leather tumbled out onto the floor. Ruth pushed them aside impatiently with her foot and elatedly showed Shaul the basket.

"You are light, and the basket is strong – I wove it myself only last Passover. In this you will be safe, and can take provisions with you. What do you say?"

There was a moment of silence. Shaul tried to suppress a terrified shudder, struggling with himself, breathing deeply, and telling himself the Lord would not call him to a great work only to calmly watch him break his neck.

For a moment he stood nervously rubbing the prickly itch on his face. The remedy Loukanos had given him was in the scrip at his waist; he would try it later, once he was safe. Meanwhile it felt as if a spitfire caterpillar had draped itself over his nose and spread over one cheek. Perhaps he should concentrate on that discomfort, in the hope it might act as a counter-irritant to his fear. Then he took hold of himself and spoke firmly.

"I think it is the only way," he said at last. "Can we test the strength of it first?"

The men underslung the basket with cords, making a kind of cradle to support it.

"Should be strong enough now," Loukanos nodded, yanking at the knots.

They tied rope to the cradle and threw one end over a beam of the low ceiling. Shaul climbed gingerly in, where he crouched, feeling rather foolish, as they pulled him off the floor. The basket spun like a child's swing. They jerked it, jolted it and swung it, but it held fast and showed no sign of giving way.

Shaul climbed out, feeling queasy, but *almost* smiling. "It will work!" Relieved laughter broke the tension.

"That settles it," Samuel said. "You must go at once. Tonight, while there's just enough moonlight but not too much. They won't be expecting us to move so quickly."

While Ananias hastily wrote Shaul several introductions to various Judaean disciples, the men busied themselves with knotting all the remaining ropes together. The women made up a bundle of provisions; dried figs, dates, raisins and nuts, flat cakes, slabs of cheese and bread were wrapped in cloth and stowed in a satchel, together with a small flask of wine. Ruth added a flat waterskin, three parts empty to save weight. Once he was well away, Shaul could fill it at the first brook he came to.

Young Sepheth slid off his sandals unnoticed and stuffed them into the satchel. They would fit Shaul, who had a lot of walking to do. Esther folded a thick cloak into the base of the basket, while Ananias handed Shaul the letters he had rapidly written, and gave him directions to a safe house in Jerusalem. There he would find someone to guide him through a hidden network of Nazarenes and their sympathisers, who might be anywhere, depending on the state of things in the capital.

"They are all extremely cautious these days, with good reason," Ananias reminded him. "Go at night, stay alert, and do not compromise anyone's safety. Remember the knock and the watchwords."

Shaul nodded, wondering momentarily whether Deborah and Simeon had returned to their home, hoping they had, and marvelling again at the change in his life.

A short, fervent prayer was made for their brother's safety and the success of their plan, then, muffled in dark cloaks, they hurried down silent streets to Samuel's house, which was built on the wall at the far end of the watchman's beat.

They ducked through the doorway and set the basket beside a tall narrow window set into the thick outside wall. The free end of the long, long rope was made fast to the ceiling beams, the slack coiled carefully on the floor.

Samuel opened the shutters. Loukanos steadied the basket on the low, wide sill and Shaul nervously clambered in, his arms clinging to the tall physician's neck while the others ensured nothing could strangle him if the basket tipped the wrong way. The network of cords would keep him in, at least, if he hung on tightly enough. Nobody spoke. Loukanos nodded, and Shaul slumped down as far as possible, transferring his white-knuckled grip to the ropes above his head. Then, with a final brief benediction the creaking basket was forced through the narrow opening into sickening space.

The darkness swinging dizzily around him, Shaul closed his eyes, clutching the ropes, trying not to think of the hard ground so far below, hearing last faint whispers from above.

"Goodbye, my brother!"

"God be with you."

"Lord Jeshua bless you, my friend!"

"Go with God!"

Above him, the team of men squeezed around the window paid out the knotted cords as steadily as they could. At one point the line slid faster than they intended. Instantly Sepheth snatched at the skidding rope, saying nothing as it burned the skin off his hands. Control of the descent regained, the basket continued to lurch down the wall.

Inside, Shaul was sickeningly jounced and spun, but the ropes were good, the knots secure, and the basket strong. Jolting, bumping and scraping, it neared the bottom of the wall. A last sudden slip and it landed with a heavy thud, toppling on its side. Shaul was winded but unhurt. Scrambling out quickly through the slackened cords, he pulled his bundles after him, and gave three short tugs on the rope to signal all was well. The tall basket wobbled upright and was quickly hauled out of sight, its dark shape rising to melt into the dull black shadows high above.

Shaul listened for an anxious moment to determine that he was still undiscovered – then ran off into the night.

Chapter Fifteen

IN a shadowy Jerusalem street, a weary traveller rapped carefully at a shuttered window, measuring out a particular rhythm.

"Who is there?" A bearded face peered out uncertainly through the gloom.

"A friend – a fellow traveller on the Way."

"So you say. But where is *he*?"

"He is not here, he is risen."

The watchwords thus safely exchanged, there was a muffled bumping as the heavy door was unbarred. It immediately swung open. "Welcome!"

Shaul slipped gratefully into a warm room, where a small fire cast flickering light on the expectant faces of a woman and several children. He turned to the husband.

"You are Matthias? Forgive me for intruding at such a late hour, my brother. The disciples at Damascus told me to seek you first, and that –"

"Damascus!" the woman gasped, shocked into interrupting. "Oh no! Pray God that mad Cilician has not taken any there! I heard he had returned! I always *said* his conversion was not real!"

The man's friendly face changed at once. "Tell us quickly – who is it this time?" he said grimly.

A shock went through Shaul. "Who is it?" he repeated, confused.

"Yes, yes," Matthias said fiercely. "Just tell us the worst at once. We've had no word from the brethren there for weeks … oh, may God destroy that fiend … may he be blasted with the breath of His anger!" He covered his face.

"Hush, Matthias," said his wife faintly. "Vengeance belongs to Almighty God. He will repay, not you. Bitter words will not restore your parents."

Shaul grew cold with misgiving. He took a step backwards. "I … I bring no bad news," he stammered awkwardly.

Matthias let out a sigh of relief. "Praise the Eternal for that! Forgive my outburst, we have all suffered here. Judith, some hot soup for our brother, even before water for his feet. Yes, yes, at once, see how he falters. He is hungry and faint from travelling."

Judith took an earthenware bowl, carefully filling it with spicy vegetable soup from a pot beside the fire. "We have forgotten our manners," she said, smiling apologetically. "We have not even asked our brother's name!"

There was a long pause. Judith raised a questioning eyebrow, surprised at the silence. She and Matthias exchanged glances, suddenly alert.

Shaul's heart sank. With a wry attempt at a smile, he answered slowly, "You could call me *ben* Benjamin the Benjamite."

"Ah," Matthias answered warily. "Your father either had a strong sense of tribe, or a good sense of humour."

"Both, in fact." There was no way he could soften the shock. They would have to know. "But I am known as Shaul – Shaul of Tarsus."

Instantly the bowl smashed on the floor, spattering steam and soup. Judith seemed unaware that she had dropped it. "Oh! God have mercy on us!" she cried. "We are betrayed!"

Matthias sprang at Shaul, dragging him away from the door, driving a knee into his thigh, pinning him fast to the wall.

"Run, Judith!" he shouted. 'Take the children and run!"

"No! No!" Shaul struggled to free himself. "I am one of you now! I have letters from the Damascus assembly, from brother Ananias …"

Matthias gripped him even tighter, ignoring his words. "Go, woman!" he cried over his shoulder to his wife. "Warn the others! There may be men awaiting his signal – go now!"

"No!" Shaul pleaded. "Wait! It is not true!"

Deaf to his protests, Judith swung the youngest child on her hip and dragged the other children out through the back of the house.

"Till the Kingdom, Matthias!" she cried out in anguish.

"Till the Kingdom!"

The frightened wails of the children, the running footsteps, rapidly faded into the night.

There was a moment of silence. Matthias released his grip. "Do your worst," he said roughly. "God forgive me for laying a hand on you – but I am not perfect. Call your men – I am ready."

Shaul limped to the door then turned. "You are not betrayed, Matthias," he said painfully, "but I do not blame you for doubting me. When the Master confronted me with my own blindness, my conversion was as much a shock to myself as to anyone else. But in his boundless mercy, my eyes were opened and I was baptized into his saving name. I am in truth his disciple … and I – I cannot express my grief at what I have done to the brotherhood."

"*Your* grief!" Matthias swung round. He laughed harshly. "Do you expect me to believe you? I believe you not, Rabbi Shaul, murdering Pharisee! Do not play your cat-and-mouse games with me! Return later with your band of ruffians if you will, but we will be gone. May God forgive you!"

"God has forgiven me," Shaul answered quietly. "But I may never forgive myself." Wearily, he stepped out into the blackness of the silent, empty street.

In the days following, he again attempted to meet with other believers, but all were suspicious of him. What was a lull of a few years? Just enough time for his past actions to be more fully realized in their crippling, far-reaching consequences to those in the Way. It was hard for them to trust that their fanatical persecutor was not duplicitously concealing his true self within their ranks; hard for them to believe he was not still bent on hauling them to trial, and inwardly panting to see them excommunicated, dispossessed, gaoled or stoned. Ananias's hurriedly scrawled letters to pillars of the Nazarene community made no difference. They could have been forgeries; it had been done before.

It was a bitter, lonely time for Shaul. His former friends were now his enemies, and those he had expected to befriend him were too afraid to

A Time To Act

do so. Left to himself, he searched for Deborah and Simeon, but without success. None who had known them could, or would, tell him anything of their whereabouts. How he would have rejoiced in their company now! Even if Simeon doubted him, Deborah would have faith in his sincerity – she of all people knew and understood him! Yes, if she could only hear his story, surely she would trust him – but it was too late.

Frustrated, baffled and depressed, Shaul often slipped into the Temple to pray. Afterwards he would walk the city, sometimes for hours, to ensure he slept soundly that night. In the streets he escaped public gaze under his head cloth, drawing it across his face to hide the rash blooming across his face in a rough stripe from nose to cheekbone. He had overheard graceless youths sniggering about it. One said it was surely the imprint of a woman's slap, another that he had been struck by a jealous husband, and a third pronounced it to be the mark of Cain, whereupon they agreed it was probably all three and went off into paroxysms of gargling laughter. Shaul was not vain, but this kind of foolish talk blistered his soul.

One evening he was returning to his lodgings when he felt a sudden desire to see again the spacious home which had once enveloped him not only with physical comfort, but also with an emotional and spiritual comfort he had taken for granted. There he had been loved and supported, secure in his precious studies, amid the warmth of his small, affectionate family. He wondered if they would ever know that he now shared their commitment to the Way of the Nazarene which he had once despised. Never had he felt so friendless and alone. Now it was too dangerous to return to Damascus, the Jerusalem brethren were mistrustful and afraid of him, he had driven away his own kin by his misguided, uncompromising zeal – and the High Priest was only looking for him to show his face …

Where now was that great work promised for him to do? He could see nothing for him in Jerusalem. The only thing left of his old life was the still-deserted shelter crouched on a sandy spur which overlooked the Kidron Valley – the place where he had once sought to free his mind from an unnamed and unnameable burden. He had not realised at the time what that burden was. He knew now. The neglected booth in an unclaimed plot had been a place of escape, a nowhere place, a place to distance himself from the many long hours in a miserable room where he assiduously plotted and planned much evil. Now the stones were loose and crumbling, the palm frond roof was shredded and stripped by piercing winds, and he turned his back on it almost with a shudder, allowing his feet to find their own path, almost forgetting where he was headed, losing himself in his cheerless thoughts.

His echoing steps halted. He stood before the large whitewashed house which had once meant home. Cautiously he pushed open the courtyard gate. The place did not seem to be occupied but a carved *mezuzah* was still attached to the right hand doorpost. Was it the same one he had given Deborah? He looked away, not wanting to know, hoping it was not. It would pain him to realise she had never returned to retrieve it, unreasonable as that might be. Silently he mounted the moonlit stairs to the flat roof. Here he had meditated and prayed during noontides; here he had spent convivial hours talking and laughing on long summer evenings; here he had dizzily contemplated the magnitude of the night sky; here he had praised his Creator in those eerie, pristine moments before first light – and struggled with his concentration when a cacophonous dawn chorus of birds blithely added their voices.

Leaning on the parapet he gazed unseeing into the night, motionless, as if to catch these lingering fond memories. A salty drop slid down his cheek, stinging a raw patch near his nose. Wincing, he blotted it hurriedly with his sleeve. A wooden creak down in the darkness made him start – he was not alone.

A bar of light flashed out below and a voice called up quietly, "Is that you, Cephas?"

"No, sir," Shaul answered soberly, as footsteps and a wavering light mounted the murky stone steps. "I am a stranger, but I mean no harm."

A tall figure appeared out of the shadows, setting down the lamp on the parapet, where it guttered feebly in the night air. "What brings you here, friend?"

Even a stranger was better than nobody to talk to. Shaul gestured wearily with his hand. "My sister and her husband once lived in this house. They became followers in the Way of Jeshua the Nazarene, but my violent opposition caused them to flee the city. The irony is this ... now a disciple myself, I cannot find them. I – I came here to remember them – and to pray for them."

The tall man reached out to touch Shaul's thin shoulder and asked excitedly, "Your name?"

"Are you sure you want to know?" he replied wryly. "It is a reproach among all men, it seems." He steeled himself for more rejection. "My name is Shaul Benjamin of Tarsus."

"Shaul!" cried the man. He flung his arms around him, nearly crushing him in a bearlike hug. "Praise the Eternal! Shaul of Tarsus! Shaul, my friend!" he cried with great emotion. "I heard of your conversion to the Way, but also that you had disappeared soon afterwards, and then I did not know what to think, and one report contradicted another. Now I can dismiss all rumours for truth! Shaul, my old friend, praise God you are now my brother in the name of the *Christos*! Don't you know me? Have I changed so much? *You* have not! Unlike me, you still have all your hair."

"It is dark ..." Shaul stammered in utter confusion. He felt an absurd desire to laugh and cry at once at this strangely effusive and unexpected reception.

"Joseph! Cypriot Joseph! Joseph of Salamis – we were at school together!"

"Joseph!" Shaul was stunned. "You! My friend the debater – you also follow the Way?"

"I do indeed," Joseph laughed, though tears stood in his eyes as he hugged him again. "But they call me *bar Nabhas* here, Shaul! I can't think why, but it's stuck now."

"*Son of comfort* – and so you are." Shaul returned the embrace joyously, swallowing his own tears as he did so. From misery to consolation in such a short time was completely overwhelming. "Especially to me, right at this moment! It suits you."

"Come down into the house," Joseph urged him. "It shelters many of us these days but so far tonight I am the only one here."

Holding the lamp high he guided them down and through the door. Shaul's heart missed a beat as a ray of light fell on the *mezuzah*.

"My wedding gift to Deborah and Simeon!" It was the same! He touched it and kissed his fingers with fresh tears in his eyes.

"Yes, my friend!" Joseph smiled at him compassionately. "This is still their house, you know, though practically speaking it is more what you might call common property these days. Simeon made it clear to Nakkai the night they left, that everything should remain as it was and be used for the good of the brethren. Unfortunately we have not heard from them now for more than two years, and nobody is sure where they are. Come, sit! We have so much to speak of, and so many years to reconcile! Now, tell me, have you come across any of the Twelve yet? Those who were our Lord's special companions? Mind you, their work for Christ takes them far and wide. They are rarely in one place for long and not many of them are still in Jerusalem. Those who are, need to be cautious about advertising their whereabouts these days. But I know where to find them."

Shaul shook his head. He knew these men were deeply respected as the *Shaliachim,* the Master's emissaries, whom the Hellenist brethren called his *Apostoloi* – those sent on a special mission. Was it likely that any of them would welcome a man who had once savaged their community? "The disciples here flee from me. They find it impossible to believe I am sincere – and I do not blame them. What I did is too raw, too recent, to be forgotten. For those who daily live with the grievous consequences, it may even be an insult to call it the past."

Joseph grew thoughtful. "Yes," he admitted. "But Lord Jeshua himself has called you, and forgiven you, and you have thrown away everything to follow him. Your former life means nothing now except that the love of Lord Jeshua goes beyond all human expectation. I will vouch for you, Shaul."

With the kindly, loyal Joseph *bar Nabhas* – or Barnabas, as Shaul learned to call him – as his mentor, the humbled young Pharisee gradually became accepted among the believers at Jerusalem. He first spent an intense fifteen days with Shimon bar Jonas, now known as Cephas, the chief spokesmen of the Twelve, and also sought out Jacob bar Joseph, the half-brother of the Lord himself. He asked them many searching questions, listening greedily to their account of living and working with the Master, treasuring all they told him. Greatly uplifted by their words, he threw himself into preaching boldly in the Jerusalem synagogues, especially those attended by Hellenists. Surely as a Hellenised Jew himself, he might more easily persuade them!

But Shaul's meticulously reasoned arguments met with resentment and anger. The conservative Jews were outraged that such a shameless defector should come preaching the very ideas he had once been so driven to destroy. How dare he call himself a Pharisee, as if he still had a foot in their camp! He was a danger to Judaism, a traitor to their cause – the cause of wiping out wicked heresy. As a traitor, therefore, he must be dealt with! And so he became the target for threatening letters, slanderous rumours and mysterious minor accidents, until the disciples had confirmation that the danger was real. Sympathisers within the homes of high officials urgently passed the word – a hand-picked group of unscrupulous men was plotting his assassination.

Shaul had delighted in preaching in Jerusalem, countering the arguments of his countrymen in the Greek-speaking synagogues; rejoicing in speaking of the love of God and His Son in the very places where he had once waged campaigns of hate. But now, realising his life once more was under threat, he found himself cast down and dismayed, not so much out of fear, but because he was unable to do what he passionately felt was right.

Going to the Temple, as was his habit, he threw his problems before God, praying for guidance. So deeply did he immerse himself in his prayers, that he no longer heard the bustle in the echoing courts, or felt the hard marble beneath his knees, or smelled the burning of incense and sacrifices … and as he prayed, the veil which hid the Divine world from the mortal was briefly swept aside. Falling into a trance, the troubled young man saw Lord Jeshua himself addressing him. A great calm flooded his mind, as the authoritative, reassuring voice instructed him to leave Jerusalem. Not because of the plot against his life, for that would fail, there being much work for him ahead. But he could do no more here, at this time.

They will not believe you, Shaul.

This, Shaul had to accept, hard as it was. Despite his best efforts, the Jewish elders were condemning his preaching and trying to undermine his efforts to spread the gospel. This he had striven earnestly to change, but he now acknowledged to his Lord that it was beyond him. No matter how eloquent his words, his infamous part in the execution of Stefanos, and his equally infamous recanting had destroyed trust on all sides. Now there were enemies both before and behind him. But the risen Lord had not appeared to Shaul to encourage him to wallow in guilt. He gave him clear directions.

You must depart, and my plan for you must be accomplished. You are to travel far away to bring light to the Gentiles.

It was a timely reminder of the words he had heard in Damascus and in Nabataea, and yet he felt confused that he seemed no closer to fulfilling them, or understanding how to go about his mission. Deeply frustrated by his inability to support the apostles effectively in Jerusalem, a dejected Shaul told Barnabas of his vision. His warm-hearted friend was understanding.

"Had you hoped to complete the work begun by Stefanos in the Hellenist synagogues? There are others here to do it, Shaul. But there is none so capable as you – an educated Hellenised Jew, a learned Pharisee, and yet a Roman Citizen – to travel the world as an ambassador of the Saviour, and of the Kingdom of God."

Shaul was quiet for a few moments. Then with a deep breath, he stood up and embraced his friend. "My dear *bar Nabhas*! Again and again you prove how aptly you are surnamed. You are right, of course. Every part of the body cannot perform the same function. If I may not be a hand, then I will be a foot!"

"Oh surely not a foot," Barnabas rejoined with a droll look. "Surely someone as eloquent as yourself should be a *mouth!*" which made Shaul laugh, and lightened the mood, as he had intended.

For all that, Shaul was silent and sad as a company of Jerusalem brethren escorted him safely to the splendid white limestone harbour at Caesarea, where he boarded a small, cargo-crowded ship. Once more he stood with a spray-dampened deck swaying and heaving beneath his feet, hearing the creak of sails, clump of wet ropes, and unintelligible bark of seamen's orders. As the clear turquoise waters foamed white behind the helm, he stood in the stern, arm raised in farewell, watching the cluster of disciples, still waving on the dazzling beach of the inner harbour, slowly shrink from sight. Gradually their blurred forms became indistinguishable from the dark rocks and straggling trees at its edges and all he could see was the massive curving arms of the outer breakwaters, until they too finally disappeared.

Having rigged himself a shelter among the barrels of salted fish stowed on deck, he slipped under his scrap of tenting with resignation, and prayed. He thought of all that had happened during the time he had been back in his spiritual homeland. It was very hard to leave Jerusalem, where he had finally found so much to rejoice in. But in one thing at least he was glad – that he might yet trace Deborah and Simeon. For Shaul was returning to Tarsus.

Chapter Sixteen

SHAUL stepped onto the familiar wharf with mixed feelings. He looked around him – there were changes, a few new buildings ... he felt a tug at his coat sleeve and looked down into the grubby, impudent face of a well dressed urchin who was trying to appear servile.

"You new here, sir? I can show you the city, cheap! You want to see the University, sir? Very fine, very famous! Or I can show you whatever you wish – what is your interest? Stadium, horses, women ..."

Shaul twitched his sleeve free with annoyance. "I was born here, you pest," he said severely, though he was about to flip the boy a coin when he stopped. "Wait! Don't I know you?"

The boy's eyes dropped quickly. "No, sir, I'm just an orphan, sir."

Shaul held him gently by one ear. "You ungrateful brat, Gaius Minimus, your father is not only rich, but alive and well and still leasing my family's warehouse. You've grown a lot, but I recognise you, I'm afraid. Are you playing truant from school?"

Gaius reddened and squirmed. Shaul laughed, giving the captive ear a tweak before releasing it. "If you want to play at poverty you need more than dirt on your face. Wear rags next time, and go barefoot! Why the begging act?"

Gaius rubbed his ear and shrugged. "My old pedagogue is sick and mother made him rest instead of taking me to class as usual – which isn't fair, because when *I* feel sick I *still* have to go. Anyway she didn't trust me to go without him, so I stayed home after all, which was good, but then father got angry just because I accidentally broke a silly old vase, and said I ought to pay for it, so I thought ..." He rambled on, but Shaul did not hear him. His playful mood dropped away before a mental image of delicate black and red fragments in a corner, an expensive vase lying in pieces, the only evidence of a hurried flight so long ago.

"Will you take me to your father?" he asked abruptly.

The Honourable Gaius Maximus received Shaul in his private *tablinum*, an elegant office where he might work at his desk while still enjoying the fresh air from the adjoining *atrium*, and the soothing play of light on its shallow pool which collected rainwater from the open roof. He was delighted to see Shaul again, but regretted he had not seen the merchant Simeon ben Gabbai and his wife for a long time. Yes, they had visited Tarsus a few years ago, after an unexpected departure from Jerusalem.

"Something to do with family matters," said the Roman vaguely. They had not stayed long, and he had no idea where they were headed. As a prosperous trader in luxury goods, Simeon might be seeking new suppliers anywhere around the Great Sea from Italy to Egypt.

Determinedly, Shaul enquired of all his old acquaintances and friends, but without success. All he found was veiled hostility among members of the synagogues who had heard of his new way of life. How was he to achieve anything at all in the face of such indifference? His spirits sank once more, but now there was no warm-hearted *bar Nabhas* to encourage him. Here he was, ready and waiting for the Master to reveal that it was now time to act, and charge him with how and where to start his campaign of converting the wider world to the Way of Life – but there was only silence. The Call had not yet come.

One bleak day he found himself walking aimlessly, while conflicting thoughts swirled around in his mind like wraiths in a fog. No doubt he still had much to learn, and if only he knew what it was he would set about it at once, but life lessons were not as clear-cut as those he had learned at school. It seemed they emerged out of chaos more often than out of some neat equation of right and wrong, cause and effect. As he wandered past the University buildings, he could not help remembering how the young Joseph ben Asa Nahath had first befriended him there, and of the widely different paths they had taken in life both before and after the Son of God had entered their lives. Whoever would have believed they would meet again, and in such circumstances as they had! And that Joseph again would take him under his wing and ease his way. Yes, he owed his good friend a great deal.

Thinking of him now, in this place, it was unexpectedly hard to remember the change of name. Joseph, that is to say, Barnabas, had always exuded an avuncular manner and a kindly, generous personality and seemed genuinely interested in everyone. Perhaps it came from having a large extended family, but perhaps not, for Shaul knew that his friend had been very independent as a young man, and with commerce on his mind had determined early in life to make his own way. Still, everybody liked him, and found him easy to talk to. People warmed to him, they confided in him, they trusted him. Shaul however lacked the common touch, and he knew it. Barnabas could move through a crowded room, radiating good will and encouragement, leaving smiles and relieved faces in his wake, while Shaul invariably found himself holed up in a corner thrashing out something deep and meaningful with people who had a point to prove. It was not intentional, it was just the way people responded to him. An insinuating doubt intruded – was it possible that Barnabas was far better fitted for spreading the gospel abroad than himself? Was this why he still had received no further instructions from on high?

Shaul shook his head impatiently. The road to Damascus! He had been chosen – plucked from his destructive life like a burning stick from a campfire. Of course the Master knew what he was doing! Suddenly he remembered that Barnabas too had endured his own scorching moment of truth. His friend had related with deep humility how Lord Jeshua had also challenged *him* to his face, by stripping away all that he had believed about himself, and forcing him to see reality.

"I asked how I might secure eternal life. His response was simple – that I should stop seeking to secure *this* life! He asked me to give up everything I could be certain of, all that kept me safe … and I could not do it. He had laid bare in me a fault I had not known was there, and it shook me so badly that I turned tail and fled. It was a very long time before I recovered."

Barnabas had paused in his quiet recital of the painful incident. "Levi told me much later that had I been present a little earlier on that day, I might have never asked such a question in the first place. You see, people had brought small children for him to bless. As a widow's eldest son he had been a father to his younger siblings for years, you know. I think he must have missed them, and all his young nieces and nephews too, no doubt."

Shaul had interrupted with a degree of impatience. "What have children to do with anything?"

"Ah! That's more or less what his men said too! But he was almost angry when they tried to prevent the little ones from getting near him. *Let them come to me*, he said passionately. *In truth, if you do not receive the realm of God like one of these children, you will not enter it!* And holding out his arms to them, he lifted each into his lap in turn, from youngest babe to the oldest child, and with words of blessing he embraced every one. And each child sat contentedly in his arms - some hugged him tightly, and some kissed him, and even the infants smiled into his eyes, and they all went away happy. You see?"

Shaul had sighed. "Not really."

"Well, Levi put it this way: the children came to him with nothing to offer. They were not buying a blessing. They wouldn't know how, most of them were too young to understand much anyway. But they were drawn to him, accepting his affection without a second thought and with complete trust. They simply received what he gave, responding with a spontaneous warmth which touched him deeply and made him glad. That is how we will enter the realm of God, you see. By *receiving* his love with the heart of a child."

"Yes. Now I see. You had come to him full of what you might do to gain the Kingdom. But none of us can earn it. We can only receive it as a child receives, and a small child does not think of earning or paying back gifts from the giver."

"Yes. And only empty hands can receive such a gift – but I could not see that at the time."

Shaul valued this insight from his oldest friend, and was humbled by realising that they had experienced similar heart searchings. Now he tried to reason things out with himself. He had no difficulty in admitting he still had much to learn, and that he must trust and receive as a little child, but the fact was that he *had* been called to *action*, so what was he to do about that?

The words of the Master which he had heard in the Temple, words so full of import concerning his future … yes, they would come to pass – but when? Were his years in Arabia and his labours in Jerusalem *still* insufficient preparation for the work before him? Yet, surely he had taken some kind of a first step, for he was here, away from the Homeland, already in Gentile territory – and there must be a purpose in it. Confused, impatient, he prayed for guidance, spending long hours carefully formulating the most effective preaching plans, until very late one night, suddenly it hit him – it was not Shaul of Tarsus who would convert anyone, but Lord Jeshua himself! He had it the wrong way around.

Shaul groaned – *Ach!* That execrable, insidious natural pride was still lurking in his soul! He confessed himself to his Lord, and fell exhaustedly into bed, fully expecting as he snuffed the lamp that he would toss and turn for hours. The next thing he knew, it was daybreak, with birds raucously welcoming a tentative sun, and a gecko in the rafters gulping and chirping over an early breakfast of flies. Surprised, Shaul sat up, deeply rested. As he unlatched the shutters to admit the first light, he realised something he had not known the night before … something humiliatingly, almost childishly simple, even obvious, before which all his self-imposed pressure to accomplish great things, evaporated like morning dew.

Divine reckoning of time was not to be measured by the limits of human patience.

It was not up to him to determine the Divinely appointed pace of events. A servant did not need to know how and when and where his Lord might use him next. All he had to do was make a start – now, wherever he found himself. Shaul drew a deep breath of the sultry morning air and praised God. With renewed heart, a few hours later he went in search of the tentmaker for whom he had worked after Benjamin's death.

"Will you let me work for you again, old man?" he asked respectfully. "I may be somewhat out of practice, but I have not forgotten my trade."

Wiry, wrinkled Sempronius gladly stretched out a calloused hand to his former apprentice. "There's plenty to do here!" he said, nodding happily. "And you were always my best worker! Ah, but the young ones these days are lazy and have less respect for their craft. And surly with it. Look at this piece, eh? Crooked weft, loosely tamped – sloppy work! I dismissed that young waster last week, and lo, here *you* are! Truly the goddess Fortuna smiles on me today!"

The master weaver was very happy. Not only had the young Pharisee been a trustworthy and painstaking employee, but a good listener too. And once you got him going, he could talk about all sorts of subjects for hours – even recite poetry. It had varied many a monotonous hour at the loom, and it would be delightful to have him back again. As well as this, Sempronius had recently heard much curious talk about how Shaul Benjamin had changed, and his ears were itching to hear more.

"Sit, sit! Prove you remember what I taught you, eh? And while you work, tell me of this *Christos*! So many things happen so fast in this modern world of ours, and no one has the time to talk to an old man who is going a little deaf!"

Shaul's eyes lit up. "I have plenty of time."

Throwing off his coat, he sat at the upright loom, swinging his legs into the square pit in which it rested. The rhythmic toss of the shuttle formed a steady accompaniment to Shaul's careful words, punctuated by slight grunts as he tugged down the tamping board to force the threads together. Thus was the clipped wool of headstrong goats painstakingly woven into a material which would give lifesaving shelter in harsh weather. Shaul's agile mind could not fail to see some kind of allegory. As a headstrong young man he had also been clipped of his natural pride, and now the Divine Weaver was fashioning him into something useful. Of course it would take time.

His spirits lifted. Here at last was a start. Here was work to be done! It was not the ambitious preaching to large synagogues that he had once imagined, but the quiet enlightening of one old man. To instruct Sempronius, patiently repeating words loudly for his deaf ears, was a joy and privilege. The elderly tentmaker became Shaul's first convert in his home city. Others followed. And so little by little he began, in a small way, his life's work, labouring at his chosen trade and preaching to any who would listen. Time slid past, and more time. The months became a full year, and then another, and another. His fellow Tarsians were not particularly responsive, but delivering tent-cloth and taking commissions took him to neighbouring parts of Cilicia, and he made the most of these opportunities. Wherever he went he spoke of Jeshua the Saviour of mankind, who brought hope of life for all who would believe and obey.

His efforts met with varied success. Some communities received the gospel gladly, others were dismissive, and several were downright hostile. There was no telling how people would receive his message. Just as he had decided that one little group, too few in numbers for a synagogue, was too dulled by isolation, tradition, and hardship to rouse themselves to take an interest; another, equally small, isolated and poor, would be excited by the message. By the same token, a prosperous assembly of devout Jews might meet his words with enthusiasm – or cold stares and anger. As for his consistent attempts to preach in his home synagogue in Tarsus, these met with increasing resistance and hostility, until the day came when he was judged to be in contempt of Judaism, and after an eloquent but fruitless appeal to the elders, he was turned over to their Chazzan for discipline.

His sinewy body stripped to the waist, wrists lashed to a pole, Shaul was beaten with rods like a criminal. The pain shocked him, the humiliation burned deep, but he set his teeth, reminding himself how many believers had suffered as much and more because of him. When one particularly zealous blow cracked three ribs, he lost consciousness – a mercy which spared him further punishment, for the elders stayed the Chazzan's rod, according to their lofty principles!

A young proselyte boldly stepped forward to succour him – it was Gaius Minimus, no longer a schoolboy. He took him home to his family, where the compassionate Gaius Maximus immediately called in a physician to attend him. That same night there was an almighty thunderstorm, roaring down from the Taurus ranges, howling through the city, lashing trees and ripping awnings, toppling wooden statues, and crashing and flashing around the quivering doors and window shutters of houses with such violence that some even suspected an earthquake.

Shaul's late-born fear of such storms having vanished after his conversion, he now found exhilaration in the earsplitting thunderclaps, the heavily rolling, menacing rumbles, and staggering glory of the lightning – for this was the raw power of the Eternal at work! In place of the old terrors was a strange, deep comfort, for in these moments, it seemed that God Himself reached down and touched the earth. Now he was in sore need of such comfort, and as the storm raged he was grateful for it, welcoming the sound and the fury which distracted him from severe pain as he lay, immobile, in the rich house of his Roman friends.

In the midst of the storm Gaius Minimus came running in excitedly to tell him a tree in the garden had been struck by lightning. Defying the weather he threw open a shutter so Shaul could see the strange sight from his couch – the tree burning like a giant torch in the rain, the red and yellow light of flickering flames dancing through the narrow window to weirdly illuminate the room where he lay so helplessly. Shaul could not help thinking of Moses at the burning bush – called to a great task after a false start and years of waiting, protesting his inadequacy, and being reassured by God before going forth to speak His truths to a mixed multitude. The parallels with his own situation were striking. Whether sign or coincidence, this sight too was of considerable consolation in his hours of agony.

It was not until the next day that he attempted to stir, only to find it almost a worse punishment than the original beating. Having stiffened up all over, flesh torn and blackly bruised, with his feverish sweat stinging the lacerations at every twitch of his skin, head throbbing, and ribs stabbing with every shortened breath, he was imprisoned in his own body. One part of him could scarcely believe it was possible to suffer so much pain and still live. Yet in his heart he had no doubts, for had not Lord Jeshua himself told him that there was great work for him ahead – and that he must suffer many things for his sake?

"Eternal God, I know this is just! Should the Master suffer and not his disciples? Should not I in my turn fill up the measure of his suffering? I, of all people – who have hurt and destroyed so many! Give me strength, I pray, and courage! Courage to endure, to go on, to overcome in the name of Lord Jeshua, the *Christos*, Thy beloved Son – and, Great God, I pray thee, increase my faith!"

Slowly the wounds healed. Shaul returned to his own house, and resumed his life as if nothing had happened. He did not speak to anyone of how cruelly he had been treated in his home city – not for many years, and even then, it was but a passing reference. Trials would come, trials would go. It was not important how much he suffered, only how much he loved, even as Lord Jeshua had loved! Even in letters to Barnabas, he said nothing. His friend had his own griefs to bear, having written only recently that his beloved older brother Asa, a stalwart pillar of the Jerusalem ekklesia, had reached the end of his full and well spent days.

Shaul had not known him personally, for the family had been visiting other parts of the Land when he was in Jerusalem, but he knew that good-hearted Asa had not only been a wise and loving influence in the lives of his own daughter and stepson, he had also stood *in loco parentis* to Barnabas and his sister Mari in their youth, and later to Mari's own fatherless son. Barnabas had enough sorrows to distress him. Shaul would not write of his own.

In the beginning, the two friends wrote frequently to each other, but eventually their correspondence dwindled to annual salutations at Pentecost and New Year. News from Jerusalem and Antioch was spasmodic. From time to time Shaul came across Jewish disciples who had fled from Judaea or other territories in the Homeland, bringing the gospel with them to various Cilician communities. Though he was glad to find such staunch believers, he felt deep remorse when he saw the grinding poverty to which persecution had reduced them. He had been so much to blame! Later though, came a sense of healing. For these brethren in Christ the past was over – there was no bitterness, no division.

Nevertheless, Shaul sold his spacious old family home for a good sum and buying himself a very humble dwelling, quietly distributed the surplus funds to those most desperately in need. Families once reduced to destitution, even begging, could now repair dwellings, plant gardens, stay warm, feed and clothe their children, and most importantly of all, redeem crippling pledges on their tools of trade, and start to support themselves once more.

As time passed, through the efforts of Shaul and other disciples, many small assemblies of believers became dotted throughout the regions around Tarsus. These little ekklesias were a great comfort to Shaul, and their fellowship was dear to him in replacing the family he had lost. He may have been more educated than any of them, but from them he learned much about living as part of a community rather than above it, about giving and receiving and respecting others, and about Godly compassion amidst human weakness.

He was quick to observe how the dramatically enforced restriction of their lives affected these believers for good and not evil, according to their positive faith and attitude. Inspiring him further to curb his natural impatience, this realisation formed a conviction which was to uphold him through the rest of his life – that to those who loved God, and responded according to His purpose, *everything* worked together for their ultimate good.

When old Sempronius died several years later, the little workshop became Shaul's. By day he continued his craft, by night he studied, reading and thinking, praying and meditating, and copying from the sacred scrolls. He had quiet satisfaction in weaving the cilicium cloth; and whether selling the heavy material, fabricating whole new tents, or repairing old ones, he found that the hours of repetitive work with his hands freed his mind to meditate. He reminded himself, not for the first time, that David of old was anointed years before he took the throne - years he spent largely as an outlaw! And even the great Moses himself had to spend forty years leading sheep before he was fit to lead people. The Kingdom of Heaven was eternal and God was just. Therefore, if a man was called, no matter how much or how little time he had, it would be enough.

So the tentmaker Pharisee wove and stitched and travelled and preached both in and out of synagogue, assiduously avoiding all traps made by calculating mothers of hopeful daughters, and accepting his situation – even finding contentment and fulfilment in his occupation and simple life. Shaul of Tarsus, from a fiery beginning, was settling down comfortably into the steadier warmth of his thirties. Lines deepened on his forehead, grey sprinkled his close-cropped brown curls and beard, and his shoulders stooped a little more from constant bending over his work.

What of the promised witnessing before kings? Still the Call to greater service had not come! But Shaul was learning patience. Not until nearly ten years after his dramatic escape from Damascus did life take a new direction, and when it did, it took him completely by surprise.

Chapter Seventeen

UNCOMFORTABLY seated astride a borrowed donkey, Shaul was jogging back home from a visit to several remote villages. Absorbed in thought, he was deaf to the monotonous clicking of hooves on the stony road, and barely noticed that the city gates were already in sight. Suddenly there was an exuberant yell a mere stone's throw away. Startled, he jerked up his head.

"Shaul! Shaul Benjamin, is it you? Shaul!"

Shaul squinted in vain to see who was hailing him. His eyesight was poor, a frustration he tried to accept as a reminder that he had once been totally blind in more ways than one. He was still squinting as a tall figure dashed up the road, shouting and waving wildly.

The donkey was most alarmed by this noisy apparition. Honking indignantly, it danced and shied back, unseating Shaul, who was not much of a rider at the best of times, and none at all when distracted. The tall man flung himself forward to save him, misjudged the distance and knocked the skittering animal off balance. With confused cries and braying, men and beast together ended up in an undignified jumble on the thistly roadside, while two small sacks tied to the cloth saddle tore free – and one split, powdering the donkey liberally with freshly ground flour and causing him to sneeze. Highly exasperated and covered in flour, dust, and prickles, Shaul glared fiercely at the cause of this accident (now groping in the dirt for a toppled turban) but almost at once his knitted eyebrows leapt up into disbelieving arches.

"Shaul! It's me!" panted the bruised stranger, who had suddenly turned out to be no stranger at all.

"Barnabas? Barnabas! Here? I don't believe it!" Struggling, Shaul shoved the sneezing, outraged little donkey off his leg. "Why, you're quite bald! And your beard is turning grey!"

"And so is your hair! But at least you still have it." Laughing, Barnabas jammed the bent turban back on his head, pulled Shaul to his feet, and hugged him joyfully.

"Shaul, Shaul, my dear old friend! Where have you been? I've spent days searching Tarsus for you. The synagogue was most unhelpful, I must say. I take it you must be a kind of outlaw. Then I heard you might be over in Saglikli, so I was on my way."

"I left it only a few hours ago," Shaul explained cheerfully, rescuing the remains of his flour before the donkey could poke his nose right into the burst sack. "I had business there after visiting some disciples further inland. It was a relief to get back to a decent Roman road after all the goat tracks! We're not too far from my place now. Hop up behind me on the donkey."

Barnabas eyed the little beast doubtfully. "No, thank you. Unlike yours, my legs are considerably longer than his. I'll walk."

The two talked without ceasing all the way home and for many hours afterwards. Shaul had very occasionally received letters from the

Damascus assembly through Gaius Maximus (though not through the synagogue, which refused to pass on anything to a heretic), but he had not heard from anyone at all for a long time. Now he was saddened to hear from Barnabas of the death of the former Elder, Rabbi Joseph. The Judaean disciples had called him *Joseph Ari*, Joseph the Lion – in deference to his courage so many years ago, when he and the once-cautious Rabbi Nakkai together had saved their Master's body from the ignominy of a smouldering rubbish heap. Gehenna! Where dead animals and the carcasses of criminals were cremated together with the city's refuse; a fiery, filthy place; a cursed place, where apostate Jews had once burned their own children to propitiate the pitiless idol Moloch. The sinless Son of God was not to be thus thrice defiled! Without regard for their own reputation, position, wealth or safety, bold Joseph and Nakkai had taken it upon themselves to bury him with an honour befitting who and what he was – a scion of the royal house of David, a true prince of Israel. This much Shaul already knew.

Now, Joseph related that Joseph Ari had been laid to rest only after a fast and furious discussion in the Jerusalem assembly. The brave old man's death had posed something of a question as to whether his fine family sepulchre in which the Lord's body had lain, should still be used for its original purpose – or not. Some felt uneasy about it, others said that of course it should, lest the tomb from which the Christ was raised became a shrine and a snare even as did the brass serpent which Moses lifted up in the wilderness.

In the end, Joseph's wife, daughters, and four beloved sons-in-law united to have the last word. That particular empty tomb was an enduring and potent symbol of the Resurrection, they said firmly, and empty it would remain as a witness to all men! Joseph Ari was therefore buried in a more lowly part of the rambling garden, where the sepulchres were small and roughly hewn, where many other believers lay awaiting the reviving call of their Master. And so it was that the rich man made his grave among the poor who were his true brethren. Shaul nodded thoughtfully, remembering his own baffling visit to that tomb in the days of his ignorance. He liked this apposite solution, and was sure that Joseph Ari himself would have approved.

The night drew on as the two old friends exchanged their stories. There was so much to talk about, so many years to fill in, so much to ask, to tell and to hear; particularly about the individual welfare of those Shaul knew in Damascus and Judaea, where a severe drought was now entering its second year, and causing deep concern. It had had always been a struggle to care for the poor, the widows, the orphans – not just in money, goods or housing but in their equitable distribution, and matters pertaining to this continuing crisis occupied the friends' discussion for some time.

It was long after they had reached Shaul's little house that Barnabas came to the real reason why he had come looking for his friend. It was after midnight. Only one or two mosquitoes were still persisting with their high-pitched attacks from shadowy lurking places, and though the air outside was cold and damp, within the little house the two men were warmed by a small fire, now burning down nicely to a steady heat. A few faint blue wraiths were still dancing over the coals, slowly crusting the glowing lumps with ash, and the effect was comfortingly soporific, but by now, some distinctly audible hunger growls were preventing either man from sliding into a contemplative state. With a grin, Barnabas apologized handsomely and began rummaging in his belongings for anything edible, while Shaul excused himself with a laugh for being such a poor host.

Thus made aware of the fact that it had been a very long time since either of them had last eaten, he set about remedying the situation at once, glad there was a handful or two of the fine wheat flour left after the mishap with the donkey. It would lighten the heavier barley flour, anyway, of which there was plenty, since *that* bag (of course!) had remained intact. To him, food was food, but Barnabas he knew to be a fastidious eater. Now he was mixing both flours busily with salt, oil and water, flattening his dough into thin rounds which would cook quickly. Meanwhile he offered his guest the internal warmth of a Tarsian wine which he assured him was very famous.

"Famous?" Barnabas tilted the cup of blackish liquid to the light, demanding suspiciously, "For what?" Cautiously he sipped, and put it down in a hurry. How Shaul could drink this sweet stuff was beyond him!

"I could not possibly deprive you of such precious nectar," he said solemnly, and tipped the rest into Shaul's own cup.

Shaul grinned at his friend's grimace. "I should have known better than to offer it to a former vintner, of all people," he laughed. "No doubt it is an acquired taste. If you drank a little every day as I do you might grow to like it."

"There are not enough days left in my life to acquire such a taste, believe me. But it is surely potent enough to have medicinal qualities – perhaps if I anoint my scalp with it I may regrow some hair."

The two laughed again. It had been a long time since Shaul had laughed so much. He had forgotten what good company Barnabas was. Suddenly he caught himself halfway to regret, and shook his head – his oldest friend had only just arrived, and already he was thinking how he would miss him when he went! What kind of madness was that? Turning his attention back to the food he crouched over the flat cooking stone, frying the cakes, while Barnabas contentedly poked the fire, and munched on his own contribution of furrily unripe almonds sprinkled with salt, enjoying their milky crunch and velvety texture.

"A lot has been happening in Jerusalem," he said at last, licking the salt from his fingers. "Some of the former Zealots in the assemblies are growing impatient with the Lord's delay in delivering us from Rome.

There is pressure from other Zealots to abandon the Lord as a lost cause, to leave the Way and join with them in their various attacks and schemes to overthrow the occupation. Anything to reclaim the Land."

"Reclaiming the Land is secondary to reclaiming people who are also 'occupied' by matters foreign to Godliness. Delivering men from internal evils is the Lord's first work, and the rest will follow in the Eternal's good time."

"We can see that, but not everyone can. Some Zealots clearly have espoused the Nazarene cause because it seemed closest to their own, and now their goals have not been furthered as they expected, they are wavering. The apostles in Judaea have many battles to fight, and I tell you this so that you may pray for them. But that is not the reason I came seeking you. A lot has also been happening over in Antioch. Among many of its synagogues good work has been done, and the community of Nazarenes is growing. But it's a very long way from Jerusalem, in more ways than one."

Shaul poured a little more olive oil into the greasy clay lamp and trimmed the wick. "Indeed it is. Such a mixed population, and such a multitude of gods! Tell me then, is it trouble?"

Barnabas considered. "Not exactly, not yet, anyway. We've received many Gentiles into the brotherhood there, which has caused some strain. There is a need of more understanding on both sides, especially in relation to cultural differences. Our Jewish brethren have been subject to a God-centred law all their lives, and it's hard for them to be patient with those who are unused to any regulation. Some used to obey no law but their own pleasure – so of course, the Gentile converts have their own struggles. You know what a sink of iniquity Antioch is."

Shaul did know. In Syrian territory, some three hundred miles north of Jerusalem, it was the third largest city in the Roman Empire, and much admired by the elegant and well-to-do. It was arty, outrageous, fashionable, a place where living for the moment was all that counted – where people sauntered along marbled walkways to lavish spas and gymnasiums, discussing their favourite racing stable, or boxing matches, music, tragedies, comedies, or dance – together with much gossip about the most notable performers of these arts – and whatever was the latest extravagant spectacle in the amphitheatre. Street lighting and floodlit terraces allowed night-time entertainments; the rich lived in centrally heated houses with running water, sluice lavatories, bathrooms, fountains and swimming pools. And yet with all this emphasis on physical cleanliness, moral grime was ingrained; sin, corruption, lust and vice lurked at every corner. In the middle of this bright, glossy, deceptive and artificial world was a single clear light ... the light of the Word ... the ekklesia of the living God.

Shaul flipped the barley cakes onto a wooden plate. He could well imagine the problems Jewish disciples had in mentally adjusting themselves to accept Gentiles who had once flourished within the permissive atmosphere of Antioch. Historically, devout Jews had always attempted to keep themselves apart from Gentiles as much as possible.

Barnabas continued. "For Jews it is a more straightforward matter of accepting that the risen Jeshua of Nazareth is the true Messiah prophesied of old – descended from King David, and yet the holy Son of God. They rejoice in their deeper understanding of redemption, glad to serve God in a more meaningful way than superficial legalism. But for Gentiles it is different – they are earnest and sincere, but the concept of everyday holiness, or 'walking with God', is foreign to them. Their former religions involved bribing silent deities with offering, and encouraged immoral self-indulgence. They were never challenged to change their own behaviour, still less their entrenched habits of thought and speech."

Shaul nodded. "It is only natural that there are difficulties. Let me guess – the Jewish brethren are easily offended by them, and the Gentile brethren are offended that they are offended!"

"Precisely! There is much work to be done to establish harmony. My friend, you are a Jew and a Roman citizen. You are a Pharisee who knows the Law backwards, and yet had a foreign education. You know intimately our ancient and holy city Jerusalem, but you live in cosmopolitan, Gentile Tarsus – a great and modern capital. You of all people can understand the problems of both sides ... we need you, Shaul!"

The barley cakes slid slowly off the plate and dropped onto the floor unnoticed. Shaul's eyes shone. At last the way was being made clear!

Once more, Shaul sailed away from his home town, selling most of his possessions, which were never numerous, leaving behind him little physical trace that he had ever been there. Only the old warehouse was still his, though Shaul was under the impression he had sold it to brother Gaius Maximus and his son. The two had indeed given him a very fair price. Half of it, Shaul laid by, praising God that now he might freely serve the Antioch ekklesia for many months without either burdening anyone else or having to spend most of his time working to support himself. The rest of the money he requested the Gaiuses to deposit in the ekklesial Poor Fund, ready to distribute to the needy as they saw fit. Recently a series of minor earthquakes had damaged brethren's homes in one of the outlying regions, and the vicissitudes of life meant there was always a call on the ekklesial purse.

Rising from his desk to rub his hands before a cheerful brazier which warmed the sparsely furnished *tablinum*, Gaius Maximus promised solemnly that such would be done. Leaving the room, Shaul did not see him turn and wink at Gaius Minimus, and for many years afterwards had no idea that behind his back the document of sale he had just signed had been neatly filed inside the smouldering brazier. Their generous subterfuge having thus ensured both an immediate and future provision for a good man who made none for himself, the Gaiuses took the precaution of noting the matter in their wills, and promised each other that should they ever learn he was incapacitated or unable to support himself, they would confess. Neither of them could ever have guessed how far away the comforting warmth of that brief blaze of parchment might be felt. Certainly they could have had no idea that one day it would reach a cold prison on the other side of the Empire. But all that was far in the future, and meanwhile the unsuspecting Shaul was fit, strong, and eager to plunge into the pastoral and preaching work awaiting him in the huge city of Antioch.

Disembarking at the Syrian harbour of Seleucia Pieria, he and Barnabas headed east. As the arrow flew, it was not a daunting distance from prosperous Seleucia to the great city of Antioch, but the rugged terrain was far too steep to permit a direct route. The two men were glad of the well-trodden Roman road which painstakingly wound through the rough, hilly country. A day later they came upon the wealthy metropolis sprawling luxuriously beside the Orontes River, its outlying suburbs encroaching upon a nearby plain. Everywhere they looked was evidence of lavish living. Near the entrance to the city, ferryboats toiled to and from a large island in the middle of the river, where a grand citadel peered over a massive hippodrome which was audible if not completely visible. It was race day, and floating over the water came the excited roar of massed spectators cheering on their favourite charioteers.

Shaul paused as they traversed the city, staring at the main *stoa*, an impressive thoroughfare which ran east and west and seemed to go on forever.

"I thought Tarsus was the epitome of luxury, but Antioch outstrips it!" he exclaimed, shaking his head at the sight before them. Paved in marble, the entire street was roofed with a double height portico so that anyone enjoying the sights and indulgences of the city might saunter along the *stoa* for more than a mile, comfortably sheltered come rain or shine. "Had they put the same effort into helping the poor … but of course, this is not a place which pretends to follow Moses."

Barnabas nodded. "Amazing, isn't it? But not so many are desperately poor here and mercifully the Judaean drought has not reached this far. Look around – here there is plenty of water and fertile country. As the hub of major trade routes it is presently untouched by hardship and business is prospering; artists and musicians have as much work as artisans and labourers; and with no lawyers enforcing heavy religious taxes, Jews are flourishing, Nazarenes and non-believers alike."

Flourishing they were, for good or evil, in the free and easy atmosphere of Antioch Orontes. But as Barnabas led the way to the suburb of Kerateion, the densely populated Jewish quarter, Shaul wondered how his fellow Jews would regard him. He was unknown by sight in this place, but his name had once been inextricably associated with violence, reproach and infamy. For his own sake he did not care so much, but he was anxious about how his old reputation might affect his ability to communicate the gospel. Would the believers fear him as a former persecutor? Would the non-believers deny him the synagogue because he had, in their eyes, betrayed the establishment? But to his relief it was soon apparent that here his past was not a subject for discussion – to his face, anyway. There was nothing to fear here from either the brethren in Christ or the more conservative inhabitants, whether of Kerateion or elsewhere among the diverse population. Praise God! It was a new beginning.

It was also the beginning of a new name for the disciples of the Way. With the influx of so many Gentile converts, a distinctive title was needed which was free of totally Jewish overtones. 'Nazarenes' was no longer appropriate. While the brethren thought about the problem it was solved for them. The citizens of Antioch were renowned for their irreverent readiness to nickname everything, and even the Emperor was not exempt from their wit. The brotherhood's insistent efforts to spread the teachings of the Saviour, or the *Christos*, as was the Greek word, began to earn them the title of the 'Christ-people'– the *Christianoi*. So it was that the name 'Christian' was adopted. The disciples realised it could not have been bettered, as it proclaimed to the Gentiles that a Saviour of all mankind existed, and to the Jews that this Saviour, their own promised Messiah, had finally come.

Used first at Antioch, the word *Christian* rapidly spread as an instant identification of those who believed in the sinless, crucified and resurrected Son of God, the One who would save from eternal death all who followed him in the Way of life.

The work at Antioch was absorbing, occupying Shaul and Barnabas for the next year. It was, as Barnabas had intimated, a testing time. The grip of Pharisaism on the Jewish population was far less than in Jerusalem, but the self-indulgent, cynical spirit of Antioch was a different kind of enemy; more invisible but just as insidious as the open temptations of the city's pleasure resort – the Park of Daphne, where the god Apollo was worshipped with unspeakable lewdness.

Antioch was the last place anyone might expect the gospel to survive, but the ekklesia thrived – nurtured, guided and built up by its core group of Spirit-gifted elders, including Barnabas and Shaul.

First granted to disciples in Jerusalem, the various Gifts of the *Ruach* – the Holy Spirit of God – were of vital assistance in this diverse population of believers, immediately bestowing upon the recipients skills which would otherwise have taken years to acquire – and some were rare powers which no mortal could ever learn. Just as the Master had promised, they were a great comfort in this strange time of flux and upheaval, when the Jewish and Gentile worlds which had always been so far apart, were being so rapidly and sometimes uncomfortably meshed together in Christ. By the authority of Lord Jeshua, these extraordinary abilities were prayerfully distributed as the Christian community grew, so that no assembly of believers need be without the aid and encouragement of sound teaching or effective administration; the understanding of wisdom or possession of knowledge; the ability to heal infirmities, to translate or speak another language; and various other such tools with which to help their members and witness to their wider communities.

However, although the individual Gifts were greatly prized, they were not everything. What was invaluable was the ministry of a devout person of many natural talents and wide experience in life, and so Barnabas rejoiced that Shaul proved to be all he had hoped for in the work of their very mixed congregation. Many a time he thanked God for his learned friend's ability to penetrate to the heart of a misunderstanding, for the way he could clear up confusion, and for his easy straddling of different cultures. The long years in Cilicia, as well as taming his impatience, had taught him much about harmoniously marrying *learning* with *living*.

The ekklesia flourished. Cosmopolitan Antioch might mock the *Christianoi*, but for the sake of comfort and commerce – the city's main passions – its many mingled races and religions must coexist pragmatically. Here, nobody really cared what anybody believed as long as it did not disrupt anyone else's business or pleasure. As a result, there was no question of persecution, and the brethren had peace.

Back in Judaea, however, the situation was very different.

Chapter Eighteen

TIME had not tempered the aggression of non-believers towards the mushrooming groups of *Christianoi* in the Land.

The ascetic Essenes alone singled out the Christians for no special disdain. Isolated by choice, adhering to their own complex code in which abstaining from meat and continual bathing for purification figured largely, they abhorred Herod's Temple, and rarely set foot in Jerusalem. In their eyes, apart from themselves, the entire national worship was corrupt – aberrant Nazarenes in that degraded mix made no difference either way. One day a great Teacher of Righteousness would come and make everything right – but only once they had first cleared the way for him by creating the holiest possible community of purified souls, by which he might enter the world. To this esoteric sect, the Christian claim of a Messiah who had *already* come – and to save *sinners!* – was beneath contempt.

The fiery Zealots had no such aloof capacity for shrugging off followers of the Way. They heartily and hotly despised them for claiming that the long-prophesied Saviour had come without liberating them from Rome, which to them was a flat contradiction in terms. The very idea of a Messiah who talked about the Kingdom of God in the same breath as *blessing peacemakers* was insufferable! Why, the only time he had mentioned people wielding swords was when he pronounced that a man's foes would be – not Romans – but those of his own household! No, it was unthinkable – ridiculous. It was somewhat ironic that this man of peace had been executed just like any war-mongering Zealot – but they were glad to see the back of him. Deliverers who failed to deliver only made things harder for the next Zealot to raise enthusiasm. These Christians did the nationalistic cause no favours by meekly transcending the whole issue of true freedom!

As for the cool Sadducees, they were deeply offended by claims of the Nazarene's resurrection, but no more or less than his disciples' stand against covetousness, worldliness and political corruption. Shocked and infuriated by the believers' independence of the Temple, they hated them all the more for portraying aristocratic priests and Herodians as dishonourably involved in the Nazarene's crucifixion. This was more than insulting, for the Sadducaic creed held that, should a person be put to death because of the testimony of false witnesses, then the perjurers ought likewise to be put to death. If Christian witnesses to their leader's unfortunately *ad hoc* trial were believed, what then?!

The Scribes and Pharisees meanwhile continued to gnash their teeth over the accusation that they had rejected a 'Messiah' who was in their eyes a mere Pretender. They were furious that ever-growing numbers of the common people no longer looked up to them with awed and deferential respect. Rather, these ignorant commoners were rejecting all their sagacious works, their weighty pronouncements on lawful precedents, and their demonstrations to the rabble of how to show correct piety, as irrelevant!

Particularly outrageous to Pharisees – indeed to all men with a proper passion for national purity! – was that *any* Jewish sect should openly invite Gentiles to share the blessings of Abraham. Of course they believed Gentiles would *one* day be blessed in faithful Abraham because

God had clearly said so, but in their eyes it would have to be the very last on His list – to be fulfilled only once the *true* Messiah had come, driven out Gentiles and sinners (meaning Romans and Sadducees, and assorted heretics), elevated the truly righteous (meaning themselves), restored the Kingdom and made Israel the head of all nations!

The hatred of these factions within Judaism, once directed mainly at each other, intensified as they found a common enemy in Christianity. Added to this, a changing political scene now increased their ability to punish dissenters without interference. The situation of believers was now more precarious than ever, and it was largely due to the steady rise in power of Herod Agrippa, grandson of the Herod called 'Great' – a title equally befitting his grand public works and outstanding evil – the king who had inflicted so much wanton violence upon so many, including his own family, that even his infamous slaughter of Bethlehem infants was but a footnote to a heinous list of other bloody crimes.

But the Herods were a dynasty noble in rank if ignoble in nature, and so Herod Agrippa was connected to men in high places. Educated in Rome, he was a personal friend of both the erratic Emperor Gaius, better known (to his annoyance) by his childhood nickname of Caligula – *Little Boots* – and his under-rated uncle Claudius. Closer to home, Agrippa also had two useful uncles of his own – Herod Antipas, the Tetrarch of Galilee and Perea, and Philip, who was Tetrarch of a handful of north-eastern territories: Iturea, Gaulanitis, Trachonitis, Batanaea, and Auranitis.

After a reckless and turbulent youth, Agrippa had at one time been imprisoned for speaking carelessly against the Emperor Tiberius, but when Caligula took the throne, he was released with tokens of honour. Granted the enviable title *Amicus Caesaris*, 'Friend of the Emperor', Agrippa had returned triumphantly to his homeland, where his fortunes continued to improve thanks to him staying on the right side of Caligula. When Philip the Tetrarch died, Agrippa was appointed to succeed him, ruling his group of territories while his other uncle Herod Antipas, ruling Galilee and Perea, was venially carving out his own dishonourable place in the national memory.

By the time Barnabas had brought Shaul back from Tarsus however, the villainous, adulterous Herod Antipas was no longer in power. A few years earlier, an ambitious Agrippa – forever *Amicus Caesaris!* – had denounced him to Caligula. Consequently Antipas found himself banished, stripped of both his fortune and his territories, which were immediately added to those of his nephew. *That fox,* as Lord Jeshua had called him, had been outfoxed!

Thus having enlarged his domain by political cunning, Agrippa intended to retain it – even enlarge it further – by the same means. Now, if he could only get his hands on Judaea! Comprising the Jews' ancient tribal areas of Judah and Benjamin together with Idumaea and Samaria, Judaea would be a prize worth having! Not only would he then have the Jews' precious Jerusalem in his grasp, but the heart and core of the country – the key piece which would lock all his other territories together into a powerful whole. But since at that time Judaea was still under the administration of a Roman Procurator, the newly enriched king bided his time.

Meanwhile he courted and won popularity by zealously adopting Judaism as his religion and staying firmly on the right side of the influential Jewish hierarchy. Aligning himself with them in many a public show of Godly humility and piety which belied his private immorality, he also conspicuously earned everyone's gratitude by persuading Caligula not to enforce the cult of emperor-worship upon the Jews.

Shortly afterwards the violently unstable Caligula was slain by his own Praetorian Guard, who set his limping uncle Claudius on the Imperial throne. In a culture where physical weakness was equated with a man's character, the sickly new Emperor's position was initially precarious, and he was quick to reward men who promoted his cause – among whom was his good friend Herod Agrippa.

By supporting Claudius as carefully as he had supported Caligula, Agrippa now reaped his reward. A grateful Claudius recalled the Procurator of Judaea and handed over the prized territory to his old friend, thus effectively granting King Herod Agrippa a larger, more coherent Kingdom of Jewry than any one man had ruled since Herod the Great.

Herod Agrippa was not disliked by the conservative Jews; far from it, as he continued to show benevolence to the nation and sensitivity towards their religious observances. But this arch-manipulator knew he could not afford to be complacent, nor take the Jews' allegiance for granted. Neither did he underestimate the power which resided in the spiritual leaders who had such a firm grip on passionate national sympathies. The last thing he needed was religious conflict damaging the Emperor's confidence in him as a firm ruler, one who could keep the peace in this notoriously volatile corner of the Empire. It was vital to please the 'establishment' – therefore, to prove his fidelity to Judaism, Herod Agrippa must needs be against all of its sworn enemies. And that meant anyone and everyone who followed the Way, or even sympathised with it.

Now, suddenly, like the striking of a viper in the desert, the King lashed out at the Christians when they least expected it – shocking them all by imprisoning and executing the faithful apostle Jacob Zebedee. One of the Sons of Thunder, as the Master had affectionately nicknamed Jacob and his brother Johanan, was silenced.

Throughout the Land, and beyond – to Damascus, Antioch, and as the news rippled out, to small scattered communities in Nabataea, Cilicia, Cyprus, Alexandria, Cyrene, and further – believers were devastated with grief, and many trembled. It had not seemed possible that such a thing could happen! No Divine deliverance for one of the Lord's own Chosen! One of his beloved men, one of the three who had always been closest to him! The close-knit Jerusalem assemblies were left reeling, while their enemies rubbed their hands with satisfaction. These Nazarenes were not as invincible as they thought!

Seeing that this unprovoked violence had highly gratified the important Jews who were so politically valuable to him, Herod, forever adept at seizing opportunity, soon determined to despatch another of the chief apostles. This time it was Cephas himself who was arrested, right in the middle of the week before Passover, and thrown into prison to await execution immediately after that feast. Given that the executions of both Lord Jeshua and Stefanos so long ago had also occurred at Passover, it appeared Herod was making a significant point. The national celebration of Deliverance was again to be mocked. It was a dark time which tested the courage and faith of every believer in the Holy City.

Barnabas's nephew in Jerusalem, Johanan Marcus, wrote to him of these grim events in his usual blunt style, writing also to his cousin Loukanos in Damascus – in his haste however forgetting to inform each that he had written to both of them. As a result, the letters read aloud to keenly attentive assemblies in both Damascus and Antioch were immediately redirected to each other. The subsequent arrival of what initially appeared to be more news aroused fresh dread, followed by great relief when it was found they were only copies. But though the original letters had shattered them with the tidings of Jacob Zebedee's tragic death, a jubilant postscript dashed across the page had also given them cause to rejoice, to sing joyfully to their risen Lord, and to praise the Eternal's mercy – for Agrippa's plan to frighten believers by a second, very public execution, had been thwarted the very night before it was to have taken place.

The usually neat hand of Marcus had become an untidy scrawl in his excitement. Eagerly the recipients drank in his words as they were read out, hearing how a multitude of believers had assembled at his mother Mari's house to pray for their beloved elder, when Cephas himself had astounded them all by appearing at the door. No one was more dumbfounded than Marcus's own wife who answered his knock. So flustered was she that she ran back to tell everyone but forgot to let him in – an amusing detail which raised quiet smiles. Anyone who knew Rhoda – and Barnabas and Loukanos had known her from a child – could not help laughing, it was so like her. She had left Loukanos himself standing at a gate before now.

Once their dear brother Cephas, half smothered with embraces and tears of joy, had been given a chance to speak, the excited disciples listened avidly to his story. They had been awe-struck to hear that he had escaped from shackles, chains, and a heavily guarded dungeon by means of nothing less than a visible, angelic intervention. The chief apostle's rock-steady faith was evident as he reminded believers to trust in their Master's words, *Remember I am with you, always.*

Back in Antioch, hearing of these momentous events and discussing them soberly with the other brethren, Shaul was deeply moved. His own life had been threatened before, and he too had escaped, but this deliverance was through a direct miracle, not the contrivance of man. More than ever now, he found comfort in Lord Jeshua's promise, *I will deliver you from the Jews, and also from the Gentiles to whom I will send you.* Even so, Shaul still could not help wondering from what awful dangers he might be delivered, and prayed that he would meet them with that same unshakeable confidence as Cephas. Meanwhile, the Christians rejoiced, and in Jerusalem, for a time breathed more easily.

Herod, baffled and angry, put the luckless prison guards to death, and sought for consolation and glory in another direction. A perfect opportunity to reassert his power and soothe his wounded vanity soon presented itself when diplomats came to him from Tyre and Sidon, territories out of favour with the King. Sorely affected by the widespread famine, they needed to re-establish trading relations, and supplicate Herod's generosity, if their own people were not to starve. They entreated his good will, and the proud King was far from displeased.

Graciously condescending to these timely peacemaking efforts, Herod arranged a lavish and spectacular ceremony in the massive seaside amphitheatre of Caesarea Maritima. Sumptuously dressed in clothes extravagantly woven of silver thread, and surrounded by symbols of his power, he gave the principal oration from his throne. Behind him translucent blue wavelets sparkled like dancing mirrors, his ornaments of gold and precious gems threw off gleams of colour, and bright rays of the morning sun reflected off his shining silver robes, surrounding the king with flashes of light as he gesticulated gracefully throughout his stirring speech. Few reminded themselves that the vision of glory before them masked a man who was inwardly corrupt. It was breathtaking, and the huge audience responded with awe.

Dazzled by such splendour, and anxious to flatter the king upon whose favour they depended, the people cried out that he spoke with the voice of a God. "Henceforth we will reverence thee as superior to mortal nature!" they shouted. Uplifted with triumphant gratification, Herod revelled in the praise which elevated him to divine status, but a moment later God struck him down for that tacit blasphemy. He died soon afterwards, a lingering and horrible death that sickened all who heard of it. One of Christianity's most powerful enemies now removed, the work of the gospel continued to flourish, even in the midst of the harsh drought.

After the death of Herod Agrippa, there was no immediate successor to his throne. Emperor Claudius, a thoughtful administrator, decided that Agrippa's son was far too young for the responsibility of kingship. He went so far as to make the young man the Head of Temple Affairs – infuriating the Jews – but for the time being Agrippa's kingdom reverted to direct Roman rule. Not needing to placate Jewish leaders, the succession of foreign Procurators who governed for the next several years left the Christians alone. The blood-soaked reign of the Herods was thus interrupted for a period, much to the relief of the brotherhood.

Chapter Nineteen

THE recent events in Judaea had been sobering to those hearing about them in Syria, so when they learned that several Spirit-gifted elders from Jerusalem were on their way to Antioch, one of whom was divinely charged with a message for them, the disciples there took heart. Very gladly then did everyone gather to welcome them and hear what brother Agabus had to impart, but to their dismay he told them sombrely he did not bring good news.

His prophecy was met with alarm and lamentation as he revealed there would be no immediate end to the drought which was already crippling the countryside further south. Worse, it would be prolonged. Already its grievous natural effects were irremediable, and he was there to warn them all that before long the shortages presently inflating food prices would rapidly turn into severe famine and cause sore distress throughout the entire land.

Greatly concerned for their brethren everywhere, the Antioch Christians, surrounded as they were by so much wealth, immediately began a relief appeal while individual disciples sought ways and means to contribute as generously as possible. To this end, putting his commercial acumen to good use, Barnabas organised various successful enterprises which reminded Shaul of their student days, dedicating all profit to the famine fund.

Meanwhile Shaul himself, having immediately donated what remained of his warehouse transaction, worked hard as a tutor to one of the wealthier brethren's three oldest and most obstinate sons (his hard-won patience standing him in good stead), laying aside a hefty proportion of his well-earned wages for the fund. Others did likewise.

Over several months, contributions poured in until they had amassed a large sum, whereupon Shaul and Barnabas were chosen to safely carry it to Jerusalem, over three hundred miles away. With them went Titus, a young Greek, keen to assist his Jewish brethren in Christ, staunchly refusing to be concerned about the danger. Highway robbery was a fact of life, and conveying money was not a safe mission to undertake, but as Shaul said, they would just have to "Pray the Lord and take precautions!"

Taking the example of the ancient patriarch Joseph, the three undertook their mission with the precious silver stowed in sacks of grain, and by the grace of God made the long journey to Jerusalem without any loss or damage from either wild men or wild animals (which were just as dangerous to travellers.) The impoverished Judaean Christians were grateful, not just for the money which would buy their daily bread, but for the services of these dedicated men who stayed on to assist in its distribution.

Meanwhile, despite the strict rationing of food, Barnabas was very happy to be in Jerusalem again, where he, Shaul, and Titus stayed with the small family of his widowed sister Mari, and a large floating population of disciples, friends and relations.

Wealthy Mari's very spacious and ever-hospitable house had long been a central gathering place for the apostles and Jerusalem believers. Shaul entered it with mixed feelings. Years ago he had personally raided this very home with a band of guards and captured many of the Nazarenes sheltering there. But now he was one of them, welcomed and accepted by those within.

Who Shaul was, and who he had been, had long been something of a byword among the Christian community but now their response was that if Lord Jeshua himself had forgiven and chosen this man for his purpose, who would dare to doubt him?

Finally meeting him face to face, the Judaean brethren could see the man and not the legend. They could see not only his sincerity and his passion, but also his humility, and they warmed to him at once. Praising Heaven, they glorified the astonishing work of God through Christ, in the one who had once attempted to destroy them.

Even Mari's plain-speaking son Johanan Marcus seemed to bear Shaul no grudges. Like everyone else, he was too concerned with present challenges to dwell on those long past.

On his part, Shaul liked Barnabas's energetic nephew and equally hard-working wife, and was quietly impressed by their commitment to helping the less fortunate. Though childless, a sore trial for a Jewish couple, Marcus and Rhoda quietly accepted it as God's will, turning their private sorrow into a blessing by making full use of their greater freedom to serve others. Their selfless attitude was typical of the uplifted spirit of the believers at that time. Born rich or poor, Christians were known for living simply and sharing for the common good, and these two were a fine example.

Though trained as an architect, Marcus sought to increase neither the social standing nor personal wealth with which his family was already blessed. Instead, responding to the increasingly pressing needs of the Jerusalem brotherhood, he had recently left his profession to work with the busy elders and deacons of the fast-growing ekklesia. As a youthful eyewitness to many incidents in Lord Jeshua's life, his testimony was always invaluable for preaching, but now much of his time was spent in pastoral care, getting his hands dirty, assisting distressed families in a hundred practical ways.

With the continuing failure of the life-giving rains, bewildered livestock chewed at dust and stubble and twigs, nosed for water under rocks of dry creek beds, licked at empty troughs and sucked dampness from the cracks of what once were dewponds. Amid the exhausted landscape crops shrivelled, and suffering was on every hand.

Bodies of emaciated creatures both great and small lay bloated or dying on the tinder-dry ground, pillaged by scavengers which feasted regardless of whether tongues or staring eyes still twitched. Cruel decisions were forced upon struggling households concerning life or death for beloved animals which had lost their milk. Should they become meat to save the family now? Or be spared – at the family's cost – to save the family later?

Men dug deeper wells, women walked ever further for water, children scavenged far and wide, and precious stores of seed grain began to disappear into hungry mouths. Gaunt-eyed tillers of the ground watched grimly as hot winds skimmed the once rich soil into useless powder, and, swirling up dancing burdens of dust in a mockery of dark clouds, carelessly blew all their hopes away.

As dire famine stalked the land, faithful stewards such as the tireless Marcus and his family were like angels of heaven to the growing numbers of poor and desperate people both within and without the community of believers.

Scarcity relentlessly forcing up the price of food, it was the unprotected who suffered most – the widows and fatherless, households without breadwinners, or those who scratched along barely able to feed themselves at the best of times. With cisterns emptying and water courses drying, only the deepest wells and springs still gave water, and even for those with the means to buy, food was increasingly harder to obtain.

In Jerusalem and throughout the whole land, even up to Syria and its coasts, the catastrophic drought bit deep, and then deeper. Pestilence ravaged the weak, the old, the children. The hungry began to starve, and the starving began to die.

God-fearing individuals with private means did all they could, but no matter how much they gave, a handful of worthy people could not feed a nation when there was nothing left to buy.

Yet a welcome degree of succour arose from an unexpected quarter – from a notable, if unusual, Jewish proselyte – the pious Helena, queen of Adiabene, a small Assyrian kingdom. A generous woman already respected for her lavish gifts to the Temple, she sent servants to buy great quantities of dried figs from Cyprus and grain from Alexandria. These she immediately distributed to the poor of her adopted faith, while her son gave a large sum of money to the Jerusalem elders for famine relief. Thus did two Gentiles save many Jewish lives.

Even so, throughout the suffering land many died of starvation, while everyone lived with its spectre. Never was the Christian commitment to having all things in common more needful, and the deacons of the ekklesias had their hands full with ensuring proper equity in all matters.

An unforeseen outcome was a surge in new converts. Conversely, the ruinous dearth had also swelled the numbers of reckless men resorting to highway robbery, especially on the stark Jericho road which led down to the Jordan. Once, penitents had gladly braved the gruelling, full-day's journey, flocking to the river to be immersed by the great Johannes the Baptiser. But in these faith-testing days, a visit to the sluggishly flowing Jordan was more perilous and less practical than ever. As a result, in Jerusalem it was not uncommon to see large groups of people seeking baptism at the Pool of Siloam, which being spring-fed was one of the few places with a reliable water supply. There they patiently awaited their turn, sometimes for hours, while processions of Pharisees took precedence with their own lengthy rituals of purification.

Was this unwavering resolve to become affiliated with the Nazarenes wholly due to the caring example of the community of Christ? Was it because they demonstrated his love so well that it powerfully convinced others? Or was it because some were determined to qualify for all the help they could grasp, by whatever means?

Reluctantly it began to dawn on some of the brethren that whether due to fear of starvation or other reasons, false converts were beginning to creep into the assemblies. It was a distressing thought, but unavoidable.

Now it was becoming even more clear that certain Holy Spirit Gifts granted to various believers years ago, had been given with a compassionate and wise eye to this future. Men and women who had been blessed with a Gift for discernment of intentions or skill in administration, began to be called on more often than ever before, to resolve many an awkward issue.

In the midst of these difficult times, came trials of a more personal nature for Shaul. Although, even here, nobody openly dredged up his history, gradually he began to be aware of a disturbing undercurrent of hostility, too subtle to challenge, from several brethren of standing among various assemblies of the Jerusalem ekklesia.

Something was affecting brother Titus, too. Marcus, with whom the young Greek was often paired for pastoral work, was the first to notice that the formerly enthusiastic, open-hearted youth smiled less and less often. Increasingly tense, he seemed to be withdrawing into himself. And it was far more than the mere wasting of flesh which affected them all.

"Something's eating him," Marcus said bluntly to his uncle. "He won't say what it is, not to me, anyway. But you've known him much longer than I have."

"I'll see what I can do."

Barnabas immediately alerted Shaul, and that night after evening prayers on Mari's quiet housetop the two of them persuaded the stony-faced young man to confide in them. Afterwards they looked at each other in dismay.

"Lord Jeshua commanded us to baptise all men, not circumcise them. That makes nonsense of the entire gospel message. Who had the temerity to interrogate you about this?"

"Nobody asked," Titus responded tersely. "They just observed when opportunity came."

Shaul gave an exclamation of disgust. "So are men now to be followed to public baths and latrines and spied upon for the marks in their flesh? This must be stopped! I say again, who are they?"

Somewhat reluctantly, Titus named several brethren of note, and Shaul's eyes narrowed.

"Very revealing!" he said slowly. "These are the same elders who, when we converse, fix their gaze on a point just over my head and do not meet my eyes – and before you say a word, Barnabas, it is something rather more than my lack of height! What else have they said to you, Titus?"

"Oh, they have never approached me directly – just firmly expressed their opinions in my hearing. They blame what they call 'the Antioch Influence'."

"Meaning us." Shaul looked thoughtful.

"You in particular," Titus admitted uneasily. "They say this is what comes of outsiders preaching the gospel without the direct instruction of the chief apostles. They say it is a disgrace to baptise someone without completing the process of conversion. I don't even know what they mean by that."

"I do." Shaul leapt up to pace the room, frowning. "Oh, yes, now I perceive what this is all about! You remember Marcus telling us what the Master said about new wine in old wine skins? Only new vessels are supple enough to stretch with the ferment of a recent vintage. When stiff old skins are stubbornly retained there is bound to be a rupture. *Ach!* I should have seen this coming."

"You mean, *we* should have seen it coming," Barnabas corrected regretfully. "We've had similar misunderstandings in Antioch from time to time."

"This is far more than a misunderstanding, Barnabas. Putting it all together, it's clear there are several serious matters here, all related. Any one of them puts the gospel work at risk."

"I can see only the one which most concerns myself," Titus confessed humbly.

Barnabas patted his shoulder comfortingly. "Understandably so. Shaul, set out your thoughts in order and enlighten me as well."

"Very well. To me the starting point is not the questions so much as who is raising them and to what end. The brethren concerned are well regarded by many, but ask yourself– *why* is that so?"

"No doubt because they were chief men in synagogues, learned Pharisees such as yourself, respected for their piety. Their reputation has not been lost in their conversion to the Way, nor has their air of authority."

"From whence *is* their authority?" Shaul demanded. "Not Christ, or they would not be troubling his ekklesia. Especially not when people are struggling to stay fed! No, indeed! You see, I know something of these men, and I know their branch of Pharisaism. They belong to the School of Shammai!"

Titus looked blank. "I'm confused."

"Let me explain. If a Gentile wants to embrace the Jewish faith, what must he do? After satisfying the elders of his sincerity he must repent of past sins, be washed in the *Mikvah* – the ritual bath – and be circumcised. Now, followers of the School of Hillel, such as I was myself, will tell you a proselyte's baptismal washing is the most important rite of conversion because it speaks of spiritual cleansing, and making a new beginning."

"Then is that very different to Christian baptism? Or that of Johannes the Baptiser many years ago?"

"In a sense it is very like the baptism of Johannes – except that he was not making proselytes – he was chiefly calling *Jews* to be baptised for repentance! Can you imagine how offensive that was to men who thought repentance was strictly for *Gentiles*?"

Remembering how offensive it once had been to himself to hear of such things, Shaul gave a wry smile. "However," he continued, "as you know, the baptism into Christ which washes away our sins, is far more than a ritual cleansing. Our immersion in water – as into the grave which all mankind deserves – acknowledges this and identifies us with the Lord's death, burial and resurrection. But these brethren who are steeped in Shammai's teachings are treating Christian baptism and the proselyte ritual as one – and again I have to ask, Why?"

"Why indeed?" Barnabas frowned. "Compounding the two just creates confusion – deliberate or otherwise. Perhaps they only need to be shown that elevating rituals above the spirit behind them has inevitably lead to error."

"You are too charitable, Barnabas – past wisdom, in fact. I believe it is quite deliberate."

Titus sighed. He was still confused. "Brother Shaul, I fear my question has made you digress."

"It is of no matter, Titus, never be afraid to ask questions. A digression is often necessary to lay the groundwork for a complete answer. Where was I?"

Barnabas smiled. He was used to his learned friend's 'digressions' and if no question was asked, Shaul would often pose one himself to clarify a line of reasoning.

He prompted, "Converting to Judaism. A proselyte's *Mikvah* cleansing. Pharisees of the Hillel School emphasising baptism as the most important ritual of a proselyte's conversion."

"Ah, yes – the most important for various reasons, not the least of which is that it applies *equally* to both men and women, which circumcision does not. However, the *Shammai* School, being far less liberal, believes that *circumcision is the efficacious rite,* and far more significant than immersion! I don't know what that says about their respect for female proselytes, but leaving that aside, why do they hold this view?"

Titus had no idea. "Who knows?" He looked at Shaul hopefully. "Do you?"

"Oh, I think so!" Shaul raised a finger to make his point. "Just consider this – under the Law a man is *forever* bathing for one reason or another. Ceremonial washing leaves no evidence once you are dry – but cut the flesh and you have irreversible physical proof, you see? So, if brethren who revere Shammai demand that you as a baptised Gentile must *also* be circumcised, what are we to infer?"

"That they would make me a full proselyte Jew before they accept me as a Christian!" Titus's jaw dropped. "So in their eyes Lord Jeshua did not go far enough! The baptism of Christ is insufficient and must be subordinate to the teachings of this Shammai!"

"Yes, this Shammai – this hoary old scholar noted for his rigid interpretation of the Law, to which our freedom in Christ must be completely opposed. What? Is our unity to be destroyed? Is the body of Christ to be segregated like the Temple courts? Jewish ekklesias here and Gentile ekklesias there and no concourse between them? *Me genoito!*"

Finding himself shaking, Shaul leapt up to pace the room with quick, stalking steps, determined to walk off the annoying tremors.

"I tell you, such well educated men have no excuse for 'misunderstanding' the gospel so plainly preached to them! No – we have been infiltrated! These are false converts, spying on our community from within – enabling them to sow discord and doubt, to weaken the influence of the gospel and draw people back to their control. Violence has already failed to destroy the community of Christ – but if we tear ourselves apart, their work is done."

"Could this be true?" Titus asked incredulously.

"Without doubt. It is a well known ruse of warfare to side with the enemy in order to destroy it. As a Pharisee who once planted spies in many assemblies for the same purpose, believe me, I know how it works."

"So it is not just about me – or attacking you as an interloper."

"No – both are merely parts of the whole plan. But that last must be addressed without delay. My commission did not come second-hand, not even through the twelve Chosen – it came directly from Lord Jeshua himself, just as theirs did. I admit to my late spiritual birth, but in no way am I illegitimate! However, it seems we are dealing with strategists. If they successfully discredit my authority to preach, they effectively block opposition before it arises, shrugging it off as 'the Antioch influence' you already mentioned."

"They do not know *your* skill at strategy," Barnabas mused, remembering many a hard-fought board game at university. "Whether at *Calculi* or *Latrunculi* you beat me far too often for my self-respect."

Titus grinned but Shaul looked serious. "Human strategy is a carnal weapon. These men must be withstood by other means – the very unity and authority which they seek to destroy."

He stood up, pulling on his coat, shaking the last of his agitation from his fingertips as if shaking off water.

"This is why I went privately to Cephas and Jacob when we first arrived here, to explain exactly what and how I preached during my years in Cilicia – to fully assure them that we promote the same gospel. I knew very well that if anyone viewed me as a rival to the pillars of the ekklesia, it would undo much good. And my preaching would be in vain."

He took a deep breath, calmer at last, and beckoned to the others.

"Come, we must bring these agitators before the chief apostles and resolve the matter. For now, anyway. I fear this is a problem which will keep recurring as long as there are old bottles holding new wine."

In the course of the next week, the threat to the believers' harmony was duly averted in the manner Shaul had proposed. Cephas, Jacob bar

Joseph, and Johanan Zebedee asserted in the presence of the trouble-makers that brother Shaul, his mandate to teach, and his teaching, had their full confidence. As an acknowledgement and demonstration of this, ceremoniously they gave Shaul and Barnabas their right hands, signifying unity of fellowship.

"You have given faithful service here, brethren," Cephas said warmly. "Soon however, I believe you must return to your fruitful work among the Gentiles, because there is no doubt that you, more than any of us, are ideally suited to the task. As for us, we will continue to preach to our fellow Jews," – here he looked piercingly at the outraged elders who had urged circumcision – "but let there be no doubt that all of us preach exactly the same gospel to all men!"

Shaul agreed firmly, reiterating that immersion was the sole essential rite for anyone to become a Christian – whether Jew or Gentile, bond or free, male or female. At this point the Shammai sympathisers threw up their hands and left, some of them muttering threats.

With sadness the others watched them go. Splinter groups were inevitable where human designs were at work. They could only pray that at best these men would see the error of their ways, and at worst that they would not corrupt others.

Cephas turned back to Barnabas and Shaul. "Wherever you may go in future days, my brothers – do not forget the poor in this place!" he said quietly. "Hungry people do not reason well and are prey to stronger wills. This famine hurts everyone, but savage as it is, it will pass. The poor, however, have it always at their door."

Of this they were well aware, and Shaul felt it acutely, knowing that in many cases he was witnessing the sad fruit of the destruction he had sown years before. So many had lost everything in successive waves of persecution – livelihoods, breadwinners, possessions and homes. Among the Christians was an abundance of struggling widows and orphans and their lives were precarious. Not even the merciful Law of Moses came to their aid, being administered by unmerciful men who denied them gleaning rights and synagogue relief on the grounds that Jews who were Christians were heretics outside the Law.

So, very readily did they promise to remember the poor – a promise Shaul would honour all his days.

Chapter Twenty

THE legalists in the assemblies had been silenced, for the moment. The famine fund had been distributed; many friendships had been forged in the fires of affliction. Shaul and Barnabas realised that Cephas was right, and that they should now return to Antioch where their particular abilities were most needed. Their work in Jerusalem was over, and to stay longer was only to tax the ekklesial resources.

The long journey back to Syrian territory, though it had the usual share of hardships which travellers must expect, was made somewhat easier by the added companionship of the ever-willing Marcus increasing their original party of three men to four. It had been his own suggestion, and they welcomed it, especially as he had offered to stay with them for several months, for there were many ways he could be valuable among the assemblies there.

Knowing his restless spirit, both his mother and his wife unselfishly had encouraged him. They could see he was itching to serve in fresh territory, and surely he would learn much from the experience. Not only that, but the fine architecture, public works and municipal planning of the place would fascinate him – and he could not find a greater city in the world to study such grandeur than Antioch unless he went all the way to Alexandria in Egypt, or sailed off to Rome.

Another fact favouring his proposal was that both he and Barnabas (whom his older relatives still called Joseph) had another family connection in Antioch. Rather a disjointed connection now, admittedly, but a warm one, for together they had once shared and endured many things in the days of the Saviour's earthly ministry. Of course Marcus must go! Though they would miss him, both wife and mother-in-law were very happy in each other's company, and would be kept busy with their own work among the families and poor of their community – for as Lord Jeshua had once reminded them from the Fifth book of the Law, *"The poor will always be among you."*

News that the likeable Marcus was coming with them went ahead of the travellers by several weeks, and no sooner had they arrived, with Titus having returned to his own home and the other three newly settled into their humble lodgings, than a message arrived from the Antioch cousins – an invitation to dine with them. Marcus read it at a glance, and privately showed it to his uncle.

"What do you think? Do we bring him, or will it be too awkward?" Marcus fingered the note indecisively in his short stubby fingers. "Have their paths crossed yet?"

Barnabas rubbed his jaw thoughtfully. "No, he hasn't seen them at all. They were visiting Galilee for half of last year, then went up to Jerusalem."

"Yes, they were with us for Passover and Pentecost. After that they went down to Nabataea, but I thought they went home after that."

"Not directly. They went back through Galilee – Banayim again of course, for Dan and his family, and a final round of all their old friends in the Lakeside ekklesias, not to speak of those in Cana. Even afterwards they did not go directly home but spent a considerable time in Damascus. I think Loukanos almost demanded it of them."

Marcus grinned. "Sounds like him. So, what do you think?"

"Bring him," Barnabas said decidedly. "He's invited, isn't he?"

Shaul nodded absently when informed. If anybody had ever told him Marcus had a cousin (and Barnabas a niece) in Antioch, he had long since forgotten.

Barnabas cleared his throat. "You remember that abortive raid you told me about years ago? The one in Cana that went horribly wrong?"

Shaul grimaced. "The one I try to forget? Only too well. If ever a fool spoke unwisely with his lips it was I that night – ruining a wedding, forgetting my own name in an excess of pride, dredging up the forgiven sins of a courageous scribe, frightening an old bridegroom and his wife nearly to death, losing control of my men, being routed by a courtyard of shepherds, and ending up with a handful of feeble prisoners who did not deserve their rough treatment. Then I had to leave them in charge of a guard with a ridiculous name – Kaf – Kafshash – or something. That alone should have told me he was a few olives short of a pot-full."

"His name was Kafshalosh!" Marcus corrected with relish, trying not to laugh. Eye-witnesses had faithfully passed on the whole story until over many retellings it had become something of a legend. "*Fork-spoon!*"

"Well, I ask you, what kind of a name is that? Maybe he was a cook before he turned soldier. Did you ever hear how they later escaped?"

"I did. They were rescued by a flock of goats!" Marcus chortled triumphantly. "How I wish I'd been there to see it! Good old Dan must have been an impressive sight. He told me he was simply yelling his head off the whole time, and all he could think of was saving Meia."

Barnabas nodded, smiling faintly. Now that the terror of the raid was far in the past, and it seemed nobody had been hurt, there was no harm in recalling the funny side of the tale. Yet it was not true that no ill had been done that dark night, for there had been private anguish, a hopelessly premature birth, and many tears. But a little life which came and went like a fleeting sigh – such things were not spoken of.

Shaul's face had changed. "You knew these people?"

"Yes, my friend," Barnabas said gently. "Mordecai of Antioch, that brave scribe of whom you spoke, is married to my niece Anna." He indicated the folded papyrus on the table. "That invitation, which includes you, was sent by him."

Hesitating for barely a moment Shaul squared his narrow shoulders. "Praise the Eternal," he said firmly. "Then I have a chance to ask their forgiveness."

The undeniable tension of meeting those he had wronged so long ago was soon dispelled. Tall silver-haired Mordecai and his almost equally tall wife accepted Shaul's quietly sincere words with warm assurances that the past was done with. Inevitable tears were wiped away, and before long comfortable laughter reigned in the house as they exchanged news of Jerusalem, in particular, of Mari's household, and the latest from friends and family in Galilee.

The famine had not hit them quite so hard there as elsewhere, since in Banayim the fresh water of the Lake, though diminished, was still at hand, to seep up through the bottom of the village well for drinking and to bucket from the rocky shore to keep vegetable gardens alive. This plentiful supply in a time of severe drought had encouraged the village to sprout many such gardens over the last couple of years; therefore, like many of the smaller Lakeside communities it was actually holding its own in the midst of adversity. Growing grain however was another matter, and bread, their staff of life, was seen less and less.

"Speaking of food, when are we eating?" complained a youthful voice of uncertain pitch, and they looked around to see a lank-haired, gangling boy slouching easily against the door frame.

"Uriel, my son! Is school over already?" Mordecai asked, beckoning him inside.

"Yes, dear Father, just as it is at this time every day. Clearly with your head in your books you hardly notice my absence, for you seem astonished every time I walk back through the door."

"My dear boy, where are your manners?" Anna reprimanded quietly, indicating their guests.

The boy bent to kiss her, playfully tweaking a grey-streaked braid in her stately coronet of hair. Then he looked up, opening his arms extravagantly to the visitors as if he had only just spied them.

"Uncle Barnabas! Cousin Marcus! How good to see you again!"

Next he gasped at the sight of Shaul, and made a flourishing gesture, raising his hands exaggeratedly.

"Won't someone introduce me, *please*!" he said grandly, though he knew perfectly well whom his parents had invited.

Mordecai looked rather exasperated at these antics. Marcus, however, grinned back at his young kinsman. His own uncouth days were not so far in the past that he had no sympathy with the age which he had heard described as *All Hair and Horseplay*.

The introductions and greetings being properly made at last, Anna was satisfied. At a sign from Mordecai the steward performed welcome ministrations with water and towels and before long young Uriel had stopped theatrically vacillating between over-casualness and over-formality, and was behaving more naturally.

Shaul was agreeably surprised to discover an extremely keen intellect under the untidy flop of black hair and the two of them were soon huddled in a corner, happily engrossed in discussing two topics at once, while unravelling a confusing lineage in the book of the Kings. Barnabas and Marcus, looking somewhat blank, left them to it. Meanwhile a relieved Mordecai and Anna exchanged a private smile. It would do their son good to whet his wits against a sharper blade for a change! At times, he really was quite exhausting to live with.

The steward murmured in Anna's ear. The meal was waiting to be served. She nodded, and excusing herself, slipped out of the room and upstairs, where she tapped lightly at a door.

"Danya? Our guests are here, and the meal is ready. Will you come down?"

The door opened quickly, and a pair of rebellious wet eyes met hers. "Must I change?"

"No, my pet. You are beautiful just as you are. But I see you are still unhappy. You need not join us unless you wish to."

"I do wish to. I am so sick of crying." The dusky-skinned girl snatched up a cloth from a basin and bathed her hot face, dabbing crossly at her long-lashed, jade-green eyes. "I am ashamed to be such a baby. I was all right in Jerusalem."

"No, no, my love, there is nothing to be ashamed of! You were not in Jerusalem long enough to be homesick, and then there was Galilee, with new friends to make in Banayim, and Dan's children to amuse you, and all the hard work and fun of the shearing feast. You were too busy to mope."

"I was very happy to be helping with such fine animals, though it was sad to see them so lean. I miss ours. I wonder if they miss *me*." Danya stared out of the narrow window, teary all over again at the thought of the sheep and goats in her family's herd, and Anna hastened to distract her.

"I know somebody who will be missing you in Damascus," she sighed forlornly, while her twinkling eyes belied her tone.

The girl tossed her head, and a stray shaft of sun flicked a raven-wing gleam from her hair.

"That horrible boy in the souk? It was disgusting how he kept following us. Every time I turned around there he was with his vegetable barrow, ogling me up and down with his tongue hanging out. If Uncle Loukanos hadn't explained he was a patient of his, and touched in the head, I might have crammed one of his own miserable cabbages down his throat."

She fished up a cord which hung around her brown neck, revealing a tiny wooden camel, a whimsical gift from Loukanos to remind her that there would always be a way home.

"If this was real I could almost gallop home for a week and be back again before new moon."

"Brace up, my pet. No doubt it's that letter from home which has given you a fresh dose of the miseries. I was much the same when I first came here. Antioch is overwhelming at the best of times and I missed my home dreadfully. Now put away your trinket and tidy yourself up before the men start without us."

Danya blew her nose with determination, and gave it a cursory inspection in a bronze hand mirror. At least it hadn't swollen! And fortunately she was too swarthy to worry about it turning pink. She picked up a brush and gave her rippling mass of dark hair a few violent strokes, biting her red lips with vexation as she tugged through hidden snarls.

"I warn you, Aunt Anna, if Uriel annoys me tonight I will kick him hard under the table."

"Don't worry," Anna laughed. "If he does, I might do the same!"

That brought a half smile, at least. Taking over the brush she drew back the lustrous locks from the young woman's flushed face, deftly twisting the sides into two ropes and securing them at the back with a tortoiseshell comb.

"But you must not be over-sensitive, my darling. Boys are clumsy brutes as they struggle out of boyhood, and really have no idea of how girls feel. They catch up much later. Meanwhile, you must try to remember that while you are already a woman of marriageable age, he is still an awkward, overgrown child."

"I know that, Aunt." Danya lifted her head proudly as Anna affectionately smoothed the hair cascading from under its twisted bands. "That is why *I* intend to marry an older man, just as my mother did. She is not half my father's age and they live in perfect harmony."

At the thought of her beloved parents her lip quivered again and she ducked her head to hide it.

Anna gently tilted the dimpled chin with one finger as a more serious thought occurred to her. "Danya, dear, forgive my asking, but you are not *afraid* of meeting brother Shaul, are you?"

"N-no, not exactly afraid, but uncomfortable, yes. It will be so strange, after all I have heard of him, and – well, everything…" She gestured vaguely. "You know."

"Yes, my darling. But remember how much good has come out of it – especially your own lovely family." She hugged her, and the young woman stood up, taking a deep breath, shaking out her simple dress. Lithe and slender, she was almost as tall as the older woman beside her.

"Ah, how beautiful is youth!" Anna thought tenderly. "Not a trace left of those tears already. If it were me, I'd be a sodden wreck and not dare show my face all day!" She stroked Danya's cheek with a look of enquiry, and the young woman nodded.

"I'm ready."

"There's my brave girl."

The men were already seated when the two walked in.

"Ah, there you are," said Mordecai mildly.

"Danya, my dear child! Is it really you? How you've grown!" said Barnabas, genuinely startled. He had not seen her for years. Marcus, who had seen her only a few months before, greeted her with a warm smile, and Uriel merely winked.

Danya hardly noticed them. Standing beside Anna she had immediately fastened her searching eyes on the unfamiliar guest at the end of the table: a wiry, slim-shouldered man with tight dark curls sprinkled with grey, and a neat crinkled beard. In an instant she noticed his thick eyebrows, his strong nose, his lean cheek, firm mouth and sensitive hands, and she felt her heart quicken. So, this was the man.

Had it not been for him, a thousand things may never have happened, including herself! It made her head whirl to think of it. But she must not appear to be a foolish and shy goat girl in this company; she must have courage! Exerting herself with an effort, she bowed respectfully and managed a formal greeting, forgetting she was no longer in her home country.

"Greetings, brother Shaul, blessings and peace to you and all yours," she said in Nabataean, looking at him as calmly as she could manage.

Shaul, who had been momentarily distracted by the steward filling his cup, looked up politely – to find himself steadily regarded by a tall dark girl with clear eyes the colour of new olives. Suddenly, he could not even blink. A rhythmic clapping seemed to troop through his head in time to an old, muffled chant.

"Your pardon, sir." Flushing with vexation, Danya repeated her greeting in Aramaic.

"Greetings, daughter of Mordecai," Shaul responded stiffly, with equal formality. He could not think of anything else to say.

The graceless Uriel hooted. "She's not *his* daughter!" he blurted out in amusement, earning himself a sharp look from his father. Chastened in an instant, he mumbled, "Sorry. She is my sister, though – well, sort of."

Mordecai smiled at the girl, inviting her to sit. "We carried away our dear Danya from Nabataea. Her parents felt it was time she had more experience of both her Jewish heritage and our Christian community than they could provide."

"So now I am playing at having a beautiful daughter." Anna patted the girl's hand, and Danya flashed a smile for the first time, revealing overlapping front teeth, one of them chipped – an oddly charming irregularity in her otherwise flawless face.

"Thank you, Aunt Anna. And *I* am pretending to have no brothers."

"Ouch!" Uriel pulled a face, knowing he had brought that on himself, while everyone laughed except Shaul, for whom the whole tangle of relationships went right over his head.

With a grin, Uriel promised an explanation once they were eating their frugal meal, and after Mordecai gave the blessing he began, much to the amusement of the others, who watched him flounder hopelessly.

"Danya's oldest brother is, in fact my – no, he isn't exactly ... wait, I'll start with his parents. My mother is his – bother, I mean, Danya's father was her –" Laughing at himself, he shook his head. "You see, it's all a bit complicated."

"Not to me." Danya looked directly at the somewhat blank face of Shaul. "When my father married my mother, he already had a grown up son, whom Aunt Anna had adopted years before. So I was born with an older brother, and I now have seven who are younger, as well as Uriel here, whom I count as another."

Mordecai beamed at her. "Well done, young lady. There now, my son, take a lesson from that. When it comes to explaining matters of kinship, the women run rings around all of us."

"I see," Shaul murmured. "You are connected by virtue of relationship, not mere genealogy."

"That's right," Marcus nodded. "An odd mixture, but all family."

The rest of the evening passed in pleasant harmony, comfortable to all except Shaul, who was feeling unaccountably disconcerted, and unsure why.

Once Danya's initial shyness had passed she proved to have something of her Aunt Anna's unselfconscious ease in mixed company, perhaps because she had been brought up with so many boys. Yet there was nothing bold about her, despite a natural warmth of disposition, and her modesty was uncontrived. After supper, when Mordecai read to them from the scriptures, her ardour for the Faith was unmistakeably revealed as she joined eagerly in the discussion which followed, her intelligent questions and brief, pertinent comments revealing a retentive memory and a lively spiritual mind. With all this, Shaul could not help but be strongly reminded of his own sister.

Where was she now? Was she alive and well? The dribbling red-haired child Joshua would be a young man now. Were there other children? Perhaps there were girls, learning the games she had once taught him. Clapping games. Deborah with daughters. Would they be good looking, would they look like her? Not that he had the slightest idea whether Deborah herself was good looking or not. He had never thought about it. But if they were plain no doubt she would worry they might not marry well. If they were as striking as the girl in this room, they might attract too much attention, which would be worse, perhaps. How strange such a thought had never occurred to him before.

Irritably he told himself to stop such pointless speculations. Imagining her with daughters, no doubt, had resurrected that silly childhood rhyme from the dusty crypt of memory, and very annoying it was. With an effort he roused himself to become more sociable, but his underlying mood remained restless.

As the talk eventually moved on to more general matters, Uriel teased the girl to explain how she had chipped her front tooth, and Danya burst out laughing, a full-throated, womanly laugh, very unlike the high-pitched giggle Shaul had half expected to hear.

"It happened in the most ridiculous way!" she said, her eyes sparkling with fun. "One of our little kids, Kedar, went exploring and became wedged in a crevice – right on top of a steep crag – bleating his little heart out. He was quite frantic and so was I, for at first I could not see how I would ever get up to rescue him. So I girded my skirts up tightly – yes, cousins, you may well look askance, but try chasing goats when you are tripping over your robe and see how *you* like it – because all I could do was pray for firm handholds and start climbing.

"Just as I began, Hagru his mother came leaping to the rescue from the next hill, bounding clean over my head to land in front of me. Well, I knew she might reach him, but what then? Someone had to extricate him! In a flash I snatched at her tail as she bolted up the slope and off we went, with me hanging on for dear life, scrambling behind as best I could while she towed me along." The girl laughed again and everyone joined in, enjoying the comical image conjured up by her words.

"We were nearly at the top when my foot twisted out of its sandal and I slipped. I must have hurt her poor tail as I fell, for she jerked it out of my grip with a last almighty leap – and smack! a hoof clipped me right in the mouth. Luckily I was panting so much it was wide open or I might have ended up with a nice scar on my lips as well as a chipped tooth!"

"Poor darling." Anna's infectious, gurgling laugh broke out again, making everyone chuckle all the more. She knew the story, of course, but it was a treat to hear the girl tell it herself in such an entertaining way. There was not a scrap of vanity about her.

"Did you reach the kid?" Shaul asked politely, but he already knew the answer. Of course she did. Such an indomitable spirit would not have been quenched by a minor mishap.

"I did – he had wriggled himself in tighter than ever but I soon had him out. He and his mother took off at once without even a snicker of thank you, leaving me to struggle back as best I could. I had to slide, slither, and scrape all the way down. Ouch! Mother was *not* impressed by the state of my clothes when I came home, while poor Hagru was careful not to turn her back on me for days. No doubt little Kedar thought it was all a lovely game. He is a big buck now, but still just as silly."

"I think we all know someone like that," Mordecai murmured amusedly to his wife, looking affectionately at their son.

Much later that night as the three walked home through the broad torch-lit streets, they were accosted by a rowdy group, half-dressed in overpoweringly perfumed and tawdry clothes, staggering home from the Park of Daphne. How they had managed to walk so far in their condition was a puzzle to sober men. Now with ribald hilarity they addressed the quiet trio of Jews, both men and women pawing at them drunkenly with slurred and brazen invitations. It was a common enough incident in this massive city of selectively lax morals, and the dishevelled group was easily shaken off, but Shaul glanced at the heavily painted faces, slack mouths, and unfocussed eyes with a stronger revulsion than usual.

"What kind of a place is Antioch for a fresh-faced innocent from the desert?" he demanded with sudden asperity, abruptly lengthening his stride so much that the others had to hurry to catch up with him.

"Young Danya? She is well protected, Shaul," Barnabas said in surprise. "She will not be exposed to this type of filth."

"She will not be able to avoid it, if she so much as sets foot in the market-places."

"She is not a child, you know. She is a capable young woman who has been shepherding with her family for years, and regularly frequents Petra, which, as you have told me yourself, is a market-place which caters for everyone and every whim."

Marcus looked with faint amusement at the scowling man beside him as he strode fiercely on. "I am afraid you are turning paternal, brother Shaul," he remarked sagely.

As Shaul threw himself almost angrily on his bed that night, the distant clapping and chanting were still whispering in the back of his head. He plunged immediately into prayer. He was not at all afraid that he was turning paternal. He was very afraid that he wasn't.

Chapter Twenty-one

MARCUS and Barnabas were frequent visitors to the comfortable house of Mordecai and Anna, but Shaul just as frequently found reasons to stay away, pleading that he was far too busy to be sociable. He reminded them that with limited means at his disposal, he must earn a living, and outside of his work pastoral care and preaching took up every available moment. This was true, for he made certain that it did, though Barnabas quietly pointed out that a few cordial hours a week with hospitable fellow travellers on the Way was hardly a waste of time.

"Has it occurred to you that our work involves receiving as well as giving?" Even as he spoke the words Barnabas felt something of a pang, for he had been forced to learn that lesson himself, and a hard one it was too. Belatedly Shaul recalled a past conversation about receiving as a little child – something he had applied to receiving from his Lord, but not in relation to receiving from his brethren. It was a valid point, even obvious – how had he missed it!?

But Barnabas was continuing to remonstrate. "Must people have a problem before they are worth your congeniality? Were you this frantic when first you arrived here from Cilicia? I do not think so. Or have you become vain?"

"Vain?" Shaul was astonished.

"Yes – that rash on your face is back. So, it troubles you, then."

Shaul half smiled. "Only when it itches, I assure you. After all, I never see it, though I know it is not an endearing feature. It is only fine fellows like yourself who are in any danger of vanity. Fortunately I have never been handsome, it saves a lot of trouble."

"Aha, I thought that would provoke you! Now that I know you are listening I will restate my concerns; when we first arrived you were quite sociable. Now you are not."

"Perhaps not. Well, yes, it may be that lately I have become too centred on problem solving. But I take the correction. We cannot expect people to receive graciously what we have to offer, if we are not willing to accept that they too have something to give."

Whereupon he made a point of spending his time somewhat less exclusively with the troubled or troublemakers, and found that as usual Barnabas had given wise advice; to be with people who gave rather than took balanced his perspective, and was more helpful than he had expected. It was pleasant to sit outside in a courtyard and appreciate the fresh air, the sound of a breeze softly rustling leaves above, the play of shadows flickering across relaxed faces, the warmth rising from sun-steeped steps where people sat talking and laughing – and more than pleasant to enjoy uplifting conversation with fellow Christians who were not at pains to emphasise either their holiness or their sinfulness, but who lived cheerfully and in steadfast hope.

Yet for all this he did not appear much more refreshed. He shrugged off his friends' concern, blaming various minor ailments for the shadows deepening under his eyes. Since he maintained a cheerful demeanour none suspected that his physical weariness bespoke a disturbed spirit and troubled nights full of unsought dreams and wrestlings in prayer. Meanwhile he still resolutely sidestepped many an invitation to the home of the kindly Mordecai and Anna. He was acutely aware of his own contradiction in this, for though he would not deliberately put himself in their company for any length of time, he knew very well (and did not avoid) the places and times he might come across Anna and her young charge and exchange a nod, a smile, a brief salutation as he hurried past. At ekklesial gatherings, aghast at a distractibility which had always been utterly foreign to him, he struggled to pretend to himself the tall girl was not there, yet the very effort of doing so exasperatingly seemed to make her presence all the more palpable, even if he did not see her. It was the kind of heightened awareness of another which had once belonged only to his God, and it dismayed him deeply. What else could he do but look away ... and drown out with higher, louder thoughts the silent words of an old and foolish rhyme.

Long-legged Uriel, however, he was always genuinely glad to see and in fact he saw him often, as the boy frequently ran in to visit his cousins and Shaul at odd hours, chattering idly and amusingly about his family and sometimes discussing his studies – but most often bent on extracting all he could from the trio about their personal experiences with the Lord and his chief apostles in Jerusalem.

One morning Shaul was on his hands and knees rolling up a finished rug at the busy carpet bazaar where he worked, one part of him ironically amused that he had ended up in the same business as his unknown grandfather Asahel after all, when he heard a familiarly enthusiastic voice hailing him through the thicket of upended rolls all around. Yes, it was Uriel. He smiled to himself. The irrepressible Uriel was always a breath of fresh air – a welcome diversion from unwelcome thoughts – and exchanging occasional banter with the boy took him back to schooldays with Barnabas.

"Brother Shaul? Are you here?" A rather spotty face peered around a teetering stack of small mats and grinned down on him. "There you are. Hiding?"

Shaul straightened. "No, but now that I've seen you, I realise that might have been a good idea. What do you want here? Don't tell me you want a carpet."

"Not me, but Danya wants a nice *khilim* for her mother."

Distant clapping. He would not listen. So, the girl would be going home soon. Good.

"She trusts you to choose one for her?" Shaul queried drily.

"No, she doesn't," answered a feminine voice, and there was Danya herself peering over Uriel's shoulder, her green eyes luminous above a gauzy face veil, and mercifully the phantoms and fears in Shaul's head fled in the presence of reality. "But I do trust you, brother Shaul, to show me good quality and see I am not cheated. My father's money is too hard earned for me to waste it in a bad bargain. If *you* sold it to me, I know you would not load the price and put the change in your belt."

"Alas, that is not possible. Since I am incapable of dragging defenceless people off the street to buy, I do not handle sales. I am permitted to sort, clean, stack, fetch, carry, take orders, make deliveries, wind endless shuttles and set up the warp thread on looms; that is all. But I am profoundly grateful for that. I would rather *eat* a carpet than have to sell it."

Danya and Uriel immediately burst out laughing. Uriel honked and brayed like a young donkey, so Shaul thought, unable to resist a grin himself, but his sister – half-sister – step-sister – or whatever she was – crinkled up her eyes, and her laugh was a throaty chuckle.

"Would you at least advise me?" she asked, her eyes still dancing.

"More than that. Tell me what you have to spend, I will help you choose, then I will do the buying for you. Take your time. You will not be cheated."

As she thanked him, Uriel groaned. *Take your time!* It was downright cruel of his mother to insist he must accompany Danya to the bazaar on a day when he had so many other things to do for so many other people. Girls were hopeless, taking half a day to decide on the simplest things. He began to fidget and sigh and cough and complain of the dustiness, until Danya told him quite briskly to go.

"Finish your errands, then come back for me. That will save us both time. I don't like to be rushed and you will only annoy me. I may stay here in perfect respectability until you return, as long as you don't dawdle."

Uriel needed no second bidding and he was off. Danya gave a satisfied nod and turned her attention back to a low stack of colourful woven rugs; toying with the little camel around her neck, tapping it thoughtfully to her veiled lips, finally dropping it back down the bosom of her dress as she bent over her choices.

At once Shaul busied himself with rerolling a carpet. "You sound very maternal for such a young woman," he remarked, then bit his tongue. What kind of a comment was that? Clumsy? Patronising? In any case, it was none of his business. However, Danya merely shrugged.

"I know. It comes of having so many younger brothers. Uriel is not very different to them really, just bigger and more noisy. When he is too impatient I tease him with his Greek name, but we like each other very well. When he is not being an *Ignatius* he has a kind heart, and doesn't mind my manner, for all we are much the same age. I have great respect for his passion for the Faith."

"Yes, I have seen that passion in him too. He has told me how determined he is to meet Cephas, Johanan Zebedee and Jacob bar Joseph one day, so he can learn directly all they can teach him of Lord Jeshua. I understand that desire, for I did much the same at the first opportunity I had."

"Yes, so I heard from cousin Marcus." She glanced at him. "You must be alike, then, for Uncle Joseph told me that when it comes to the gospel, Uriel is 'as fiery as Shaul himself' underneath his gawkiness."

Shaul raised a questioning eyebrow as he lifted down another stack of rugs.

"*Uriel's* gawkiness, that is!" she corrected hastily with a blush, suddenly taking a great interest in the designs and colours spread before her.

"Then gawky or not he was well named *Fire of God.*"

"Yes." She knew just how deliberately chosen it was, for it was no secret in their family that it was the scorching flame of this man's persecutions which had caused Uriel's parents to leave their home and supplant themselves to Antioch. However, that was not her story to tell, but theirs. Absently she fingered an intricately patterned *khilim* in red and black, and after a moment's indecision added it to the small pile of favourites.

"Your own name is akin to it, perhaps. *God is my judge.*"

"You might say that. I was named partly for my father's son Dan."

"Then you should be Dana, surely?"

"No. There was more to it than that."

"I do not wish to pry." Squatting down, Shaul fanned out her choices in a business-like way.

"Then I shall tell you no more."

She looked down at the man conscientiously busying himself with the goods at her feet. Of course he had no idea, and she could not tell him. But perhaps one day he would know that had it not been for his determination to hunt the Nazarenes out of Jerusalem, her father and brother would not have been fleeing up the west bank of the Jordan to reach Galilee. Had they not, they would never have come across her own desperate mother, fleeing from persecution of another kind, despairing of finding justice among men. How differently their stories might otherwise have ended was anyone's guess. Despite the muffled closeness of the air, she shivered slightly. Yet all at once she felt she would like him to understand how it was.

Impulsively she opened her mouth again, but, "Is it not strange how good may come of evil things?" was all she said, for it was enough – and she must not prattle!

Shaul looked up at her with an appreciative glint in his intense dark eyes. How strange that now they were virtually alone he was no longer afraid. "Yes, and no, my young sister. Evil is never justified, but this much I have learned – that all things, good or evil, work together for good, for those who love the Eternal and His Son. Nothing is impossible with God. We must hold on to this, hard as it is to grasp at times."

Danya nodded, feeling suddenly light-headed. *Nothing is impossible.* How amazing. How wonderful!

Outside in the street the proprietor was shouting the quality of his goods and relentlessly importuning passers-by to come in and inspect them. At the far end of the long, narrow, stuffy shop, looms creaked and weavers chattered, while before her, in the centre of piles and forests of rolled carpets, was the flip and thud of smaller rugs being unrolled and stacked before her by a short, slightly built man – who himself seemed to be an impossibility, a part of some strange dream.

Surely it *was* impossible that the terrible scourge of the Nazarenes, Rabbi Shaul, who had provoked so many momentous events in her far-flung family, should be *here*, in a *carpet shop* in *Syria*, of all places, crouching casually at her feet as he worked, and talking to her as easily if there was neither distance nor difference nor years between them.

Giving herself a little shake, she recalled herself to the reason she was here. "I like this one. Will it wear well on an earth floor?"

The discussion turned business-like, the final selection was made, and by the time Uriel had returned, his arms laden with bundles, Shaul had been as good as his word and obtained the smart red and black *khilim* for an excellent price. He had an uneasy feeling that his good-natured employer had been under something of a misapprehension about the whole thing, from the number of clumsy jokes he made about mothers-in-law, while waggling his eyebrows at Shaul behind Danya's back, but that could not be helped.

"Can't possibly take that as well," panted Uriel. "Come to supper tonight and bring it with you. Mother's orders."

The two left well satisfied, and Shaul turned back to his work, giving his head an occasional shake as if trying to dislodge something. At the back of the shop the hardworking weavers began to sing a popular nonsense song about catching fish in a pond and the pond was in a field and the field was by a wood and the wood was on a hill and so on it went. Gratefully he joined in, somewhat to their surprise, as he restored the shop to order with hands that suddenly trembled, singing louder than the rest of them. Anything to stop the chanting in his head, which now she was gone, had returned with a vengeance. Like a wave on the shore it had retreated only to rush forward with greater force.

Who shall I marry? Who is for me?
Find my love and you will see.
A tall brown woman with blue-black hair
A foreign tongue and a green-eyed stare.

"Oh, this is perfect!" Anna said admiringly later that evening when Shaul, determinedly crushing his inner discomfort, appeared with his delivery. "Dear Mahalath will be delighted. How thoughtful of Ammiel to arrange a surprise gift like this! Danya, my love, you have made a good choice – this will not even show the red dust which your little brothers wear like a garment."

Oh, that familiar red dust! Those loveable scamps of brothers! Darling Mother! Dearest Father! And all the dear animals she knew by name! Here, there was not so much as a fat little puppy to cuddle! Suddenly Danya's eyes filled again and Anna reached out to hug her gently but the girl squirmed free with a desperate gulp.

"No, no, don't be kind to me, Aunt Anna! I'll only howl like a baby again, after being very grown-up all day." And she fled upstairs.

"Poor child," Mordecai said compassionately. "She is used to hard work, not city idleness, and she misses her family so much. It seems to come over her in waves."

"But she is going home very soon, is she not?" Shaul enquired. "Hence this purchase today?"

"Oh, no. That is being sent down with friends who are going to Petra. Danya is to stay with us till Pentecost. The homesickness is hard to manage at the moment, but only to be expected now the excitement of a new place has worn off. She told us herself that she firmly instructed her parents not to allow her to come home too soon, or she will never learn to adapt to new circumstances."

"I see. An unusual young woman!"

With a wink to his wife, Mordecai cheerfully agreed. "All the women in our family are somewhat unusual!"

Anna caressed his silver hair. "And the men," she said fondly. "If we find our lovely Danya a match who is anything like the rest of you, I will rejoice with cymbals and dances."

"But remember what Loukanos says about your musical abilities!" Mordecai chuckled.

"I know, I know!" Anna's unusual eyes, one brown, one hazel, twinkled as in unison she and her husband imitated her brother's anguished tones, *"For pity's sake, Anna, don't sing!"* and laughed. It was an old family joke.

Shaul saw the look they exchanged and suddenly felt very much out of place – even alone. He would have liked to hear more about Loukanos, now that he realized Danya's, that is, the *family's* connection. Loukanos was a very interesting man, and he had never had enough time to get to know him. But, thanking them for the invitation to supper, he excused himself. The elders were meeting at Simeon Nyger's that night and he must not be late.

He and Barnabas strode to Nyger's in silence, both of them preoccupied. Many of the initial difficulties in the assemblies had settled down, and tonight's meeting was to decide what next they should do to further the cause of the gospel, particularly in light of Antioch's approaching autumn festival of athletic games. Held a few miles outside the city at the well-watered Park of Daphne, and therefore known as *Daphnea* the games were a crowd-pleasing event which attracted many people from all over the region. It was not surprising that some of the brethren regarded them with trepidity as yet another disturbing and ungodly influence, but others believed they provided excellent opportunities to preach the gospel to a wider field.

Either way, the forthcoming athletics festival – and no doubt its effect on the Christian community – would be even more significant than usual, because it was now to be a mere adjunct to a slightly earlier and much greater event. In fact, it was not yet clear that *Daphnea* would take place at all in its old form, since this year it was to be entirely overtaken by the famous Games which began the next Olympiad – the four year interval between Olympic contests. City of Antioch officials having successfully petitioned the Emperor, Claudius had directed the Eleans, guardians of the sanctuary of Olympus and traditional hosts of the Games, to permit Antioch to purchase them – or rather, the right to hold them in their own city. The Antiochians were wildly excited by the prospect of staging the historic Games, and it seemed that people could talk of nothing else except all things athletic – contestants, trainers, venues, and the enormous financial benefit in store for the region as a consequence of the huge influx of visitors who would be drawn to the city.

The ekklesial elders had much to think about. The Antioch Olympics would affect everyone whether they liked it or not, and the question was, how best to promote the gospel in a city going mad over physical contests? This however was only one of the matters they wanted to discuss this evening. The primary issue was that while the Games might bring thousands to this hub of the gospel, what then for any future converts among them going back, unsupported, to their own worlds? To their own towns, cities, territories? To be sure, there were Jews and synagogues scattered all over the Empire, but how receptive would they be to Gentile followers of the Way of the Nazarene? Would they welcome their association, would they share the reading of their holy books? It was all very well for some to say that individuals in Christ must stand firmly on their own two feet, but human nature had a bias against being alone. And lately Shaul had found himself acutely conscious of it, in a way he had not known before.

Now, as the two friends strode along towards the meeting at Nyger's, Barnabas was mulling over various ideas, but Shaul had already decided to propose that they should first individually prepare themselves by fasting, and only afterwards meet as a group to seek Divine guidance. Till then, he could see no point in making plans. In any case, tonight he was finding it very hard to concentrate. Praying as he walked, he tried to keep his mind on the meeting ahead. Please God that the incessant words in his head would quieten!

The meeting took place, the brethren readily assented to the suggestion of fasting, and the two walked home again. The wretched chant was still repeating at the back of Shaul's every thought, but had now shifted to the second verse.

Oh no, my boy, you pay good heed,
A Jewish wife is what you need.
Turn around and flee away
She won't be worth the price you'll pay!

He told himself many things. He told himself he was ridiculous. He told himself she was half his age, that she towered over him, that she was a Nabataean. And in the same breath he told himself she was as Jewish as he was, regardless of a Nabataean mother. Next he told himself she was a sister in Christ, so her bloodline, even her culture, was completely irrelevant. Then he told himself he was making pathetic excuses. He told himself that he had – not sworn, exactly – but determined long ago that he could not afford to entangle himself, to be fettered in any way. He told himself he had once tried to destroy members of her family. He told himself to remember the youthful wisdom of one Cypriot Joseph of long ago, *There is more to life than domesticity and begettal!*

He did not tell himself that she was fresh and lovely, that she was strong yet vulnerable, that she was intelligent and different and intriguing. He did not tell himself that she was full of Godly faith and Christ-like virtue, and he did not tell himself that she was both youthful and womanly, both sweet and desirable. He simply knew it, and felt it, and ached with it, deep in the marrow of his bones.

Chapter Twenty-two

ON a set evening, following their agreed period of fasting, the brethren who were the chief Antioch elders returned to the humble house of Simeon Nyger, just as they had arranged.

The five men praying in the lower room of the simple mud home, though all Spirit-gifted prophets or teachers, were an unlikely mixture with very little in common, by worldly standards at least. There was the intense, slightly-built Shaul, a Roman citizen and Pharisee; compassionate, tall Barnabas, a well-educated Levite; and the quiet, imposing Simeon of Cyrene himself. His surname Nyger, *'Black One'*, was a reference to his dark skin, but there were times when a different kind of darkness roiled silently inside him, the haunting memory of dragging the heavy cross upon which his Lord had been so cruelly crucified. Large and powerful, with crinkling soot-black hair, Nyger's impassive bulk dominated his smaller companions.

At his elbow was his faithful manservant Lucius, also from Cyrene, hundreds of miles away on the North African coast. The extraordinary levelling influence of the *Christianoi* was gracefully demonstrated in the cooperation of these two, for here it was the old servant who had the

Gift of prophecy and his words were valued by his master. No single Gift stood in isolation, and Nyger's own Gift of teaching assisted in communicating the deep spiritual insights of Lucius to many others.

Lastly there was Manaen, perhaps the most unlikely disciple of all, a man whose early life had been spent amongst royalty. Hard as it was to believe, he had been a foster-brother of wicked Herod Antipas. Nobody could have imagined that any relation of the ruler who slew the Baptiser and was complicit in Messiah's death would ever end up as a Christian teacher. Yet there he knelt with the others, his plump face pale with the fatigue of fasting. Years ago he had boasted of having a son in the guards who had assisted none other than the famous Pharisee, Rabbi Shaul, to arrest Nazarene believers. Now Manaen too was a believer himself. Such was the power of the gospel to change lives!

Their prayers over, the brethren meditated in silence. Moments later, their thoughts were suspended – forgotten – as there fell upon the room a profound, shimmering stillness, striking all present with awe ... and a Voice spoke, pure-toned, angelic. Not a man there could have said whether he heard it in his ears or in his mind, but there was no question that it spoke – every word distinct, clear, and compelling.

SET APART FOR ME BARNABAS AND SHAUL TO DO THE WORK FOR WHICH I HAVE CALLED THEM.

The strange celestial stillness withdrew, and the room returned to normal. Shaul's heart hammered wildly, sweat poured from his face, something like a sob clutched at his throat. The Call! At last! After so many years of preparation, of waiting, of wondering, of fearing, of growing older, of temptation – it had come! And just in time to save him from himself.

Later he would weep in mingled grief and gratitude, but for now all that mattered was that his beloved Master had reclaimed him as he had begged him to through so many troubled and sleepless nights, and set his feet back on the road which began so long ago in Damascus. And he was not to go alone – dear, faithful, steady Barnabas would be by his side. Shaul caught sight of his friend's face, which like his own was a study in mixed emotions – amazement, elation, thankfulness, and joy. By divine directive they were both now commissioned as *Shaliachim*, as *Apostoloi*, ambassadors of the Kingdom of Heaven, chosen to carry the message of Life to the wider world.

The news spread quickly, and many were the well-wishers – and prolific the advice – from excited friends in the brotherhood.

At once they began to prepare, though much of their planning could only be done in outline. There were no certainties in travel, subject as it was to so many vagaries from weather to politics, and every separate stage of a journey must be arranged at its point of departure. They could only settle upon key destinations, and for the rest would have to be guided by the promptings of the Spirit. In every place their first appeal must be to their own brethren. From the days of the Babylonian captivity Jews had been dispersed far and wide, some by choice, others by compulsion, and there was no shortage of provinces with a Jewish presence. Synagogues of all sizes could be found in many towns and certainly in all major cities.

Therefore, in every place they would begin with these assemblies of Jews and Gentile God-fearers, then reach out by whatever means possible to the pagans – for as God had promised centuries ago, through the Christ, the descendant of Abraham, Patriarch of the Jewish nation, would **all** nations be blessed. That promise had always held good for any Gentile who individually sought after Israel's God and became a spiritual Jew, but only now had the time come to reveal this privilege in a clarion call of invitation to the whole world. Only now would the purpose of God be thrown open to the view of those who had not been seeking it, nor even known there was anything to find. And the responsibility fell heavily on these two men, each henceforth designated an *apostolos* of the *Christos*, to make it known!

In conference with the Antioch elders, the two newly appointed apostles settled that they would start close to home, and in a very familiar territory for Barnabas – the island of Cyprus. In that place there were many synagogues and also a core group of Christians (some of whom had fled there from Shaul's persecutions) who could do with their support both pastorally and in preaching. Then, from Cyprus they would sail to the vast region of the Roman Empire known as Asia, sowing the seed of the gospel in remote communities of Diaspora Jews among the Gentiles.

As Barnabas and Shaul burned their lamps late into the nights, discussing everything from funding to food and making endless lists of essentials and unessentials with regard to packing and portability, Marcus – listening to their adventurous plans with more than a touch of envy – importuned them to take him too. Far from quieting his desire for change, his experiences in Antioch had only made him hungry for more. He admitted that there may not be much call for his *Ruach* Gift of Sahidic in a place like Asia – but you never knew when it might be needed. Even here in Antioch it had proved invaluable in preaching to a family of Egyptians – household slaves of a rich proselyte – who appreciated not having to grope their way through Aramaic. Also, his Greek was good, and though not fluent in Latin, he could get by. Finally he pointed out that neither Shaul nor Barnabas were particularly young men, and that a strong, willing travelling companion would lighten their load. This could not be denied, nor could his value as another eyewitness to significant events in Lord Jeshua's ministry. All in all, his qualifications for the task seemed ideal.

The two told him that they had already decided that it would be only practical to take just such a companion with them, and since they had not yet fixed upon exactly whom to ask, his offer was most timely. But they would be away a long time – at least a year, probably longer. Was he sure? He was. Therefore, with Marcus so keen to serve and his loyal Jerusalem family giving their blessing, the decision was easily made to include him rather than seek for another, and before long all was ready. Final invitations and little gifts for the road poured in. Among them was a small wooden camel on a silken cord. Mordecai had penned the note tied around its neck.

"Danya asks that I send you this, her favourite little talisman. She has a fanciful idea it may remind you that no matter how far you go, there will always be a way home. No doubt a bit of Nabataean folk-lore yet clings to her. She is still a child in some ways."

As Shaul untied the note from the neatly carved trinket, words about graven images ran unbidden through his head, but he brushed them aside almost with impatience. The letter of the Law should not mask its spirit, and there was nothing cultish about this simple ornament. He already knew from Barnabas why Danya always wore it, and it was clear that neither she nor her family saw it as anything but a little toy affectionately given to comfort a homesick girl.

Shaul stared for a long time at the small object. It had meant something to her. Yet, she had parted with it for his sake. He knew where it had nestled. He could smell the faint perfume of a sweet oil and see its sheen where the wood had absorbed it from her warm, silken skin. If he gave in to the temptation, even now, to keep it … wear it … carry it with him … it would be a step backwards. A mistake. But how could he spurn such an innocent gift?

It remained in his possession while he, Barnabas, and Marcus tramped the length of the steep winding road which brought them to the port of Seleucia Pieria. With them was a group of Antioch disciples who had come to see them on their way. It was another three days before they could board a ship, and during that time, the brethren supported them in prayers and fasting.

At first light on their last day, Shaul rose quietly from the huddle of sleeping men around him and slipped into the cold fresh air of the street. Picking his way down to the ragged edge of the harbour where a few twisted trees were well rooted in the rocky soil, he sat there, meditating, with only the sleepy swish of grey wavelets for company.

The moment had come. The time was here. He was finally about to board a ship, to sail away, to fulfil the charge of Lord Jeshua, revealed to him so long ago. What lay ahead was real enough – even real enough to give him occasional qualms – but at this moment it seemed formless, half-realised, like the indistinct objects under these dull waves, shapes blurred by the quiet water crumbling over them. What was behind was still vivid. Too vivid.

He leaned back on a gnarled trunk, feeling the rough, salt-cured bark digging through his clothes into his skin. He welcomed the discomfort; it was physical, a literal distraction from one which was phantasmal. All his adult life, he had been disciplined, controlled, sure of himself. Only at his sudden conversion had that confidence been completely thrown into chaos, and of course that had been necessary. Afterwards, the old habits of internal mastery and discipline were still there, and he was glad of them. A follower of Christ might be free from the Law, but when external constraints of obligation were done away with, internal constraints imposed by Love were vital. Yet he had never felt constrained, for his will had always been to follow his convictions and therefore, though subsequently he had endured many physical hardships, he had suffered very little inner conflict. Until the unthinkable had happened.

What had it all been about? Was it truly about what he felt for Danya – or just about what he felt? Those sweats, that hammering heart, that nameless longing, the involuntary thoughts – and those disturbing, repetitive words which would not leave him alone! From the blessed night when at last the Call had come, the torment finally had left him. But it had left him shaken. What had been the point of it? Had it been a test? A punishment? Had it made him a better person? It had mocked his confidence in himself … perhaps that was a good thing. No doubt, for only by acknowledging his own weakness would his work glorify Christ, rather than himself. Was there more to it? Was it that he had to face the fact that he was not above other men, that he too had a man's susceptibilities, against which all his single-mindedness and devotion gave no immunity?

He stared unseeingly at the first glimmer of silver stroking the grey waves which crisped gently at his feet. Behind him a tentative pink dawn was breaking.

I have always thought I was different. Forgive me, Lord, for my wretched pride. You have shown me I am no different to any other man. For this I thank you.

Tied to his girdle was a small rolled pouch containing leatherwork tools – his awl, short-bladed knife, beveller, waxed thread, triple-pronged lacing punch, a tiny lead-weighted mallet, bodkins, a folding bronze measuring rule, and a few stippling stamps. With these he could earn a crust if no other work was available, and just as importantly, keep their own leather items in good repair. As such, they were too precious to risk losing in his jumbled canvas swag of necessities. Now he untied the thong, unrolled the bag, laid it flat, and from one of its various pockets extracted the toy camel. He fingered it for a moment, looking seawards over the gentle waves which were just beginning to shrug gleams of the rising sun from their sleek backs. Their dullness was dissolving, the shallows were turning translucent in the strengthening light.

Getting to his feet he drew back his arm, intending to cast the trinket far out into the deep, but even as he did so a loud chittering noise came from just over his head. Startled, he looked up, to see an anxious bird warning him away from her nest in a hollow branch. At the same time a bigger bird swooped from the stumpy tree and landed in front of him, trailing an apparently broken wing, hopping and crying, attempting to lead him away, while unseen nestlings undid the father bird's best efforts by revealing their presence through hoarse little cheeps.

Shaul stood perfectly still, the carved camel in his hand, its cord dangling, as he watched the feathered parents protecting their young. A single tear scalded its way down his cheek, as slowly he rewound the cord neatly around the wooden trinket. Now he understood.

It had not been about weakness or chastening! Nor had it been some lesson in discipline which he had been learning the hard way. It was about unforseen vulnerability, and it was a lesson in love.

He already knew what it was to love, first as a son, then as a worshipper of God, and later as a follower of Christ, responding joyfully to love first shown to him when helpless. He already knew what it was to love as a brother, a friend, a neighbour – whether in reciprocal warmth of affection or as a choice to act lovingly toward others. He was no stranger to the inconvenient impulse of lust either, but was long practised in disassociating mere physical responses from any thought of indulging them … just as he had learned to ignore the pangs of hunger while fasting. And from an early age he knew the glory of loving soul-soaring ideals in all their abstract beauty.

But he had known nothing about being struck with a whirlwind which seem to spin with every kind of love at once, a fury which buffeted a mere man till he was breathless and bruised against his own bulwarks. He had known nothing about tumultuous and unreasonable emotion, about the fear and helplessness of feeling passion which struck uninvited, about the extraordinary way it could swamp rational thought in a dizzying and oft-deceptive fog, or provoke wild, mad scheming over the simplest actions all in the hope of tasting again – be it ever so briefly – the agonising thrill of just being near that one special person – no matter how unconscious of his struggles she might be. And that she *was* unconscious of it, he was certain. For her sake as much as his own, he had not betrayed himself, and he was profoundly thankful for that.

He was about to bring the gospel to people afar off. Not just to Jews but to Gentiles, people for whom the scope and passion of human experience, not divine law, was the sole arbiter of their reality. He had seen the difficulties of the Antioch converts at first hand, and had to admit that he had not fully understood just how hard it was for many of them. His abilities had been valued, but when it came to dealing with people's hearts, he could see that he had approached many problems academically, as if untidy emotions could be neatly reasoned away to smooth a Christian's path.

But from this time on it would be different. As a man who had experienced confusion and temptation and heady human delirium, he would have a more genuine fellow-feeling, a deeper compassion, a more profound patience. It was so obvious now. How could he help others if he had no empathy with their struggles? No comprehension of their strongest emotions?

And there was one more thing. Now he knew what it felt like … and he would never forget it.

"Thank you, my blessed Master, for your protective hand which has brought me through a trial I never thought to be mine. Praise to the Eternal for the glory and beauty of Eden, for I have tasted the wine of the human heart and it is sweet, as the Father created it to be. Yet you have given me clear visions of what lies ahead, when Eden is restored, and it is high above all human desires! So I shall walk in your footprints, my Lord, a eunuch for the Kingdom of Heaven's sake. And may I do my part in bringing many sons to your glory!"

Taking a deep breath, he drew his sleeve across his eyes and looked up. Morning had broken, the dawn sky was streaked with delicate rose-tinted clouds. The struggle was over. The tide had crept up, and the sparkling water was tentatively licking his feet. So still had he been that even the birds had stopped worrying about him.

He turned, glancing up at the nesting hollow. An impulsive step and a stretch – and he strode off, tool pouch in hand, leaving a puzzled bird pecking at her solid new chick.

Several hours later he boarded the ship with his two companions and a feeling of immense relief. Then, with smiles and a few tears and earnest prayers, the Antioch disciples sent their two Ambassadors of truth, and their younger assistant, on their way.

Thus they began their seemingly impossible mission – to spread the pure doctrine of Christianity across a continent of superstitious pagans. Apart from a few codices of notes, and a small bundle of scrolls, their only library of scriptures was written in their memories. They had no helpful works of explanation by clever scholars, no way of publicising their intentions ahead of time, and must be their own heralds. No swift carriages would bring them in comfort from one place to another – these emissaries of the Kingdom of God had only slow, uncertain transport, and their own feet, to carry them.

Still, they were undaunted. They had a courageous faith, and the Christ, their Master, had invested them with a portion of the Spirit Power of Almighty God. What more did they need?

So they set out, bearing the enlightening torch of the gospel – and slowly began to change the world.

Chapter Twenty-three

THE three men leant on the ship's bulwark, watching the harbour of Seleucia dwindle, and the shoreline slip away.

"Goodbye to Antioch," said Marcus, a trifle wistfully, thinking of his soft bed on land, and comparing it to the bare planks on which they must now sleep. "Farewell to civilisation!"

Barnabas cleared his throat loudly. "How dare you, young man!" he protested with mock indignation. "We are going to the city where I was born – an extremely civilised place, even compared to Antioch!"

Shaul was not inclined to joke. "Antioch, civilised?" he murmured, watching the dark blue water heaving below. "Marble streets and colonnades, coloured fountains and gilded statues, lustful rites of idol worship, and everlasting prattle of sports, scandals and theatrical entertainments! Does a craving for sensual gratification make a people civilised?" He shook his head, unseeing as a gleaming fish flip-flopped out of the water for an instant. "The heart of Antioch is no different to a brute beast's – I don't call that civilised."

"You are right, of course," Barnabas agreed thoughtfully, idly watching the square sail bucking in the stiff breeze. "The place is completely amoral – outside of the synagogues and our colony of Christians."

Marcus followed his uncle's gaze to where the mast swung a dizzying arc across the blue sky. Then wished he hadn't.

"Speaking of colonies – I hear that Roman settlers are trying to colonise wild Britannia," he said with false brightness, trying to keep his mind off the uneasy feeling in the pit of his stomach. "Now that's a place *I'd* call uncivilised. Give me Antioch any day, civilised or not."

For a fleeing moment Shaul felt an uneasy qualm. Surely this young man realised that they were themselves intending to traverse some very wild and comfortless country, where they would experience many hardships! But he dismissed it at once – clearly Marcus was trying to distract himself from a woeful onrush of nausea. Shaul observed with compassion his set pallor. You could talk yourself out of it for only so long!

"I wonder what Emperor Claudius hopes to gain from such a far-flung conquest," he responded heartily. "It is said that the land is continually shrouded in cold mists and rain. It hardly sounds fit to live on, yet some say the savages there run around covered in nothing but blue paint."

"Blue paint!" Barnabas began to laugh. "You can't believe everything you hear in Antioch, my friend! You should know that by now."

Shaul smiled and shrugged as he swayed to keep his balance on the lurching deck. He didn't believe it for a moment, himself, but it might favourably distract their unhappy companion. In this, he almost succeeded – but not quite.

Gripping the bulwark rather more tightly than necessary, Marcus gritted his teeth and swallowed stickily before replying, "At least we will not be sailing as far away as Britannia! That would be a lot of ocean to cross ... and far too many waves ..." His voice trailed away and he took a desperate breath, his face turning even paler.

Barnabas, who had made the crossing to Cyprus many times, eyed his nephew with some amusement. "Doesn't this fresh sea air and the rolling, *heaving* motion make you feel –" he began, but Marcus had already dashed to the other side of the boat, where he hung, groaning, "–wonderful?" Barnabas finished with a grin.

"Stop, Barnabas!" Shaul nudged him in reproof, rather surprised at such heartlessness from his usually warm-hearted friend. "That's downright cruelty to a man on his first voyage! Obviously you've never suffered the same affliction."

"True, to both statements. I repent in dust and ashes."

Chastened Barnabas was genuinely apologetic as he went to the assistance of his forlorn nephew. For once, irrepressible high spirits at the prospect of returning to his beloved island had got the better of his good nature. In that unguarded moment, the mature *bar Nabhas* had shown that *Joseph*, his teasing younger self, was still very much alive.

Remembering the anxious misery of his own first voyage, Shaul had more sympathy. It had taken him a long time to be convinced that every steep roll of the ship would not end in it turning turtle. The compulsion continually to rush to the higher side and somehow rebalance the boat was strong, but when a man was doubled over the edge, busily disposing of his breakfast while attempting not to nose dive into the awful depths, he was utterly helpless. All he could do was dolorously watch its evil billows rising to mock his fears. Even now, sailing was not Shaul's favourite way to travel, and a heavy swell could still turn him queasy. Ugh! Sea-sickness was a loathsome thing!

He was not sorry to have his mind taken off the unpleasant subject as his tall companion returned to his side. Having apologized and vainly attempted to comfort his unhappy nephew (who being not the slightest bit interested in sympathy at that acutely miserable moment, implored him just to go away) Barnabas was unable to resist a final impish remark.

"Oh, no, Shaul! I've just thought of something, my friend! I'm so sorry! Brace yourself for a disappointment."

"What?" Shaul looked startled.

"I know how much it means to you," Barnabas shook his head, attempting to look glum, "but we're going to miss the Antioch Olympics!"

For only the briefest of moments an indignantly incredulous Shaul was taken in – before the two of them burst out laughing.

The sea had calmed and Marcus had recovered by the time the little ship neared the Isle of Cyprus. The long brown coastline came wavering into view, backed by dense woods and misted mountains. Spicy land smells wafted towards them over the warm turquoise water which slid noiselessly along the dark planks of the ship, creaming in their wake. Orders were called, sails trimmed, ropes readied.

Barnabas caught Shaul's eye and smiled. "My home!" he said gladly.

As they joined the few other travellers straggling down the crude gangplank, Shaul looked about him.

"It looks far grander than I had expected," he commented, following Barnabas on to the wharf. "Almost as impressive as Sebastos Harbour at Caesarea, possibly not Tarsus, though."

"Has to be. It's our commercial capital," Barnabas reminded him over his shoulder. "One of the most important in the Great Sea, in fact. With so many Jews here, it's a perfect place for us to start."

He beckoned encouragingly to his nephew, who was unsteadily negotiating the bouncing plank. "As soon as we have visited my household and friends, as we arranged, then we will make ourselves known to the synagogues."

Marcus stepped onto the wharf with relief. "Plenty of Jewish ears around to hear, then."

Shaul gave a satisfied nod. "Where the commerce is, there will the Jews be also! Some of my father's shipments used to come here – though to me it was just another name on a list."

Barnabas had brought with him a bulky chest filled with presents for old friends, which included the household of loyal servants who worked his property. Once he had ruled over many vineyards and olive groves, but these he had long since sold, donating the proceeds to the apostles to use as they saw fit for the community of believers. Now he could hardly wait to see again the familiar old house and fertile swathe of land which still provided him with a modest living.

He was even more impatient to see the friendly faces he had left behind and to give out his gifts. He watched the chest anxiously as sailors hauled it up from the hold in a well tarred cargo net, while Marcus tried to find his land-legs again. After so many hours at sea, he had the peculiar feeling that the solid ground was moving under his feet. This was most disconcerting, especially as earthquakes were not uncommon in the area, but his well-travelled uncle merely chuckled, assuring him the rocking sensation would eventually pass.

"Just don't shut your eyes!" he warned. "That makes it worse!"

Experimenting, Marcus discovered to his alarm that it was quite true – and his eyes flew open at once in astonishment, whereupon the bizarre feeling subsided, much to his relief.

Meanwhile, Shaul went in search of the harbour master. When he came back he found the others patiently sitting on the chest watching seagulls squabbling over a fish. Barnabas raised his eyebrows enquiringly. Shaul shook his head, and helped them lift the awkward luggage.

"They passed through this port not long before the famine," he reported, panting with the weight. "That means Deborah and Simeon were here when I was at Antioch. Close, but not close enough."

Marcus grunted as he tugged the rope handles of the chest. "Did you have to be so generous with presents, Uncle?" he groaned in mock despair. "I hope everyone hasn't decided to retreat to the mountains this summer. We'll never manage to drag it up the tracks."

"Fear not, they will be there! It's not so far," Barnabas grinned, nodding nevertheless to a lanky, grimy fellow with a battered handcart, who was harassing them for business. "You can admire the scenery as we go and be glad the only thing swaying in the breeze will be vegetation. Now, let's find a water carrier, I'm parched!"

Salamis was a grand place, showing off its prosperity in the lavish use of marble – in flights of steps, market-places, temples and, for the wealthy, splendid Roman houses which boasted bathrooms and central heating for the cold winters. All appeared fresh, clean and sparkling in the hot sunlight, but so strong was the glare they were not sorry to leave the bustling city.

Once clear of some untidy little suburbs of squat dwelling places amid prolific vegetable gardens, they enjoyed a shadier tramp along a well-trodden white track, as it led them deeper into the ragged green countryside. It was hardly quieter, though, since the wooden cart rattled and clunked noisily behind them, while the odiforously sweating carter hoarsely croaked tuneless dirges the whole way.

They did not meet anyone else on the road, though they came across one unexpected interruption – a tangle of sleepy brown snakes, sunning themselves in the dust. The carter jerked to a stop, Marcus paled, and his companions judiciously paused.

"Yes," Barnabas answered the unspoken question. "These are poisonous, but not enough to kill you. Just a nasty bite. Anyway, they will be more afraid of us than we are of them."

"Oh really? How is that possible?" gritted Marcus, shrinking back to Shaul's side as Barnabas and the carter slapped the road with branches, banged rocks together and created noise. Slithering magically out of their knots, the snakes slid away into the scrub, and the quartet continued on their way. Barnabas cheerfully gave them a lesson on what snakes they might expect to find, and in which particular places, in future. Distinctly unimpressed to be told at this late stage that the island was infested with them, the others were not particularly reassured to hear that only *some* were venomous, and out of these only one was actually *deadly*.

"It's the blunt-nosed viper you need to avoid at all costs," Barnabas warned. "It likes shade, wells, and running water, just like us, unfortunately! But it will only attack if you disturb it, and at least it will hiss loudly first."

"How much warning would that give us?" Marcus asked cautiously. "Enough time to avoid it?"

"Ah, no, not really," Barnabas admitted. "But remember what our Lord said, Marcus! I was there when you wrote it down, just as the Twelve told us, at Mari's. He said that when believers went into all the world to preach the gospel, signs would follow them – not only speaking other languages, but also being able to heal sickness whether in minds or bodies. And that they would be unharmed by drinking anything poisonous. And what else?"

"Yes – of course – and that they may handle snakes without being injured," Marcus said, rather ashamed of himself. "I need to reread some of my own notes."

"There you are, then," Barnabas said confidently. "Snakes everywhere here. A bite will still *hurt*, of course, and quite a lot too, so use your commonsense, but there's no need to be afraid."

Shaul and Marcus exchanged a rare look of mutual relief. "Thank you, my friends!" said Shaul gratefully. "That was a very timely reminder for us all, and has cheered me up immensely. Praise and thanks to our Lord Jeshua for his very *practical* care of those who serve him!"

They marched on in a very good mood after that, and less than an hour later they saw sprawling vines crouched low against a rocky slope, a grove of bushy olives flashing green and silver in the breeze, and behind it, a large, neat white house peering over the trees. They had arrived.

They paid off their wiry carter and he trotted away at a surprising speed. He had barely rattled and clunked and croaked himself out of sight when a shout of recognition went up from the housetop, and Barnabas's old home seemed to erupt with bodies pouring out to envelop them in a warm and emotional welcome.

The well-loved disciple had not seen any members of his household since leaving Cyprus to help form the ekklesia at Antioch many years before. Since then, partly through his faithful steward Linus and estate manager Mnason, and partly through believers who had fled there from persecution, a sizeable group of disciples had become established on this part of the island. Now it seemed they had all had gathered to meet them. Delightedly, Barnabas introduced his nephew and his oldest friend, and soon both Marcus and Shaul felt very much at home.

It was a noisy, happy time as everyone talked at once, eagerly enquiring about friends and relatives, exchanging news of the Homeland. Some remembered the brief visit of the merchant Simeon ben Gabbai. He had spent only a day with the disciples before his ship departed. No one had seen his wife Deborah. She had remained on board with a sick child. Even this small fragment of news was treasured by Shaul. There was hope yet!

Shaul and Barnabas began as they had planned, proclaiming the glorious truths of the Messiah's ministry to their fellow Jews in every synagogue they could, preaching the gospel to the general population wherever they might gather a crowd, teaching in houses, on rooftops, in gardens, educating anyone with ears to hear. The Salamis disciples did everything they could to help the visiting missionaries, spreading the word, inviting all their acquaintances to come to their homes and hear the good news.

Many responded with curiosity, some with enthusiasm, and several more households were baptised each week as people realised that these men were independent eyewitnesses of the very things the Salamis Christians had been telling them all these years. A few of these disciples had been present at the first outpouring of the Holy Spirit upon the believers after Lord Jeshua's ascension to Heaven, and had returned to their island with the ability to speak languages they had never learned. But none of them could pass on their Gift to others.

Yet now, Barnabas and Shaul were doing just that, passing on a variety of very practical *Ruach* Gifts to those in the Christian assemblies, powerfully attesting to all that the Spirit of God was with them, and that the good news they preached of the Messiah of Israel, was true, trustworthy, and way beyond mere religious supposition.

The stir created by these events was considerable, but all too soon it was time to move on. Having appointed several new elders to help those already serving the Salamis ekklesia, the apostles left. The brethren farewelled them with many thanks, rejuvenated by their visit, praying for the continued success of the apostles' work on the island, and vowing to keep up the refreshed interest in the city. It was a wonderfully heartening start to their tour.

After leaving Salamis, Barnabas, Shaul and Marcus made their way along the Roman road which ran across the southern breadth of the island. It was high summer and the heat was punishing, but at least, as Barnabas said cheerfully, they were spared lashing winds, drenching rain, flooded paths and calamitous landslides!

The glare on the white road was intense. Shaul's head ached with squinting. He thought about a strip of thin black veiling he had found helpful in Nabataea, where the burning light had often troubled his eyes. Hadn't he used it to tie up his parchments? He had! Deputising a spare sandal-lacing to that task, he shook out the fine cloth and gratefully draped it over his head. Instant relief!

Barnabas smirked, and Marcus collapsed in kinks of laughter.

"You look like a leper! Promise you'll take it off if we meet anyone!"

Shaul did not care how he looked; the cruel glare was gone, and he could see very nicely through the loose weave – and it kept off the flies, well, *most* of them. Of course it made his face even hotter, but it was that or the headache. After a while his companions stopped laughing at him and even began to wonder whether they might try the same remedy, if they could find suitable stuff in the next market.

The sun was high, the light as achingly bright as liquid crystal in a glassworks. All around, the dusty grey-green shrubs shrilled deafeningly with cicadas, gnarled olive trees shimmered darkly on the steep hills, and twisted vines crept over dry cleared slopes as if exhausted by the effort.

The highway stretched ahead, its smoothly worn paving polished like water-worn rocks, bearing testament to the steady river of travellers which had flowed along it over many long years. Cartwheels of iron and wood had also left their trace, over time grinding into the thick stone a dual scar of shallow grooves – a curse to any vehicle of dissimilar size, and a hazard for travellers who did not watch their step. Here and there, the heavy air thickened with the unmistakeable stench of carrion, upon which large black crows hopped, uttering their weird, creaking, languid groans … as if despairing over the repulsive morsels at which they pecked and tugged. Outcrops of limestone, weathered to a dirty grey, limped up and down the rugged hills, looking somewhat like sea monsters frolicking through dull green waves, while ribbon-like tracks ran in all directions to sagging little settlements and farms.

Among these habitations, travellers – armed with stout sticks to keep off the inevitable dogs – might obtain refreshments such as eggs, curd, soured milk, bread, olives, or figs, even a cooked meal, if they were willing to deviate from the level highway to trudge the hilly paths … strewn as they were with rocks the colour of melted butter and rancid cheese. Sometimes the food was worth the effort. Sometimes not.

Shaul held that all such disappointments must be shrugged off as minor annoyances within the grand scheme of things, Barnabas blithely adding with supreme optimism – considering his own fastidiousness – that they should be shrugged off *cheerfully*. But as Marcus bitterly said one day (deeply regretting a boiled egg he had unwisely wolfed without sniffing first), by the time a man's insides had tried to become his outsides, he was physically incapable of such philosophy.

Apart from such lamentable incidents, however – similarly dire moments being common among travellers – their journey was mostly a pleasant one as steadily the two apostles and their faithful (now wiser) assistant worked their way along the main Roman road.

Preaching the gospel wherever they could, with varying degrees of success, slowly they travelled west – through Ammocostos, Kition, Amathus, Neapolis, and Curium – towards the administrative capital of Paphos, a hundred and fifty miles away at the western tip of the Island. Behind them they left tiny groups of excited believers, a husband and wife here, a household there, a congregation of five or six somewhere else.

Upon two or three or more in these humble little assemblies, the ambassadors of Christ laid their hands according to the guidance of the Spirit, conveying to the new believers whichever Gifts were the most suited to their unique circumstances. The language Gifts so valuable in preaching were the most fascinating to curious outsiders, but to the joyful new brothers and sisters in Christ, the Gifts of understanding, wisdom and knowledge were even more greatly prized.

Their mission on Cyprus so far had been hard work, but they had risen above all petty discomforts and trials, and there was no doubt that Barnabas's familiarity with the island and its customs had smoothed their way many a time. Now the trio walked the coastal road in good spirits, talking about people they had baptized, making a joint effort to remember names and relationships, and occasionally arguing cheerfully about who went with whom.

By this time they were a practiced team, working well together, having established a pattern which they expected to repeat in Paphos. Starting in the synagogues as usual, there they would preach, baptize, teach, establish a group of disciples, invest them with appropriate Gifts, and appoint elders. Then, after encouraging their new brethren to hold fast to the faith and continue the work begun, they would move on.

Now with the capital so close, they felt a pleasurable sense of accomplishment. The first section of their missionary journey had been well blessed, and their time on the island was drawing to a close.

Paphos was the final city on their tour of Cyprus, and at last they were almost there.

The white road was dusty and hotter than ever. Shaul snatched off his stifling veil to cool his face for a while, flapping thirsty flies away from his dripping sweat with a bunch of leathery leaves. As usual his purposeful, oddly efficient stride – rising high on his toes in a manner Barnabas rather rudely called 'stalking' – had outstripped the others.

Through the scrubby sandhills to their left came the soft sound of gentle surf, an inviting flash of blue sea, and the intriguing glimpse of a massive pillar of rock.

Barnabas licked a finger and held it up. "A breeze!" he said triumphantly.

"Where?" Marcus looked around hopefully.

Barnabas laughed. "Well, you won't *see* it. But I think the sea breeze is in at last. You can even smell it!"

Shaul drew a deep breath, rather unwisely, as he inhaled a fly. When he had finished coughing it out and the others had finished laughing, he tossed away his leaves and declared impatiently, "Enough of this road – it's hot enough to fry cheese. Let's go as far as we can with cool feet! Come on!"

Scrambling through bushes at the side of the road, they found a rocky, overgrown track towards the water they could so tantalisingly hear and smell. Once they were through the shrubby, tangy-scented hills, the sea breeze caught in their hair and ruffled their tunics as they crunched over a rough shingle beach, where the rugged obelisk they had spied from the road stood like an impassive giant up to his knees in the sea.

"Ahh!" Marcus tore off his sandals and sighed with satisfaction as his toes sank into cold, sloppy sand, small waves splashing and frothing blissfully around his ankles. He waded out a little further. "This is the way to travel!"

Shaul winked at Barnabas. "You prefer your feet *in* it, to *on* it, eh, young man?"

Marcus laughed good-naturedly, not minding that the others referred to him as if he was still a youth. He was in fact over thirty, but he would always be 'young' to the older men.

"At least this way I can feel the bottom!" he agreed, then winced as his bare soles met a slimy cushion of seaweed and a sharp shell in quick succession. "Ugh, I can also feel too many other things! Wait, I'm putting my sandals back on."

"Antioch has made you soft!" his uncle scoffed, but after treading on the spiny body of a dead fish he quickly did likewise, and the two recklessly waded through the shallows fully shod. Shaul shook his head, knowing a little more about leather than men who could afford to be careless with it.

"Seawater will rot the stitching," he warned them, swishing barefoot in their wake through the welcome shadow of the rocky column. He had only one pair of sandals and intended them to last as long as possible.

"Too late now," Marcus laughed with a shrug.

They continued for a while in a contented silence, enjoying the respite from the stifling road until Marcus suddenly pointed.

"Look there!" A walkway from the beach had just come into view, and buildings could be spied further along. "Paphos! Journey's end!"

Barnabas shook his head regretfully. "Not yet, not until nightfall. We're still about ten miles away. This is *Palai Paphos* – Old Paphos. Pilgrimage centre for Aphrodite, Goddess of Love, who was supposedly born on this very beach, arising from the foam of the sea. You'll be sick of the sight of her before we get through the city. Shrines everywhere. And an elaborate sanctuary. Fortunately, that is some distance out of the city itself," he added hastily as Shaul's heavy eyebrows met above his nose in a scowl.

"If it was at the other side of the world it couldn't be too far away," he growled. "But this whole island is infested with the wretched cult."

"True," agreed his friend, "so let's pray that one day the whole island might be infested with the gospel instead."

"Amen to that! And with God all things are possible! But is there a synagogue here?"

"I'm not sure. Last time I was on the island it had been severely damaged by an earthquake, and I believe there have been more tremors since then. But we have to pass through this place to rejoin the main route to the new city, so we will soon know. It may have been repaired by now, or even replaced."

Shaul brightened. "There must still be Jews here with livelihoods they could not leave – with or without a place of worship. Let us stop here tonight and seek them out! And if they have a synagogue after all, why, today is Second Day so there will be a service this evening. A perfect opportunity."

The others readily agreed, and so taking the walkway up to the old city they passed through its crowded streets. Barnabas had been quite right about the proliferation of images. Shrines to Aphrodite were everywhere and in the distance a huge temple complex could be seen, while all around the city many of her carved images in wood and stone were brightly painted and startlingly life-like.

CHAPTER TWENTY-THREE

Marcus blinked at one particularly graphic statue.

"If this is what they're like in the street, I'm glad we can't see inside the temple," he commented bemusedly.

His uncle shrugged. "Oddly enough, in the temple itself, elaborate as it is, the goddess is simply represented by a sort of conical pillar of basalt. That is, so I've been told!" he hastened to add to their significantly raised eyebrows.

Making enquiries of an elderly passer-by, the trio were gratified to discover that the Jews' old synagogue, like many other damaged buildings, had in fact been fully restored with the concerted aid of Jewish communities from all over the Island and even abroad. Of course, Jews always stuck together, didn't they, the man shrugged, and not everyone was so lucky as to get a hand-out from strangers. But, occasional earthquakes were a fact of life and unless the whole town should be laid waste – *me genoito!* – here in *Palai Paphos* people would always repair and carry on as usual.

Thanking the proud old fellow who had imparted this information so readily, Barnabas immediately turned down the next street. "Come on, it's this way! Let's hope the Chazzan here is as hospitable as our good synagogue keeper was in Salamis."

"Offering us lodgings *there* was easy merit," Marcus pointed out with a grin. "He already knew we were staying at your place!"

As they approached the rebuilt synagogue they heard the massed voices of children in school chanting the last lines of their lesson for the day. Inside, a sing-song voice droned a benediction as the academy was dismissed. A scramble of boys scampered out into the sunlight, noisily laughing and pushing, dashing off like escaped prisoners.

The three dusty travellers entered to introduce themselves and found the lowly official tidying up. It was soon clear however that regardless of the traditional requirement that a synagogue Chazzan should be a humble, worthy servant of the congregation, brawny Hadar did not regard himself as particularly lowly. He gave them a rather bland reception and did not offer hospitality, only a neutral stare from his darkly pouchy eyes.

However, on hearing that one of them was a rabbi, a Pharisee, he scratched his bristling beard and scraped up some belated enthusiasm.

"H'm – we do need ten men for a service this afternoon, and I happen to know that while there will be plenty of women and children, we may be several short of a quorum."

"That surprises me!" Barnabas said before he thought. "Is there not a goodly congregation of men here?"

"Certainly. But yesterday over in *Nea Paphos* – New Paphos, you know – there was an important wedding which most of the synagogue are attending, and naturally they will stay several days for the full celebrations. Families are very tightly connected at this end of the Island," he added proudly.

"You did not wish to go yourself, then?"

"A respected Chazzan desert his duty? Of course not!" Hadar replied, shocked. "I take my position here very seriously. But even I cannot multiply myself into three or four men, so your attendance today will be useful and ensure we have the needful *minyan* for the prayers."

He paused, looking them up and down for a moment, and frowned to himself as if trying to make a decision. Drawing himself up with a slight grunt and a nod, he continued.

"Rabbi, if you have no objection to addressing an audience of more women and children than men, I will invite you to speak. The only other I can call on today is very aged and feeble. His voice is too weak to hear, and the last time he stood before the *bema* to read he collapsed through lack of breath and fell onto the elders in the chief seats. Facing the congregation as they do, they had no idea what was happening until they were knocked to the floor."

Hadar shook his head so disgustedly that he narrowly escaped spitting. "It made a shambles of the service!" he added sternly.

"I would be honoured," Shaul replied courteously, inwardly thanking Lord Jeshua for once more opening the way. After a few more words, the disciples took their leave and went to find lodgings.

Marcus laughed about the self-important official enough to make him forget the offensive shrines, and Barnabas shook his head wryly, but Shaul felt vaguely disturbed, thinking instead of the struggling old man whose efforts to serve in physical weakness had earned him contempt rather than compassion.

Chapter Twenty-four

AT the due hour, washed and refreshed, the three returned to the synagogue, where Shaul spoke with powerful simplicity concerning the Messiah prophecies, and how they were realised in the extraordinary life, death, resurrection and ascension of Jeshua bar Joseph of Nazareth, whose lineage could be traced back to Solomon and David. After the service both Shaul and the others were besieged with questions about the gospel and drawn into many lively conversations. It was a most encouraging response.

By the end of the day, Marcus was laughing again. "All that fuss about his duty, and our pompous friend Hadar did not even stay past the opening benedictions!"

"I don't think he had a choice about that," Barnabas said reasonably. "He was pale and sweating and by the rather desperate way he rushed out, I would say he was most unwell. Probably something he ate."

"If you say so." Marcus did not sound convinced.

Shaul frowned slightly. "Anyone can be stricken with a bad belly, especially in hot weather. It might explain his irritability this morning."

"I held my breath when that poor wheezy old Phineas tottered up to take over the serving," Marcus confessed with a grin. "It was a relief when he managed those heavy scrolls without dropping them."

"He found the right passages easily, at least," Barnabas pointed out, "and asked some good questions later. He may be weak-winded, poor fellow, but there's nothing wrong with his ears."

"Yes, he has an enquiring spirit," Shaul agreed with satisfaction, "and a perceptive mind, as have many of the women. If they are a true representative of this congregation it would be a shame to leave before the absent members return. Even more of a shame if they left New Paphos before we got there, and then we missed them altogether."

"I heard they will be back by Sabbath," Marcus offered.

"Good," his uncle nodded. "Meanwhile, we have a lot to do. Hadar's married daughter Galia has invited us to address a large group of women tomorrow. Her husband is presently on business in Kition, where we were some days ago. I wonder if we met him?"

"Perhaps." There had been so many faces, so many names. Shaul resolved to make lists in future so he would not forget who they had met, and where. "The only name I can remember from Kition is *Zeno* – probably because we learned about him at university!"

Barnabas burst out laughing. "Zeno, the founder of the Stoics! Well, he had some worthy ideals about virtue, peace and harmony with nature, I admit, and perhaps he was a good man. But as he died about three hundred years ago, you would be better off remembering the living!"

"I agree," Shaul said ruefully. "I wish I had your knack for recollecting names and faces, but then you have always been at ease with strangers. I mistrust my memory as much as my eyes until I am better acquainted with people."

"Ah, but you remember the best of them, and the worst of them, well enough!" Marcus pointed out with a grin.

"Alas, that is true. But everyone is equally worthy of notice, and I see I must make more of an effort. I won't forget Hadar in a hurry, that is certain, but I will remember his daughter for better reasons. She strikes me as a sincere and thoughtful woman."

"And hospitable. She told me whenever her husband is away she fills the house with devout women – all fatherless or widows – children and all. I said they were fortunate to have her as a friend and she just laughed, and told me it was the other way around. Meanwhile, old Phineas begs us to dine with him tonight, and there are other invitations as well. Praise God!"

"Praise God!" the others rejoined gladly.

For the rest of the week the three worked steadily, proclaiming the gospel to groups small and large. Astute Phineas was not slow in understanding and accepting the truth of their words. As an aged man in uncertain health he had no time to waste in prevarication, so he told them plainly, and he was the first of the synagogue to be baptised according to the commandment of the Saviour. The very next day, his wife, daughters, and household servants lined up to follow his example, and soon there was a large group of excited people at the public washing pool, attracting staring onlookers both Jew and Gentile. Galia, the proud Chazzan's daughter, was one of many women who came there to be baptised. Her humble spirit, tempering a quick intelligence, showed that she did not take after her father.

Having heard her earnest confession of belief in the gospel, Shaul helped her into the water and was just reminding her to take a breath when there was a stern shout. Startled, they looked up to see an angry Hadar pushing himself through the crowd, waving his arms.

"Stop!" he barked, still pale from his recent malady. "Stop this at once! What do you think you are doing with my daughter? You may have thought me safely out of the way, but I have heard what you are doing here, and it is heresy!"

"Father!" Galia protested, dismayed. "You are interrupting the most important moment of my life! This act will wash away my sins before Adonai God!"

"What?" he spluttered. "Is the Day of Atonement not efficacious enough for you?"

"No longer," she responded quietly. "The Messiah has truly come at last, Father, and through his sacrifice we have atonement every day. But first, we must acknowledge our need of him, and this immersion is what he requires of us."

Hadar stabbed a finger accusingly at Shaul. "What *he* asks of you, more likely! Are you making vows to this person? Are you? Then I disallow them!"

"You may not do that, Father, I am married."

"What? Do you know the law better than your own father, an appointed custodian of the synagogue? Your husband is not here and I stand in his place. I forbid you this ritual!"

"Not so. His absence does not make me a widow."

"Then delay this heretical nonsense until he returns next month. Let him decide."

"Excuse me, Father, I have no wish to delay and it is not my husband's decision to make but my own. Much as I honour you both, I must obey Heaven before either of you."

Hadar looked as though he had been slapped. He shook his fist in Shaul's face. "Subverter of women! Opportunist! I will have no serpents in my congregation! I will have you stopped!" Scarlet with fury he stormed off while the onlookers busily expressed in emphatic tones their diverse opinions.

Shaul waited silently as a trembling Galia stood motionless in the water for a moment longer. Then she sniffed away a few hot tears, and lifted her chin with determination. "I apologise for my father. Please proceed."

By Sabbath the synagogue was crowded. All the regular congregation were back again after their festive week, as well as a number who were less regular, and more than a few Gentiles. Everyone was looking forward to exchanging views on what had happened in their absence, and to see what might happen next. Shaul, Barnabas, and Marcus walked to the service with high hopes, but before they had even entered the building were taken aside by the returned elders, who looked coldly at Shaul.

"Our Chazzan has told us you dealt falsely with the holy scriptures, and bathed publicly with our women," they said shortly. "Consider this your first warning."

"Hadar was not present when I spoke," Shaul replied quietly. "I am a Pharisee, brethren, and can assure you I respect the holy scriptures as much as anyone."

"A rabbi? Well, he did not mention that, nor that he was absent. But we are fair men, so if you will keep your words brief, we will hear you for ourselves and judge."

So again Shaul was able to address the synagogue. This time he read from the scroll of Isaias, explaining to the intent crowd how it was that the passage about *a lamb led to the slaughter, silent as a sheep before its shearer,* referred to the Nazarene prophet Jeshua – who though innocent as a lamb, was condemned by the Jewish leaders, and crucified in Jerusalem nearly fifteen years ago. "He was a willing sacrifice for his people," Shaul asserted boldly. "What greater love can a man demonstrate? He was – he is – our Passover Lamb, and by his blood we are saved."

"Amen!" croaked old Phineas loudly, while a sibilant rustling up in the gallery betrayed that the women were whispering excitedly to each other. Confused, the rest of the congregation listened almost in a trance, until Shaul proclaimed that this Nazarene Jeshua was no ordinary prophet, but the Christ, their Messiah, and that God had raised him from the dead! A sudden agitated hubbub burst from the audience – and with Hadar hissing angrily into their ears the elders rose in their seats as one man, commanding Shaul and his friends to leave.

"This is your second warning!" they said sternly. "Is this what you call respecting the scriptures? Claiming that Messiah came only to be condemned as a criminal?!"

"Condemned as such, yes, but unjustly, brethren, as I have been attempting to show."

"If he was unjustly condemned, then you make criminals of those who condemned him. Priests! And the High Council – the holiest men in Judaism!"

"Many of those priests have since repented and accepted that Lord Jeshua is indeed the Son of God," said Barnabas. "They are now some of his most devout disciples."

"Now we know you lie! All priests are Sadducees and none would believe a resurrection."

"Sirs, they, like many, have been convinced by the multitude of miracles and signs God has given to verify our words."

"We have seen no wonders but we see clear signs that your sect is a divisive force in our religion, and that you are spiritual imposters who have no respect for the traditions."

"I have great respect for tradition," Shaul replied quietly. "Mindfully practised, it reinforces our faith, and encourages unity. And when we are inwardly struggling, it supports us with sound habits of worship until we are stronger. Undisciplined man is reminded by rituals and comforted by ceremony, else God would not have given us the high days, holy convocations and festivals. But tradition is an aid only, not an end in itself."

"Surely, brethren," put in Marcus impulsively, "you understand that when traditions of men contradict God's word and obscure truth, we must chose which to serve."

"We understand only that you are very determined to overthrow our authority in this place," Hadar spluttered. "Claiming unprovable events. Creating confusion. Stirring up silly women and old men! Preying upon the weak minded!"

"On the contrary, Chazzan, I believe they have shown great strength of mind," Shaul said honestly.

"What do you hope to gain? That is what we want to know!" Hadar demanded belligerently, before he was silenced with a look from the elders for too freely asserting himself. After all, they were the shepherds of this congregation, and he was only a minister.

"What do we hope to gain?" Barnabas smiled. "Nothing material, I assure you. Only the joy of bringing light to those who sit in darkness."

It was an unfortunate choice of words. The chief elder gestured widely to the idolatrous city around them. "*There* is your darkness!" he said scathingly. "Go and 'enlighten' these filthy heathen and see how far you get! But do not attempt to corrupt Godly men in this city again, upon pain of synagogue discipline. And stay away from our blessed place of sanctuary. We will tolerate no more disruptions. We will have enough work as it is with undoing the mischief you have already caused."

With that, the elders marched them out of the synagogue porch and down the steps.

"I understand your anger and your fear, brethren," Shaul attempted to reason with them. "I was once myself a fierce opponent of the Nazarene sect, persecuting them from one end of the Land to the other. But once the risen Lord himself appeared to me, I could withstand the truth no longer."

But the men were already forcing them into the street, so without further argument, the disappointed trio left. Behind them, with the service broken up in disarray, the congregation, all agog, was crowding out of the building. Old Phineas hobbled, gasping and panting, as fast as he could after the three disciples. Struggling painfully for breath, hoarsely he implored them to come back to his home. Accompanied by his household together with Galia and her friends, they did so, gladly, slowing to his feeble pace and helping him along. But even so, by the time they reached his house sweat was pouring from his ashen face, and his steps were tottering.

Scarcely had they been shown inside his neat courtyard when the agitated old man collapsed, wheezing pitifully, his lips turning blue. At first he feebly waved off their concern but it was quickly obvious this was no fleeing breathlessness. Women and servants swarmed over the helpless form on the paving, bringing cushions and rugs, attempting to help him, rubbing his wrists, giving him water and wine, anointing his temples; his wife weeping, fanning him and half apologising to her visitors all at the same time.

"He has these terrible attacks," she sobbed in explanation as a servant ran out with a smouldering herb to wave its vapours in the greying face.

"Each one we fear may be his last." And indeed it looked as though her words were being fulfilled at that very moment.

Her husband's frightened eyes were bulging but he made a supreme effort. "Baptised – just – in time!" he gasped. "Praise Jeshua!" The quivering eyes rolled up in his head as his wife screamed, "No!"

Amid loud lamentations all around, the two apostles dropped to their knees beside him, each with a hand on the frantically struggling chest. Their eyes met as they appeared to listen to something inaudible.

"There is a fatal canker here," Shaul said briefly. "And this man has much to do for the gospel." Silencing the others with a quick, commanding gesture, he nodded slightly to his friend.

"Brother Phineas," Barnabas spoke clearly, his voice ringing with authority. "In the name of Lord Jeshua the Christ, you are healed of your disease."

Instantly, fresh, healthy colour flooded into the sagging, leaden face, and the agonized mouth relaxed, drawing a long, sweet, deep breath. The old man shuddered, blinked, opened his eyes and sat up in one swift movement, looking a little confused. Flinging her arms around his neck his wife shrieked with astonished joy, and Phineas flinched, rubbing his ear.

"Wife! My ear!" he protested heartily, his voice strong and unwavering. "Would you deafen me?!"

Whereupon she laughed wildly and burst out crying, hugging him tightly, kissing the apostles' hands – and suddenly everybody was kissing and crying and hugging everyone else in sight, trembling and marvelling at the apostles' astounding gift. Chorus after chorus of praise burst out spontaneously, until throats were dry, and Phineas waved a hand for attention.

"Enough now. I do not wish to become hoarse again," he chuckled, still dizzy with the heady sensation of breathing with sound lungs, and feeling thirty years younger. "Go and gather all your friends! Tell them what you have seen today. Everyone must hear that the hope of all Jews has been realised – that Messiah has truly come! Yes, he who is our sun of righteousness, with healing in his beams! To these men, who are his servants, he has given the Divine power to prove it! Go, spread the word!"

Taking him quite literally, the neighbours and friends at once ran willingly to do his bidding, while Phineas turned to Marcus with sparkling eyes. "And you, young man – how long do you think it will be until the Christ returns to restore the Kingdom of Israel, eh? Till the power of Rome is broken, and we live in peace under our Saviour's hand?"

"That is something we cannot tell," Marcus shook his head. "I know only that we must live as if in his Kingdom already. In that sense, it lies within us."

"We *can* tell you this," Barnabas added soberly, "that for each of us it will not be longer than our own lifetime – and none of us knows how long that is."

"As today has shown!" Phineas replied fervently. "How the Lord has blessed me, brethren – and how wisely we must use the time we have left to prepare!"

Chapter Twenty-five

THE next few days were chaotic, bringing so many people to Phineas's house that the disciples took to teaching in the public forum. Here they were defied by devotees of Aphrodite, mocked by sarcastic wits, besieged by professional beggars, taunted by sneering children, and continually harassed by Jews from the synagogue who resented their doctrines, their influence, and their popularity. Despite this generalised disdain, many others sought them out, intrigued by their words; and so much private hospitality was pressed upon them that Marcus declared if they ate many more of the enormous rounds of flat bread which were the specialty of the city's womenfolk, they would soon be just as circular, while nowhere near as thin.

In the evenings they went from house to house, preaching, baptising, and confirming a steady influx of converts, answering many questions, relating their own experiences, and passing on the precious words of their Master. Old Phineas in particular was so anxious to preserve a record of these sayings that he paid two public scribes to follow the apostles everywhere, working in tandem to write down as much as they could.

"How else will we remember when you are gone?" he said to Barnabas. He put an arm around Marcus and shook him gently. "Now, if only you could leave this fellow behind, eh? How helpful that would be! An eyewitness to so much!"

"Indeed, he saw more of the Master's ministry at first hand than I did," Barnabas replied with a touch of envy. "But that was my own fault. No, don't ask – it's a long story."

"And as for me, I was a late-comer by comparison," Shaul admitted. He did not say that during his time in Arabia he had perhaps communed more with the risen Lord than anyone. So sacred was that time that he kept it to himself. He added with a wry smile, "Though I was a premature birth in the natural sense, spiritually my birth was definitely overdue, and I too can only blame myself. Marcus, however, has little reason to reproach himself, and he has been duly privileged."

"I am very conscious of that privilege, I assure you," Marcus answered, uncomfortably aware that the first part of Shaul's commendation was less than accurate. "Though many others saw as much and more."

"Ah, perhaps," said Phineas. "But for we who are so far away in time and place, that does not feed our hunger to know more of the Master, our greediness for detail! See now – you are all educated men – another rare privilege! I urge you to set down all you can, before your memory fades like mine."

"You will have no argument from us on that," Shaul replied warmly. "Without a written record it is far too easy to add or subtract detail through continual retelling, too easy to confuse one incident with another."

Barnabas agreed. "Memory can be a slippery thing."

Phineas nodded regretfully. "Oh yes, I know. Just ask my wife, who is always indignant that I forget which of our children was the first to talk, or the last to walk! I tell her at my age she is lucky I still remember their names – or hers!"

He chuckled briefly before continuing more seriously, "But there is no place for vagueness when it comes to matters of our faith. The record must be preserved with clarity and accuracy, and who better to do it than eyewitnesses! So waste no time, brethren, I beseech you, for the sake of all your fellow disciples. You especially, young Marcus, before the greater responsibilities of age swamp you. Meanwhile, I ask all of you to be compassionate on my scribes – and do not speak too fast, eh?"

"My uncle and I have already made a collection of many of the Lord's sayings," Marcus assured him. "Some he heard, some I heard for myself. And my cousin Loukanos has even more. He followed Lord Jeshua's group for many months in the days when he was searching for truth, and he made careful notes of what he saw and heard. As a physician, he was particularly intrigued by miracles of healing."

"We have copies of some of his notes with us, as well as our own," Shaul put in. "Phineas, with your permission, we might make very efficient use of your scribes. Will you allow them to work with Marcus? If they make copies of each other's material, others later in our mission will benefit from it too. And of course you will circulate what you have to the other believers on the island?"

"Of course!" Phineas echoed enthusiastically. "That is an excellent idea, indeed! How wonderful that you have already compiled written records – and I assure you they will be devoured by me as soon as the ink is dry, and read to everyone regularly. Besides myself, there are two others here in our group who can read, and everyone will soon have their favourite sayings by heart."

Barnabas snapped his fingers. "Another thing! Some have been set to music by my niece's husband, brother Mordecai of Antioch."

"Excellent! We must get everyone here tomorrow and you will teach us all you can. The children will learn faster than anyone, of course, and that will be helpful when the rest of us struggle."

Accordingly the daily discussions now ended on a musical note, so to speak, as Barnabas and Shaul's resonant voices, assisted by the lighter melodious tones of Marcus, taught the Paphos disciples the songs their brethren sang in Antioch. Many were recitals of the Lord's words, yet the one which always affected Shaul the most was based on the prophet Isaias.

Who has believed our report? To whom will God show His power?
God's Son, despised and rejected, bearing our sorrows and griefs.
His life he gave for our sins, yet he shall prolong his days
The Eternal's pleasure shall prosper in his hand.
Who is God's righteous servant? Who will make many righteous?
Lord Jeshua, see the fulfilment of your life long travail!
We are healed by your wounds, and you will bring us life
The Eternal's pleasure shall prosper in your hand!

The tune was an ancient one, known to most Jews, a melody haunting enough to bring a lump to any throat, but to Shaul, Mordecai's setting of the prophet's words would forever bring back that dark night in Cana … the night he had first heard Nazarenes singing joyfully of their Master … the night when *"My name is Shaul bar Shaul!"* was no longer a schoolboy joke, but a shouted declaration of angry pride …

Less than a week later, the disciples' buoyant mood was checked, when the gospel workers were again confronted at the public pool where they were conducting baptisms. A frail old woman had just been immersed, and Phineas and his wife, enveloping her in a large blanket, were insisting she must come home with them for dry clothes. As they led her away, there was a restless movement at the back of the chattering crowd – Hadar and five elders had arrived. Forcing their way to the front they beckoned imperiously to the trio in the pool. Shaul, Barnabas, and Marcus obligingly stepped out, dripping in their wet tunics.

"Have you changed your minds about us?" Marcus asked cheerfully. He did not really think so, but given what had happened to Shaul on the road to Damascus, anything was possible.

Discounting Marcus as merely an impudent servant, the elders ignored him, and sternly eyed Shaul and Barnabas. The leader raised an authoritative finger.

"You were given two warnings, and this is your third offence."

"*What* is?" Barnabas asked, genuinely surprised. "We have not set foot in the synagogue since you ejected us."

"You are still subverting the faith of the fathers, you are still engaging in rites not prescribed by Moses, and now we hear you are dabbling in sorcery. Do you deny it?"

The apostles were momentarily baffled. "Sorcery?!"

The elders pointed accusingly towards hearty old Phineas, walking comfortably, talking and laughing easily with his wife as they assisted their elderly new sister down the street.

"You invoked the name of the Pretender to cast out *shedim* from an old man at death's door."

"You cannot have it both ways," Shaul challenged, his eyes flashing. "If he is a pretender, then his power is not real, and we have not healed anyone. If we *have* healed by the power of his name, then he is not a pretender but the Son of God as we claim."

"That was your third warning," the chief elder said, ignoring Shaul's argument, which he could not quite follow. "But I see you are set in your sins." He swung around to address the wary new converts behind him. "You have been deceived and misguided by these base fellows! Repent and return to the ways of Moses which you have forsaken, lest you share their punishment."

Galia was hurriedly weaving her way to the front of the crowd. "But we have forsaken nothing," she protested. "We revere Moses! Did he not write in the Fifth Book that God would raise up a prophet like himself, whom Israel would ignore at their peril? Lord Jeshua *is* that very prophet, and so we do well to heed him."

Hadar spluttered in his beard. "What – at the expense of Adonai God?!"

Galia laid an appealing hand on his arm. "Father, do you serve God less because you honour Moses His prophet? Of course not. The one requires the other. Then surely you understand we do not serve God less because we honour Jeshua His Son!"

"Go home, or be silent before your elders, daughter!" he commanded, flicking her hand away. "You disgrace me with this unfeminine conduct! It is not for women to debate the Law with their betters! Yes, and it shames your poor husband that you do this behind his back! Beware he does not return home only to divorce you!"

Galia stood her ground, her eyes glowing. "I think not, Father." She plucked a letter from the bosom of her *chiton* and kissed it impulsively. "This came from him today! I had it read only an hour ago – and never was I so glad to pay the fee. He has made some wonderful new friends over in Kition – yes, read it! – and they baptised him into the name of the Christ five days ago!"

Immediately the exultant woman was overwhelmed with congratulations from fellow believers as they praised God for this unexpected blessing.

Snatching the letter from her hand, Hadar hurriedly cast his eyes over it before savagely tearing it in two, muttering angry words.

"Enough of this!" barked the chief elder impatiently. "Chasten your wayward daughter in your own time. We are not here to argue with foolish women, but to discipline men who are renegades. Their teachings are corrupting Jews near and far, and they must be stopped. Now, Chazzan, do your duty!"

Checking himself with an effort, Hadar took a few deep breaths. Very deliberately he began to remove his long striped coat. Ostentatiously he rolled up his flowing sleeves.

Shaul gripped Marcus by the arm, speaking quietly but very rapidly. "Get everyone out of here at once – there's nothing they can do except inflame matters." He snatched his precious document case from around his neck and threw it over his younger friend's head. "Keep this safe for me. Now run. Tell Phineas what's happening, and prepare for a shock when you next see us. We'll need salt water, oil and clean rags."

"And strong wine!" Barnabas added quickly, his face very pale. He too had just seen what was hanging from Hadar's belt. "Leave now!"

Following his eyes, Marcus exclaimed sharply, and stunned as he was, instantly obeyed. "We'll pray for you!" he flung over his shoulder and vanished into the thickening crowd.

Even as the warning leapt from one alarmed Christian to the other like wildfire, Hadar strode forward, roughly seizing Barnabas with one hand and Shaul with the other, manhandling them to a clear space away from the hazards of the pool. It would never do if any of the accusers accidentally tripped and fell in! By the time the officials closed back in around the arrested apostles, the rest of the believers, obedient to the urgent words of Marcus, had extricated themselves from the press of bodies and melted away.

Now the swelling market crowd pushed closer, intrigued, relishing the conflict. These Jews were such a proud lot, holding such lofty opinions of themselves, and yet here they were, treating two of their own like common criminals – such a fuss did they make over their religious rules and regulations! But they were generally a law-abiding people, so a public Jew-beating was rare excitement, and the people of Old Paphos were going to make the most of it.

Bets were already being laid. Which would take it best? Would the short one or the tall one cry out first? Would they call on their God, or would they curse their elders? They nudged each other to silence as the chief ruler formally announced the sentence.

"By order of the Synagogue Council, this Shaul of Tarsus, and this Barnabas of Salamis, being members of a sect outlawed by our Sanhedrin, having been three times warned, and having persisted in their rebellion against our spiritual authority will receive the discipline of the lash."

Barnabas set his teeth. "Is it worse than the rod?" he whispered huskily to his grim-faced friend.

"There is not much to choose between them, believe me," Shaul replied in a terse undertone. "The one will rip your flesh, the other will break your bones."

Jostling expectantly, the pagan crowd wagged mocking fingers, shouting crude comments and jeering rudely as the two were bound face to face on either side of a nearby pillar. Nerving themselves for their ordeal, the apostles were oddly grateful that they could still partially see each other. A fleeting thought even crossed Shaul's mind that they were positioned strangely like the Cherubim over the sacred Ark.

Barnabas muttered grimly, "I have had no practice at this sort of thing. I was not even whipped as a child."

"Nor I."

"My father indulged me."

"Mine did not. But he was an amiable man."

The elder's voice again. "The sentence is forty stripes. One to be withheld, that the Law of Moses be not accidentally transgressed."

"Have you seen this done, Shaul?" Barnabas whispered hoarsely. "I have not."

Shaul winced. "I have seen it done, I have ordered it done, and I have done it myself – God forgive me!"

The clothes were torn from their backs. Out of the corner of their eyes they could see the Chazzan positioning himself between them, ceremoniously uncurling not one but two whips– one for each of his big, practised hands. In a prideful display of strength and dexterity he was going to flog them simultaneously from where he stood – a cut to the right, a cut to the left, one for this man, one for that man. He spat on his palms. Barnabas drew a sharp breath and turned his head away.

"No, no!" Shaul's voice was urgent. "You must face him! At this angle he will do most damage to the far side of the body. The lash will curl around when it strikes and may take out an eye. Better that it cuts the back of the head."

Barnabas obeyed, though it was not easy to accept. "I hope you are right," he gritted tensely, pressing his cheek against the cool stone, staring with horror at Hadar grimly flexing his arms as he shook out the leather coils. "I am not good with pain. Forgive me if I do not suffer in silence."

"Courage, my brother. These are drover's whips and there are no barbs in these thongs. Our Master suffered far worse."

"Lord Jeshua help us!"

"Amen!"

Thwack! Thwack! Two agonised gasps. The savage beatings had begun, and the crowd gloatingly kept count.

Chapter Twenty-six

"WELL?" Shaul stretched cautiously as Marcus finished swabbing.

"Crusting over nicely," his companion answered slowly. "But no infection, thanks be to God!" He stared grimly at the mottled red and dark purple welts.

A synagogue beating was thorough, with miscreants turned part way through to receive blows both front and back. Angry stripes covered not only each man's back, chest and stomach, but had licked around to his neck, his flanks, legs, and arms. The ordeal had been all the more terrible for having been administered with a long single-thonged whip. The shorter three-stranded flail kept by most synagogues for such discipline, required only thirteen blows. Clearly the Cypriots of Old Paphos made their own rules.

Barnabas tenderly felt the back of his head. Shaul had been right about the curling lash. At least they still had their eyesight, even at the cost of lacerated ears.

"How is the pain?" Marcus asked almost hesitantly.

"Painful," his uncle replied with the ghost of a smile, very carefully drawing on a light robe. "But somewhat better now my clothes don't stick to me. The stiffness is almost worse."

Shaul stood up slowly and nodded, cautiously easing the leather thong of his document case to a more comfortable position on his smarting neck.

"We can't give in to it," he said firmly, grimacing as reached for his tunic. "We need to move, and keep moving, for our brethren's sake as well as our own. Tonight we will ordain elders, and bless whoever our Lord appoints to receive the Gifts. Tomorrow we must leave." He put a kindly hand on Marcus's muscular shoulder. "We are thankful for your ministrations, my brother. And your strength. Carrying belongings on our backs would not be pleasant right now."

"That's my job," Marcus responded absently, his mind busy elsewhere. Should he include this horrific incident in his next letter home, or would it only worry the life out of them? He was not even sure about including it in his personal journal of their travels.

Why record the pain and humiliation inflicted upon servants of the Lord? Would it not discourage others from preaching in far-off places? And he felt faintly uneasy about what he had seen on Shaul's back. He could have sworn there were old scars among the new injuries. Had this happened before? But Shaul had said nothing and it was not his place to press him.

As it was, Marcus could only feel thankful (if slightly guilty, which he knew very well was unreasonable) to have escaped the lash himself – if for no other than purely practical reasons. Had he been whipped as well, he would not have been much help to his companions. Please God there would not be a next time!

The next day the newly ordained elders, Phineas among them, formally farewelled the determined missionaries with prayers and blessings, but this was not goodbye, for the entire congregation of disciples, rejoicing in the Gifts now among them, insisted on accompanying their teachers to bring them on their way. Slowing their steps to accommodate their wounded brothers, the massed group walked beside them, singing all the songs of praise they had recently learned. Phineas had been right, the children had learned them first and knew them best, and the adults were glad to be prompted when they faltered over unfamiliar words.

For the three companions travelling in the Master's service it was a heart-lifting, unforgettable farewell, a wonderful affirmation of the love of Lord Jeshua which so warmly bound together people who so lately had been strangers. At the second milestone the procession halted. Regretfully everyone said goodbye. There were few hearty embraces – the apostles were still too damaged to be touched without pain. With tears in their eyes, the singing ekklesia turned and walked home, and the three men slowly continued on alone.

At first the sun's heat on their throbbing backs was a boon, but by the time the harbour of New Paphos came into view, trickling sweat had begun to sting the apostles' wounds and make them itch. Finding a way down to the beach, thankfully they left the road to refresh their hot dusty feet in the sparkling cool shallows, with Marcus, packs and all, crashing through the scrub after them. With relief they squelched and splashed along, absorbed in their own thoughts, until Barnabas, who was leading the way, turned and broke the silence.

"We have company!" he said, indicating a figure waving up ahead. The others looked up.

"A soldier!" Marcus was surprised. "Are we trespassing? Surely this whole coast isn't sacred to Aphrodite?"

CHAPTER TWENTY-SIX

"Ridiculous!" Shaul snorted.

"Hey!" the soldier bellowed, tramping through the rock-strewn sand towards them. "Are you the preachers? The travelling preachers from Antioch Orontes?"

Shaul and Barnabas glanced at each other, rather puzzled to be hailed in such an unexpected way.

"Yes, we are," called Shaul, wading out of the water and painfully struggling into gritty sandals.

Barnabas asked, "Who wants to know?"

The soldier looked the bedraggled trio up and down for a moment, then squared his shoulders.

"Proconsul Sergius Paulus sends you his greetings," he said formally. "He has heard reports of you and your preaching and wishes to hear you speak."

Marcus put down his heaviest bundle. "I wonder if he heard reports of your beating, too!" he muttered darkly to the others.

Shaul caught Barnabas's eye. "We will be honoured to meet him," he answered courteously, "as soon as we have found lodgings. The Governor may not care for us shedding sand all over his courtyards."

The soldier grinned suddenly. "The Governor would think nothing of it," he said. "But his favourite, Elymas, is a great one for ceremony!"

He gestured to a flight of sandstone steps leading up to the higher level where the city streets began. "Follow me," he said, scrunching over the shingle.

"So, who is this Elymas?" Barnabas asked as they obeyed.

"A Jewish mystic," replied the soldier, "though not so Jewish as you'd notice. Known also as *bar Jeshua* – he's a prophet, magician, astrologer – whatever you want. Sergius Paulus keeps him around to satisfy his everlasting questions on the universe, the meaning of life and such like. Always wondering, is Sergius Paulus – probably why he's sent for you. But Elymas bar Jeshua has a comfortable following up there at the Residence. Don't cross him if you can help it!"

"You don't seem exactly awed by his talents," Shaul said, amused.

The soldier laughed as he led the way up the steps. "Not me!" he admitted. "I was never one for worrying over the mysteries of life! Give me something obvious – strong, sweet, and simple – like Aphrodite, for instance."

He jerked his thumb to the east where a flowered walkway led towards a distant temple. "Now, that's something a man can understand, all right."

Shaul touched the soldier's arm. "We bring something far more lasting than the self-serving lusts of such worship," he said soberly. "We bring a hope of bodily resurrection after death, and the gift of eternal life."

The soldier looked at him queerly. "Never heard that one before! Not the same as dying and going to Hades, then? Or Olympus?"

"Not at all. Come and hear us when we address the Proconsul!" said Barnabas encouragingly.

The soldier shifted his gaze. "Reckon I might!" he muttered.

Later that day, Barnabas and Shaul, now looking considerably cleaner and tidier than they had on the beach, rather stiffly mounted the dazzling steps that led to the Proconsul's reception hall, and hoped they would not have to sit for too long. With their bodies a mass of painful lacerations, at the moment it was more comfortable to stand.

They were ushered into a long high-ceilinged room with an intricate mosaic floor depicting colourful scenes from Greek mythology. Rather *too* colourful, as Barnabas murmured to his companion, who muttered curtly that in his opinion, underfoot was right where it belonged.

Sergius Paulus was seated at the far end of the room, holding audience with several appellants. Short and studious in appearance, his face was shaven in the Roman fashion and his hair was as close-cropped as a soldier's, though he wore the white senatorial toga. Also present was a row of attentive men sitting on plain benches along the walls. Most were civilians, and the purple stripe on their tunics marked them as government officials. Some were accompanied by their wives, languid women in flimsy draped dresses and elaborately braided hair styles. A number of soldiers were there too, as well as the usual guards.

In their simple tunics and plain coats, the apostles looked rather out of place in this formal setting, as they stood quietly awaiting their turn. Barnabas noticed the soldier from the beach and nodded to him without receiving a response. Like the others, he stood staring straight ahead, while public petitions, judgements and matters of administration were dealt with by the Proconsul and his officials. At one corner of the room silent slaves replenished various tiny refreshment tables from baskets of golden quinces and ruby pomegranates, clearly more for show than consumption, since no one with any self respect would risk their dignity by eating such awkward fruits in such a gathering.

Government business now concluded, the audience looked up and murmured appreciatively as a tall old man sidled into the room. He stroked a long, forked beard, and greying locks of hair, carefully curled, swung to his stooped shoulders. His dark, elaborate turban was twisted with bands embroidered with mystical signs, and his expensive robes rustled as he slid into a seat behind the Proconsul. There he sat, Elymas the sorcerer, leaning on a painted staff, his ferocious glance darting jealously around the room.

Beckoned forward, Shaul and Barnabas now approached, and were presented to the Governor.

"So you are of Tarsus – and a Roman!" he said interestedly to Shaul. "You are the more welcome – we share the same name, I believe! Is not Paulus the Roman form of Shaul? You are in Rome's territory now, my fellow citizen, and must take the name which entitles you to her protection!"

There were murmurs of approval from around the room. Shaul bowed in acknowledgement of this compliment from the Governor, who continued, "So, Paulus, as we must call you, and Barnabas, compatriot of this glorious island, you see a ready audience before you! Tell us, what is this message you bring? Speak up, for all we know is that it has caused great dissensions among your people, especially in Judaea – and being so far away, how can we enjoy intelligent debate on the subject if we remain ignorant of the particulars?"

Underneath the polite compliments and formalities, Shaul sensed a keen interest. This thoughtful man was not merely seeking a diversion for a long afternoon. The soldier's words on the beach had revealed as much. Here was a man of understanding and intellect, who was seeking for something and could not tell what it was.

Encouraged, Shaul began to tell those assembled of the One God, the Creator of all, Who cared for His creation as a father cared for his children, and was grieved when they turned away from laws which He had made for their well-being. Man's estrangement from Him was the cause of mortality and all the world's evils, but God in His loving kindness had a plan of redemption. This plan had previously been revealed only to Jews, but now was to be made known to all people.

Gesturing enthusiastically as he spoke, Shaul told of Lord Jeshua, the Son of God, the long-promised redeemer, the Jews' Messiah who had finally come, being born of a royal lineage, and living a sinless life. Though crucified by wicked men, he had been raised from the grave by his Divine and loving Father. Granted immortality, he was now a perfect Mediator to reconcile mankind to God. The way to life had thus been opened to all who would follow him.

Excitedly, shaking a little in his enthusiasm, Shaul explained that he himself had seen and spoken to the resurrected Lord! But at this point, he became aware of a faint tittering among his audience.

Barnabas whispered, "That creature Elymas is mimicking you behind your back. Everyone is distracted."

Shaul stopped speaking and Barnabas continued. With his calm manner and smooth flow of words, he was not so easy to imitate. Elymas began interjecting with sarcastic comments. The Governor did his best to ignore him, drawing his seat closer to Barnabas that he might hear more clearly. This enraged the sorcerer, who was accustomed to being the centre of attention.

Shaul now resumed speaking, trying to explain the purpose of Lord Jeshua's sacrifice, but he was halfway through a sentence when the sorcerer interrupted contemptuously.

"My lord," he muttered in the Governor's ear. "This is fool's talk! What is this clumsy contradiction of which he speaks – being cleansed by a man's blood?!"

Sergius Paulus looked over his shoulder at the magician. "It is not a literal washing in blood, Elymas. It is a figure of speech for an atonement such as your own people make with their continual animal sacrifices – a very interesting concept, sirs!" he added, turning back to the apostles.

Elymas dismissed these words with an angry gesture, and tossed a hand into the air so that his wide sleeve fell back, exposing a stringy arm.

"Wash – in blood!" he scoffed loudly. He raked his pointed nails down his bare arm and long red streaks appeared. "Behold – blood!" he cried, as the fascinated audience held its breath. "Let us wash in blood!" He mopped his arm with a white silk cloth and waved the bloodied article above his head. "Is this clean? Is it pure? Is it washed white in blood?"

The audience waited delightedly, wondering what would come next. The magician screwed the cloth into a ball and waved his fists in the air with wild incantations. "Can a dead man wash you clean in his blood?" he crooned. "Can anyone?"

The people muttered, "No! Of course not!" and shook their heads.

"Hah!" cried Elymas. "But as truly as my name is *bar Jeshua*, I tell you all Jeshuas are not the same! Witness this!"

He tossed the crumpled ball into the air, caught it by the corners, and waved it triumphantly. There was a gasp, and a round of spontaneous applause. The silk square was pure white again.

"So much for *your* Jeshua!" Elymas said with overdone politeness. "It is a thing I can do with a snap of the fingers! But to wash *sins* in blood!" He spoke with heavy irony, and the people laughed.

"Elymas!" Sergius Paulus spoke crisply. "You are conjuring nonsense from the explanation of our guests – what you are saying is just a confusion of words and has nothing to do with their arguments. Pray let them continue!"

Elymas stooped over his Governor and whispered loudly. "Their words *are* nonsense! One God? No underworld? No demons, spirits, dryads, no pantheon of beings who control the world in its every complex function? My lord, I believe these men may be sent by the gods to test your loyalty to the mighty ones on Olympus! Be careful lest they put the evil eye on you!"

"Be silent!" demanded Sergius Paulus with annoyance. "What did you expect from men preaching a new development of Judaism? I find their words of great interest!"

"Then I must protect you from yourself, my Governor!" spat Elymas, "for my amulets tell me they are indeed evil spirits in the guise of men! The amulets do not lie! Behold!"

He drew from his robes two strangely shaped pieces of stone threaded on beads around his neck and rubbed them vigorously on his silken sleeve. He held them up high.

"See them shine!" he hissed, and the amulets did indeed seem to gleam strangely with a cold greenish light.

There were rustles of alarm from the people. Even Sergius Paulus looked taken aback. Barnabas was dismayed to see their once interested audience being weaned away by the magician's tricks. But Shaul was more than dismayed, he was furious! He turned on Elymas.

"You!" he cried boldly, pointing straight at the sneering sorcerer. "You monster of cunning and deceit!"

The assembly gasped. Elymas's jaw dropped, but he recovered in an instant. He drew himself up to his considerable height so that he seemed to tower over them all, but Shaul faced him, unflinching.

"You offspring of evil!" he thundered, speaking now with the authority of the Holy Spirit. "You enemy of anything righteous! Would you confuse these people by twisting the straight teachings of the Lord in heaven? Would you blind them to his mercies? Would you darken the light of truth? Now feel the power of the one you mock!"

Suddenly, the sorceror's imposing figure seemed to dwindle. His face became a mask of horror. Ashen-faced, he stumbled forward, tripping on his elaborate robes, clutching the air for support, knocking into one of the delicate tables. Pomegranates and quinces instantly tumbled in every direction, bouncing and rolling all over the beautiful inlaid floor and he staggered again as he trod heavily on them, his long black sleeves flapping impotently, like broken wings. Frantically he rubbed his eyes.

"Help me," he quavered. Transfixed, nobody moved. "Help me!" he shrieked. "I cannot see! I am blind! Blind!"

"And so you will remain – at least, for a season," Shaul said more quietly. The chastisement was from the Lord and not himself, but Shaul felt a shudder within as he recalled the road to Damascus. What effect the same affliction would have on this backsliding Jew he could not predict.

The stunned audience shrank back fearfully, but Sergius Paulus sprang to his feet, eyes glowing, astonished.

"I *will* hear more of what you have to say! You must finish telling me of this gospel! No mere man can rebuke in this fashion! Your words must be true – you have proved it – for such divine power is a solemn witness to their veracity!"

Sergius Paulus became the first convert at New Paphos, where the apostles found receptive hearts. The divine retribution on the sly sorcerer, coupled with the enthusiastic response of the Governor, provoked many to realise a greater God existed than those of their mythology. Marcus too had been affected by the incident, though in a different way. He had not been present when Elymas had been blinded, but when Barnabas related what had happened he looked taken aback.

"The *Ruach* rebuke is a fearful thing," he said soberly. "I did not know Shaul had the authority to exercise it."

He said no more at the time, but succinctly recorded the matter in the account of their travels which his cousin Loukanos had urged him to keep.

"Write something every day, while events are fresh and vivid," he had instructed, as one who had long been accustomed to the practice. "Time will sort out which are valuable and which are trivial, and either way, you'll have memories to share forever, instead of having them fade out of mind. When you get home, have our old friend Nathan Hill-and-Dale make me a copy and I'll pay for it. If he's on a hill he will refuse payment and you'll have to smuggle it into his purse somehow, and if he's in a dale he'll refuse to do it at all, but one of his copyists will, so let there be no excuses."

What would Loukanos think when he read of Shaul and Elymas? Would he too be reminded of that sickening day in Jerusalem – in the very home where Marcus lived! – when the *Ruach* rebuke had first been demonstrated? Unexpectedly invoked by the apostle Cephas, it had left two Spirit-gifted disciples dead, with no time for repentance. The shocking event had caused much heart searching, but the outcome was salutary, precipitating a far greater respect for the apostles, their authority and the seriousness of their message.

Shaul's reproof of Elymas, though milder by comparison, seemed equally efficacious, but it disturbed Marcus, though he could not say why. Was it that Shaul blinding someone (even temporarily) as Lord Jeshua had blinded the Pharisee himself, seemed too personal, almost retaliatory?

Even as he asked himself the question Marcus was forced to discard it. Honesty compelled him to admit that the *Ruach* moved in ways they could not comprehend, and how much of its operation was either the initiative of those gifted, a response to its promptings, or even an involuntary act, was impossible to say. But from that point on, as the three companions spent considerable time instructing Sergius Paulus and his household, as well as many synagogue Jews and interested God-fearers, it seemed that Barnabas deferred to Shaul more and more.

When the time came to leave Cyprus the apostles were well pleased.

"The Lord has greatly blessed our work here!" Shaul was cheerful as they clambered into the small craft which would take them to their ship moored in the harbour. Nodding, tall Barnabas folded himself carefully into the narrow stern. Neither of them mentioned their cruel beating, Marcus noted. He tossed their belongings on board, splashing in the salty shallows as he lost his footing.

As the brawny sailor at the oars swung the boat around, they spied their Roman soldier striding along above them at the city level, whistling as he headed towards a floral grotto of Aphrodite. Barnabas called to him and waved. The soldier saw him, stopped whistling, turned on his heel and walked very fast in the opposite direction.

Shaul smiled wryly as the others burst out laughing. "Who knows?" he said. "He may yet accept the true Way!"

Upon boarding the sailing ship, Barnabas and Marcus went below, thankful that the boat was large enough for them to find shelter, down with the cargo, out of the weather. The ship rolled out into the wine-dark sea and the evening air grew chilly. Shaul stood a long time on deck watching the sunset smudge the sky with fiery pink and terracotta clouds, fading to smoky greys and purple reds.

The glowing ball of the sun dropped suddenly into the sea, and Shaul straightened up with a sigh. Sergius Paulus was right – from now on he should adopt his Roman name. Painfully he remembered the last time anyone had used it – then, it had been an endearment.

"Paul-Shaul!" his sister had pleaded tenderly. *"No!"* he had shouted at her. Now he was taking that name again in the task of spreading the very gospel he had then despised and rejected. If only he could hear her say it once more – what a different response he would give! But there was no use in repining. Henceforth the name must facilitate his work, and remind him that the mission was far bigger than the man.

Paul, as he became known from then on, sent up a silent prayer for the family he had driven away, and joined the others below.

Chapter Twenty-seven

"UNCLE – Uncle, wake up!" whispered a voice in the heaving blackness of the ship.

A long bundle of blanket grunted and turned over. "What's the matter?" he said sleepily, then jerked bolt upright. "If you're going to be sick – get on deck quickly!" he hissed.

"Ssh – I'm not sick – don't wake Shaul. I have to talk to you."

Barnabas groaned and shuffled further down into his blanket. "We find a spot under cover and finally get to sleep, and *now* you want to talk?"

"Please, Uncle!" Marcus put his mouth close to his uncle's ear. "I can't sleep – I must talk to you now. I don't want to wake anyone else."

Barnabas rubbed his ear. "Stop that whispering – it tickles!" he grumbled. "Oh, very well – come on deck."

Up on deck and huddled in thick cloaks, they settled themselves on a big coil of rope. The sharp night wind, the harsh slap and gurgle of the rocking sea, made everything seem larger than life. Barnabas, now fully awake, leant resignedly against a cage of chickens.

"Now, what's troubling you so much that we have to sit up here and freeze before you can tell me about it?"

Marcus spoke in a low voice. "It's Shaul."

Barnabas gave a start of surprise that jerked the chicken coop. A sleepy hen clucked disapproval.

"Oh, I knew you wouldn't take it well!" Marcus muttered.

"How can I take it well or ill unless I know what you're talking about? What's this about Shaul?"

Marcus stared straight ahead. "He seems to have taken over," he said slowly. "When we started out, you were leading the mission. Now he is making decisions and you follow. Ever since the business of Elymas, it's been happening. Was that his way of showing who was in charge? Now he's even changed his name in deference to the Proconsul! Of course, a Roman name will give him more respect from Gentiles – more than you, at least. Yet if it wasn't for you he'd still be an outcast in Jerusalem!"

Barnabas took a deep breath, but before he could speak Marcus added roughly, "And what made you consent to go so far into Galatia, instead of keeping to the coastal towns?"

"Since our new brother Sergius Paulus gave us introductions to his relatives in northern Pisidia, we could do no less. This is the Lord's work and we must allow ourselves to be guided."

Marcus did not seem to have heard him. "What of the route you've agreed to for the sake of speed? Ask around – anyone on this ship will tell you going directly north through the Pisidian mountains is worse than hazardous. It's sheer recklessness! And what do we know of the Via Sebaste from there onwards? Nothing! But we do know any highway gives easy pickings to violent men. *Pax Romana* or not, it's hardly safe."

"No road is safe, you know that yourself. It is perilous just going down to Jericho, yet you have been there and back many times without turning a hair. You are no novice, Marcus! Over the years you have travelled extensively within the Land, as well as up to Antioch. And I seem to recall a certain boy, many years ago, who ran away from home – all the way from Jerusalem to Cana – just because he was in trouble at school."

"I was far too young to realise how rash that was! In any case, it's different in home territory. If we disappear in a foreign place who will even realise we are missing? Several men on this ship have already told me the region is so wild and sparsely inhabited that mountain lions, bears, and wolves roam freely. And everyone knows the inland roads are steep and treacherous, and crawling with criminals. I just say it's fool-hardy to take dangerous risks. We can't preach the gospel if our throats are cut."

"Johanan," Barnabas interrupted quietly, using his nephew's boyhood name. "This grudging attitude is not like the wholehearted and fearless young man I used to know. Were we called to preach Christ only to provide fodder for desperate men and hungry animals? Next you will be demanding, *Were there no graves in Egypt?* Are you homesick?"

"What?" Marcus was surprised into meeting his uncle's eyes. "No, of course not," he faltered.

It was several months since he had left Jerusalem and the secure warmth of his family's bustling household. He had set out with a keen desire to serve in a new field, to be doing something useful and significant, and nobody had tried to hold him back, but he had not realised how long or how far away he would be.

For a while there was silence, with only the creak of ropes, the flapping of sail, and the occasional swish and slap of water below. Barnabas was considering what he should say next, and silently praying for wisdom. Marcus, with lips compressed, was searching his own heart.

Was it homesickness? Was he a coward? As his uncle had intimated, he was no stranger to risk and daring. He had as a boy boldly set out on adventures and as a youth had endured the terror of persecution. He had even wriggled free from the clutch of soldiers one dark spring night in an eerily torch-lit Jerusalem garden, and fled for his life. But though he had been utterly panic-stricken, had he truly believed anything would happen to him? Every escape from danger had only made him feel that he *was* protected, that the next time would also bring an escape.

Perhaps back then – feeling that he was so strong, so alive, and always would be – he had not yet grasped that he was as vulnerable as the next person. Yes – typical youthful conceit and inadmissibility of his own mortality! – that might have been part of it. He could see that now. As a stripling, even in the midst of quaking fear, he had deep down been confident that in the end – somehow – surely he would come through alive, if not unscathed.

At only one other time had he been confronted by very real and immediate danger – in his boyhood – and it had happened so fast and was all over so quickly that he had not thought of it for many years. Not until recently, that is – not until that idle conversation with a few hardened mariners, which had stirred up the old memory ... one which now haunted his dreams and made him sweat with a fear he had not felt at the time ... trapped in a rank, dim cave ... two boys and a man ... caught between a furious wildcat and her mewling kittens ... Oh, suddenly he remembered as if it were yesterday!

Everything happened in a heartbeat. Ammiel leapt towards the snarling beast, roaring and waving his arms, but the wildcat in vicious fury sprang for his face – just as Dan wrenched his cache of stones from his bosom, and darting in front, hurled them with all his might. The creature dropped in midair with a scream, twisting round and lashing her long tail as she fell with the heavy stones scattering at her chest.

In a flash Ammiel whipped off his cloak and flung it over her head. She fought her way out in an instant, but it was long enough for Johanan to scoop up the struggling kittens and pitch them straight past her, far outside the cave where they squalled lustily in the scrubby bushes. The outraged mother darted after them, coughing and screaming her anger and distress. Ammiel snatched up the cloak, roughly bundling the boys out before him, and they all ran into the sudden twilight, stumbling over the rocks and back to the slate coloured river which lapped idly at their feet.

Marcus shuddered and rubbed the gooseflesh from his arms. Why did it affect him so much so long after the event? With a sinking feeling, he gradually recognised the answer. It was not just that he was a heedless boy at the time, able to dismiss danger with a laugh and a shrug once it had passed. It was because back then, he had nothing to lose – and no concept of what others might lose if harm came to him.

But now he was a grown man, with a beautiful, loyal wife whose heart and hand he had laboured long and patiently to win. And now, as a man with no offspring, he better understood how his ageing, widowed mother must feel about her precious, only son.

He squirmed uncomfortably on his makeshift seat. It was not so much for himself that he feared, but for those he loved – he was all they had!

Apart from his uncle, of course, still sitting here so quietly and patiently beside him. And his cousins. But that was hardly the same thing, and besides, none of them lived in Jerusalem.

He stared unhappily at the pinpricks of shore lights so far off on the black coastline, appearing and disappearing like coruscating stars as the boat rode the waves. How was he to go on with such a conflicted mind? As the forthright apostle Jacob ben Joseph had reminded the Jerusalem brethren more than once, a double-minded man was unstable in all his ways – like this detestable boat – lurching one way with the wind, tossed another by the waves.

Marcus dropped his head into his hands. *Lord Jeshua, I deserted you once because I was afraid. I am afraid again. Is this another test of my loyalty to you? Or merely a test of my pride, in that I should not be ashamed to act more responsibly for my family? What should I do? Show me a sign, I pray, and let none influence me but you!*

With a deep breath he lifted his head and opened his eyes, wrapping his cloak more tightly around him against the cold wind. Barnabas also stirred from his reverie, ready to resume the conversation, wriggling his shoulders more comfortably against the chicken coop.

"Let me ask you a few things," he said carefully. "Which of us three was called out by the direct intervention of the Master himself, especially for the work of the gospel? It was not me, and it was not you, though we were devout believers from the beginning. No, it was Pharisee Shaul the heretic-hunter who received that special calling. Have you ever asked yourself why?"

"I suppose, to prove that with God nothing is impossible," came the reluctant reply.

"True – and that the saving power of Lord Jeshua goes beyond all reason, perhaps. Yet I think it is more than this, and even more than the unique education and upbringing which fits him for the work. Willing as we are to serve, I like my comfort, and you like your security. But Shaul in his zeal does not even *try* to accommodate such things. He has a passion which disregards all else but his cause. I believe our Master saw that it only needed to be redirected. And so he opened the man's eyes to reality, and our fiery Pharisee has never looked back."

The younger man stared at the moon wavering on the inky sea and did not answer. His uncle continued more gently.

"What if I had *not* found him in Jerusalem? Would the gospel work have stopped just because the great and mighty Joseph of Salamis had not stood up for him? And does it really matter who is 'leading' this mission? We are all *following* the Master and work together for Him, remember – each at what he does best. You're surely not jealous on my account? Cyprus was my own familiar territory, and it was only practical that I should guide our travels there. I didn't hear Paul complaining."

Marcus changed the subject. "Are you really going to call him Paul?"

Barnabas sighed. "Why does it worry you? My name also was changed! A follower of the Way changes many things in his life, and that sometimes includes his name. In any case, *Paulus* has always been his registered *praenomen* just as Marcus is yours. How often are you still called Johanan these days, if it comes to that? Remember we are striking deep into a superstitious heathen world of deities and religions for everything. As Shaul Benjamin, a Jewish rabbi, he may seem to be teaching just a variation of Judaism. But as Paul of Tarsus, citizen of the Roman Empire, he brings a message for the whole world. It is the gospel he is promoting, not himself."

Marcus shrugged. "You always think the best of everyone."

"So did you – once. But wider experience often makes for sadder men."

CHAPTER TWENTY-SEVEN

Marcus knew it was true. "Perhaps Antioch has turned me cynical."

"Do you really think it's a matter of his pride?" Barnabas uncurled himself from his cramped position and stretched, swaying a little with the motion of the ship. "Was he not royally named, not just for his grandfather, but for a glorious giant of a man? Our Shaul may not look as impressive as King Shaul of old, but he has a strength of heart which the king himself never had. Wouldn't you say that to give up a name that means *Asked of God* for one meaning *Little*, speaks rather of humility?"

"Oh, I suppose so. Don't preach, Uncle, you make me feel petty."

"Then stop sounding so, eh?" Barnabas patted his nephew's shoulder, adding shrewdly, "You miss your family, I know, and nobody can blame you for that. But Mari and Rhoda are proud you are here; and doing without you is their own willing sacrifice for the cause of the gospel. Remember Paul has been without the comfort of his family for far longer than either of us."

He yawned. "Come now, let's get some sleep. Tomorrow we'll reach the coast, and once we get up the river to Perga things will look better. There may even be letters from home waiting for us at the synagogue."

In Perga, the large and attractive capital of Pamphylia, the afternoon sun blazed cheerfully and the scent of wild lilies sweetened the air, but the steamy heat drained the three companions of all energy – and things did *not* look better.

Exhausted after a hot, seven mile tramp from the busy Attalia harbour, they put up at the first *stabula* they came to on the outskirts of the city. Its rubbish-filled, overgrown courtyard and broken steps did not hold much promise of comfort, and a mosquito-ridden swamp wallowed nearby, but they were too overheated and in need of rest to care one way or another.

The watered wine they gulped down their parched throats was lukewarm, the water they washed in was tepid, and neither afforded refreshment in the oppressive conditions. The air was like soup. Their clothes clung stickily to their skin, and thirsty flies tormented their faces. The innkeeper gave them a small room which was more stifling than the open street.

Outside, however, a stream of townspeople went to and fro about their business unconcerned by the weather, whilst the many ornate temples to the goddesses Venus and Diana were not short of visitors.

Barnabas flung himself full length on a grimy sleeping mat, hoping against hope that it did not contain lice, and groaned. "What a climate! How do the locals bear it!"

Squinting through an acute headache, Paul answered, "They might like it." He shut his eyes and lay back. If he had ever imagined that life in Tarsus might have immured him to mosquito-ridden humidity he was sadly disabused of that notion now. This was the worst he had ever experienced.

Marcus, gloomily mopping his sunburnt neck with a wet cloth, peered through the grass blind which hung at the narrow window. "The sun won't set for hours yet."

They should have found a boat going up-river from Attalia, he thought irritably. The Kestrus was navigable almost this far up – all but the last hour's walk – and it would have been an easier, cooler way to reach Perga, even if no faster than the sweltering road. But Shaul – *Paul* – was always trying to save money.

Paul bundled his coat into a pillow. "At first light tomorrow we must find the synagogue!" he murmured drowsily.

The stupefying heat overpowering them, they all slept. A few hours later the sun set, and a chorus of frogs in the swamps and marshes about the city began their monotonous, lugubrious chant. As darkness fell, the heat of the day quickly died, and a dank chill crept into the room.

Barnabas woke, suddenly cold. He flapped his hands to disperse the irritating whine of hungry mosquitoes. "Let's find some supper and a good fire," he said, shaking Marcus. "Paul, wake up."

A mosquito stung Paul half-awake before Barnabas had finished speaking. He slapped sleepily at his forehead and felt the stickiness of blood. Suddenly it seemed that rocks – *flying stones – blood-spattered dust* – swam before his eyes. He sprang up, shaking off clinging dreams. Pulling on his coat, he followed the others out of the room.

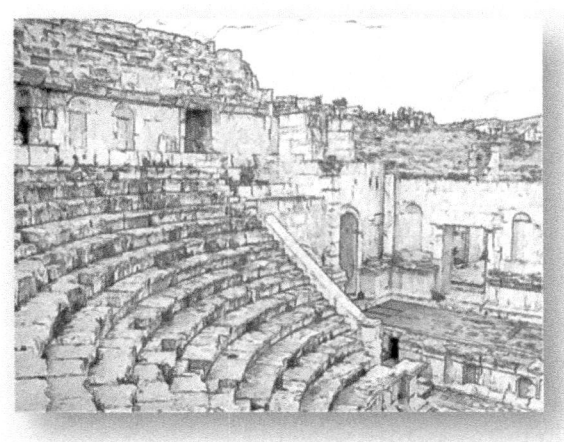

Chapter Twenty-eight

THE small fire in the lamp-lit crowded hall seemed a long way from the dim draughty spot where Paul, Barnabas, and Marcus sat eating their supper. The room was rowdy with pleasure-seeking sailors from Attalia, all looking forward to the next day's big animal fight – arguing over their favourites and placing bets on everything from whether bears would win over lions, to whether the theatre had nineteen upper rows and twenty three lower, or the other way around, and whether it held twelve thousand spectators, or thirteen, or ten.

In the midst of this raucous noise, a sharp jangle of brass instruments accompanied a weary dancing girl close by. Marcus resolutely turned his back and sat staring at the wall. Paul ate mechanically, lost in thought. He wondered uneasily why he should feel so hot in such a chilly room.

Barnabas glanced shrewdly at the girl's strained face. *She's worrying about the money they throw. Adding it up as she dances – is there enough to pay the landlord … to feed the children tomorrow …*

The tired dancer missed her footing and stumbled against a table, upsetting a jug of wine which stained her thin, tawdry costume. Laughs, curses, jeers – she was hustled roughly away. She barely had time to snatch at her few coppers before she was elbowed past the little group of Christians.

Barnabas caught her hand as she passed. "Buy them bread."

Amazed, the girl clenched her thin fingers fiercely around the hard coin she found in her palm. "How could you know…!" she burst out.

"No begging!" the innkeeper bellowed across the room. Pouncing on her as she shrank past him, roughly grabbing her scrawny arm, he gritted, "Next time dance as though you like it, you whey-faced drab, or don't come back!"

She turned and fled into the night – and immediately another, much older dancer sprang forward to take her place, cheered on somewhat sarcastically by the jaded men.

"I'm surprised at you, Uncle," Marcus said stiffly. "Giving money to such a woman."

Barnabas pushed his cup away. "Even tavern dancers need to eat, Marcus."

He had to raise his voice. Coarse jokes were being yelled to and fro across several groups of sailors, all drunk, all trying to outdo each other in offensiveness, and all roaring with laughter. The mature dancer, her age artfully disguised with khol, chalk and carmine salve, was working hard to regain their attention – which meant their money. Snapping her fingers with false gaiety to the musicians behind her, she urged them on to a far more rousing pace until her increasingly energetic gyrations began to win over her audience. The arguments and betting were forgotten as she worked the room, flaunting herself to one man after another, deftly snatching their coins as they flipped them her way; stowing them in tantalising places within the diaphanous draperies which emphasised her remaining charms while hiding the flaws of age, maternity and ill treatment.

The stony-faced trio of Jews holding themselves apart was a challenge – always good for creating more hilarity, and with it, more reckless generosity. Therefore, she sidled deliberately into their view, singling out Marcus as the one most likely to give good entertainment value. Rolling her shoulders invitingly and holding out graceful arms, she shimmered voluptuously towards him with a practised smile, eyes bright with provocation, circling their table until she was shaking her hips almost in his face; while the sailors whistled and gestured and stamped, boisterously chanting in unison a word which if unintelligible was still unmistakeable in meaning.

Scarlet-faced, Marcus leaped to his feet. "This is an unholy place," he said angrily. "It is unfit for bearers of the gospel!"

"Those who are well do not need a doctor." Paul looked up for the first time since giving thanks for the food. "These are the people who *need* the gospel." He rose slowly from the table, unsteady on his feet, his head swimming – fever again!

Marcus stalked away without answering, pushing blindly past the dancer, who shrugged with disdain, winking slyly at her noisy audience. Barnabas hardly noticed him go. He was too alarmed by the sudden slurring in Paul's speech, his clumsiness and the hot flush on his face. He helped him out of the room, ignoring the jeering hilarity thrown at their backs. In this place it was not surprising that such symptoms indicated only that a man could not hold his wine.

The small room which had been like an oven only that afternoon was now cold, damp and draughty. The night mists curled in at the roughly shuttered window. Barnabas led their evening prayers, and Paul crawled, shivering, into bed. He lay there tossing uneasily in and out of feverish dreams.

Barnabas also slept badly, worried about both of his companions, though for different reasons. He was taken aback by the growing tension in his nephew, whose increasing moodiness was uncharacteristic of the willing, confident person he had once been. He was also very concerned for Paul's health. The wonderful feeling of purpose and adventure that had uplifted them on the Cyprus tour, even after their flogging, had gone completely flat.

That night was long and miserable. Marcus huddled in his hard bed with many private thoughts chasing around his head. This was a fine time for Paul to be ill! They were stuck in this place with an exhausting climate, completely without friends, about to go inland for hundreds of miles up mountainous roads where many dangers lurked, and to places they knew nothing about. He knew Paul was determined to visit the main commercial and religious centres in each area, and he flinched to think what they might be like.

Back in Syria, Antioch on the Orontes was also an unholy city, but Marcus had never felt daunted by its challenges. The Christian community there was large and well supported both from Jerusalem and from within, with every difficulty shared among many Spirit-gifted brethren. Here there were just the three of them, and now they were in a vast territory which was familiar to none of them. He could see nothing but dangers and difficulties, both physical and spiritual. Every tormenting thought which had assailed him on the ship from Cyprus was still churning over and over in his mind.

He thought with a shudder of the savage animals which would tear each other apart in the city's arena the next day, all for the entertainment of godless men. Where had those animals come from but the wildernesses through which the apostles so rashly intended to travel? He could not have been more explicit in warning that lions, bears, wolves and boars were known to prowl the mountains and plains of this daunting, massive landscape of Asia. It had not moved his uncle one whit – and it was clear these were perils of which both the older men were already very well aware. Snakes were one thing, but Lord Jeshua had said nothing about ravening beasts.

He thought again of his precious wife and his ageing mother. For the hundredth time he agonised over whether his enthusiasm to serve the ekklesial family had blinded him to his spiritual responsibilities towards his own; towards *their* needs, their dependence on a supportive, caring husband and son. Had he deserted his first duty by leaving them?

Anxiously he prayed for guidance, earnestly he prayed for a sign, until sheer fatigue overwhelmed him in a fitful sleep which brought no relief … only nightmarish recurring dreams in which he told Rhoda he was never coming home, and as he took her in his arms her cries of grief became the harsh hacking cries and screaming of a wildcat, while she turned into a snarling beast, tearing and ripping at his throat.

Again and again he awoke with a sharp gasp, trembling all over, feeling the petrifying wave of terror subsiding, leaving his skin prickling cold and clammy, his heart hammering wildly.

Repeatedly he attempted to return to the refuge of prayer, but feeling himself inexorably sinking into the horror of sleep, he forced himself to stay awake by mentally reconstructing a large ruined *columbaria* he had seen on Cyprus … visualising every detail, guessing its measurements, drawing its plans, rebuilding it to perfection – anything to swamp the phantom recurring images in his head – until finally in the middle of repopulating the fascinating and elegant structure with grateful doves … suddenly he dropped into a dead sleep mercifully free of dreams.

At the end of that disturbed, unhappy night, the sun rose, the mists melted and sudden warmth warned of the heat to come. Leaving the other two sleeping heavily, Barnabas rose quietly and went to find the synagogue. Inside, the Chazzan, a talkative and cheerful man quite unlike Old Paphos's surly Hadar, was preparing for the morning service.

"Yes, yes, we do have something for you. Only a month ago we received letters from Jerusalem by the hand of young Tychicus, one of our proselytes. Most enthusiastic fellow. First, though, if you will forgive me, I must just finish sweeping these steps, some of the older members arrive so early and are most offended if all is not as it should be. No, no, there is nothing you can do to help, thank you."

"He has family in Jerusalem? Perhaps I know them."

"No, he knew nobody there at all, when he left. You see, it was not to visit family that he went, but for his first Passover pilgrimage. He had been saving up for some time, determined to celebrate it at the Temple! Of course everyone here loaded him with messages and gifts to pass on to anyone they knew either on his route or in the Holy City. He complained that he felt like a pack mule, but just between you and me I think he was very proud to be entrusted with the task. It gave him many useful introductions too, of course. Oh, have a care, brother – mind the broom! I would hate to trip you up. It would not look good for the regulars to find you crumpled at the bottom of the steps." He chuckled apologetically, as Barnabas with a grin obligingly jumped out of the way.

Chazzan Efram swept on busily, both literally and conversationally. "If only Rome did not reserve the *Cursus Publicus* for government business, it would make life so much easier. Even the meanest towns are not short of scribes to read and write letters – but finding someone to deliver them in the first place is another thing altogether. We were very fortunate to be able to send things with Tychicus. He tells us Jerusalem has what we would call a *Cursus Privatus* which *anyone* may use for a fee! That made us feel quite envious."

"Yes, Shalal's Jerusalem Post has been very successful. He carries letters and small packages to and from various parts of the Land, though of course his service does not extend outside it. It is not cheap but the convenience is invaluable. No doubt your obliging messenger returned home with almost as many letters to pass on, as he took with him."

"Ha-ha, yes indeed he did and not a word of complaint this time either. In fact, now I come to think of it, apart from his amazement at the glory of the Temple itself, about which he said much, he said very little about anything else, oddly enough. Only that many things are happening in Jerusalem, both good and bad, and that he found ready hospitality in the Freemen's Synagogue. You know it?"

"Very well. He would have come across quite a few Christians, then?"

"Just enough for him to come home feeling very confused, I'm sorry to say. I think that is why he has been so quiet ever since. I'd like to know more about it, myself. So many rumours get about, it is hard to know what to believe, especially at a distance of so many years, eh? I mean, who has actually *seen* this man whom they claim was raised from the dead to be the Christ?"

"I have, and so have both my friends who are with me," Barnabas said quietly to the man's astonished face. "He is real, and we follow him gladly. I would like to meet your proselyte. My friends and I would be glad to put his mind at rest one way or another, and yours too."

"*You* are Christians? Well! I am sure he would like to ask you many questions, as would I, and perhaps a few others too. I think we should always hear people before we condemn them. But of course, in my position I must tread softly, and there is no hurry. I will ask him and let you know next time you are in synagogue. Now, my tasks are finished at last, so thank you for your patience, and now let us go inside for your letters."

As he ran back up the steps with his broom, he glanced up and gave a half-amused exclamation. "See – three of our oldest members are already walking up the street! They sleep light, the old ones. They tell me that at their advanced age they do not have time to waste in dreams. I declare they arrive earlier every month and before long I will be sweeping steps at midnight. I must hurry."

Quickly he fetched a small box with a heavy clasp and was soon rifling through it.

"Let me see – ah, here we are. Yes, two letters, they've been here for some weeks, as I said. See, they are marked *Please hold for Travellers* and your names. One for a *Joseph Barnabas of Antioch Orontes*, and one bound to the back of it and sealed for a *Johanan Marcus* who I take it must be travelling with you. None for your other friend, though. Praise the Eternal that you arrived here safely to collect these, eh? We have been looking forward to having fellow Jews visit from so far away. Quite a shock to find you are *Christianoi,* mind you! That will keep us all talking. How long will you be with us?"

But Barnabas was not sure. He returned to the inn, to find Marcus, with dark shadows under his eyes, eating a scrappy breakfast alone, with his back to the general sprawl of other travellers among the rough benches.

"Paul?"

"He's hardly moved, yet." With alacrity Marcus snapped the seal and tore open his letter, and Barnabas left him to it. He hoped the news from home was good and would lift his nephew's spirits. Meanwhile he was too concerned about Paul even to glance at his own letter, except to note that it was from his sister Mari.

In the cramped chamber, Paul – his woollen tunic soaked with sweat, hair tangled, and with great shudders shaking his body – was a frightening sight.

"My friend," Barnabas said quietly, "you are getting worse, not better – tell me what to do for you."

Paul clenched his jaws to stop his teeth chattering before he spoke. "T-t-too humid – the s-swamps," he managed at last.

"Then we will not begin here after all, but venture on directly into Phrygia and Galatia as we planned," Barnabas suggested. "Once we get to higher country the air will be more pure. There may be opportunity to return in a cooler season."

Paul nodded and squeezed Barnabas's hand gratefully.

As hourly he grew worse it became clear that they must move on immediately. It also became clear that Marcus had other things on his mind. His letter had indeed greatly affected his spirits – with a great rush of heady excitement mingled with a kind of awed apprehension – for it brought him amazing, wonderful tidings from home. After years of disappointment, he was to be a father at last! He had prayed for a sign – and what greater could he have?! Now, returning was all he could think about.

"We praise God and rejoice with you in this great blessing," Barnabas said warmly and sincerely, "but the child will not be born for many moons yet. If you will only stay with us a little while longer, even just a month or two, it would help us greatly. Once we are safely into Cilicia, you can continue into Cappadocia without us."

Marcus remained silent, and though feeling his resistance, his uncle persevered in the most encouraging tone of voice he could muster. "You will have plenty of time to find other travelling companions for safety, and once you've reached Cybistra, the Taurus mountain pass will be in view. Up through the Cilician Gates and down to the plain is only around five days, and then you'll be in Tarsus, and can choose your route home. If you should find a ship heading for Caesarea right away, you could be in Jerusalem only a week later. Even if you go overland through Syria, God willing you'll still get there with many weeks to spare."

Marcus shook his head firmly. He had grown up without a father. He would not risk the same thing happening to any child of his if he could help it. And what if the new life came at the expense of the mother's? Nothing was certain in this matter, except that he must be back with his precious Rhoda as soon as possible!

"I've made up my mind," he said steadily. "I'm going home. At once."

Paul struggled onto one elbow. "You b-begged t-t-to c-c-come!" He spoke with difficulty, but the disillusionment in his voice was plain. "I w-w-will not b-beg you to s-s-s-stay!"

Marcus turned away, chastened by Paul's weakness, yet he did not waver. His turmoil of spirit had been growing ever since the flogging, and had been all the more painful for being unshared – and, he felt, unshareable – with his companions. Now his silent pleas had been heard in Heaven. The Master had plainly shown him where his greater duty lay! That being his conviction, he would not be dissuaded.

However, he could not shake a certain feeling of guilt, despite all his rationalising. Perhaps it was to assuage this, that he allowed himself to feel slightly nettled by his companions' unspoken reproach. All through their many weeks in Cyprus, he had given them ungrudging service as their faithful assistant – yet suddenly that seemed to amount to nothing in their eyes.

In his present mood it did not occur to him that, particularly so far as Paul was concerned, he had committed the sin of putting his hand to the plough and then looking back. And it was not just that he had done so, but that now the apostles were left at the most distant point of their journey without an assistant, in a place where there were no other Christians to help them.

Had Marcus told them plainly at the start that he would not accompany them any further than Cyprus, they still would gladly have taken him, but they would have brought another willing brother from Antioch as well; one physically, mentally and spiritually prepared to continue on to the end, ready to face the unknown without flinching. Meanwhile Marcus would have had valuable experience of missionary work, been extremely useful, and then returned home with their blessings on his head. But what was the use of hindsight!

Barnabas was greatly disappointed, but did not press his nephew any further. After all, childbearing was a hazardous business from start to finish. It was only natural that a man should be anxious for his beloved wife, and it was not as if anyone could have anticipated this news, in the circumstances. Resignedly he helped the younger man find a passage home on a trading ship and reluctantly said goodbye.

Paul said nothing more on the matter, but he felt strongly that Marcus had betrayed their undertaking. Sometimes (he knew to his cost) it turned out that a man had sworn to his own hurt – but how valid were his intentions if mere distress changed his mind? Of course, Marcus had not exactly taken a vow, but the man had pressed them to use his services and accepted the blessing of the ekklesia, so what was the difference?

Surely, any man whose many prayers had at last been so miraculously answered – who had been so divinely blessed! – should have shown his gratitude by finishing the Godly task he had put his hand to, regardless of his own feelings, and regardless of his own safety?

Barnabas felt Paul's agitation, and tried to excuse his nephew. He read out part of his own letter from Mari which confided, *"I have not alarmed my son by telling him this, but his dear Rhoda is quite unwell, poor girl."* So perhaps it was just as well Marcus had gone home.

Paul did not trust himself to reply. It seemed obvious to him that to be tied to a wife and children, was to risk hindering your service. Well, he would not again make the mistake of trusting to a companion whose loyalties were likely to be divided.

The subject of Marcus was now closed, but there was no doubt that his practical assistance would be very much missed, all the more so because of Paul's illness. Still, the work must go on, and they must recover their good humour and positive spirit to do it well.

Earnestly did the apostles pray that night as they privately struggled with their deep dismay – and took courage. Lord Jeshua was with them and *he* would not desert them. He had said so. *"I will never leave you."* Yes – their immortal, unchanging, faithful Master could be relied upon!

Chapter Twenty-nine

NOW they must head north, towards another Antioch – almost a hundred miles away – a large military colony in the region of Pisidia. There were in fact sixteen towns in the Empire with variants of this same name, all founded by an ancient ruler in honour of his father Antiochus, but fortunately they were too far away from each other to be confused. Leaving Paul undisturbed in his semi-stupor, Barnabas checked their supplies, made himself a list, and thought hard about how they might get there.

In this land of precipitous ranges there were no truly direct routes and while there was no shortage of roads linking settlements and scattered villages, many were little more than tracks. Well constructed Roman roads also served the region, allowing ready movement of supplies and forces between various strongholds built to keep the Imperial peace. There was a lot to weigh in the balance – speed, safety, reliability and practicality.

The shortest route from Perga was rough and unpatrolled. Much of it fit for nothing more than foot traffic, it staggered through mountainous terrain which only a robust man might risk– and then only if he could join with a large enough company to deter the notorious bandits which infested the region. It might have been purpose made for lawless men – this daunting place of terrifying chasms, deep canyons, and rushing rivers into which a tell-tale body might too conveniently be dropped.

Still, perilous or not, it also had several supply stations, at one point merged with the ancient King's Road from Babylon to Ephesus, and was the most direct way to Pisidian Antioch, officially known as Colonia Caesarea Antiochia. Once there, a traveller could join the Via Sebaste running east and west across Galatia, having saved himself – if he were both strong and fortunate – valuable time.

It was ironic that this punishing route which had been the apostles' original choice, and concerning which Marcus had been so agitated, was now out of the question due to Paul's illness. They would have to take a far longer way around, and that meant a choice of two other Roman roads, both part of the great Via Sebaste.

From Perga, this major highway began its circuitous approach to the northern region of Phrygia. Heading northwest, after some forty miles it divided into two branches. One swept wide, keeping as much as possible to the gentler highland plains and skirting the western edge of the great central lakes. The other, shorter and steeper, curved up through the mountains, stringing together an uneven chain of significant fortress towns, before climbing down to cross an extensive stretch of rough country between two vast lakes and edge its way round the next set of ranges.

There the two branches of the highway met again, merging and veering east to crawl over another twenty rugged miles of mountain ridges to the town of Apollonia. From this point, with Antiochia a mere forty miles away, the way became easier. Descending once more to a long sloping plain, at the northern end of the vast Lake Akrotiri, the reunited highway ran more comfortably past various outlying settlements and through the fine city gates of Antiochia itself to become part of the ancient Silk Road from the orient.

An important trade route, and accordingly well maintained, the shorter arm of the Via Sebaste nevertheless still stretched over many long, steep, and dangerous miles. It too was notorious for brigands, and criss-crossed by ravines and swift rivers. Nevertheless it was studded with important fortified towns and supply stations, and had been built wide enough for marching troops, and strong enough for the continual traffic of heavy wheeled vehicles. Paul's frailty obliging him to be carted like a piece of merchandise into crisp mountain air without delay, this therefore was the road upon which they must set forth. The first would take too long.

Feeling guilty about being unable to follow up his conversation with the Chazzan, Barnabas scribbled an apologetic note explaining their need for a sudden departure to Antiochia, and paying a street urchin to deliver it, went in search of transport at once. Enquiring of porters and carters at the bustling *agora,* a noisy confusion of market-place activity, Barnabas was directed to a *khan* where travellers with vehicles and beasts of burden sheltered in stalls and bays around a large dung-strewn open courtyard.

Their funds being only just adequate and certainly not plentiful, now he must weigh up the cost of being carried compared to the time it would take. The dubious privilege of perching on a wagonload of goods drawn by oxen might be the cheapest, but would take more than twice as long as walking and would hardly improve Shaul's health.

After some hard bargaining he finally settled with the owner of a donkey cart going to Cremna, shrewdly insisting on paying only half the money down and the other half on arrival. From there they should easily be able to find another such carrier to take them to the next big town, or even the rest of the way.

Though no faster than foot travel, the two-wheeled cart at least meant Paul would be spared the exhaustion of more than a week's strenuous uphill trudging with a pack on his back. The donkey's hooves clopped monotonously like the faraway beats of a badly made drum, accompanied by the relentless skirring of iron bound wheels over stone.

The teeth-jarring sound overlaid all quietness and pierced all noise, and whenever they stopped the silence was deafening. Still, though this unmusical refrain gradually ceased to fret Paul's nerves, the rattling and jolting of the cart could not be escaped. It was a bone shaking experience which did nothing to ease the sick apostle's aching body.

The bags of wheat which the carter was transporting with them belied their cushioning appearance and continually slumped their sluggish weight into the narrow space where Paul huddled out of the wind. Barnabas invariably walked, it was no slower, and gave Paul just enough room to lie flat – at least until the hard sacks encroached again.

When the cart juddered sickeningly over narrow viaducts which bridged dizzying chasms far below, Paul turned face down and refused to look while Barnabas got out and walked behind with an odd, shuffling gait, staring straight ahead so steadily that his eyes ached. Meanwhile the driver and his donkey casually meandered along as if the road was ten times its width and a gleefully gusting wind was not attempting to push them over the edge.

Two days into their travels, the cart became bogged in a creek bed and they narrowly escaped being swept away in a flash flood. Scrambling out so fast he wrenched an ankle, Paul lent his feeble strength to the efforts of the others and they hauled it out just in time, at the cost of four drowned sacks of wheat, a soaking for all of them, a relapse for Paul, and three snapped spokes for the cart. The driver splinted the damage with swift and enviable skill but insisted they pay him "up front" the full cost of a new wheel before he would continue.

The fact that a replacement could not be obtained until they had reached the heights of Cremna, deep in the mountains, made no difference to his demands. A new wheel would cost what he said it would cost, and if they disagreed, well, he would just whip up the donkey for a mile or so, that's all, and leave them standing. It was all the same to *him,* he shrugged, casually picking his teeth with a dirty thumbnail. But if they thought he would risk them decamping at the next town without compensating him for damages, well, they were dreaming.

His price was outrageous, but they had no choice, and resignedly Barnabas paid up.

"We were warned about thieves ambushing us on the road," he muttered, "but it seems some of them around here drive donkey carts."

Paul laughed weakly, "Only in their spare time! The rest of the time they lurk behind the rocks in the approved manner! But seriously, we should praise the Eternal for such a safe journey. So far, at least."

"I praise Him for every safe *hour,* you may be assured of that," his friend answered, furiously swatting at a cloud of tiny flies humming around them. "But I won't be sorry to be rid of this fellow." Wrapping his headcloth determinedly over his face, he added glumly, "Or these flies!"

Paul had already draped himself in his useful black veil, but he was not thinking about the flies. He was thinking of his parents, who so long ago had thoughtfully given him the shabby old leather cylinder with its contents carefully sealed in waxed linen. He fished it out from inside his wet clothes, shook out the last drops, and laid it on his chest for the sunshine to dry the leather. He had never yet had occasion to open it and prove his citizenship. But if he ever did, it was good to know that their foresight meant such dunkings as they had just undergone would not have harmed it.

The fortress city of Cremna was reached at last. High on a hill overlooking the Kestrus River it was well placed to guard this vital section of the Via Sebaste which not only gave entry through the mountains to the inland wealth of Galatia, but deep beyond to the mysterious lands of the far East.

At this point the apostles paid off their driver, who attempted to extract from them a further twenty-one *sestertii* for every sack of his lost wheat, but all his vociferous arguing and bemoaning of his ruination were in vain, for Barnabas told him flatly that if he thought he was getting more than the second half of their fare as originally agreed, well, he was dreaming.

Muttering about the insult of having his own words thrown in his teeth by unscrupulous Jews, the carter clopped away with a thunderous scowl which melted into a sunny grin as he turned the next corner, to buy two new cartwheels, pay off his latest fine imposed by the *Duoviri* for public brawling, and decide in which of his favourite *tabernae* to spend the change and no doubt soon incur another fine. Such was the happy cycle of his days!

Meanwhile, in a small but busy khan Barnabas had finished counting their money on the dirt floor of a dim chamber while Paul lay watching, his head pillowed on a lumpy pack; and now they were having an argument, and Paul was losing.

Attempting to move with casual ease, he raised himself up on one elbow and tried to reason with the stubborn friend who was inflexibly enumerating every one of his ills.

"But I *am* getting better! Forget my face, it is not infected and the rash will go, it always does with time. If it was in my beard you'd never even notice it. I do feel stronger, and look, even this ankle isn't so swollen now. If I walk we save around two hundred *denarii!* Is that anything to sneeze at?"

He lay back with a flushed face and an itching cheek which he dared not scratch, attempting to breathe evenly and appear full of well-being, but Barnabas was not deceived, and shook his head.

"We are not saving money if it costs more in the long run!" he said firmly. "See here, Paul, it is not just your health, but a question of time. We're losing enough going this way round as it is. You're not fit for hard walking yet and every day we wait is a day lost from the sailing season on the return trip. And if you collapse on the road, what then? We save neither time nor money and merely invite the attention of cut-throats."

"You have no mercy." Paul sank back with a groan, clutching his aching head. "You fight unfairly with a sick man!"

Barnabas burst out laughing. "*Getting better,* you said? Oh, Antiochia's in sight already, then! Come, cry *Pax!* – you know I am right – and I will go in search of transport this instant."

"*Pax!*" Paul grumbled reluctantly, and with a grin Barbabas tossed him the money bag for safekeeping.

As he emerged from their narrow stall he almost tripped over a small bandy-legged man with a greasily pocked face, who materialised from the shadows.

"Looking for a ride north? Couldn't help overhearing."

Barnabas eyed him with suspicion. "I'll wager you couldn't," he replied stiffly. "Not with your ear so close to the partition."

Unabashed, the man gave an oily grin which revealed a shining pair of gums, and jerked his thumb towards a four-wheeled wagon in the wide bay opposite.

"Army contract, shee? Haul shtuff to Shagalashosh, Sheleukia, all the way through to Antiochia and back. Frog on a rock, hop here, hop there, hop, hop, to and fro, that'sh me. *Bufo*, they call me, ha ha. Closhe enough. Light load tomorrow, *and* a fresh mule each shtop."

Looking at the unfortunate fellow, for whom *Sagalassos* was impossible to say without spitting, Barnabas agreed privately that 'Toad' was indeed a most appropriate nickname, whichever way you looked at it. Suppressing a grin he said blandly, "Antiochia, how much?"

"Two hundred *denarii*. Sheat on the back board. Cheap."

"One fifty," Barnabas said coolly, "and my friend lies down comfortably the whole way."

"One ninety. Guaranteed shafety for pashengersh."

"Not for our goods?"

"Not likely. Againsht my other contract, shee. Friendsh of the road. Shtuff always fallsh off the back of a wagon. Shafer than getting your throat shlit, but."

"Yes, I do see. Which *Armicustos* gets a cut for turning a blind eye to your 'other' contract? The one here in Cremna or the Supplies Officer at other end?

"Neither. What they don't know won't hurt them, but. One ninety, then?"

"What they find out might hurt you, though. Let alone your business. Did I mention who we are visiting in Antiochia? The family of one

Sergius Paulus, a good friend of ours. And a *most* conscientious Proconsul. One fifty five."

Blanching, Bufo threw up his hands. "One shixhty!" he said quickly. "Guaranteed shpashe for both!"

"Done."

As they moved on through the higher, fresher air of the inland, Paul slowly began to recover. The bigger wagon did not jerk and sway as much as the two-wheeled donkey cart, and lying on a couple of wool bales on top of several flat bundles of army blankets, he was well cushioned and able to sleep – despite a miscellany of other small packages and army supplies, including a row of striped melons packed in with greenstuff to avoid bruising.

"I've counted thoshe melonsh," Bufo cautioned. "And I'll count them again in Antiochia, sho don't shay you weren't warned."

In another two days, though still weak, Paul insisted on leaving the relentlessly rattling wagon for short spells at a time, limping beside it on a firmly strapped ankle while holding the tailboard to help him along. Barnabas walked with him, equally insistent on hoisting him back to his makeshift bed at the first sign of any dizziness, discomfort or returning fever. His vigilant care was rewarded, there were no more relapses, and Paul's appetite began to return.

Meanwhile the tireless mule plodded its way uphill, prodded by the laconic Bufo, who seeing that he had to deal with men of scruple, behaved himself wisely. This was evidenced by the fact that if anything did 'fall off the back of the wagon' at certain points prearranged according to his 'other contract', the apostles knew nothing of it, for he made sure it happened only while his passengers were otherwise occupied in attending to the call of nature.

Yet knowing the violent reputation of these mountains, they could not help feeling a certain underlying tension the whole time they were on the road. They were torn between wishing they had more company while at the same time being wary of any which approached. Any group of strangers might be the local *sicarii* – dagger-men – greeting them with deceptive smiles and weapons concealed in their cloaks. Bufo's private *modus operandi* might not be honourable, but they could understand it.

It was a relief when the sternly steep and wild slopes suddenly opened out to reveal the notable town of Sagalassos in all its terraced splendour against embracing hills. Standing sentinel over the fertile, undulating plain, it was watered by a slender tributary of the Kestrus and on cold mornings with river mist rising at its feet and low cloud stroking its marble brow, appeared to have been spun out of vapour. But despite its ethereal appearance at such times, this was a solid, no-nonsense place. Centrally placed near the western border of Pisidia, it was a significant staging post for wagons, oxen and mules transporting military equipment, imperial wheat and other provisions to various key cities in both the Pisidian and Phrygian regions.

Efficient as it might appear, however, the Army's system of supply was compromised by widespread abuse. In the rugged fastness of the mountains lived many violent inhabitants, whose brutal lawlessness hundreds of years of empire builders had failed to subdue. Meanwhile, apparently law-abiding contractors continued to serve two masters. That is, while the Army might employ a man, giving him a mere pittance upon which to support his family, once alone and unobserved that same man might help himself, in more ways than one. As a favourite witticism of the wagoners put it, *Rome for Home, and Self for Pelf.*

A scoundrel he might have been, but Bufo was helpful enough when they entered the city. Once he had pointed out the khan from which he would leave the next day, he led them to a noisy *taberna* in the lower acropolis where they were served a hearty bowl of leek and barley

344

pottage, with a leathery slab of flat bread for a spoon, for the price of two copper *asses* each.

"Bargain!" Bufo assured them, giving the vendor a private wink.

"Special deal for travellers," the vendor added genially as he busily wove his way around the cluttered shop collecting an armful of empty bowls. "Extra bread, with wine, and an extra pinch of salt thrown in, for only another two *asses* each. Half a loaf, half a jug."

"For each man?" Barnabas asked quickly, and the vendor gave him a pained look.

"Between you!" he said indignantly. "A man must live!"

Barnabas looked at the diminutive size of the loaves and the short jugs on the bench below a small array of wall-mounted shrines to various *Lares* – household gods – and exchanged looks with Paul, who pretended to count on his fingers.

"Special deal, Barnabas," Paul said solemnly. "That's only eight *asses*! Four *sestertii*, all found! For double the price of buying our extras separately, we get half the food. How can we refuse?"

"My friend, I accuse you of complex arithmetic," Barnabas replied with equal solemnity. "You are indeed a *Shaul bar Shaul* after all, and your grandfather would be proud of you."

Refusing the 'special deal' they burst out laughing, knowing that Bufo, who was already finishing up his own extras of bread and wine (and several *large* pinches of salt), had paid one *semeses,* which was only half an *as.*

Unsurprisingly their banter, leftover nonsense from their school days, went over Bufo's head. He tried to persuade them to take the 'extras' (since by longstanding prior arrangement these neatly subsidised his own), but they told him the pottage was quite filling enough. In any case, they intended to buy bread and wine and a few provisions for the road from producers down the other end of the *agora*, where they could be more assured of a fair market price.

They did not say this last to Bufo, and he remained affable. Tucking the last chunk of bread into his capacious cheek, he waved at the public baths just opposite the square.

"Nothing like a hot shoak. Doesh you good after a long haul," he said, champing vigorously with his gums and gulping several times, thereby increasing his toad-like resemblance. "Don't drink there, but! Cut-purshe pryshesh."

Tempting as a hot soak might sound, Paul and Barnabas had no intention of visiting the baths. Instead they would have a cold wash as usual, courtesy of their little leather bucket, filled at the public fountain. Stripping off was done piece-meal and in privacy, for devout Jews were modest people who did not glorify the human body as Gentiles did. Quite apart from this cultural consideration, public baths were generally renowned for lewd paintings and licentious behaviour.

Seeing their expressions, Bufo leered sympathetically as he stood up.

"Forgot you're Jewsh! Well, no bathing, then. Nobody wantsh their privatesh mocked, eh? Shee you back at the khan. Unlesh you fanshy the night-life. Roomsh upshtairsh here, only half a *shestertiush*. Shum with company – ekshtra charge, but. If you know what I mean. Enjoy yourshelvesh."

He winked, and off he went to transact his business, throwing over his shoulder a final piece of advice as he stumped away briskly on his bowed little legs.

"Get drunk at your own rishk, but. Leaving firsht light – regardlesh!"

The next morning, as the suffused early light brightened the open courtyard of the khan, it was with a sagging, heavy countenance that Bufo hitched up a newly hired mule to the reloaded wagon, clearly not having heeded his own warning of the night before.

The apostles were not in the best of spirits themselves due to lack of sleep, for not only had a contingent of soldiers earlier tramped noisily past for a head start on their march, but in the khan itself a group of cameleers had been carousing half the night. Nevertheless they greeted their driver with amusement tinged with a modicum of respect, for though Bufo was plainly suffering a queasily throbbing head consequent upon a riotous night, yet he was a man of his word – and duly left, regardless.

The mule was as morose as his handler. Having enjoyed two days rest after hauling grain along gruelling roads, that morning he had been woken by a stable hand far too early for comfort, rudely interrupted while attempting to finish his breakfast (which was promptly eaten by his ravenous replacement), and then clumsily handled by a surly Bufo who several times had pinched him carelessly while yanking at the harness buckles. Therefore, the mule being both fresh and bad-tempered, the wagon jerked and lurched unpleasantly as it clattered over the road at an uncomfortable pace.

Bufo was in no mood to argue with a hired mule. Instead he shrugged crossly. The stupid animal would pay for it later, especially in the steepest stretches, and then they would lose whatever time they gained now, and more. He did not bother with reassuring his rather startled passengers. Bufo was not inclined to be conversational, squinting through bleary eyes and wincing at every bump, until his torrent of Phrygian swear words was spent, and thirsty swigs from his private flask refreshed him, and after a while he began to cheer up.

Once the mule had finally settled down into a steady walk, being encouraged by a number of disciplinary whacks from a long cane in

Bufo's freckly hand, the rumbling of the wagon added to the soporific effect of dappled sunlight and a caressing breeze. Though very little had been offloaded at Sagalassos and sundry items had been added, encroaching on the 'guaranteed space' and giving Paul even less room than before, he was nevertheless well settled on the consignment of wool and blankets.

Lying comfortably with his face upturned to the mountainous white clouds in a piercingly blue sky, he was able to forget the lingering pain of his ankle and the smarting weal on his face, while the continual vibration of the vehicle masked the bodily tremors which frequently disturbed his rest. Before long, he gratefully drifted off to sleep, leaving his tall friend to pass the time with Bufo as best he might.

Now that the mule was moving slowly, Barnabas walked beside the wagon rather than perching on the rattling back board where dust swirled up from the heavy wooden wheels. He might squeeze in beside Paul, but that would disturb him, and he was still unwell enough to need all the sleep he could snatch. With their packs on board, walking was no hardship; in fact, at times it was a good sight more comfortable than riding.

Once he had recovered his temper, Bufo doled out snippets of information regarding the next town, two days away.

"Old folk shtill call it Sheleushia Shidera. Courshe, it'sh Claudiosheleushia now."

"Shidera, you said?" Barnabas asked, and coughed suddenly. "I mean, Sidera," he corrected, trying to distract himself from Bufo's regrettably risible way of speaking by assuming a lively interest. "From *sideros*? So, was there iron mining close by?"

"Ironworksh, yesh, not sho much now though. Handy for knife-makersh, but, harr harr, ash my friendsh alwaysh shay."

Barnabas preferred not to think about knives in such uncomfortably close association with Bufo's friends, who might at this very moment be watching the road from the dark depths of the forest around them, or hiding around the next bend in the road, yes, *that* one, just there where the trees hung low!

As if to confirm his uneasiness, now he could hear tramping footsteps and voices up ahead, and for a moment Barnabas held his breath. The mule rounded the bend – and he relaxed.

"Many a *gladius* blade started there too, no doubt," he rejoined rather more loudly than necessary, indicating the group of soldiers marching almost half a *stadion* in front of them.

Bufo shook his head. "You're wrong there. It'sh no good for shwordsh. Nothing good enough ekshept Noric shteel. Hauling that'd be a good contract I bet. Pity Noricum ishn't closher. They shay it'sh on the other shide of the Empire. Mushn't grumble, but. I do well enough. Better pay than thoshe fellowsh!"

Bufo raised his stick in casual acknowledgement as several soldiers glanced over their shoulders at the sound of their approach.

"How many would you shay there are?" he asked with studied casualness, his eyes darting to and fro as the wagon jingled and rumbled past a rock formation familiar to him.

Barnabas shrugged, but stared hard at the group up ahead, obligingly attempting to count. Behind him Bufo reached back into the wagon with his long cane, over the top of the oblivious Paul, and with one swift and dexterous move, neatly jabbed a small bundle over the side. There was a crunching sound in the undergrowth as the wagon clattered on. It *might* have been a fox, had the bundle not mysteriously vanished a moment later.

CHAPTER TWENTY-NINE

"Thirty, maybe?" Bufo suggested carelessly to the back of Barnabas's head.

"Twenty, I'd say," he responded good-naturedly, unaware of Bufo's stealthy movements. "And a civilian with them, by the looks. Does it matter?"

"Not really. Nishe to know who we'll be sharing the night with, but."

"I would say they will outstrip us long before nightfall."

"We'll catch them up. Reckon it'sh my friend Juliush. Transhferring shome new recruitsh with a couple of veteransh. More than the eight he'sh entitled to push around ash a shimple *Decanush*, but he'sh alwaysh after higher dutiesh. We shee a bit of each other on thish road."

The wagon creaked and plodded on.

Chapter Thirty

CATCH them up they did as dusk was dissolving into night, coming to a clearing under the firs just nicely in time to appreciate the soldiers' good fire, the light of which was flickering through the trees. It was a pleasant change to avoid the laborious business of coaxing a flame out of sparks struck from flint, or teased from the whirling end of a stick. Having woken a few hours earlier, Paul stiffly clambered down from the wagon, refreshed by his heavy sleep, looking around with interest. Thickly blackened stones encircling the fire showed this site was regularly used. Several dark tents had already been erected beside a trickling creek, and sprawling on a carpet of pine needles, tired men were chewing hard bread and cheese with salt, washed down with water scooped from the rivulet.

Beside one enterprising group, the spoils of forage sat in a tin pannikin, adding to their monotonous fare a welcome relish by way of variety – a knob or two of wild garlic, a head of fennel, a handful of pine seeds knocked out of old cones. Some men were nibbling on tender shoots of green bracken, and a few were inspecting a handful of tiny brown mushrooms, sniffing the thumb-like caps and arguing over their edibility. They beckoned an old veteran to their side, and the leathery fellow poked the glossy skins and thready stalks with a wary finger.

"You'd be a fool to eat these," he rasped, shaking his head firmly, "unless you want a nasty visit to the underworld. Or maybe you'll be trying to fly off the next viaduct. Remember what happened to poor old Acacius. Went off his head and disappeared."

With a disappointed grunt, the others tossed the rejected delicacies into the bushes and resigned themselves to their hard bread.

Meanwhile, stationing the wagon under a tree, Bufo chocked the wheels and began to unbuckle the sweating mule.

"Greetingsh, Decanush Juliush!" Affably he hailed the tall officer in charge, raising his hand in a lazy salute. "Fortuna and Dishiplina shmile upon you."

"I would say, you too, Bufo," Julius responded without enthusiasm, "though judging by the way you fleeced me at dice last night, I would say Fortuna has smiled upon you quite enough already. As for Disciplina, excuse me while I laugh."

Bufo was not at all put out by this rude response. "I do not ashpire to worship shuch a goddesh," he said with mock humility. "I leave it to better men shuch ash yourshelves. For your devotion she will reward you with a Shenturion'sh posht one day."

Julius grinned. "You're not called Bufo for nothing, are you? Come, introduce me to your passengers and I'll introduce you to my cousin Epaenetus over there. I'm seeing him safely to Claudioseleucia, along with this bunch of wasters. He's a great devotee of Disciplina. Even wants to join the army, foolish fellow. Rather painfully high-minded, but means well. Let's hope he grows out of it."

The introductions made, the men talked around the fire as they ate their own meal, which was much the same as the soldiers' rations, with the welcome addition of some dried apple slices which they shared with the Decanus and his cousin. In return Julius urged them to share his own generous pot of beans, which was simmering invitingly over the fire, sending out mouth-watering wafts of garlic.

"*The property of friends is common*, as the saying goes," he quipped with a wink, and as if to demonstrate his maxim, commandeered a few mess tins from his men and doled out the hot mixture. Epaenetus sighed – Julius could never be made to see that such showing off was hardly in the appropriate spirit of Disciplina.

"You know something of Menandros, then," Paul commented with interest. "How so?"

"My first centurion was an educated man, very fond of Greek ways. A bit too fond, according to some of my fellow recruits. Fortunately I was spared his attentions. But he was a voracious reader of the Greek writers, and a great admirer of Menandros. After a few drinks it was like opening a spigot – he'd spout the fellow for hours. We didn't care, except when he harangued us with his favourite: *Bad company corrupts good morals,* which we considered insulting, even if it was true."

"Ah, that is one of my favourites, as well. The poet was an astute observer of men, I think, though I don't care for his plays. And speaking of astute observations … Barnabas, I believe I saw you – or rather, heard you – with some almonds this morning … are there any left?"

Barnabas obligingly foraged in a capacious pocket tied to his girdle, and handed around the last of his favourite toasted almonds, well salted, which were pronounced very good. Young Epaenetus took only five, in accordance with his creed of frugality. It was clear he was full of idealistic ambition.

"Of course I would have to serve my time as a regular, but once I have proved myself, then I can seek promotion – and security," he said earnestly, sucking the salt off an almond to make it last longer. "As a skilled carpenter I have every chance of becoming an *immune,* you see, where my trade may better serve my Legion. Seige engines, accommodations, bridges – where would the army be without carpenters?"

"Lazy devil," Julius mocked him with a wink at Bufo. "No latrine duty, no rampart patrol, all for the glory of Disciplina and higher pay. Some people are so selfish."

Epaenetus flushed. He knew he was being baited, but he took his beliefs seriously.

"You value Disciplina's creed yourself," he retorted warmly, crunching his last almond and swallowing it long before he had intended to. "*Frugalitas, severitas* and *fidelis* are no joke, Cousin, but a standard all men would do well to heed."

"I agree with you," Paul said quietly. "We also serve one who urges similar restraint, determination and faithfulness."

"Is that so?" Epaenetus asked in surprise. "Who is that, then?"

"What an ignorant fellow you are, Cousin!" Julius grinned. "Did you not recognise that Aramaic blessing before they ate?"

He was rather proud of his wide general knowledge. A man who must forever be knocking about the world could not help picking up such things, if he *was* a man and not a mere vegetable with a sword.

"I don't pretend to know the language," he continued with slightly false modesty, "but I believe it starts, *Blessed be thou, King of the World, who gives us bread from the earth* – or something like that – I forget the rest.

Only Jews would give their deity such a title, but he does have a name. They call him Adonai, their Eternal God."

He turned to them with a wink. "What surprises me is that you should be sharing salt with us! Are we not somewhat beneath your acceptable standards of holiness?"

Paul smiled. "No man is holy before God, my friend. As one of our own sayings goes, *What is man, to claim he is clean? Even the heavens are not pure in God's sight.* There is only one man who has ever lived a stainless life, Jeshua our *Christos*, the Son of Almighty God Himself –"

"Well, there's something new!" Julius interrupted, raising his eyebrows in amused astonishment. "I thought your God was celibate. Isn't it only *our* gods who have all the fun?"

Paul and Barnabas exchanged looks. Of course, as a heathen, the man's ignorant attitude was understandable, but it was painful to hear such levity on such a hallowed subject as the Fatherhood of the Eternal – something which was both miraculous and an astounding condescension of His ineffable grace towards sinning mortals.

"Hear me out, I pray," Paul said patiently. "Lord Jeshua came not by the will of man, but by the will of Adonai God, who through His divine powers caused a virgin to conceive and bear a son, even as foretold in our holy scriptures. That is how he was fathered, and if you think *that* was miraculous, let me tell you that God also seeks to father *us* in a spiritual sense, adopting us, as it were – elevating us to become His children through a relationship with His Son."

"What does that profit you?" Epaenetus asked curiously, struggling to comprehend these extraordinary assertions.

"It profits us salvation from the effects of sin and death. It profits us the divine gift of eternal life."

"All very nishe for Jewsh," Bufo croaked sardonically. "No joy to the resht of ush, but."

"Aha, but that's where you are wrong!" Barnabas put in quickly. "It is joy to the *world,* not just to us! The *Christos* offers this hope to both Jews and Gentiles, you see, without favour to one above the other."

Paul nodded. "That is the very reason we are here now, in this country, to spread the word, this gospel of good news to all men."

"Whew!" Julius exclaimed. *"And* we poor dogs of Gentiles? (No offence, we are equally rude about barbarians.) I never heard of such a thing! Yet, here we are, eating from the same pot, so it seems you mean what you say. Remarkable! Well, live and learn! Anyone for more beans?"

"What does he ask of you in return?" demanded Epaenetus.

Paul smiled, thinking wryly of the years and years in which he had striven so strenuously to obey in everything and offend in nothing, and the torturous lengths to which he had gone in an effort to safely navigate the Law through a myriad of ever-narrowing channels of life. Oh, surely in essence it was so simple, for the Law taught a man what to do, while the Christ taught a man who to be, and it all came down to only one thing.

"Love," he replied warmly. "Love! Genuine, demonstrated love of Who God is, and what He has done for us, in giving us His Son as a sacrifice for our sins. Genuine love of Lord Jeshua, who laid down his life for us, and has become the first man on earth ever to be granted immortality! Because of their great love toward us, we have life through his blood."

"Blood? Isn't that what mortals shed for their gods, not the other way around?" Julius clutched his head dramatically. "And a god sacrificing his own son for the sake of men? Love! What religion is driven by such a thing from gods to men? This seems all backwards to me."

"These are indeed unusual novelties," Epaenetus said slowly. "Confusing. But since your god's creed reflects that of my beloved Disciplina, I would like to understand. Tell me more, and if I am still confused, I will ask yet more questions of you tomorrow as we walk. If you are willing, of course."

Praise the Eternal! Of course they were willing, and more than willing!

The night drew on as the men talked in low tones. Bufo yawned ostentatiously but since nobody else in the campfire group seemed inclined to sleep, he resigned himself to the murmur of voices, wrapped himself up in his cloak and made himself a comfortable bed on the soft needles under the wagon where the mountain dew would not reach him. Squirming free of several knobbly pine cones which were digging into his shoulder blades, he was soon snuffling quietly off to sleep, where he had delightful visions, as he so often did, of being a fine fellow with a magnificent set of strong teeth, able to manage the toughest meat with ease, crunch whole handfuls of nuts, and chew the hardest bread without the ignominy of having to soak it first. His bare jaws mumbled and champed happily as he slept, and an unconscious, gloating chortle escaped as for one blissful moment he dreamed that he had actually bitten his deliciously plump wife with teeth sharp enough to make her scream.

The four men who were left, quietly talked on far into the night, poking the fire absently, feeding it with pine cones, until the last log, already smouldering low, suddenly crumbled into coals. Julius jumped up, cursing himself soundly as he piled on more fuel from the untidy jumble of dead branches and sticks which the men had gathered. Here he was, the Decanus in charge, almost letting the fire go out, and he had not even done the rounds of his men! That was no way to promotion! Firmly he wished the others good night and after a stern word to the soldier on watch about tending the fire, checked on the men, and retired to his own tent, dragging his cousin with him.

"We're not waiting for any sluggardly civilians in the morning," he told him pointedly. "Sleep!"

Sleep? Epaenetus closed his eyes, but how could he possibly sleep after all he had heard that night! His head was wide awake. So much was jumbling around excitedly inside it. To think that a couple of wandering Jews could disconcert him so thoroughly and make him ponder, and doubt, and wonder! There was no doubt they were very learned men, but still – *Jews!?*

At Bufo's suggestion, Barnabas had earlier toppled the wool bales from the wagon to make room. Now he and Paul stretched out on the load of blankets, thankful indeed for such an unusually comfortable bed while still on the road. Off the ground! Clean blankets! Sleeping nose to nose with melons and ticklish fronds of greenery was a small price to pay.

Their grateful prayers over, Barnabas quickly fell asleep, snoring gently (and occasionally grinding his teeth), and even though Paul had slept virtually all day he was not far behind, as the lofty pines, shushing unceasingly, soon lulled him into dreams of being once more at sea, rocking to and fro. Around them gentle rumblings and snores began to arise from the sleeping men in the tents, until even these died away.

For a long time there was only the sibilant silence of the black surrounding forest. Against a deep purple sky, shadowy tips of fir swept over the stars, like dark fingers caressing a remote, moonlit, crystal lyre. Small creatures scuffled in the undergrowth, glaring owls hooted hollowly as they glided on mute wings with claws of death. A far-off fox barked harshly, and one of Julius' men began to talk in his sleep. He was immediately silenced by a swift kick from the man next to him, but in the wagon Paul was awake at once, and stayed that way listening to the invisible life around him.

The stars above were a mere blur to his weak eyes, the treetops swayed unseen, the black tents melted into stygian trees. Rolling over and propping his chin on one of the melons, he peered over the edge of the wagon. Only the dull red glow of the campfire revealed anything recognisable – a guard who had made the mistake of sitting comfortably instead of staying on his feet, and was now nodding off beside flames which had dwindled to a mere blue flicker among the mottled crimson coals.

Paul clambered down from the wagon as quietly as his awkward ankle allowed, limped over to the sleeper, and tapped him on the foot. At once the man's eyes opened wide, his hand flying to his short sword, but with a warning finger on his lips Paul pointed to the dying fire, whereupon the soldier sprang up with alacrity. The two of them quickly built it back up, but at first the fresh wood smoked badly, blanketing the sullen light even further.

It had not quite crackled into flames when suddenly, beside the wagon a dark lump which was the hired mule snorted violently and leaped into life, ears twitching, hooves digging, anxiously throwing his head around, trying to escape his tether. Underneath the wagon a startled Bufo sat up, cracking his head on the axle, and with a muffled oath crawled out to calm the agitated animal.

The mule would not be calmed. It plunged up and down, kicking and straining, protesting at the top of its lungs in a honking, whinnying braying alarm which brought sleepy yells of annoyance from all sides. The fire flaring up at last revealed Julius tumbling angrily out of his tent just as what sounded like an answer – a deeper, rumbling braying noise – echoed lustily from the forest.

Having woken with a jump, Barnabas, bolt upright in the wagon, was just convincing himself it must only be wild asses fighting when from the same direction a harsh snarl made him freeze, and a high-pitched, squealing scream split the air, turning his blood to ice. Julius shouted to his men who scrambled out with swords in hand, looking wildly around in the murky, wavering firelight. All at once came a heavy shaking of the bushes, nearer and nearer, and with a low gurgling growl a huge spotted lynx sprang into the circle of light and tore across the clearing with a screaming piglet in its jaws. The lynx flicked its head sharply as it bounded into the night, and even before its short tail was swallowed up in the darkness the squealing had choked into silence.

Momentarily transfixed, the half-dressed men were still gaping after it – when with a mighty crashing in the undergrowth a massive wild sow burst out with an anguished roar, heading straight for the men bunched up at the fire. They immediately scattered, disclosing Paul, who with nowhere to run and unable to leap the crackling flames behind him, snatched up a blazing branch and brandished it in fiery swinging arcs, yelling for all he was worth. As the frantic creature momentarily hesitated and veered away, Julius dived forward, stabbing desperately with his blade – and skidding on the slippery pine needles succeeding only in gouging her rump before landing on his face with the sword twisting out of his hand.

Now half the men were bolting in all directions to swarm up trees or into the wagon. With a harsh barking scream the heavy sow slewed around so quickly that three more sword-wielding soldiers were felled by her body even as Julius regained his weapon – but several more thrusts had found their mark on head and flank.

Back she charged with lowered head – blood flowing blackly into her tiny eyes, long yellow tusks gleaming wickedly in the shadows – but Julius rolled and sprang aside just in time, and the infuriated animal, brought up short against the wagon, wheeled again – just as a fear-crazed Bufo, dashing out from the wool bales behind which he had hidden himself, was attempting to gain its refuge. Miraculously both snout and brutal teeth just missed him but her heavy hindquarters knocked the howling Bufo off his bandy legs and into the shafts.

In an instant, tall Barnabas and the others beside him had plucked him to safety by the hair, armpits, and whatever else they could clutch, before the beast could turn again to rend him. Thrusting the gibbering little man behind him, Barnabas appeared to have completely lost his head and was wildly snatching up melons in both hands, flinging them down with all his might.

"Come on!" he bawled, pelting the maddened sow with Bufo's cargo as she ferociously rammed the wheel spokes below, shaking the whole wagon with battering blows. "Come on, men! Help me!"

It was a strategy of sheer desperation, but the heavy missiles distracted the crazed animal for just long enough for one of the men to stab her behind the skull with a powerful, double-fisted blow from above, and as she staggered, another lunged dangerously over the side to thrust a blade deep into her neck. Tottering from loss of blood, she shook her head frantically, plunging this way and that with husky guttural bellowings and tossing tusks, as Julius roared orders and first one group of soldiers and then another ran upon her with swords as one man, and suddenly the terrifying creature which had chased away a savage predator to protect its young, was only a heavy, bloodied, quivering carcase on the forest floor.

Paul, still standing dazedly by the fire, found he could move at last, and hastily dropped his burning stick as he sank gratefully to the ground. His mouth was too dry to speak.

Julius, panting, but grinning widely, wiped the blood from his face and counted his jubilant men. One was missing, but it was not a soldier.

"Epaenetus?" he shouted, and a shamefaced body swung itself down from a branch and dropped lightly to the ground.

"Fine soldier I'd make," he muttered disgustedly, but his military cousin only clapped him on the back and assured him he'd rather face ten crazed Gauls than one mad sow any day.

He looked at his excited men, who were already arguing about who should get the tusks.

"Who wants to sleep now?" he asked meaningfully, and a burst of laughter was the reply as the men flashed their blades in gratified answer.

"We can sleep tomorrow night, sir!"

"As I thought. Then help yourselves, but cook it well – anyone who delays me for a putrid belly in the morning will be on a charge."

"What about the sucklings, sir? Pity to waste them!"

"Do you want to set the forest on fire and roast us all too? One clumsy fool with a dropped light will do it nicely. No, first light you can look for them and not before. They'll be making enough noise by then, if something else hasn't eaten them already. Here, Epaenetus, bring out that wineskin in my pack. There's not much left but enough for a swig all round." He waved imperiously at his delighted men, and raised his voice. "*Anapauou phage pie euphrainou!*" he pronounced somewhat grandly.

The men cheered and proceeded to obey forthwith, for never had they thought to hear a superior encourage them so heartily to *Take your rest, eat, drink, and be merry!*

Aside, Julius chuckled to his cousin, "It's not often a mere Decanus gets to be so popular! How many have a chance to give that kind of order, hey?"

Epaenetus frowned slightly. "You're showing off again, Julius. I know you are ambitious, but what difference does it make if they like you or not?"

"Perhaps none at all. But let me give you a word of advice, Cousin. On your way up a crowded ladder, it is wise not to grind the faces of those you overtake. You never know when you may slip down again, or when they might climb past you. Either way you will be glad to have created good will and not enmity."

"I stand reproved," Epaenetus said humbly, and sincere fellow that he was, actually meant it.

Julius's men long remembered that night as one of rare pleasure in their hard soldiering life. All the meat they could comfortably eat, plenty of fat to slather it in, and more than enough for the next day! Paul and Barnabas, however, long remembered it for what they suffered. The ugly sight of the badly butchered body and the pervasive smell of the roasting pork nauseated them to gagging point. Climbing back into the wagon and burying their noses under the blankets they tried to block it out and eventually, despite the impromptu celebrations of the others, managed to suffocate themselves back to sleep.

In the damp early morning the pungent smell of charred swine flesh hung in the air, and the hacked carcase, already buzzing with flies and crawling with ants, looked more grisly than ever, but the apostles tried to keep their discomfort to themselves. They were strangers in a strange land, after all.

Meanwhile, the easy discovery of the sow's remaining offspring hungrily squealing in the forest added to the soldiers' triumph. Nine of them! Never had they had such a delightful march! Maybe the Jews had brought them good luck! If so, what a fine joke that was – considering that the good luck came in the form of plentiful pork! Looking at the captured piglets with satisfaction, Julius ordered that the squirming little bodies be tied up alive in spare ration sacks, offering the runt of the litter to Bufo in return for carting them to the next town, and to compensate him for the ruination of the melons, the remains of which the men had already devoured for breakfast.

Paul and Barnabas's resolve to appear politely unconcerned was severely tested by this plan, but there was little they could do about it.

"I'm not ashking you to *eat* them, am I?" Bufo said reasonably enough to their strained faces. "I'll shtick them up front neksht to me, but. You'll never know they're here."

Alas, such was not the case. Not only did the unfortunate piglets continually remind them of their presence by the pitiful high-pitched yawpings and unpleasant smelling liquids soaking through the bags, but Bufo indulged in a lengthy rambling monologue of exactly how he would have his own suckling prepared, and worse, how it would taste.

They listened long-sufferingly as he described how the gently roasted skin would turn "ash shining pink ash boiled quinshesh!", and how the crackling would be so delicate that even his gums could crunch it before it melted in the mouth and oozed down the chin, until finally he rhapsodised, "The shoftnesh of the flesh will be only shurpashed by itsh flavour!"

As Bufo smacked his lips with a faraway look, Paul rolled his eyes. What was it about pork which turned ordinary men into salivating gluttons? Next they would be passing around recipes like the renowned Roman food-lover Apicius, whose god was his belly.

Julius had been just as bad while striking camp, cutting out the sow's udder – perfect for stuffing with other meats, and a great delicacy! – and expressing his regrets that the entire carcase was impractical to transport. He knew a place in Claudioseleucia which specialised in *petaso*, where his friend Draco the cook would have prepared some choice cuts to perfection, giving him a good serving in return for the fresh meat.

"Dare we ask what *petaso* is?" Paul had said warily.

"Pig And Fig," Julius answered with satisfaction. "Delicious!" He laughed at their expressions. "The meat is boiled with figs, then browned and seasoned with pepper sauce. You could make a Jewish version, I suppose! Yes, no reason why you couldn't do the same with lamb, though I never have. H'm, that might be worth suggesting to old Draco."

He turned to Bufo, who was hobbling ostentatiously as he slowly harnessed the mule. "Shift your bones, Bufo! I don't want those sucklings dying before we get there. They'll last the day, that's all."

"Can't you shee I'm shtruggling?" Limping on his left leg, Bufo rubbed the right one tenderly. "I've got thish leg, now!" he said accusingly, glaring at Julius as if the attack had been his fault. "Lucky I washn't killed lasht night!"

"Which leg, again?" Julius asked drily, and Bufo groaned as he limped on the other instead.

"Can't tell. That'sh the trouble, but. Both, I reckon."

"You'll live!" Turning his back on the little man, Julius barked an order to his men, and shouldering their heavy packs, they fell into rank and were soon marching down the road at a smart pace.

An hour later, having endured all matters porcine for as long as he could stomach, Barnabas jumped down from the slowly trundling wagon, and with an apologetic grin to the still lame Paul, stalked on ahead to walk with Epaenetus. Before long the two were deep in discussion, falling further and further behind the soldiers up ahead.

Julius looked over his shoulder. "Not waiting for stragglers!" he shouted. The marching men were tired and somewhat bloated after their feasting but he would keep them up to their four miles an hour no matter what.

It was a full day's march to Claudioseleucia and they would only just get there before nightfall. "Meet me at the barracks, Cousin! With the pigs!"

Epaenetus waved acknowledgement and with swinging strides Julius and his troop drew ahead, marched steadily around the next curve, and disappeared.

Chapter Thirty-one

THE way started out just as steep, just as alarming in its variety of vertiginous places and just as fraught with dangerous possibilities as ever, but if there were any brigands watching from the trees they were too careful of their own necks to attack Julius and his company of soldiers – who in any case would have little of value about them. And even Bufo's slower-moving group was in no danger while he and his unseen friends of the road honoured their private agreements. The sun shone fitfully through mountainous white clouds, the road crawled ahead relentlessly, the wind blew huskily through the towering pines, the mule plodded, the wagon creaked, the piglets snuffled and squawled, and Bufo warbled a mournful Pisidian ballad with far too many verses and a depressingly frequent chorus.

"O foolish Galatea, who holds you in thrall
That mine is no longer the name that you call?
So quick to turn faithless, how can you disdain
The love you once cherished, while mocking my pain!"

By the tenth time through, Paul and Barnabas (most unwillingly) knew it by rote and were heartily sick of it. They were just deciding that perhaps foolish Galatea had the right idea after all, when at once the dark wall of tall trees seemed to part, and her fickleness, justifiable or otherwise, was forgotten. There below them was a sweeping vista hedged by faraway mountains: a lumpy plain with a river worming its way through, a distant grey city brooding on a hill, the glimpse of a vast body of blue water to the east, and way ahead, steadily marching along a scratch of road, something like a small red insect throwing an occasional metallic glint from its body. Julius and his men were already more than an hour in front, and now with a steep decline slowing the wagon further, their roast suckling-pig dinners might yet end up as a midnight feast. Paul wedged himself more securely in the back of the wagon, Bufo got down and took the mule's halter, the men tightened their sandals, and gradually the white road led them down.

Once safely descended to the rugged plain, they paused to rest the mule and their aching legs. Paul gratefully got down from the wagon and stretched, glad to feel the smoothly worn limestone blocks under his feet. There was something horribly helpless about sitting in a steeply angled vehicle which at every bump threatened to run over the animal in harness, or tip sickeningly to the sheer drop side of the road and fling its contents into thin air to be skewered on the trees far below, like morsels in a cook shop. Now with that tension eased, he massaged his jaw ruefully, realising that he must have been clenching it unconsciously all the way down – no wonder it ached. From then on however the road ran easily by comparison, and for the rest of the journey he pushed himself to get out and walk beside the others for a short while every hour.

By the time they approached the city, with the late afternoon rapidly melting into dusk, he was now walking with less of his old limp than Bufo's new one. He, Barnabas, and Epaenetus were a little way ahead of Bufo in the wagon, avoiding both the dust and the imprisoned piglets, who having been jogged (or sung) into a kind of torpor, were now coming unhappily and hungrily back to life and beginning to complain about it as best they could in their weakened state.

Paul and Barnabas had no love for pigs but could not help feeling sorry for the doomed, thirsty creatures. The Law enjoined men to care for their animals, but how anyone could have aided these hapless little brutes was beyond them. Still, they would be out of their misery in another few hours, and their fresh meat would be rejoicing Bufo's family and the men of Julius's mess hall – and probably his superior officer too, since Julius most likely would grasp any such chance to attract favourable notice. For all that, his generosity seemed genuine, his pride in his scraps of second-hand learning touching rather than boastful, and taken as a whole he was a likeable man, who would no doubt go far.

Paul was sorry they could not have kept up with the marching men and continued to engage him in conversation. Despite Julius's easy geniality, he felt there was a reaching for something more in the Decanus, which had nothing to do with a centurion's helmet. Meanwhile, free of his slyly provoking older cousin, Epaenetus had been an attentive and inquisitive listener all day, asking many questions, pressing for explanations, and feeling his grasp on all his previous certainties disconcertingly slipping away. For the last hour, however, scarcely realising that he had digressed from conversation to introspection, he had been deeply absorbed in thought.

The wide, white ribbon of road rolled on towards yet more northerly mountains, but having turned east at a fork heading over the plain, Bufo's group, travelling towards the massive lake had left the main branch far behind them. Now they were on the last stretch, curving up and around to approach the heavy gates of Claudioseleucia, sternly set into the huge squared blocks of the city walls. The last fortified city on this section of the way to Antiochia, it was one of nine Seleucias in the Empire, thanks to the ancient ruler who had lavished his family's names on cities far and wide. Though Emperor Claudius had since conferred upon it the honour of attaching his own name, and had funded various works within, it was not a beautiful place. The bald northwest slope of the hill upon which it stood greeted any traveller who might be congratulating himself on surviving a perilous journey, with a dismal reminder of his mortality – what appeared to be a miniature city of cliff-dwellers, their neat doorways cut into the broad rock face … the city's necropolis.

At the sight of the tombs a slight shudder ran through Epaenetus and he spat rapidly three times, murmuring an invocation under his breath. Paul glanced at the young man's tense expression.

"You fear this place?"

"Who would not fear a place of dead men, where evil spirits may roam?"

"Yet you would be a soldier, Epaenetus, creating whole fields of dead men if so commanded."

The young Greek looked taken aback for a moment, then defended himself. "Any man at arms is careful to prepare his soul for death before a battle. And a soldier does not linger on the battlefield once the burials are over. But men buried without proper rites of passage lie unquietly in their graves and become *Lemures*. Every necropolis will contain such unfortunates, and therefore harbour these restless spirits. I tell you, this city is too close to its tombs, and just now day is too close to night. The two combined do not make me easy."

"No evil sphpiritsh have ever shcared *me* around here." The unpeturbed Bufo looked positively cheerful. "Another half hour, and you wouldn't even have sheen any gravesh. It'd be too dark, ha ha."

Epaenetus looked at Bufo rather coldly. "No sense, no feeling," he muttered ungraciously.

Barnabas had turned his face away so as not to betray his amusement at this exchange, but Paul, seeing an opportunity to enlighten him further concerning the true state of the dead, put a reassuring hand on the young man's shoulder.

"There is no awareness in death, my friend," he said encouragingly, "not until resurrection of the body. And since resurrection is only for those who know their true Creator I would say the dead buried here will remain in peace." As he gestured to the nearby tombs, an iron grip bit so suddenly into his arm that he yelped, looking at Epaenetus with astonishment.

The young Greek was standing rigidly, fingers digging whitely into Paul's flesh, trembling all over, eyes wide in horror, pointing with a quivering finger. "*Lemures!*" he said hoarsely.

"Shades of the dead?" Even as Paul struggled to make sense of this, for his eyes could distinguish little in the gathering shadows, there was a wild, terrified shriek from Bufo, who collapsing backwards into the wagon and instantly scrambling himself upright enough to clutch the reins, cut the startled mule mercilessly with his cane, lashing him into a frightened gallop. Barnabas stared from one to the other as Bufo, yammering wordlessly, tore up the road, leaving them standing – and then he saw, and finally, so did Paul.

A little way off the road, a swaddled body was emerging from a low tomb, wriggling like a caterpillar squirming out of a bad apple. For a few delirious heartbeats, even the apostles' mouths went dust-dry. Then the caterpillar swore angrily and blundered into a bush, thrashing itself free. With a low moan Epaenetus crumpled in a dead faint to the earth, as Barnabas ran over the rough ground to help the cursing man, who was clearly very much alive.

Finally extricated from a kind of sacking hood, a filthy, emaciated face was glaring with blazing eyes – not at Barnabas, Paul, or even Epaenetus, but at something, or someone, invisible further up the slope.

"You harpy!" he choked, shaking his fist. "You foul, stinking, perfidious harpy! How many times will you deceive me? Will you not let me die in peace?"

Tearing at his matted grey hair and wheeling around with an agonised moan, he spied the three travellers for the first time, and cried out again, pointing. "Ah! Like him! Like him! Why take him but not me!?"

A thick wave of grave-stench rolling from his body he dashed past the unnerved Barnabas, to pounce upon the limp form of Epaenetus, clutching him with black talon-like nails, sinewy hands working convulsively, jealously sobbing upon his breast. Instinctively springing to protect his pagan companion, Paul leapt on the wrong foot, the bad ankle gave way and he sprawled on top of both men, while Barnabas, recovering himself with an effort, stumbled back to the road to pull them apart. At that unlucky moment young Epaenetus sighed, and coming out of his swoon opened his eyes – only to find himself in the noisome embrace of a wailing vision from Hades. His mouth gaping in a soundless scream, his eyes rolled backwards and once more he was mercifully oblivious.

Paul struggled to his knees and in one swift movement swept back the filth-matted mane to raise the haggard stranger's head. "Look at me!" he demanded crisply, squarely meeting the tormented eyes. "What are you about, fellow? My young friend is not dead, but you have frightened him into a faint. Leave him alone at once."

"He is – not – dead? Ah! Then, I grieve for him! She has deceived him too!"

The wild man dragged himself off the unconscious Epaenetus and slumped down beside him. The smell was indescribable and Paul gritted his teeth, forcing himself to speak gently. "Come, there is a painful tale to be told here, I perceive. What is your name, and what is your story?"

The old man slewed his head from side to side. "The sun is almost down," he said flatly. "The city gates will shut, and I – I –," his voice rose to a despairing shriek, "I will be out here, alone – with them! With the *Di Inferi* who only mock me! And … with *her!*"

"Are you barred from the city?" Barnabas asked, hastily muffling the lower half of his face in his headcloth and praying he would not gag.

"They will force me out. She says not but it is just more lies."

Epaenetus stirred as he gradually revived, only to stagger to his feet aghast, clapping a hand to his nose in shock. Barnabas immediately drew him aside, giving him wine from the slender flask tied on his girdle, explaining to the pale, sweating young man the truth of what had terrified him. Nodding, but yet unable to speak and still trembling in every limb, Epaenetus, gulped the proffered wine in desperate, grateful mouthfuls – and was instantly violently sick.

It was almost dark. Above them, flickering in the breeze, lights winked from the forbidding walls, and a square glow hovered around the still open gates. Paul stood up, and the skeletal old man flung himself at his feet, clutching him by the ankles, crying, "Don't leave me! Don't leave me!" Paul winced. That ankle was becoming a problem.

"Barnabas, get Epaenetus into the city before the gates shut. He is badly rattled, and you must deliver him safely to Julius – and also find Bufo before someone helps themselves to our packs. I can't do it with this ankle and will stay here. Just leave me your water and wine and whatever food you have about you. I have some dried figs still, and a few crusts – and the flint. Come back for me in the morning when the gates open."

"Is this wise, Paul?"

"Yes. Lord Jeshua is with me. Now hurry."

Obeying at once Barnabas raced up the road with Epaenetus, who needed no urging. The sound of their flying feet faded away, and they reached the city just as the square glow from the slow-closing gates began to narrow. Gradually it shrank, and suddenly vanished.

The old man hardly noticed. He was watching the sun sinking rapidly behind the mountains. "You see," he whispered with foetid breath. "You see? Every day she promises I may join her in death and be with her forever. She whispers so sweetly to me that she will propitiate the *Di Inferi*, for I have nothing left to share with the underworld gods but the little mushrooms I find under the trees. Every morning and evening I perform the rituals as best I can. I prepare and lay myself in the grave, I bind up my body, I cover my head … and every day I think she has been faithful, for I quickly plunge into blessed darkness. But no sooner have I died than she joins with them to torment me with nightmare visions where I taste colours and smell sounds and swell strangely, or shrivel to the size of an ant. Then later – much later – perhaps a day, a night, a week, who knows … I awake and I am still here! She has deceived me again!"

Ready tears furrowed pale streaks through the grey dirt on his face, pooling in the filthy tufts of beard. "I do not know how I can go on," he sobbed. "But I cannot live, and I cannot die!" Suddenly he stopped crying and looked piercingly at Paul. "You have food! And fire! You can help me!"

Paul, having calmly scratched some tinder together, was now striking his flint. A wisp of smoke curled up, then a tiny flame, snaking through the dry leaves to lick at the shreds of bark above them. He carefully laid small twigs on top and dragged up a long dead branch. "I have food, and a little wine. Not much, but I will share with you gladly."

"No! No! What use is food and wine to me? You will offer it to the gods, you will do it for me! Yes, it has been all wrong, I see it now. I had no flame! No friend! And nothing for a libation! But you will do this for me, and then I will be free!"

Rolling up the long tattered blanket and hood he had dropped earlier, he scrabbled under a bush and drew out a flat stone on which perched a small pile of mushrooms. "You see? This is all I had, but now a far better offering may be made. Many times I have spied on mourners from the darkness, envying their food, their sacrifices of puppies! But now Fortuna smiles upon me. Surely I was a fool to attempt to offer for myself when the dead cannot eat with the living. Of course I could not be both the corpse and the one who paid for its soul's safety! Wait – you have coins for Charon the ferryman! Yes? Ah! surely *now* I may cross the river!"

Suddenly his excitement dropped away. He looked warily at Paul, his crusted eyes fearful in the growing firelight. "You *are* sent to me by Fortuna? You are not yet another phantom sent to trick me?"

"I would not dream of tricking you, old man, and I will help you all I can."

"No man has ever lingered in this dread place. Not with me. Why are you not afraid?"

"Because I serve one who has conquered death and it holds no terrors for me."

Paul's self possession was not as solid as he made out. Underneath it, he had not stopped praying, for he was not yet sure in what way he should proceed, only that there would be one. What was he faced with? A madman? Or something else? There was an answer somewhere, he could sense it, creeping its way up to the surface of his memory. *Lord Jeshua, I would help this poor man. Guide me!*

"Come, share my food, such as it is. You look like a hungry fellow."

The hollow-eyed face twitched in an angry grimace. "No – it is needed for my offerings! Do it now! You said you would help me!"

"I will do so in my way and in my time, not yours, old man. But see, I will save some for later and it will be enough. You have my word as a citizen of Rome and a man of Tarsus, no mean city."

His anxious companion nodded, satisfied, but could not stop glancing fearfully into the darkness even while Paul divided the food into three portions and laid one aside, covering it with his head cloth. Now Paul pronounced a blessing, still speaking in Latin, for he did not want to startle the delusional man by using Aramaic lest he imagine some spell was being cast.

"Blessed art thou, King of the World, who brings forth bread from the earth, for which I praise thee through Christ, Amen!"

"King of the World?" The confused eyes flickered with a momentary clarity. "You worship Caesar, then! Are you too a soldier?"

"You are one?" Paul countered instantly.

"Miles gregarius, Evocatus," the fellow muttered, as if reciting a lesson learned long ago.

Paul did not need to wonder why a retired foot-soldier, now in the reserves, was living among tombs when surely he would have received a pension or land. Clearly, penury was not the reason.

"Good, so you are ready to serve again when your master needs you. But you are in no fit state while half-starved. So, fall to – eat and drink!" Paul commanded briskly, and the man obeyed instantly. Stuffing a dried fig into his mouth he champed with an air of curiosity.

"No sound to this flavour," he croaked through a sticky mouthful, "nor even stripes."

Paul could not eat. Averting his eyes from maggots dropping from the man's smeared clothing, he put his own meal to the other's portion and collected more fuel. The old man did not notice. He made short work of the food and slurped the wine thirstily, seeming to find wonder in every sip, every mouthful, his demons briefly forgotten. Then Paul spoke again as he tended the fire, pushing the branch further in, breaking a dead bush into crackling dry twigs which would give good light.

"You still have not told me your name."

"Nor you yours." The red-rimmed eyes began to dart around suspiciously once more, and the knobbed grimy fingers twisted themselves nervously in the sacking hood.

"You may call me Paulus. And you are?"

"I was Acacius of Ghaziri," he mumbled. "Now I am nothing."

Acacius! Where had he heard that name? But the man's moments of lucidity were slipping away. Quickly Paul spoke in the crisp tone of authority which seemed to invoke a more coherent response.

"Acacius of Ghaziri, *Evocatus* of Caesar, I charge you, tell me your story!"

The drooping back straightened as old military habits of obedience held sway. Jerkily, the miserable man spilled out his tragedy, prompted by Paul's direct questions. A beloved yet capricious young wife, ruined from her own misadventures, fleeing back to her husband, lavish with tender vows to stay with him forever, only to be snatched away by death. An obliteration of grief and anger and regret. A deep mourning turned to darkness, confusion, and sick yearning. Mockery of nightmares amid enticing phantom visions, promises of sweet death, of safe passage over the River Styx and blissful reunion in Elysian fields. Futile beseeching and appeasing of the gods till nothing was left to offer.

The trembling skin-and-bone frame unfolded itself from its crouch by the fire, releasing a fresh waft of polluted air. "All I had left was these. Night and morning without fail have I made my offerings, but it was never enough." Reverently placing his meagre handful of wild food for the gods with the portion Paul had reserved, he added humbly, "Until you. A stranger. You, Paulus, will save me."

He dragged up the stinking ragged blanket, and pulled the stained hood over his head. "Come, her tomb awaits. I will wind myself in these graveclothes and lay myself beside her, and you will scoop a little pit for the offerings. You must be sure to partake of each morsel first, and make the prayers long enough for everything to burn to ash. Pour the libation carefully so as not to douse the fire! Then come to place the coins – on my eyes *and* in my mouth, eh? Yes, yes, to make it sure!" His voice shook and relieved tears spurted down the craggy, skull-like face to pool in the filth-caked tufts of his beard. "This time, no cruel *Di Inferi* will mock me. This time she will honour her promise. This time there will be no dread awakening!"

Paul had been staring at the glistening, thumb-like mushrooms heaped on the pale cloth. He drew a deep, thankful breath as brilliant light flooded into his mind.

"Sit down, my friend," he said firmly. "There is no hurry. To leave me alone here all night would be unkind of you, in the circumstances. You must trust me a while longer." He smiled suddenly. "Just until sunrise."

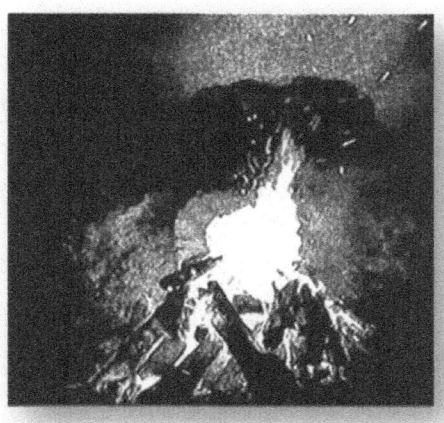

Chapter Thirty-two

"WHAT?!" Julius wheeled around from the spit where he was fussing over his roasting piglets, and glared at a still-pale Epaenetus. "That waster Bufo took off and abandoned you to a lunatic? But you have left behind your lame companion, both of you, so you are just as bad!"

Barnabas interposed. "Paul could not run, Julius, and the gates were about to close. It is imperative I retrieve our packs before they are stolen, and to that end he urged me to find you and Bufo at once. I can assure you he will come to no harm."

"You can assure me of no such thing," Julius grumbled. "But I suppose that is your affair. At least my cousin here is safe, though I must say he looks a little green around the gills, and no wonder – he stinks enough to poison the pigs." Lifting a couple of torches from a metal hoop by the door, he thrust the pitch ends into the fire and handed one to Barnabas. "Lucky for you, my recruits don't report to their new commander before noon tomorrow so till then my time is free."

He looked over his shoulder and barked, "Bernardus! Over here!"

The oldest veteran broke away from his fellows and saluted smartly. "Sir?"

"I'm going out. Mind the spit, and don't let the fattest one burn, it's for my superior – and keep the men in order till I get back. Epaenetus, get you to the baths before someone kicks you into a cess pit! Come on, my Jewish friend, let's find Bufo and your things – I know his usual haunts – and come sunrise we'll go back for your companion to see what's left of him, if anything. Stay sober, Bernardus, I'll want you with us tomorrow, just in case. Now everyone, look sharp!"

It was to be a long and worried night for Barnabas, who – despite his own prayers and Paul's earlier reassurance – still felt anxious and somewhat guilty. He did not fear that Paul might be torn limb from limb, exactly, but he might well be injured – as if he did not already have enough to try him! The apostles were promised protection in so far as preservation of their lives was concerned, but at no time did Lord Jeshua ever promise they would not be hurt. Quite the opposite, in fact, while Paul had been told very plainly he must *suffer many things*. Barnabas hoped devoutly that this would not be one of those occasions, yet he did not know what else they could have done.

Here he told himself firmly that surely for Paul to exercise the Gift of healing would be his best protection. For all this, he was very conscious that possessing a Gift did not make a man its master. A man might not cure all and sundry, nor heal himself, else Paul would have done so on many occasions before now, instead of labouring under continual infirmities. The purpose of any Gift primarily was to glorify God, to provide the stamp of Divine authority on the words of the preachers, particularly for the sake of the unenlightened, and to encourage believers with a taste of how things would be, come the wondrous new age of Christ's Kingdom. And even so, in its use the apostles must be led by the Spirit, not by their own inclinations.

These thoughts preoccupied Barnabas as he accompanied Julius on his hunt for the elusive Bufo. But the Decanus was unashamedly enjoying himself, rushing around, demanding answers from people, waving his torch with an air of command, poking his nose into several unsavoury *tabernae* and shouting upstairs to their private rooms, rousing up the posting stables, and darting into various travellers' dens. It was a satisfying diversion from the hum-drum of everyday marches and wet-nursing of raw recruits. He was almost disappointed when a very drunk Bufo was found in a small khan peacefully snoring in the wagon with his passengers' bundles safely hidden under the stack of army blankets bound for Antiochia. Barnabas had a rather unworthy suspicion that Julius might well have found him much sooner had he not so relished the excitement of a chase.

In a corner of the stall, waveringly illuminated by the brandishing of their torches, the unharnessed mule nodded peacefully. Beside him on its sack slept Bufo's piglet, the milky mush on its snout revealing that Bufo had found a way to keep it alive long enough to ensure a feast with his friends at the end of his trip.

After some abrupt words with the startled Bufo, Julius strode back to the barracks for his roast pork which by now must be done to a turn, and Barnabas, waving aside Bufo's insincerely slurred apologies, went to the still busy, torch-lit *agora* to find a water carrier, sluice himself off as best he could, and buy something to eat. As the night chill struck in, he returned to the khan to pray himself to sleep, beginning and ending with the psalmist's words, *I will lay me down in peace, for thou, Adonai, will make me dwell in safety!* while thinking only of Paul.

Hours later, as a silver-edged dawn was beginning to feather the leaden sky over the mountain tops, Julius, true to his word, marched into the warm khan with both Epaenetus and old Bernardus in tow, and ignoring grumbled curses from various other stalls, soon had everyone scrambling into life. Nudging Barnabas with his foot, he stuffed the supine piglet into its sack and slung it in the wagon, then prodding a bleary-eyed Bufo with a hard finger soon had him harnessing the bewildered mule, and in no time they were at the city gates, which were just beginning to creak open.

"Come on!" Julius urged them, lending his strength to the guards hauling on the thick wooden doors. Scarcely had they opened the width of a man when he had forced himself through, dragging the others with him with such haste that even Bufo was caught up in the mood, and slapping the reins shouted to them to get in or be left behind.

Down the dim, weirdly shadowed road they clopped, the mule crossly tossing its head, Bufo poised nervously with twitching cane, Julius fiercely gripping his sword, Epaenetus and Barnabas silent and frozen, the piglet complaining from under the blankets, and calm old Bernardus grimly watchful. As they rounded the curve of the looming, pock-marked hill, every eye strained in the half-light towards a tiny heap of smouldering coals, beside which two dark bodies lay.

"Paul! Paul!" Barnabas shouted at the top of his lungs, suddenly terrified. He scrambled out of the wagon as Bufo yanked it to a stop. Julius sprang out and everyone rushed over, yelling anxiously, except for Bufo who was calming the confused mule, and the old foot soldier who followed stealthily, hand on the hilt of his short sword. A necropolis was a dread, umbrageous place where anything might lurk, and he would tread very carefully so as to offend nothing and nobody, living or dead! He had not survived the lowly rank of *miles gregarious* all these years by taking chances.

Paul sat up slowly and stiffly, rubbing his arms, thankful for the dawn. Despite the fire it had been a very cold night and he had been awake and talking hard for most of it, all the while enveloped in nauseatingly mephitic air. But now it was over. He held up a hand to calm the wild-faced group tearing towards him.

"Softly, softly, my friends!" he said cheerfully. "You are making enough noise to wake the dead. Speaking of which ... or should I say ... whom ..." He gestured at his companion, and as the others clamoured for answers, answered the unspoken question on Barnabas's face. "No," he said with a smile. "This was a different kind of miracle."

"Who's making all this fuss and row?" the body beside him mumbled from under its grisly hood. "Some of us have a headache. Brrr, it's cold!" Rolling over, he yawned, opened his eyes, and sat up, looking around uncertainly.

"Hallo, is that you, Bernardus, you old dog?! What are you doing here? Come to think of it, what am I doing here?"

"Acacius!" the veteran stammered, startled out of his usual stolidity. "I – we – we thought you were lost – or dead – all these months!"

"Perhaps I was." The foul-smelling old man scratched his matted head. "I can't remember just now, but it will come back to me." He looked up expectantly. "Where is my wife?"

Bernardus awkwardly indicated a dark opening in the rock nearby. "She died, my friend," he said, groping for words. "And you haunted this place until we thought she had taken your soul with her ... and then you disappeared. We looked for you, but ..." he shrugged apologetically.

"He was here all the time," Paul said quietly, "hiding in the tombs from all men, scavenging remnants of funeral meats and foraging in the wild to survive. But it is thanks to *you*, soldier, that he is now in his right mind."

"How so?" Julius demanded keenly, then whistled as Paul related the warning he had overheard Bernardus give in the forest the previous evening. "And you say poor old Acacius was eating that accursed fungus night and day all this time? No wonder, that's all I can say. No wonder!" He shook his head and clapped the veteran on the back. "Bernardus – you have distinguished yourself!"

"Glad to be of service, sir," Bernardus muttered, suddenly overcome. His old friend was back from the dead! In a few more hours the poison would wear off completely and Acacius would again be totally himself. The old soldier was very glad of it, yet he shivered, and not from the cold, for this was truly a fearful spot, and he was not easy.

Julius felt much the same. Scowling at the still bemused Acacius he snapped, "You smell disgusting, Evocatus, and you need a good feed. Into the wagon, all of you. Bufo, get us out of here. There's a cold pork breakfast waiting for us – but let the Jews here have eggs or whatever they please, my treat." He grinned at Paul with genuine warmth as he helped him hobble to the wagon. "You deserve it, friend." Slapping Barnabas on the shoulder as he leapt up beside him he added, "You too, bald one."

The long-suffering mule hauled his heavy load back up the road, around the bend, and triumphantly the motley crew clattered through the gate, back to the mess hall to astonish everyone with their appearance and their story. Though news of Julius's errand of mercy had already flown through the barracks, nobody knew any of the details. Now everyone was talking at once with their mouths full, pounding the rescuers on the back in hearty congratulations and drinking their health.

The story of the fall and rise of Evocatus Acacius staggered noisily from group to group around the room, accumulating so many variations that for a week afterwards even his oldest friends were still arguing about how he had come to be in such a pitiable state.

A day later, however, Acacius was a new man. Soaked and steamed and scrubbed and shaved, wearing clean fresh clothes, and with his grizzled hair clipped to a neat stubble, he was fed, rested, and clear-eyed, though still physically feeble. Sitting beside Paul in a small goat cart, legs dangling comfortably over the back board, he was able to piece together his unhappy history. As the little cart rolled steadily along, Barnabas and Epaenetus walked alongside, listening intently, while the half-grown carter perched up front screwed his head around so often and so hard to eavesdrop on the astonishing tale that it seemed he might screw it right off and lose it altogether.

"It happened gradually," the old soldier said slowly. "My regrets, my grief, my anger on the death of my wife overwhelmed me. I spent many dark hours making offerings at her tomb, imploring the gods to take me too, for I lacked the courage to take my own life. In the self-indulgence of my misery I betrayed the creed of Diciplina, for I knew no restraint in my bitterness. One day, hungry but too spent to return to quarters, I devoured some mushrooms growing under the trees, and suddenly everything went black.

"Strange as it sounds, at that very instant I felt a kind of ecstasy in the midst of my fear, for surely I had discovered a painless way to die, and I would soon be with her again – but it was not so! I was only transported to a fearsome place of nightmares … One moment I was a giant … the next a mere grain of sand … the next, I was whisked into the air – where I heard my wife whispering, softly enticing me with honeyed words – and there she was, beautiful and seductive as ever – yet just as faithless, just as cruel."

In a low, almost monotonous voice, Acacius described some of the lurid apparitions which had bewitched him, the distortion of body, the inextricable entanglement of all his senses, the terror of any other living creature, and the driving passion to be reunited with his young wife in death.

At first friends such as Bernardus had sought him out, urging him to avoid the intoxicating fungus which he insisted could show him the underworld. They tried bringing him food, attempting to intervene, but so powerful were his hallucinations that he attacked them as enemies. From then on, fearing to be seen, he hid himself among the tombs, emerging only at dawn and twilight, to slake his thirst from rainwater pooling among the rocks.

After many hours he would slowly come to himself enough to recall why he was at the necropolis, and again attempt to perform his increasingly inadequate sacrifices. But more havoc was wreaked on his disordered mind, for subsisting on scant forest foragings and half-burnt funeral meats stolen from other graves, he began to starve. Hunger driving him to consume the only ready food at hand – the mushrooms – their noxious spell was refreshed and intensified morning and evening. His bizarre delusions deepened until he was convinced that only the correct ritual burial proceedings would bring him the peace he craved.

"Hence your morning and evening entombments beside the corpse of your wife!" groaned Epaenetus. "Ugh! What a shock you gave me, old man – my knees are still quivering."

Acacius shook his head wonderingly. "I owe my salvation to Paulus here. All night long he kept the fire high. All night long he talked to me, and held my terrors at bay. I do not remember what you said," he confessed, turning to Paul, "only that you spoke of another man who rose from the dead to a new life, and you gave me hope."

"There is a still better salvation in store for you, Acacius, and you too, Epaenetus, if only you will receive it," Paul responded.

"Ah, yes, you mean the *Christos*!" Epaenetus said eagerly. "Let us talk about him now, since he is the reason I have deserted my martial cousin for your company!"

"Gladly!" Paul and Barnabas laughed. "Did we tell you that during his life on earth our Saviour was a carpenter like yourself?"

"No! Truly? Well, then I am all the more ready to listen, since he was no mere scholar but a man who knew hard labour! But you said before he is of royal blood, and a priest. Now, a man works, a prince rules, a priest offers, and a sacrifice dies. And yet, you say this Jeshua was *every one* of these things, a willing sacrifice to save mankind, who was himself saved when he rose from the dead! How can all this be?"

"No man can save himself," Acacius grunted. "He is lost to Tartarus, without the intervention of others who perform the rites. Have I not just learned that?"

"And I agree with you in principle," Paul replied. "So lay aside all else but that fact, and let us explain how our Lord Jeshua accomplishes all these aspects, as the Captain of our salvation, to present us as acceptable before Adonai God, his Father."

"Aha!" Epaenetus tapped Acacius on a bony knee. "Yes, you see? Just as a Centurion has many functions to fulfil in preparing his legionaries, that they may stand with pride before the Emperor. A rabble of quivering recruits is no use to Caesar!"

He nodded to the two apostles. "This makes sense. Say on, or our journey will not be long enough." He grinned. "Once we are on the water I may turn seasick and past all caring."

Nothing loth, the apostles obliged, delighted by the young man's dogged interest, which had only just recovered from the shock of hearing why one who served Christ could not fight for Caesar. Epaenetus had suddenly felt dizzy, as if the entire universe was spinning around him. If these men spoke truth, what of his military ambitions? Yet he must *know*, one way or another, and so his questions kept pouring forth. His favourite goddess was already looking more and more shadowy, inadequate, and distant compared with the Jews' Immortals, who were apparently eager to be closely, supportively (even lovingly!) engaged in men's lives.

Noble as Disciplina might be, it seemed that to follow the *Christos* was a still higher calling. Clearly it required more than adopting a simple if exacting creed, and trading offerings for favours. Rather, this new religion embraced an entire process of personal metamorphosis – and how bizarre was that?

Chapter Thirty-three

IT had been a morning of rapid decisions, with all of them revising their original plans. Julius had ordered Acacius home to Ghaziri, on the far side of Lake Akrotiri, to await orders, advancing him a small sum upon which to get by, and promising to appeal to their commander on his behalf for clemency and a reinstatement of his pension.

Seeing the man's frailty, the capable Decanus, with a generosity above his station, had arranged for a humble goat-cart to carry him east across the plain to the lakeside fishing community of Prostanna, from which point he should easily find a boat to take him the rest of the way. By this means, the fatigue of doubling back to the fork of the military road, and climbing north through another ridge of mountains at the furthermost end of the lake, would be avoided.

Learning of this plan from Epaenetus, and realising its advantages, Barnabas at once went to Julius, asking that he and Paul might be included. Julius agreed readily, gratified to be of help to these intriguing and well-read Jews. Impatiently waving aside the offer of sharing the cost, he assured Barnabas that a connecting road from Ghaziri passed comfortably through a valley to meet the Via Sebaste, and so once disembarked, they would be only another day or so from Antiochia.

Now it was the turn of Epaenetus to prick up his ears, and at once he decided to go with them instead of waiting for Julius to ready his next consignment of troops. Over the last two days the goddess Disciplina had begun to pale in comparison with the robust *Christos* of these unusual men, and he wanted to know more – much more. Who had ever literally seen an Immortal? Yet these men had seen one with their own eyes, spoken to him! Not only that, but Paul's courage at the necropolis had stirred him as much as any of their words. It was clear these men spoke truly when they said they did not fear death, and he was determined to find out how he might share such rare confidence.

Not at all put out by his cousin's defection, Julius arranged to meet him at the barracks in Antiochia, and bade them all farewell. "We might bump into each other there, too, my learned friends," he said casually to Paul and Barnabas, "or we might not. If not, may your god smile upon you."

"We will not forget you, or your kindness," Paul said sincerely. "Blessings and peace be upon you, Decanus Julius. I hope we will meet again."

"Perhaps some day, hey? The world is wide!" Giving the hilt of his sword a quick polish with his elbow, Julius marched away cheerfully.

Now they only had to pay off Bufo – who complained less than they had expected. Truth to tell, Bufo was not sorry to be rid of them, for though he liked them well enough these Jews seemed to attract disconcerting events. He decided it might be best not to quibble over the revised fare– from what he had overheard so far, their Immortals were rather too ready to interfere in earthly affairs.

Anyway, he'd got a fine little pig out of it which was still doing well, for all it was the runt. Much as his mouth watered at the thought of sweet crackling and delicate flesh, perhaps it might be more prudent to fatten it up? But wait! Since it was a female, what if he should breed from it? He could sell the offspring – always keeping one for himself of course – and then he could have his pig and eat it too. *Oho, indeed! A fine idea!* Bufo now being possessed of this delightful fantasy, as well as exciting fresh tales to earn him a few drinks, he trotted away quite happily – and even said nothing about receiving an obviously shaved *sestertius* which Barnabas, in his haste, for once had not even noticed.

Shortly afterwards the rearranged party set off, heading due east on an unpaved road – Paul and Acacius loaded in the boxy cart with their bundles, a pimply driver perched up front with a fishing rod for a whip, Barnabas and Epaenetus striding alongside and the low wheels rumbling along, while the big rough-haired goat walked with quick, elegant steps, his yellow eyes peering all around and his beard whiffling in the wind.

Though they had many glimpses of Lake Akrotiri as they approached, it was not until evening, when they reached the shoreline settlement of Prostanna, that the full enormity of its size was impressed upon them. Stretching out as far as the eye could see, it was easily twice the size of the Galilean lake known as the Sea of Tiberius. Its deep blue was a refreshing sight after the glaring monotony of the dusty white road, where the only splashes of colour came from dizzy butterflies cavorting in the dull bushes and dancing through dry grasses.

As a mellow sun lowered gently over the western mountains, swarthy fishermen in small craft were returning over the wide indigo water, rounding a little island which hovered at the end of a narrow green peninsula, while waterfowl gathered in noisy expectation of a feast. Swans, cormorants, bald ibis, waders, ducks, and geese of all descriptions, advanced upon the patch of beach and took up their positions. A stone's throw away, above reedy marshes where water buffalo wallowed, black vultures rose lazily into the air, circling high above with slyly deceptive indifference. Women and children laden with baskets drifted from their lowly shacks to the water's edge, ready to help with the unloading, with the nets, and with the sorting and cleaning, the moment the boats scraped to shore.

The joy of the families over each successful catch made for a heart-lifting scene, but to the small group of men who had been travelling all day – questioning, answering, reassuring, explaining, discussing the things concerning the Kingdom of God and the saving name of *Jeshua Christos* – a still more heart-lifting scene came a little later, once the satiated birds had flown away, once the busy fisherfolk and their families had finished their back-breaking work, taken their fish home to salt vats or smoke huts, and left the beach to the rising moon.

From a crude shelter on the shore, down to the darkly lapping edge of the chilly lake they walked by flaring torchlight, picking their way carefully over the gritty shingle. On the rocks, a deeply thoughtful Acacius stood holding their outer garments, while the two Jews waded into the cold waters with the young carpenter, and there baptised him – Epaenetus the Greek, now their brother in Christ, the first fruit of the gospel in Asia.

Early next morning a weather-beaten boat, patched sail bucketing gaily in a stiff breeze, whisked them all the way to Ghaziri at the far north-east end of the Lake, covering in a single day twice the distance of their previous day's journey from Claudioseleucia. To a born lake-dweller such as Acacius it was no novelty, but to the apostles it was a welcome change from all the rattling and trudging and climbing of their last week on the road. Poor Epaenetus, however, found that his earlier joke about sea-sickness was no longer quite so amusing, and for all his spiritual elation over his baptism, huddled unhappily in the bow, growing more taciturn with every roll and plunge of the little vessel. The fisherman, laughing in his sleeve, suggested various odious cures, each more revolting than the last, until Acacius fixed him with an evil eye while suggestively flexing his hard-knuckled fingers. The fisherman desisted at this hint, but was so far from taking offence that when they disembarked that evening he took their money with cheerful if insincere good wishes, and with a satisfied grin went off whistling.

Ghaziri was a fairer place than they had expected it to be, with a fine temple of Artemis, here honoured as Diana, Virgin of the Lake. Acacius led the way to the untidy outskirts of town and forced open the warped door of his neglected dwelling, which was squashed into the side of the hill. There, storks had made untidy nests on his craggy roof, while inside various birds and small creatures had made themselves at home in his absence.

That night in the dusty hut the three Christians prayed together, sharing a portion of dry bread and wine in memory of their Lord. Acacius observed their simple ceremony with polite curiosity, but made it clear that he was not ready to join the former devotee of Disciplina in changing his religion.

"Not that I'm not grateful to you, Paulus," he said uncomfortably. "But I don't know that I have grasped all you say, exactly, for all I respect your learning."

"Hardly surprising." Paul put a kindly hand on the painfully thin shoulder. "You have had your thoughts badly scrambled of late, and this is not the best time for you to absorb new ideas. But you still have more clarity than many men, since you are honest about your doubts. The last thing we want is for you to adopt our faith from any sense of obligation. Though we might convict a man's reason, only he can persuade his own heart. But we will pray for you, regardless."

Acacius nodded, pleased. One could never have too many gods on one's side. "Well, no doubt you will wish to sleep now, ready for an early start. Perhaps Julius will give me news of you all at some future time. You will always be welcome in my home, such as it is, whether I am here or back with my legion." He gazed forlornly around the miserable room, as if recalling how it once was bright with life and promise.

Paul and Barnabas exchanged looks. Now Acacius must fend for himself, and he was still very weak. Suddenly Epaenetus spoke up.

"Old man, you must recover your strength before there is any talk of you rejoining anything. Let the others go on, but shall I stay with you a while longer? Cousin Julius will not be in Antiochia for at least another week. Meanwhile, perhaps I can help put some meat back on your bones. And even if you don't like my cooking, I can fix your door, mend that stool, fetch the water, keep you company."

"Why would you do that?" the old soldier asked, astonished. "You owe me nothing!"

"True," Epaenetus laughed. "But I owe it to my new Lord and Master. I am now a Christian, and you are my first opportunity to behave as one."

And so the evening broke up in amicability and all slept well on the hard dirt floor. Next day, Paul finding that he could walk quite well with a stick, Epaenetus at once ran out to the bazaar and soon returned with a smooth, light staff. Touched by his thoughtfulness, Paul was grateful for the gift. Now, with many thanks and warm farewells and promises to meet again, he and Barnabas continued on, walking slowly along the narrow road which skirted more everlasting hills until they found themselves once more on the Via Sebaste.

Finally, Pisidian Antioch was only a matter of hours away. Barnabas was still solicitous about his friend's health, but Paul was less patient. He assured his friend that the illness which had surfaced in Perga was over, and now it was only the ankle which slowed him down. The shaking fits which still came over him occasionally, he ignored. There was work to do!

Chapter Thirty-four

"WELCOME to Colonia Caesarea Antiochia!" Elated that they had finally arrived, Paul gestured grandly.

"Very kind of you," Barnabas grinned. "I was not aware this was your city."

Paul laughed. "Here – it's the inscription on this wall. I think old Emperor Augustus must have felt very proud of such a fine military establishment."

"And felt a lot safer, too," his companion replied shrewdly, gazing all around at its impressive situation among protective mountains and lakes. It was well chosen as capital of this part of Galatia. To the east there was even a fearsome ravine, concealing the Anthius River which rushed through its sombre depths. "No one in their right mind would attack this place!"

As Barnabas stared at the stone fortifications of the city and the imposing buildings within, he could not help thinking of his nephew, now more than halfway back to Jerusalem. Marcus would have been intrigued by the architecture, no doubt. If only he had stayed. He took a deep breath.

From somewhere behind them a gravelly voice boomed out orders. Instantly there was a smart crump-crump of feet, and a troop of soldiers overtook the travellers. They swung rhythmically down the wide street, turned a corner and disappeared into the *Cardo Maximus* – the principal north-south thoroughfare of most Roman cities, invariably lined with intriguing shops, eateries, and trade stalls.

Paul watched them thoughtfully. "A very promising mixture," he mused. "So many diverse cultures side by side, army men both active and retired, and so much commerce."

"Like most fortress cities," Barnabas agreed. "Not that there was so much commerce in the last one, which was small and out of the way in comparison, not to mention a sad lack of Jews in every one we've been through so far. But now we can really begin in earnest. Everyone travelling east or west has to come through here, so there will be a huge amount of traffic from all directions. Romans, Greeks, Phrygians, Galatians, trading caravans of all descriptions, and travellers by the hundred!"

"And – at last! – plenty of Jews!" Paul said with satisfaction. "All waiting for the gospel!"

"We hope," added Barnabas, noting an imposing temple of Cybele, the Phrygian earth-mother goddess, which Emperor Augustus had built on one of the city's seven hills.

"Of course we will begin with our own people," Paul said, dismissing the massive temple at a glance, "but just imagine if we could end by turning every pagan from that false 'mother' over there to the true Father of all creation!"

Propping his walking staff against the rough wall he sat down to rest his swollen ankle, but he was not thinking about physical discomfort. "Sabbath tomorrow night. Plenty of time to find somewhere to stay before we introduce ourselves to the synagogue. Then we can start at once! If the Lord wills, we may be here for some time."

Barnabas did some mental calculations. "We will need to work, if we are to eat as well as preach."

"How much money is left?"

"Not much. Not after all those tolls and taxes along the way – not to speak of those iniquitous money changers in Cremna. How were we supposed to know whether something with Agrippina's head was worth more or less than one with Tyche or Kestros or Claudius – I've already forgotten all the others, and I could barely tell the difference in the first place. Except for the Athena – and then only because of her helmet. We were mere lambs to the slaughter in their hands."

"I'm afraid I wasn't much help to you, either, in calculating the worth of one coin over another."

"Help? You were a positive hindrance. However, your lack of numerical skill is just one of those sad facts of life to which I have resigned myself. Meanwhile, I never thought I would say this, but it's a relief to be somewhere the Emperor's currency is likely to be accepted without quibble."

"That is a true saying, Barnabas, worthy of instant acceptance by all confused men!" Paul said light heartedly, as he tenderly rubbed his ankle. "I have strong suspicions that the exchange rate had a sudden adjustment in someone else's favour every time we needed local coinage."

"Another sad fact of life, my friend. You rest that sprain a while longer while I go down the *cardo* and spy out the land."

The efficient Barnabas disappeared into the crowds to ask around at the *agora*, and the result was that they found lodgings before nightfall, and did not have to make do with the dubious comforts of a *stabula*. It was with relief that the two men unrolled their bundles in a tiny rented room. It was not a Jewish house, but its respectable reputation had commended it to them as promising, for in such a place there might be discerning eyes to observe the way a Christian lived, and willing ears to hear the gospel.

"Bed and board at a very reasonable price," said Paul, sitting down thankfully and rebinding his ankle. It was still sore, but considering how much walking he had done that day it could well been worse, so that was encouraging. "Only four others in the house, not counting the landlady, but according to her they are out more than in. I think we had been given all their histories before we'd even drawn breath."

Barnabas picked grass seeds out of his cloak. "Portia is indeed talkative," he laughed, "but if she tells others all about *us* just as readily that will work in our favour. She's a pleasant woman and clearly proud of being household seamstress to a lady of good standing. Pisidian society, among the colonists at least, seems be unusually equitable here – Portia told me almost with her first breath that her mistress is well respected as a community magistrate."

"Who pays her so well," put in Paul critically, "that she has to take in boarders to make ends meet."

Barnabas shrugged. "What else can a childless widow do?" He paused, and added, "Better than dancing for next to nothing in some tavern."

Portia, a rather faded-looking woman of middle age, was very interested to hear why her new boarders had come to Antiochia.

"I've never thought about 'salvation'. I'm not even sure I know what it means," she said apologetically as she plied a fine bone needle by lamplight, stitching busily down a long length of linen.

398

She pulled the last stitch through with a firm tug, double over-sewed the end, and bit off the thread. "All I ask for is to be spared trouble, since I have no family to fall back on. I don't mind telling you, I don't bother the gods much and they don't bother me. Apart from the essential rituals, of course, to ensure a quiet life."

She indicated a wide niche in the wall where a host of small images presided over a few morsels of food, replenished morning and evening. "As you see, I am careful to avoid favouring one god over another. That is not the Jewish way, however, I know. I have a very good friend who is always trying to convert me to Judaism," she added with an embarrassed laugh, as she rethreaded her needle. *'One God, not many!'* dear Chloe says, but I say if we are to remain friends, we must agree to disagree. She is related to an official of the synagogue – I must tell her all about you!"

The Sabbath service at synagogue was crowded. Paul and Barnabas sat quietly on one side as passages were read from the scrolls of the Law and of the Prophets. The reader spoke carefully and monotonously, guiding his eyes with a golden pointer skimming the lines from right to left. There was a muffled rattle of old parchment as the heavy scrolls were rewound. A grey-bearded man with a deeply fringed prayer shawl leant over towards Paul and Barnabas.

"Brethren," he said politely, "the synagogue officials invite you to speak, if you wish to do so."

Barnabas met Paul's eyes, which shone with anticipation. "You speak, Paul," he urged quietly. "You are the rabbi!"

Paul stood up with a warm gesture of appeal – beckoning to the congregation as if encouraging them all to draw closer. It had become his habit to begin in this way, unconsciously inviting his audience's attention even as his own father used to invite his when he had something special to impart.

CHAPTER THIRTY-FOUR

"Men of Israel's faith, and all you who fear God, hear me."

As he spoke, the faces all around became alert. It was a customary courtesy to invite visitors to contribute to the service, but before long it was clear that this particular visitor had something unusual to say. Barnabas listened with a strange feeling that he had heard the words before. Then he remembered a cold night in Tarsus … when Paul had haltingly repeated to him the defence of Stefanos before the Council, so many years before. The fiery young Pharisee who had once been so maddened by those words, was now a new man, an apostle – and here he was, preaching the same gospel in almost the same words, the pattern of his arguments echoing those of courageous Stefanos.

Speaking plainly and clearly to his audience, Paul wasted no words, his voice carrying to dim corners, where nodding old men woke up, fidgeting boys paid attention, and women up in the gallery stopped whispering to listen. He related the history of Israel, reminding his listeners of God's promise to King David – the promise of a descendant who would be their Saviour. He spoke of Johannes the Baptising prophet who had spoken boldly of the greater man to follow. That man had come and his name was the same as his mission – Jeshua – *he who saves*.

"Men and brethren, we are here because we have been sent," said Paul earnestly, "sent by Heaven to bring you good news!" Here he leaned forward on the *bema* and casting his eyes over all the faces below him and up in the gallery, spread out his hands in appeal, and spoke with deliberation.

"This good news is for every one of you, and it is this … whether you are descendants of Abraham or Gentile God-fearers, through the sacrifice of the Son of God, eternal salvation from death is offered to you all!"

He paused to let the words sink into the startled silence. "Who would not gladly accept such a Divine gift?!" he continued strongly. "Yet the rulers and inhabitants of Jerusalem rejected it, being undiscerning of God's word and refusing to recognise our long-promised Messiah. And because of that, they fulfilled the prophecy of the very scriptures they read but do not heed, by condemning the Saviour to die!"

There was a shocked whispering along the benches where the Jews sat. In the humbler seats, the proselytes looked fascinated and leaned forward with anticipation.

Paul continued, "But unlike David his ancestor, the Eternal's holy Son did *not* corrupt in the grave. In the same sacred writings you read here every week, you will find that this too was prophesied to our forefathers. Almighty God did not abandon His Son but raised him from the dead – as many eye witnesses can attest."

The whispering became murmuring, but Paul spoke on, quoting from the scriptures to support his statements.

"The Law of Moses alone cannot bring salvation from the consequences of sin," he declared to the astounded faces around him, "but I stand here to tell you that through the risen Lord Jeshua every sin may be forgiven. By him we may be made right before God, accounted clear and sinless in His sight, to thus share in His mercies, not just in this mortal life, but for all eternity!"

By now, everyone was torn between listening to Paul's astonishing claims, and demanding in fierce undertones what his neighbour thought of this strange preacher, who was now seen to be shaking from head to toe in a rather ridiculous manner. Paul, however, was not about to abandon his speech just because another fit of tremors had caught up with him. Whether it was from sheer intensity of emotion or another onset of illness, he would ignore it. Stammering a little, he finished what he had to say.

"Take care!" he beseeched them, "Do not be like the foolish in the days of Prophet Habakkuk. Beware that his words do not apply to *you* as they did to your ancestors: *Look, you scoffers, be astonished before you perish …* *for I am doing a work in your time which you will refuse to believe, even* *should someone describe it to you!* "

When Paul and Barnabas left the synagogue, they were surrounded by both Jew and Gentile worshippers clamouring to discuss what they had heard. Some invited them to their homes in order to continue uninterrupted. Greatly encouraged, the apostles commended them for their enthusiastic interest in the word of God, and urged them all to grasp tightly the wonderful grace of God which He was extending to them through the work of His Son.

During the following week the two accepted all the invitations they could manage; in private, reasoning from the scriptures with many diverse people, and in public, seizing every opportunity to advertise more widely who they were and why they were there.

Their very first visit however was one they had been waiting to make ever since they had left Paphos. Therefore, armed with letters of introduction from their new brother Sergius Paulus, they called on his relations, and as he had asked, related to them everything that had happened during their time with him. The family received them cordially enough, and though slightly askance, all of them were intrigued to hear of their kinsman's conversion. They were amazed by what had happened to the sorcerer Elymas, but unsurprised at his reaction to losing the Governor's attention.

"It's our experience that Diaspora Jews with any kind of power guard it jealously, present company excepted, no doubt," one of them said shrewdly. "Perhaps because it is so hard to come by outside of their own circles. I wouldn't cross any of your elders here if I were you."

Though their visit seemed at the time to bear no other fruit than polite interest, the apostles were not entirely disappointed. They knew the goodwill of such an influential family might later prove invaluable to any Christians in this pagan city.

Several days later they were delighted to be discovered by the newly-arrived Epaenetus, fresh from a hurried conversation with Julius at the barracks. The two cousins had no chance for more, since no sooner had Julius arrived with one group of men than he had been sent elsewhere with another, and Epaenetus was lucky to cross his path in time.

"At least *you* are still here, and easy to find, too," he said cheerfully. "I only had to ask at the synagogue where the travelling preachers were staying. Acacius? Feeling much better. A number of his neighbours in Ghaziri have now taken him under their wing, and though he is still hoping to be reinstated with his legion, between you and me I think his soldiering days are truly over."

"And what of your soldiering days?" Barnabas asked slyly.

Epaenetus reddened. "They were over before they began," he confessed with a sheepish laugh. "That diabolical pig showed me just how brave I really was. So much for Julius attempting to toughen me up ready to enlist here! Praise God, you opened my eyes even further before it was too late. But there's no shortage of carpentry work back in Sagalassos, and my parents will be thankful to see me safely home. They might not approve of my new faith, but since they did not approve of my old ambitions either, it comes out even, in my view. They need not fear their son will die young, and now I need not fear even if I do! Julius is disappointed, though."

Paul smiled. He liked the warm-spirited Decanus and was sorry not to have seen him again. "What did he say when you told him?"

Epaenetus rolled his eyes. "He was rather taken aback at first, then he said solemnly, '*Alea Iacta Est,* Cousin! Now you have crossed the Rubicon!' He never *can* resist airing his knowledge."

Paul and Barnabas burst out laughing. In this instance, for Julius the Decanus to quote Julius the Caesar's, 'The Die is Cast,' *was* very apt.

"By the way, old Menandros said it first anyway – in his play, *The Flute Girl*," Paul pointed out mischievously. "You can astound your clever cousin with that little morsel the next time you see him!"

"I shall," Epaenetus laughed. "He will be very gratified to add it to his collection!"

By popular demand, Paul spoke again in the synagogue the next Sabbath. It was an extraordinary scene. In and around the city and up and down the *Cardo Maximus*, word had spread about these unusual Jewish teachers who had no prejudice against Gentiles, and who preached a doctrine of eternal salvation for *all* men. Almost the whole population of Antiochia had turned out to listen, as well as the regular synagogue members. Inside the building people were crammed shoulder to shoulder, overflowing through the porch and onto the pavement. Paul spoke passionately to those who had managed to squeeze inside, while in the street tall Barnabas raised his voice and preached to the sea of eager faces before him. Epaenetus, finding himself stuck halfway through the porch, tried to hear both men at once while simultaneously telling his own story excitedly to anyone who would listen.

Meanwhile the chief Jews of the city were having angry second thoughts about their invitation to the preachers. One flutter of interest was reasonable, and a little diversity in discourse was welcome, but this was too much! Never had *they* drawn such rapt crowds! Where was the gravity appropriate to synagogue gatherings? People were pushing and murmuring excitedly and the whole exercise reeked of sensationalism. These independent expositors were most definitely proving to be undesirables! After all, there was nothing orthodox or respectable about them, nor about their looks, come to that. The tall one was actually bald, so his mental powers might well be failing.

"Yet look at the fellow," they muttered amongst themselves. "He has the confidence of a politician! Standing on a kerb of the gutter, shamelessly addressing that heathen mob … and what about his awkward looking companion? Whenever he speaks with any vehemence he shakes like a drunkard! Most likely he is one, in secret. Or perhaps he takes fits! Either way he should not be teaching anyone, either in or out of the synagogue. For a supposedly learned man, he is a very poor specimen. After all –"

"I don't care what either of them does outside synagogue," interrupted the synagogue ruler sharply, "but the short sickly one is a particularly inappropriate person to address our congregation, especially as he squints horribly over the Holy Writ, *and* there are scabs on his face. Beautiful fruit does not come from an ugly tree!"

The others nodded sagely as the ruler uncompromisingly spoke his mind. "If a healthy body is the best demonstration of healthy thinking, then mark my words, no benefit will come from our congregation being forced to gaze upon such a contemptible sight peering over our beautiful *bema!* We must face the fact that we have made a sad error of judgement here, brethren, and have surely lost respect by inviting an unworthy man to stand in Moses' seat. All we can do now is to get him out as quickly as possible."

"How? The people are drinking in his words and may protest their displeasure if we attempt to remove him."

"Then we make sure the people are the ones to eject him – and his friend. That way there will be no repetition of this scandalous matter. Crowds are fickle and may be swayed with well chosen words in the right ears. There are more heathen here than God-fearers. Start with them and do it quickly."

With satisfied nods, the jealous men moved stealthily through the crowds, inciting the irreligious who had come merely to be entertained, and muttering darkly in conservative ears, causing ripples of dissent. Before long, both inside and outside the building, the listeners started to become restless, and both of the preachers began to be interrupted. To Paul and Barnabas it felt uneasily like an echo of the episode of Elymas, magnified over and over.

The people now being completely unsettled, the whisperings became murmurings, then talking, then firmly expressed opinions and loud dissenting remarks. Each individual being thus emboldened by the support of strangers, the noise increased steadily until, all in a rush, mocking shouts spurted from the once-attentive audience – interjections, contradictions, sarcasms, even jeers. Swelling with confidence the crowd grew boisterous, while those who had been truly listening tried to quieten them.

Never had the synagogue heard such a chaotic uproar, as the waves of opposing voices rose and fell. Suddenly, amidst a momentary lull in the clamour someone behind Paul savagely spat out, "*Anathema Jeshua!* A curse on this Jeshua!" Paul shut his mouth with a snap, breathing deeply.

Just then Barnabas came in from the sun, pushing his way through to where Paul, his face pale and set, was on the point of being dragged from the reading desk by stern faced officials. They paused however, as Barnabas spoke in his friend's ear, raising his voice above the din.

"It's no good, Paul, the elders are stirring everyone up outside as well and making it impossible to be heard."

Paul nodded, the rough patch on his cheek flushing brightly through his pallor. As the inwardly delighted officials and their troublemakers watched to see whether the two would leave of their own accord, he gestured commandingly for silence, raising his voice boldly so that all outside could hear. The audience noise simmered down to an excited hubbub – what would happen next?

"Men of Israel, listen! It was fitting that we spoke the words of God first to you, as His chosen people, but you have thrust it from you. We do not judge you, for clearly you have already judged yourselves as unworthy of the gospel of salvation. Therefore – mark this! – now we appeal directly to the Gentiles!"

Directly to uncircumcised Gentiles! An insult! Angry responses murmured and bubbled around them. Deeply dismayed, Barnabas also raised his voice as he looked around the tight-lipped faces, and put in a final word.

"Yes, and they will hear us! For even so did our Lord Jeshua the Christ command us, charging us with this very purpose – to hold up the light of his salvation to Gentiles, even to the ends of the earth!"

At once the startled synagogue erupted into fresh chaos; a mixture of yells, hisses, and wild, arm-waving exchanges – furious, malicious and indignant from fist-shaking Jews, amazed and thrilled from stunned Gentiles and God-fearers, many of them crying out to the apostles not to leave, to wait, they would listen, they would hear!

In the porch Epaenetus was excitedly shouting to the bodies around him that *he* was *proof* of their words, being a Greek yet a new, baptised believer in the Christ! Finally managing to extricate himself from the crush, he found himself almost manhandled down the steps to a quieter spot, having been pounced upon by a sunburnt Galatian farmer demanding to know more.

Now a shambles, the assembly of Antiochians both inside and outside the building broke up in confusion. It was one thing for Jews to preach to Gentiles who had adopted the Jews' religion, but to bypass the Jews and their synagogue completely was another thing altogether! For the

Gentiles it was an unheard-of innovation. For the Jews it was an unholy scandal.

The news spread, and soon the whole town could talk of nothing else, and everyone had an opinion. More than one educated person scratched his head over the coincidence that their proud city had long ago been named to honour the ruler *Antiochus Soter* – 'Antiochus the Saviour'. And here were two feeble Jews, invading their city, as it were, preaching of a new ruler, a new Saviour of quite a different kind, and taking it by storm.

Chapter Thirty-five

FOR Paul and Barnabas, it was the beginning of a long and busy time in Pisidian Antioch. Early in their stay they found employment, which stopped Barnabas doing daily sums to assess their finances and fretting Paul about the outcome. Paul's recurring rash, which had done him no social favours by turning lamentably pustulous after the near-riot outside the synagogue, suddenly cleared up not long afterwards, leading Barnabas to declare with his tongue firmly in his cheek that it must have been caused simply by laziness since it seemed to be cured by hard work.

Hard work it was too for both of them – Paul being kept busy in a workshop which made market awnings in a shabby end of the city, while Barnabas developed writer's cramp as *amanuensis* to the busy local *Aedile*, responsible for Public Works.

As Paul wove and stitched endless heavy panels of fabric, he talked of the Saviour and the Kingdom of God to any who would listen – his employer, fellow workers, customers, tradesmen, idle passers-by. Barnabas did not get far with his aristocratic master – who required that his assistant be seen and not heard except for the incessant scratching of his pens – but in his spare moments he talked with the servants and slaves, enthralling them with stories from the scriptures. Hungrily they listened as he told of *Jeshua Christos*, and a Way of Life where all men were equal in their standing before the one mighty God.

Throughout all this, Paul and Barnabas were shunned by Jewish elders. Thus prevented from participating in synagogue observances, the apostles remembered significant occasions such as the Day of Atonement in their own way, and never lost an opportunity of discussing with anyone who showed the slightest interest, the significance of the various Jewish holy days and festivals in relation to the saving work of Lord Jeshua, and the Kingdom of God.

As the days flew by and the increasingly cool nights began to lengthen, the number of Christians steadily grew. In those early, exciting days Epaenetus was a great help to them, and they missed him very much when he returned home. Two weeks later however a stable-boy from the garrison ran over with a few lines of news unsteadily scrawled by the peripatetic Julius who, being ever-aspirational, scorned to use a public scribe like normal people and had signed his name with a sputtering flourish.

"Christian cousin returning Antiochia soonest. Disowned. Your fault. Look out for him."

Barnabas met Paul's eye regretfully. Family estrangement was a common consequence of conversion, even as Lord Jeshua himself had warned many years before.

Paul took the note and wrote large underneath it. "Greetings, Julius. We will do our best. He has already found new friends here and will make many more, *Deo volente!* Blessings and peace. Paul and Barnabas."

Snatching the small coin offered him, the stable-boy happily ran off with the reply back to the barracks, from whence it would return through several hands to the garrison at Sagalassos.

Meanwhile, many a crisp evening found the two friends going from house to house, holding discussions and prayer meetings, teaching, counseling, and explaining why and how a believer must adopt a new way of thinking, a new way of living. Patiently they listened to many questions, doubts, and problems, baptising all who believed, giving vital spiritual support to the growing flock.

Like ripples in a pond, the word of God spread. Happy was the day when even the cautious Portia became convinced of its power and truth, and was baptised – along with the entire household of her friend Chloe.

Portia's conviction came about in an unexpected manner. Pleasant and kind as she was, she had maintained a steady disinclination to discuss religious matters, having a policy of never embroiling herself with her boarders' opinions in matters which might turn controversial, such as politics, religion and money. In any case, as she told them firmly, she was a very busy woman and did not have the time.

She certainly was busy. Every night she seemed to have work to finish by lamplight before morning. Every morning she rose early to do her household tasks and give breakfast to her boarders before setting off to sew for long hours at the house of her demanding mistress. And every afternoon, with knotted shoulders and a headache from eyestrain, she hurried home to the poorer side of the city by way of the *cardo* where (if she was not kept late by her employer) she would buy her daily provisions.

Several weeks after she had taken in her Jewish boarders, (*Such nice quiet men,* she mused, *and so helpful with it! Such a relief after those drunken Cappadocians who made my life a misery all last year!*) she was walking purposefully down the *Decumanus Maximus* – the east-west street which intersected the *cardo* – intent on reaching the *agora* before the stallholders began closing down. She did not mind the late afternoon rush, it was a good time to shop – just late enough to beat down prices on anything which would not keep another day.

It was raining lightly if steadily, but the street was still full, and here and there in alcoves tucked out of the weather, old women armed with big bowls of dough and small bundles of sticks crouched over their mushroom-shaped ovens, turning out freshly-cooked rounds of warm flat bread to tempt hungry, tired workers.

Wagons, carts and carriers were everywhere, porters yapping occasional words of warning as they rushed through the rain. Men of business strode purposefully towards the wine shops for a sip of something to fortify themselves against less than welcome homecomings. Rich men's wives in closed litters were carried home through the wet from important consultations with their hairdresser or dressmaker. Larking apprentice boys released from irksome labour scuffled with each other and shouted insults as they darted carelessly through knots of pedestrians. Watchful, sly-eyed wantons sauntered in the drizzle that it might dampen their clothes to cling more enticingly.

Ignoring the weather, those anxious to placate or persuade the gods hurried towards their temple of choice to pay their daily homage before afternoon dulled into dusk. Temples and shrines with colourfully painted statues abounded in the city, but the busiest and most impressive was the great temple of the earth goddess Cybele, and a little further out, the spectacular sanctuary of the moon god Men Askaenos.

Standing tall amid a broad courtyard flanked with grand colonnades, the sanctuary covered a vast area, and formed a complete world of its own. As well as the main temple, it boasted its own stadium, an additional smaller temple, and rooms for assemblies and banquets. How Jews (or Christians) could fail to be moved by such omnipotent centres of devotion – such manifest magnificence! – puzzled many Antiochians.

Portia, however, gave the matter little thought, preferring to reserve her judgement for the sake of maintaining the essential peace of her paying guests. Right now religion was the last thing on her mind. She had shopping to do, and here was the *cardo* and yes, there was her favourite vegetable stall just across the *agora*, still trading, with plenty left to buy.

A chorus of little voices called her name from the other side of the intersection and she glanced up and smiled. There among the preoccupied crowds, women of all ages (laden with purchases and hung about with small children) lingered in the sheltering *stoa*, enjoying a last bit of gossip as they waited for the rain to ease.

One of them was Portia's friend Chloe, chattering obliviously on the kerb with her back to the street, while her children swung off her skirts and stamped their feet joyfully in the gushing gutter, shouting to Auntie Portia to watch them. As she cheerfully waved back, Paul and Barnabas emerged from the *cardo* behind her, having met on their way home. They were about to greet their landlady themselves when several things happened at once.

The two smallest children sprang from the kerb to scamper excitedly into the road towards Portia, just as a wagoner coming too fast down the street lost control of his oxen. Hooves skidding on the slippery wet paving, the beasts plunged and bellowed, staggering as the heavy load drove the yoke hard against their necks, forcing them to their knees. As people leapt back from the kerb, warning shrieks pierced the pandemonium. Petrified where he stood, the littlest boy was knocked off his feet by the desperate dive of a passing porter. The amphora of wine the man had been carrying on his head flew into the air and smashed with a crimson splatter. Nobody complained of cuts or ruined clothes – the child was safe!

But in the middle of the road, time seemed to have congealed.

Barnabas saw it clearly and it haunted his dreams for weeks. The second boy, oblivious of danger, rushing ahead with oustretched arms and laughing eyes only for his Auntie, was felled even as he smiled – trampled by the stumbling oxen, crushed by the cruel iron wheel which passed over his chest. The warning shrieks had been in vain. Born deaf, he had heard nothing.

Other carters came running to help the sobbing wagoner regain mastery of his terrified, gory-kneed beasts, while frantic men and boys strained every muscle to roll the vehicle off the broken little body which lay underneath, its sightless dark eyes staring in surprise.

Forcing his way through the crush, urgently propelled by Paul, Barnabas felt his knees shake violently at the dreadful sight sprawled in the blood and ox-dung and water which glistened wetly on the paving. Women collapsed, men vomited, utterly speechless children were hustled away. The confusion, the horror, the wailing, was overwhelming.

A knot of aghast women, along with an ashen-faced Portia, struggled to hold back the hysterical mother, shuddering all over, trying to block her view, pleading with her not to look. At a nod and a look from Paul, Barnabas commandingly waved back the crowds as he ran to the women's assistance, and putting his strong arms around the screaming mother, buried her face in his broad chest.

In the wet, bloody road, kneeling by the child, Paul felt a gut-wrenching surge of deep, painful emotion. All the children his mother had buried seemed to pass before his eyes. All the brothers and sisters he never had the chance to know. The little sister who had laughed, just once, and just for him. He bit his lips.

"Show them Thy power and Thy mercy, Father," he murmured fervently. "Show them what it means to have life from the dead!" Suddenly demanding silence, he was instantly obeyed by the shocked onlookers. He looked intently at the distraught faces all around, meeting one frozen gaze after another.

"In the name of Lord Jeshua the Saviour of mankind!" he cried with authority, "I call you all to bear witness, that through the power of the Holy Spirit of God Most High, this boy will live."

The distraught onlookers held their breath as the forceful Jew bowed himself over the child, covering the ghastly body with his own – what strange ritual was this?

But now Paul lifted his head, several passionate tears spilling from his brimming eyes onto the pale, baby-soft face below his. "Hallo, little one," he said gently.

The wide eyes blinked and the child sat up, astonished. "I can hear things!" he said, smacking his ears in bewilderment. "Where's Auntie?" He looked confusedly around at the awe-struck, stunned faces in the trembling crowd, and began to cry loudly, instantly covering his ears in distress at the strange sounds he was making. "I want my Mother!" he wailed.

The astounding news of the miracle flew through the city. Portia declared afterwards that she and Chloe did not stop crying for weeks, firstly because they were so thankful, then because they were so frustrated by sceptical rumours that the child had never been truly injured.

"When the poor darling baby had been virtually cut in half!" she shuddered, tears dropping again at the terrible memory. "And do none of those scoffers wonder why suddenly the boy not only hears but *speaks*?"

Notwithstanding the doubters, if the gospel previously had spread like ripples on a pond, now it spread like a flood in spate.

Also spreading, however were strenuous efforts of the city's most influential Jews to discredit Paul and Barnabas, and put an end to their preaching altogether. It was into this tense atmosphere of conflict that Epaenetus returned from Sagalassos, his few worldly goods following by courtesy (and payment) of Bufo on his next supply trip.

Bufo was much the same as ever, and being very gratified that his new piglet was thriving, had obliged his erstwhile companion with a very special price for cartage of his belongings (or so he said). Hearing from his drinking companions of the exploits of his former passengers, he betook himself very nervously away without renewing the acquaintance. There was something too other-worldly about anyone (let alone Jews!) who could sleep in a necropolis without harm – and as for putting mangled bodies back together?! Bufo shuddered. All very well, indeed, if it was true. (*Enough to make a man's flesh creep, but …!*)

As for Epaenetus, glad as he was to be reunited with the apostles who had so dramatically changed the direction of his life, the ardent young man was at first quieter than he had been. It was obvious he felt the pain of his family's disapproval. However, with a determined effort he soon put this behind him, and from then on he remained unswayed by any difficulties, whether physical or spiritual.

As a jobbing carpenter he was not short of employment, and upon being virtually adopted by a large family of enthusiastic converts, he soon felt surprisingly at home. Whenever he had opportunity he accompanied Paul and Barnabas, learning all the time, lending valuable support to them in the work of preaching, teaching, and pastoral care – even as Marcus had done.

Everything the apostles preached grated harshly on the chief elders and those who held them in honour. For hundreds of years Jews both in the Homeland and throughout the Diaspora had been waiting for their glorious Messiah – and were they supposed to believe he had turned out to be nothing but a humble workman? And surely the *proof* that their Jeshua was an imposter was that he had done nothing except talk! (For of course they were not going to give credibility to any fanciful reports of his imputed miracles!)

What sort of Deliverer, they scoffed, did not bring deliverance? He must have been a very poor excuse for a messiah! He certainly had *not* restored the Kingdom of Israel or made it the head of all nations. Far from it – he had died the death of a criminal! And if he *had* been raised from the dead as his followers so egregiously claimed, just where had he been for the last fifteen or more years and where was he now? It was ridiculous, they fumed.

But the undeniably awkward fact was that more and more of the populace *were* swayed by the stories of miracles – which they asserted were still happening, even right here and now. People actually believed these pestilential preachers had saved a boy's life by their sorceries, and now many Jews were deluding themselves that the long-dead Nazarene *was* the True Messiah! And once enough people believed that, the elders would be put squarely in the wrong. They would even look like fools who did not know their own scriptures. Oh no, this could not be allowed to continue!

Secretly they devised their plans, slyly they exerted their influence, and slowly the mood in the city began to change. What started with baleful stares, anonymous threatening letters, and a shunning of the shop where Paul worked, escalated into a state of open persecution. More than once he arrived to find the workroom broken into and lengths of cloth slashed or trodden into the mud outside. Next, his loom was damaged. He worked night and day to mend it and salvage the time lost, but soon afterwards the head weaver asked him to leave.

"I have nothing personal against you," he said apologetically, as his best worker removed yet another skewered rat nailed to the shop door, "but I have my family to consider."

"At least one of us still has work," Barnabas said that night, "but for how much longer I don't know. Someone today approached me rather furtively, wanting me to copy a few documents for him. Birth records, citizenship papers and so on."

"No harm in that, surely?"

"None at all, except that they were not to be marked as copies, and I was to substitute other names for the originals! The fellow offered an excessively generous sum. He assured me I would be using the right inks on government quality parchment, and that he has a master craftsman who creates official seals which are indistinguishable from the real thing."

"Very efficient of him!"

"Yes, that's exactly what I told him myself, but he didn't seem to understand my tone of voice, and seemed to take it as a compliment! He also confided that no one person in the operation was ever told the name of another, so I was quite safe, especially since he knew I was not likely to remain in this city for much longer! On the grounds that a soft answer turns away wrath I told him what I thought in a *very* quiet voice, and he disappeared in a hurry."

Paul frowned. "Many people might expect us to leave sooner rather than later in the face of the malice hounding us on every side, but we have made no mention of doing so. Either he is a genuine forger, if you will pardon the contradiction in terms, who knows that plans are afoot to eject us, or –"

"Or he has been commissioned to entrap me into criminal activity for which I may be exiled at best or executed at worst."

"Both of us would be implicated, you may rest assured of that. Well, either way, we are not leaving until our work is done."

Only several days later Barnabas was accosted on his early morning way to work by a softly spoken, eager-eyed man who drew him into a quiet alley and offered to pay him handsomely for a small copying task.

"I've heard tell the councillor's new *amanuensis* writes a fine Latin hand. Just a bit of inscribing in wax, you see, sir? With a nice sharp stylus. From this old thing into this little folding tablet here. A few minor changes. That's all."

Barnabas took the faded wooden diptych in one hand and the new one in the other. They were identical. He did not even need to open the old one to know what was in it.

"Why?" he said bluntly. "Do you have a child you wish to legitimise retrospectively?"

"No indeed, sir, this is for myself. My father was well-to-do but he died intestate in another province, and as the son of a concubine I have no claim on his property. I am not known in those parts, so if I present myself with the correct records all will be well. You are a stranger here, you will depart richer, and nobody would ever know."

"*I* would." Barnabas tapped the new diptych thoughtfully. "Do you seriously expect to deceive anyone with this? The wood is not even aged!"

"I have ways of achieving that, don't you worry, sir."

Barnabas handed them back. "Let me tell you that this will only compound your problem. Your father's concubinage would be already registered with the state, and showing a birth record which contradicts your mother's status will convict you at once."

"Ah! No, I have thought of that! You see, my father's *wife* died childless, so I simply wish to posthumously bless her with his son. I assure you, my father had always intended to adopt me, to perpetuate his family name and secure peace for the souls of his ancestors – but he hesitated, still hopeful that his marriage would bear fruit – then suddenly, when their carriage overturned on a viaduct, it was all over for them. Since there are no legitimate heirs, your conscience need not trouble you. I will be depriving no man of his rights."

"You are a very sharp fellow, no doubt – so sharp you may cut yourself one day and bleed to death. But I fear God and respect the laws of Caesar. Therefore I do not make forgeries. Be off with you before I report you to the magistrates."

Chapter Thirty-six

THAT night Barnabas and Paul talked freely as they helped Portia make the flat rounds of bread upon which all her boarders breakfasted. Her busy hands worked quickly, pulling off lumps of dough from a big bowlful, patting and shaping it between her palms before deftly rolling each to an enormous size with a long narrow rolling pin and slapping it on her pair of wide clay ovens. "Helping" was a polite fiction of Portia's, since it involved nothing more than feeding the right sized sticks into each oven, and a kind of pleasantly hypnotic watching of the flames crackling inside it.

Portia was impressed by Barnabas's intelligent interest in preparing food, and was always ready to try out any variations he suggested. Paul, however, she saw as a cook's hazard, since when talking he was easily distracted from the task at hand, and was more adept at scorching first the bread he was supposed to be watching, and then his fingers while attempting to rescue it. Nevertheless, it was a pleasurable way to end the evening before their prayers, and it was soothing to drift off to sleep with the smell of fresh bread filling the house, not to speak of the lingering taste of those untidy little crusty fragments which Portia made them "eat up out of the way" because they came from the last scrapings of the bowl.

As they exchanged news of their day around this companionable activity, Barnabas reported the curious matter of the hopeful yet illegitimate son who had sought his assistance.

"H'm." Paul pursed his lips dubiously. "It all sounds suspiciously glib to me. If anyone was to consult local government archives and find there was no child registered to his father's marriage, surely the deception would be obvious. Just as obvious as if he had falsified his mother's status. It doesn't make sense."

Portia gave a comical shrug. "Unless he planned to arrange for a convenient fire in the record chambers!" The others chuckled, and she added, "Maybe he was just stupid, or blinded by his ambitions."

"Sheer avarice, more likely," Barnabas replied dismissively. "He looked extremely well off already – why, the fellow had a gold-wired eye tooth!"

"Really?!" Portia looked askance. "Well, it does sound like sheer greed, then, just as you say. When my mistress lost a tooth, poor woman, her husband told her she must learn not to mind the gap, for while he did not object to the cost of the ivory, he refused to allow her to pay iniquitous amounts for the fitting and gold wiring. And they are *very* comfortably situated in life."

"Well, I don't know what to think," Barnabas yawned tiredly, flexing his ink-stained fingers. "It could have been yet another trap, I suppose – but perhaps it was just a coincidence."

Whichever it was, subsequent days left no doubt that the resentment of the city towards the apostles was intensifying, until daily life became something to be endured. Only prayer and the consolation of the growing band of disciples, kept their spirits from slumping into misery.

In the city, scornful words turned into spiteful actions. Missiles were hurled at the two men from upper stories, tradesmen and street vendors refused to serve them.

Unable to find more work, and harassed in the streets, Paul took to preaching in outlying settlements, tramping the damp countryside and spending quiet hours in communion with his Master. One unfortunate day he found himself festooned with leeches after unwisely prostrating himself for too long near a creek. He suffered much in detaching them, and parts of their jaws remained to fester under his skin. He then sought drier sanctuary out of the cold incessant wind, a ruined hovel on a scrubby hill, where he found solace in the silence, broken only by the passing of a well-wrapped-up shepherd with a mixed herd, leading his animals to a new pasture. The shepherd's voice and the answering honks of his lone donkey, the bleats and whickerings of his flock faded into the distance and Paul resumed his prayers undisturbed. Rising from deep meditation an hour later, he felt an itchy lump high on his leg. Investigation revealed there was a fat black tick half buried in his thigh.

Several days later, every muscle aching, his stomach revolving with nausea, he came down with fever, his body prickling with tiny purple spots. No doctor could be found willing to attend him, and it was Portia who tirelessly nursed him back to health, though nothing would clear the recurring rash across his face which, after years of quietude in Tarsus, had during these last months, intermittently returned with a vengeance.

Meanwhile Barnabas worked long hours to support them, and a trickle of new brothers and sisters in Christ visited whenever Portia would allow. All brought their spiritual problems, their trials, and difficulties to Paul's sickbed, where notwithstanding his weakness he listened, counselled, mediated disagreements, exhorted and prayed with them, encouraging them to do the same for each other as members of the one family.

Epaenetus ran in as often as he could, cheering Paul with reports of the growing faith of the believers in the face of injustice, ill treatment and even persecution. Despite everything their mood was high. The miracle of sister Chloe's son had witnessed to scores of people that the apostles had divine authority, the seal of heaven stamped on their words and deeds! What greater proof did they need that Lord Jeshua had fulfilled his promise never to leave them, and to send them a Comforter, the Holy Spirit working among them! Even leaving aside miracles, this they had experienced for themselves, as their hearts and minds had thrown off superstition and embraced the Saviour. As the enthusiastic Epaenetus firmly asseverated, "This is not the work of persuasive tongues of men, but the work of Christ through the great power of God!"

Unexpectedly, further confirmation that the apostles possessed strange powers had begun to seep into the conversations of Antiochians from a secondary, unlikely source, causing more than a little alarm in some quarters. The extended family of Sergius Paulus had kept themselves aloof from the doings of the Christians, but not so their servants, many of whom had been baptized, counting themselves very blessed to meet no objections from their noble *pater familias*. As members of the household they had heard of everything that had happened on the Isle of Cyprus – the revived wave of the Christian gospel which had swept through the towns and settlements, the keen interest of the intelligent Governor, and in particular, the terrifying miracle of chastisement worked on Elymas the sorcerer, followed by the baptism of Sergius Paulus himself!

Rejoicing in their spiritual kinship with the other believers, these servants were not slow in spreading what they had heard to their new family in the Lord and any other Antiochians who would listen. Thrilled with the story, disciples both Jew and Greek had the apostles repeat it over and over. It was a strange contrast to Paul's own account of being blinded, which had such a different outcome. Barnabas had also related the shocking fate of the deceptive Hananiah and his wife Shapira in the early days after the Resurrection – disciples who had been blessed with the *Ruach* in the first great outpouring of linguistic Gifts upon the believers. Yet in their self-centred folly they had underestimated this honour, treating it with a complacency that amounted to contempt.

In their greed – both for money and for honour in the eyes of men – they had conspired to present themselves to the Chief Apostles as generous and humble people. Having sold a plot of land they gave a portion of the proceeds to the Jerusalem ekklesia, each asserting virtuously that they had donated the entire sum. This deception they had carried out with cool deliberation, in disregard of the holy Gift within them, thinking to deceive men who were the Chosen of Lord Jeshua himself – men who had been his closest companions, upon whom he had breathed, and upon whom he had bestowed an even greater measure of the Spirit!

Barnabas was agitated even in the retelling. "I was there, you see," he said grimly. "It was in my own sister's house. I will never forget … that terrible morning … I saw him die …"

"Brethren," Cephas spoke heavily to the motionless men in the silent room. "This man was our brother. He was counted as one of us in the Way of the Nazarene. Yet in seeking the praise of men, he sought to deceive those of us who are endowed with the Spirit of the Living God to shepherd Lord Jeshua's flock. He had full opportunity to speak truth, but he persisted in his lies. This man, our brother, was also blessed with the Ruach as many of you have been, but it was not enough for him. He despised the gracious Gift of God, a gift given to him for only one purpose – to speak Truth! His actions were arrogant blasphemy against that Spirit of Truth, and the Eternal has allowed him no more time for repentance. Hear this, remember, and take warning."

He turned away. "Cover his face," he said, his voice shaking.

"It did not end there, you know," Barnabas continued quietly. "His wife came to the house a few hours later, confidently expecting to receive the Chosen's thanks for their generosity ..."

She glanced at the parchment and tapped it with a smile. "Why, I see you have already noted our gift on your list, with our names beside it and all! Very efficient. And most important, to keep clear accounts when dealing with a public purse, of course. My Hananiah always keeps very careful records."

"Tell me, sister Shapira, is that amount correct? Is that the sum for which you sold the land?"

"Yes, yes, that is perfectly correct," she nodded, wiping her moist fingers on a large fine handkerchief, and mopping the sudden beads of sweat on her upper lip ...

"However has this come about, sister, that the two of you have actually conspired to cheat the Holy Spirit of God?" he asked her wearily.

Gulping drily, stammering soundlessly, she turned in wild, impotent panic towards the door.

"Yes, look there, where the feet of those who have already buried your husband are on the threshold! Now they will carry you to his side."

Immediately, in came Mordecai's students ... Casting one fleeting, agonised look at their tense young faces – and without even a cry – the stout woman crumpled to the floor.

Suppressing a shudder, Barnabas gratefully accepted the cup of water which someone quietly passed to him and drank it in three gulps, as the shocked disciples tried to absorb the awe-inspiring tale. He had given them much to think about, and think about it they did, discussing what he had told them and comparing it with what they had heard concerning Elymas. Two apostles of the Lord Jeshua – each beginning their ministries with such devastating rebukes! It was a clear warning that no one should underestimate the responsibility of possessing a *Ruach* Gift. It was indeed a deeply sobering thing for them to realise that the Spirit could chasten as well as uplift, but despite everything, it did not daunt the Antioch brethren, which both Barnabas and Paul felt was a healthy sign of their faith.

"After all, surely rebuke – even punishment – is necessary if good and evil are to be distinguished. And wickedness is a corrosion which should not go unchecked, any more than wood rot should be gilded over," Epaenetus said feelingly as they talked it over at Paul's bedside. "But human chastening is fallible. How blessed we are to have the power to rebuke *justly*. Truly the Spirit works among us only for our good – therefore it gives every believer here comfort, and fills us with confidence and a great joy which all the petty persecutions of man will not quench!"

Paul was almost back on his feet again, when one notable day Epaenetus came with some cheerful news – the new Christian community was soon to see its first wedding, that of Aemilia, eldest daughter of the generous family who had taken him into their home. Paul quickly rifled through his mental list of names and faces, a self-imposed discipline he had been improving upon for some time. Ah, yes, Aemilia was the capable one in that family, thoughtful, with a rare gift for managing people without them feeling organised. She was a small, fine-boned girl, with limp brown hair so stick-straight and glossy it was forever slithering out of whatever constraints she attempted to impose upon it. Her wide attractive smile and grey-green eyes sparkled with an enthusiasm which reminded him, however unwillingly, of Danya.

"Well, that is pleasant to hear. She is sure to make an excellent wife for her lucky bridegroom." Paul thumped his cushions into a more comfortable position. "Do I know him?"

"Very well indeed!" Epaenetus began to laugh. "You're looking at him."

Congratulating his young friend warmly, Paul praised God with a full heart. The gospel, having united these two in faith, had brought them together in love.

Meanwhile, though Paul was finally recovering, Barnabas was having his own problems. A campaign of whispers accused him of subverting his master's staff. Then his meticulous work was mysteriously undermined by a slew of blots and smudges, altered figures, and the disappearance of important papers. To his dismay suddenly he found himself unceremoniously dismissed as an incompetent scoundrel. Resolving not to touch the travelling funds they had so carefully apportioned, the two friends tightened their belts, determined not to be a drain on their new brethren. Not many mighty or wealthy folk had accepted the gospel, and everyone's resources were limited.

However, Barnabas did manage to bring in small sums as a common scribe, tramping regularly to various outlying hamlets where the city's antipathy had not taken root, reading and writing for villagers, who mostly bartered humble items for his services. It might be a handful of raisins, a shared meal, a lump of cheese or dried figs, a small bundle of firewood, a cattle bell, even a scrap of leather for patching sandals. Making use of his old commercial knack, Barnabas would trade with his takings whenever possible, anything he could turn into coin going straight to Portia for their bed and breakfast (often their only food for the day). The apostles would not defraud her on their account, and she had her own rent to pay.

Paul now having regained some of his old strength, he hired himself out as a drudge in a less than salubrious eatery, the only place willing to employ him. There he was daily insulted by rowdy customers and paid with leftover food, which at least enabled them to eat an evening meal - most nights, anyway. The apostles suffered it all in silence until one day they found Portia surrounded by baskets and belongings, tearfully packing her water-pots in straw. Her other boarders, who had taken not the slightest interest in the apostles' preaching, had already left.

"They've all got together," she sniffed from the depths of a basket. She stood up and stretched her aching back. Whiskers of straw clung to her cheap amber beads, and she plucked them off impatiently. "All the committee women, all those with the ear of the city council, even my mistress – the Jews have put pressure on them, of course. Particularly the women with synagogue influence, I would say."

Barnabas picked up a document that was lying on a bare scrubbed shelf and showed it to Paul. One glance was enough. Portia's lease had been cancelled. She had lost her house. Paul impulsively took Portia's rough hands in his.

"My poor sister," he murmured. "We should have foreseen this – we should have found somewhere else to stay."

Portia snatched her hands from his warm grasp and dashed away her tears. "Do you think I care about a house?" she demanded angrily. "It's you they're after! You can't stay in Antiochia any longer – soon it will be blood they want – can you not see that?"

Outside came a scuffing of many feet, and a swelling of voices, direct confirmation of Portia's words. She peered from a window. "A whole mob of them!" she gasped. "City officials! Quickly – get your things, quickly, quickly!"

Paul and Barnabas needed no second bidding. They dived into their room for their possessions; there were precious few of them but they were essential, especially the parchments. Portia pounced upon a large empty basket and threw into it any food she could sweep from the shelves, recklessly tossing in a small wineskin unhooked from the rafters. The murmuring outside became a rumble, then a many-throated chant.

"Jews – out! Preachers – out! Liars! Charlatans! Stirrers! Out!"

The two dashed back clutching a jumble of linen, parchment, cloaks and old sandals. As they flung them into the basket and slammed down the wicker lid there came a heavy, formal thumping at the door.

"This is goodbye!" said Portia firmly, impatiently brushing away a straying wisp of grey hair. "May God go with you!"

"Goodbye, dear sister Portia!" Barnabas tried to smile. "Whatever happens here, hold fast! We will write to you and all our brethren here, I promise!"

Outside, a formal declaration of eviction from the city was being read in loud, important tones. Regarding Portia's tense face with affection and regret, Paul thanked her humbly. "Everything you have done for us, dear Portia, you have done for our Lord Jeshua. May his peace ever be upon you." He put his fingers to his lips and lightly touched them to her lined forehead. "Excuse the liberty, my sister. Were you a man I would embrace you."

"Were I a man there would be no need for such a fond farewell," she answered stoutly, "for I would go with you."

Crash! The door was kicked open and light streamed in. Portia put the basket in Paul's hands and pushed him gently towards the door. Roughly seized by official hands, her two friends were swallowed up by the chanting mob. A flash of gold in one of the shouting mouths caught the eye of Barnabas, and he looked coldly into the eyes of the supposedly illegimate son. The richly-dressed man merely laughed in his face, yelling as vehemently as the rest as they marched victoriously down the street to run the apostles out of town. The door banged emptily behind them, and only then did Portia sit down and cry.

At the boundary stone on the outskirts of the city, the two servants of the Lord pulled off their sandals and shook the dust from them in protest at their unjust treatment.

"We disclaim any responsibility for your fate at the Judgement Seat of God!" Paul shouted to the jeering crowd as it flung a few last insults before returning triumphantly homewards.

There was a sudden clap of thunder and it began to rain. The two men turned their backs and began to walk, trudging soberly down the steep highway, heading south-east towards the city of Iconium. Thankful that the basket had strong handles, they trudged on with it swinging unevenly between them. Meanwhile, the rain poured down in steady streams, running in rivulets from their heavy hooded cloaks. Barnabas huddled gratefully inside the thick woollen fabric, which Paul had woven himself. It was dense and matted like felt, the natural oiliness of the goat's hair keeping out rain as well as wind.

A stiff breeze sprang up and the rain scudded in flurries across the road as if impatiently urging them to hurry along. It was a relief when finally it eased to a dismal drizzle. They splashed silently through the cold puddles, feeling the tension within them slowly ebbing with the passing miles. Both were devoutly thankful that they had not been evicted from the city while Paul was still sick. They were, however, very regretful that they would miss the forthcoming wedding of Epaenetus and Aemilia.

At dusk they sheltered beneath an ancient olive tree. Its gnarled branches stooped almost to the ground, giving protection from the wind. There they prepared for a cold, miserable night. Paul opened the basket and looked at the muddled contents, which were clammy from the rain which had blown through the wickerwork. The whole thing smelled of sweating cheese, wet wool, unwashed linen, squashed olives, stale bread, leaked wine, and dirty leather. Suddenly he began to laugh, rather ruefully at first, and then with increasing hilarity.

Barnabas stared at him. "What's so amusing?" he growled, wrestling the stopper from the uncooperative wineskin.

Paul shook his head. "Nothing!" he admitted, trying to compose himself. "It's just me … and this absurd little basket!" He kept laughing, his shoulders shaking helplessly.

"Well?" Barnabas demanded irritably.

"It's just … I'm just … so thankful …" Paul gasped, unable to stop, "that this time, I'm not *in* it!"

Barnabas tried to glare at him, but after a few moments, his sense of humour got the better of him and he too threw back his head to laugh.

Chapter Thirty-seven

AROUND four days and over sixty miles later they came to Iconium. For once, the journey had been pleasantly uneventful. The morning after their expulsion from Antiochia they saw in the distance a large group of men, women, and children trooping towards the highway from one of the smaller tracks which ran into the countryside, and it was not long before they caught them up. They were a cheerful band in holiday mood, travelling to the wedding of some well-to-do cousins in an outlying settlement not far from Iconium. Over the next few miles two other related farming families joined them with several mules in tow, laden with possessions. After the growing strain of the last weeks, Paul and Barnabas were relieved to be in the company of people who had nothing more on their minds than celebrations and good wishes and the carefree prospect of a large, rowdy reunion with friends and relations. To be among such good-natured friendliness was in itself a blessing.

Travelling with such a large group was inevitably slower than travelling alone, but it was reassuringly safe, and though cold, the weather had not quite turned. As they walked along, they came to hear many farming tales – usually from the men. The women and girls mostly avoided them, but the boys rampaged around with enviable energy, running and chasing, goading each other into scraps and scuffles, aggravating their sisters, disobeying their mothers, quick to brag about anything and everything, and full of questions, the answers to which they rarely stayed long enough to hear. A sharp word from their fathers, however, and they became meek as lambs.

"Were we ever like that?" Barnabas muttered askance to his friend. "Our poor mothers! Aren't you glad you avoided all this sort of thing?"

Paul half smiled. "I don't know," he said truthfully. "These children have been raised in utter ignorance so perhaps we should not judge them by our standards. But I will admit, that just occasionally there are times – rare times – when I wonder whether a son would not be a comfort – a son with a passion for learning, a son to teach as my father taught me, an affectionate son to bring warmth to my old age …" His voice trailed off and he flushed, rather annoyed at sounding sentimental.

Barnabas gave a yelp of laughter. "That's *three* sons! I doubt you'll find all that in one."

"I won't find it in *any*, thank you," Paul retorted quickly, all wistfulness instantly banished, especially as the peasants were now singing a raucous folk song and the boys were punctuating the chorus with some unpleasantly expressive gestures. "Now stop asking personal questions, and as soon as this noise stops let's sing something of our own and give these people something else to think about other than domesticity and begettal."

Barnabas laughed again as Paul quoted ruthlessly from his younger days. They did eventually manage to sing, teaching the gratified company an equally exuberant song from the Psalms, with plenty of vigorous mimed action for the children.

O Praise God in His Sanctuary, Praise Him for His sovereign power,
Praise Him for His mighty deeds, He sustains us hour by hour.
Praise Him with a bugle blast! Praise Him with the lyre and lute,
Praise Him with the drum and dance! Praise Him with the strings and flute!
Praise Him with the tinkling timbrels, Praise Him with the clashing cymbals!
Praise Him every living thing! Lift your voice and to Him sing!
Hallelujah! Hallelujah! Hal-le-lu-jah!

Precisely to *which* God the group imagined they were singing was anyone's guess, as despite Paul's custom of tempering his preaching to the mood of the listeners, the farming families were completely disinterested in anything but the music itself, and resisted all the apostles' attempts to explain who this God was, and what was His plan of salvation for the world.

Nevertheless, the women sang the song softly to their babies, the girls chanted and clapped it at play, the boys whooped it with glee as they blew imaginary trumpets and banged makeshift instruments, and the men sang snatches of it as they worked, and so it was that a tiny rivulet from the inspired scriptures of Adonai God came to trickle its way around farming communities in the region for many years. Would any of it eventually water a stray seed of the gospel? Would any of it later bear fruit? Who could say? One man might sow, another water, but only God would give the increase.

Such musings were in Paul's mind after the wedding party with blessings and good wishes expressed on every hand finally branched off on a well-beaten track, waving goodbye until they disappeared around the curve of a hill where long dry grasses rustled and rippled under a playful wind.

On the two walked alone, striding the road in good spirits, slowly traversing the great, softly-hued plain with its endless swards of muted green and gold, enjoying its profound peace after all their recent sociability. Out here in this immense land, nothing small or delicate could catch the eye, fine detail was engulfed by sheer expanse, and everything took on a tinge of unreality – the sweeping open spaces so fresh and clear all around them, the dizzying height of the heavens so blue and shining above them, and the vastness of the brooding purple distance stretching out so far and wide before them. It seemed that here all creation was holding its breath, empty, full of promise, waiting for them – two emissaries, ant-like in a boundless landscape – to bring new Life to places yet unseen, where lives were full and souls were barren.

In companionable silence they walked, each occupied with his own meditations. But after some hours, signs of human occupation gradually intruded on the eye, until the outskirts of Iconium itself came in sight at last. With the friends' attention thus drawn to the man-made mass, the natural landscape seemed to shrink and the vault of heaven contract as the city loomed nearer – then before they knew it they were overshadowed by its walls, passing through its gates, fumbling for coins, groaning over the rates of exchange, and paying the usual tolls.

All around were fertile slopes where grain was grown, orchards flourished, and patches of forest lingered. Late in the year as it was, the last autumn fruits were being picked, and stubble fires lent a smoky tang to the chilly air. Like Pisidian Antioch, Iconium was a bustling city of traders and merchants, thanks to its location on the old Silk Road which linked important trade centres right across the Empire and way beyond to the exotic East. However no soldiers were garrisoned here, and many of the inhabitants were democratic Greeks. There was also a strong Jewish presence. Some had been attracted to the city by its peaceful prosperity, but many more had been there for generations and were of standing in the community. These were descended from over two thousand Babylonian Jews who long ago had been resettled both here and in other cities across Galatia, by edict of the ancient ruler Antiochus Magna. With such a well established Jewish quarter, and a central synagogue full of devout Jews and God-fearing Gentiles, it was ideal soil in which to sow the gospel.

Paul soon found work with a busy sack-maker. Weaving, stitching, and mending rough sacks was a dull occupation in itself, but full of interest because of the number of traders who came to the workshop, often with news and adventures to tell. Paul invariably added a traveller's tale of his own – particularly concerning a certain dramatic journey to Damascus. Many a trader went on his way with new ideas centred around the word '*Christos*' turning over in his head.

Barnabas meanwhile set himself up in the market-place, under the *stoa* beside other public scribes, all of them reading and writing for the busy populace everything from short notes to long letters and business documents. Literacy being an uncommon accomplishment, he was not short of work. This gave him many opportunities to engage in conversation and talk about the gospel message. It was an encouraging start.

Equally encouraging was the reception they found in the synagogue, at least, at first. Their words created a great stir among the Jews and God-fearing Greeks, and many believed, including a pious Jewish butcher and his wife. They were quick to offer the apostles accommodation, which the two friends accepted upon condition that they paid fairly for their bed and board. They knew protracted hospitality could turn sour if not on a businesslike footing, and from the positive response of the community, they expected to be here for some time. This settled, the two became part of the household, and many were the lengthy, lamp-lit discussions they shared around the holy scriptures as the winter set in. One evening, with all but two of the five children in bed, conversation turned to the family's history.

"Our forefathers were transplanted here over two hundred years ago," Jacobi told them, "It must have been a great trial at first – trying to establish themselves among an alien society while keeping strictly separate. I believe my ancestral grandfather tried harder than most, for he was accused of being more holy than righteous many a time ... so the old family legend goes, anyway! It can't have been easy for any of them, but we Jews are nothing if not adaptable, and the next generation flourished. Now, as you see, there are so many of us that we seem to have our own little Jerusalem here – or so my dear Elishabet claims, don't you, my dear?"

His wife shook her head with a little smile. "No, Jacobi, that's what *you* say, and some of your fellow elders at the synagogue too. But it is true enough, and I am thankful. Unlike smaller communities scattered afar off, here we have no hindrance to our way of life, and the synagogue is blessed with a very large congregation."

"True enough," Jacobi said. He pinched the cheek of his attractive little daughter. "That will stand our dear Johanna in good stead later, hey? No shortage of suitable young men."

Turning pink, Johanna tossed her head rather petulantly and whispered to her mother, "Why is Father always so embarrassing! Why doesn't he single out Tomas for a change!"

"Hush, my dear," her mother smiled. "It is already settled that your brother will marry Anais, the daughter of Petros and Stella. He told me so the other day."

There was a burst of laughter, for Tomas was four years old.

"Your youngest son already has very domestic ambitions, it seems," Barnabas chuckled.

"Yes." To the apostles' surprise, Jacobi's brow darkened in an abrupt change of mood. "Unlike my eldest, who has no ambitions at all except for wanting to escape both his childhood faith and his comfortable lot in life. I fear we utterly spoiled him with too much indulgence."

Flushing, his wife bit her lip and immediately sent the children off to bed, looking at her husband in mute appeal. Jacobi dismissively waved a brawny hand.

"Yes, I know, I sound very harsh," he said rather defensively, "but there is no use in pretending things are otherwise than what they are." He turned to the apostles. "You have not met him, since he has left home to lodge with less than desirable companions. He takes no part in family life and neglects the synagogue. He even works for a rival butcher. Using the skills I taught him from childhood!"

Jacobi's voice thickened and he cleared his throat. "I do not know what the younger generation is coming to," he said wearily.

There was a moment's silence, broken by Barnabas. "I am sorry for your distress," he said quietly. "Is he very young?"

Jacobi shrugged. "Not in my view. He is of age, and no longer under my roof, so what can I do? As I say, no doubt we spoiled him as a child. I am learning that too late."

"Hindsight gives all honest men cause for regret," Paul said soberly. "There are fathers equally regretful of their severity."

Jacobi gnawed at his greying beard. "It is hard to strike the correct balance with a firstborn."

"Yes, my dear," his wife responded tremulously. "And even with experience, I find each child responds differently to correction."

"By the time we learn wisdom, it is all over." Jacobi rose to stare out of the darkening window. "Blink twice and we'll be grandparents. A pity we must be parents first, eh?"

"Oh! Do not say so, Jacobi! You love your children, and Fabius too!"

"Of course I do!" he said impatiently. "That is the problem. My father was harsh, I was determined to be gentler, and then the boy's infirmity made me over-kind. Well – there is no help for it now. Clearly extremes are a common pitfall for new parents – we are all so much in earnest, with too much to prove!" Making an effort to recover himself, he gave a wry smile. "I have learned a great deal about God, from being a father. How we must try His patience at times!"

"Indeed," Barnabas agreed. "We are blessed above measure that our Heavenly Father is infallible!"

"You say the boy had an infirmity?" Paul asked.

"Little Fabius was born with a cruel tongue tie," Elishabet explained with downcast eyes. "The worst the midwife had ever seen. He was fretful and difficult to feed. Later, because speech was so frustrating for him and hard for us to understand, it was easier to anticipate his wants and needs. It seemed the best way to avert many a painful struggle and stormy tears all round. When not provoked, he was a dear, sunny child who loved to make us all laugh with his silly antics. But then he changed," she added wearily.

"He can make himself understood well enough these days to get by," Jacobi snapped, "and there is nothing wrong with his mind. He knows right from wrong. But he avoids us. Not even his mother can draw him out. A sure sign of a bad conscience."

"His eyes are sad, Jacobi, not defiant," Elishabet protested with a flash of independent spirit. She gestured helplessly as she rose to light the lamps. "I think he is troubled."

"Troubled!" Jacobi spluttered. "Is he not troubling us? Our family reputation?"

"I should like to meet him," Paul said mildly. "Where does he work?"

Jacobi jumped up to close the shutters, slamming them shut with a bang. "In the shambles!" he said bitterly.

Very early next morning – long before the sackmaker had unbarred his workshop – Paul set out into the cold grey drizzle, pulling a warm cloak firmly around his body. The city streets, powdered with snow, were silent and empty, but in the market-place early workers – stamping cold feet and blowing clouds of steam into cold fists – were setting up for the day, lighting little braziers, preparing food in their tiny shops to tempt workers with a hot breakfast. Already steam was rising from the large kettle of a *thermopolium* selling warming mugs of dark, watered wine laced with spices. Known as *calda,* the hot drink was understandably popular. One or two labourers in hooded cloaks were already standing around, warming their cold hands on the thick mugs, dunking their slabs of coarse bread and wolfing it down before they strode off to work. All around busy traders were unloading produce from baskets and hand carts or stacking their wares temptingly, and some were putting up awnings to protect their goods from the weather.

Catching sight of a long-haired man setting up his stall, Paul reminded himself again that his own hair was badly in need of a cut. Barnabas had castigated him several months ago for hacking at it himself, but Paul was always reluctant to spend their limited money on something as trivial as barbering. Only last night Barnabas had frostily told him to be grateful he had any hair to cut, reminding him that since one of them was bald they were *already* saving on haircuts, and if he could not work that out for himself, truly he was no Shaul ben Shaul but a shaggy-pated disgrace to his nimbly-numbering grandfather's memory. Recalling this nonsensical raillery with good humour, Paul now grinned sympathetically as the long-haired, middle-aged man struggled ineffectually with a heap of stiff canvas, his endeavours to fling it over a rickety wooden frame succeeding only in burying himself. Muffled oaths came from within the heavy folds, but in two strides Paul had come to his assistance, and together they finished the task.

"*Todah rabah!*" the fellow grunted, pushing the hair out of his eyes and blowing on his stained, chapped fingers. "Thank you, very much."

He rubbed his left arm and shoulder, wincing. "Rheumatics. Cold mornings are a curse."

With a friendly nod Paul was about to go on his way, when suddenly he turned back. *Todah?*

"Do I address a fellow Jew?" he asked in Hebrew, surprised.

"*Ach*, a mere slip of the tongue." The man looked slightly uncomfortable, but answered in kind. "I do not put it about much. I have been out of the Homeland for many years."

Paul's curiosity was aroused. "A slip of the tongue, perhaps, my friend, but that would mean Aramaic for most Homeland Jews. You must be an educated man."

"Some might say so. Much good it has done me."

"I have not seen you in synagogue. Of course, it is a large congregation."

"Nobody sees me there. *Yom Kippur*, is all. Just in case. Haven't you got somewhere else to be?"

"Yes, the shambles. I am looking for a young butcher named Fabius. Do you know of him?"

"I should say so. He shares my household of misfits. In trouble is he?" Looking Paul up and down in a not unfriendly manner, he reverted to Greek. "Odd errand for one such as you, isn't it? Your Hebrew is flawless, so you too are an educated man. Oh yes, it takes one to know one. Is the synagogue appointing learned strangers to reclaim sinners these days? Who are you, anyway?"

"My name is Paul, and I am new in this place. I hope we meet again, as I would like to hear your story, friend!"

"It's a long one. Not very believable, either. Shambles, down that alley." He nodded at a dark opening in the wall on the other side of the square, turned away dismissively, and sheltered by the tenting began to set out his spice pails with care.

"Wait – will you tell me your name?"

"Malchus. Good luck with understanding young Fabius. You won't get much out of him."

With a word of thanks, Paul strode carefully across the frosty square into the narrow lane, suddenly flattening himself against its greasy wall to avoid a hulking porter with what looked like half a goat slung over his shoulders. A few moments later he ducked as a short man followed with a wide basket of raw bones. Already he could hear the noise, and finally as he emerged into the broad open meat market, he was hit with the unmistakeable smell of the shambles. The greasy odour of rank fat and raw meat, the thick aroma of blood and offal, the pungent stench of dung, the gut-churning stink of rotting flesh heaped at the far end, where dogs, rats, foxes, carrion birds, and a few brave chickens hopped and scavenged. Paul averted his eyes, almost gagging at the thought of the foul host of crawling things which would be gorging themselves within the heap, only thankful that at this time of the year it was too cold for flies. The central strip of paving was slippery underfoot with mud, icy slush, blood, and fat, and reminding himself forcefully of his weak ankle he trod cautiously.

Already busy, the shambles was becoming busier and noisier by the moment. A stream of cattle handlers, shepherds, goatherds, swineherds and poulterers were converging on the chaotic market from various well-beaten tracks, shoving assorted livestock into holding pens, controlling it with the aid of snapping dogs, cracking whips, jabbing rods, and the help of numerous darting, dirty, accomplished children. Voices argued, bargained, shouted, laughed, and roared in warning; heavy bells clanked dully on animal necks throbbing with fear; distressed bellows, bleats, squeals, and animal cries filled the air. Along one side strongly-muscled, blood-splashed butchers worked with grim efficiency, almost ankle-deep in gore, slaughtering, flaying, hacking and slicing. Their sharp knives flashed in the thin morning light, while assistants with long-practised contempt for danger pounced on each part as it came away from the fast-moving blades, sorting and hanging the red lumps on large hooks. Others caught fresh blood in basins as it spurted from stuck throats and hurried it over the way to the stalls manned by wives who would sell it on for sauces, puddings, sausages, charms and beauty treatments.

Every butcher had his own stall, displaying body parts of all descriptions; large masses of dark flesh and slabs of pale fat, ribs, hocks, and haunches; tails, ears, hooves, tongues, and entire heads, some split in half with the single blow of a huge cleaver and displaying white brains like walnuts curled in their shells. Everywhere hung strangely twisted, fleshy trees of windpipes and lungs with hearts attached like single grotesque fruits, and ribbed throats with waxy tubes from which dangled pouchy stomachs. And on every hand, stalls were festooned with long cloudy loops of dark entrails large and small, ready for stripping and washing to become sausage casings, pudding bladders, protective sheaths for amorous men, medicinal aids, and translucent membranous panels for small windows and lanterns.

While the butchers worked, assistants scurried to and fro, and several knife grinders did the rounds of them all, the buyers poured in. It was still too early for the women of the town to be out marketing, and at this hour the shambles seemed strictly for those sent on business. Cooks from wealthy houses quarrelled over the best cuts, while servants buying for their mistresses fingered the meat, sniffing it, picking it over, greedy for a bargain, that they might pocket the difference in price.

Some of the customers went directly to various booths where smaller quantities of choice cuts were available, not exactly fresh, but attractively laid out with flowers and herbs before small shrines honouring a random selection of *Lares* which hung on the canvas walls. By way of supplicating daily protection from adversity the dressed meat had already been offered to one or other of these gods, whose figurines appeared to cast an approving eye over those who bought their leavings. Brought in from various temples where it had lain for at least a day and sometimes more, it was considerably cheaper than freshly butchered meat. For this reason it was particularly popular with owners of the *agora* food stalls, who moved up and down the displays, choosing rapidly and with a practised eye before striding off to begin preparing for the breakfast rush, when still-tired, hurrying workers would snatch a welcome hot bite to eat on the run.

"Out of the way, fool!" yelled a busy drover, and a somewhat dazed Paul shrank back against the wall, sickened by the smells and sights before him. At Passover, he had always managed to attach himself to another Jewish family and avoid killing a lamb for himself – his theoretical knowledge ever being too tenuous a bridge to the act itself. Still, in the Temple he had many times seen animals slaughtered before now. Only recently had he watched Jacobi similarly at work in the Jewish quarter, but that had been on a far smaller scale, and all was done according to the Law of Moses. There, each animal was first carefully examined before being passed as fit for meat. Led in quietly and with kindness, a beast stood puzzled but unconcerned as the butcher thanked God for its life before wielding a long, freshly sharpened knife with great strength and expertise. In one precise and sweeping blow he would cut the animal's throat in such a decisive way as to render it immediately unconscious, whilst the simultaneous severing of vital nerves and blood vessels ensured that death quickly followed. Hung to drain away its lifeblood, the carcase was prepared – stripped of skin, internal fat, and offal, the meat was finally washed, and ready for purchase. Somehow it seemed less like thoughtless slaughter and more like mindful sacrifice.

Of course butchery was a bloody business by its very nature, but faced with the unholy chaos of the pagan meat market before him, Paul silently thanked God for the Divine laws which regulated the practice, and reminded a man to have respect for the life of a mere brute beast. Perhaps this was important – he had not thought of this before – just as much for the man's own sake as for the animal itself.

The pale sun had now risen high enough to strike into his eyes, recalling Paul to himself. Time was wasting, and how in all this gruesome nightmare would he find Jacobi's son? A hefty butcher striding past with a dripping haunch of who-knew-what on his shoulder turned to shout to someone, and the grisly end of the meat slapped into Paul's head. Hurriedly scrubbing face and hair with his sleeve, Paul shuddered with repugnance. That did it! This very day he would have a barber mow the lot down to stubble! Just in time, he jumped out of the way of a scrofulous-looking boy staggering under the weight of a fresh pig's head. What it must cost a young Jew to work in this place after being meticulously trained according to the requirements of the Law, he could not imagine.

Doing his best to avoid treading in steaming dung and trampled gobs of congealed grey meat which seemed to adhere to everything, he headed across the meat market, weaving his way past the central pens of anxious animals, to make determined enquiries of some peasant women with dripping noses and cheeks stung red with the cold, who sat efficiently wringing necks and plucking poultry, amidst a cacophony of doleful clucks and squawks from caged birds awaiting their turn. Their hands never ceasing in their work, the women were quick to respond, if hardly kind.

"Oh, you mean the gecko boy! You know, can't talk, just gulps and clicks. Good worker, though. Never gives any lip. Wouldn't be worth the bother, would it now?" And cackling shrilly amid their flying feathers, they directed Paul to the far corner of the shambles.

446

Chapter Thirty-eight

"YOU are Fabius?"

The lanky, tow-haired young man looked up with weary eyes and nodded, raising his brows at the stranger who accosted him so unexpectedly.

"The spice seller Malchus told me you were here."

Fabius nodded again with a faint smile, and with one eye on his employer who was flaying a carcase only a few paces away, invitingly indicated the meat he was cutting on a well-worn plank.

Paul shook his head. "No, I'm not here to buy. I am a friend of your father Jacobi."

Fabius scowled and brought down his cleaver with a sharp chop. Paul immediately chuckled which stopped the young butcher short, and he stared at Paul in surprise.

"Very expressive!" Paul said, his eyes twinkling. "Come now, young man, I am not here to plead your father's cause with you, but because when he told me about you, I was immediately interested."

Fabius grunted suspiciously, clearly questioning Paul's motives, but the older man met his guarded eyes with candour. "You see, we have something in common, I think. Like myself you were raised in the Faith yet now you have changed, as I did, even alienating your family. Nobody does that lightly, only out of much turmoil and pain. I am still a Jew, but nothing like the kind of Jew I once thought I would be. Oh yes, there are many ways to be a Jew! The question is, what is the right kind?"

With a cautious ear out for his master, now arguing with another stallholder, Fabius, looking exasperated, exaggeratedly raised eyes and hands to heaven as if in prayer, pretended to hunt through a scroll and scribble notes with an imaginary pen, and then with a long face mimed beating himself on the back. It was clear he was being sarcastic.

"Is that the only way you know, Fabius?"

The butcher shrugged sullenly, and with a dismissive flap of a hand turned back to frowningly concentrate on his work. Chop! Chop! Chop! He looked up. Paul was still there. Fabius laid down the cleaver and folded his arms in resignation.

"If you are as unhappy as I was, you will be almost beside yourself," Paul said quietly. "Confused, miserable, guilty, wretched, wondering which way to turn. Your friend Malchus told me he only turns up to synagogue on the Day of Atonement. You too? Ah, good!"

Fabius looked startled, and Paul smiled. "It tells me, if nothing else, that both of you want a wager each way. You still believe in God?"

A decisive nod, then a determined struggle to get the words out. "Buh noh ih *meh!*"

"I rejoice to hear it! The scripture agrees with you there, for the Psalmist says, *Do not put your trust in mere men.* I do not ask you to trust me, Fabius, but will you tell me your story sometime soon? You and Malchus? I know what it is to be conflicted to the point of desperation, and there is an answer which may astonish you. No," he laughed, as Fabius sardonically rattled coins in the takings basket. "It is nothing anyone can buy. It is a gift, nothing more, nothing less. May I call on you?"

Fabius scratched his forehead with a bloodstained thumbnail, clearly astonished, but nodded. He held up six fingers, then twinkled them skywards.

"Very well, Sixth Day, in the evening? Thank you. No, I will say nothing to your father. Now I must hurry, I can't be late for work. I will ask Malchus for directions."

Somewhat grudgingly the long-haired spice seller obliged, and so the chilly twilight introducing Sixth Day found the apostle, having first prayed with Barnabas, making his way to a very dilapidated and overgrown gate opening on a cramped, brambly courtyard at the other end of the town. Within crouched a house with a dim light in an upstairs window, and a warm glow stealing through chinks of the downstairs shutters.

Fabius opened the rough door. The room was lit by several small lamps, and the flickering of a low fire played over a fine, inlaid mosaic picture which adorned a narrow stone hearth. It looked oddly out of place in a house with a beaten earth floor.

Malchus was not home yet, but the young man beckoned Paul in, ducking his head awkwardly to thank him for the gift of spice cakes which he had, perhaps unwisely, brought with him. Paul admired the hearth, where with great artistry a prancing horse was depicted in many shades of red, black, white, and terracotta, the dancing firelight lending it a warm vitality.

"This is a most unusual thing to find in a Jewish house," he commented mildly. "Beautiful, though. He almost looks alive."

Fabius smiled a little and pointed upstairs, mimed the careful placement of the tiny coloured blocks, and pointed upstairs again. Paul guessed that the artisan must be one of the boarders there and Fabius nodded, pleased. Wiping stray flakes of ash off the decorative hearth with a perfunctory sweep of his sleeve, carefully he laid out the cakes in a row.

Just then the door banged open and Malchus stamped in. He seemed agitated. Flinging himself down beside them without a word of greeting he scowled at Paul, and bit into the spice cake offered.

"Cheap rubbish!" he said disagreeably after one mouthful. "Or a poor recipe. Come to me next time you want spice and I'll give you the good stuff." He glared at the somewhat bemused Paul. "Or maybe I won't," he added brusquely.

"You seem upset. Have I offended you, brother?"

"Don't 'brother' me, Pharisee, I've been asking around, and now I know why you're here. If you call this upset, you haven't seen anything yet."

Fabius flinched at the word Pharisee, and looking anxiously at Malchus, began to tremble. The spice cake he had been enjoyably mumbling fell into his lap.

Paul laid a reassuring hand on his arm. "Do not let that word alarm you, young man. It belongs more to my past than my present and has very little to do with the future."

Malchus plunged straight in. "You are here to tell us the Messiah of Israel has come. Actually, come and gone. But he did not deliver Israel, and we are still scattered like sheep all over the Empire. We are still living under Roman rule. We are still dispossessed. We are still struggling to make sense of our religion! For every law we are supposed to obey, there is a reason why it is impossible. And why? Because we are *here*, not there.

"We have no Sanctuary here, and even in Jerusalem the priesthood is corrupt and the Sadducees have a stranglehold on Temple commerce. Commerce! I have seen it first-hand and it disgusts me. But what did your precious Messiah do about it, eh? Tell me that! Preached peace, that's all. Good to those that hate you! Miracles at sword point, eh?! What use by all the demons of hell is that to *us*? So we can't go forward, we can't go back!

"Here they all sing the psalms about mourning for Zion by the waters of Babylon, while the old ones regard Babylon with a second-hand nostalgia inherited from their grandparents who inherited it from theirs! It makes no sense! Nothing makes *sense*! I want honesty! *Honesty*! Tell me, you Christian Pharisee, where will it *end*? Is it any wonder the young lose their way?"

The angry spice seller raked the grey-streaked hair back from his face with impatient fingers as if he was about to yank it out in sheer frustration.

Paul, who had listened silently to this tirade, suddenly bent forward, raising a hand to the man's head. Malchus grabbed it in an iron grip. "No!"

"Too late, my friend," Paul said quietly, lifting the lank hair with his free hand. "I heard of this from the lips of one who was there and saw it happen! You say you want honesty. Good. Explain to young Fabius here why you hide your right ear. Could it be because it is so strangely unblemished for a man of your age? Could it be because of *a miracle at sword point*, as you put it? Could it –"

Angrily Malchus jerked his head away. "I don't believe in miracles!" he shouted, his face reddening. "When that hot-headed Galilean went for me I staggered from the blow, but maybe I was only nicked! Ears bleed easily! And I couldn't *see* it, could I? In the torchlight that thing at my feet might only have been a mushroom.

"So the prisoner touched me, maybe in sympathy, what of it? He was that sort of person, wasn't he? I felt warmth that's all, then it was as if nothing had happened. So *did* it happen? I refuse to believe it! If he was truly a miracle worker, why did he not save himself? With such powers, what was the sense in dying?" His voice was frantic.

"He was a willing sacrifice, Malchus, accepting death to acknowledge God's just sentence on all mankind."

His outburst over, Malchus slumped against the wall, speaking almost to himself. "There were witnesses to what supposedly happened in that garden. *I* could not explain why one ear had turned pink and fresh like that of a child, and so I kept it covered. Even so, the unthinkable, the unbelievable, could not be true! I trembled lest I – a disciple of Sadducees! a servant of Caiaphas! – should be counted as one of the Nazarene's followers. After all, how could – why *would* anyone work a miracle on a disbeliever!"

"Because he first loves us, even while we are yet sinners. The same was done for me and I will tell you of it later. What happened next?"

Malchus, agitated again, threw up his hands. "Everyone knows! The execution, an eclipse, an earthquake, an empty tomb, disgraced guards, furious rulers, outrageous claims of resurrection – of course I scoffed at all of it. Sadducees accept resurrection? Pah! Then six weeks later came more confusion than ever. Dead or alive, he had vanished from the face of the earth – and no sign of any Restoration of the Kingdom either.

"Even so, the Nazarene movement swelled, while Jerusalem erupted with miracle tales I could neither countenance nor contradict until I thought I was losing my mind. When priests began going over to them in droves Caiaphas was almost insane with impotent fury – and I ran. In a sense, I have been running ever since."

Paul waited. The man had not finished, and was now making an effort to speak more calmly.

"I came here, determined to forget the whole thing, knowing there were many Jews in Iconium, glad to be an unknown in a place so far away, yet still among my own people. I had no desire to be another rich man's servant, it would raise too many questions, so I set up, in a small way at first, as a purveyor of spices from the passing caravans. I told myself now I was safe, that I had out-run my panic."

He hesitated, collecting his thoughts, absently handing Fabius another of the despised cakes.

"What I did not bargain for was the increasing hollowness of synagogue worship in this place so far from Temple rituals and sacred soil. Yet what else was there? (Paganism? *Me genoito!* I swear by its demons only because they are safely spurious and sometimes a man must swear or choke!) Synagogue services seemed dry and lifeless, giving me no comfort. I began to lose my faith – and there was nothing to replace it.

"This young man here understands that emptiness. He may be tongue-tied but his mind is agile enough. He heard me defying his father and other elders on several occasions and sought me out, hard as it was for him to confess his own struggles. Others have joined us. Now at least our misery has company. But this is the first time young Fabius – or anyone here – has heard all my history."

CHAPTER THIRTY-EIGHT

There was silence. Paul nodded slowly.

"I see. Curiously, I came hoping to help him in his spiritual crisis, having been through similar pain myself ... but it seems I have even more in common with you, Malchus. I know what it is to be confronted with the impossible, with something that defies all your inner certainties. The turmoil of soul is indescribable ..."

There was another silence. Malchus stared with narrowed eyes at the fire, as if unwilling to meet the apostle's gaze lest he give away more of his soul. He had already said more to this man than he had ever confessed to another – and perhaps even more than he had been willing to confess to himself.

He twisted his clasped hands together in a spasm of mortification. No doubt tomorrow he would wish he had never laid eyes on the fellow. What was the use of talking, anyway? Did it change anything? It was a fact of life that some things were incomprehensible – irresolvable – and a man who wished to stay sane had to learn to live with it. He was not going to believe the impossible, and he was certainly not going to believe anything on the strength of another man's conviction, and that was all there was about it.

But now Paul was speaking again, quietly. "As for you, Fabius, I suspect yours is a somewhat different conflict, though with similar effects. I will not judge you. Will you tell me about it, and let me help, if I can?"

Having finished his crumbly morsels Fabius was scratching his wispy beard, very confused by the somewhat cryptic tale related by his landlord, and the equally cryptic questions posed by their visitor. Now he nodded definitely, making inarticulate sounds.

"*You* won't understand him," Malchus growled. "You'll need me to interpret."

"You might be surprised." He paused. "Do you still disbelieve in miracles?"

Malchus buried an agonised face in his hands. "I don't know!" he said thickly, shaking his head. "I don't know anything anymore!"

"Let me tell you then, what you do not know. Let me tell you that the Nazarene who so disturbed you will now bring you peace. *Let me tell you that in the name of Lord Jeshua the Christ all things are possible!* Now – look up, my friend and take a deep breath. Your life is about to change."

"What – what do you mean?" Malchus lifted his head, bewildered.

Turning to Fabius, Paul said calmly, "Young man, you have made such a mess with that cake, there are crumbs all over your whiskers. Better lick them off."

Fabius obediently swept a long, pink tongue around his lips, and then froze – with it still hanging out – his eyes dilated with shock. Malchus went very pale.

"What have you done here?" he faltered, trembling in every limb. "What – what do you call this?"

Paul smiled a little. "Why don't you ask Fabius? What do you call it, young man?"

A stunned Fabius came back to life with a gasp. "I call it a miracle," he said very carefully and clearly.

He sprang up with a burst of wild, ecstatic laughter. "I call it a *miracle*, Malchus!" he shouted, leaping on his shaken friend, hugging him, hugging Paul, yelling and weeping, prancing madly in his joy. All at once another three boarders clattered noisily down the stairs demanding to know what in the world was going on and where the fire was. Fabius pounced on them too, babbling away at the top of his voice.

"Look at my tongue! Look, I can lick! See how long it is! I can find poppy seeds in my teeth! I can touch the tip of my nose! Hear my lovely words! Listen! La la la la la! It's a miracle! Isn't it, Malchus? Isn't it!"

Malchus staggered to his feet, his face stricken. "Yes," he said with a deep sob. "A miracle. God forgive me! God forgive me!"

Chapter Thirty-nine

THE excited household of 'misfits', as Malchus had described them, had finally simmered down. Malchus himself was still stunned, no longer unable to deny that when the arrested Nazarene had touched him so long ago, it was to undo a real injury, not just a scratch, impetuously inflicted by one of his own men. And if that was true – and it must be – it *was* – then he had seen the Messiah with his own eyes, and not known him. *Seen* him! And undeservedly received his compassion! He, the same Malchus who had fled from confronting the truth, all this time had been a reluctant, silent witness to the power of the Christ! And he must never be silent again! What now? He had many questions for the disconcerting Christian Pharisee who had turned his world upside down! But they would wait until later. First, he reminded himself, the apostle was here for the sake of young Fabius, who must be allowed to tell his story with his newly-loosened tongue.

The neglected fire had been rekindled, wine and water poured, basket of cakes demolished (with no more remarks about their inferiority), and now, warmed by the glowing hearth – and somewhat in awe, still – they were all listening soberly as Fabius described the growing disquiet which had led him to isolate himself from his family and synagogue.

"I'm not really sure how it began," he said slowly, tracing his fingers gently over the bright mosaic on the hearth, as if he found comfort in the liveliness of the animal there depicted. His voice, freed from the nasal tones and constraints which had strangled it since birth, was soft and expressive. "I loved synagogue, I felt safe there. As a child I stood beside my father among a forest of men, listening to the readings, the prayers, the responses murmuring above my head. I thrilled to the singing because I could join in with notes if not words, and it made me feel joyful – tightly woven in with everyone, all the same before God."

Interlocking his restless fingers to illustrate his words, he looked up, and his fellow boarders, Jonas, Ariel and Ezra, nodded in understanding. "I was proud to be a Jew in this city – grateful. One of the chosen people! All the promises, the words, the customs, just – oh, I don't know, just the *rightness* of everything. I was happy, despite my impediment. My mother would tell you I was a demanding child but as I grew, I did try to temper my frustrations. Father was my example, so patient as he taught me his trade – well, most of the time – and the work suited me. After all, a butcher needs to listen more than talk. I did a lot of listening." He stopped, staring at his entwined fingers, and sighed as if gathering strength.

Malchus stirred the fire, and a stream of sparks danced upwards, giving an angry red glint to the eye of the horse set into the hearthstone. "That's what hurt you!" he said sternly. "Fool gossips at the meat market, cackling that your father need not look to *their* daughters to find a wife for his defective son. That you were touched in the head. That your children would be idiots. That nobody would want you. Saying it in front of you as if you were deaf."

"I did not know people thought of me that way," Fabius said painfully. "I had assumed I was liked for myself, now I saw all their kindness was false and only to earn merit. I felt humiliated, alone, shut out. I went on as before, but in my heart trusted nobody. Not even the daughter of

Petros who had always smiled at me. My secret hopes about her were in ashes."

"When you stop being a participant and become an observer," the thickly bearded Jonas put in roughly, "everything begins to look different."

"Yes! Exactly so! It is the strangest sensation. I seem to have walked all my life clothed in a protective cloud of incense, and now the cloud was thinning, clearing – against my will. Suddenly it had all gone, leaving me naked in a barren landscape."

"A good description," muttered Malchus under his breath.

"I sat in synagogue and felt *nothing*. I listened and my heart was not uplifted. I sang and the thrill had gone. The – the *power* had gone out of everything! I wondered, is this what outsiders see when they look at us? A strange people who hold themselves aloof, who recite ancient words and revere old scrolls and mumble through prayers to an invisible God, convinced they are the centre of the universe? I am aware that the very antiquity of our faith gives us respect among pagans, but among *ourselves* suddenly I felt it was stifling. Surely we should look *forward* as well as back, with eagerness for what is ahead – the Messiah, the Restoration of the Kingdom of Israel, the Kingdom of God in the Homeland!

"All at once I felt that in our own lives this supposed passion was not real at all, just lip service to something which we had to keep telling ourselves out of tradition. I was oppressed with the sense that everything continued as it had from the beginning, limping on for thousands of years with no end in sight, and I could not breathe. I was aghast to find that listening and looking around me, all seemed *empty* – even, almost comical. I asked myself again and again, 'What is *real?*' and I was afraid. I could not go there again, feeling this way. Once stripped of genuine feeling, I felt too much of a hypocrite to be in synagogue at all."

"That game we played as children," Jonas spoke harshly, "where you heap up sticks and must pull one out without collapsing the pile. It is like that! All your life you are heaping up the sticks, one by one – then one goes, and everything is lost."

"A good foundation is never lost," Paul said quietly. "The question is how we build upon it. I take it you have not let go of God."

"No, indeed!" Jonas said strongly. "We are all utter failures in this house, but as Solomon said, only a fool says in his heart there is no God – we fear only that *He* has let go of *us*, for though we revere Him as Creator, we are lost – not knowing where to go from here. Governed by our sins we have no way to atone, especially far from the Temple, in a foreign land. Even if we were good men, the Law is impossible to keep."

"The Eternal never lets go of His children. It seems it is not God you doubt, but yourselves, and the relevance of the way we worship in a world which is no longer as it once was. You are also right when you say the Law is impossible to keep, and so it always has been, Tabernacle, Temple, or no. Yet there is one man who did, who asks us to worship in a temple not made with hands. But first let me hear the rest of what Fabius has to say."

In a low tone Fabius continued. His sense of alienation, his loss of confidence in everything – in himself, in the sincerity of others, in the synagogue, even in his faith – grew daily. Now convinced he could never marry, he was all the more tortured by a hopeless longing for the daughter of Petros, which robbed him of sleep. The very innocence of his younger brothers and sisters seemed to mock him, while his parents, who could neither reason nor punish him out of his refusal to attend synagogue and his increasing moodiness, seemed to be very far away. To them he explained nothing, fearing to shock and disappoint them all the more, but as they alone understood his garbled speech he could share his burden with no-one else. Yet he could not dissemble forever,

460

and unable to find answers he sank into a misery so deep the pain became unbearable.

He had heard Malchus challenge the elders with similar questions, but it brought him neither resolution nor reassurance. It only made him wonder whether *everyone* was equally unsure – and worse, whether the whole system of Judaism was a mere pretence. It was an even more excruciating thought. Fabius was too afraid of the answer to directly question the spice merchant, but in any case, by now the effort of communicating his inner conflict to a virtual stranger was getting far beyond him. Sleepless, restless, anxious day and night, he wept and prayed one moment, wept and cursed the next, and was exhausted from hiding his state of mind. When his family went to evening services he would defiantly visit a particularly rowdy *taberna*, where raucous laughter, loud relentless music, and strong wine filled his head and numbed the endless cycle of his increasingly agitated thoughts. Finally there seemed to be only one way out.

Fabius took a gulp of wine, ran his fingers through his untidy hair, and looked appealingly at Malchus, who nodded.

"Luckily for him I was there myself that night, in a foul mood too, though I always say drink of itself solves nothing. When I stepped outside I nearly fell over him, dead drunk and mumbling in the gutter. I knew where he lived, so I propped him up and offered to see him home but he shook his head, raving and crying like a madman. When he pulled out a knife and stuck the point under his ear I don't mind telling you I went weak at the knees." He cleared his throat. "Any butcher knows where the sacrificial vein is, and I had no doubt it was no idle threat. I grabbed his wrist and slammed it against the wall so hard I nearly broke his bones, then hauled him back here to talk sense into him. And here he stayed."

"I would not allow Malchus to tell my Father," Fabius said huskily. "If he was ashamed of me before he would now be doubly ashamed that I would use a knife he gave me for my work, for such an unholy purpose.

Now I earn a living in the common shambles; no slaughtering, just cutting and selling. Maybe it's fitting – what I see around me reflects how I feel inside. But at least in this house I do not suffer alone."

"All too true." Ariel, the second boarder, agitatedly twisted his slender fingers together. "In this house of misfits we all grapple with inner demons, and though they have different faces, they are all hateful to God-fearing men."

"I do not count doubt or fear as hateful," Paul replied. "It is only *wallowing* in them, allowing them to justify ungodly behaviour, which is hateful. Honestly faced they provoke us to examine ourselves and our beliefs and may lead to confidence and peace."

"Peace! I have forgotten what that is." Ariel poked the fire savagely and the charred wood crumpled. He blew on it fiercely, coughing on the smoke as the flames recovered. "And don't talk to me about honesty. If I was honest you would not sit in the same room with me. Some of us must live a lie, there is no help for it. But what is the alternative?" He rubbed an agitated hand over his face, leaving a dark smear of ash on his clean-shaven cheek. "I am a proselyte – I took the name Ariel in faith and hope that I might find redemption with the people of God – and how can I go back to gods I know are false?"

"We three have the same problem," Jonas said impatiently. "What is the sense in not naming it? We all struggle with overwhelming vices while being cursed with a conscience and belief in God's judgements. Abstinence tortures our bodies, and capitulation tortures our souls. We are utterly miserable either way!"

"Come, this is hopeful," Paul said, to their surprise. "If you are miserable, those consciences have not yet been deadened. Lust of all kinds is so common to men it seems to have a life of its own. But to acknowledge a habitual weakness is a courageous start."

"Mine is for another man's wife," Jonas said abruptly. "She is a pagan beauty, fearless, and very free with her favours, which does not help. What sacrifice do I make for that? I can't even pray without her getting in the way of the words."

"Mine is for wine," Ezra, the quietest boarder, said wearily, and for the first time Paul noticed that his bony, trembling hands, ingrained with chalky dust, held only a cup of water. "Once I was a cook, a good one too, but now I am a pathetic sot for whom one drink is never enough, and so I grub out my days doing the rough cutting in an alabaster workshop, earning just enough to keep me in bread, but not wine. Just a joke to many people, but it is no joke to drink away your money, your livelihood, your friends and family – and become a common thief. Had it not been this good Malchus who caught me in the act ..." His voice trailed away. "I dare not even drink the wine at Passover. Not that I have kept it for a long time."

Now it seemed to be Ariel's turn. He compressed his sensitive lips, looking levelly at Paul. "Since you have the powers of a prophet of God, perhaps you have divined everything about me already."

"Just enough," he answered with compassion. "Yours is a very difficult path, my friend."

"You healed Fabius. What about us?"

"I am not the master of the Gift, only a vessel. The Holy Spirit moves as Lord Jeshua the Christ sees fit to direct. Fabius had an obvious defect but there is nothing wrong with the rest of you."

"You say that, knowing what we are – what I am? What I have always been? Cursed?"

"Cursed? *Shall the pot say to Him who made it, Why have you made me this way?* God's strength is glorified when men acknowledge their

463

weakness, and in Christ overcome it. You did not chose to be as you are, but you may chose to be a eunuch for the kingdom of heaven's sake. To be as Job, to make a covenant with your eyes that you will not think unseemly thoughts about another. Even as I have. Oh yes – I am not entirely indifferent to women, and I know what it is to be swamped with a wave of longing I never saw coming. Old, ugly, and crusty as you may see me, I am still a man with warm blood coursing through my veins, but I have learned governance, even as did the young Lord Jeshua himself, for he too was celibate."

"My life is then to be without love, lonely, and bare as a winter bough."

"Only if you choose. *Let not the eunuch say, I am a dry tree!* Do you not have good friends here in this very room? Give and you will receive – do not hold yourself apart, for there are many good and holy ways to love, and you will need them all."

Paul looked around the silent room. Only the crackling and snapping of the fire could be heard. "I can do all things, not of my own power, but through Christ, who strengthens me," he said. "And this surety may be yours. Believe this, for belief is peace! He did not come to condemn, but to save us."

"Everything you say must be true, since divine power shown here in this very room has testified to your authority!" Malchus spoke for the first time in a while. "But if he was – is –the Messiah, why has he not restored the Kingdom?"

"Because that will come in God's good time, when all things are ready for it. Messiah's first mission is to do with *personal* restoration, not national! It is to *individuals*, restoring hope, restoring hearts, minds, and souls. Washing away all past sins in baptism, presenting us to God as forgiven, and therefore faultless before Him. He offers to all men the gift of new life, whether Jew or Greek, bond or free, male or female. A rebirth."

"To wipe the slate! To be free of tormenting thoughts, to break the grip of sin, to sweep it out of the door," Jonas muttered. "*Then* I may serve God again."

"That is not how it works, Jonas, you have it back to front. Put God first and the rest follows. Lord Jeshua spoke a parable of a man who swept his house clear of one demon, only to find seven more flocking in to fill the empty space! Baptism expunges old sins yet not our nature, which, having a bias towards gratifying self rather than the Creator, will very soon reassert itself. But the more space we give Christ within our lives, the less room we leave for old habits and new sins to crowd him out. Of course we will fail, constantly. Show me a man who says he has no struggle with sin and I will show you a liar! But *intention* is everything, and if that is genuine, we need have no fear, for with every sin confessed and forgiven through Christ, we have a fresh start every time. For the rest of our lives! This is true liberty!"

"What about the Law?" Ezra demanded. "What about offerings for sin? The Day of Atonement? What about the synagogue?"

"His death is an enduring offering for sin, Ezra. Lord Jeshua *embodies* our atonement, being the ultimate and willing sacrifice to which every offering pointed forward. The Law was like an inflexible pedagogue marching us down a long weary road to school, prodding and lecturing us all the way. Now it has brought us to one who teaches with love and not a rod. Now we are released into our new Master's care, learning from him how to live loving and sanctified lives in joyful service to God, how to pick ourselves up despite our failings, how to think as he did. The Law has been fulfilled, and we are free to serve as adults, not mere children whose behaviour must be hedged about until they learn maturity!"

He looked around at each man present – shut up as they were by sin, would they turn the key of the door to spiritual freedom and bravely venture its higher path? "Come the Restoration, or come the Resurrection of our bodies – whichever is first – we will be even more free, for then we will receive the greatest gift of all – sinless, perfect, eternal life. Bring *that* thought to synagogue and see how it changes your point of view! Whether we look forward or back, how much richer is our worship there when we see God fulfilling His promises under our very noses? Grief is inescapable in this short, mortal life, but before us is everlasting joy. Make a start, and eternal life, in a sense, has already begun."

"What rites must we then perform to ensure this eternal life?" Malchus demanded. "How does this *work?*"

"Baptism is the only rite. Nothing mystic, simply an act of submission – full immersion in water much as Ariel here will have undergone in converting to Judaism, though with far more significance than a ceremonial cleansing. Baptism into Christ is an acceptance that we need Divine forgiveness, that we are not in control of our life, and that without the death, burial, and resurrection of Christ we are dead in our sins. The glory of it is this: in acknowledging our sins, in acknowledging that God alone is righteous, we have his righteousness imputed to us. If counted sinless, in God's mercy, we too may triumph over the grave, even as Lord Jeshua himself. Did the Eternal create man only to feed graves? No! He created us to share His everlasting love!"

With a degree of exasperation Paul became aware that he was again shaking with the sheer intensity of his emotion, and gritting his teeth, leapt up to pace the room. There were times he simply could not speak passionately and stay still or he became a shuddering wreck. But it was frustratingly and peculiarly unpredictable. Waving off their concern he continued earnestly, "We are His offspring, conceived for His glory. Let Him not grieve over us as stillborn babes or sickly children who die before maturity. Let us rejoice, holding out our arms to Him in confidence, as we grow up to the full measure of His Son who has gone before us!"

"You said, we are not in control," said Ezra. "Does this not contradict what you said earlier about making a choice in how we live?"

"Of course we are in control of our individual choices, but not things outside of ourselves, for these are in God's hands. In the end, it is not what happens to us which matters, so much as how we respond to those things. None of us is perfect, none is without sin, except the Son of God. Now he is our High Priest, who continually mediates for us in heaven. Every sin sincerely confessed and regretted is forgiven. In this way, being justified through our faith, we are thus credited morally with a divine perfection which humanly is unachievable. Having this, we will be literally, *physically* bestowed with divine perfection when he returns to claim those who love him! That is the unearned gift of the gospel, which as my friend Barnabas could tell you, is free, but not cheap. It costs us many things which naturally we cling to. The question is, do we think it is worth it?"

There was a stunned pause.

"At last! This makes sense!" Malchus said slowly. "Yes, it finally makes *sense*." Fiercely he demanded of the others, "Doesn't it? Doesn't it!" and they nodded slowly, hope dawning in their eyes.

Silence again. Then, "Is there a contract?" Jonas said gruffly. "If so, show me where I sign."

Laughter broke the tension, and everyone rushed into speech, all talking at once, loudly, and over the top of each other. Malchus rustled up some more food, everyone suddenly feeling ravenous. They hunted out more cushions, made up the fire, and for some hours longer, Paul preached earnestly to the misfits in the tiny room, answering their many questions, reassuring them, explaining clearly to them what it meant to take on Christ.

Early next morning, Jacobi staggered to the door of his house, grumbling mightily in his snatched blanket. "Is there an invasion?" he growled as he jerked open the door upon which some inconsiderate fool was hammering. In the morning mist an exhausted Paul grinned amid an orderly group of tired, glowing, semi-familiar faces.

"Good morning, brother Jacobi," he said cheerfully, his breath forming clouds in the freezing air. "Break the ice on your courtyard pond, will you? And rouse the household! We have five baptisms to perform before people hurry off to work. But I'll let this young man tell you all about it."

Gently he pushed Fabius forward, as Elishabet and a group of wide-eyed, tousle-headed children came crowding to the door, followed by a sleepy Barnabas. Then Fabius smiled at his family and opened his mouth and as his triumphant, clear words poured out, all semblance of order was entirely lost.

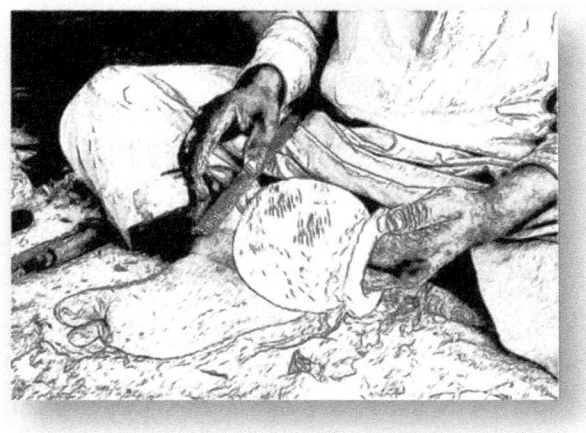

Chapter Forty

THE redemption of the house of misfits and the miracle worked upon young Fabius, brought people from far and wide – in defiance of the bitter weather – seeking the apostles wherever they were, whether at home or at work, or teaching from house to house wherever groups of believers gathered in turn. Malchus and his boarders also found themselves sought out to tell and retell their stories, even the reclusive Ezra finding that he was no longer left in peace to rasp and hack at his lumps of alabaster, but must talk and answer questions half the day. This caused him some extra trials, as the more he talked, the more the fine white dust which pervaded the workshop and powdered his hands and feet, got into his lungs – and the more tempting was the impulse to wash it down, as the other workers did, with lashings of hot spicy *calda*. Privately he resolved to start looking for another kind of employment.

Meanwhile, the work of spreading the gospel and building up the believers in Iconium went on. In the beginning Paul and Barnabas had been able to teach in private houses, talking to a family here, a group there, but as the numbers increased this became less practical. There were not enough hours in the week to visit everyone in this piecemeal fashion, but at the same time it was difficult to collect the growing body

469

of believers together in the one place. The synagogue was no longer available to them. The rulers by now had made it very plain that those who promoted alien interpretations of the Holy books were not welcome inside unless they agreed to stay silent about their private beliefs. This injunction being somewhat unclear, a few accepted it with the mental prevarication that they would not be silent *outside* the synagogue, while others stayed away altogether. Social connections thus weakened, and traditional habits of worship fractured, Jewish believers had lost a central place of refuge and affirmation of their culture – which despite their joy in the gospel was a cause of grief to many, even as it was to Paul himself. Regardless, with the synagogue building no longer available for a spiritual schoolroom, they had to find somewhere else to meet, since at this time of year open air teaching was out of the question.

The solution came, just as it had in other responsive cities, from one or two of the wealthier converts. Their spacious villas were well designed for entertaining visitors, and ideal for holding large assemblies for prayer, scriptural education, and celebrating the Lord's memorial supper. The massed gatherings were more than a practical answer to a problem of space. Meeting with so many like-minded disciples created a powerful sense of community for new believers, and a feeling of support and encouragement. Particularly in the weekly Thanksgiving service, their united orderly worship, whether expressed in prayers, reverential silences, or heart-felt songs of praise, fostered a respectful sense of solemn occasion.

Not every ekklesial gathering was a solemn one, however. That year, while the synagogue held special services for the Festival of Lights, the Jewish Christians who were denied entry celebrated among themselves, with many of the Gentile Christians adopting *Chanukah* for the first time, with great exultation and equal exuberance.

From whatever background they had been drawn, whether Judaism or paganism, the festival seemed to symbolise the miracle of their own rededication, their own redemption from the destroying enemy of ignorance and sin. They had so little to offer, just a small flame of tremulously new faith, but now against all odds it burned steadily, brightly, continuously, shining its light forth to challenge the surrounding darkness. And this was evident to everyone, when not only Jews but many Greeks, ever keen to hear of some new philosophy, likewise sought out the Christians – Paul and Barnabas in particular, for Fabius was but the first of many others touched by the healing hands of the apostles. The Iconians now had clear proof that a supernatural power was with them. These preachers worked miracles and genuine cures on impossible conditions no physician could touch. And they did so – not in some secretive corner of an exclusive temple before accolytes sworn to esoteric mysteries, but publicly – in plain view of everyone, even doubters. Awed men, women, and children were full of wonderment, and many questions.

The city was astonished, even a little afraid. Wandering wise men, healers or magicians were not novelties, but nothing like *this* had ever been seen in Iconium before! How was such a thing even possible among men who were virtually atheists? Yes, *atheists*, and how they slept peacefully in their beds on wild thunderous nights was anyone's guess! Any fool knew that since there were literally hundreds of chief gods, minor gods, and demi-gods, whether *di superi, di terrestres,* or *di inferi* – celestials, terrestrials or of the underworld – to worship only *one* god was tantamount to worshipping none at all!

These Christians were worse than the Jews, who might also worship only one god, but at least their religion had the *gravitas* of many centuries behind it, and they did not force their views down other men's throats. But as for devotees of this new religion (*new* and *religion* being surely a contradiction in terms!) they were not content to live and let live, but actively preached that all other deities were a man-made fantasy and not true gods in the first place. Such assertions were dangerous and subversive. What disasters might fall upon men who abandoned the faith of their forefathers? If they no longer worshipped in the temples? If they no longer placed twice-daily votive offerings for their household gods? If they no longer burned incense to the Emperor? Who would protect them then?

As the apostles' words continued to create a great stir in the streets and in the synagogue, and there was a fresh surge of new believers among both Jews and God-fearing Greeks, perhaps it was inevitable that all this provoked the ruling Jews and city officials alike. As in Antiochia, so in Iconium – men who felt they were losing control of their subjects, whether religious or municipal, hastened to stir up bitterness against those who accepted the Way of Truth.

All winter the whole city raged with controversy, and every inhabitant had an opinion. Those on the rulers' side quarrelled fiercely with the opposition, claiming that the Christians were trouble makers – wandering faith-healers at best, and dangerous sorcerers at worst. Those on the apostles' side protested that any message of hope and healing could be no threat to anyone. Their gospel promoted harmony and good morality. How could it be a bad thing for the Jews' God to offer all men a place in his kingdom? Especially a kingdom which seemed to be spiritual rather than physical, insofar as it was still more of a promised ideal, than a tangible reality. After all, where was it? Not here, not yet, but prophesied to eventuate some time in the future! Well, that was vague to say the least, and need agitate no one. *Cras non est,* they shrugged. Tomorrow never comes!

Meanwhile those who could not make up their minds feebly protested that this could *not* be true Judaism, being neither of the Jews' God, nor His people, for nothing like it had ever been preached by Jews before. As for the extraordinary outcrop of supposedly supernatural events at the hands of these most *unlikely* people, that was simply too disconcerting to understand, let alone accept.

For a long time the population engaged in a verbal tug-of-war in true democratic style, until the city officials and Jewish rulers alike decided that things had got out of hand, and it was time something was done. Spring was on the doorstep, there was an urge to sweep away the dross from the winter-weary streets and from the soul of the city; to have affairs neatly and tidily run as they had been before itinerant preachers compromised its model harmony and complacency. In Iconium any majority decision by its citizens had real power. Now they only had to agree on what must be done to reclaim and preserve the peace of their agitated city.

A private meeting was arranged and grim decisions made. Nobody noticed an insignificant slave woman, her eyes dilated with alarm, slip from the room.

In another half hour, frozen to the marrow, she had found Malchus, who had found Barnabas, and now Barnabas had found Paul, who was working late. In a dusty hovel of a workroom on the other side of the city, Paul put down his coarse needle, rolled up the last rough sack, and stared at the steady flame of an oil lamp with a weary feeling. Again – a plot on his life!

"What do they plan for us, my brother?" he asked, his eyes fixed on the flame. So cold was the room that their breath hung in clouds, misting across the tongue of light to vanish in a moment, as if to remind them that man's life was but a vapour.

Barnabas answered softly, "Stoning, Paul."

Wincing in sudden pain, Paul saw the flame flare white hot at the back of his eyelids. The whiteness hardened and hurtled towards him – *a rock – a battered body – young, muddy, bloody* ... With a gasp he shook the image free and once again saw Barnabas quiet and grave before him, awaiting an answer.

"The Word of Life has been planted here," Paul replied slowly. "Now we must trust to our Lord Jeshua to make it grow."

That same night, they packed Portia's well-used basket and fled the city. This time Paul did not feel inclined to laugh at himself. A cold feeling of dread had descended on him like a fog. They sheltered that wild, windy night, as had many before them, in a filthy, musty cave near the eastern roadway. Barnabas rolled up in his thick cloak and somehow managed to sleep in spite of the cold and a yowling spitting scrimmage of wildcats under a tattered moon, but Paul spent sleepless shivering hours in an agony of prayer. Could he never forget what he had done?

Yet even in his distress, he found a reason to thank Lord Jeshua – thanking him yet again, as he had done many times before, for the unknown girl in the crowd at the stoning of Stefanos. The girl whose distraught shriek had distracted him as he flung that first accusing stone ... and made him miss.

Chapter Forty-one

STIFF and cold next morning, Paul and Barnabas resolutely chafed the sluggishness from their reluctant limbs, and trudged on for many dreary hours. They were thankful the winter had passed, but early spring was still a miserable time to be travelling, with snow still thick on the mountains, the rough ground windswept and bare, and every creek and river glazed over with ice each morning.

Complaining of chapped lips, Barnabas dug out their little pot of wool fat and screwing up his face dabbed it inexpertly on his mouth, making a nice greasy mess of his whiskers. Paul dared not laugh at him – he merely held out his hand for the pot and coated his own lips, thickly daubing the troublesome patch on his nose and cheek, which had broken out afresh overnight. Then he saw Barnabas glance at him sideways, obviously struggling to return the courtesy of ignoring his smeared face, for solemnity was far from his eye. Both of them gave up all pretence, and their spirits lifted as they chuckled at each other's appearance, ruefully agreeing that their pot of ointment was in dire need of replenishing, for it was definitely beginning to smell.

As darkness gathered with a heavy shower, they made camp under a shallow rocky outcrop hovering over a bleak stretch of the road. Grateful to be out of the wind and rain, they lit a good fire and agreed that there was nothing more blissful after a wretched day. They were engaged in inspecting their feet, anointing various scrapes and blisters with the odiferous cure-all, when the dull clop of hooves and rattle of wheels alerted them to the fact that they were about to have company. Before long they were being hailed cheerfully by the driver of a very small donkey cart, a rather shabby, gaudily-dressed man, who asked if he might share their shelter for the night. Seeing his eyes wandering hungrily towards the pannikin of beans on the fire they invited him to share their meal as well, which he did with great gusto, talking and bragging non-stop between (and during) mouthfuls.

His name was Plato the Puppeteer, an Athenian born and bred, or so he said. Paul was momentarily sceptical. Athenian? He suspected that Plato's physiognomy was as Jewish as his own, but as Plato had never known his parents, who could say?

"I've been doing the rounds," Plato mumbled vaguely through a mouthful of beans. "Lystra next – it's easy takings there. They're not very sophisticated, you know. Oh, some are, of course, the usual bunch of aristocrats. But most of the natives are barbarians at heart!" He belched loudly and wiped his mouth with the back of a hairy hand.

Barnabas caught Paul's eye and winked. Plato nodded towards his cart.

"All my things are in there – tell you what! How about I run a little rehearsal and you watch! Return for hospitality, hey?"

Without waiting for an answer, he darted out and rummaged around, coming back to the fire with an armful of large stick puppets. Barnabas noted the soiled, threadbare costumes and worn paint, and guessed that business had not been very good for Plato lately, for all his earlier boasts about entertaining the rich and famous.

Assuring them he would explain anything they might not understand, Plato was almost pathetically keen to entertain his captive audience, so they sat quietly and watched.

"The Lystrans just love this one!" Plato popped his head over the crumbly rock he was using for a stage. "It's their very own mythology, you see. Happened right in their territory, they say." He disappeared and began the play.

He was good, there was no doubt of that, and very accomplished in the use of different voices, but something about the whole situation struck them as so comical that Paul and Barnabas dared not catch each other's eyes. As it was, Barnabas sat with his shoulders shaking, chewing his cloak, half choked with suppressing what could only be described as guffaws.

The little tale unfolded: disguised as poor humans, the gods Zeus and Hermes ("That's Jupiter and Mercury around here, mostly," Plato obligingly interrupted himself) came to visit the people of Phrygia – in fact, they came to the town of Lystra itself!

"That's my version of it, anyway," Plato explained helpfully, his bulging, earnest eyes reappearing over the rock. "Of course, I tell *every* town theirs was the one." He ducked down again.

Nobody would give hospitality to the two shabby strangers, except an old man called Philemon, and his wife Baucis. The gods then revealed their true shape and promptly drowned all the unhelpful villagers in a flash flood. Philemon and Baucis were made young again and had their humble shack turned into a magnificent temple – "I can do this much better with my props, you know," Plato's tousled head, grotesque in the firelight, popped up yet again to explain – where they were made priests, and lived happily ever after.

Paul and Barnabas applauded loudly. Flushed with delight, Plato sprang up, bowed exaggeratedly and packed away his little characters in the cart. While the puppeteer was busy attending to his donkey they could hear his voice rumbling away to him all the while, and to their amusement it seemed he was attempting to mimic their own accents, presumably for the benefit of another play.

Paul nudged his friend. "Control yourself, Barnabas! You'll offend the poor fellow!"

Obediently stuffing the cloak back in his mouth, Barnabas could only shake his head helplessly. He was sure that if Plato's eager face had bobbed up one more time to "explain", he would have burst out laughing, cloak or no cloak. The only thing that was not funny was the taste of the cloak.

That night there were no wildcats to disturb their dreams – only some wild asses which blunderingly nosed around in the moonlight, grunting and snorting, and agitating Plato's donkey to bray after them, whether through fear or loneliness was impossible to tell. It was a relief when the rhythmically snoring Plato woke from his slumbers, and uncurling himself from a comfortable hollow in the cave, curled up instead with the little beast, draping his blanket over its head and murmuring to him soothingly.

In the morning, Paul and Barnabas again shared their food, and in return, the puppeteer generously offered to give them a lift in his cart. Thanking him warmly even as they eyed the rickety little vehicle with doubt, they suggested it might be easier all round if he carried their basket instead. Thus blissfully unhampered, and feeling much happier since the wool-fat treatment of the previous day (despite its odour) had effectively soothed their painfully chapped skin, they walked beside the tiny jolting cart while Plato loudly sang tragic love songs to his peevish donkey, which did not seem at all grateful for his evident affection, and they entered Lystra much earlier in the day than they had anticipated.

Paying the tolls at the gate, for once they received some small change, a few unrecognizable copper coins, which they gave to a cripple sitting silently nearby. Unlike many beggars who never took money but they whined for more, the man met their eyes and thanked them with a nod and a smile. Meanwhile Plato went off happily to try his luck in the market-place, leaving Paul and Barnabas to enquire for the synagogue, but there was none. Lystra was out-of-the-way, uncommercial, an awkward sort of town that did not attract Jewish interest. There was only a handful of Jews and they met in private houses.

A street urchin directed the pair to a narrow alley, where most of the doors displayed a *mezuzah*. They stopped at the first house they came to, a neat place with plastered walls and a most unexpected feature for such modest Jewish quarters – a stone lintel over the door, beautifully carved with pomegranates. A boy of perhaps fourteen answered their knock. His grey eyes surveyed Paul cautiously from under a strangely lopsided mop of tight black curls. Damp clumps and crescents of hair clung to a cloth draped over his narrow shoulders.

"Eben!" a woman's voice called impatiently from inside the house. "Come back here! I haven't finished."

A stout woman trotted up behind him, brandishing a pair of shears. The front of her gown was also sprinkled with hair clippings. Suddenly she saw the men at the door.

"I beg your pardon, sirs! I did not hear your knock ... please excuse my appearance! How can I help you?"

Paul smiled. "Blessings and peace be upon you, Lady, and upon your household. We are fellow Jews from –" but he got no further. The woman pounced on them with a cry of delight, showering them with hair clippings, and almost dragged them through the door.

"Men of Israel!" she exclaimed. "Peace be upon you and blessings from the Eternal! You are welcome here! We have so few of the True Faith pass this way. You will spend this Sabbath with us? And Passover next week, too! Yes? Oh, how wonderful! Mother!" she called, hardly pausing for breath. "Here are two of our kinsmen! Eben, Eben, my son, have that lazy Felicitas bring water for their feet, quickly. I'll finish your hair later."

Overwhelmed with hospitality, Paul and Barnabas soon felt completely at home with this small family, and the two women not being shy of talking, before long the apostles knew all about them.

Young Eben's father was a Greek artisan who travelled wherever the work was. A skilful stone carver and sculptor, he spent long periods away from home, and it appeared that Eben had been raised chiefly by his mother Eunice, and grandmother Lois. Both were thoughtful, pious women, and the boy's knowledge and love of scripture, which never failed to delight Paul, revealed that they had brought him up with great care.

Life had not been easy for them. Eunice's husband Kyros had been a Greek proselyte, an intelligent, hardworking man, but of a tempestuous disposition. Once so devout that he had chosen a name for his hoped-for son which signified '*honouring God*', by the time the babe was born Kyros was already wavering enough to forbid the circumcision ... and even before the child was out of swaddling bands, he had impatiently revolted, throwing off the shackles of Judaism to return to the gods of his people. The little boy's name now objectionable to him, with smug humour the sculptor renamed him Lithos, meaning '*stone*'.

Deeply dismayed as she was, his Jewish wife was a match for him, however. Hiding her grief, she congratulated him on his wit in choosing such a fitting name, calmly adding that, nevertheless, she would use only its Hebrew form, Eben – short for Ebenezer, *'stone of help'*. It was plain to see that this was equally an act of obedience and an act of defiance – both an assertion and affirmation of her faith! And yet, as mercurial as he was charming, Kyros only roared with laughter at her cunning, cheerfully accepted the substitution, and went off to his next commission delighted at having such a clever wife and such a fine tale to tell his friends, even if it was at his own expense.

Though they did not miss his unpredictable outbursts, his wife and mother-in-law always spoke kindly of Kyros. They were grateful that he generously supported them and that being absent more often than present, he did not further interfere with the boy's upbringing, except (to their delight) to insist that his son learned to read, write, and figure.

Kyros's occasional lavish spurts of beneficence were a God-send to Eunice, who saved every spare coin, running her household with the utmost frugality so that she might gradually acquire, book by precious book, expensive copies of the holy scriptures from Antiochia and Iconium. There being none other in their circle who was literate, the young boy was appointed their scribe by default, daily reading from the *Septuagint* - the Greek translation of the Hebrew texts - to his mother, grandmother, and Jewish friends, just as soon as he was capable of the honourable task.

Eunice bore Kyros five more children, but there was no tussle over what they should be called. None of the unfortunate infants survived long, and their jaundiced little bodies were laid in the grave without individual distinction – for such was the custom. Meanwhile, as the years passed and Eben grew in understanding, he determined in his young heart that one day, when he reached manhood, he would reclaim his true name. Until then he must try to live up to it.

In Lystra, the apostles found work hard to come by, since nobody wanted to pay a man to do what a slave would do for nothing. They were not in dire need, for after their lean time in Antiochia, Iconium had well replenished their purse, but to make the funds last as long as possible they now had to create their own employment. Fortunately, with Barnabas plying his pens and Paul his leather tools in the *agora* on market days they could earn just enough to pay their way, (and, so Barnabas averred, keep firmly at bay Paul's 'rash of laziness'!)

While Paul fashioned small leather articles such as belts, sheaths, shoe lacings and document folders to order, Barnabas sat busily writing such vast quantities of manuscript that he seemed to be in great demand as a copyist. The truth was however that he had very little to do that was lucrative, and was in fact writing up a journal of their travels, or rather, continuing the one which Marcus had begun. This task he had taken over at Perga and later his notes too would find their way to Damascus to be shared with Loukanos, who had urged the undertaking.

After all the tension they had experienced lately in Iconium they found the phlegmatic folk of Lystra congenial by comparison, and were glad to settle down at once to preaching the gospel in the town and outlying villages. Boarding with Eunice, Eben and Lois, the apostles were introduced at once to the tiny Jewish community, with whom they joyfully celebrated Passover. To their new friends they explained that, as *Christianoi*, they no longer regarded it only as a memorial of Israel's deliverance from Egypt. Instead they celebrated it in deep and reverent acknowledgement of the deliverance of all mankind from eternal death, through the saving blood of Jeshua of Nazareth, the Saviour promised since the foundation of the world.

Thus they were soon provoking many lively discussions on the full meaning of Passover, in relation to the Messiah, the perfect Lamb of God, who had indeed come as promised, sacrificing his own life that all might live. This led on to further explanations concerning the

Christ's extinguishing of the power of death, the forgiveness of sins, the importance of holiness in head, heart, and hands as a way of life honouring God, what the Law of Moses could and could not achieve, the confidence of resurrection, and of course, the vital importance of baptism as a first response to the command of the resurrected, glorified Son of God.

To their surprise, Eunice's young Galatian maid Felicitas became something of a follower, traipsing after them whenever she could sneak away from her duties. Paul was somewhat oblivious, but Barnabas shrewdly noted that never was she so keen a listener, never were her staring blue-green eyes so attentively fixed upon them, as when Eben was present. How genuine was her interest in the gospel was hard to tell.

In the absence of a formal synagogue, whenever they had opportunity the two disciples preached outdoors, with the enthusiastically supportive Eben invariably in attendance – in the *agora*, one or other of the city's little gardens, or near the gates where there was a square with a fountain – anywhere they could find an audience.

It was rather slow work. The Lystrans were not particularly interested in listening to itinerant preachers, especially those with such bizarre ideas. Everyone knew the gods had their own areas of influence! Yet these fellows seemed to believe that theirs was not only above all others, but somehow portable from place to place, equally careless of arousing the wrath of either the immortals of Olympus, or more local supernaturals. Well, perhaps the preachers were travelling mystics, and such were always hard to understand – speaking in riddles and meaning the opposite of what they appeared to say. Busy people had better things to do than bother their heads with such stuff.

Still, the pair were inoffensive in all other respects … so the Lystrans tolerated them, but there was no doubt they preferred to watch entertainments like Plato's puppets when they had time on their hands.

The legend of Philemon and Baucis was very popular, especially when played outside the temple of Jupiter. Plato nodded cheerfully whenever he saw the two preachers, unaware that he was making things difficult for them. After all, his business was improving!

Paul and Barnabas continued their efforts, however, and with the whole-hearted conversion of Lois, Eunice and a handful of others, they felt their stay at Lystra was well rewarded. When Eben came rather timidly to Paul, asking if he was too young for baptism, Paul's heart gave a great leap. This boy had become very dear to him.

"Not you, Eben," he answered gravely. "You have known and loved the scriptures since you were very small. I think you fully understand what baptism is all about. Are you ready to accept the trials that following the Way can bring?"

Eben looked him straight in the eye. "Yes, if God gives me the courage."

Paul lay awake for a long time that night. "Barnabas?"

"M'mph?"

"I think – if I'd ever had a son, I would have wanted him to be just like that boy."

"He could almost pass as your son as it is." Barnabas wriggled his shoulders deeper into the blankets, thinking how much Eben's quiet, keen intensity mirrored the schoolboy Shaul of many years ago. Of course it was sheer coincidence that the boy's original name was so similar to the cognomen of Shaul's own father, but perhaps that had unconsciously evoked a warm sense of family. Despite the gap of years the two were kindred souls. "Not only is he small, dark and scrawny like you, but you are oddly alike in other ways. He even walks on his toes."

"Trust you to remember that! I grew out of it and so will he. I was referring to his attitudes. The boy has a spiritual depth beyond his years. Something any father would be proud to see in a son."

Barnabas smiled in the darkness. He would not remind Paul that when barefoot he still trod lightly as a cat, especially if lost in thought, as if unconsciously shrinking from the touch of earth. Instead he gave a stifled yawn. "I think he does regard you as a father, in a way – not as a replacement, but as a stand-in, you know."

"You could be right," his friend said offhandedly, turning over. He gritted his teeth. Stupid to have allowed that out. Self-indulgent.

"There's still time," Barnabas mumbled sleepily, giving his lumpy pillow a lazy thump, and Paul could hear the grin in his voice. "You could yet settle down, marry, raise a son, call him Eben ..."

"I *am* settled down – I am married to my work," Paul's tired voice answered roughly, but at once he regretted his abruptness. Raising himself on one elbow, he added impulsively, "Don't think I am without natural feeling, Barnabas, for I am no more immune than the next man to the lure of that vision! But I cannot afford to indulge it. Of course, to serve Christ requires that a man acts honourably by his family, and *vice versa*, as they say, but I *know* my personal limitations. I *must* be unhindered, or I would be continually torn between earthly and spiritual responsibilities." And he bit his tongue before the shadowy thought, "*Like Marcus*," could escape in words.

Yet, even as he did so, he wondered uneasily, and for the first time – had some part of him actually been *envious* of that young man? "*Speak truth in your own heart, Shaul Benjamin!*" he warned himself wearily. Yet truthfully, he did not know the answer. *Search me, oh God, and know my heart!*

But Barnabas was quietly responding, "You are preaching to the converted here, my brother. I am too selfish and you are too passionate for either of us to divide our allegiances, no matter how well others may succeed in uniting them."

Paul snorted. "You are the least selfish man I know." Now it was his turn to thump his pillow, and as he lay down again, he added, "Quite apart from all that, can you imagine asking a young woman – I should say, *any* woman – to share the kind of life – the kind of hardships – which the Master himself prophesied for me?"

Barnabas sighed as he felt sleep retreating before awakening memories. "And he too was a eunuch for the sake of the kingdom of heaven."

"Yet he will bring many spiritual sons to his glory," Paul murmured, his brief flare of agitation subsiding as he reminded himself of this belief, for belief was peace. There was a pause, then a few more words, almost to himself, "Anyway if I had a son I wouldn't call him Eben…" His voice trailed off. He had already said more than he intended.

"You wouldn't?"

"No," Paul's voice was muffled. "I'd call him S–something else …"

Barnabas sighed again. He also lay awake for a long time, but he was thinking of Marcus.

Chapter Forty-two

THE trickle of interest in Lystra was enough to keep Paul and Barnabas persevering, and they made it a habit to preach at certain times in particular places. One of these places was a wide open square near the city gates. Here was a public fountain where in the mornings people fetched their water, surrounded by many stalls where they did their marketing, and although everyone was busy, the essential nature of these occupations ensured a regular audience, whether it was keen or not – and admittedly, mostly it was not. However, as Paul said to Eben, perhaps they might not persuade even one more Lystran – but you never knew who else might come through that gate from other parts, and have eyes to see, ears to hear, and a heart to understand! So they persisted, and Eben accompanied them.

For some time Paul and Barnabas had been aware of the keen attention paid to them by a cripple stationed at the gates – the same man who had thanked them for their few coppers when they first arrived. Leaving his usual position he began to make a habit of shuffling as close as possible to wherever the apostles happened to be speaking in the square. It was disconcerting to see the gaunt, hungry-eyed man dragging his body around by rowing himself backwards on his calloused hands, his stunted, deformed legs trailing in the dust, but it was clear he did not pity himself. He seemed far more intent on observing and listening closely to everything they said and all the discussions that went on around them. Once they realized this, Paul and Barnabas made sure they stayed near the fountain so he did not have to struggle far from the safety of his niche by the gates. Unlike other beggars the cripple did not clamour noisily for alms. People tripped over him, flung him coins or ignored him as the mood took them, but he stayed at his self-appointed post, listening, thinking. He seemed to grow more animated as the days passed, his dark face lighting up as the apostles spoke of the One True God, Creator of the Universe, who had sent His own Son to change men's hearts and save them from everlasting oblivion in death.

"A god who is our father!" he muttered to himself. "A deity who does not merely toy with men, but loves them?"

Eben overheard and squatted beside him. "Yes indeed," he affirmed. "He created us for His pleasure, you see. He desires all men to come to Him through His glorified son."

"*All* men, you say. Not just a chosen race? Not just those who can afford fine offerings? What of a beggar who has nothing to give?"

Eben grinned. "Paul says the best thing a man can give is his love. Without it, any offering is worthless. You see, it's the only thing we have which God doesn't already own."

"So he loves us – and wants us to respond! To return that love. To love him and also love his son ..." The man rubbed his hardened grimy hands together anxiously as he tried to grasp the scope of this idea. "Yes, yes, I see that must be so, for of course to love any man truly is to love his offspring, just as to love any man truly is to love his father also, for his sake. But one who is Creator of the Universe must be too far above mere mortals. So then, I perceive we should love them as a slave loves a good master and his master's heir."

"Oh, but far more than that!" Eben said enthusiastically. "He wants us as adopted children, who may share in the inheritance of His own Son. He wants us to be part of their divine *family*."

"Part of a divine family!" exclaimed the lame man, dumbfounded. "A benevolent deity as *pater familias* of adopted men, mortals he did not even sire? Why, then, surely there can be no other gods like Him! Blessed be His name, and blessed be His Son!"

"Amen!" Eben agreed happily. He looked over at Paul and caught his eye, nodding towards the lame man with a pleased smile. Paul stared intently at the helpless cripple on the pavement. With a flash of insight enabled by the Spirit, he read the man's yearning heart. Here was fledgling faith.

Immediately taking a step towards him, he held out his hand and demanded loudly, "Man, stand up on your feet!"

The rest of the crowd looked at each other, surprised and amused. They nudged each other with knowing looks, murmuring that the preacher could not have been taking much notice of his audience all this time. Hadn't he noticed this luckless beggar was lame? Julius the Cripple had worn a smooth patch on those flagstones over many years, and expecting him to stand was laughable.

But to their astonished consternation, Julius the Cripple was already scrambling to his feet! Almost shrieking with awed delight, he was feeling the weight of his body through the soles of his feet– revelling in the sensation of putting one foot before the other – the joy of moving effortlessly! – something he had never before experienced. Ecstatically he hopped and skipped on well proportioned, straight-boned, firmly-muscled legs – wriggling obedient toes! rotating strong ankles! – staggering slightly with the unfamiliar change in balance, delighting in the glorious, tingling sensation of it all. With child-like clumsiness he pranced and cavorted, laughing hysterically, flexing his knees, lifting them too high, unused to feeling so light – and he was comically unsure of what to do with his arms, which now they were no longer his means of propulsion, dangled awkwardly at his sides.

On every side the crowd was gasping, clapping, laughing, and buzzing with awed speculation. Eben's deep grey eyes widened with shock. The apostles had told him of their acts of healing, but he had never thought to see it done right in front of him! He tugged Paul's sleeve.

"That man was *born* lame!" he gabbled excitedly. "You haven't just cured him, it's like you made his legs all over again – the way they were meant to be!"

Paul shook his head, smiling. "Not us!" he reminded him. "The grace of God has done this, not just to help him, but that others may see, and wonder, and be moved with confidence to believe our message of salvation."

The amazed beggar grasped Paul's hands and kissed them, stammering out his gratitude. "I thank your God for showing me He has the power to heal! Now tell me more of His power to save! And I, Julius Petronius, no more the Cripple, will bear Him witness all my days!"

Paul and Barnabas, unheeding of the sensation rippling through the astonished crowd, were about to reply when Eben gave a cry of alarm. Lystrans were flocking towards them from all over the square, chattering excitedly amongst themselves, pointing and arguing, their voices rising higher with every gesture.

Barnabas reassured the nervous boy. "Don't worry, Eben, agitation is a natural response to what people do not understand. Miracles often have that effect on bystanders. Sometimes they doubt the evidence of their eyes, or they suspect trickery at first, but the Lystrans will soon realise that God is working through us for their benefit."

"Not this time!" Eben said anxiously, concentrating.

Paul listened hard, frowning, then shook his head. "They've dropped their Latin – and that's not Greek they're speaking, either!" he said in exasperation. "I can't understand a word of it. What tongue is it?"

"Lycaonian! And they're not giving God the glory at all!" Eben despaired. "I just knew they weren't paying proper attention to you!"

The gathering crowd had begun acting in a most peculiar manner. People were bowing and chanting, others were kneeling with outstretched arms, singing strange, high-pitched songs, while many ran shouting with alarm to the temple of Jupiter where there was an answering flurry of activity.

"What are they saying? Have we frightened them? Offended them? Tell us!" Paul demanded.

The healed Julius had stopped leaping around and was looking perplexed. He translated rapidly. "The gods have become like men and have come down to us. Praise to Jupiter. Praise to Mercury."

Paul gave an exclamation of dismay. "What are they thinking of?"

As the dense crowd thickened around them Barnabas looked around wildly for escape, and caught sight of a faded, ornamental box with a tousled head peering over the top. "I should have known!" he cried. "That wretched legend – Philemon and Baucis!"

Light dawned on Paul. "This is ignorant, superstitious folly!" he groaned. "They don't want to risk another flood!"

491

"Look!" Eben yelled above the commotion of the seething crowd. In vain did Paul and Barnabas rapidly retreat, being brought up short by the city gates and hemmed in by clamorous townsfolk. As they turned around, suddenly they saw what Eben was shouting about, and stared in consternation.

A hastily-assembled procession was marching determinedly down the street to the square, the crowd parting hastily before it – an anxious priest of Jupiter leading a yoke of oxen, followed by dazed girls waving garlands of flowers snatched from the temple altars. A native Lystran scraped up his Latin and pushed forward to prostrate himself in front of the disciples.

"Hail, Great Jupiter!" he cried with trepidity to tall Barnabas, his words attempting pomp and achieving only panic. "And hail, Mercury, Messenger of the gods!" he added quickly to Paul, his voice beginning to quaver. "Your devoted subjects await your pleasure – the sacrifices approach – and –"

He never finished. "No, no, no!" cried Paul. "You must not worship us!" Shaking their heads insistently and making frantic gestures of refusal he and Barnabas quickly raised the trembling man to his feet, then dived into the ever-growing crowd with urgent appeals, tearing their clothes in dismay. "Stop! Stop this!" they shouted. "We are not your gods! You must stop! Please stop!"

Eben and the newly long-legged Julius ran to the priest to halt the procession. The oxen lowed bad-temperedly as the pair tried to turn them around. The people were puzzled, but the gods were no doubt entitled to behave strangely. They smiled reverently and tried to place wreaths of flowers over the heads of these very animated deities. Trembling with outrage Paul tore the tainted flowers from their grasp and dashed them to the ground, trampling savagely on the petals, yelling for silence. Taken aback by this reaction, the anxious crowd stopped hailing them with assurances of allegiance, and the noise simmered down enough for Paul's voice to be heard above the din.

"Sirs – why are you doing these things to mere men?" he shouted pleadingly. "You must not sacrifice to us, for we are as mortal as you are! This miracle you have seen here was not done of our own powers, but through the power of the one true living God. Will you not listen now you have seen His merciful hand at work? It is He Whom we have been preaching to you ever since we came to your city, imploring you to turn from your vain idols to acknowledge Him as the great Creator – the Originator of all life. It is He who makes the rain and brings the seasons – it is He who cares for you and blesses your crops, and brings you joy, filling your hearts with gladness – not these false and powerless gods of wood and stone!

"It is He who fashioned the world; the heaven and earth, the sea and all it encompasses. In times past He allowed all nations to go their own way, though the goodness and bounty of creation has always been His silent witness. But now the Creator has sent us here to witness to you in words – clear, plain words about Him and His Son and His purpose. He is reaching out to all men to create in them a new heart, a new life, to bring you more abundant blessings than you can ever imagine. Only hear us out!"

Whether the Lystrans understood any of this was doubtful. They had got hold of the idea that these men were gods, and for all they knew, this protesting might just be another of those tricks and tests that Celestial beings used to test the loyalty of hapless mortals. The Lystrans were stubborn in their determination not to be wrong twice. With gods, you could never tell ... they were a capricious lot, by all accounts. It took an exhausting amount of begging and pleading and arguing before they were convinced that, for whatever reason, their homage was not required. Their hysterical excitement rudely interrupted, they were baffled, disconcerted, let down, and upset.

Someone kicked sullenly at Plato's puppet theatre, where Philemon and Baucis were woodenly waiting to go through their routine. The flimsy canvas stand swayed, toppled, and collapsed, one of its snapped supports stabbing through the fabric. Muffled roars and curses came from Plato, who was inside it. He scrambled to his feet with his prominent eyes glaring.

"Troublemakers!" he bellowed across the square to Paul and Barnabas, who were still trying to placate the agitated Priest of Jupiter. His young priestesses had turned petulant and tearful in their confusion, and now he was angry … but not as angry as Plato. "Why did you have to come here and stir people up!" the puppeteer roared. "Leave us in peace!"

There was a ragged cheer to support his heated words. "Stirrers!" another voice repeated fiercely. "Disturbers of the peace!"

Startled by this vehemence, Barnabas stared into the crowd – recognising a face, and then another, and another, and a glint of gold in a wide, accusing mouth. "Paul!" he said slowly, incredulously. "These men – surely we know them! Yes! Synagogue rulers and their supporters, from Antiochia! And from Iconium! They have followed us all the way here!"

Paul's weaker eyes could not make them out. The old, cold feeling began to settle around him once more. The shouts continued over the rumble of the crowd.

"They made sad trouble for us in Antiochia!"

"We had to throw them out!"

"They preach another king, Jeshua the Jew – they're traitors to Caesar! Don't believe the lies they tell you! They're frauds!"

"Frauds?" Some in the the downcast crowd brightened up, looking hopeful.

"Yes – frauds and agitators!" Stepping boldly in front of the confused people the newcomers began to harangue them skilfully. "They nearly caused a civil war in Iconium! Divide and conquer is their creed! Do you want that to happen here?" They spat contemptuously, and the crowd shuffled forward a few steps, looking expectant as the men continued.

"But we have travelled far for your sakes! Yes, we have come to you people in honesty, to prevent you accepting seditious ideas which might expose you to the Emperor's displeasure! We make no secret of the fact we are Jews and do not share your beliefs – but among you we know our faith is respected for its antiquity. Whoever heard of such a thing as a *new* religion with any merit? If it is genuine, it would have stood firm throughout centuries! Even as your own practices of worship have done! Would you allow these to be swept away by dangerous religious novelty and incur the wrath of not only Caesar but also your own deities?

"And to our fellow Jews here present, we say, would you risk the judgements of Adonai God upon your heads, and those of the good people of this city among whom you are privileged by the grace of Caesar to freely worship? Do not be deceived by poetic words and market-place cures! Do not be taken in by promises to sprinkle you with occult skills! These cunning fellows only think to practice upon your credulous simplicity. Show them you are not the dullards they take you for! Show them you are discerning men of wisdom, who will not be swayed from the faith of your fathers, and your loyalty to your Emperor!"

During this scathing speech the Lystrans had become more and more unsettled; first disturbed, now they too were angry. They would show these Jews just who was credulous and simple! Menacingly pressing forward, the bravest shook their fists, shouting their support – immediately the rest vociferously joined in, and suddenly the whole atmosphere had changed.

Paul gripped the cured man's arm urgently, "Take this lad home, friend – make sure he keeps out of danger – hurry! They haven't come so many miles just to voice their opinions."

Julius nodded, tugging Eben away by the arm. "Let me go!" the boy shouted. "I want to stay! Paul – let me stay!" But sensitive to the fickle mood of the crowd, the former cripple dragged him off with arms strong from years of exercise, obedient to Paul's plea.

"You may need my help!" Eben shouted, unreasonably.

"Go, boy!" Paul shouted back anxiously. "Stay home!" The taunts of the crowd grew louder. People were hurling abuse at the tops of their voices.

"Let me go, will you!" Eben struggled to free himself. "How can you desert him after what he did for you! Are you a coward?!"

His yells of protest were swallowed up by the growing noise of the crowd. No longer benign and slightly foolish, it had become a roaring mob which rushed forward, bearing down upon the apostles until Barnabas was swept away by the pressing, eager bodies and Paul was trapped in the centre. Jeering, accusing chants thickened the air as the hustling crowd noisily swept him down the street like flotsam on a tidal race. Still yelling and shouting they came to a place where men were preparing ground for a new road running through a thistly overgrown wasteland. The men at work saw them coming, downed tools and vanished at once. As if by a pre-arranged signal the crowd retreated all around like a wave on the shore, stranding Paul alone in a rough arena where stood various mounds of road materials – slabs, rocks, stones, and chippings. The Jewish ringleaders sprang into the circle, shouting with furious gestures to the townspeople, inciting them to action.

Now an ugly roar swelled in Paul's ears; malice, spite and blood-lust glinted in eyes all around. His mouth went very dry. He shut his eyes. How many chilling dreams of such a scene had haunted him over the years! Only this time he was in the middle of it, it was real, his turn had come as he had always felt it would … and he could hear, faintly, far away, Barnabas screaming to him, "Paul! Look out! Cover your head!"

Smack! A broken piece of paving crashed at Paul's feet. The first stone. It was like a signal – the pent-up fury of the crowd was unleashed and the stones flew thick and fast in an unrelenting hail of hate. So often had he had seen this in his mind's eye, and yet nothing had prepared him for the immediate reality of incredible pain – the stunning force of the sharp rocks as they battered the breath from his body, which gasped and moaned and staggered out of his control – and the humiliation! How horribly strong was the primitive, screaming urge to retaliate – to snatch up a murderous missile and smash it cruelly back into the attacking mob!

Reeling, Paul was struck by a heavy rock in the stomach. He doubled up and dropped to his knees, vomiting, tears and blood streaming into his beard. The howls of the crowd boomed in his ringing ears. He was trying to speak through broken teeth and blood, "Father … forgive …" when a violent blow on the head smashed him into the filth and dirt, and swinging blackness roared over him. Then – nothing.

A few more stones thudded into the motionless body, and the crowd thinned. Rough hands dragged away the tattered, bloody, dust-covered creature that had been a vigorous man only an hour before. They dumped it outside the city near the rubbish heap where sinister black crows hopped and chuckled.

Suddenly a slight figure darted from the city gates and ran, stumbling and staggering towards the sad heap on the ground, calling Paul's name over and over. Behind him others came running, Barnabas, Julius Petronius, Eunice, Felicitas, the handful of new disciples, and last of all, grandmother Lois. In agony of mind, nobody even stopped to help the older woman over the uneven ground.

Eben had flung himself on Paul's body and was wailing like a baby. Felicitas was hovering behind him, wringing her hands, agitatedly blowing on her thumbs, spitting left and right over her shoulders. The distraught disciples gathered round, as Barnabas knelt and picked up one limp hand. He pressed the cold skin to his cheek and kissed it. Blood and dust smeared his mouth. The others openly wept, while the cured Julius seemed to be in a state of shock. Barnabas remained on his knees.

"I know that my Redeemer lives," he whispered, unable to control his voice. *"And that He shall stand at the last day upon the earth."* He bit his lips, shaking tears from his eyes. *"And though worms devour this body –"*

"Oh – *don't*!" Eben moaned. "Leave that part out!"

"Yet in my flesh shall I see God!" Barnabas finished with difficulty, and a great sob burst from his chest. He could restrain himself no longer. "Shaul, Shaul! My beloved friend, my brother! Oh, Paul, my faithful companion!"

Lois stepped forward and laid a wrinkled hand on his shoulder. "We could not save him," she said gently, her old eyes brimming over. "Let us at least give him a decent burial."

Barnabas, overcome, pulled Eben away. The body coughed. Everyone froze.

"Don't ... bury me ..." came a weak, hoarse whisper. "I'm not dead ... yet."

"Paul!" Eben shrieked, flinging his arms around him rather thoughtlessly. Paul groaned sharply and painfully rolled over, his face a dreadful sight – lacerated, dirty, bloody, and swollen. Eunice unhelpfully fainted and added to the general confusion, whereupon Felicitas promptly fainted as well, only far more artistically, at Eben's feet. With the help of the other men, Barnabas lifted Paul gently, sobbing now with relief. Meanwhile old Lois revived her daughter and matter-of-factly prodded Felicitas out of her dramatic swoon – and the motley group, overwrought and still slightly hysterical from the whole experience, staggered back into the city.

Carefully washed, bandaged, and anointed with all the healing remedies the women could concoct, Paul was grateful for the solicitous refuge of Eunice's house. By the grace of God, no bones were broken except for his right thumb. Many heart-felt, thankful prayers were said that night by the small group of Christians at Lystra.

Later Barnabas took a lamp and went to see how Paul was faring. He was awake but groggy from the hot spiced wine they had given him to dull the pain.

"Any better?" Barnabas asked quietly.

"Yes, better," Paul muttered, but he was not thinking of his wounds. In a strange way he knew that his nightmare visions of Stefanos would not return. He had paid the price.

The next morning Paul insisted on climbing out of bed at dawn, protesting that he was only stiff and sore, and they must move on before he stiffened up any more and became immobile. He was battered, bruised, and bandaged, yes, but he was capable of walking, and walk he would and must. Barnabas knew Paul too well to argue with him. Besides, he was right. They must leave at once for a safer place before they brought trouble to the other believers. They had not stayed half as long as they would have liked, and nowhere near the time they had spent in Antiochia and Iconium. Perhaps it was because there were so few of their countrymen here, and they were all equally strangers in a strange land, that their warm bond of national kinship was so compelling. Nevertheless, leave they must, though it would be a wrench, especially for Paul who had found in young Eben not only such a kindred spirit, but also something of a spiritual apprentice.

Once more they took to the road, where the springtime early-morning wind buffeted and howled as mercilessly as the crowd which had attacked them. Barnabas, shocked by the bruising which bloomed darkly on Paul's body, would not let him carry anything except his staff and insisted on frequent rests. Paul regretted that Barnabas had to carry their belongings on his own, but as even the simplest tasks made him wince with pain, and his thumb throbbed incessantly, he did not protest. Neither of them voiced the thought which was at the back of both their minds, that if only Marcus had stayed with them, how much easier it would have been in this time of trouble. Solomon the wise had written, *A man can overpower one who is alone, but two can withstand him, and a threefold cord is not easily broken*. But their threefold cord had unravelled, and now they were down to only two.

Trying to temper emotions as distressing as his injuries, Paul resolved to stop tormenting himself with that proverb, but the more he tried not to think of it, the more the words kept running through his head. *A threefold cord is not easily broken*. Suddenly it came to him that he and Barnabas were *not* merely 'two', for the Lord Jeshua had said plainly, '*I will never leave you*'. With or without Marcus, they still were a threefold cord, one which nobody could break! Comforted and uplifted by this fresh understanding, he let the revolving thought repeat itself without resistance, and pushed on through the pain with renewed determination.

Chapter Forty-three

ONCE more they took to the Via Sebaste, heading south and east, so deep into the loneliness of Galatia that the highway was no longer paved. The first few days were necessarily very slow – a sore struggle for Paul, who leaned heavily on his staff, but if he felt any qualms at the length of their journey he did not voice them. The ancient trade route was hardly a direct line to their destination, but it was well trodden, and the only way which was safe, relatively speaking. No traveller in his right mind would blindly set out across the bare, forbidding wasteland of the vast Lycaonian plains.

From time to time the two companions were glad to be joined by others passing between various farming settlements and small towns scattered throughout the region. Travelling in bands was some deterrent against the ever-present threat of bandits, though Barnabas joked that the sight of Paul's battered face was enough to frighten off the bravest robber. Once or twice a local inhabitant –having compassion on the wounded wayfarer – pressed the pair to accept hospitality, welcoming them into homes sometimes more wretched than a roadside cave, if only to give a cup of water, a sip of wine, a few dates, a roof for the night.

Conversation however was difficult as Lycaonian was not a language with which the apostles had been gifted, and the few native inhabitants who had Greek or Latin submerged it in such a mangled dialect that the travellers found it almost impossible to communicate. Uproarious laughter, puzzled shakes of the head and extravagantly apologetic shrugs greeted their attempts. As Paul said regretfully to Barnabas one wakeful night when gymnastic fleas leaped thickly from a host's dirty blankets – smiles, nods, bows and gestures sufficed to share agreeable social exchanges, but were hardly adequate to share the gospel. Barnabas, scratching furiously at several places at once, testily rejoined that if this was what Paul called sharing agreeable social exchanges, he must have taken too many blows to the head.

Almost a week after leaving Lystra they came to Derbe, where cold winds swooped down across the raw Lycaonian landscape from the snow-capped Taurus Mountains. Derbe, one of Rome's frontier cities, was perched on the inhospitable southern edge of Galatia, but it was no backwater. Presiding over the great highway which linked Pisidian Antioch in the west to the Cilician Gates in the east, it was a large town where customs were levied on all trade entering the province. It was a gateway not a destination; it was business-like, steady, with none of the lively interest of Antiochia or Iconium. But Paul and Barnabas had taken enough excitement by then to last them a long time, and were relieved to be able to preach the gospel in a calm atmosphere.

Paul had arrived having walked through the worst of his pain but was still a fearful sight with ugly lacerations scabbing over his beard, and grotesque black eyes which had become infected along the way, making him look worse than ever. Now they were burning an angry red amid the puffy purple bruising, crusted with discharge and so swollen he could barely see. It did not bode well for his reception by the resident Greeks, for their culture equated physical beauty with nobility of character. Nor would it endear him to the Jews of the city, as such a blighted appearance was enough to bar a man from congregational worship if the elders found it too offensive.

Such fears however proved to be unfounded. The mixed population of Derbe – Romans, Greeks, Jews, Cilicians, Phrygians, and Galatians of all ethnicities – lived in pragmatic harmony. Though urbane compared to the native peasantry, few were so coldly over-sophisticated that they would assess a man's character purely by his appearance, especially one damaged by assault or accident. This was quickly apparent when the apostles made their way to the busy *cardo* in search of eye salve – which they did immediately after paying the inevitable traveller's toll at the imposing city gates.

"Here, Paul." Barnabas led him to a neat shop over which hung a sign proclaiming *Gaius the Apothecary*. "I rather like the sound of this fellow."

Gaius was a common enough name, but given its meaning of 'happy', it was an apt one for a man who sold soothing remedies for bodily ills. Paul, privately recalling the two Gaiuses who had succoured him after his first beating, was cheered by the coincidence. There was something to be said for the belief that a good name fostered an appropriate character.

Undeterred by the dusty traveller's disfigurement, the stout little apothecary bathed Paul's eyes, examined them with care, and applied the salve himself.

"Laodicean, you know," he told them, as he gave further instructions. "It has a very fine reputation." Upon hearing the reason for their visit, the man's own eyes widened with interest. "Ah! Yes, yes, we have heard of you! Is it true that you, being Jews, preach a strange new religion, even to Gentiles like myself? No wonder you were punished by your own people – oh, yes, news travels fast in these parts. So this will be your opponents' work, then! Very thorough, worse luck for you. As for that thumb, I have to say I don't much like the look of it.

"Let me finish here and then you must come home with me – given the state of your face, and the awkward way you are walking, I had better inspect the rest of the damage. A visit to the baths should be efficacious once your eyes clear, I think – alternating *frigidarium* and *caldarium* is a fine treatment for most things … No? Ah, of course, not really a Jewish practice, is it. Well, never mind, meanwhile I do have some excellent ointments, so let's start with what I can see here. Keep still, now. Aha, what's this among all those wounds, eh? That's a nasty little rash you've got there, and needs attention too. Comes and goes, does it? Tell me more about it … H'm … Yes … Emotional strain, I'd say, so you're probably stuck with that, but I'll give you something to soothe it anyway. Don't worry – I won't cheat you – just tell me more of your message! You don't mind if I invite my friends to hear you too? I am in desperate need of fresh conversation. All people want to discuss with me is bad bellies, extortionate taxes, and how to treat the pox."

Laughing, the two agreed with great pleasure, and later that day found themselves talking to a whole houseful of people hastily gathered by the loquacious apothecary. More than a few of them knew of devout Jews from the north-east region of Cappadocia, who a number of years before had gone on pilgrimage to their holy city and come back with strange talk of a sacrificed and resurrected Saviour. This story they had heard in Jerusalem from fellow Jews who, though neither educated nor widely travelled, had unaccountably and fluently addressed them in the native tongue of Cappadocia. Some of the returning pilgrims had even set up small communities, calling themselves *Galileans*, or *Nazarenes*. But nobody here had given them much thought all these years. Many intense and demanding questions flew around the room until the lamps, refreshed more than twice, sputtered out in oily wisps of smoke, and reluctantly the visitors went home. The kindly Gaius however refused to let the apostles leave, and their host he remained for the rest of their stay.

The very next day, introducing themselves to the Chazzan of the small synagogue, Paul and Barnabas were very encouraged to find a little bundle of grubby and well travelled letters which having passed through many hands and various routes from Perga, Antiochia, and Iconium, had been awaiting them for some time. To their surprise one addressed to *"Paulus, travelling preacher"* was enclosed in a brief missive from Epaenetus. Paul, his eyes still swollen and bleary, asked Barnabas to read this first, and was touched to find that the grizzled old soldier Acacius had sacrificed a few precious coppers on scribal services in the Ghaziri market just to send him personal greetings.

The old man's news was simple but joyful. Finally having left the reserves he was now fully retired. His lingering doubts having been overcome by the attentions of the faithful Epaenetus, who visited whenever he could (and kept his hut in good repair), Acacius was now a baptised brother in Christ, much to the amusement of the worldly-wise Julius, who these days was bragging of his recent promotion from *Decanus* to *Optio,* and declaring a centurion's helmet would yet be his, and the prize of citizenship with it. No doubt he would go from strength to strength, rising up through the various ranks of centurion with equal confidence – so Acacius wrote, but whether out of admiration or sarcasm was not clear. At the end of the letter, he had made the scribe reopen it, to add an irritable post-script complaining that he had done his utmost to convert his friend Bernardus, who had visited him recently, but the interfering Julius had undone all his good work as soon as the poor old veteran had got back to barracks.

The covering note from Epaenetus was even shorter and to the point. Despite continual undercurrents of resentment towards the Christian community, he and his hard-working Aemilia were kept busy with pastoral work in the ekklesia and were hoping to persuade their new brother Acacius to move to Antiochia to be nearer to other brethren.

From Iconium came tidings of Jacobi and his family. They were all safe and well; Fabius was once more happily working with his father, and excited to be creating solid friendships among other Christians both Jew and Greek. Meanwhile Malchus had cut his hair very short, thus successfully provoking comments on his unusual ear, and was now making something of a name for himself in the market for dispensing the gospel as he dispensed his spices, while shrugging off all opposition. As for the three other young men baptised the same day, Jacobi reported that they were still with Malchus who kept a fatherly eye on them, encouraging them to be useful in the ekklesia and foster healthy friendships with those who would help and not hinder them. Malchus himself had beckoned over a market-place scribe to his busy stall, dictating a note while he worked, for Jacobi to include in his letter. He said only that in the evenings the four of them prayed together, and each morning joined in reciting a psalm Paul himself had recommended, taking it as their daily pledge:

Adonai, who shall ascend your mountain? Who shall stand on your sacred hill?
He who walks blamelessly, who works righteousness, and who speaks the truth in his heart!
He speaks no slander, does no evil to his neighbour, nor bears a grudge against him.
He despises the vile but honours God-fearers.
He swears to his own hurt and does not change!
He does not charge usury, or accept bribes against the innocent.
He that does these things shall never be moved!

"It helps," Malchus wrote succinctly.

Reading this, Paul reminded himself to keep praying for them all. Once the first glow of temperance had faded, none of them would find their pathway easy.

The last letter, redirected from Perga by way of Antiochia, Iconium, and Lystra, was addressed to Barnabas. He snapped the seal and read the contents with mixed feelings. Among other necessarily belated news of home, his sister Mari had proudly written that she was now the grandmother of the dearest baby girl in Jerusalem, born somewhat ahead of time and still quite ugly, but in God's mercy doing very well, and after all, Marcus had been an ugly baby too and just look how handsomely he had grown up. And since his darling wife was as beautiful as the rose she was named for, good looks would surely win out for their blessed little Charron.

Silently thanking God for this happy news, Barnabas folded his letter without comment. Yes, no doubt it was just as well Marcus had gone home when he did, after all. But he sensed it had left a raw spot in Paul, and he would chose a better time to tell him. Mari had said little of the state of affairs regarding the famine, and he suspected nothing much had changed. Knowing his sister, she would not trouble him with bad news while he was so far from being able to do anything about it.

At this moment Paul was already urging him to sharpen the pens and take his dictation, being very intent on writing to the Christians at Lystra. Of course Barnabas obliged at once. Not only did they both want to let the Lystran brethren know they had come safely to Derbe, but each of them felt concern for the tiny ekklesia, which they had left in such a hurry that no *Ruach* Gifts had yet been communicated and no elders appointed to oversee their welfare. Paul then and there decided they should write regularly to nurture the ekklesia in general and Eben in particular, and this he was to do faithfully during the whole time they were in Derbe. In every missive he urged them to visit the brethren at Iconium whenever possible, the two ekklesias being very blessed in being only some twenty miles apart.

All the good news in their letters, and the blessing of hospitality from the cheerful Gaius, was a very heartening start to their lengthy mission. To their great relief, and not a little amazement, in this place their untroubled way continued smoothly, and for a long time afterwards peaceful Derbe shone in their memory like a warm sun on a wintry day. No civic or religious controversies undermined the work. In both synagogue and market-place they found receptive listeners and a certain amount of interesting debate.

Some who were native Cappadocians had been influenced by one Apollonius of Tyana, a fellow countryman and wandering philosopher of the school of Pythagorus. His ascetic life was well respected, people claimed he could heal the sick, and he had some novel teachings about a beautiful god who was indifferent to worship but who might be reached by means of a disciplined intellect. Comparisons between Apollonius and the *Christos* preached by Paul and Barnabas were inevitable. Gaius and his wife Aletheia discussed it at length with their two boarders.

"He may well have healing abilities," Gaius admitted, "for faith-healing and wonder-working are not unusual. I have seen mere children charm themselves out of warts many a time! Not to speak of women cured with potions I concocted of mere bitters and coloured water. No, no, my dear," he said hastily to his wife's raised eyebrows, "I have never done that to you."

"I should hope not, Gaius! And don't tell me women are the only ones with such blind faith in your nostrums. Speaking of which, I must say, *I* never put much store in the god of Apollonius. Such a superior being, who only deigns to notice the mentally gifted of his creation, is a little too much like the man who invented him, in my humble and *un*intellectual opinion."

Like Gaius and his outspoken wife, who were the apostles' first converts, the people of Derbe were generous and compassionate people, scandalised by Paul's stoning, not at all repelled by his initially shocking appearance, and always solicitous for his well-being. Not that they needed to be concerned for long. The bracing air kept his fevers away, and under the solicitous care of the happy apothecary, the infections, bruises, and wounds soon healed – even the unsightly recurring rash faded and disappeared. The broken thumb, however, set crooked and ever afterwards made wielding a pen awkward, at times painful, especially in cold weather. Aside from this, Paul felt healthier than he had for a long time – apart from one agonising episode when he had two lower teeth, broken by the stoning, pulled out by one of the town's blacksmiths.

Finding work was more difficult than they expected, however, especially for Paul, who was at first limited by his injuries, and unable to do the continual arm-work and heavy lifting of a weaver. Flatly refusing to allow their new friends to provide their daily necessities apart from the roof over their heads, for a while the two scratched along, hiring themselves out in the market-place, Barnabas with his pens, and Paul with his leatherwork tools. The occupations of public scribe and self-taught shoe-mender were hardly lucrative, however, and Gaius and his wife would have been shocked to realise how many times their two houseguests went hungry from dawn till dusk, rather than draw on funds they were reserving to ensure completion of their long journey.

It was Aletheia who unwittingly changed things for the better when she complained about the state of several rush mats which her husband had promised to take to the market for mending, "Before Someone catches a toe in the holes and Breaks Her Neck!" as she said very pointedly to her husband. Jacobi, who had forgotten (yet again) to take them to be mended, gave Paul a mock-anguished look and a wink as meekly he offered to mend the mats with his own hands. Aletheia sniffed scornfully, turning away quickly to hide a chuckle at the very idea. Amused, Paul immediately offered to take this task upon himself, and so neatly did he accomplish it, despite the unfamiliarity of the material, that Aletheia was delighted and proudly showed off his handiwork to her friends.

"Oh, I do wish he would mend mine, then!" exclaimed her nearest neighbour. "They are a disgrace, and I am still waiting for three new ones from the rush-weavers at the river. They cost a little more, but I won't touch those loose flabby things you get cheaply in the bazaar, woven with somebody's elbows, by the look of it. Sheer false economy in my view, and meanwhile I'd rather get the old ones fixed. But the river folk are also the only ones who do a decent repair, so I'll have to wait, either way."

"Are they as busy as that?"

"Not busy so much as very far behind. They buried their father two weeks ago – *Zoi se mas!* – so they are sadly short-handed."

"*Zoi se mas!*" the others responded automatically. "May life be granted to us!"

"*Zoi se mas*, indeed," Aletheia said firmly. "And if you hearken to the man who mended *my* mat, you will find that there is a God in Heaven who *will* grant life – to all who hear His Son!"

On that note, off she ran to the market-place to tell Paul about the struggling family of rush-weavers. Before long he had sought out their spot by the river. There he found them working in the shade of curious little thatched shelters, curved like upturned coracles, which they seemed able to throw up in no time whenever they needed one. Introducing himself, his trade, and his need for work, he was pounced upon with gratitude.

"Fortuna smiles upon us!" exclaimed the haggard widow, her leathery face working with emotion. "My husband … such a good man … without him I have been at my wits end…"

"He was not a good man," a boy's voice contradicted roughly. "But he was a very good pig."

Instantly the woman turned and smacked him in the head. "Hold your thumbs! Do not speak ill of the dead unless you want worse to come upon us," she said harshly. "He was a good man at his trade, the best, no matter how many beatings he gave us."

"And what about the rest?" Defiantly the boy made an obscene gesture before sulkily tucking his thumbs under his fingers to keep away the dead man's spirit. "His fancy for yellow-haired Germani!"

Her grimy hand dealt him another hard whack. "Do you think I cared about his harlots at the *lupanaria*? Better he spent a few coppers on them than gave me more brats than we could keep. You were fed and clothed. What more do you want? When you are a man you may judge your father and not before." Here she looked pointedly at her new worker. "Ask this fellow! He is not a Galatian, but he will tell you the same, eh, Paulus?"

Paul shrugged. "The Romans have a saying, *De mortuis nil nisi bonum dicendum est* – of the dead speak nothing but good," he replied. "But I know of only one man to whom that could honestly be applied."

"My brother speaks no more than the truth," one of the younger girls said angrily, hobbling on a twisted foot to his side. So terrible was the defect that she must walk painfully on the turned, calloused ankle. She could not have been more than fourteen, but her unchildlike expression added years to her dark little face. "Our father made our lives a misery."

"Silence, *locusta*! At least you *have* a life to be made miserable. With that foot you should have been smothered at birth as the midwife advised. Now get back to work or taste the back of my hand."

"I don't care. What is life without truth? We were all afraid of him and now we are free."

"Free?" the woman replied bitterly, her stained hands never ceasing their work. "Who is ever free in this life?"

"I am," Paul replied quietly, and they stared at him.

"Oh, I do not think so," the woman said, controlling her scorn with an effort, remembering that she had just thanked the goddess Fortuna for finding her a desperately needed extra pair of hands. "Else why do you ask me for work?"

"I am free because I serve Lord Jeshua the *Christos,* the Son of God who dwells in Heaven, and I trust in him. He has the power to right wrongs, to heal ills, and to grant us life everlasting."

"*Free* because you *serve*?" an older boy said scathingly, taking a heavy bundle of reeds from the back of another child and throwing them on the ground. "That makes no sense."

"You trust in him?" the woman said incredulously at the same moment. "I have never heard of this *Christos,* still less any heavenly being who would concern himself with mortal woes, but who can trust the gods?"

Paul had gathered an armful of trampled reeds and was repairing gaps in the sparse thatch of her shelter. He smiled.

"I trust anyone who shows he can keep his promises," he answered, working busily.

"You say he can heal ills?" The girl sorting the fresh reeds at their feet looked up with weary eyes. "What offering does he demand for that? Something too costly for rush-weavers, doubtless."

"Only trust. And that is equally costly for everyone, I think."

"*Pah!* Then you go in circles!" the older boy cried dismissively from his own shelter, where he was lacing thick stems to a stick frame. "You must first trust him to heal! But how do you trust before you see it?"

"Oh, I have seen it, young man, many times. And I have been healed myself."

"Of what? Lovesickness?" the woman retorted sardonically, making a rare feint at humour. "Marriage is the best cure for that."

The whole family laughed loudly, all except the lame girl who did not look up, but twitched her muddy hem to cover her deformity. Paul squatted beside her.

"I was half mad, back then – and trusted only in myself," he said quietly to the downcast face. "And I was blind. My Lord reached out and touched me, and now I see."

"Oh, I would trust such a Lord," she said passionately. "If only he might be found in this place!"

"He is everywhere, child. He is not constrained by hills and rivers and man-made boundaries."

She looked around half fearfully. "Show me his shrine, then, and let me beseech him for myself!"

"His shrine is here, in my heart. And if you receive and obey him, he will be in yours. Only believe."

"What strange superstition is this?" the mother cried nervously, spitting on her fingers and flicking them three times right and left. "Gods do not dwell with men!"

Ignoring her, the girl blurted out, "Sir, I know nothing of your *Christos*! Show me, and help me to believe!"

"You permit?" Gently he drew out the foot half hidden by her ragged robe, holding the cruelly bent ankle in both hands. Closing his eyes, he drew a deep breath, released her and stood up. "In the name of Lord Jeshua the *Christos*, Son of the Living God," he said quietly, "henceforth you are free to walk without hindrance." He held out his hand, adding warmly, "Up you get!"

A look of astonishment flashed across her face as she clutched the proffered hand – and instantly she sprang up on two perfect feet, screaming with half terrified joy. Wincing, Paul put his fingers in his ears as startled shrieks erupted from the family around him. Gaping with shock, they stared at the ecstatic girl who was hopping and skipping, laughing wildly, and sobbing praise to Lord Jeshua and Paulus his servant. He smiled as silently he offered his own thanks. When they had all calmed down, they would hear what he had to tell them. They would listen with wide open ears to the gospel message. There would be plenty of time as they worked. Meanwhile, he went on thatching the roof.

From then on every day found him labouring away on the low grassy slope cutting and sorting reeds, learning from the hard-working children how to do tasks they had done since they were tiny, and adapting his old skills to the new occupation. Barnabas too soon adapted some of his old skills, continuing his work as a public *amanuensis* while sitting on a stack of the sweet-smelling mats, and promoting their sale to all who passed.

The rush-weaving family's understanding of the gospel grew apace with Paul's mat making abilities, and it was not long before the river bank where their violent father had drowned, was witness to the rebirth of the mother, three daughters, and two sons. The family's legacy of communicating through aggression would remain a habit to resist, but gradually it began to dwindle as a first response, as they learned more about living prayerfully and in Christian love.

So continued a very uplifting sojourn for the two missionaries, and they remained there contentedly and busily working among a small but growing community of new believers until waning summer days reminded them of how much time had passed.

Chapter Forty-four

PAUL and Barnabas were reluctant to leave Derbe, where life was so peaceful and fulfilling, but they could not live there for the rest of their lives. They had a mission to complete. Paul looked longingly at the misty blue and white Taurus Mountains which loomed so near the city. Just a hundred miles over those mountains, up and through the steep, rugged, ancient pass known as the Cilician Gates, was the Tarsus he knew so well! His gracious home town! There, apart from the severe treatment dispensed by his old synagogue, his life in the main had been quiet and comfortable, among people who knew and loved him – and there, still, hovered the chance that Deborah and Simeon may finally have returned. Perhaps even settled there with their family! Even after so long, Paul had not quite given up hope that he would find them some day.

The temptation to complete the round trip and return to Syrian Antioch via Tarsus was very strong – and the Cilician Gates would be passable for several weeks yet. But in the wake of their hasty departures, Paul and Barnabas had left behind them small groups of new disciples both Jew and Gentile, inexperienced and immature in knowledge. "Babes in Christ," Paul called them, wondering how they had managed on their own, anxious for their welfare, worried about persecution, concerned for their newborn faith. They could not be left without means to nurture, deepen, and sustain that faith. The only place they might hear God's holy word was in synagogue – and what help would that be to a Gentile who had not previously attended as either a proselyte or a God-fearer? In towns like Lystra, not to speak of various small villages, there was no synagogue. Even where there was one, Christians – whether Jew or Gentile – could scarcely count on a welcome.

Acutely aware of this, right from the start the apostles had done what they could to sustain their new brethren along the way. In every spare moment throughout their journey they had worked steadily with parchment and pens, sitting up late at night, copying until their hands ached, their eyes blurred, and the lamp sputtered so low that Barnabas grumbled he could hardly tell an *alpha* from an *epsilon*. The collection of parchments they had brought with them from Antioch Orontes – consisting of parables and sayings of the Master together with the small, closely-written codices of notes made by Loukanos and Marcus of various incidents concerning his life, death, and resurrection, as well as some personal recollections of Barnabas – all these were valuable records, to be copied with care and accuracy. And thanks to the hired scribes of old Phineas at Paphos, now the two apostles also had some notations of their own words, taken down during exhortation and preaching, not to speak of some of Paul's own notes and the journal Barnabas was keeping so faithfully. All of these would help the new brethren.

It did not matter that few could read and fewer could write. The documents would be read in the ears of each community even if a public scribe must be paid to do so, and they would be memorised, shared, copied and referred to as each new ekklesia rehearsed the factual accounts originally presented by the apostles, reminded themselves of what had been done for them, and refreshed the hope of the gospel which was within them.

The pressing need to support the oral accounts with the written had driven the two apostles on through cold, discouragement and fatigue, and in most places they had been able to present copies of their records on parchment to the new ekklesias. Lystra, so hastily left, was an exception. They had only been part way through the task, still scraping together the funds to buy enough materials to complete it. Now, with his badly healed thumb, Paul struggled to write for more than a half hour without agonising cramp, and many a blot and smudge marred his work. Forcing himself to write left-handed, after much effort he eventually managed to make his letters readable, as long as he wrote them large enough. It sufficed for Hebrew, which was written from right to left, but these copies must be made in Greek ... and writing from left to right he continually smudged what he had just so laboriously scrawled. When he began to shake with frustration, Barnabas intervened.

"Stop that for now, and help me instead, will you? If you dictate I will get on faster."

Hearing Paul dictating, the helpful Gaius their host soon discovered their occupation, and insisted on doing his part. Two men could take dictation as fast as one, he said, and the result was twin copies produced simultaneously and with greater accuracy than a piecemeal approach. The apostles were relieved and thankful. Gaius being as quick and neat as Barnabas, the method worked so well that parchments for both Lystra and Derbe were completed in another couple of weeks – and then they could delay no longer. Once the sailing season closed with the approach of winter, lonely roads would become almost impossibly dangerous to travel, wild rivers would roar in torrents through the mountains – and they still had many hundreds of miles to traverse before they reached the deep dark perils of the Great Sea.

Hard as it was, the two friends, praying for strength and courage to face any more troubles that might come upon them, resolved to steadfastly set their faces away from the haven which was Derbe, back towards the places which had used them so badly.

Before they left this city, and in every place to which they returned, they must appoint overseers among the believers, fasting and praying with them, ordaining them in a simple ceremony of dedication, commending them to the care of Lord Jeshua in heaven. Laying their hands on the new elders and other selected disciples, the apostles would pass on specific Gifts, conferring upon a core group in every ekklesia various abilities most suited to each community's situation; for a witness to the world, for the well-being of their community, and for the furtherance of the gospel. Whether it was a Gift of wisdom, of understanding scripture, of an aptitude to teach, to administrate, or to lead others, to speak or translate a foreign language, or to heal the sick, every individual's Gift was given for the one purpose – to authoritatively communicate the blessings of the gospel. These extraordinary Gifts – valuable skills which they had not learned and miraculous abilities no man could ever learn – demonstrated to all men that an Almighty God was working among ordinary people for their ultimate good, and for the glory of His name.

The newly bestowed abilities of these converts would have a profound effect on the ekklesias and outsiders who observed their manner of living. Who could not be amazed when unschooled men overnight became quick of understanding? When timid women became fearless in communicating their faith? When an unlettered disciple interpreted the most difficult dialect, and worked alongside another who could speak it with ease? When simple people grasped profound lessons and encouraged each other to live in joyful service before a God of Mercy, through a High Priest ministering in love?

The apostles knew very well that the wonder of miracles would wear off, just as they had in the days of Israel's wilderness wanderings. When life and its problems still had to be faced, even daily miracles could soon be taken for granted. But the Gifts were the fulfilment of a prophecy of God and the specific promise of Lord Jeshua himself ... giving new Christians the best possible start and valuable support in their isolated situation amid a huge pagan world. The rest was up to each man, each woman, each family, each community.

And so it was in this way that the apostles would confirm the faith of the disciples of the Christ, as they retraced their steps.

Emotionally they farewelled the staunch band of believers in the haven of Derbe with heartening words of exhortation, giving a final charge to the newly appointed elder Gaius and his fellow pastors to build up the ekklesia and do all they could to keep their faith strong. Sad as the apostles were to leave, they rejoiced to see that the precious Gifts they had passed on, though communicated only to a select number, had been welcomed by the whole ekklesia as if entrusted to them all – as in a way, they had. Every member was in awe, deeply touched and humbled by the honour of the blessing in their midst, and greatly uplifted in spirit. The apostles were satisfied. Gaius with his Gift of preaching would, along with others, continue to spread the good news of the Kingdom of God and the name of Jeshua the Christ; his Aletheia would work at his side using her Gift of languages.

Among the other Gifts given at Derbe was that of encouragement. Nobody was more amazed than the young woman who was chosen to receive it. Once, the cruel epithet 'locust' had been flung at her because of her clumsily hopping gait. Now, sister Locusta, being cured of her infirmity, had adopted the name with pride, taking every opportunity to speak of the healing power of Lord Jeshua. Now she – a lowly rush weaver! – would be able to help others, to communicate kindly and effectively with people of all ages and social standing, to uphold weary hands, to strengthen feeble knees, to cheer sad hearts, and – most difficult of tasks for any mortal – to speak quiet, sweet reason to angry and bitter souls and brighten their vision of things eternal. Even so, as she told Paul and Barnabas with tears in her eyes, even so had they done for her!

Surrounded by sad faces and full hearts the apostles embraced all their fellow Christians for the last time. They did so with confidence however, knowing they had fully accomplished their work in this place, sure of the faith living in those they must leave behind. Now they set out for Lystra.

This they reached with speed, if not exactly with ease, for a brother who was a cameleer had managed to talk them into a place in a friend's west-bound caravan, and soon afterwards, somewhat to their discomfiture the apostles found themselves mounted on an alarmingly tall pair of dark, shaggy-haired camels of a rather moth-eaten appearance. Swaying along the road, at the dusty end of a string of ten heavily loaded beasts with a disconcerting tendency to kick, spit, and lunge at each other's rear ends with bared yellow teeth, the two friends were grateful that the disturbingly small wooden nose pegs, by means of which the camels were roped together nostril to tail, did at least prevent them from turning around to bite a piece out of their riders.

Imitating the imperturbable cameleers up ahead, the two friends found their cloth saddles were best ridden with one leg slung over the front of the animal's hump, but neither of them was much of a rider and it was not an enjoyable experience – especially during mounting and dismounting, when it seemed they must surely pitch forward and break their noses on their animals' heads. Both men deeply mistrusted their gargling, supercilious steeds; their height made Paul nervous, and their gait turned Barnabas queasy. These, however, were minor inconveniences when compared to the speed and safety of a journey which they could now complete in a matter of only a few days instead of a week.

Passing through villages where they had struggled to make themselves understood, they once more received hospitality from one or two of the same folk who had given them shelter on the outward tramp. After a long hot day on the road, the cameleers were not inclined to weary themselves with playing at interpreter, and so there was little the apostles could profitably exchange in the way of conversation, but they left behind much goodwill.

Having staggered safely off their camels in Lystra, they farewelled the obliging head cameleer very thankfully and – once they were sure they *could* walk again – went to seek their friends. It was a very glad, if quiet, reunion they had with a somewhat taller Eben – like Paul he would always remain slight. He was almost awed by the manuscripts they had prepared, neatly folded and stitched for convenience into codices. Taking the precious records entrusted to him, he promised to care for them faithfully, read and share them regularly and use them wisely. The boy had grown in more significant ways than his height, for his clear grey eyes were darkened with responsibility. In the last few months, he had suddenly become the man of the house. Sorrow still shadowed his mother Eunice's face for the handsome, passionate Greek she had married; for the loss of all he had been, and all he had vainly promised to be, and for the tragic way he had died – crushed by a toppling *caryatid* on a construction site in Laodicea.

Tactfully enquiring of grandmother Lois in private, Barnabas was able to reassure Paul that the tempestuous Kyros had nevertheless made good provision for his small family and they would not face hardship. Sparing Paul's paternal concerns for Eben, he did not mention that Lois was anxious for her grandson's health. Since the sad news had come, the boy had begun suffering from stomach cramps. Well, grief took people in different ways, and no doubt it would pass. He and Paul would pray for the lad in any case.

Paul needed no reminders to pray for Eben. Even he had been surprised when moved by the Holy Spirit to ordain the youth as an ekklesial shepherd, and bestow him with the Gift of prophecy – an ability to communicate the deep truths of God. These were huge responsibilities for such a young man, but since the Lord himself had directed the choice it could be no mistake. Together with older men Eben would have to fulfil his portion, guiding and educating others to understand divine matters which did not come naturally to anyone. Yes, he would need their prayers – they all would, but Paul would pray in particular that the boy's strength and courage would not fail.

A more cheerful reunion was made with the other believers, including Julius Petronius, who had since been baptized and was now working as a porter in the market-place where once he had begged. Even the flighty maid Felicitas professed extravagant delight to see them, and just as soon as Eben was comfortably within earshot, confided to them in a penetrating whisper, that she was *considering* turning Christian herself. Eben had told her that Christian men must treat their wives with respect, since they believed before God they were equally important. Fancy that! "Praise God!" she added piously, modestly dropping her glittering blue-green eyes and shooting Eben a calculating look from under her lashes. She turned away with a simper, wondering how much Eben's father had really left him.

An exhausting week later, fatigued with unceasing labours in speaking and visiting, for the time was short, Paul and Barnabas had fulfilled their mission. Having ordained other pastors, one of whom was an astonished Julius Petronius to whom they also gave the Gift of exhortation, they passed on several other spiritual Gifts, mostly to the sisters who formed the bulk of the small ekklesia – and then they took to the road again, urging them all to be strong and of a good courage. Refusing to farewell them at the city gate, Eben accompanied them as far as the first milestone, then embraced them fiercely.

"Go with God, my friends, my brothers!" he cried after them, swallowing desperately as he raised his hand. Unable to restrain their emotion, the two waved back and resolutely walked on, though water stood in their eyes. A moment later and Paul's tears overflowed, spilling unchecked into his beard. Pray God the boy would not faint under the burden of responsibility which was now on his slender shoulders! Suddenly they heard flying footsteps crunching on the road, and as they turned, the young man impetuously flew into Paul's arms.

"Paul! Paul!" he wept. "I have no earthly father now but you, who have fathered me in Christ! You won't forget me?"

"God be with you, young man," Paul said huskily. "I shall always think of you as my son in the faith. And I will never forget you."

Along the highway they walked steadily towards Iconium, preoccupied, saying little for a long while. Mercifully they travelled without any incident more dramatic than an ugly fight between two rogue camels, which had inconsiderately chosen to wage their vicious battle outside a cave in which the friends had been sheltering from a sticky thunderstorm. It was the same cave which had sheltered them from a springtime downpour on their dismal flight from Iconium nearly six months before. Fortunately its entry was too low to admit warring camels, and the hideous noise eventually died away to low groans. By then the fierce lightning which had rent the dark sky was also dying away, until it was no more than a fine silver crazing intermittently etched on grey, grumbling clouds.

Once the heavy rain had finally ceased, the two men ventured to peer outside, where lay a panting, tattered, ancient, staring-eyed creature, steaming in the newly-emerged sun, expiring from a mighty kick to its skull, and bleeding from a score of savage bites. Much as they disliked camels, it was a miserable sight to see. There was nothing they could do to put the beast out of its misery, so pouring a little water over its horribly gasping muzzle, they strode off quickly down the road.

Paul looked sick. "I hate nature!" he said forcefully, with a shiver. "Oh, don't look so shocked, I know it is the Eternal's handiwork and beautiful in its time. But this kind of thing – the savagery of it, the cruelty and suffering, the pointlessness, the ugliness – I hate it! Bring on the time when the lion will lie down with the lamb, I say! Restore Eden, Oh Sovereign God on High, where peace and glory and love will reign, and not teeth and claws and blood!"

His passionate outburst over, he stalked ahead, his eyes burning, telling himself he was a fool to feel so much over a disgusting, ferocious old camel. But felled like this it was so helpless, he could not help but see it with pity. Surely this was the world without the enlightenment of the gospel!

Behind him Barnabas murmured, "Restore Eden, indeed, we pray, Great God!" and ran to catch up. "Come on, Paul, don't mope. Let's sing instead. How long is it since we sang our heads off with nobody to care how bad we sound?"

Paul recovered himself with an effort. "Ah, dear old Joseph Barnabas, my ever-faithful, ever-comforting friend and brother! Whatever would I do without you? You start."

At once Barnabas opened his mouth and blared, "*O foolish Galatea, who holds you in thrall, that mine is no longer –*"

"Stop! Stop!" Paul groaned. "A psalm of Zion, please!"

Barnabas obliged very gladly. He had made his best friend smile, at least.

Chapter Forty-five

SOON rousing hymns of praise and songs of affirmation echoed through the landscape. Contrary to Barnabas's self-deprecating words, both of them were very fair singers, and with the welcome change of mood carrying them along the last hours of their journey, they reached Iconium that same evening in good spirits, despite a nasty skirmish with a pack of dogs which set upon them as they passed the last farm. The two men laid about them with their staffs until they slunk off, and the only damage done was when Paul – flailing with more energy than accuracy – gave his friend an accidental crack across the shins. Barnabas instantly forgave him, though – aggressive dogs were a constant menace as they travelled, and counter-attacks had to be fast and fierce. An unlucky whack was a small price to pay, far preferable to being bitten by an animal which may or may not give them hydrophobia. No doubt it was better to be slightly maimed than find out the hard way whether or not the Lord's promise concerning *snake*-bites extended to *dog*-bites … so Barnabas said kindly to his very apologetic friend. Nevertheless he took care to engage in some exaggerated limping whenever Paul looked his way, which entertained them both.

Dusk was falling as they entered the city. Immediately they sought out Malchus, and word of their arrival quickly spread. The next week was spent in encouraging and reassuring the ekklesia, and passing on the latest news of their brethren and sisters in Lystra and Derbe. It was a wonderful time of reunion with all the men, women and youngsters who had been part of their lives and shared their trials.

The opposition which had previously fermented in the city had settled down. With time the municipal officials had grasped that the *Christianoi* were not troublemakers but law-abiding citizens. Losing interest in the conflict they advised the resentful leaders of the Jewish community to beware of further disturbing the city with their religious schisms. The patience and sufferance of the Christians under trial had thus brought them peace, for the time being.

At the welcoming house of Jacobi and Elishabet, Fabius told them proudly he was now betrothed to the sweet-natured Anais who had once seemed so far out of his reach. The only fly in the ointment was young Tomas. "He's not speaking to me just yet," he said laughingly. "Apparently my Anais was supposed to be *his* bride."

Malchus had moved from his flimsy market stall into a small shop in which he and Ezra worked together. On one side Malchus sold his spices and on the other Ezra used them to great effect, cooking delicious food over a range of small braziers on the low stone counter, all the while diverting onlookers with entertaining instructions about what he was doing, how, and why. The young man's former quiet misery and air of defeat were nowhere in evidence. Now his amusing remarks enticed people to listen and his skills encouraged them to watch and learn. At the same time, clouds of aromatic steam wafted from the pots, tempting them to buy and eat, before making their purchases from Malchus (who dispensed every spice with a good pinch of the gospel) that they might attempt the dishes themselves at home. Of course, Malchus and Ezra cautioned their customers to use only meat from

Jacobi and Son, since being slaughtered according to Jewish law, it was never tough! So it was that the combined skills of the former misfits made the place an attraction to market-goers, enjoyed by Jews and non Jews alike. Sampling the tasty dishes, Paul and Barnabas congratulated the pair on this successful venture. But it was not so much the business they referred to, as its outcome, for Ezra confessed that he had relapsed more than once, but with the prayerful help of the others, ever since Malchus had come up with the brilliant idea of the cookshop he had stayed fully sober.

"I could not have done it without my brothers," Ezra told them with emotion. "They have been the voice and the hands of Christ to me, you see? I was a worthless misfit, we all were, but we thought about it a lot after you left, and realised that this is no longer how we should see ourselves. Malchus was talking to me about rare spices one day and he said that *you can tell the value of something by how much someone is prepared to pay for it.* Then it struck me – the Eternal God valued His creation so much He was prepared to pay the price of giving His only Son. And Lord Jeshua valued *us* so highly he was prepared to pay the ultimate price of his own life – yes, for we misfits! That being so, we have no right to loathe ourselves or say he made a mistake – or surely we make him either a fool or a liar. We are sinners, yes! But we are sinners who are loved! And he came to save sinners – so we are no longer misfits, but perfect fits."

"I like that," Paul responded quietly, as with feeling he and Barnabas in turn embraced the earnest young man. "I like that very much."

As for Jonas and Ariel, they too had formed an alliance, rather unusual in regard to their work, for burly Jonas was a woodcutter, and lithe Ariel a tesselator. The one cleared land and managed woodlots, felling trees, chopping, splitting, and sawing, preparing wood for fuel and building materials. The other painstakingly created beautiful mosaic decorations for houses and gardens of the rich. A contrast of supplying basic needs as opposed to artistic luxuries, the two occupations did not appear to be compatible, but they had made them so, as Ariel explained.

"I had to remove myself from working long hours in houses ruled primarily by the indulgence of pleasures and a craving for novelty," he said matter-of-factly. "These days I make only portable pieces, for which Jonas supplies frames and backing boards. At first I was not sure they would sell, but the small ones in particular have proved popular. A man who might not otherwise afford a tesselated floor or wall can buy one or two of my creations and have them plastered in or hung up anywhere he pleases, even set in furniture. Now I am also getting commissions for work made to order, which is quite lucrative. Jonas had the idea of my using one end of his barn for a workshop, we recommend each other's business to our customers, and it has worked very well."

With the muscle of one and artistry of the other they had achieved a good working partnership, yet the two made it clear it was primarily one of moral and spiritual support rather than of business.

"We keep each other honest," Jonas told the apostles frankly when Malchus took them to visit the barn on the edge of the woodland. "And if need be, we each call on the other to accompany us anywhere we know there may be temptations, since ours are mutually exclusive. You once told us that our bias to sin is part of man's natural, self-serving instinct to survive in this life – but that Christ asks us to develop against nature, a God-serving instinct to survive *beyond* it. We remind each other of this, and it helps."

"And we need that help, each one of us." Malchus gave a decided nod. "No man finds it easy to sacrifice his instincts."

Jonas agreed. "Yet, a change of habits makes a surprising difference to one's thinking, if only one finds better habits to adopt – even as you once told us, brother Paul. For my part, it has taught me to appreciate another kind of beauty than the obvious – though it is still true, just as Malchus says, that it is hard to sacrifice our instincts."

"Sacrifice is a profound subject," Ariel said soberly. "Especially the sacrifice Christ made for us, and those we are required to make for him. Feeding idols food and drink and calling that sacrifice as I did in my pagan days is laughable in comparison! Jonas and I have often discussed what it really means, and how King David of old said, *I will not offer to Adonai God that which costs me nothing!* It occurred to us that anyone might die a swift death for another in a sudden, heady moment of self-sacrifice – a mother for her child, a soldier for his king, even a man for his friend, or his wife – but enduring years of a daily death of many small things is quite another thing, intolerably harder. Ten thousand thousands of relentless, slow mosquito bites compared to one quick punch, you might say! And yet our Master suffered both. If he did this for nearly thirty-four years, for *our* sake, then how else can we respond but to give him all we can?"

"The parallel with mosquito bites is one we can understand all too well," Barnabas said wearily, having endured a sleepless and stuffy night with several trapped under the blanket he had pulled over his head in order to keep them out.

Paul nodded thoughtfully. "A very striking word picture, my brothers. On the one hand a brave man who dares to die, perhaps on impulse, to save a life he values above his own ... and on the other our Saviour, sacrificing his own impulses, deliberately and slowly moving towards an excruciating death, that he might save the lives of countless unknowns. The one is noble, but the other is utterly sublime and beyond human comprehension. If that does not impress us with the value Lord Jeshua has placed on our salvation, nothing will."

"And so here we are today, by his grace," Malchus said cheerfully. "All of us men who were spiritually down in the gutter, men whom most devout Jews – and certainly most Pharisees, begging your pardon, Paul – would probably want to tread down even further."

Paul laughed. "As a former Sadducee, don't you think you're a little biased about Pharisees? We are gentle in comparison, have you forgotten? My father was also a Pharisee, and he taught me that no one can help up another with a clenched fist, only with an extended hand."

"I stand corrected," Malchus grinned. "Now speaking of hands, poor old Ezra will be over-run if I don't get back to the shop, so you must excuse me and find your own way home. Jonas and Ariel will show you more of what they do here."

With a wave, Malchus disappeared, while Jonas took Barnabas and Paul through the wood-lot, describing with enthusiasm how he managed his section of the forest so it would sustain his occupation for many years. With his previous background in olive-growing and viticulture, Barnabas was a particularly appreciative listener, and even Paul found it more interesting than he had expected. Back in the barn, he turned to Ariel with a smile. "Well, I have learned a few things today! Perhaps you and Jonas also learn from each other practically as well as spiritually?"

Indeed they did. The two explained that from time to time they would trade skills – Ariel had taught Jonas how to make the special mortar he used, and Jonas in his turn had shown him how to whittle, by way of variety. To the surprise of them both, Ariel had soon outstripped his instructor and now his favourite recreation was making toys with odd bits of wood scavenged from the floor of the barn.

"I want to try putting wheels on them, next. Children love to pull things along on a string, you see," he told them. "People do like them just as they are, though, and they're easy to sell." He shook his head when Barnabas suggested that perhaps it might overtake his existing business.

"I am not going to become a toymaker," he said firmly. "Otherwise it would no longer be an idle pleasure which aids my meditations, but a chore. Not that I have much time for it in daylight hours – Jonas sees to that, for whenever I have a lull in my work, he insists I help him with his."

Ariel grinned through the beard he had chosen to grow. It was scruffy and untrimmed, and the apostles guessed rightly that this too was a choice, a discipline undertaken to curb vanity and old habits of self-absorption and attention-seeking.

"I'm proud to say I can handle the other end of a large saw these days, though I do *not* appreciate it when this black-hearted brother here makes me stand in the pit to be showered with sawdust. But I am growing a nice set of callouses, and it tires me enough to sleep soundly." Almost absently he picked up a forked lump covered in rough bark, turning it this way and that, tossing it thoughtfully in his palm. "There's a nice plump hare in here, you know, twitching his ears. I must let him out."

Jonas rolled his eyes. "Don't mind him. This barn is full of creatures 'waiting to be let out' of his scroungings!"

Paul wondered briefly whether the man who had carved Danya's camel had looked at his work the same way. Or maybe he had just set out to carve yet another camel. He looked at a rough, low table of neatly arranged animals in a corner of the barn which was floored with woodshavings and sawdust. "Two by two?" he asked with interest.

"That's right, and see, here's the ark. A bit odd-looking, definitely unseaworthy, I'm sure, but the youngsters won't mind. Finished just in time, too. Get the rope up, Jonas!"

As Jonas roped off the corner, a growing chatter of excitement came up the path and into the barn ran a collection of many small children.

Pouncing on Ariel they vied for his attention as they dragged him to the corner and scrambled all over him.

"Get down, you pests!" he said severely. "You're strangling me! If you are going to be such nuisances there will be no story – and no songs!"

A burst of laughter greeted this wholly insincere railing, as the mothers and grandmothers who had brought them appeared in the doorway, and greeted him affectionately.

"Dear Ariel, you are such a life-saver," said one tired looking sister thankfully, putting down the small girl in her arms. "Go to Uncle Ariel, Ephrona, there's a good girl, and give your poor mother some peace." With a giggle the child toddled over, and giving him a smacking kiss, crawled into Ariel's lap and began sucking her thumb, her free hand toying with his light beard, and her large eyes looking up at him expectantly.

Smoothing the untidy black curls, Ariel met Paul's eyes. "You gave me good advice, my brother," he said with a quiet smile, as he snuggled the small creature to a more comfortable position in his arms. "I keep a reminder close by. I had Malchus write it for me, so I can see it every day – not that I know letters, but I know what it says, and that's all that matters."

He nodded to a board hung on the wall behind him, which Paul now noticed for the first time. On it was chalked a passage from the psalms: *God sets the solitary in families, He brings out those who are bound with chains ... it is only the rebellious who dwell in a dry land.*

The thumb was removed with a slurp. "Story!" The thumb was re-inserted.

"Patience, young lady. Now, is everyone sitting quietly? Today's story is about Noah's Ark ..."

The barn serving as a workshop in all weathers, the sheltered back wall was boarded only half way up for the sake of light and air, and against it most of the women now settled themselves to listen as expectantly as the children, occupying themselves with handwork taken from their capacious baskets. Meanwhile, comfortably seated on logs outside the wide doorway, the visiting apostles conversed quietly with the rest, but inside the barn an elderly sister lingered at the far end to discuss firewood with the ferociously bearded Jonas, who was sharpening his axe with a whetstone. Beside them hovered Ephrona's mother, flushed and ill at ease.

"That poor girl, so young, so pretty, so sad." One of the grandmothers sentimentally shook her head. "Widowed with four children, all such a handful. She must miss her husband so much."

"Not so much that you'd notice," another said sharply, "considering he beat her black and blue most days. He nearly killed her the day of her baptism, didn't you *know*? Said the old gods knew their place, and this Christ was too demanding. He positively forbade her to turn Christian and said the only person she had to serve was her husband."

"She was a good and faithful wife to that monster, nevertheless," said a brisk middle-aged sister, breaking off as some noisy youthful protests reached their ears. "Oh dear, is that my Josiah who is making a nuisance of himself in there? He knows ducking under the rope is strictly forbidden! All those sharp tools – and he upset a whole tray of sorted *tesserae* once – Ah! It's all right, brother Ariel has dealt with him nicely, bless him."

"I rejoice to see Ariel so well loved, sisters," Paul said sincerely. "Accepting the gospel fractures many old relationships and our ekklesias are full of such disconnected people. Mere words are scant consolation for solitary souls. Including them wholeheartedly in our lives, finding their talents, and making them feel *needed* is vital to their survival, and it seems that you recognise this – for which I thank and commend you most heartily."

Barnabas agreed. "I like his reminder, *God sets the solitary in families*," he commented thoughtfully, "but unless those families truly embrace them, being with others can feel lonelier than ever. Nobody wants to be floating around merely as the subject of other people's good works."

"True, brother Barnabas," said the first sister. "You have taught us the ekklesia is all one family in Christ. A strange one at times, and like any family its members are not always who we might choose to love as brothers and sisters. But Christ has chosen them, and therefore who are we to dismiss any as not worth our affection?"

"Speaking of affection ..." murmured the mother of the recalcitrant Josiah who was still keeping an eye on him from a distance. She nodded happily towards the far end of the barn, where a scarlet-faced Jonas was scrabbling for several tools he had unaccountably dropped. She turned to Paul and Barnabas with an air of triumph. "That will be a match very soon, if all our prayers are answered," she laughed with satisfaction. "Poor brother Jonas is smitten with her, while she can hardly speak to him without trembling, she is so frightened. Look how she hangs back in there, letting the others do all the talking."

Barnabas protested at once. "Jonas is a brawny fellow, but surely he is not violent!"

"Oh, she's not frightened of *him*," Josiah's mother replied thoughtlessly, "only of herself. He has what we women call animal attr– ouch!" A sharp feminine elbow in her ribs recalled her to propriety and she coughed. "I beg your pardon, brothers. Never mind what we call it, but we know it when we feel it."

Just then Ephrona's mother and her elderly friend came out, and the tantalising conversation was dropped. Josiah's mother being roundly scolded by her friends later that day, she was somewhat ashamed of what she had let slip, but Paul went away with a very light heart, and that night he and Barnabas rejoiced together in prayer. Many people in Iconium had been convinced of the power of the gospel through the miracles which they had seen with their eyes, but to the apostles, the greatest proof of its power was in the miracles working in the unseen recesses of people's hearts.

Paul was under no illusion that a change of life was ever more permanent than a person's next decision, and he prayed fervently that the good work begun, particularly in the lives of these formerly troubled men, would continue. Though as individuals people might be very much in earnest, the ekklesia as a body was still very young, and all was not sweetness and light. As a hybrid body of Jews and Gentiles born out of much debate and even acrimonious conflict, it retained some seeds of division which might yet bear bitter fruit if not wisely handled. Even now Paul saw warning signs that some of the Jewish members saw the Gentile converts as somehow 'less' than themselves, particularly those who had not first been proselytes to Judaism … as if they were apprentices who had shirked their full period of indenture and should not expect to be given the same respect as qualified men. He sighed. Experiences in both Syrian Antioch and Jerusalem had made him aware that there was a disturbing tendency among Jewish Christians to assume pre-eminence in ekklesial affairs.

For the moment, however, he and Barnabas had done all they could. They could not be perpetual nursemaids to everyone. The Way of the Nazarene, now increasingly known as Christianity, was not yet a generation old. There were no weighty centuries of custom and learning and accepted practice to cushion new converts and nurture them to maturity. Each believer's faith must stand alone, for all they were connected to the one hope. Paul was not a sentimental man, but for a moment he had a fleeting image of children learning ball games in the street, each one trustfully and clumsily attempting to imitate older playmates – who hardly knowing themselves what to do, were also learning as they went along. Thankfully the new ekklesias did not need to learn like this – the hard way. Among such raw collections of new recruits for the Kingdom of God, the *Ruach* Gifts made up for acquired wisdom – giving certainty, guidance, knowledge, comfort, practical help and spiritual nurturing – if all members only worked together with singleness of purpose.

Therefore, the ineffable impulse of the Holy Spirit having directed their choice of elders, and having entrusted various Gifts to men and women to support the still-tender young ekklesia in its isolation, Paul and Barnabas knew they must now trust to Lord Jeshua to complete his work in each individual brother and sister.

Chapter Forty-six

IT was time to leave. After fasting and prayer, the new elders had been ordained – Jacobi and Malchus among them – and presented to the brethren as willing servants. The last exhortations to courage and faithfulness had been given, and received a heartfelt "Amen!" Paul patched their thick travelling cloaks and stout sandals yet again and Barnabas packed their meagre belongings and precious collection of writings. Having managed to attach themselves to a group of men and boys taking a caravan of pack mules to sell at Antiochia, now they set out to meet them at the khan by the city gate, accompanied by half the ekklesia.

As they passed the main synagogue Paul felt a pang of regret. In another two weeks was the First of *Tishri*, when the ram's horn *shofar* would sound from this place to mark the Feast of Trumpets, but he and Barnabas would not be accepted inside to celebrate it, should they stay. The exclusion felt all the more poignant for the fact that they were all Jews together, far from the Homeland. If only they were not so stubborn, so afraid of losing what they had clung to over the centuries!

Paul loved the words of Moses, of the Prophets, the inspired words of Israel's historians, wisdom writers and poets. He loved to hear them read reverently in synagogue. He loved to hear the blessings, give the responses, sing the hymns of praise. Yet few synagogues now would admit him. In vain had he explained to the elders that Moses and the Prophets were very far from being irrelevant to Christians; it was only that the Son of God who fulfilled their words, must take precedence.

To himself, the services, the prayers, the traditions, were not utterly without value merely because now he had a greater understanding of their significance. He rejoiced in worshipping God with his fellow Jews, it hurt him to be estranged from them, and all this conflict was so unnecessary.

"Paul?" Barnabas shouted from the head of the little crowd. "Come on, Paul! Keep up."

Suppressing a sigh, Paul came back to reality and was about to hurry on when the portly Chazzan stuck his head out of the porch.

"*Paulus Christianus?*" he demanded abruptly.

Paul braced himself. "Yes?"

The man beckoned him urgently up the steps, speaking to him from behind a pillar.

"Letters just arrived for you. Take them! Lucky I caught your name! Don't tell anyone who passed them on, will you? It would be more than my place is worth. I'm supposed to lose any which come here for Christians."

Paul looked at him properly. "Thank you," he said slowly. "God reward you, my kinsman."

"Ha, kinsmen, I suppose we are, both being Jews. I heard you can trace your lineage back through the tribe of Benjamin. Lucky you. Very pure bloodline mine too, as it happens, for the last five generations, anyhow. You've created something of a monster here, I suppose you know that."

"You do not seem to be too afraid of it."

"I don't know, really," The rubicund man scratched his plump cheek thoughtfully. "See, I'm nothing important around here. People don't even see me half the time. Just the man who lights the lamps, sweeps the steps, prepares the books and so on – just the before-and-after side of the services."

He shrugged. "Don't misunderstand me, I'm proud of my job. I think it's a worthy one. But as I say, I'm almost invisible, do you see? Oh! Ha, ha, I think I made a joke. Was it a good one? My wife says I have no sense of humour."

Paul smiled. "Not bad, anyway."

"Oh dear – there's your friend shouting to you again, you'd better hurry, but I'll just finish what I was saying, very quickly – nobody really stops to listen much these days. What I meant was, a man nobody sees, sees everything nobody else sees. Do you see? And what I see in here, and what I saw and heard when you were here before – that plot to silence you, permanently – I was very unhappy about. Very. And regardless of this queer business of involving Gentiles in Jewish matters without due process and proper rituals and so forth, I see changes in people's lives that the Law could not effect. So much so that I am disturbed."

"Good man," Paul said wonderingly. "You must seek out Jacobi and Fabius the butchers, also talk to Malchus the spice merchant. They very well understand such disturbance of mind and will help you. Meanwhile, I deeply regret, I must hurry away."

The Chazzan clutched his arm. "Will you write to me? You see that I can read! You must send letters to me here, but after Passover next year I will be in Rome. My brothers are there, and an uncle has left me a living which I am now minded to take up."

"Rome!"

Paul had never forgotten that he was to declare the name of Christ *'before Gentiles, and kings, and the sons of Israel!'* He had held aloft the light of the gospel, bearing the torch high, but surely, he had only just begun! Before what royalty might he yet be brought to witness? Another Herod? Even a Caesar?!

He looked at the Chazzan with a spark of excitement in his eyes. "Then perhaps one day we may meet again! I may yet have a destiny in that place."

"Yes, yes, may it be so indeed, whatever God requires of you, but you will write to me here? You promise me?"

"I promise, friend. Thank you for our letters, thank you!"

Paul was now being sought ever more clamorously by his concerned friends. A few were already running back to fetch him, and his exchange with the Chazzan could not be prolonged. He turned. "Quickly, what is your name?"

"Herodion – unfortunate, isn't it, but blame my ancestors. My friends call me Japheth, you know, as in the invisible one everyone knows *was* in the ark, but that's all. Goodbye! Go with God!"

"And you, Japheth Herodion! I will pray for you!"

And Paul allowed himself to be dragged away.

An hour later the city gates and all the inevitably painful last words and tearful embraces were behind them, and once more Paul and Barnabas were tramping the Via Sebaste.

Though they could not help feeling grieved by the parting, both were deeply thankful for the letters so hastily stuffed into Paul's hand at the synagogue, for they had torn them open at once and shared their good tidings with the brethren at the gate, even before the muleteers had finished sorting out the best order in which to rope their animals according to which were most (or least) likely to bite or kick each other.

Titus had written from Antioch Orontes, Loukanos from Damascus, and their message was the same – *Praise the Eternal, the King of the World, the Master of the Universe! – for the Judaean famine is waning and once more may He bring forth bread from the earth!*

Desperately needed rain had fallen at last, and everywhere men had sown the dessicated country with preciously hoarded seeds, praying with tears to the Eternal that it would not be in vain. The rain had held. The first green shoots were now flushing the hills with promise of vital crops, easing the twin grip of famine and fear. Slowly the disciples in Jerusalem and further afield were emerging from the dark shadows of hard times.

Though this news was hardly fresh by the time it came to hand it was wonderful to hear, going some way towards alleviating the sadness of so many goodbyes and giving a joyful start to the next gruelling section of the road. Now they could march along with the muleteers and their animals with an extra length to their stride, and Paul – always a fast walker – did so quite literally, until even long-legged Barnabas had to trot at intervals to catch him up, while the ragged free-ranging urchins in the group scampered alongside, laughing at both of them for their uneven partnership.

The muleteers had been glad enough to have two extra men join them – the larger the group, the safer they all were, and the apostles were equally content with the arrangement. However, due to the slowness of droving and a number of delays caused by breakaway animals (which Barnabas suspected might have had more to do with the troublesome boys than anything else), the return journey from Iconium to Antiochia took longer than the outward one. The way was hot and dusty, and somehow a few mules always managed to 'escape' whenever they passed a tempting body of water, into which they unerringly bolted with the shouting boys splashing gleefully after them.

There were the usual trials of the road – the torments of small biting flies by day and persistent mosquitoes by night – but to the apostles' relief the worst which befell them was losing food to foraging animals and thieving children, and losing sleep to noisy companions, yawping foxes and swooping bats.

Barnabas later declared that by far the most displeasing thing which happened was the shock of being awoken one morning by an escaped mule which was hopefully nudging his bald head with its velutinous nose before trying to nibble his eyebrows with its whiskery lips. Paul on the other hand, who had very callously laughed until he had a stitch in his side, said it was the most pleasing thing *he'd* seen for a long time.

Some of the company were willing enough to while away the monotonous hours of travel in listening to what the two men had to say about the Creator of the Universe and His Son, the Saviour of mankind, but it was soon clear that the gospel message was regarded by most of them purely as a form of entertainment to enliven the journey. Nevertheless, Paul and Barnabas preached regardless, for the seed must be sown, and who could say when or in what strange circumstances in the most casual hearer's future it might germinate?

Their most attentive listener shambled to their side whenever he could, escaping the cruelty of the smaller boys who taunted him for his ugliness. The unfortunate Goreme was a raw-boned, vacant-looking youth with tiny ears, drooping lacklustre eyes, and incipient whiskers fringing a rather slack mouth through which he breathed stertorously. Barnabas had at first dismissed him as somewhat simple-minded, but Paul was not so sure.

"He asked me today how a man as ugly as himself could be of any worth to any god," he said that night after their prayers, as he rolled himself into his blanket, squirming in a vain attempt to extract more comfort from the crackling leaf litter and dead bushes he had heaped together.

Barnabas was so preoccupied in making similar crunching sounds as he wrestled his own awkward bed into submission that he had to ask Paul to repeat himself.

"H'm, that's rather a sad question, isn't it?" he said thoughtfully, once he had heard it properly. "He must have had some cruel things said to him. It's not as if he would ever have possessed any mirror other than a muddy puddle, and that wouldn't reveal much. How did you answer him?"

"I said it is inward beauty not outward which matters to God, which is why He asks us to change our natural thinking and become more like His Son."

Turning over, and pulling the blanket over his head to keep off dew and insects, Paul continued in a rather muffled way, "I told him, if we only try sincerely to be like Lord Jeshua in our hearts, God will one day complete the transformation; and then we will have not only perfect, beautiful Godly minds but perfect, beautiful, immortal bodies like our Lord himself."

"H'm. That was a lot for the poor boy to understand, wasn't it?" Barnabas grunted. "All you had to say was that you are a fine illustration that looks are not everything before God."

"Or that any young man with hair will always be far less ugly than one who is old and bald?" Paul quipped sarcastically, trying not to laugh, for in the way of boyhood friends, such jibes were mere exchanges of affection. "Maybe he would have found that encouraging, poor lad."

Loftily ignoring that remark, Barnabas again attempted to wriggle himself into some semblance of comfort. "Do you think the fellow took in anything you said?" he wondered, his twiggy bed crunching and snapping under his weight.

Suddenly he slapped sharply at the side of his head, hoping that what had just tickled him was a stray leaf and not an earwig, or worse. "Ow! Wait a moment, my ear is ringing, I can't hear anything now. Look here, is your bed as bad as mine? I am being stuck all over with a thousand sticks, for my sins!"

"I jumped on mine first to break them up a bit." Paul's thick eyebrows emerged from his blanket, his crinkled eyes revealing that there was a grin lurking below. "And *don't* ask, 'the sins or the sticks?'"

He covered his head again, his high hooked nose conveniently keeping the stretched blanket clear of his face. "But never mind our beds, they're no worse than yesterday. I'm telling you about Goreme. He asked me by what magic a man could change."

"I hope you kept it simple!" Barnabas yawned, following Paul's example and muffling his head in blanket. A bald scalp was not only cold, but far too inviting to mosquitoes.

Thus enveloped, they lay side by side like talking corpses, much to the amusement of the muleteers, some of whom were more comfortably cushioned against the warm bodies of their beasts and like them, seemingly impervious to all biting insects.

"I did. I said it is not magic, but just like a caterpillar spins a cocoon and turns into a butterfly, it happens through the power of the Creator. His eyes lit up then, so maybe he understands more than we think."

"I didn't think you knew such things as butterflies existed," Barnabas mumbled rudely. "Moths around a candle, maybe, since they are right under your nose. And mosquitoes. Astonishing how a single one of these little beasts can keep a man more awake than a bad conscience."

"Speak for yourself," Paul retorted witheringly, and with another smothered chuckle or two the conversation died away.

Goreme approached Paul unhappily the next day – showing in his hard leathery palm, seamed with dirt, a torn chrysalis with a creamy grey blob oozing from it.

"I opened it to see the butterfly," he mourned, scratching his lice busily with his free hand. "Where is it?"

Paul patted his shoulder regretfully. "It takes time, you see?" he said gently. "This one was not ready yet, that's all."

He thought of the other young men they had left behind, each a caterpillar in the process of change. They had spun what many would imagine was just an imprisoning shroud around themselves, but they were now in a state of submission, allowing their previous lives to dissolve into something which many would see as senseless chaos.

He prayed no careless hand would tear open their protection before the new creature had been fully formed within – and patiently he turned back to his crestfallen admirer, who was now asking hopefully whether he *had* to be a butterfly, or could he not rather be something stronger and safer, like a bear or a wolf, perhaps. Paul sighed. Using analogies had definite limitations when dealing with a mind totally unused to abstract – let alone spiritual – thinking.

Nearly a week after leaving Iconium they came safely through the imposing gates welcoming them to Colonia Caesarea Antiochia, having made no further progress with Goreme's spiritual education, but the gangling youth himself was quite happy. He had been treated with respect and kindness, they had made him feel special and worthwhile, and now he knew all about butterflies. These Christians were strange, but very nice people. So, apart from a few thumbed noses from the youngest boys, the apostles and the muleteers parted with good feeling on both sides.

Chapter Forty-seven

AS before, the two friends called first on the relations of Sergius Paulus, who again received them courteously. They were careful to give no indication that they would ever care to emulate their illustrious kinsman on Cyprus, but for his sake – and also because some of their own valued servants and family slaves had followed his lead – they would afford to other Christians whatever protection they could, should it become necessary. This much they hinted broadly, at least, and the apostles were thankful to hear it. Jews historically had been exempted from the compulsory cult of Emperor-worship, but not every Christian was a proselyte of Judaism and could not count on sharing this exemption. There was bound to be conflict sooner or later. The apostles took their leave of the gracious family, promising to heed their judicious warning to avoid the synagogue for the sake of peace.

Next they went happily in search of Epaenetus, finding him bristling with new and proprietal airs as he showed off his astonishingly fat son. The new father seemed torn between prodding him proudly to show his fine condition, and expressing various paternal anxieties about the amount he screamed, snored, dribbled, ate, or excreted. Paul and Barnabas managed to hide their amusement, which the serene Aemilia seemed to share, if her twinkling eyes and gentle admonitions to her husband not to fuss were any indication. The biggest surprise came when she ran upstairs to fetch 'Grandfather' who now lived with them – and who should come down but a beaming Acacius! It was the happiest of reunions, after which, armed with Aemilia's clear directions, they set off to find their former landlady.

To their delight they found Portia was now married to a soft-hearted knife-grinder, stepmother to his seven boisterous children, and apparently just as astonished as her two old friends by this turn of events.

"Never was a man more well named," she told them, beaming as if she could still hardly believe her blessings, "for my Theodorus has indeed been God's gift to me!"

Her husband's thin, careworn face creased in an affectionate smile. "As you are to all of us, my dear Portia." His aquiline nose lifted proudly as he added, "Not one woman in a thousand would have taken on this unruly brood of mine, for they all ran wild after their poor mother died – and truthfully I was at my wits' end. But my Portia is a woman in *ten* thousand, whose worth is far above rubies as your wise Solomon said. Or wait, perhaps he said coral, or was it, pink pearls … I am not yet well enough acquainted with the Hebrew scriptures and tend to mix them up. But priceless is what it means, and so is my Portia in this household. I am certain she had no idea how hard it would be to be a second wife, let alone a second mother to so many half grown boys and girls. But do you know what this remarkable woman says about that? *Theodorus*, she says to me, *Theodorus, my dear, when I married you, I married the whole family.*"

Swallowing hard he sniffed fiercely, just as the whole noisy tribe burst in and clambered all over the two of them, clamouring for attention. Portia extricated herself with difficulty and set the girls to helping with supper, while the boys besieged the visitors with questions about what were their *most dangerous* adventures. Afterwards, Theodorus insisted on sharpening Paul's leather tools, Barnabas's stumpy little folding knife reserved for cutting pens, and the pair of stout bladed knives they used for everything from cutting food and chopping fuel, to digging holes and scraping mud off their sandals. Steadily pedalling his heavy grindstone, Theodorus told them happily what a useful occupation his was for preaching purposes.

"A man must talk to his customers if they like to watch him work, eh? And I can start many a conversation by musing about how a man's character is honed by life and adversity to a keen edge. People like that, you know, yes, indeed, they always like a bit of philosophising from an uneducated fellow so long as it's just a morsel and tidily put. Then they are keen to tell me their own stories, and so I watch for my chance, you see?"

He held each knife up to the light, squinting along its length, then selected a long, fat strip of leather from his tools, and expertly stropped the blade, testing the whetted edge with his thumb in a casual manner that made his friends' blood run cold.

"Once they know I am a sympathetic fellow, then I confide something of the distress in my own life – and how it all changed when I learned there is a God in Heaven Who is above all other gods." He began on Paul's tools, his thick fingers delicately stroking them with small whetstones before buffing them with soft leather and pinches of powder-fine sand.

"There, you should get a nice clean finish when you use these now." He blew away the last specks of dust and wiped the tools with a scrap of oiled rag, then opened the wooden-handled pen knife which he eyed dubiously.

"I've seen worse," he said unconvincingly. "Never mind, this won't take long," and in no time Barnabas's most important tool was in fine shape to slit nibs in quills and cut reed pens with precision.

Not to be outdone in usefulness, Portia took charge of their filthy, mud-splattered cloaks and demanded they hand over all the rest of their washing. Washing?! The two men could not help chuckling to hear their few spare clothes described in such domestic terms. Barnabas humbly surrendered several stiff and grimy items retrieved from the old basket, which was battered to an almost unrecognisable shape.

"That's never the one I gave you?" she asked, shocked and amused at the same time.

"It is indeed," Paul replied solemnly. "When it's not in use as a wash-basket, I use it as a sun hat."

Laughing, Portia promptly claimed it back and presented them with a new one. The children finally asleep, in came the neighbours and other brethren; the lamps were lit and the adults talked long into the night.

The next evening was the Sabbath. As the conservative Jews of the city flocked to their synagogues, the expelled Christians, Jew and Gentile, made their way towards a grand and beautiful house standing at the corner of a wide and well-kept street. Built in the Roman fashion, it was the *domus* of a wealthy brother of many talents and just as many interests. Ten years ago he had been a humble wagoner, and by dint of hard work, commercial skill and various sleight-of-hand dealings in army contracts, had elevated himself to the ownership of a very profitable transport business – a rise to riches which earned him the name of Crescens – *Growth*. Since those early days however, Crescens had risen in morality as well. Having married a Jewish wife, he became first a God-fearer, then a full proselyte – and now here he was, an eager brother in Christ. With wealth and time on his hands he had been able to indulge many passing enthusiasms over the years, and though his friends of the old days cynically waited for his pursuit of Godliness to wane, thus far they waited in vain.

The genial generosity of brother Crescens and sister Liora his wife in throwing open their home for such occasions, at whatever hazard to their beautifully painted walls, gracious garden and lovely furnishings, was a valuable asset to the Antiochian brethren. There were now so many of them that they rarely managed to be together in one place at the same time, and the ekklesia habitually met in various smaller groups, from house to house in turn. Even the house of Crescens would not hold them all for a meal, and tonight there was standing room only. Cramped as it was however nobody was willing to miss out on seeing and hearing their beloved apostles, and some of the more recent converts would be meeting them for the first time.

So in they poured, up the street, around the corner and past the shops at the front, where during the day the servants of the enterprising Crescens sold surplus household food and drink to passers-by. Now the same servants ushered the eager visitors through the large door. Some of the more lowly families entered with wide eyes, especially the children, drinking in all they saw, still not quite used to the privilege of being inside such a rich man's house. Into the vestibule they came, then through the *atrium* with its tiled pool reflecting the streaky sunset sky visible through the open roof. (Some of them had been baptized in this very pool, and they could still hardly believe it.) Next they passed through the *tablinum*. From this open-ended office Paul and Barnabas were to address the congregation, its central position in the house allowing them to be heard not only in the rooms behind and beside it, but also across the entire colonnaded garden enclosed by the *peristylum*, to the cushioned benches of the *triclinium* and the adjacent *exedra*, a large garden room used for entertaining. Every single available space gradually filled up, as steadily the ekklesia came together, many having brought curious friends, family, or the rest of their households.

Meanwhile Crescens, Liora and their servants seemed to be everywhere at once, finding places for everyone. The entire portico of the *peristylum* being soon smothered in people, Liora crammed its neat central garden with children, and even had the servants set wide the doors of the chambers which opened on to the courtyard, so that all the old people could sit in sheltered comfort, without missing anything. Eventually, somehow, the whole assembly was present, everybody fitting in one way or another. After they had sung glad praises to God and to His Son, Barnabas led them in prayer, and then they were all ready to listen. It was to be a long night, but the apostles were to stay barely a week, so what were a few extra hours of sleep compared to a few extra hours of encouragement?

All listened attentively as Paul and Barnabas exhorted them, explaining how how the atoning work of Lord Jeshua should spur them on to love and good works, and warning them against the influence of Judaisers.

"Brethren, do not be distracted by the works of the Law. If you have opportunity, by all means celebrate the feasts if you are so minded, but not as a duty which will earn you merit, only as a glad recognition that they have now found their fulfilment in Christ, whose Way is, being the substance and not the shadow, better than the ordinances of Moses. The life he offers us is a gift, this we all understand, and one does not earn a gift else it is no gift, but payment. You may ask, do we then sit and do nothing except wait for our gift of salvation? *Me genoito!* It is held out to us, but we must walk fearlessly towards it, and the way is not easy," Paul said earnestly. "Under the Law, fear of judgement held men in check, but never-ending fear is an unsustainable emotion which dulls to exhaustion, then stubbornness takes its place. It is natural to fear God, for what mortal does not quake when faced with an immortal being? I speak from my own experience of being confronted by the risen Christ! But our God is a loving Father, and as such does not want His children to be obey simply because they are terrified of Him. There is only one way to serve, one way to overcome, the same way in which our Christ was able to overcome – and that is through Love!

"Unlike Fear, Love is never exhausted, never surfeited; it grows, gathering strength. Love and faith together promote loving, faithful actions, and if not, then they are neither love nor faith but a counterfeit of them. Remember, brethren, that faith is not an object to be purchased, a set of beliefs to be put on a shelf to be admired while we go about our daily lives doing other things. Faith, like love, is a living, growing thing, which requires nurturing to sustain it, or it wilts and dies. Look for the work of God in your life, watch, pray, learn, and do good to others – and above all things, love each other as Christ loved us and gave his life for us."

As in the other cities, the apostles now elected overseers, Epaenetus and Theodorus among them, solemnly charging them to shepherd the Master's flock of believers. Next they laid their hands on a select number of men and women who would be vessels for particular *Ruach* Gifts – among them old Acacius, who was staggered to find himself with the Gift of interpretion, across a range of dialects and tongues he had not even known existed. To Epaenetus went the Gift of knowledge and to his Aemilia the Gift of understanding. Portia was amazed to receive the Gift of ministry, while Theodorus was overcome by receiving the Gift of discernment. Almost twenty in all were blessed in this way by the Holy Spirit of God, directed by Christ through the hands of his apostles. Paul and Barnabas rejoiced with them all. The family in the Lord in this place, which they were so soon to leave, was now well equipped to nurture itself and those around them.

Loud choruses of joy and thanksgiving rang in the air that night, and the hymns so passionately sung seemed to hang above the *domus* of Crescens and Liora like a blessing – thereby amazing their neighbours, who enjoyed their *gratis musica* so much they did not even complain of the noise.

The next day, the ekklesia of Pisidian Antioch gathered to partake of the Lord's Supper, the memorial ritual he had enjoined, often referred to by believers as the *eucharist* – the Thanksgiving. Gratitude was indeed a heightened emotion among them that evening as they came together to share the bread and wine, to speak of his love, to hear words of instruction and encouragement, to sing songs of praise – and excitedly to discuss the many spiritual Gifts now in their midst!

From all over the city and surrounds, groups of brethren and sisters and their families assembled, meeting in various houses according to location and practicality. In the wealthy part of town Crescen's grand *domus* accommodated many in comfort, the bread passed around was the best white *panis siligineus*, fine wine was served from a silver pitcher, and even the water with which the wine was cut (for this was the Lord's Supper and there must be no hint of drunkenness) was poured from a decorative jug made of glass. It could not be avoided that many of the poorer brethren must arrive late after their long, hard day's work, and these quietly slipped in to take the last places left, which were invariably under the portico of the garden. There they and the others with them had a good view of the comfortable *triclinium* where Crescens sat to preside over the Thanksgiving.

He was however, an unusually considerate host, as equally concerned for the comfort of others as for himself. Not one person was ever made to feel inferior in *his* house no matter where they must sit, how humbly they were dressed or how late they came. The lamps were equally as bright for them, the food and drink equally good. His servants being well instructed, they also ensured that those in the courtyard were given water for their hands and faces, and in chilly weather were warm, being provided with mats to soften the cold tiles, and blankets to wrap around cold shoulders. It was plain to see that brother Crescens had very much taken to heart the saying of the Master, *Whatver you do for one of my little ones, you do for me.*

Meanwhile in an outlying field three shepherds who could not leave their animals, sat crosslegged in a crude hut on a beaten earth floor, while the wives and daughters who had joined them for the *eucharist* lit tallow candles, unwrapped from a napkin a coarse dark loaf of *panis plebeius,* and poured the water for their rough wine from a lumpy earthenware pitcher, carefully carried from their shabby dwellings. Let it be said, however, that in these heady, early days of the Antioch ekklesia, any contrast between these two gatherings was purely superficial. Their motive was the same, and morale was high, and their worship hearty. So was it also wherever the brethren met, regardless of their social standing. As for the house of Theodorus and Portia, where neither poverty nor riches were apparent, it was so full that people spilled over through the doorways into all adjoining spaces.

Paul looked around the crowded room with a heart swelling with joy. Jews and Gentiles, one in Christ! Some of them were now elders, overseers chosen by guidance of the Holy Spirit, ordained by the hands of Barnabas and himself. Others had been given precious Gifts, to nurture their brethren and to show the world that the One they worshipped was living and powerful, that this was not an airy construction of human conceit and mere philosophy. Perhaps in later years a regrettable jostling for the 'best' seats, for pre-eminence, would come, even as it had in other places – in Syrian Antioch, and Jerusalem. It seemed inevitable that human nature would assert itself – but how earnestly he hoped and prayed it would not! For now, gazing at the uplifted faces he rejoiced in their earnest faith, and as he raised his voice in unity with his beloved family in the Lord, not a single wistful thought of the synagogues – their hush, their unique scent, their polished wood and ornate scroll cases, the formality of their services, the prescribed prayers, the thrum of voices echoing responses – even crossed his mind.

A very busy week later, Portia's new basket was packed with nourishing provisions – along with some very sharp knives and some very clean clothes – and they passed through the stout portal of the city. A large group of the brethren walked through with them until they were clear of the noisily congested gates. With them were Theodorus, Portia, and their children, as well as Epaenetus and Aemilia with pudgy little Linus held up to wave goodbye in Acacius's stringy old arms. Now came the hard part, where throats choked and eyes stung, but finally with all the goodbyes, the prayers, and exhortations to courage by all sides expressed, Paul and Barnabas turned and walked away. Behind them the disciples, Jew and Gentile in unison, lifted up their voices in song, singing an ancient blessing from the synagogue which had rejected them.

The Eternal bless you, and keep you.
The Eternal make His face to shine upon you
And be gracious unto you.
The Eternal lift up His countenance upon you
And give you peace!

They sang it again and again, the gracious words floating down the road, growing fainter and fainter until the two men strode around a bend and were gone. Neither of them spoke, being filled with emotion. They could not have asked for a more suitable farewell than such a blessing, for they knew that once out of sight of the imposing aqueduct which carried spring water to the city, civilisation was behind them and they were in for a difficult journey.

Chapter Forty-eight

PREPARED as he was to face the road, Paul could not help a slight misgiving at the thought of Perga, still so far ahead. There he had been so sick on the outward journey, and there Marcus had left them, and not one word of the gospel had been preached. This had to be put right, and now time was alarmingly short.

Almost overnight the summer heat had passed. The days were already colder, the nights longer, and they must complete their mission before the sailing season closed with the onset of winter. To miss it would force them to make a difficult decision – to stay put for another half year till the next season, or slowly work their way back to Antioch Orontes, overland. That in itself would mean either doubling back again through the regions they had only recently left, or struggling through unknown coastal territory to which they had not been specifically guided by the Lord – all while battling winter storms and treacherous snows. Each of these choices was equally unthinkable.

They must push forward towards the coast, do as much as they could in the time available, and sail before the season closed and cut them off, that much was clear – but they still had to weigh up the various merits and disadvantages of ways to get from Antiochia to Perga, and the decision was not easy. It came down to a matter of the days *versus* the dangers.

The easier but longer western sweep of the Via Sebaste they ruled out at once, but should they return by the way they had come – the shorter arm of the highway – or venture upon the hazardous, most direct route through the mountains, the prospect of which had so disconcerted Marcus nearly fifteen months ago? Though neither of him voiced his name, his flushed, grim face came clearly before their mind's eye. Younger, stronger, and no coward, still he had refused to risk it.

Asking around the khans had not helped them. Every traveller had a favoured route, complete with his own variations, and each man contradicted another on how long it would take and how dangerous it was or wasn't, until Barnabas threw up his hands in exasperation. Praying for guidance, they had found their answer the next morning when Paul woke up with a saying from his student days on his lips: *It's easy to make decisions when you know your values.*

"That's the heart of it, Barnabas, not dithering over details. What do we value? Our safety? Or the work we have to finish? There is only one thing to take into account and that's the gospel. We must not stint on preaching in Perga."

"The fastest way, then, regardless!" Barnabas had leaped up at once with an air of relief. "And I can even see a short cut already – Lake Akrotiri again. A march to Ghaziri, then sail clear across the Lake, past Prostanna, as far as we can. From there we should be able to find a trail to the Kings Road, and work our way down through the gorges. Let's pray we find a guide or a party going our way."

Devoutly thankful that this time they were both fit, healthy, and well toughened by adversity, they faced the long, daunting journey with determination. So now, here they were, setting out towards the shorter, more dangerous route from the southern tip of Lake Akrotiri, from which point on they would need serious stamina and courage to traverse the Taurus ranges through to Pamphylia. Retreading the path to Ghaziri by the Lake, they sheltered overnight in the old hut of brother Acacius, who had urged them to use it if ever they passed that way again.

The next day they had no trouble finding someone who (if they crossed his palm with silver) would sail them the full length of the Lake, for the strange story of the preacher who had found poor old lost Acacius had already become part of local folklore. The thickset Ghaziri fisherman took the money which would compensate him for losing a full day's work, delighted that he could now boast of meeting the legendary Paulus for himself and resolving to hear the whole tale again from his mouth. A grey and sullen sky threatened misery, but the boisterous wind which roiled down from the grim encircling mountains was in their favour, smacking the sail at such a rate across the choppy water that even the hours of nausea felt like a small price to pay for the considerable saving in time and shoe leather.

Listening hard whenever he could spare the concentration, the fisherman asked many questions as Paul and Barnabas obligingly retold the tale of Acacius – it helped keep Paul's mind off his rebellious stomach – and of how it came about that the bereft old soldier had found a new family in Antiochia. It was one way of preaching, though it seemed their interrogator was more interested in storing up some fresh, dramatic, strange-but-true stories for long winter nights. But – who knew? If the fellow retold them faithfully, he was helping to spread the gospel one way or another, whether he realised it or not.

The westering sun slanting through the parting clouds, the slate-grey waves began to take on a tinge of colour as finally the scudding craft passed some recognisable landmarks. Here were the little islands, there was the long spit, and now they were beyond the shore of Prostanna where they had baptised Epaenetus the previous year. The wind was gradually easing, the end of the long lake was in sight, the easiest part of their journey was nearly over. Soon afterwards they were bobbing on a pale green fringe of shore, the bottom of the boat bumping gently on the gritty shingle. The burly fisherman wished them well, even making them a present of several fish caught along the way. Thanking him sincerely the apostles shouldered their bundles, hitched up their tunics, hopped overboard and splashed through the freezing shallows to a rocky beach.

"Heus! Amicus!" A friendly shout hailed them from under some scrubby trees, where five native Phrygians were gathered around a small fire. Paul and Barnabas smiled and returned the salutation.

"Salve! Quid agis?" they replied cheerfully, and would have said more, but the one who had greeted them waved his hand self-deprecatingly.

"Mea lingua latina est mala!" he said, his Latin thickly accented.

Assuring him that they could understand him very well, the apostles were rewarded by a proud smile and an invitation to warm and dry themselves, which they were very glad to accept. Wayfarers together, all seven of them were soon companionably sharing the night, the fire, and the fish, and (notwithstanding the peasants' hybrid dialect) exchanging the usual travellers' tales – those of Paul and Barnabas being regarded as the most peculiar of all. The son of a god, sacrificing himself for mere mortals? Sending them to the wilds of Asia to spread the news? It was all too fanciful, and clearly must have been invented for their entertainment.

"An unusual tale indeed. Yet it is also unusual for us to come across strangers here – especially Jews! This is not a good place for those who do not know our territory, and wise men do not venture it without a stout company of protectors. *Quo vadis?"*

The apostles told them where they were headed, and the Phrygians shook their heads at once.

"Perga, taking in that stretch of the Kings Road? And through the canyons? Not safe on your own. Two words – no, three. Mad. Mountain. Marauders."

"They won't get much out of us," Barnabas said, a little too pointedly. "Maybe our clothes."

"That would do," they shrugged, taking no offence. "That and the pleasure of slitting your throats. Murder is mere sport to them. No, better come with us, if you're up to it, and that will get you most of the way. We know this region and have our own tracks, down past the smaller lakes, following a feeder to the Kestrus mostly, wherever we can that is. It's hard, though, not much relief with the river valleys, and even then it's tough going. Hope you're not scared of heights, there's plenty of mountain-goat footwork. And snakes, of course. But as long as you're sound of wind and limb ..."

Paul and Barnabas exchanged glances. Neither of them was overly concerned about snakes, Cyprus had been swarming with them, and as Barnabas had reminded them then, the Lord himself had been very specific that they need not fear them. Since then they hardly even noticed snakes any more, though they had come across plenty in their travels – so solid was their assurance that they were no threat! But men were another matter. Could they trust these affable peasants, or were they being lured into even more danger? Barnabas thought wryly of what Marcus had said on the ship from Cyprus, *"We can't preach the gospel if our throats are cut."* Very true! But since Lord Jeshua had sent them to preach, it was unlikely they were going to end up dead before the job was finished. Meanwhile Paul was thinking much the same thing in relation to his private fear of tumbling brokenly to a chasm far below. A moment's reflection, a silent prayer for guidance, they made up their minds this was a blessing not a trap – and accepted the offer.

Their new travelling companions turned out to be all of one family, on their way to claim two brides who were sisters, being cousins promised from childhood. The prospective grooms, still very lightly equipped as far as both whiskers and depth of voice were concerned, at first were subject to much coarse ribaldry from their older brothers, and though this was rather tiresome, Paul and Barnabas ignored it by singing with an equal enthusiasm their favourite songs and psalms. But once the climbing became serious, nobody had the breath for either singing or joking. The way was indeed more suitable for mountain goats. Barnabas lashed Portia's new basket firmly on his back, Paul did the same with various smaller bundles, and tightening their sandals, they did their best to keep up with the younger men's relentless pace. Never did a trail so aptly illustrate, they agreed, the struggle of mortal man to keep his feet on the narrow, rugged path to the kingdom of God!

Much of the terrain was so rough there was no time for looking around them; every step must be watched and calculated. Would this rock turn underfoot? Would this ledge crumble? Would this branch steady the next jump or pull out of the cliff? Scrambling up and down, now on a mere scratch of track, now pushing through scrub ... clambering on smooth boulders, splashing through icy streamlets ... ducking under this, weaving around that ... As they worked their way through the towering Taurus ranges, it seemed at times as if The Watchers of ancient rabbinic lore had descended to capriciously stir up many landscapes into a confusing jumble.

Soaring, cedar-clad heights broke into slippery scree-covered slopes, grey-faced craggy ridges gave way to abrupt canyons where the glittering river roared between its narrow banks; dry gravelly creek beds crunched underfoot near sudden springs, from which sly trickles gathered together to leap down the mountain in unexpected waterfalls, plummeting to crystal green pools in gorges far below. Sharp peaks jostled with tabletop plateaus; cypress, oak and juniper forests collapsed into scruffy little steep-sloping meadows where wild goats grazed and a few wild horses shook their manes in the cold wet air. Occasionally they spied a lone shepherd and his wary dogs, or a tiny settlement tucked away in a crook of the hills, but mostly there were few signs that men had ever set foot in such untamed, tumultuous and inhospitable country.

Every now and then the shut-in walls of rocks and trees would open out to give sombre views of far-off mountains wrapped in layered shawls of soft blues and purples, crisply capped in luminous snow. Then down the next steep decline the determined travellers would plunge, clambering across to scale yet another ridge, with no eyes to spare for beauty and grandeur, only for the next safe spot for a foot, a knee, a hand. In such awful places, Barnabas made his mind a blank, while Paul did not even attempt to look down, but gritted his teeth, glad he could not see well at a distance. Surely those new brides were in for a shock on the return journey – but then, perhaps not. As mountain dwellers themselves, they would be as hardy and agile as their men ... even as Danya, and no doubt her mother, fearlessly shepherding together with their menfolk in the wilds of Nabataea.

Strange to think he might once even have seen her – or rather, *them*, he corrected himself, for of course back then she would have been a mere baby, what a disquieting thought, was he really so old? – but it was not unthinkable that he may have glanced their way in that stark, strange place ... sometime ... somewhere in the distance, perhaps ... But he must not think of that just now! He must only think of climbing, up, down, across, under, over! Again and again the track criss-crossed the narrow river, forced from one side to another, makeshift bridges and boulder-strewn fords taking travellers from obstructions on this bank to a passable stretch on that one, then back again, and again, in the continual hunt for a safer, easier trail, and surer footing. Again and again Paul had to repair their tortured sandals – a continual reminder that they would have been far better off with tough boots like the hob-nailed *caligae* worn by Julius and his men.

Day after day, their long woollen tunics firmly girded up for safety, well clear of clinging wet vegetation, they attacked their route until the dark mountain tops sucked the light from the sky and it was too dangerous to continue. A fire was lit, food was chewed eagerly but wearily, and then they were thankful to tug down sleeves and unbind tunics, loosening them to full length and tucking up their cold feet inside them for warmth, before winding themselves about with their thick cloaks. Night after night, every man slept, if not the sleep of the just, certainly the sleep of the truly spent, too worn out to complain about the freezing cold or the hard ground – just so long as he was safely wedged where he would not roll into the campfire, the closely rushing water, or over a ledge into thin air! The apostles rarely slept solidly, continually half-waking to sounds which pierced their dreams … sharp coughing barks of foxes nearby … far-off, blood-chilling howls of wolves in the high timber … strange rustlings and noises in the bushes, and sometimes when the wind was right they could even hear distant, eerie echoes of night creatures growling and snarling in unseen canyons where the main track ran – the track they were avoiding, and for good reason.

One spine-tingling night it was not animals they heard but the fearful sound of men fighting, screams, and shouts. In alarm Paul and Barnabas started up from their sleep, but the brothers pushed them down again, warning them there was nothing to be done. If it was a brigand attack, there would be no one left alive. If it was a mere wayfarers' quarrel then they were better off minding their own business. The canyon was nowhere near as close as it sounded, and even if they did not break their necks in the pitch blackness before they got there, they certainly would afterwards, only to be found by the next lot of travellers, stark and stiff and torn by beasts at the bottom at the chasm.

Paul and Barnabas subsided into their blankets, feeling the horror, deeply sobered. From then on they were extra vigilant while on watch. Wrapped against the cold, penetrating damp, steeped in the smothering mountain blackness, they took their turn with the others to keep the fire blazing against wild animals – listening through the night noises for stealthy footsteps of men, comforted by their small crackling beacon of fire, the ghost of a moon, and the occasional promise of stars.

Each day they eked out their dried foods as best they could, while the brothers supplemented theirs by setting overnight snares and eating whatever they caught – rabbits, squirrels, dormice or hedgehogs, none of which the two Jews – regardless of their Christian conviction that all food was permissable – could bring themselves to touch. As Barnabas said gloomily, old habits died hard and he just could not stomach the thought of eating a hedgehog no matter how lawful it was. Paul had to admit he felt much the same.

"Look on the bright side," he said, trying to and nearly succeeding. "It just means we are not hungry enough. Therefore we are not starving – yet!"

One joyful morning however, the brothers caught several quails and a partridge, which being roasted on a juniper spit provided a tasty meal for all of them, even if there was more flavour than fullness in the eating thereof. At least they did not wake hungry the next day, which was some comfort to Paul, who had already woken in the bitter misty dawn with his ankle aching. Crouched in his blanket, he bound the offending joint firmly with the old black cloth, now rather worse for wear, but which had shielded his sensitive eyes on many occasions. Barnabas huddled beside him, inspecting his own injuries. In the matter of blisters, scrapes, ripped nails, cuts and insect bites they were about equal. Paul spat in his hand, added fine ash from the dead fire and stirred it into a paste to anoint the sores on his long-suffering feet. Watching, Barnabas said morosely, "Now, that is truly an ugly sight for a man to bear on an empty stomach."

With difficulty Paul kept a straight face. "I have it on good authority that my feet are in fact, very beautiful," he replied loftily. "And hard as it is to believe, so are yours."

Catching his meaning in a flash, Barnabas began to laugh and to the surprise of their companions without another word the two of them broke into a stirring song. It uplifted their spirits that morning, and ever after held special meaning for them – *How beautiful upon the mountains are the feet of them that preach the gospel of peace!*

That day it rained dismally, making every step dangerously slippery, but to the travellers' relief, as the hours went by the landscape began to soften, losing its ruggedly stern look … the river imperceptibly broadened below them, and gradually the way became less taxing. Next morning, turning a bend in the river they came upon a group of swarthy peasants – a welcoming party of the brides' family – camping by another offshoot of the Kestrus. As they greeted them boisterously, the brothers explained that the brides' menfolk would now escort them to a mountain village (with an unpronounceable name) where awaited the beauteous Oljai and her pretty sister Gilli – descriptions which the grooms hoped were still true, since they had not seen the girls since they were children. Why not go with them and share the festivities?

Expressing their honour at the invitation, Paul and Barnabas declined with polite regret. They must reach Perga without delay, but would greatly miss their agreeable guides, and hoped that without them they would not lose their way. Reassuring the apostles that they were now a good two thirds of the way there, and definitely past the worst of it, the brothers directed them to continue on the trail by the river. Before long the mere track would become a path, they said, and very soon after that, a recognisable road, which would bring them to the city in less than a day. And already, so the men assured them, they were in far safer territory. This was very good to hear, and the apostles felt tension lifting from their brows almost at once.

"Gratias multas!" they said sincerely, after wishing them well for their celebrations. *"Gratias multas! Vale!"*

"Vale!" the peasants shouted their goodbyes happily as they left. *"Salutatio! Vale!"*

So with spirits undampened by a cold drizzle of rain, the apostles turned to go, and continued on alone with great cheerfulness. They did not notice that one of the welcoming party had melted into the shadows of the overgrown riverbank – a rat-faced man, watching them behind his eyes. Had they done so, they may not have been so shocked when an hour later they were attacked as they sat down to rest for the first time that day, with their backs against a boulder, and their belongings at their feet where the ground dropped away to a tangle of nondescript bushes buzzing with foraging bees.

When wild-eyed men sprang from their hiding places with fierce yells, the apostles had no time to be frightened. As they scrambled to their feet to face their attackers, Paul with great presence of mind sharply kicked the smaller bundles over the ledge into the scrub below, while Barnabas deliberately made much of protecting their less-valuable basket. This the men ransacked, taking what little they had – money, cheese, dried fruit, a flask of oil and little bag of flour stowed in a leather bucket, with two thin blankets, a few spare clothes, and their all-purpose knives – before vanishing, basket and all, into a heavily wooded gully.

Considerably shaken, the apostles took stock of what was left. Barnabas, once so well-fleshed, urbane and elegant, had over the years become lean, practical and far less fastidious, but he had never abandoned the habit of wearing breeches under his robes. Inside these were sewn their emergency funds, tightly wrapped so as not to chink. As well, under his clothes he, like Paul, had also tied sundry pockets of various sizes containing spare rations of dried apricots, figs, and nuts, together with essential flints and dry tinder for striking fire. So there was still balm in Gilead! Paul's quick thinking had saved their most prized items – the bundles containing their pens, several precious codices and tightly rolled manuscripts, and his leather tools, all bound up in their heavy cloaks. Retrieving these with great relief, at the cost of being stung by a number of disturbed bees, they continued on their way, giving thanks for the preservation of their skins, and keeping a nervous eye and ear out for unusual sounds and movements.

567

In the back of both their minds was a determination that should they ever again have opportunity to revisit the ekklesias of Asia, they would manage their time so as to avoid the faintest likelihood of needing to take this punishing route or any variation of it. The Via Sebaste arm through Cremna, Sagalassos and Claudioseleucia had been far less stressful, not to speak of productive, and even though it took longer, they would stick to it. At least now they knew from experience where and how they might travel, how long it would take and how much it might cost – and could make more efficient plans in future!

Striding along discussing these matters, actually laughing at themselves for planning the next trip before they had finished the one which had already exhausted them to the marrow, that very same afternoon they were suddenly accosted by a second, far more aggressive group of bandits – grotesque inbreds of reptilian appearance, all chinless faces, bulging eyes, protruding teeth and ugly goitres – roaring foul-breathed, unintelligible threats in their faces, chopping at the straps of the bundled cloaks with long, wicked-looking knives.

Angered that inside there was nothing worth stealing except Paul's tools – pens and closely written manuscripts they had no use for – they stripped both men of all their outer garments, tearing off the concealed waist pouches which might contain valuables, and furiously beating the unfortunate pair with fists and sticks before disappearing into the landscape. With them went the apostles' now slashed but still precious weatherproof cloaks, their much-mended footwear, and clothes, patched and torn as they were. Turning in a last gesture of contempt, the most villainous of them sneeringly flung the shabby tunics into the icy river tumbling along below, then he too, was suddenly gone.

Dazed and bleeding, Barnabas slumped down in his breeches, thankful he still had them, and shiveringly eyed a passing tortoise with envy. Right now he would not mind being a tortoise, warm and protected in its shell! Paul however was incensed. Springing to his feet, all but naked as he was, he leapt and scrambled to the river bank and scoured the rocks for a good way down, finally returning triumphantly to his goosefleshed, teeth-chattering friend. He had rescued one sodden tunic, at least! And luckily it was not his own, but the far more capacious and definitely over-sized one belonging to Barnabas. Taking an end each, together they wrung it as dry as they could and shook it out, agreeing soberly that if ever they wanted proof they were protected, they had it now! There was no earthly reason why those knives had not been planted in their bodies – only a heavenly one. Profoundly did they give thanks to Lord Jeshua!

The afternoon was waning, the air growing colder. Deprived of their flint, which had been in a pocket of Paul's cloak, they had no fire, and even had they managed to fashion a fire-drill they had no dry tinder, and all the wood around them was too wet to raise even a wisp of smoke. It was going to be something of a desperate night, but a big damp woollen tunic was at least more than they had an hour ago, and that was something else to be thankful for.

Paul had even found a pouch of dried apricots which had been ripped from the narrow cord around his waist. In the bandits' brutal haste they had dropped it, unnoticed. It was almost worth the rope burns.

"A pity they snapped the cord and took that too – it might have been useful," he said to Barnabas. "However, speaking of snapping cords – help me hunt for my leather sheath, will you? I tore it off the instant they ran at us, and threw it somewhere in the hope of retrieving it later. But I'd rather lose it altogether than have it stolen for crimes to be committed in my name."

Barnabas knew that the small object was precious to Paul not merely for the document it held, but because it was the parting gift of a beloved father, whom he had never seen again since that day. While they were travelling it was never off his person.

"Ah!" he answered sympathetically, vainly hugging himself against the creeping cold while poking around hopefully in the wet scrub with one foot. "I wondered why you were waving your arms! I could only suppose you were trying to be ferocious. Let's see. We were *here,* so maybe we should look over *there* ..."

But the two searched in vain, and soon were forced to give up under the greater pressure of needing to get warm and stay that way overnight. As they chafed some temporary heat into their half frozen arms and legs, Paul firmly put the loss of the case out of his mind for the time being. He could worry about it tomorrow, he said. Barnabas approved. Right now they must stay as cheerful as they could, and even laugh at themselves if at all possible! He had learned over the years that healthy laughter was better than any medicine. Come to think of it, hadn't Solomon said it first?

"Something like that," Paul replied briefly. Neither of them felt particularly cheerful just at that moment but since feeling sorry for themselves would get them nowhere, they got to work.

Cobbling together a shelter of torn branches propped against a large boulder, they heaped the ground inside with the driest vegetation they could scrape together from under various dripping bushes. Then they crawled inside to shiver through their evening prayers with the single damp woollen garment spread rather inadequately across their bare shoulders. At least there was hardly any breeze, which was a blessing.

Another blessing was having the pouch of leathery apricots – though in the past Barnabas had always complained they made him think of dried baby ears. Now in the fading light he opened the little bag and peered inside, all such gruesome associations the last thing on his mind. "They look nice and snug in there," he growled enviously, fishing out one each. "I wish *I* was an apricot, right now."

This was so ridiculous they both burst out laughing, which did them good, and then suddenly Paul had a flash of inspiration. "Barnabas, what an excellent idea! Look, your tunic is hopelessly inadequate as a blanket for two grown men – but what if we use it as a bag to sleep in? Remember what Solomon said – *Two together have heat: but how can one be warm alone?*"

Barnabas admitted it was worth trying. So, one at a time they carefully squirmed in through the wide bottom hem (with Paul's feet poked into one of the sleeves and Barnabas's sticking out of the neckline), and dragging it up around their shoulders huddled together as best they could for warmth, piling over themselves every spare leafy clump in reach ... and there they lay, chewing their dried apricots by way of dinner. Apart from icy draughts around the feet, much of their body heat stayed trapped inside, and very gradually they stopped shivering. It was, as Barnabas mumbled bravely, his nose buried mournfully in the back of Paul's head, better than nothing, and far be it from him to complain but would Paul kindly move that sharp elbow out of his ribs?

Paul grinned in the darkness and tried not to chuckle, knowing it would irritate his friend who must be far more uncomfortable than he was. With them both munching away amid the greenery, and only their heads poking out of this upside-down garment they must have looked like a couple of caterpillars sharing a cocoon. The figurative language he had tried to explain to the puzzled mule boy Goreme had suddenly turned ludicrously literal. It was a bizarre situation but there was a definite funny side, and besides, being small, he had the best of the bargain, while poor tall Barnabas must suffer cold legs all night for the sake of keeping the hem pulled up to his neck.

Well, cold legs or not, at least they would not freeze to death, even if they could feel every pointy twig and scratchy piece of shrubbery on which they lay. Barnabas had even had his own stroke of genius, ripping open one side of the empty apricot bag to tug it over his chilled, hairless scalp. This he did with a faint air of defiance, but sympathetic Paul, whose hair was still thick, even if receding, smiled only on the inside. The bag made a very small hood, rather too tight for comfort, but in their situation warmth was a necessity, while comfort was a mere luxury with which they could dispense. This they told themselves firmly, even while thinking wistfully about just such a luxury!

Barnabas, who always lay like a log, felt that Paul's incessant fidgets were an added and quite unnecessary trial. Meanwhile Paul, a light sleeper accustomed to thrashing like a water wheel, hoped that Barnabas (who smugly and erroneously believed himself to be a *silent* sleeper) would tonight not grind his teeth or snore directly in his ear. Engrossed in these private thoughts, as well as trying to ignore the pain of their injuries on top of many smarting itches from the earlier bee stings, they said nothing more for a while … until finally poor Barnabas could take no more.

"Will you keep *still*!" he barked, startling the drowsy Paul into a violent flinch which cracked his head against his friend's chin.

"Sorry," he mumbled, and with various exasperated mutterings the two managed after some struggling to rearrange themselves back-to-back. This proving to be more comfortable as well as warmer, soon afterwards they both fell sleep, notwithstanding their many other discomforts. So exhausted were they after their nerve-wrenching day, that Paul twitched unrebuked and Barnabas snored and gritted his teeth unnoticed, for the rest of that freezing, drizzling night.

Next morning, after extricating themselves from their cocoon and shaking life back into their clumsy, cold-deadened limbs, they found a couple of sharp stones with which they managed to rip open the side and shoulder seams of the big tunic. Having thus torn it in two, they fashioned with the help of strips from Paul's ragged loin-cloth, some kind of covering for each of them. Paul however would not surrender the old black cloth around his weak ankle, saying that without it he may never arrive at all. Sitting down carelessly to rebind it, he jumped up with an exclamation – and a tear of relief sprang to his eye as he praised God – for there was the little round sheath, the embossing worn almost flat by now, but well oiled, as he always kept it – looking for all the world like just another damp stick on the ground.

Barnabas caught his glad expression and smiled. "If God is for us, who can be against us!"

"Who indeed! Neither the highest of the high nor the lowest of the low!" Joyfully Paul knotted together its broken thong and rehung the slender case around his neck. Happy as he was to find it, though, he could not help thinking of the day he would no longer need to wear it for safekeeping, but having finished his travels would be able to take it off at last, and pack it safely away – until next time! But there was no use daydreaming – they were not there yet.

Picking their way carefully, the two moved on. Without their sandals there were frequent grunts of pain and the occasional agonised yelp, but there was no help for it, and fortunately it was not long before the rough path began to widen, and finally, just as their erstwhile companions had assured them, they found themselves once more on a paved road, its well-worn stones blissfully smooth by comparison.

In this manner, barefoot, more than half naked, frozen, famished, their bodies throbbing all over with welts and bruises, the ragged apostles trudged into Perga, Paul with a long, clotted cut matting the hair on one temple, Barnabas with a split lip and menacing black eye, and both of them blotched with bee stings. In this deplorable state they headed straight for the synagogue, hoping and praying that the friendly Chazzan – the only person they knew in the city – was still there.

He was. Horrified at their appearance and shocked, if hardly surprised, by their misadventures, the kindly Efram was full of solicitude. Hastening them to the guest chamber he succoured them nobly, fetching them water to wash with, insisting they take some medicinal spirits of wine (hidden in a basket of cleaning rags, "for just such occasions as this!") and providing them with the only food he had about him – a handful of date-and-sesame balls to keep him going until a late dinner, and a little box of dried figs stuffed with walnuts which he had bought as a treat for his children – before unearthing some clean clothes from the Poor Box. Apologising that he must hurry away to prepare for the next service, he ran out, only to hurry back in again.

"I forgot! Here – letters for Barnabas! I was in two minds about sending them north to catch you at Antiochia – I wasn't sure whether or when you'd be back this way, but now I'm glad I hesitated. Praise God you survived to receive them!" And off he ran again, promising to return later.

The precious letters were tantalizing, but they could wait a little longer. First, being now warm, clean, clothed, fed, and as comfortable as they could be for their many hurts, the apostles bowed in prayer, extolling God for the compassion of a fellow Jew in a strange land, praising and thanking Lord Jeshua that they had been protected even as he had promised, that they might continue his blessed work and finish what they had begun! In particular they prayed for Chazzan Efram – that the kindness he had shown them might be rewarded by the gift of life in Christ, through the gospel they would preach to him and his family.

Only after this did they begin to wilt, and feeling the effects of Efram's strong wine, they rolled up in blissfully warm blankets, on deliciously soft couches, to fall asleep almost at once, while murmuring from the other side of the thick stone wall, the comforting sound of familiar Jewish prayers filled their dreams.

Chapter Forty-nine

SOME hours later a shaft of sun struck through the single window onto their faces, and they woke, very hungry and at first struggling to remember where they were. They rose, stretching their stiffly aching bodies, again giving thanks for the safety, comfort, and shelter they had found after their gruelling journey. But now they must stir themselves. They must find clothing so they could return the borrowed garments ready for the next person in need, as well as footwear – and food. What a blessing they had not lost their hidden money!

Rubbing his growling stomach, Barnabas handed Shaul a small knife from a pile of useful utensils sitting in a wooden platter, and waved the essential garment rather helplessly at him.

"Can you unpick these? With this? I will only hack them to pieces and then you will have to make more for the voyage home. Believe me, I'm very grateful for your stitches, but they are so small."

"And believe me, I am very grateful for your breeches, but they are so big!" Paul answered with a grin. Sitting in the window the better to see, he began deftly unpicking various little inner pockets with the sharp point of the knife. "You read your letters. I'm just as anxious as you are to free our funds – grateful as I was for those sweetmeats I feel hungrier now than ever."

"And I! They have only reminded my stomach of what it's missing."

Snapping the black and brown seals, Barnabas opened his letters, greedily running his eye over the crackling papyrus sheets. The first was the oldest, as evidenced by the once-black ink having rusted to brown. It contained much news from Mari but disappointingly little of ekklesial matters, being rather too full of the prodigously advanced progress of her small granddaughter. This he put away for later, guessing that it would not interest Paul. He did however share with him the second letter, its firm neat writing still very black, which was from his niece in Antioch Orontes.

"From girlhood Anna was always my most faithful correspondent, you know," he smiled happily, "and still is. Unlike my dear sister Mari, she has a remarkable economy of words. See here – she has even managed to tell me all about young Danya's betrothal without a single mention of clothes, jewels, gifts, or number of guests at the celebration. Paul? Are you listening? But, perhaps this doesn't really interest you. It's not as if you knew them intimately."

Paul was staring out of the window. He sucked the finger he had accidentally stabbed and taking up his work again said casually, "No, no, go on by all means. So they found her a husband in Antioch, after all."

Barnabas grinned. "Not really, that's the funny part. Of course, they had promised to keep an eye open for a suitable match, but with Danya protesting she could never live in such an overcrowded and unwholesome city as Antioch, nobody was seriously looking. But someone *else* was – a travelling smith from Galilee. He had been visiting family in Banayim when Danya was there, and was immediately smitten. As soon as he had opportunity he pursued her to the metropolis – just after we left in fact – and laid steady siege to her affections. Apparently he was prodded into action by Old Etta, Dan's elderly aunt! Bless her, I didn't realise she was still in the land of the living."

Barnabas chuckled as he skimmed down the page.

"Anna says Danya's early resolve to follow her mother's example and marry a much older man simply tumbled like Jericho once young Shuni made his intentions plain – and no wonder. She writes, '*He is a strapping fellow, as handsome as his mother, as tender-hearted as his father and a fine Christian with it. And he has a rollicking sense of humour which Danya finds irresistible and keeps her laughing all the day. He has done very well for himself here in Antioch too, with smithing of all kinds so much in demand, but to Danya's relief he is not at all tempted to transplant himself, and Galilee will be their home.*

"*Both sets of parents were not slow in giving their blessing, and everyone is delighted, for our two families were very close back in the old days. They are to be married in Banayim at the end of next year, and what a celebration that will be for all of us, for dear Dan and Meia's Michal is to marry Shuni's brother Obed at the same time.*' Well, well, they're all so terribly *young*, of course – but I'm happy for the girl. She will have another shepherdess for a sister-in-law, be near her own relations, and will be much loved by Shuni's family." He sighed rather sentimentally.

"You knew them?"

"Oh, yes, we became well acquainted during Anna's Banayim days, and I could tell you many tales of those times. Ittai and Marta were excellent parents – and they were very young themselves, back then. How the years fly!"

"I congratulate them all and wish them God's blessings and much joy," Paul said quietly, and his pale lips smiled. For a moment he was silent, as if harkening to a fading whisper, then, turning from the window, abruptly he changed the subject.

"Speaking of time," he added with unusual heartiness, "we may not remain as synagogue guests more than two or three days, so –"

"Yes, too true, we must find lodgings, of course, or be seen as reprehensible wasters. Ah, you've finished? How much do we have?"

"Enough to be adequately shod and dressed, if we buy from a dealer in used goods. After that, apart from our passage home, which we daren't touch, about five days' food, maybe two days' shelter. Nowhere enough for the time we need here."

"Ah, *ben Shaul,* my arithmetical brother! I am truly impressed with the improvement in your calculating skills!"

"So kind," Paul said drily. "Necessity is the best teacher! But you see how it is. We can hardly apply for synagogue relief if we run short, especially once we start preaching, since they will probably bar us anyway. Another reason to return these borrowed robes quickly, in case our good-hearted Efram should find himself in trouble over it. So – we had better buy clothes and then set about finding work at once."

"This also is true – but not tonight, my conscientious friend. Like Esau, I am starving right here and now! Lead me to the nearest cook shop!"

"The *nearest?*" Paul snorted incredulously, bantering to lighten his mood. "Since when were *you* ever satisfied with the *nearest?*"

Barnabas laughed. "Well, the nearest with good food at the best price, of course!"

He was firmly of the opinion it was no use leaving decisions about food to Paul, who was more often than not regrettably indifferent to what he ate, just as he was usually indifferent to the weather, or indeed, any of his physical surroundings, though admittedly there were times when this had advantages. Barnabas had once asked him as they tramped along a mountainous mile, what he thought of the view. Paul had looked at him with a slightly puzzled expression, and squinted to where Barnabas was pointing.

"Very nice," he said obligingly, adding, "Very green."

At the time Barnabas had chided himself for forgetting Paul's weak eyesight. Afterwards however he could not help wondering whether there was too much landscape inside his friend's head for him to pay attention to the one outside it. Most likely, sharper vision would not have made the slightest difference.

With alacrity Barnabas now scooped up some of the coins Paul had just freed from their bindings, and feeling much better after their rest, back into the street they went, making their way straight to the *agora*.

There, lining the broad public terrace were scores of shops and tiny stalls selling goods and services of every description. In one corner a trio of barbers sat idly chatting between customers. Shears and razors, together with combs, brushes, and tweezers were laid out on cloths beside their stools, with soap and oils, pomades, towels and bowls of water standing by. Beside them, a neat-bearded hairdresser was braiding an elaborate edifice from a mass of unruly hair belonging to a girl who twitched and yelped at his every move, while at each squeak her glaring mother threatened to reduce his price.

The mother herself was twitching a good deal, for she was ticklish, and the hairdresser's wife was crouched at her feet manicuring her toenails – meekly risking a kick in the nose for the sake of the few copper *quadrans* she would earn. However, she did it with a glint in her eye, for when her stint as manicurist was over she would be hurrying around the back to another stall over the way, where, darkly veiling herself in a gorgeous garment, she would reappear as the fortune teller to whom the sulky pair resorted weekly. There she would throatily whisper of interesting times soon to befall them, and more than recover the price of the insults she and her husband had endured.

Here and there one or two people peered over the shoulders of public scribes and notaries, who perched at their portable writing desks taking down dictation in swift, neat script, drawing up contracts, or concocting wooing missives for the lovelorn. Occasionally one turned his head to snap a warning or slap away pilfering fingers tempted by his intriguing boxes of supplies. Children especially were drawn to these boxes, equipped as they were with a variety of reed and plume pens and sharpening knives, smoothing stones, lead sticks and neat rulers, red and black inks, coloured waxes and seals, crayons, crackly sheets of papyrus, and soft clean rolls of parchment.

On either side other stalls vied for attention – displaying everything from clothes and cosmetics to cooking pans and cucumbers, and an array of tempting places to eat. The question of clothing was deferred for now as Barnabas literally followed his nose from one tiny barrel-vaulted *taberna* to another as he sniffed the tantalising aromas wafting their way.

"Here – this smells good!" Hovering over the counter of a *thermopolium,* Barnabas lifted a lid on the nearest *dolia* – a hot dish set into a hole in the stone top. "What's this? Stewed carrots, or are they parsnips? And that fried stuff?"

"Carrots with scallions and mushrooms. Too late in the year for parsnips, friend. And that *there's* a juicy bit of crackling," the vendor replied smartly. "Does you good, but a lot of crunch, so suck it if your teeth are bad and save the rind for later, eh? Good for a teething babe, my wife says. Good value! And speaking of teeth, if you have a sweet tooth here we have sour cherries with curds and honey. Now, what will you have? Any *dolia* – all the same price – only one *as* each. With bread, two, with wine two and a half. *Garum* extra," he continued. "No?"

He snatched up the other lids at random, whacking them down again like a conjuror moving a pea under a cup as he recited rapidly, "Stewed cardoons? Or cabbage for that black eye, eh? Some for a poultice and eat the rest, now that's value for money! Well, never mind – mixed greens, then? Hot peas? Boiled eggs? What about baked fish? Nothing like a bit of nice fresh fish!"

Barnabas gave a limp-looking specimen a judicial poke. "Looks a bit dry," he said, rather critically for such a ravenous man.

"Nice *dried* fish," the vendor agreed quickly. "Nice, freshly dried fish, er, freshly cooked," he added, that there be no mistake. His shoulders sagged as Barnabas shook his head and moved on. Fresh or not, the fish had no scales and looked disconcertingly like an eel.

Paul, eyeing its leathery flesh with disfavour, had much the same thought. He frowned thoughtfully at the small shrines to Mercury and Dionysus and various other favoured gods which hung on the smoky walls of the shop, but he was not thinking about the fish – or idolatry. As a man who must live in godless places he had long since learned to glance over such objects without really seeing them. Just now he was remembering their first visit to this city – and even in the midst of those thoughts, being grateful for the fresh, cool weather, such a contrast to the feverish, breathless humidity which had assailed them on the outward journey. How long it had been since they were last in Perga, since Marcus had deserted them – more than a year and a half!

And speaking of a long time, why must Barnabas always take so long when deciding about food? Just buy it and eat it, no questions asked! It was right that since they had so little to spend, they should spend wisely, but Barnabas was always determined to ensure whatever he bought should be as delicious as possible, whereas Paul only cared that he should not eat anything too unpleasant. Though his stomach pleaded, he curbed his impatience. After two days of true hunger, a few moments either way made no difference.

"Ah – do you smell that?" Barnabas's eyes lit up. "Garlic and coriander! Over here! Come on, Paul, don't dawdle."

He dived into a *taberna* beside a small jewellery and trinket stall and a moment later looked out again, happily beckoning to his slower friend. "This is more like it! Look – lentil stew with asparagus and peas, a millet loaf and a jug of wine, only four *asses* for the two of us."

Paul's eye had been caught by the trinket stall, where amid a bright selection of coloured glass beads hung a few toy wooden animals. No camels, though. Suddenly he wondered whether Danya's was still where he had so impulsively put it. That he had left it there at all, and not thrown it into the sea as he had first intended, no longer made him reproach himself for foolish sentimentality. Reluctant either to keep or destroy it, he had merely honoured the intention of the gift. Stowing it in the nest of protective and innocent creatures seemed to embody everything he had come to realise from the whole agonising experience, and unless someone else had discovered it, Danya's keepsake would still be there in the hollow of the tree – in which case, should he retrieve it or leave it?

He followed his friend into the busy shop and gratefully ate everything put before him, but even the relief of satiation did not stop the question of the camel preoccupying his mind.

It was not until after their evening prayers that his thoughts finally cleared, even as – so long ago! – the dull waves on the Seleucian beach had cleared to translucence in the gently probing light of dawn. He had been through a very private fire of affliction; he had been well and truly scorched. Residual pain was inevitable and would fade with time. The important thing was that the fever had burnt itself out. Of course he should see if the trinket was still there! Its whimsy could not hurt him now, and perhaps when Danya bath Ammiel married Shuni ben Ittai, she would be amused, maybe even touched, to receive back the little gift, returned with his thanks for her good wishes, as a friendly token of his own.

Somewhat to their surprise, within the week, despite the traces of injury still visible on their faces, Paul and Barnabas had found work to support themselves, thanks largely to the kindly Efram, who was full of helpful information. His was not a lofty position, but he was proud of it in a way which was quite different to that of puffed-up Hadar in Old Paphos. The apostles liked him very much, and to them he seemed to embody the sentiments of the ancient psalm, *I would rather stand as a doorkeeper in the house of my God than sit at ease in the dwellings of the wicked.*

To Efram fell no crumbs of importance, not even from teaching the youngest boys, since here they were taught by men of higher standing. He was humbly content to take care of the building and its contents, counting his service an honour. He cleaned, filled and lit the lamps, swept the floors inside and the steps outside, maintained the guest chamber, distributed alms, fed the poor, lovingly tended the ark of sacred scrolls, polished the golden pointer which guided the readers, prepared for services and opened the doors.

Less pleasant was his obligation to administer punishment decreed by the synagogue rulers, and for his sake as much as their own, Paul and Barnabas hoped their message would cause no anger in this quiet place, such as had led to their thrashing on Cyprus.

To their relief, in Perga they were able to preach freely, both in the synagogue and at work – Barnabas as yet another humble copyist among others buried in the municipal offices of the local *Aedile*, once more wading through documents relating to Public Works, and thankful indeed that unlike in Antiochia nobody here was interested in covertly injuring either his work or his position.

Unfortunately Paul could not say the same when he began tutoring five insolent sons of the provincial *Quaestor*, who privately admitted that being Municipal Treasurer did not bring him appropriate respect from his ungrateful offspring or indeed any respect from them at all. Vexedly he told Paul that his deplorable sons seemed to think that the city's purse should be *his* to lavish as *they* would like. Refreshingly, Quaestor Decimus had no illusions about them, or himself. He confessed he could do little with them, and had dismissed too many incompetent tutors already.

"Had I been elected as *Praetor*," he said darkly, referring to the position of Officer of the Law, "it might well have been another matter! Well, do what you can with them, you can't make them any worse. Boys! How my father survived ten of us I will never understand. Give me girls any time, though I wouldn't say that in public of course, even though my three have me where they want, but at least they are far less uncivil about it. As for the boys – I will say they are very sharp when it comes to numbers. Their last tutor claimed to be a descendant of a famous *mathematikos*, but my boys outstripped him in calculating, for all that. No doubt you have heard of Apollonius of Perga?"

"The Great Geometer?" Paul hoped he did not sound as faint as he felt. "I must tell you at the outset, Quaestor, that I have absolutely no knowledge of Conics!"

Decimus snorted. "Who does? Certainly not I, nor that useless tutor, for all his boasts, nor my boys. It is not what *I* would call a practical subject.

The fact is, I don't even care very much about their basic *arithmos* – in my view they're rather too clever with figures already, especially when it comes to elaborate justifications of how to spend money which is not theirs." (Here Paul privately breathed a sigh of relief.) "But their reading and writing is far below competence, especially in Latin, and at this rate they'll never get a public office."

Reassured as to the Questor's expectations, Paul very gladly promised to do his best, and began the very next day, with his new pupils eyeing him with private and gleeful expectations of their own concerning his downfall. Much to their confusion these expectations did not eventuate. His previous experience with teaching stubborn boys standing him in good stead, he calmly and with the utmost consistency thwarted their best efforts to overthrow him, with a resolve his dismayed students found more steely than their own.

Having made them understand he was there to stay, and there to teach them against all their endeavours to the contrary, he made their lessons lively, interesting, and full of spirited discussion, and even noisy debates. Their father's eyebrows went up and down many a time upon hearing reports of the raised voices and laughter from the schoolroom, but though his sons never became real scholars, they did at least stop plaguing him about their tutor and whining about lessons – and they rapidly improved past all expectation.

It was not long before the Quaestor realised Paul was using Greek texts of some very exciting portions of Jewish scripture as a basis for many lessons in reading, writing, and reasoning. At first he said nothing. The main thing was that the boys should not be as ignorant as peasants!

But the boys themselves could not resist relating 'the best bits' from these classes, and soon a frankly curious Decimus surreptitiously began to listen in whenever he could spare the time. Eventually all pretence was abandoned, as the pupils' insistent questions and demand for more thrilling stories in their dictation and reading led to an open schoolroom shared with their father in the evenings. From encouraging the youngest boys to learn their letters and the older to improve their written Greek and Latin, Paul quickly progressed to teaching the whole household about *Jeshua Christos,* thus opening the door of faith and salvation to this slightly chaotic family of Gentiles.

Both in the city and further afield in small settlements and villages, the gospel message provoked many lively disagreements among – and between – both Jews and Gentiles, but in this place, at least the arguments were fought (however clamorously) with words rather than physical force. The biggest obstacle seemed to be not the message itself so much as the baffling simplicity of Christian worship.

To pagans, worship of deities was associated with tangibility – things you could see and hear and feel. Invocations, offerings, atmosphere, priests, interpreters, mysteries, forms, and prescribed rites, the more elaborate the better. Whatever gods or goddesses a person chose to honour, pantheism offered the spice of *variety* – temples, shrines, grottos, groves, and as many differing rituals as there were gods to worship. As for these Christians, scoffed devotees of Artemis and Zeus and Aphrodite, they had no foothold at all in this country! They could not claim (nor even invent for themselves) a single stand of hallowed ground where a sacred event took place – not in Pamphylia, nor anywhere else in Asia. Their aloof deity, by their own admission, had confined himself to Jewish home territory!

Many in the Jewish community were equally taken aback by the starkness of Christianity. Jews might also serve only one God, and an invisible one at that, but their religion was rich in ritual and tradition, enmeshed in complex legalities, ordinances, and customs governing everyday life. For those who saw Jeshua the Nazarene as an interloper, the Way of the Christians was not even a twisted branch of Judaism, being decidedly cut off from what they claimed were their roots, and therefore lacking the credibility of antiquity. In their self-governing isolation there could be no true connection between them and the synagogues! And speaking of synagogues – why, every stone and pillar was weighted with the reverence of centuries. There were special furnishings, appointed seats for the chief men, holy books, and solemn forms of service with prescribed prayers and responses. Inside a synagogue, you *knew* you were somewhere holy – you could see it – you could feel it!

What had Christians to offer in comparison? No temples. No special sanctuaries. No venerated sites hallowed by legend. No priests. No holy artefacts. No *ceremony*. Once they had been initiated by a single, uncomplicated act of immersion in water (anywhere, any water!) – what sacred thing was required of them when they gathered to worship, except to share a bit of bread and wine? *Everyone* ate bread and drank wine! If you had a bath and then went home for dinner, had you made yourself a Christian by accident? And if you were a Christian on purpose – how would you even know when you were worshipping and when you weren't?

Thus the wits both low and high enjoyed themselves while the arguments went on. *Everything* about it was invisible – so how real could it be? It was all far too simplistic for people who saw worship as an act, and not a state of mind.

In the absence of outright opposition, however, the apostles continued undaunted. One unexpected thing happened – they bumped into their old acquaintance, Plato the Puppeteer. He was astonished, embarrassed, and relieved to see them.

"I really thought I'd started the whole riot and got you killed back at Lystra," he said uncomfortably. "I didn't mean you any harm, you know. Just my temper. People don't realise how much work goes into my props and my booth got torn, so I was angry. I never thought they'd all go wild like that! No lasting damage, I hope?"

"Only a crooked thumb," Paul shrugged, his tongue regretfully feeling the gap where two of his back teeth had been. Hard bread or almonds still caused him discomfort.

Plato looked at the awkwardly bent thumb and grunted with genuine sympathy. "I'm sorry. Looks painful."

"Only in cold weather," Paul assured him with a rueful smile, "and there is one compensation – it's very good at foretelling rain. Very useful for travellers!"

He and Barnabas assured the puppeteer that they did not hold him to blame for the riot.

"It wasn't your fault," said Barnabas. "The Jews from Antiochia and Iconium were determined to make it happen. They didn't pursue us all that way for nothing. It wouldn't have made any difference whether you'd been there or not."

Plato blew out his breath, pleased. "Well, that's all right then!" More cheerfully, he continued, "I heard a fair bit of your speeches while I was there, you know. You told some good stories – I've worked some of them into my act – that one about your holy man walking on the water is always popular!"

In spite of their efforts to enlighten him, Paul and Barnabas never managed to convert Plato to the Way, and he continued to gather "good stories" from the Christians and use them in his little theatre wherever he went. However, out of respect for his learned friends of the road, as he called Paul and Barnabas, he would always finish such shows by announcing loudly to his audiences that the local Christians would be very happy to tell them more about the stories he had just shown. "There's more in this than meets the eye!" he would declare mysteriously. Nobody would have been more astonished than Plato himself to know the number of people who met the "local Christians" because of his puppets.

And now by the grace of God and Lord Jeshua, there were around thirty Christians in Perga – among them Efram and his family, his devout proselyte friend Tychicus, and the entire household of Decimus the Quaestor – wife, mother, daughters, servants, slaves and all. His sons were still careless young boys, but he had hopes that as they grew they too would understand and accept the gospel.

Meanwhile, guided by the Holy Spirit, the apostles had laid their hands on several chosen men and women, bestowing upon them appropriate *Ruach* Gifts to serve the ekklesia, and the necessary overseers had been ordained, including both Efram and young Tychicus. The humility of the one and the zeal of the other boded well for the new community, as did the attitude of Decimus, who, far from being put out, was rather relieved that he had not been appointed to such a responsible position.

"Finance is my skill, not people," he said firmly. "Numbers behave themselves, people do not. I believe an elder's position must be a paternal one, and as brother Paul knows, I am not the best example of a man wisely managing his own family. It would be insufferable conceit for me to pretend otherwise. But ask me to start a Poor Fund, or whatever you like, and I will manage it faithfully."

Paul commended him warmly. "Everyone has something different to offer the Lord's ekklesia, my friend, whether a *Ruach* Gift or a natural talent, and all are needed. Yours will be equally valuable."

"The value of any gift lies in how wisely it is used," Decimus replied thoughtfully. "You see, I know how it goes in the civic service, and surely men are the same everywhere. In my experience, recognising your limitations saves much distress. *Nosce te ipsum* as the philosophers say. When people strive to be recognised for a talent they do not possess, but which seems to have more honour than their own, that is when discord arises!"

"Ah, yes indeed," Barnabas agreed. "*Know thyself* is excellent advice, and our King David said something akin to it. *Search me, O God, and know my heart!* Though God knowing, and ourselves knowing, are often, sadly, two separate things."

"Well, that is my point, you see. But remember the passage we discussed with the boys the other day, *How shall a young man cleanse his way? By taking heed to it, according to God's word!* So it is the word of God which reveals to us the truth about ourselves, if we are honest enough to look into His mirror."

"I like the way you put that," Paul nodded. "You might also say that when we read the scriptures they read us, for they reflect back, as you say, what we truly are."

"Yes – however," Decimus shook his head gloomily, "the trouble is that the more of a mess we are in ourselves, the harder it is to see even what is staring us in the face. We think we can see clearly, but it's often distorted." He picked up a favourite glass goblet and peered through it. "Aha, I can see you perfectly, brother Paul, though rather darkly. Your face is blue and has a twisted nose and green hair."

The others burst out laughing. "A neat analogy," Paul grinned.

The new little ekklesia was on its feet. The work at Perga was done. The sailing season was drawing to a close – soon the tempests of winter would howl over the seas. Paul and Barnabas arranged for their passage, and had only to wait out the days which the ship-master's soothsayer had declared were inauspicious for a voyage.

The morning before the day determined as most pleasing to the captain's gods, the two rolled up their bundles and prepared to leave the lodging they shared with Tychicus, for the ship would sail from Attalia very early the next morning, and they must be on board that night. Very forlorn indeed was young Tychicus as he shared their early breakfast. He had now succeeded to Paul's position as tutor to the Quaestor's sons, yet he would have given anything to be free to join the apostles in their work.

"Perhaps another time!" they said warmly, touched by his genuine feeling. "For we will return, if the Lord wills! Meanwhile, you have much good work to do here, brother, and the Gift of teaching to help you. Do not neglect it."

"I will not!" he said, cheering up. "I have so much to learn still, and we will all learn together, thanks to the Gifts of our Lord Jeshua!"

In company with Tychicus and the entire household of Decimus (the boys being delighted to have a rare release from lessons for a few hours) as well as the good-hearted Efram, his family, and as many of the other disciples as could manage to join them, the apostles walked down to the wharf on the Kestrus. The farewells were draining, as always. Paul found each goodbye seemed to be harder than the last, yet suddenly he was aching to leave. Fortunately the scampering sons of Decimus had wasted no time in finding a small fishing boat which was about to cast off, and after some rapid hard bargaining with the owner, eagerly waved Paul over, very proud of their catch, and proud of the grateful words he gave them as he and Barnabas clambered in.

Now the two were under way at last, waving goodbye, hearing the shouted blessings of the Perga ekklesia drift over the green water, until they rounded a bend in the river and were out of sight.

It was hard to believe that the time in Asia was over, at last – that there was not yet another place to tramp towards, yet so it was. It was a strange feeling. One or two imperceptible sighs escaped as the apostles settled back as best they could, their mixed emotions tempered to some degree by the practical discomforts of the short voyage – during which the fishermen allowed them to sit uncomfortably on a damp heap of barnacled nets, and enjoy the smell of rotting fish *gratis*, all the way down to the Attalia harbour.

How long it had been since they were last there! How much had happened! And there, sitting in the choppy green water before them, was a fast corn ship, furled sails ready to spread like wings in the wind ... just waiting to take them home ...

Chapter Fifty

THE freshening winds of approaching winter hurried the *Sea Dove* through the deep water. Gone were the sparkling billows of translucent turquoise, topped with the crystalline colour of the sky, which belonged to summery seas. Now the waves rolled heavily as if their sombre colours of dark green, slate grey, and deep indigo weighed them down – and the mariners had a certain narrow-eyed watchfulness about them which was absent in men who did not race the calendar with Imperial grain aboard.

As the days passed, Paul and Barnabas felt increasingly restless, pacing the swaying deck, too tense to talk. For so many seasons, so many months, they had never once lost sight of their mission – every moment had been filled with a sense of purpose, a need to drive themselves relentlessly. Paul in particular had woken every morning with the conviction that today was all a man ever had, that – not yesterday, not tomorrow but right *now* – a man must choose whether he would use *this* day as a time to indulge himself for his own ends, or a time to act for the glory of God. Now, cooped up on the ship, both he and Barnabas were forced to rest, and it was so alien to them that far from enjoying it, they found it almost uncomfortable.

Day after day Paul watched the great sails straining at the seams as the wind bellied them strongly, listening to the voice of the large vessel – the creaks of timber, snaps of bucking canvas, the groaning and thrumming of ropes. They seemed to express the tension within himself – an urgency, a longing to say, *It is finished,* to feel their mission had been completed. Had they left anything undone? Could they have done more? No, before God, he knew they had honestly done their best.

He thought of the hungry, lonely feeling that had engulfed him at Derbe, when he had looked up at the towering, frosty peaks of the Taurus ranges. How difficult it had been to turn his back on them! How thankful he was that he had been given the strength to do it! He could not have forgiven himself had they not retraced their steps to weave in the loose threads of their work. Now they could rest assured that they had not only *witnessed,* but also *ministered,* as the Master had charged. Paul knew he would never forget the wonderful, brave people they had left behind them. He would pray for them, think of them, write to them and encourage them … he drummed his fingers impatiently on a large crate beside him. From inside it came an annoyed squeal. Paul jumped back hastily when he realised he had been leaning all over a pig-pen.

Behind him, Barnabas smiled. "Still a Pharisee, Paul. Still a Pharisee."

Paul relaxed. He gave a wry grin. "I know it. Well, my aversion to unclean meat will neither save me nor condemn me! Just think of some of the strange meals we have eaten during the last few years!"

Barnabas shuddered. "I'd rather not – sometimes it was better not to ask questions!" He added wistfully, "Remember those honey cakes Portia used to make?"

"M'm." Paul gazed into the deep grey troughs of the waves below as the boat lurched along. "My mother used to make honey cakes every New Year," he murmured. "Father loved them – Deborah and I had to fight him for the crumbs." He laughed, but the smile faded quickly. Barnabas had just opened his mouth to reply when a faint cry floated down from the mast head.

"Land! Landfall!"

The coast of Syria was ahead! Barnabas leaped up to the nearest vantage point – on top of the pig's cage – with never a thought to what was inside it, waiting for the first moment when a hazy green and white strip would flicker on the horizon.

"I see it!" he yelled at last, leaping down and joyously flinging his arms around Paul, and thus rendering his shorter friend incapable of seeing anything except an uninteresting expanse of cloth.

"I believe you! Now let me go!" Laughing, Paul struggled free, but he knew it would be a while before his weaker eyes could make out the smudge of land ahead – the long coastline that meant the end of their journey. Nevertheless, it was there!

"Praise be to God in Heaven, and to our Lord Jeshua," he breathed, "for bringing us safely back!" Pensively he fingered the leather cord around his neck. He had worn his father's gift for so long, it would feel strange taking it off. Barnabas looked at the approaching coast with affection. "Tonight we will eat the Lord's Supper in familiar territory!"

Eating supper of any kind however suddenly seemed less attractive as the wind got up, freshening alarmingly, blowing off the coast and turning the water uncomfortably choppy. But the sailors were skilful and though the ship yawed heavily, still it progressed steadily, and slowly, slowly the rocky promontory of Seluecia's upper city became visible on the horizon. At last, after what seemed an agonisingly long time, they were close enough for the towing boats to draw alongside and attach their ropes. Like a giant beetle dragged by busy ants, the bulky ship slid past the two imposing breakwaters at the harbour mouth. The strong oarsmen pulled together under the watchful eye of the harbourmaster, expertly guiding it through the channel to safely berth at the sheltered inner basin.

While the passengers busied themselves with retrieving their belongings from the jumble on deck, Paul disappeared ashore, and Barnabas was curious to spy him heading for a clump of trees fringing a rough little beach which crouched beside one of the breakwaters. He soon returned, the sleeves of his coat wet around the edges. Barnabas raised his eyebrows in unspoken query and his friend smiled briefly, showing him what was in his hand by way of answer.

"Just something I picked up, you might say."

"Off those rocks?"

"No, but that's where I cleaned it. It was covered in bird lime."

"I see there is a story behind this riddle. Am I to hear more?"

"Maybe one day."

"As you wish." Barnabas looked thoughtfully at his friend as he shouldered his bundle, then shrugged. Every man must keep his own counsel at times, especially when a matter was even not his to discuss.

The gangplank was now being overrun by men unloading the hold, but neither Paul nor Barnabas was in a mood for waiting. Recklessly they tossed their bundles over the side onto the wharf and seizing their first opportunity to safely dodge the laden workers, darted down the plank and sprang ashore. Even so, by the time they had finally disembarked, reclaimed their scattered belongings, paid various taxes, and debouched into the busy streets of the lower city, it was late afternoon. Barnabas squinted at the sun.

"We had better get food quickly, while we can still see what we're buying. Just as well we're in Syria not Judaea or everything would still be shut for the Sabbath!" He looked around. "Over there!" He pointed to a small bakery on the opposite corner of the street.

"I'll go." Paul ran over the street and into the shop. With a painful thud he collided heavily with someone who had chosen the same moment to dash out of the narrow arched doorway. Automatically beginning to apologise, Paul was quickly interrupted.

"Oh, no, no, sir, but it was *my* fault, I'm sure! Please forgive me! I was in too much of a hurry, as usual. Mother says we lived in Alexandria *far* too long and complains that nowadays I have the manners of an Egyptian." The long-lashed brown eyes looked up at his stunned face in sudden concern. "Oh, but are you winded, sir? Did I hurt you?"

"Pardon? Oh! Yes, I mean, no! Thank you ... I'm sorry," he responded, trying to laugh. "For just a moment I thought I knew you. My mistake."

"I am *forever* doing just the same!" the girl confessed with a giggle. "Father brings so many strangers to our ekklesia I can never be sure who I've met and who I haven't. It can be quite embarrassing. I still don't know many people, we haven't been here very long."

Paul's eyes lit up. "Did you say ekklesia? Here in Seleucia?"

"Oh, not a *political* gathering!" the girl explained hastily, in case he had the wrong idea. "We are a religious assembly – Christians."

Paul swung around. "Barnabas!" he shouted. "This girl is a Christian!"

"And proud to be one," she said defensively, "but please excuse me now – the assembly meets at our house tonight and we must have this bread for the Lord's Supper. *Shalom!*"

"Please wait!" Dodging an ox-cart, Barnabas ran to join them. "We are Christians ourselves, just off the *Sea Dove*, on our way to Antioch Orontes. We had no idea there was now a group here. Won't you please introduce us to your family?"

Her face broke into a delighted smile. "You also follow the Way? Then praise the Eternal that I bumped into you! Come on!" she said happily. "Of course you must join us for the *eucharist*, and afterwards my parents will insist you stay with us tonight, of that I am certain! This way."

They followed her along the winding streets, elated at this chance meeting, though Paul shrugged ruefully. How many times over the years had he made the same mistake! Of course Deborah would no longer be a young woman, let alone a mere girl. How could he forget the long years that had passed! For years he had carried around a mental image of his sister when she was young, and now he may not recognise her at all. It suddenly struck him with a sense of wonderment that of course he too was no longer young. How strange he had never thought of it before. His skin was creased with age, scarred by accidents and punishments, sallowed by illness and weather-beaten from travelling – though at least, apart from a brief flare-up in Perga, that wretched recurring rash had been banished since Derbe – oh, and his hairline was receding! So, there was not much of the young Shaul of Tarsus left for anyone else to recognise, either.

The only thing about him which was the same was the old leather case which he was looking forward to taking off his neck at last, and even that had worn smoother – while he had become more wrinkled! But there was no help for the changes wrought by time and trouble, and no doubt Deborah would have had plenty of her own, too, wherever she was. They could even have crossed paths without ever knowing it. It was a painful thought, and he blocked it quickly.

The girl pushed open a courtyard gate and led them up a short flight of steps.

"You're late, Melissa!" a young man called reprovingly from a window.

"Be quiet, brother mine – we have visitors!" she answered pertly, letting them into the house. The young man immediately ran to meet them, and polite salutations were exchanged.

"Please excuse us calling on your family without ceremony," said Barnabas, as at his invitation they set down their bundles and removed their coats. "We are also disciples of the *Christos*. We have just disembarked after a long voyage, and this young woman informs us that the Thanksgiving supper will be held here tonight."

"Trust my sister!" the young man said, with a teasing glance towards her. "With her talkative tongue she is a kind of walking *graffiti* announcing our gatherings!"

The girl rolled her eyes. She had heard this before. "The other members will be arriving soon," she said. "Meanwhile please do not allow my inquisitive brother to pester you with questions until I fetch our mother and father! They will be very glad to have you join us and will have many questions of their own, I am sure. They are always so eager to hear about brethren in distant parts."

With a cheerful smile she excused herself, and in a few moments, a comfortable, middle-aged woman entered the room. She smiled warmly at the two strangers, looking them over with a kindly expression – and then the smile froze on her face. Suddenly trembling, Paul took a step forward. The room spun before his eyes. He could not breathe.

"Here she is," said the young man cheerfully, not noticing that his mother's face had suddenly paled. "Mother dear, this is –"

"Paul-Shaul!" the woman shrieked. *"Oh!* Paul-Shaul!" She flung herself across the room and into his arms, crying convulsively.

"Deborah!" Paul sobbed, crushing her to his heart. "Deborah!"

In the midst of this outburst, a stout grey-haired man appeared at the door, staring in astonishment at the stunned and tearful faces all around. Barnabas met his startled eyes and gestured vaguely in Paul's direction.

"The prodigal returns!" he said lamely, and laughed.

Simeon, for of course it was he, stood utterly astounded for but a moment, then with a cry of joy he folded wife and brother in his brawny arms, weeping like a woman. Barnabas, feeling suddenly unsteady, sank into a chair and hastily wiped his sleeve across his eyes, while the faces of small, staring children and anxious servants seemed to peer in from every direction, before hurriedly melting away again. For a while, all was confusion, then the words tumbled out.

"I tried so hard to find you both!"

"We heard of your conversion ... we scarcely believed it – not at first ... but by then you had disappeared ... we feared the worst..."

"I looked for you, wherever I went ... hoping to find you in Cilicia ... praying I might be only three steps behind ..."

"We were always so far away ... Rome ... and Carthage ... and so many years in Alexandria ..."

Eventually calm was restored. Deborah clutched her brother's arm tightly as if afraid he would vanish, while Simeon, with much throat-clearing still, introduced his family. He put a fond hand on the shoulder of the young man who had greeted them at the door.

"This is Joshua."

Paul's eyes were still wet, but he grinned at his nephew. "The first time I met you, young man, you nearly bit my finger off. I will feel a lot safer if you close your mouth."

Joshua obediently shut his still-gaping mouth, his short reddish beard bristling with confused emotions. His legendary uncle! Here! All those stories, contained in this very room! The infamous firebrand Shaul of Tarsus! Lifted up to be a torchbearer of the gospel, by the express command of Lord Jeshua on high! With a gulp, he snapped out of his trance and pounced, embracing Paul with rib-straining enthusiasm.

"Young Deborah, our busy little bee, you have already met – but we use her Greek name to avoid confusion."

Melissa dutifully kissed her long-lost uncle on both cheeks, and gave herself up to hopping up and down with excitement.

"I'm *so* glad I *wasn't* looking where I was going!" she giggled triumphantly to him, delighted with her part in the matter.

"And so am I," he responded shakily, still hardly daring to believe what had happened. "Yet another accident in my life which has proved to be no accident at all, but the loving hand of Lord Jeshua at work!"

"Oh, Uncle, do tell us about all the other times!" Joshua interjected enthusiastically.

"Yes, *please*," begged Melissa. "We want to hear *everything*!"

"And so do we," Simeon laughed, "but everyone will be here soon, so it must keep until later. But then we'll burn the lamps all night if we have to, I promise! Now, Deborah, my dear, what happened to the little ones? Are they hiding? I saw them only a moment ago."

"I think all our noise alarmed them – and the servants!" Deborah confessed, eyes laughing through a sheen of tears. She peered around the door and beckoned reassuringly. "Come out, my darlings, and meet your uncle," she encouraged gently. "This is a happy occasion!" Nevertheless, she looked somewhat hesitantly at her brother.

A pair of very small, bright-eyed boys sidled out, identical from unruly brown curls to stubbed brown toes. They marched up and stood silently before Paul, gravely looking him up and down.

"*Shalom*, little men," he said genially, squatting down to their level. "Blessings and peace to you both."

"*Sh'lom*," they said dutifully, then, "Did you bring us any presents?"

"Only one," he replied, thinking fast. He smiled, very happily. *Oh, yes – this is even better!* "It's old, but very special. So I hope you are good at sharing."

They nodded earnestly, and he showed them a weathered wooden toy on a faded silken cord, still damp from its very recent scrubbing with wet sand.

"You know, a strong camel can take you anywhere, even through a lonely desert without water. So look after him, and this little fellow will remind you that when you grow up, wherever you go, no matter how far, there's always a way home."

"Thank you, Uncle! What's his name?"

"Anything you like. Now, what's yours?"

"I'm Shaul," the first boy announced.

"I'm Stefanos," said the second.

There was the briefest of stunned pauses – then Paul scooped up both of his twin nephews into an impulsive hug, his full eyes lifted to Deborah's in sudden comprehension. "Was that for me, my sister?" he murmured.

Deborah bit her lip and nodded. Releasing the children, he kissed her and removed himself to a small balcony at the side of the room, his heart overflowing.

"That is not distress," Barnabas said gently to Deborah's concerned face, "You could not have done him a greater kindness."

She smiled with relief and took the little boys' hands. "Come now, my darlings, time for bed."

There was a knock at the door. The other disciples were arriving. Barnabas joined Paul on the balcony. The sun was setting in a splendour of cloud and colour, and the seaside air of Seleucia Pieria was growing chilly. Below, people were filing through the courtyard gate for the evening meeting around the Lord's table. Barnabas watched the shadowy figures walking up the steps. Strangers, yet brothers and sisters. Jews and Gentiles, yet one Family in the household of God. They were united in faith and hope, gathering here in gratitude to remember His beloved Son, their faithful Lord Jeshua, the one who loved them enough to die for them, even before they knew him.

Paul broke the silence. "Our beloved Master has been with us every step of the way," he said quietly, "exactly as he promised."

Barnabas nodded. A feeling of peace settled within him. "Well, Paul, my old friend?" He leant comfortably on the stone balustrade, inhaling with pleasure the faint scents that rose from the little garden beneath. "A happy ending?"

Paul lifted his eyes to the sunset and nodded slowly. "Happy, God be praised! But not so much of an ending, Barnabas – by the grace of Lord Jeshua, more of a new beginning!"

"I stand corrected," replied his friend with a warm smile. "In one sense, every ending is a new beginning, especially when families are reunited."

"Yes."

Paul's thoughts were still spinning with the wonder of it all. After all the bleak years without his own kin ... after all his painful wrestlings with that sudden, acute and belated desire not to be alone ... after all that ... when he had finally accepted with no lingering regrets that his path would remain solitary! That morning, he had stepped off the ship knowing that he had won a deep certainty far beyond mere resignation – that the greater love of Lord Jeshua the Christ was beyond all earthly longings. Truly, that love, that hope, that *reality*, was all the comfort, and all the consolation he needed – more than enough.

And now, on this very same day ... he had been given back, doubled, the precious family he thought he had lost forever. Oh, God was good, and greatly to be praised, and great was the love and the hope which He gave mankind through His Son!

Paul gazed unseeingly into the darkening sky, looking at something beyond. How true, and how wonderful were the words of Isaias: *Eye has not seen, nor ear heard, nor the heart even imagined, the things which God has prepared for them that love Him!* But how could men love Him when they did not know Him? And how could they know Him unless they were taught?

He straightened up, already seeing far distant lands and peoples before him, kings and commoners, Jews and Gentiles, men and women, bond and free ... still in shadows ... all unknowing ... all awaiting the glorious light of salvation through Lord Jeshua the Christ.

"They are waiting for us, my brother," Barnabas reminded him gently, indicating the room fast filling with people.

Paul turned from the window, and a resolute smile was in his eyes. "Yes, I know."

There was so much yet to do.

A Time To Act is the fourth book in a series by S. J. Knight.
All available by contacting: sjknightworks@gmail.com

Book One

A Time to Hear

"Father, is there always an answer for every question?"

Ammiel considered. "No," he said finally. "Not always. Not for now, anyway."

"Why not?" Dan dared to ask, holding himself very still, as he felt again that slow, new, faint stirring of awareness within. Answers!

But every new answer only provokes more questions as Dan gropes for understanding – about himself, his family, his nation and his faith.

Book Two

A Time to See

THE Nazarene is working miracles, so where is the promised Kingdom? Life goes on as usual.

But impatient Dan is no longer a child, and his growing confusion is shared by many.

"I don't know where Loukanos is. I don't know if he's even alive. I don't know how the Messiah will bring deliverance ... Or when. Or what comes first. I don't know enough about anything that matters."

The answers will astonish them all.

Book Three

A Time to Speak

ONCE it had been so simple. The flock, the family, the faith. But now Dan is a young man, and everything is complicated. Messiah has come, and gone, leaving them to continue the work begun.

"So how should we go about it?" Johanan asked bluntly.

Dan had not thought that far – a noble idea was one thing, carrying it out was another.

And life kept getting in the way.

Also *A Time To Hear*, a musical stage play based on Book One

A TIME TO HEAR

In the tiny lakeside community of Banayim, Galilee, the villagers long for the promised Messiah to save them from poverty and Roman rule. Meanwhile their work, quarrels, and gossip go on as usual. Young Dan, the motherless son of Shepherd Ammiel, is confused. Who is the Messiah? When will he come? And what does it all mean? However more immediate worries crowd his mind. Will his father remarry? What about Aunt Etta and her lazy brother-in-law, Bukki?

Suddenly Dan's narrow world expands as he meets his father's first love, the gentle Anna of Cana, her scornful Greek brother, Loukanos, and irrepressible young cousin Johanan, and the enigmatic Blind Mordecai.

When startling news comes of a bold prophet preaching in the wilderness of Judea, the family are determined to discover whether this is indeed their Messiah. They set out on a journey – a journey which will change everything. Each of them will hear more, learn more and lose more than they could ever have expected.

All of them will find more than they ever could have imagined.

Based on the novel by S.J. Knight, this uplifting musical stage play is a pleasure to read for its own sake. Written for a flexible number of participants of all ages, it is particularly suitable for production by youth, church, and amateur groups. The book is thoughtfully arranged with script on right-hand pages, accompanied by sketches, comments and personal note space on the left. Directors will find the optional cuts helpful. Music scores are included.

Script and lyrics by S.J. Knight. Music by Elizabeth Burke.
Additional music by Meg Green (music & lyrics), David Alexander & Laura Terrell.

Lightning Source UK Ltd.
Milton Keynes UK
UKOW01f0416140717
305306UK00001B/98/P